OXFORD WORLD'S CLASSICS

TWENTY THOUSAND LEAGUES
UNDER THE SEAS

JULES VERNE was born in Nantes in 1828, the eldest of five children in a prosperous family of French, Breton, and Scottish extraction. His early years were happy apart from the drowning of his cousins and an unrequited passion for his cousin Caroline. Literature always attracted him and while taking a law degree in Paris he wrote a number of plays. His books, *Journey to England and Scotland* and *Paris in the Twentieth Century*, were not published in his lifetime. However, the publisher Hetzel accepted *Five Weeks in a Balloon* in 1862, to be followed by sixty other novels covering the whole world and beyond. Verne travelled over three continents, before selling his yacht in 1886. Eight of the books appeared after his death in 1905—although in fact partly written by his son Michel.

WILLIAM BUTCHER studied at the University of London and the École Normale Supérieure. He has taught languages and mathematics, notably at the École Nationale d'Administration and the University of Hong Kong. He has published *Jules Verne: The Definitive Biography* (2006) and *Jules Verne inédit: Les manuscrits déchiffrés* (2016), together with many annotated editions, including *Journey to the Centre of the Earth*, *Around the World in Eighty Days*, *Salon de 1857*, and *The Adventures of Captain Hatteras*.

T0019649

OXFORD WORLD'S CLASSICS

*For over 100 years Oxford World's Classics have brought
readers closer to the world's great literature. Now with over 700
titles—from the 4,000-year-old myths of Mesopotamia to the
twentieth century's greatest novels—the series makes available
lesser-known as well as celebrated writing.*

*The pocket-sized hardbacks of the early years contained
introductions by Virginia Woolf, T. S. Eliot, Graham Greene,
and other literary figures which enriched the experience of reading.
Today the series is recognized for its fine scholarship and
reliability in texts that span world literature, drama and poetry,
religion, philosophy, and politics. Each edition includes perceptive
commentary and essential background information to meet the
changing needs of readers.*

OXFORD WORLD'S CLASSICS

JULES VERNE

The Extraordinary Journeys

Twenty Thousand Leagues under the Seas

Translated with an Introduction and Notes by
WILLIAM BUTCHER

OXFORD
UNIVERSITY PRESS

OXFORD
UNIVERSITY PRESS

Great Clarendon Street, Oxford, OX2 6DP,
United Kingdom

Oxford University Press is a department of the University of Oxford.
It furthers the University's objective of excellence in research, scholarship,
and education by publishing worldwide. Oxford is a registered trade mark of
Oxford University Press in the UK and in certain other countries

First published as an Oxford World's Classics paperback 2019

Impression: 4

Published in the United States of America by Oxford University Press
198 Madison Avenue, New York, NY 10016, United States of America

British Library Cataloguing in Publication Data

Data available

Library of Congress Control Number: 2018944467

ISBN 978-0-19-881864-9

Printed and bound in Great Britain by
Clays Ltd, Elcograf S.p.A.

CONTENTS

CONTENTS

ACKNOWLEDGEMENTS

THIS volume benefits from the publications of Miller and Walter, Destombes, and Gagneux (see the Select Bibliography). Frederick Walter provided many invaluable suggestions for both editions, and Wim Thierens offered judicious feedback. Angel Lui, finally, has given her support and affection unstintingly.

LIST OF ABBREVIATIONS

MÉR *Magasin d'éducation et de récréation*: without other reference, *MÉR* refers to the serial publication of *20T* (1869–70)

MS1 the earlier of the two manuscripts kept in the French National Library

MS2 the second of the two manuscripts in the French National Library

20T *Twenty Thousand Leagues under the Seas*; references are of the form II 7 (Part Two, ch. 7)

'1869' refers to the first book edition of *20T* (1869–70).

'1871' refers to the first illustrated book publication of *20T*, the basis for this edition.

INTRODUCTION

IF you ask people for the name of probably the world's most translated writer,[1] the popular writer to have increased in reputation the most over more than a century, you will get some surprising answers. If you further enquire as to the identity of the only Frenchman apart from Napoleon to have achieved universal renown, some odd looks may be forthcoming.

Verne, Nemo, and the *Nautilus* have entered the world's collective unconscious; but the only visible signs of their existence, dragged up from the murky depths, are invariably confused. These apologies for a reputation need to be put out of their misery. Thus Verne cannot be considered a science-fiction writer; he did not wish to write for children; the poor style often associated with him is not his. And Captain Nemo does not speak with a mid-Atlantic drawl.

In order to understand how such ideas came to life, primarily in America and Britain, we should start by briefly examining the author's life and the publishing history of *Twenty Thousand Leagues under the Seas*.

Jules Verne was born and brought up in Nantes, studied and worked in Paris, and spent the rest of his life in Amiens. His first known foreign visits were to Scotland in 1859 and Norway in 1861, experiences which deeply marked him. From about 1870 Verne displayed an increasing pessimism about many of his early enthusiasms, with the admiration for technology replaced by apprehension on social and political issues, and with the 'Anglo-Saxons', the heroes of his first novels, sometimes now the villains. The Franco-Prussian War may have been one of the catalysts for the change. *The Chancellor* (written in about 1870, but published in 1873) was the clear turning-point; but signs of uneasiness are already visible in *Twenty Thousand Leagues*.

At the beginning, recognition for the series of the *Extraordinary Journeys* was slow in the English-speaking countries. The first novels to be translated appeared after Verne had already written most of his best work. It must have been disappointing for the author of *The British*

---

[1] On a cumulative basis since 1850; Unesco's *Index Translationum* lists the number of new translations appearing worldwide each year.

at the North Pole to see this book unavailable in Britain itself. But when the works did begin to appear, it might have been better if they had not.

The books were sometimes radically altered. The translators, frequently anonymous, were not always fully competent in French. In the process, they produced some wonderful howlers: the hero visits the 'disagreeable territories of Nebraska' or 'jumps over' part of an island; reference is made to 'prunes' or 'Galilee'; and Napoleon dies broken-hearted in 'St Helen's'. Verne himself wrote of 'the Badlands', 'blowing up', 'plums', 'Galileo', and 'St Helena'. If we examine in particular *Twenty Thousand Leagues* (written in 1868–9, published in 1869–70), there have been thousands of editions of this work, possibly making the English version the most frequently published novel of all time. Lewis Mercier's 1872 translation was typical of the time: adequate on 'style' but extremely weak on details. Also, about 22 per cent of the novel was missing! Since then, the majority of editions have reproduced Mercier, many of them making further minor changes, unfortunately without referring back to the French.

There has also traditionally been a low level of critical commentary on the *Extraordinary Journeys* in the English-speaking world, sometimes the result of monolinguals studying these inaccurate translations. Nor has the basic textual work been done, in either English or French. The different original editions of *Vingt mille lieues sous les mers* have hardly been compared; to date no one has studied the manuscripts in detail; and there is no established text, meaning that we should be wary even of modern French editions.

Twenty Thousand Leagues is Verne's most ambitious work in terms of themes and psychology. (Readers who do not wish to learn details of the plot are advised to omit the rest of the Introduction.) It recounts a circumnavigation of the globe by submarine, with Nemo ('nobody' in Latin) as the sombre hero. It includes many dramatic episodes: the underwater burial of a dead crewman, an attack by Papuan natives, a battle with giant squid, a passage under the Antarctic ice-cap, a farewell to the sun at the South Pole, and a vision among the underwater ruins of Atlantis. But much of the interest comes from the intense if distant relationship between Nemo and his passengers, Dr Aronnax, Conseil, and Ned Land, and from the anguish gripping the captain. Nemo seems to have an unhealthy interest in shipping lanes and vessels in distress. On one occasion he imprisons Aronnax in a cell. Further mysteries are the portraits in his room of nationalist figures and of a woman and children, later revealed to be his murdered family. At the end of the novel the captain is attacked by an unidentified ship, and responds by sinking it. The three guests escape as the *Nautilus* fights the Maelstrom.

Verne's mastery of the genre is demonstrated by the interlocking and superimposing literary devices and the many vibrant episodes presenting new settings. The number of themes is also impressive: technology of course, biology, the study of the seas, exploration of unknown areas, life on desert islands, history, biblical themes, mythical ideas, even international politics. The characters, too, are more complex than in many of Verne's works.

Inspiration

Much of the inspiration for *Twenty Thousand Leagues* came from Verne's own experience. He was born on an island in a major slave port; and while preparing the book he consulted his brother Paul, a retired naval officer. In the late spring of 1868 he bought a fishing-boat of 8 or 10 tons, which he claimed to use as a study while sailing along the Normandy and Brittany coasts. In September he sailed to Gravesend, where he wrote: 'How beautiful [the scenery] is and what fuel for the imagination!' [19 August 1868].[2]

For two scenes, Nemo's elevated surveying of the ruins of Atlantis and his claiming of the new continent of Antarctica, the author may be drawing inspiration from the King's Park in Edinburgh. On Verne's second day outside France, the volcanic Arthur's Seat dominating the park was the first mountain he had visited. Imbued as he was with Scott and Romanticism, in love with this exotic land, he generated a sublime vision from the classical and marine view. Equally surprisingly, Nemo's plumbing, furnishings, and general life-style in the heart of the raging depths may be drawn from Verne's visit a couple of days later to a rain-swept but luxurious 'château' in Oakley, Fife. Verne seems indeed to be hinting at the Scottish source when he shows Nemo at

[2] The correspondence cited—in abbreviated form—follows Olivier Dumas, Piero Gondolo della Riva, and Volker Dehs, eds, *Correspondance inédite de Jules Verne et de Pierre-Jules Hetzel, 1863–1886*, vol. 1 (Geneva: Slatkine, 1999); the dates they attribute are sometimes subject to caution.

the organ, 'only us[ing] the black keys, giving his melodies an essentially Scottish tonality'—in *Journey to England and Scotland* (1859–60), Verne's friend 'Amelia', a young hostess who guides and enchants him, had similarly recommended 'play[ing] using only the black keys' (ch. 24).

Verne's other sources are wide-ranging, taken from literature, science, geography, and history, and are often openly acknowledged. In 1865 the novelist George Sand suggested to Verne that the sea was the one area of the globe where his 'scientific knowledge and imagination' had not yet been put to use. There is clear influence from the Bible, Hugo, Michelet, Scott, and Poe. *Moby-Dick* presents many affinities in details and plot (see Appendix 2: Sources, which includes full references).

The most important non-literary sources are the scientists and popularizers Maury, Figuier, Mangin, Agassiz, and Renard. Many of the naturalists *Twenty Thousand Leagues* quotes, including Buffon, Gratiolet, Lacépède, Milne-Edwards, d'Orbigny, Quatrefages, and Tournefort, were researchers at the Museum of Natural History in Paris, like Dr Aronnax. Although the novel cites one contemporary encounter with a giant squid (at the time dismissed by science), an unquoted source, Denys de Montfort, is probably the main origin of the captain's epic battle. The life of Nemo himself may be based partly on Gustave Flourens, a French scientist and international freedom-fighter.

Many commentaries have concentrated on the originality of the *Nautilus*, but it should be emphasized that Verne's technology was not innovative. The captain's presentation of his vessel provides more than enough information about its length and girth, but his only explanation of its motive power is in terms of an electricity which is 'not the commonly used sort', multiplied by 'a system of levers'! Submarine craft had in any case been used in the American War of Independence and Civil War; and there were even submarine vessels named *Nautilus*, including one the author must have seen on his visit to the Paris Universal Exposition of 1867. At least three books with titles like *Journey to the Bottom of the Sea* and *The Submarine World* were published in France in 1867–9 alone. So crowded indeed were the deeps that Verne feared being accused of plagiarism.

The novelist himself was categorical: 'I am not in any way the inventor of submarine navigation.' He even claimed he was 'never particularly interested in science', only in creating dramatic stories in exotic parts. Amongst the tales of submarines, only Verne's has survived—undoubtedly because of the living nature of his text. His originality lies in his unbridled *literary* imagination.

Inception

The book seems to have been planned over a considerable period. The correspondence, predominantly with his lifelong publisher, Jules Hetzel, shows what Verne considers the novel to be about, and reveals his mounting excitement:

I'm also preparing our *Journey under the Waters*, and my brother and I are arranging all the mechanics needed for the expedition. I think we'll use electricity, but it's still not completely decided. (10 August [1866])

After 15 months of abstinence [while writing *Geography of France* (1867)], my brain greatly needs to burst: so much the better for the *Journey under the Waters*, there will be abundance, and I promise to have myself a great time. [29 July 1867]

In about March 1868, Verne began writing his most ambitious book. Over the next few months, his excitement continues to grow at the idea of what he called the 'unknown man' and the 'perfect' subject:

I'm deep in *Journey under the Waters*. | I'm working on it with tremendous pleasure . . . I very much want this machine to be as perfect as possible. [10 March 1868, to his father]

This unknown man must no longer have any contact with humanity . . . He's not on *earth* any more . . . the sea must provide him with everything, *clothing and food* . . . Were the continents and islands to vanish in a new Flood, he'd live the same way, and I beg you to believe that his ark will be a bit better equipped than Noah's . . . I've never held a better thing in my hands. [28 March 1868]

What is difficult is to make things that are highly implausible seem very plausible. [23 July 1868]

Oh the perfect subject, my dear Hetzel, the perfect subject! [11 August 1868]

It is certainly serious, very unexpected, and no one has ever done anything like it before. [14 August 1868]

In addition to the novel as 'machine', we may note the metaphor of what Verne heatedly holds in his hands and the 'abundance' of his textual production. But we can also observe the emphasis on sea-based self-sufficiency and the biblical reference.

In the autumn of that year, Verne submitted the first volume to Hetzel, with the proofs ready at year's end. From the end of April until mid-June 1869, however, the publisher sent a series of harrowing letters about the second volume, very critical especially of the ending.[3]

The number and severity of the changes the publisher proposed or imposed can be seen by reading the second of the two manuscripts. These complex questions, which go to the very heart of the novel, and which mean that the published version must be considered fundamentally flawed, are studied in the Explanatory Notes and Appendix 1.

The Nautilus

One initial way of coping with the complexity of the novel is simply to study the behaviour of the submarine. Its very freedom and power mean that, to create tension, it must encounter dangers of some sort. Most of the threats to its shiny self-containment fall into four categories: perforation, invasion, immobilization, or suffocation. (Mechanical problems are out of the question. That the hatch might let in water never seems to cross anybody's mind, either.)

Thus it risks rupture by man's most advanced ballistic technology or by massed sperm whales and intrusion by giant squid. The most frequent problem, however, is that the 'cigar-shape' has an uncontrollable desire to slip into passages for which 'it's too big', as Farragut's sailors put it. This enables it to reach its home base via an underwater tunnel and to find the passage connecting the Red Sea to the Mediterranean, and hence to visit the seven seas without retracing its steps. But under the ice-cap its bold thrusting creates dangers, as the submarine manages to get into a tunnel which is not only closed at both ends but shrinking by the hour. In another episode, potentially involving all four dangers, it chooses to pass through the 'most dangerous strait on the globe', duly gets stuck on the rocks, and attracts hundreds of natives.

---

[3] Another irritation was that, after Verne had finished the book, Hetzel casually suggested adding a new volume to increase its length by half, rather like a butcher measuring out sausage. To achieve this, he wrote on 25 April 1869, episodes could easily be added, such as the escape, capture, and reconciliation of one of the guests, an episode involving John Brown (the abolitionist murdered in 1859), or a scene where Nemo could save a few Chinese boys from Chinese pirates and keep one on the *Nautilus*, thus 'cheering things up on board'! Fortunately, the ideas were not implemented.

Getting into so many scrapes does imply that something is going on. At the beginning, when the *Nautilus* keeps exposing itself to ships, rubbing up against them, or even penetrating them, the captain may indeed be drawing attention to his marvellous equipment. But Nemo also has a secret agenda that will become slightly clearer only at the end.

The *Nautilus* conditions the whole structure of the novel. Because of its hothouse atmosphere and Nemo's aversion to setting foot on land, those occasions when he does leave the submarine are all the more heightened. During such episodes, Aronnax has to be there as well, to tell the tale; but Conseil and Ned are often excluded. Typical is Nemo's sudden night-time invitation to visit the underwater realm in diving suits. This poetic adventure is worth studying in detail.

Atlantis

Aronnax is fidgety from the start. He jumps when he hears rain pattering on the surface and feels acutely conscious of his leaden feet crunching a 'bed of bones'. He wonders at the giant furrows on the ocean floor, the distant glow, and the clearings in the petrified forest. His over-excited mind starts imagining castles and cities—even seabed friends for the captain. His photographic vision sees everything in fine black-and-white silhouette and his movements are light: leaping tree trunks, snapping creepers, flying over chasms. Aronnax's exaltation, Nemo's pace, and the imperfect tense produce a strange mood. A metaphor converts the sea back into land, the living into the man-made, tentacles into brush, and crabs and lobsters into suits of armour. After a climb up a volcano, after the vegetable and animal kingdoms have led the way up the Great Chain of Beings, Aronnax again imagines human works.

But an eruption suddenly steals the scene—revealing a glowing sunken city. In an elegiac vision and the longest sentence of the book, teasing glimpses appear of technology and religion, Greece and Tuscany, triremes and temples, even a sea within the sea. All this provides an unusual chance for Nemo and Aronnax to communicate in depth, for although they cannot talk, they do touch, speak through their eyes, and even use the intimate second-person singular form; above all, Nemo uses a convenient piece of chalk and rock-wall to write the briefest of messages: 'ATLANTIS'.

Feverish as he is, Aronnax runs through the whole gamut of legends about the lost continent. He conjures up, pell-mell, biblical and pre-historic scenes, a land bridge to America, the giant contemporaries of the first man. He conflates geological, biblical, and mythological time to return to the origins where, paradoxically, man was at his most evolved. But he is careful to leave his mark on the living past, subtly smudging the backdrop so as to prove to himself that it is not a dream. The transcendental scene closes with the footlights on a rare relaxed Nemo. He is 'leaning on a mossy stele', as if on his reading desk, contemplating time past, empathetically 'turned to stone' in 'his' landscape. 'Was it here that this strange being came to commune with history and relive ancient life—he who wanted nothing to do with modern times?'

And this is the Verne who has been argued to be a positivist, a scientific apologist, a blind technological anticipator! He is in fact a high Romantic, with his poetic language, nostalgia, and mystical yearning for significance. The grandeur of the novel comes not only from the many 'privileged' locations the submarine takes us to but from its reference to a higher destiny.

Lists

The structure of *Twenty Thousand Leagues* is punctuated—punctured?—by many long lists. Even the paroxysm of Atlantis is interrupted at the vital moment by the eruption of names of authors on the lost continent. The lists apocryphally made the poet Apollinaire exclaim, half in admiration: 'What a style! Nothing but substantives!' There are indeed a bewildering number of common and proper nouns in the novel.

In the carefully crafted opening chapter about the 'monster' terrorizing the seas, ambiguity is already maximized between fact and fiction, persistent legend and documented reports, authorial information and the narrator's misinformation. The lists are similarly a massive importation of real-world documentation, proof that Verne has done his homework, a guarantee of seriousness or plausibility. On another level, nevertheless, they are devoid of significance. A procession of obscure fish hardly advances the plot. Scientific knowledge does not consist merely of the names of scientists, nor exploration, of those of explorers.

Although Verne's lists may no longer have the resonances they had for a contemporary French reader, some do provide an archaeology of knowledge. The substantives often come from Verne's sources, to which he adds adjectives and context. The resurgence at the South Pole of Nemo's romantic, rebellious ecstasy is again suspended by the quoting of authorities on the question. Complete with date, nationality, and successively greater latitudes, they provide a structured but reductionist history of Antarctica.

Hidden amongst the names of the pro-Atlanteans are allusions to Bailly's notions of a tropical Atlantis at a North Pole heated by exhalations from the Earth's core; and to Malte-Brun, from whom Verne undoubtedly derived the idea of going 'around the world in eighty days'. His passing mention of George Sand may acknowledge an inspiration for the novel; his reference to 'Edom' again points to biblical influence, and thence to a brilliant short story of that title published in 1910 under his name.

Characters

Another way of approaching the complexity of *Twenty Thousand Leagues* is to study the characters themselves. Their number is severely curtailed: apart from the four main protagonists and Captain Farragut, no speaking part survives for more than a paragraph or so. Nor does a single woman feature in the work, apart from Nemo's dead and nameless wife: the painter Rosa Bonheur and a painting of a 'courtesan' were deleted at proof stage. Even the ships' names, including the submarine's, are in masculine mode.

As Roland Barthes has brilliantly noted, Verne's vehicles provide a near-absolute division of the world. On the exterior can be interplanetary space, flowing lava, or murderous savages, but within all is calm, security, food, and—in *Twenty Thousand Leagues*—the world's 12,000 best books. Nemo, Aronnax, Conseil, and Ned inhabit a closed universe. As in Pinter or Beckett, the submarine is the *in camera* locus for the intensive interaction of the four possible threesomes and the five pairs: only Nemo and Conseil never communicate with each other.

Verne's first-person narrators seem shadowy sorts of people. They are generally middle-class and comfortably off, a similar age to the author, and long-term travellers without family or attachments. Most come from hard-nosed professions like journalism or science, with their work their publication. They exist to narrate, and narrate to exist.

Aronnax is no exception. He is practical, serious, cautious, detached, unimaginative, characterized indeed by what he himself calls his 'cowardice' and 'complete negativity'. Or, as Nemo tells him, 'you only see snags and obstacles'. The doctor mainly serves to organize knowledge, to ask naïve questions, to act as a foil, and to transcribe Conseil's classifications. Even his manservant is sometimes livelier, with his acrobatic ability to ascend and descend the biological hierarchy; he alerts his master when unduly hypocritical or intellectually lazy.

If nothing else, Aronnax is systematic. He is an adept of Linnaeus's binomial taxonomy, with its 'phyla, divisions, classes, sub-classes, orders, families, genera, sub-genera, species, and varieties'. His deductions follow sequences of branching alternatives, separating the known knowns from the unknown unknowns, order from chaos. He considers many objects whose shape is a branching 'arborescence': spiders, squid, and especially coral, characterized by its multiple 'branches', 'ramifications', and 'arborizations'. His science, in other words, has the same positivistic structure as many of the objects it studies.

Just as Aronnax's lists attempt to cram everything in, so his classifications go down to the finest detail. Everything inside is neatly labelled, as in Nemo's museum; but the unintelligible or uncontrollable are banished. His systems give up in panic on encountering the new. The good doctor exhaustively picks over the meagre details of Nemo's visible life, often revising his perceptions, but cannot answer any of the essential questions about him. What he lacks is the ability to connect, to go beyond. Creativity is absent from his reproductive, convergent mind-set. He is almost schizophrenic in his attempt to abolish the murky subconscious and to conceal his lack of invention. Perhaps his real problem is a fear of writer's block?

Aronnax exploits his position as narrator. Thus he only notices the body being carried on the crewmen's shoulders after two hours underwater; and he does not spot the portraits of Nemo's heroes and family until his second and third visits to his bedroom. In his discussion with Ned about the monster, the uneducated sailor is a model of accuracy while the scientist's affirmations are dubious. The naturalist is conditioned by his immediate impressions, which he does not correct when he records his notes or writes them up. An unreliable narrator is an unusual feature in the popular literature of the nineteenth century. Many readers will give Aronnax the benefit of doubt—but may have to think again before the end of the novel.

The plot may leave the reader confused on first reading. All information is filtered through Aronnax's first-person narration, and although his observations attempt to be scrupulously exact, his forecasts are invariably wildly out. Many of the events of the novel are indeed beyond the ken of a naïve bachelor from a sheltered background. The episodes of Atlantis, the underwater burial, and the Maelstrom are typical in being misinterpreted by him until nearly the end—when it is too late to study the evidence. The central enigma, above all, remains unsolved, for we never know Nemo's real name or nationality, his past life, or his reason for going round sinking ships—apart, that is, from self-defence.

Verne thus has the best of both worlds. Aronnax's stolidity lends credibility to his fantastic descriptions. But his unreliable interpretations conceal the captain's nature until the end. Nemo's wish not to be 'judged' is respected, for we only see him tête-à-tête with Aronnax and so never have an objective basis for assessing him.

Nemo

What we do know about the captain is that he shares many of the characteristics of Verne's heroes, who emulate Renaissance man in the variety of their intellectual, physical, and cultural qualities. Evans neatly sums these up as: 'courage, aesthetic sensitivity, idealism, devotion to justice, humor, thirst for glory, compassion, love of freedom, and "grandeur" in general'.[4] But Nemo and other heroes also have paranoid and self-destructive tendencies: abrupt withdrawals alternating with impassioned speeches or cold anger.

From the beginning, conflict is probable. Aronnax, Conseil, and Land arrive uninvited on the submarine, indeed as part of an attempt to destroy it. As Nemo explains, his only choices are to betray the secret of his life, throw them back into the sea, or take them in for ever. One reason for his decision is that he already knows Aronnax from his learned work, *The Mysteries of the Ocean Deeps* (c. 1865?). But he appears disappointed by the man behind the book. In any case, the two have opposing interests: Nemo's, to conceal information about his mission; Aronnax's, to gather it for his next book.

---

[4] Arthur B. Evans, *Jules Verne Rediscovered: Didacticism and the Scientific Novel* (New York: Greenwood Press, 1988), 75.

The Frenchman gets off on the wrong foot. Nemo intones: 'Our voyage of underwater exploration begins at this precise moment.' Aronnax (or perhaps Hetzel) replies: 'May God protect us!' The remark is unflattering for the submarine, untactfully religious—and results in the captain taking his leave. Nemo will repeat his sharp exit after his ardent speech about an under-sea utopia, and indeed whenever his guest appears lacking in understanding.

Aronnax apparently embodies Nemo's social life, for the captain seldom goes out—and Conseil and Ned never come in. His only external contacts seem to be wordless signs to a diver, dreams of launching a message-in-a-bottle, and violent interchanges with passing ships. Outside his submarine he is only too aware of humanity's depredations and unprovoked attacks; within his bedroom he appears anguished, lost in mathematical calculations or memories of his heroes or family. Even on the platform Nemo is less than welcoming, perhaps because it is part of his workplace or because Conseil and Ned are often there. Although Aronnax visits him in his room, with unfortunate results, the captain almost never goes to his and rarely seeks out the naturalist's company.

One exception is when Aronnax is about to escape, having already put on his coat. On this occasion Nemo takes deliberate pleasure in spinning out the conversation, leading even the doctor to wonder whether his plans have been discovered. The captain chooses this precise occasion not only to reveal his financial contributions to the 'oppressed races' and especially the Cretans, but also to invite him to visit Atlantis—which persuades Aronnax to stay after all.

Stretching out on the sofa is Nemo's only relaxed posture. The huge ship's library is the only place where he and Aronnax can freely meet. Unlike later heroes, Nemo has none of Verne's books, despite his collection of 'the modern and ancient masters': indeed, there are virtually no nineteenth-century novelists. The library—the true control room of the submarine—may contain hints of Verne's father's study or of Hetzel's bookshop in the Latin Quarter; in any case it symbolizes established authority. Hetzel was himself a well-known writer, older than Verne. The presence within Nemo's library of Aronnax's volumes reflects this complex relationship. It also focuses two connected tensions: change and stasis; and reproduction and creativity.

The yellowing newspapers are a sign of the problem. Like the prehistoric but nineteenth-century cavern in *Journey to the Centre of the*

Earth, Nemo's library is both brand-new and classical, contemporary and *passé*. New books are of course no longer arriving. Nemo claims that the concept of 'modern artist' no longer exists for him: they are out of time or else 'two or three thousand years old'; he is an exile in time or a time-traveller. His decision to halt his world is a conscious one: 'I would like to believe that humanity has thought or written nothing since then' (I 11—Part One, chapter 11). The captain uses 'you' to mean Aronnax or France but also for 'terrestrial' or 'living' objects. Everything is perfect in his library, the perfection of death. His timeless existence means that he too is 'dead', as he himself implies. And the tragedy of the living-dead is that, although eternally young, they are prone, like Rider Haggard's She, to topple over into exponentially accelerating decay.

The library is stranded uneasily between the 1865 newspapers and an adolescent or artistic eternity. The only disruption to the sterile stasis would be by creative works. Aronnax asks Nemo whether he is an 'artist', who seems to reply in the affirmative, but then paraphrases it as being a mere collector: creation is tantamount to accumulation. But in fact Nemo does write. For a start, he annotates Aronnax's book, but this was perhaps done in the past. As in a Beckett endgame, however, the slightest sign of change must be sought, the most round-about route out of the existential cul-de-sac. The notes may form an embryo of Nemo's story or even of Aronnax's next book, for both men eventually admit to writing first-person sea tales. Both authors look as though they might have no readers (except each other?); both books may indeed end up in the sea whence they came; and neither volume can admit to its title or its author's name. Writing is a secretive, even shameful activity.

Other aspects of Nemo's character develop more slowly. Although most of the incidents initially puzzle Aronnax, many are in fact connected: hindsight (and a good memory) are required to put the plot back together again at the end.

More of Nemo's deeds are going to be influenced by Aronnax's presence than he will admit. One example is the decision to open the hatches when the submarine is grounded and covered with aggressive-looking Papuans. The result, predictably, is an invasion, soon repelled by administering an electric shock. But there is little reason to open the hatches so soon before leaving—apart from a wish to impress the Frenchman. The scene is more surprising when juxtaposed with

Aronnax's pompous but humane remarks about merely retaliating against 'savages'. It anticipates the killing at the end of Part Two, which in turn echoes the incidents with the liners in the opening chapter. 'A pure accident,' says Nemo of the collision with the *Scotia*. Possibly, but he omits to account for those with the *Moravian* and the *Etna*.

Equally unclear is Nemo's attitude towards Aronnax. He often ignores his presence; and at the end knocks a telescope out of his hand. Aronnax decides that he is not the object of the hatred, on the debatable basis that Nemo is not looking at him. Common sense will tell us that when confronted with an unwelcome guest, a man without friends or intellectual equals is likely to oscillate between extremes, that any apparent indifference may be feigned. On the other hand, there are occasions when the captain does seem unaware of the naturalist; and his last words, 'God almighty! Enough! Enough!', sound sincere enough. But does Nemo dislike his guest enough to wish his death? If we think Nemo is aware after all of the evasion plans, is it impossible that the captain hopes his captives will go, but chooses for them the spot 'from which no ship has ever been able to escape'?

The ultimate mysteries, carefully built up in the episode when Aronnax is secretly drugged, are the motive for Nemo's attacks and the nationalities of his adversaries. Revenge may possibly be at work, but in the published version the rest of the evidence is inconclusive.

Nemo thus remains an enigmatic figure—we do not even know who he eats with. His chosen crew reflect him in being anonymous, mute, repressed. Only at the end do we discover that these blank, interchangeable ciphers actively support Nemo's campaign. But it is still not clear why many different nationalities are apparently represented on board.

In sum, we know very little about Nemo. In an interview in 1903 Verne described him as 'a misanthropist', and, in a letter in 1894, as 'confining himself in his [*Nautilus*]'; but this does not get us much further. What determines his route? Why has he not visited either Pole before? Does he try to influence his depiction in Aronnax's ongoing book?

Like the number of Lady Macbeth's children, questions as to Nemo's nature and the meaning of the novel are virtually unanswerable, because of the narrator's very presence on board. As with a married couple, Aronnax and Nemo's behaviour cannot be separated out: each action is modified by those of the other half, each variable in the interactive equation is fed back in, each conclusion seems undermined by its complementary opposite. Narrator and narratee are in symbiosis. Nemo-as-seen-by-Aronnax cannot be broken down.

Many of the enigmas of course serve to displace the author's unanswered questions on to the characters. What seems probable is that Verne himself feels torn between the captain and his guest. He identifies with Aronnax in his logical and systematic aspects, but with Nemo in his imagination, energy, and freedom. Equally probable is that the clash of personalities reflects the slightly incestuous relationship between Verne and Hetzel. The intense but secretive writing activities on board the submarine ultimately result in an overabundance of manuscripts, proofs, and letters flying forth between the two. Hetzel's blue pencil may be connected with Aronnax's literalness and 'realism', but his exile in Belgium may correspond to Nemo's political idealism.

The Question of Nationalities

Like Phileas Fogg, who flies over France without a single mention, the submarine crosses the Mediterranean without giving it a single glimpse. Then in another flash we are transported past Verne's beloved northern France. The only indication, itself ambiguous, is: 'we were passing near the mouth of the English Channel' (II 22). But even this short remark is unusual, because Verne never depicts France or its surroundings in his novels published with Hetzel.[5]

Admittedly, Aronnax climbs aboard the *Abraham Lincoln* with the thought of heading to his native country; Nemo goes so far as to mention 'the ten billion francs of France's debts' (I 13); the Marquesas and the Gambier group are described as French, although Aronnax hardly sees them. Certainly metropolitan France is mentioned several times in the novel, but as a distant past or an impossible dream.

This absence is linked to another, that of the nationality of Nemo and his crew, the secret key to his campaign and his exile from inhabited lands. In the novel many clues are strewn, which however point in every direction.[6]

---

[5] Among the rare exceptions is chapter 2 of *The Begum's Fortune* (1879), whose original manuscript was not by Verne.

[6] In *The Mysterious Island* (1874), Verne, under great pressure from Hetzel, claims that the captain has been Indian all along, but the idea simply does not make sense at this stage.

The exception is the climax. In the published version of II 20, the *Nautilus* passes Land's End to port. It eventually locates the *Vengeur* and Nemo declaims the glory of the scuttled ship's cause. In the waters west of Nantes, a 'great warship with a ram: an armour-plated double-decker' (II 21) attacks the *Nautilus* for no apparent reason, which lures it eastwards. Nemo intones 'I am the law, I am the justice! . . . I am the oppressed, and they are the oppressor!'—then sends his submarine clean through the vessel. As a horrified Aronnax watches the sailors' death-throes, the chapter closes.

The doctor belatedly raises the question of the warship's national-ity. The position of the sinking seems significant; the captain himself attributes the ship to 'an accursed nation' (II 21), appearing amazed that the doctor does not realize which one. Indeed, the only warships in the world to comply with this description are of French construc-tion and nationality, with an instantly recognizable shape.

If the attackers are French, what nationality would Nemo be? At the end of the 1860s, the Franco-British wars are a distant memory. Perhaps the obvious opponents of Napoleon III's Empire are French-men, among them famous personalities, like Hugo, Hetzel, or Verne himself. In sum, the closing chapters indirectly imply the same nation-ality for the captain.

Nemo claims to know French, English, German, and Latin, in that order; his declamatory soliloquies are in the language of Racine. His books, fiction or otherwise, as well as his musical taste and his quotations and allusions, are predominantly French. He studied in France, among other places. He emphasizes the existence of the Paris meridian; the crew member lifted aloft by the giant squid cries spontaneously in French. The captain seems to be especially inter-ested in the French navy at the Battle of Vigo Bay; his sympathy for the *Vengeur* is evident; the submarine's route seems to be designed to culminate in the Channel.

In sum, Verne's intention in the published version of the book could be twofold. On the one hand, according to its description, the frigate is French, as is perhaps Nemo himself.

But, on the other hand, by scattering contradictory clues through-out the novel, Verne tries to avoid any clear identification of national-ity and thus create a stateless, or universal, captain, like his name and his ship. His life is devoted to the last areas without a master, perhaps without God, in any case without a flag—except his own.

Conclusion

Exile, intertextuality, atemporality. The 'unknown man' yearns for both the future and the past, but stands outside his own period. The captain's technology is well in advance of its time, enabling him to discover a new continent or two. His social vision seems futuristic, his causes espouse the tide of history. He is anti-slavery, internationalist, individualist, rationalist, against entrenched privilege and intellectual sloth. But if he is so much of a modern, why does a whiff of nostalgia still hang about him, an air of things we shall not see again? Part of the answer may lie in the all-embracing nature of his talents, but also in his unwillingness to use social means to effect change, his reluctance to get involved. Even at the time, his mysterious cause could be seen to be a losing battle, his way of life a dead end.

But part of the answer may also lie in our own ahistorical perspective, our post-everything-ness. We no longer believe that an individual can change the world, or even defy humanity for long. The *Nautilus* would have been reverse-engineered or turned into a tourist attraction. Nemo is a prisoner of his era. He has a Quixotic and classical soul, but we feel we have got past all that. We believe we have absorbed the Byronic and '68 rebellions: we are all post-revolutionaries now, at least in stylistic externals.

Nemo's principled refusal to set foot on the inhabited continents exemplifies the *Extraordinary Journeys*. The series can only prosper by visiting virgin territories; but the quicker they are deflowered, the sooner the subject will be exhausted. *Twenty Thousand Leagues under the Seas* occupies the fatal point of no return: the dark continent and the North Pole have already been done, snapshots taken of the dark side of the moon. The ocean deeps and the South Pole form the ultima Thule of a certain mode of being and writing. The *Nautilus* can only be the end of the line.

Nemo is the last outlaw. He is in a geographico-historical cul-de-sac, and the absolutism of his fight cannot be permanent. He is suspended between George Stephenson and R. L. Stevenson, born too late or too early, post-Romantic but pre-modern. The captain's oceanic freedom is a mortgage on things to come. Technologically-inspired rebellion forms a rapidly shrinking option for meridionals in the 1870s, but Nemo's passion for music and the sea are surely destined to be eternal.

NOTE ON THE TEXT AND TRANSLATION

For this edition the translation has been systematically revised. The Introduction, Note on the Text and Translation, and many of the Explanatory Notes in the original 1998 edition have largely been retained; but the Chronology, Select Bibliography, and Appendices have been updated or replaced.

The Three Main Editions

Twenty Thousand Leagues under the Seas first appeared in fortnightly instalments in the *Magasin d'éducation et de récréation* (*MÉR*) from 20 March 1869 to 20 June 1870, with the subtitle 'Submarine Tour of the World' ('Tour du monde sous-marin'). Its structure seems to reflect its initial publication; however, Verne complained that the novel was 'fragmented' by the serialization, which often changed length. What is more, Hetzel used the pretext of the juvenile audience of the *MÉR* to impose changes to the text.[1]

The *MÉR* publication of 1869 had a dedication on the first page, which was never reprinted. Although signed 'Jules Verne', it is rather patronizing, and Hetzel may have contributed to it.

The first volume of the first book edition, 18mo without illustrations, was placed on sale on 28 October 1869, but the second one only on 13 June 1870. The large octavo edition, with 111 illustrations by Riou and de Neuville, appeared on 16 November 1871.

Astonishingly, there has never been an attempt to explicitly identify and publish the canonical Hetzel edition, in the sense of the text most revised by the author (and astonishingly, this is probably not in fact the celebrated octavo edition, the basis for all modern publications).[2]

---

[1] In the *MÉR* of 5 September 1867 it was falsely announced that 'M. Jules Verne is putting the more or less final touches to a book which will be the most extraordinary of all, a *Journey under the Waters*. Six months spent beside the sea, in total retreat, have been necessary for the conscientious and dramatic writer to collect together the materials for this curious book.'

[2] The occurrences of typographic symbols [in the second manuscript, to indicate the ends of successive typesetters' work, invariably correspond to the ends of lines in the octavo edition, which shows that the first proofs were also in the octavo format. The *MÉR* and 18mo editions, although published first, must therefore have been

Again, there has been no systematic initiative to identify mistakes in the various editions, often in the spelling, but occasionally touching on the syntax.

The Present Translation

The text here normally adheres to the Presses Pocket one (1991), which generally follows the 1871 edition.[3] This translation is an entirely original one, benefiting from the most recent scholarship on Verne and closely following the French text.

There are perhaps 2,000 rare words and proper names in the French edition, but more than 100 are incorrect. The policy here is to amend clear spelling mistakes in real-world names and dictionary words, plus simple arithmetic mistakes—in other words, changes that can easily be made within a single word or number—often noting such changes. However, substantive information will not be amended, even when clearly erroneous, although generally identified in the notes.

Verne often Gallicizes proper names and words. Thus he (or his editor) writes 'the *Castillan*' for 'the *Castilian*', 'the *Albermale*' for 'the *Albermarle*', 'oaze' for 'ooze', or 'ice-blinck' for 'ice-blink'. Even some of the French terms he uses have not been located, such as 'déponté' ('with its cover off'); others seem to be erroneous, such as 'crécelles' ('screechings') for 'crécerelles' ('kestrels').

Geographical Information

Verne is not always consistent, using for example 'Bourbon' and 'Réunion' for the same island. In many cases obsolete names have been replaced here.[4]

---

produced from the descendants of these proofs—and as a result are often more intensively corrected.

[3] Although modern French editions have invariably followed the illustrated 1871 edition, its text seems on balance slightly inferior to the unillustrated 18mo editions.

[4] 'Propontis' by 'the Sea of Marmara', 'the Asphaltite Sea' by 'the Dead Sea', 'the Sandwich Islands' by 'Hawaii', 'New Holland' by 'Australia', 'Viti' by 'Fiji', 'the New Hebrides' by 'Vanuatu', 'Lazarev Island' by 'Matahiva', 'Clermont-Tonnerre' by 'Reao', 'the Friendly Islands' by 'Tonga', 'Navigators Islands' by 'Samoa', and 'Edo' by 'Tokyo'; but not for instance 'Ceylon' by 'Sri Lanka'. A relatively traditional spelling system is used.

A number of Verne's names are erroneous, like 'Liarrov' for 'Lyakhov', 'Hadramant' for 'Hadramaut', '*Paramatta*' for '*Parramatta*', 'Kittan' for 'Kiltan', or 'Arfalxs' for 'Arfak'. This is confirmed by variant spellings (both 'Tikipia' and 'Tikopia') and what must be total misreadings, such as 'Captain Bell on the *Minerve*' for 'Captain Bellingshausen on the *Mirny*'.

Despite emphasizing the political importance of the difference between the Paris and Greenwich meridians (I 14), Verne often uses one or the other indiscriminately. In any case many of the coordinates quoted are approximate or simply wrong, such as those for Fiji and Vanuatu (I 19). Other information is occasionally as unreliable. Thus a direction cannot be 'east-north-easterly' and then still 'north-north-east' (I 14–15); the '476-fathom-high Mount Kapogo' (I 19) reaches at most 810 metres; 'Mannar Island, whose rounded shape loomed to the south' (II 3) should probably read 'the north'; 'the eastern point of the Gulf of Carpentaria' (I 23) should read 'western'; and the crater above Nemo's home port is described as '500 or 600 metres high' but then 'not . . . more than 800 feet' (II 10).

Verne says 'The British foot is only 30.40 cm long' (I 1), but this seems to be a slip for 30.48. In any case, he uses both French and British feet and miles. (Perhaps as a result, the depth required to increase underwater pressure by 1 atmosphere is quoted as both '30 feet' and '32'.) He uses leagues 'of four kilometres' (II 7)—French land ones (whereas an English league is three miles, or 4.8 kilometres). No adjustment has been made here to measures, since otherwise the title would become something like *Sixteen Thousand Six Hundred and Sixty-Seven Leagues under the Seas*!

Marine Terminology

Verne often uses the vague term of 'poulpe', corresponding to the obsolete English 'poulp' or 'polyp' and including both squid and octopus. However, the contextual information indicates that he is probably thinking of squid. One exception is when he says that 'Bouyer's squid' has eight, rather than ten, tentacles: a perhaps understandable slip, for the animal was not even recognized by scientists at the time.

The long lists of names of marine life in *Twenty Thousand Leagues* (*20T*) are a translator's nightmare. The lists are occasionally mixed up without regard for habitat; many of the names quoted are Latin ones, but Gallicized to some degree. They also contain some spelling mistakes.[5] Spelling occasionally even varies within the same passage, with both 'hyales' and 'hyalles' ('hyales'), 'pirapèdes' and 'pyrapèdes' ('pirapedas'), and 'coryphèmes' and 'coriphènes' ('coryphènes' or 'dolphinfish'). In other cases, Verne writes just half the binomial name, for instance 'parus' ('*Pomacanthus paru*' or 'French angelfish'). Sometimes hyphenated names are not really compound: Verne often conjuncts a French version with a learned or foreign variant of the same name, or attaches adjectives like 'American-' simply to mean 'found in America'.

Implausibilities

The text of *20T* contains a number of implausibilities, where the translator and editor has to be especially careful not to further obscure the situation. A select list of textual mysteries might include the following. Why are the *Scotia*'s passengers having 'lunch' at 4.17 p.m.? How do you 'push' someone along when he is floating 'motionless on his back, with arms folded and legs extended'? How do people stay dry on a platform only three feet above the sea? How is Aronnax able to describe his own facial expressions? How does the *Nautilus* manage to remain motionless in the depths using just its inclined planes and the thrust of its propeller? Why does lightning strike fish, and not the much larger metal submarine? What happens to the fragile displays in the salon when the submarine lists dramatically or collides with objects? How are pitching and rolling avoided? Why do Nemo's apartments take up so much space, when his twenty crew members have a living space of 5 by 2 metres? How can the disappearance of footprints in the sand be caused by water pressure? Can a boat that two men are able to remove carry ten people or ship 'one or two tons' of water? How does 'an unbearable sulphurous smell' reach 60 feet

---

[5] Thus Verne writes 'gymontes' for 'gymnotes', 'chrysostones' for 'chrysostoses', 'thétys' for 'Tethys', 'xhantes' for 'xanthes', 'molubars' for 'Mobula', 'albicores' for 'albacores', 'aulostones' for 'aulostomes', 'munérophis' for 'murénophis', 'melanopteron' for 'melanopterus', 'thasards' for 'thazards', 'spinorbis' for 'spirorbis', 'dauphinules' for 'dauphinelles', 'cacouannes' for 'caouannes', 'alariées' for 'araliées', 'Rhodoménie' for 'Rhodyménie', 'pantacrines' for 'pentacrines', 'dorripes' for 'dorippes', 'chrysaores' for *Chrysaora*, *Iamettosa* for *lamellosa*, *Cyproea* for *Cypraea*, *Laurentia primafetida* for *Laurencia pinnatifida*, 'apsiphoroïdes' for *Aspiphoroides*, and 'phyctallines' and *Phyctalis* for *Phyllactina* and *Phyllactis*.

down? If Nemo loves the sea so much, why does he avoid contact with sea water?

Gagneux also poses a number of pertinent questions. How does the sun shine brightly at 100 metres depth, and how does it produce a rainbow underwater? How does Aronnax hear rain 300 metres down? How does Nemo extract sodium from salt water, which requires a temperature of 3,000° C? How does a compass work inside a metal hull? How does an 8-metre wide cylinder resist a pressure of 1,600 atmospheres? How do you reverse a submarine at 20 knots through a narrow ice-tunnel? Where does the *Nautilus* find the power required to do 50 knots? Does the 16,000-metre rise in four minutes not equal more than 120 knots? What about the bends? What happens to the inclined planes when the submarine goes clean through the ship? And finally, where are the toilets?

SELECT BIBLIOGRAPHY

Hachette, Michel de l'Ormeraie, and Rencontre represent the main complete printed editions of the *Voyages extraordinaires* since the original Hetzel publication, although 44 of the books have also appeared in Livre de Poche. Since the 1980s, a vast literature has been produced on the life and works of Verne, of which only a small selection can be mentioned here.

Few monographs have appeared in English, most notably: Andrew Martin, *The Mask of the Prophet: The Extraordinary Fictions of Jules Verne* (Oxford: Oxford University Press, 1990); William Butcher, *Verne's Journey to the Centre of the Self: Space and Time in the 'Voyages extraordinaires'* (Macmillan, 1990); Arthur B. Evans, *Jules Verne Rediscovered: Didacticism and the Scientific Novel* (New York: Greenwood Press, 1988); and Ian B. Thompson, *Jules Verne's Scotland: In Fact and Fiction* (Edinburgh: Luath, 2011).[1]

There exist many stimulating collections of articles, notably *Science Fiction Studies*, vol. 32, no. 95 (2005), 'A Jules Verne Centenary'; *Europe: Revue littéraire mensuelle*, vol. 83, no. 909–10 (2005), 'Jules Verne'; *Jules Verne: Cent ans après*, ed. Jean-Pierre Picot and Christian Robin (Terre de brume, 2005); *Jules Verne ou les inventions romanesques*, ed. Christophe Reffait and Alain Schaffner (Amiens: Encrage, 2007); *Les 'Voyages extraordinaires' de Jules Verne: De la création à la réception*, ed. Marie-Françoise Melmoux-Montaubin and Christophe Reffait (Amiens: Encrage, 2012); *Collectionner l'extraordinaire, sonder l'ailleurs: Essais sur Jules Verne en hommage à Jean-Michel Margot*, ed. Terry Harpold, Daniel Compère, and Volker Dehs (Amiens: Encrage, 2015). In addition, many studies have appeared in reviews, notably in: *Verniana* (in English and French), *Revue Jules Verne*, *Planète Jules Verne*, *J.V.*, *Cahiers du Centre d'études verniennes*, *Bulletin de la société Jules Verne*, and *Mundo Verne*.

Comprehensive biographical information can be found in my *Jules Verne: The Definitive Biography* (New York: Thunder's Mouth, 2006; revised 2nd edition, Acadian, 2008).

More than a dozen annotated editions of *20T* have appeared in recent decades; none, however, establishes the text or contains research on the manuscripts.

Nearly all useful studies on *20T* are in French. The following are a selection in both languages:

---

[1] All places of publication are London or Paris unless otherwise indicated; publication details are often omitted for pre-modern volumes. Dates of Verne's works are those of the beginning of their first publication, usually in serial form.

Studies

Barthes, Roland, '*Nautilus* et Bateau ivre', in *Mythologies* (Seuil, 1957, 1970), 80–2 (brilliant but ultimately limited exploration of the psycho–physiology of Verne's ships and their closure and appropriation of space).

Bradbury, Ray, 'The Ardent Blasphemers', in *Twenty Thousand Leagues under the Sea*, translated by Anthony Bonner (Toronto, New York, London, and Sydney: Bantam, 1962, 1981), 1–12 (accompanying a reasonable translation, a lyrical comparison, by a long-standing admirer, of the 'American' spirit of Nemo and Ahab, with Nemo representing more positive values of curiosity and belief in historical progress).

Butcher, William, 'Les Épisodes fantômes de *Vingt mille lieues*', *Europe*, no. 909–10, 2005, 119–34, and http://www.ibiblio.org/julesverne/articles/episodes.doc (reproduces and analyses the manuscript descriptions of the English Channel).

Butcher, William, 'Hidden Treasures', *Science Fiction Studies*, vol. 32, no. 95 (2005), 43–69, and http://www.ibiblio.org/julesverne/articles/hiddentreasures.htm (reproduces and analyses unknown passages from the manuscripts).

Butcher, William, *Jules Verne inédit: Les Manuscrits déchiffrés* (Lyon: ENS éditions and Institut d'histoire du livre, 2015), 165–204 (transcribes many unknown or unpublished excerpts or chapters from the most famous novels, and interprets them in the perspective of Hetzel's many interventions, often considered harmful).

Chamberlin, Sean, *The Remarkable Ocean World of Jules Verne: A Study Guide for 'Twenty Thousand Leagues under the Sea'* (Dubuque, IA: Kendall Hunt Publishing, 2002).

Costello, Peter, introduction and notes in *Twenty Thousand Leagues under the Sea*, 'translated by H. Frith' (this is an error: the translator is Lewis Mercier) (Everyman, 1993), pp. xix–xxvii and 275–304 (old-fashioned introduction, disastrous translation, but useful notes).

Coward, David, *Twenty Thousand Leagues under the Sea*, translation, introduction, and notes (Penguin, 2017) (very good, literary, translation; readable and informative, albeit brief, critical material).

Dehs, Volker, translation and notes, in *Zwanzigtausend Meilen unter dem Meer* (Dusseldorf: Artemis & Winkler, 2007), 625–757 (competent notes, but almost no genetic or pre-1869 biographical information).

Destombes, Marcel, 'Le Manuscrit de *Vingt mille lieues sous les mers* de la Société de géographie', *Bulletin de la société Jules Verne*, no. 35–6 (1975), 59–70 (highly informative and ground-breaking study of the two manuscripts).

Dumas, Olivier, Piero Gondolo della Riva, and Volker Dehs, eds, *Correspondance inédite de Jules Verne et de Pierre-Jules Hetzel, 1863–1886*, vol. 1 (Geneva: Slatkine, 1999) (an essential tool, which brings together and completes the relevant transcriptions of the letters between Verne and Hetzel).

Gagneux, Jean, 'Le *Nautilus*', *L'Armement*, no. 66 (June 1981), 61–84 (accurate, well-informed study of the technical aspects of Nemo's submarine).

Gagneux, Jean, 'Le *Nautilus* pouvait naviguer', *La Nouvelle Revue maritime*, no. 386 (1984), 99–111 (knowledgeably studies the *Nautilus* from the perspective of modern submarine technology, finding a few slips).

Gagneux, Jean, *Sous-marin à propulsion électrique 'Nautilus': Dossier descriptive et plan de compartimentage*, distributed in typed and photocopied form [1980] (witty, scholarly study).

Guermonprez, Jean-H., 'Le *Nautilus* est-il "Le Bateau ivre"?', *Bulletin de la société Jules Verne*, no. 13 (1970), 1–5 (convincingly proves Rimbaud's borrowing from Verne).

Ishibashi, Masataka, 'Création littéraire et processus éditorial: Le Cas de *Vingt mille lieues sous les mers*', in *Les 'Voyages extraordinaires' de Jules Verne*, ed. Marie-Françoise Melmoux-Montaubin and Christophe Reffait (Amiens: Encrage, 2012), 155–72 (proposes the innovative hypothesis that the *MÉR* and 18mo editions are more intensively corrected than the octavo ones, and were therefore prepared later).

Ishibashi, Masataka, 'Les Références de Jules Verne dans *Vingt mille lieues sous les mers*', in *Collectionner l'extraordinaire, sonder l'ailleurs: Essais sur Jules Verne en hommage à Jean-Michel Margot*, ed. Terry Harpold, Daniel Compère, and Volker Dehs (Amiens: Encrage, 2015), 53–64 (article published in Japanese in 2010; description of selected documentary sources of *20T*).

Martin, Andrew, *The Knowledge of Ignorance: From Genesis to Jules Verne* (Cambridge: Cambridge University Press, 1985), 150–9 and *passim* (brilliantly ironic account of the structural foundations of Verne's imagination; explores *20T* as ark and archive).

Mickel, Emanuel, introduction and notes in *Twenty Thousand Leagues under the Sea*, 'a new translation by Emanuel J. Mickel' (Bloomington: Indiana University Press, 1991), 3–63 (thin introduction, strongly criticizing Mercier, although the translation is in fact mainly Mercier's; most of the 482 notes are uninformative).

Miller, Walter James, 'Jules Verne in America: A Translator's Preface', in *Twenty Thousand Leagues under the Sea*, translated by Walter James Miller, assisted by Judith Ann Tirsch (New York: Washington Square Press, 1966), 7–22 (useful introduction on the problems of translation; although called 'New' and 'Definitive', and castigating previous editions, especially Mercier, the translation omits portions of Verne's text).

Miller, Walter James, 'A New Look at Jules Verne', 'Jules Verne, Rehabilitated', and notes in *Twenty Thousand Leagues under the Sea*, translated by Lewis Mercier (New York: Crowell, 1976), 7–22, 356–62 (analyses Verne's strange reputation in the USA, caused partly by the poor quality of the translations; but reprints Mercier's poor translation, although restoring the deleted passages).

Miller, Walter James, and Frederick Paul Walter, introduction and notes in *Twenty Thousand Leagues under the Sea* (Annapolis: Naval Institute Press, 1993), pp. vii–xxii and *passim* (interesting introduction on the problems of translation; very good translation; often informative notes).

Noiray, Jacques, 'L'Inscription de la science dans le texte littéraire: L'Exemple de *Vingt mille lieues sous les mers*', in *Jules Verne ou les inventions romanesques*, ed. Christophe Reffait et Alain Schaffner (Amiens: Encrage, 2007), 29–50 (literary technique).

Noiray, Jacques, *Le Romancier et la machine*, vol. 2, *Jules Verne, Villiers de l'Isle-Adam* (Corti, 1983), 64–71, 103–7, 130–6, and *passim* (subtle study, with quotations, of Aronnax and the *Nautilus*).

Porcq, Christian, 'NGORA, ou les images de la folie dans les *Voyages extraordinaires* de Jules Verne', unpublished doctoral thesis (University of Paris V, 1991), *passim* (imaginatively exposes the personal and psychoanalytic aspects of *20T*, especially dreams and the subconscious).

Robin, Christian, 'Le Récit sauvé des eaux', *Jules Verne 2: L'Écriture vernienne* (Minard, 1978), 33–56 (important structuralist study of the theme of writing within *20T*).

Robin, Christian, 'Verne et Michelet, chantres de l'océan', *La Nouvelle Revue maritime*, no. 386, 1984, 59–65 (the borrowing from Michelet).

Scepi, Henri, edition established, presented, and annotated, *Vingt mille lieues sous les mers* (Paris: Gallimard, 'La Pléiade', 2012), 1313–88 (useful notes; quotes a few extracts from the second manuscript following Destombes, unfortunately including the mistakes; no establishment of the text or genetic research).

Valetoux, Philippe, *Jules Verne en mer et contre tous* (Magellan, 2005) (important biographical study, with many unpublished documents).

Verne, Jules, *Twenty Thousand Leagues under the Sea* (Sampson Low, Marston, Low, and Searle, 1872) (the first English-language version, translated by Lewis Mercier, still the most reprinted; cuts more than 20 per cent and contains howlers).

Vierne, Simone, *Jules Verne, une vie, une œuvre, une époque* (Balland, 1986), 197–218 (readable survey of *20T*, followed by extracts from the novel).

Vierne, Simone, introduction and archives of the work in *Vingt mille lieues sous les mers* (Garnier–Flammarion, 1977), 5–48, 519–35 (informative account of the background to the novel).

Walter, Frederick Paul, and William Butcher, 'Triumphant Translating: It's a Matter of Style', *Verniana*, vol. 7 (2014–15), 123–36 (reviews of two English editions of *Twenty Thousand Leagues*; evoking textual and translation questions, including the defects of the French editions).

Walter, Frederick Paul, introduction, notes, and translation in *Twenty Thousand Leagues under the Seas*, 319–537 and 663–5, in Jules Verne, *Amazing Journeys* (New York: Excelsior, 2010) (excellent translation in American English).

Wier, Stuart K., 'The Design of Jules Verne's Submarine *Nautilus*', *Extraordinary Voyages*, vol. 19, no. 3 (2013), 1–24 (thorough analysis of technical aspects of Nemo's submarine).

Principal Non-Fiction Sources

Figuier, Louis, *La Vie et les mœurs des animaux: Zoophytes et mollusques* (Hachette, 1866).

Flachat, Eugène, *Navigation à vapeur transocéanienne* (Baudry, 1866).

Frédol, Alfred, *Le Monde de la mer* (Hachette, 1865).

Gratiolet, Louis-Pierre, *De la physionomie et des mouvements d'expression* (Hetzel, 1865).

Lacépède, Bernard-Germain, *Histoire naturelle des poissons* (Saugrain, 1793–1803).

Mangin, Arthur, *Les Mystères de l'océan* (Tours: Mame, 1864).

Maury, Matthew Fontaine, *The Physical Geography of the Sea* (New York: Harper, 1855) (translated by P. Terquem as *Géographie physique de la mer* (Corréard, 1858); translated again by Zurcher and Margollé (Hetzel, 1866)).

Michelet, Jules, *La Mer* (Hachette, 1861).

Renard, Léon, *Le Fond de la mer* (Hetzel, 1868).

Vorepierre, Dupiney de, and Jean-François-Marie de Marcoux, eds, *Dictionnaire français illustré et encyclopédie universelle* (Bureau de la publication and Lévy, 1847–63).

Zurcher, Frédéric, and Élie Margollé, *Le Monde sous-marin* (Hetzel, 1868).

A CHRONOLOGY OF JULES VERNE

1828 8 February: birth of Jules Verne at 4 rue Olivier-de-Clisson, Feydeau Island, Nantes. His parents are Pierre, a lawyer and son and grandson of lawyers, and a reactionary and religious self-flagellator; and Sophie, née Allotte de la Fuÿe, Breton and artistic, from a military line traced back to an N. Allott, a Scottish archer ennobled by Louis XI.

1829 Birth of brother, Paul, later a naval officer, but who retired in 1859 and became a stockbroker; followed by those of sisters Anna (1836), Mathilde (1839), and Marie (1842).

1830 Jules hears the street battles of the July Revolution.

1833 First bucolic summer at Uncle Prudent Allotte's with the Tronson cousins—Henri, Edmond, Caroline, and Marie—all about the same age. Jules climbs the trees with Paul; he will write his dreams of travel and his 'invocations'.

1834–8 Goes to boarding-school: the teacher, Mme Sambain, is still waiting for her sea-captain husband after thirty years.

1836 Jules slips onto a three-master, breathes heady odours, and dreams of navigation. Henri and Edmond drown in the Loire.

1837 The family rent a cottage in Chantenay looking over the Loire, where they will spend six months each year. Jules hires a skiff, which sinks; he plays at Crusoe on an island. With Paul, sent to boarding-school Saint-Stanislas, where he will receive merits in geography, translation from Greek and Latin, and singing.

1839 The boy runs away, apparently on board the *Octavie*, heading for the 'Indies'. His father catches him at Paimbœuf.

1840 Boarding at the St Donatien Junior Seminary, with friends Aristide Hignard and Adolphe Bonamy. Composes prayers, pastiches, acrostics, and poems. At this time, the family move to Rue Jean-Jacques Rousseau.

1842 His father prints two poems about his son's love for the Loire, predicting a career as a 'scholar rather than a captain'.

1843–5 Attends Lycée Royal de Nantes, but falls a year behind, through illness or resitting. Is in love with his cousin Caroline; the families discuss marriage.

1846 Passes *baccalauréat* in arts ('with credit'). Studies law at home, since his father wishes to pass on his practice.

1847 Pierre does not allow Jules to sign up as a trainee ship's officer. First year law exams in Paris. Passion for Herminie Arnault-Grossetière, to whom he dedicates many poems. During this period, writes a novel, *A Priest in 1839*, and a tragedy, *Alexander VI*.

1848 Continues his law studies, sharing a room at 24 Rue de l'Ancienne-Comédie, in the Latin Quarter. His uncle Châteaubourg introduces him into literary salons.

1849 Through the chiromancer Casimir d'Arpentigny, meets Alexandre Dumas *fils* and *père*. Passes law degree and avoids conscription. Father allows him to stay on in Paris.

1850 Has composed about twenty comedies and tragedies, including *La Conspiration des poudres*. 12 June: his one-act comedy *Les Pailles rompues* runs for fourteen nights at Dumas's Théâtre Historique, and is published.

1851 Publishes 'Les Premiers navires de la Marine mexicaine' and 'Un Voyage en ballon'. Works as a bank clerk and tutor. Is hired as a notarial clerk, but his employer dies immediately. Moves to Boulevard Bonne-Nouvelle, opposite Hignard's room.

1852–5 Becomes secretary of Théâtre Lyrique. Publishes 'Martin Paz', 'Maître Zacharius', 'Un Hivernage dans les glaces', and in collaboration the play *Les Châteaux en Californie*. His co-written operetta *Le Colin-maillard* is performed to music by Hignard. Is rejected by a series of young women. Frequents brothels.

1856 Goes to a wedding in Amiens, and meets a young widow with two children, Honorine de Viane.

1857 10 January: marries Honorine; becomes an assistant stockbroker, and moves several times. Publication of art criticism *Salon de 1857*.

1859–60 Visits Bordeaux, Liverpool, Edinburgh, the Highlands, and London with Hignard, and is greatly marked by the experience. Writes *Voyage en Angleterre et en Écosse* and *Paris au XXe siècle*.

1861–2 Birth of only child, Michel, while he is on a decisive trip to Norway and Denmark with Hignard and Émile Lorois. Writes *Joyeuses misères de trois voyageurs en Scandinavie*. The juvenile writer Alfred de Bréhat introduces him to Jules Hetzel. The publisher orders proofs for *Voyage en Angleterre et en Écosse*, but then rejects the book. Signature of a contract for 'Voyage en l'air', a book about ballooning.

1863 15 January: *Cinq semaines en ballon* appears. At this time, Hetzel categorically refuses *Paris au XXe siècle*.

1864 A second contract, Hetzel again keeping five-sixths of the profits. In the newly-founded *Magasin d'éducation et de récréation (MÉR)*, beginning of publication of *Aventures du capitaine Hatteras*, from which Hetzel removes the Anglo-American duel on an ice-floe and final suicide of the hero, plus perhaps several other chapters. Publication of 'Edgar Poe et ses œuvres' and *Voyage au centre de la Terre*. Cuts back on his stockbroker activities, and moves to Auteuil.

1865 *De la Terre à la Lune* and *Les Enfants du capitaine Grant*. The endings of virtually all his famous novels will be altered by the publisher. At this time, visits Italy with Hetzel.

1866 Settles in Le Crotoy (summer home).

1867 Goes with brother Paul to Liverpool, thence on the *Great Eastern* to the United States. Visits the Paris Universal Exposition.

1868 Has a boat built, the *St Michel*. Travels with Hetzel to Baden-Baden and to the Riviera. A fourth contract stipulates thirty volumes within ten years; Verne buys shares in Hetzel. Michel is proving difficult. Joins a new musical dining club, the Onze sans Femmes (Eleven Without Women).

1869 Rents a house in Amiens. Two cruises to England. *Vingt mille lieues sous les mers* and *Autour de la Lune*.

1870 Hetzel sharply criticizes *Uncle Robinson*. Sails up the Seine to see his mistress in Paris, with whom he is madly in love. In the margin of a manuscript, logs his intimate troubles, apparently with the initial of the person concerned, 'M'. Outbreak of Franco-Prussian War: Verne is for a while a national guard at Le Crotoy.

1871 Briefly returns to the Stock Exchange. Father dies. A fifth contract stipulates 140,000 words a year.

1872 Becomes member of Académie d'Amiens. *Le Tour du monde en quatre-vingts jours*. Makes his ninth and tenth trips to the British Isles.

1873–4 Moves to 44 Boulevard Longueville, Amiens. *Le Docteur Ox*, *L'Île mystérieuse*, and *Le Chancellor*. Begins collaboration with Adolphe d'Ennery on highly remunerative stage adaptations of novels (*Le Tour du monde en 80 jours* (1874), *Michel Strogoff* (1880)).

1875 Offenbach's *A Trip to the Moon* includes unauthorized borrowing from Verne.

1876–7 *Michel Strogoff, Hector Servadac*, and *Les Indes noires*, with the publisher writing some of the chapters. Buys second, then third boat, also called the *St Michel*. Gives huge fancy-dress ball. Wife critically ill, but recovers. Places Michel in a reformatory. Encouraged by Dumas *fils*, Verne dreams of membership of the French Academy, but the feedback is not positive.

1878 June–August: sails to Lisbon and Algiers.

1879–80 *Les Cinq cents millions de la Bégum, Les Tribulations d'un Chinois en Chine*, and *La Maison à vapeur*. Verne sails to Edinburgh then travels to the Hebrides. Settles Michel's debts while expelling him, to live with an actress.

1881 *La Jangada.* Sails to Rotterdam and Copenhagen.

1882 *Le Rayon vert.* Moves to a larger house at 2 Rue Charles-Dubois, Amiens.

1883–4 *Kéraban-le-têtu.* Michel abducts a minor, Jeanne. Has two children by her within eleven months. Verne leaves with his wife on a grand tour of the Mediterranean, and is received in private audience by Pope Leo XIII.

1885 *Mathias Sandorf.*

1886 *Robur-le-conquérant.* Sells the third *St Michel*. 9 March: his nephew Gaston asks for money to travel to England. Verne refuses, and the mentally-ill nephew fires at him twice, laming him for life. Hetzel dies.

1887 Mother dies.

1888 Elected local councillor on a Republican list. For the next fifteen years attends council meetings, administrates theatre and fairs, opens Municipal Circus (1889), and gives public talks.

1889 *Sans dessus dessous* and 'In the Year 2889' (signed Jules Verne but written by Michel).

1890 Stomach problems.

1892 *Le Château des Carpathes.* Pays debts for Michel.

1893–4 Sales drop.

1895 *L'Île à hélice*, apparently the first novel in the present tense and third person.

1896–7 *Face au drapeau* and *Le Sphinx des glaces*. Sued by chemist Turpin, who recognizes himself in *Face au drapeau*. Successfully defended by Raymond Poincaré, later president of France. Health deteriorates. Brother dies.

1899 Dreyfus Affair: Verne is anti-Dreyfusard.

1900 Moves back to 44 Boulevard Longueville. Sight weakens (cataracts).

1901 *Le Village aérien*.

1904 *Maître du monde*.

1905 Falls seriously ill from diabetes. 24 March: dies, and is buried in Amiens.

1905–14 On Verne's death, *L'Invasion de la mer* and *Le Phare du bout du monde* are in the course of publication. Michel takes responsibility for the remaining manuscripts, and publishes *Le Volcan d'or* (1906), *L'Agence Thompson and Co.* (1907), *La Chasse au météore* (1908), *Le Pilote du Danube* (1908), *Les Naufragés du 'Jonathan'* (1909), *Le Secret de Wilhelm Storitz* (1910), *Hier et Demain* (short stories, including 'L'Éternel Adam') (1910), and *L'Étonnante aventure de la mission Barsac* (1914). Michel wrote considerable sections of these works.

TWENTY THOUSAND LEAGUES
UNDER THE SEAS

CONTENTS

PART ONE

A SHIFTING REEF

THE year 1866 was marked by a strange event, an unexplained and inexplicable occurrence that doubtless no one has yet forgotten. Without mentioning the rumours which agitated the denizens of the ports and whipped up the public's imagination on every continent, seafaring men felt particularly alarmed. The businessmen, ship-owners, sea-captains, skippers, and master-mariners of Europe and America, the naval officers from every country, and finally the various national governments on both continents—all became extremely worried about this matter.

For some time already, sea-going ships had been encountering an 'enormous thing': a long spindle-shaped object, sometimes phosphor-escent, but infinitely larger and quicker than a whale.

The facts concerning this apparition, as noted in the respective logbooks, agreed quite closely as to the structure of the said object or creature, its extraordinary speed, its surprising ability to get from place to place, and the peculiar vitality it seemed to possess. If it was a cetacean, then it surpassed the size of every whale classified by science until then. Neither Cuvier, nor Lacépède, nor M. Duméril, nor M. de Quatrefages* would have accepted that such a monster existed, unless they had seen it—really seen it, that is, with their own scientific eyes.

Taking the average of the observations made at the various junctures—rejecting both the timid evaluations assigning the object a length of 200 feet and the exaggerated opinions making it three miles long and a mile wide—it could be declared that this phenomenal being greatly exceeded any dimensions the ichthyologists had acknowledged until then—if indeed it existed at all.

But it did exist, there was now no denying it; and given the inclination of the human mind to seek the fantastic, it is easy to understand the worldwide sensation this supernatural apparition created. As for dismissing it as a myth, such a position was no longer tenable.

The reason was that on 20 July 1866 the steamship the *Governor Higginson*, of the Calcutta and Burmah Steam Navigation Company, had encountered this thing, moving five miles east of the Australian coastline.* At first Captain Baker thought he was facing an unknown reef; and he was even getting ready to calculate its precise position, when two columns of water,* projected from the baffling object, shot 150 feet into the air, whistling. Hence, unless the reef was subject to the intermittent jet of a geyser, the *Governor Higginson* was well and truly dealing with some hitherto unknown aquatic mammal, whose blowholes were blowing columns of water mixed with air and vapour.

A similar phenomenon was observed in the Pacific on 23 July of the same year by the *Cristóbal Colon* of the West India and Pacific Steamship Company.* This extraordinary cetacean was thus able to move from place to place at surprising speed, for within three days the *Governor Higginson* and *Cristóbal Colon* had observed it on two charted spots at more than 700 leagues' distance.

A fortnight later and 2,000 leagues away, the *Helvetia* of the French Line and the *Shannon* of the Royal Mail,* sailing on opposite tacks of the Atlantic between the United States and Europe, signalled to each other their sightings of the monster at 42° 15′ N and 60° 35′ W of the Greenwich meridian. From these simultaneous observations, it was claimed that the mammal could be evaluated as at least 350 British feet long,[1] since the *Shannon* and the *Helvetia* were both smaller, although measuring 100 metres from stem to stern. Now the biggest whales, the *culammak* and the *umgullick** frequenting the waters around the Aleutians, have never exceeded 56 metres—if indeed they have ever reached that.

These reports arriving hot on the heels of one another, fresh observations made on board the transatlantic liner the *Pereire*, a collision between the monster and the *Etna* of the Inman Line, an official memorandum drawn up by officers of the French frigate the *Normandie*, a very solemn statement by Commodore Fitzjames's senior staff on board the *Lord Clyde**—all this greatly thrilled public opinion. In countries of a light-hearted mentality the phenomenon was joked about; in the serious, practical countries of Britain, America, and Germany, it became a matter for grave concern.

---

[1] About 106 metres. The British foot is only 30.40 centimetres long. [JV]

The monster came into fashion in all the big cities: it was sung about in the cafés, made fun of in the newspapers, acted out in the theatres. The *canards* had a golden opportunity to lay whoppers of every hue. Each gigantic imaginary creature resurfaced in the newspapers, admittedly short of good copy, from the white whale, that awe-inspiring 'Moby Dick' of the polar regions, to the enormous kraken,* whose tentacles can strangle a 500 ton ship and drag it down into the depths. The formally attested reports of olden times were even reproduced, the views of Aristotle and Pliny conceding the existence of such monsters, the Norwegian tales of Bishop Pontoppidan, and the account of Paul Egede.* So, lastly, were the reports of Captain Harrington, whose good faith could not be questioned when in 1857 he declared that, while on board the *Castilian*, he had seen that enormous serpent which until then had frequented the seas only in the pages of the old *Constitutionnel.**

There soon broke out in the learned societies and scientific journals an interminable argument between the credulous and the incredulous. The 'monster question' inflamed people's minds. Those journalists who professed science battled with those who professed wit, spilling oceans of ink during this memorable campaign; some of them even two or three drops of blood, for from the sea serpent they moved on to the most offensive personal remarks.

For six months the war raged back and forth. The weighty articles of the Geographical Institute of Brazil, the Berlin Royal Academy of Sciences, the British Association, and the Smithsonian Institution in Washington, the discussions in the *Indian Archipelago*, Abbe Moigno's *Cosmos*, *Petermanns Mitteilungen*,* and the scientific sections of the quality press in France and abroad—all were driven back with untiring repartee by the popular press. These facetious journalists, punning on a saying of Linnaeus's quoted by the monster's opponents, argued that 'nature does not proceed by the lips of bounders',* and so adjured their contemporaries not to give the lie to nature by admitting the existence of krakens, sea serpents, Moby Dicks, or other lucubrations of crazed sailors. The last straw was an article written for a much-feared satirical newspaper by its most popular writer, who pushed his spurs in like Hippolytus* and delivered a fatal blow to the monster, putting it out of its misery amidst universal laughter. Wit had proved mightier than science.

In the first few months of 1867 the question did indeed seem dead and buried, without hope of rising from the ashes, when fresh information reached the general public. There was now in fact a genuine and serious danger to circumvent, rather than simply a scientific question to resolve. The problem took on a different complexion. The monster became an islet, a rock, a reef once more; but a reef that was shifting, elusive, and slippery.

On the night of 5 March 1867 the *Moravian* of the Montreal Ocean Company was sailing at 27° 30′ N, 72° 15′ W* when her starboard quarter struck a rock unmarked on any chart. She was making 13 knots under the combined effect of the wind and her 400 horsepower. Doubtless, had it not been for the quality of her hull, the *Moravian* would have sunk from the hole produced by the collision, together with the 237 passengers she was bringing back from Canada.

The accident happened at about 5 a.m., just as dawn was breaking. The officers of the watch rushed to the stern of the vessel. They examined the sea with the closest attention. They saw nothing but a powerful eddy breaking at about three cables' distance, as if the waters were being violently thrashed. The position was carefully calculated and recorded, and the *Moravian* continued on her way without visible damage. Had she hit a submerged rock, or else the enormous wreck of some half-sunken ship? There was no way of finding out; but when the hull was inspected in dry dock,* it was realized that part of the keel had been broken.

This collision, extremely serious on its own, would perhaps have been forgotten like so many others, had it not happened again in identical circumstances three weeks later. This time the event had a tremendous impact because of the nationality of the ship involved and the reputation of the company operating the vessel.

The name of the celebrated British ship-owner Cunard* is known to all. In 1840 this far-sighted industrialist set up a postal service from Liverpool to Halifax using three wooden paddle-steamers of 400 horsepower and a burden of 1,162 tons. Eight years later the company added to its fleet four ships of 650 horsepower and 1,820 tons, and two years after that, two further vessels of still greater power and tonnage. In 1853 the Cunard Line, which had just had its mail-carrying monopoly renewed, successively added the *Arabia*, the *Persia*, the *China*, the *Scotia*, the *Java*, and the *Russia*, all amongst the fastest and the largest ships, after the *Great Eastern*,* ever to have sailed the high seas. In 1867 the company owned twelve vessels, eight being paddle- and four propeller-driven.

If I give these succinct details, it is so that everyone realizes the importance of this shipping line, known worldwide for its intelligent management. No ocean-going company has been run with greater skill; no business crowned with greater success. During the past twenty-six years, Cunard ships have crossed the Atlantic two thousand times, and not once cancelled a journey, arrived behind schedule, or lost a letter, man, or vessel. This is why, in spite of the strong competition from France, passengers still choose the Cunard Line more than any other, as is apparent from reading the official registers of recent years. Consequently no one will be surprised at the uproar produced by the accident involving one of its finest steamships.

On 13 April 1867, in a fine sea and moderate wind, the *Scotia* was at 45° 37′ N, 15° 12′ W. Under the thrust of its 1,000 horsepower, it was moving at 13.43 knots. Its paddlewheels were striking the sea with perfect regularity. Its draught was 6.7 metres and its displacement 6,624 cubic metres.

At 4.17 in the afternoon, while the passengers were in the main saloon taking their lunch, a blow, hardly perceptible in fact, was felt on the hull of the *Scotia*, at the section just behind the port wheel.

The *Scotia* had not run into something: something had run into it, and a cutting or perforating implement rather than a blunt one. The blow seemed so slight that nobody on board would have worried, but for the shout of the hold-workers, who rushed up on deck shouting:

'We're sinking! We're sinking!'

At first the passengers were terrified—but Captain Anderson* quickly reassured them. In actual fact the danger could not be imminent. The *Scotia*, divided into seven compartments by watertight bulkheads, was guaranteed to resist any single leak with impunity.

Captain Anderson headed immediately for the hold. He observed that the fifth compartment had flooded; and the speed of the flooding proved that the hole was a large one. Very fortunately, the boilers were not in this compartment, for the fires would have been instantly extinguished.

Captain Anderson had the engines stopped at once, while one of the sailors dived to assess the damage. Shortly afterwards, the existence of a 2-metre hole in the hull was confirmed. Such damage could not be repaired and the *Scotia*, its wheels half underwater, had to continue its journey in the same condition. It lay 300 miles off Cape Clear,*

and was three days late sailing into the company docks, having greatly
worried Liverpool.

The engineers then carried out a dry-dock inspection of the *Scotia*.
They couldn't believe their eyes. Two-and-a-half metres below the
waterline appeared a neat incision in the form of an isosceles triangle.*
The break in the plate was perfectly clean, and could not have been
cut with greater precision by a punch. The perforating implement
in question had therefore to be of uncommon temper—and, having
in this way been propelled with prodigious strength through the
4-centimetre-thick metal plate, it must then have withdrawn in
a reverse movement that was truly inexplicable.

Such was the most recent event, which resulted in public opinion
being stirred up once more. Starting from that moment, maritime losses
from unknown causes were simply attributed to the monster. The
fantastic animal shouldered the blame for all such shipwrecks, which
unfortunately occur in considerable numbers; for, out of the three
thousand ships whose losses are recorded each year by the Bureau
Veritas,* the number of steam or sailing ships presumed lost with all
hands through lack of news reaches two hundred!

It was now 'the monster' that was being blamed, rightly or wrongly,
for their disappearance. Because of this, and because travel between
the various continents was getting more and more dangerous, the
public spoke its mind and categorically demanded that the oceans be
finally rid of this formidable cetacean, whatever the cost.

2

PROS AND CONS

At the time of these events, I was returning from a scientific
exploration of the Badlands of Nebraska, in the United States. The
French government had attached me to this expedition in my capacity
as a part-time lecturer* at the Museum of Natural History in Paris.
After six months in Nebraska, I had arrived in New York towards the
end of March, laden down with my precious collections. My departure
for France was scheduled for the beginning of May. In the meantime,
I was attending to the classification of my mineralogical, botanical,
and zoological treasures—when the *Scotia* incident happened.

I was perfectly aware of the topic in the news, for how could it have been otherwise? I had read and reread the European and American newspapers without getting any closer to a solution. This mystery fascinated me. Unable to form an opinion about it, I had drifted from one extreme to the other. That there was *something*, there could be no question, for doubting Thomases could be invited to touch the wound in the *Scotia*'s side.*

When I reached New York the question was a hot one. The theory of a floating island or elusive reef, put forward by a few unqualified individuals, had been totally discredited. And in truth, unless the reef had an engine in its belly, how could it move around with such awesome speed?

In the same way, the idea of a floating hulk, an enormous wreck, was rejected, and again because of the speed at which it moved.

This left two possible answers to the problem, which in turn produced two very distinct groups of supporters: on the one hand, those who swore by a monster of colossal strength; and on the other, those who argued for a 'submarine' vessel* of immense locomotive power.

Now the latter theory, admissible after all, failed to survive the research carried out in the Old and New Worlds. That a private individual had at his disposal a mechanical contrivance of this sort was improbable. When and where could he have had it built, and how could he have kept its construction secret?

Only a government might have possessed such a weapon of destruction, and in these disastrous times, when humanity endeavours to increase the power of its weapons of war, it could not be thought impossible that a country had tested this formidable device unbeknownst to the others. After the chassepot rifles came floating mines; after floating mines, underwater rams;* then . . . a reaction. At least, I hope there will be one.

But all the same the idea of a war machine had to be abandoned, in the light of what the governments declared. As it was a matter of public interest, since intercontinental communications were suffering, the governments' truthfulness could not be doubted for one moment. In any case, how could it be imagined that this submarine vessel's construction had escaped public notice? Keeping a secret under such circumstances is very difficult for a private individual, and certainly impossible for states, whose every act is continually observed by rival powers.

Consequently, after research had been carried out in Great Britain, France, Russia, Prussia, Spain, Italy, America, and even Turkey, the hypothesis of a submarine *Monitor** was rejected once and for all.

The monster therefore surfaced once more, despite the constant witticisms that the popular press showered on it; and people's imaginations soon followed this path and allowed themselves to culminate in the absurdest dreams of fantastic ichthyology.

At my arrival in New York, several people had done me the honour of consulting me on the phenomenon in question. In France I had published a two-volume in-quarto work entitled *The Mysteries of the Ocean Deeps*. This book, particularly relished in scholarly circles, had made of me a specialist in that relatively obscure field of natural history. My views were sought. So long as I was able to deny the reality of the fact, I cloaked myself in total denial. But soon, with my back against the wall, I was forced to explain unequivocally. The *New York Herald* even challenged 'the honourable Pierre Aronnax,* lecturer at the Paris Museum', to express a view of some sort.

I complied. I spoke, since I was unable to remain silent. I analysed the question from every angle, whether political or scientific; and will provide here an extract from a very comprehensive study that I published in the newspaper on 30 April:

As a result of the above, and having successively examined the various hypotheses, and since every other supposition is precluded, we are necessarily obliged to accept the existence of a marine animal of immense power.

The great depths of the ocean are totally unknown to us. Sounding lines have been unable to reach them. What transpires in those remote abysses? What beings live or can live 12 or 15 miles below the surface?* What is the constitution of these animals? We can scarcely even guess.

Nevertheless, the solution to the problem which has been submitted to me can be formulated in terms of a two-pronged alternative.

Either we know every variety of beings which inhabit our planet, or we do not.

If we do not know them all, if nature still holds ichthyologic secrets for us, it is quite acceptable to recognize the existence of fish or cetaceans of unknown species or even genera, of an essentially 'deep-based' composition, which inhabit the depths inaccessible to the sounding line and which some event, a whim, a caprice as it were, brings to the top of the sea at infrequent intervals.

If, on the contrary, we know all living species, we are necessarily compelled to seek the said animal amongst marine beings that are already catalogued, and, in this case, I should be disposed to accept the existence of a Giant Narwhal.*

The common narwhal or sea-unicorn often attains a length of 60 feet. Multiply this dimension by five, by ten even, endow this cetacean with a strength proportional to its size, enlarge its offensive weapon, and you will obtain the required animal. It will have the dimensions ascertained by the officers of the *Shannon*, the instrument required to pierce the *Scotia*, and the force necessary to breach the hull of a steamship.

The narwhal is armed with a kind of ivory sword, a halberd in the terminology of certain naturalists. This is a principal tooth with the hardness of steel. Some of these teeth have been found embedded in the bodies of whales, which the narwhal attacks with unvarying success. Others have been removed, not without difficulty, from the hulls of vessels that have been pierced through and through, like a drill through a barrel. The museum of the Faculty of Medicine in Paris possesses one of these tusks that is 2.25 metres long and 48 centimetres wide at its base!

Now imagine a weapon ten times as great and a creature ten times as strong, launch it at a speed of 20 knots, multiply its mass by its velocity, and you obtain a shock capable of producing the required catastrophe.

Accordingly, until further information becomes available, I shall vote for a sea-unicorn of colossal dimension, armed not with a halberd, but with a genuine spur, like the armoured frigates called 'war rams', whose weight and motive power it would also have.

Thus the inexplicable phenomenon would be explained—unless there is nothing there at all, which is always possible, in spite of what has been glimpsed, seen, felt, and experienced!

These last words were an equivocation on my part; but I wished to a certain extent to protect my dignity as a scholar and avert the danger of becoming a laughing-stock for the Americans, for they laugh wholeheartedly when they do laugh. I left myself a way out, but, in the final analysis, I admitted that 'the monster' did exist.

My article was hotly debated, and produced quite a stir. It won over a number of supporters. But in any case, my proposed solution left full scope for the imagination. The human mind enjoys grandiose conceptions of supernatural beings. Now the sea is their best medium, for it is the only environment that can produce and develop such giants: beside them the land animals, the elephants or rhinoceroses, are mere dwarves. The liquid masses support the biggest known species of mammals, and perhaps harbour molluscs of extraordinary size, crustaceans terrible to contemplate, lobsters 100 metres long, crabs weighing 200 tons! Why ever not? The land animals of long-gone geological eras, the quadrupeds, quadrumanes, reptiles, and birds, used to be built on a gigantic template. The Creator cast them in a colossal mould which slowly reduced with time. Why could the unknown depths of the sea not have conserved these vast specimens from another age, that sea which never changes, unlike the terrestrial core which is almost continuously being modified?* Why should she not conceal in her bosom the last varieties of those titanic species, whose years are as centuries and centuries as millennia?

However, I am allowing myself to be carried away by these musings which I no longer have the right to entertain! Enough of these chimeras which time has changed for me into terrible realities! I repeat: at that time people made up their minds on the nature of the phenomenon, and the public accepted without question the existence of a prodigious being that had nothing in common with the sea serpents of legend.

But if some saw a purely scientific problem to be solved, others of a more positive nature, especially in America and Britain, agreed to purge the seas of this redoubtable monster, in order to safeguard cross-ocean communications once more. The industrial and commercial journals treated the question chiefly from this point of view. The *Shipping & Mercantile Gazette and Lloyd's List*, the *Paquebot*, and the *Revue maritime et coloniale*,* together with every newsletter devoted to the insurance companies, who were threatening to raise their premiums—all were in agreement on this point.

Since public opinion had come to a decision, the States of the Union were the first to speak out. Preparations were made in New York for an expedition to hunt down the narwhal. A fast frigate, the *Abraham Lincoln*, made ready to sail at a moment's notice. The arsenals were opened up for Captain Farragut,* who spared no effort to arm his frigate.

But as it happened, as it always happens, once it had been decided to hunt for the monster, it disappeared from sight. For two months it was not heard of at all. No ship came upon it. It seemed as if the unicorn knew about the plots being hatched against it. It had been discussed so often, even over the transatlantic cable! The wags claimed that this sharp customer had intercepted some telegram in transit and was now turning it to its own advantage.

As a result, although the frigate was armed for a distant campaign and equipped with formidable fishing tackle, nobody knew where to send it to. Impatience was building up to a bigger and bigger head, when, on 3 July, it was learned that a steamer of the San Francisco–Shanghai line* had again sighted the animal, three weeks previously in the seas of the north Pacific.

This news caused tremendous excitement. Captain Farragut received less than twenty-four hours' notice. His provisions were on board. His bunkers overflowed with coal. Not a crew man was missing from his roll-call. He only had to light his fires, stoke up, and cast off! Even twelve hours' delay wouldn't have been forgiven! To get going was all Captain Farragut wanted in any case.

Three hours before the *Abraham Lincoln* left its Brooklyn pier,[1] I received a letter couched in these terms:

Dr Aronnax
Lecturer at the Paris Museum of Natural History
Fifth Avenue Hotel*
NEW YORK

Dear Sir,
If you would like to join the expedition on board the *Abraham Lincoln*, the government of the Union would greatly appreciate having you represent France in this enterprise. Captain Farragut has a cabin at your disposal.
Very cordially yours
J. B. Hobson*
Secretary to the Navy

3

AS MONSIEUR PLEASES

THREE seconds before J. B. Hobson's letter arrived, I no more dreamed of hunting the unicorn than of attempting the Northwest Passage.* Three seconds after reading the letter from the honourable Secretary to the Navy, I realized that my real vocation, my only aim in life, was to pursue this disturbing monster and to save the world from its clutches.

However, I was returning from a difficult journey, tired and longing for rest. I pined only to see my country again, my friends, my small

---

[1] A sort of individual quay for each vessel. [JV]

lodgings at the Jardin des Plantes, my dear and precious collections! But nothing could hold me back. I forgot everything, tiredness, friends, collections; and I accepted the American government's offer without further thought.

'In any case,' I mused, 'all roads lead to Europe, and the unicorn will surely be so good as to lure me towards the French coasts! This kind creature will let itself be captured in European waters as a special favour to me; and I wish to bring back no less than half a metre of ivory halberd for the Museum of Natural History.'

But meanwhile I needed to search for this narwhal in the northern Pacific Ocean; which was tantamount to heading for France via the antipodes.

'Conseil!'* I cried impatiently.

Conseil was my manservant. A devoted lad who accompanied me on all my journeyings; a good Fleming whom I liked a great deal and who reciprocated; a creature phlegmatic by nature, ordered by principle, and eager by habit: astonished by few of life's surprises, very good with his hands, suited for any service, and, despite his name, never giving counsel—even unasked.

By rubbing shoulders with the scholars of our little milieu at the Jardin des Plantes, Conseil had come to know a thing or two. I had in him a specialist, very well up on natural history classification, with an acrobat's agility at working his way up and down the whole hierarchy of phyla, divisions, classes, sub-classes, orders, families, genera, sub-genera, species, and varieties. But his scientific knowledge stopped there. Well versed in the theory of classification but little in its practice, he couldn't, I think, have distinguished a sperm whale from an ordinary whale! And yet what a good and honest fellow!

For the past ten years, Conseil had been following me everywhere science had led. Never a comment on the length or fatigue of a journey. No objection to packing his suitcase for any country whatsoever, China or the Congo, however distant. He travelled far and wide, without expecting anything else. Besides, his robust health thumbed its nose at every illness; he had powerful muscles but no nerves, not even the appearance of them—mentally speaking, I mean.

The fellow was thirty years old, and his age was to his master's as fifteen is to twenty. May I be excused for saying in this way that I was forty.

Conseil had but one fault. A rabid formalist, he only ever spoke to me in the third person—to the point of becoming annoying.

'Conseil!' I repeated, while at the same time feverishly beginning preparations for departure.

Certainly, I felt sure of this fellow of such devotion. Normally I never asked whether or not it suited him to accompany me on my travels; but this time it was an expedition which could last indefinitely, a hazardous enterprise in pursuit of an animal capable of sinking a frigate as easily as a nutshell. There was food for thought in that, even for the most impassive man in the world. So what would Conseil say?

'Conseil!' I cried for the third time.

Conseil appeared.

'Did monsieur call?'

'Yes, my good fellow. Please get me and yourself ready. We're leaving in two hours' time.'

'As monsieur pleases,' he replied calmly.

'Not a moment to lose. Squeeze into my trunk my whole travel kit, coats, shirts, and socks, without skimping and as much as you can, and hurry!'

'And monsieur's collections?' enquired Conseil.

'We'll deal with them later.'

'What! The archaeotheria, hyracotheria, oreodons, chaeropotami,* and monsieur's other dead bodies?'

'The hotel will look after them.'

'And monsieur's live babirusa?'*

'They'll feed it while we're away. In any case, I'll give instructions for our menagerie to be shipped to us in France.'

'So we're not returning to Paris?' Conseil enquired.

'But of course . . . most definitely . . .' I replied evasively, 'but after a slight detour.'

'Whichever detour monsieur wishes.'

'Oh it hardly makes a difference! Not quite so direct a route, that's all. We're sailing on the *Abraham Lincoln*.'

'As monsieur requires,' replied Conseil calmly.

'You know, my friend, it's the monster . . . The famous narwhal . . . We're going to rid the seas of it! . . . The author of the two-volume in-quarto *Mysteries of the Ocean Deeps* cannot refuse to sail with Captain Farragut. A mission full of glory, but also . . . dangerous.

We don't know where we'll end up. Those creatures can be awfully flighty. But we're going all the same! We have a captain who's got guts!'

'Wherever monsieur goes, so will I.'

'Please do think it over. I don't want to hide anything from you. It's one of those journeys you don't always come back from!'

'As monsieur pleases.'

Quarter of an hour later, our trunks were ready. Conseil had packed them standing on his head, as it were. I could be sure that nothing was missing, for this fellow classified shirts and coats as proficiently as birds and mammals.

The hotel lift* dropped us at the mezzanine lounge. I went down a few steps to the ground floor. I settled my bill at the huge desk, always besieged by a large crowd. I left instructions for my packages of stuffed animals and dried plants to be shipped to Paris, France. Having opened a well-provisioned account for the babirusa, with Conseil following, I jumped into a cab.

The vehicle, at twenty francs a trip, went down Broadway as far as Union Square, followed Fourth Avenue until its junction with the Bowery, turned into Catherine Street, and stopped at Pier No. 34. There the Catherine Ferry took us, men, horses, and cab, to Brooklyn, New York's great extension on the left bank of the East River. Minutes later we stood on the quayside where the *Abraham Lincoln* was spewing torrents of black smoke out of its twin funnels.

Our bags were immediately transported on to the frigate's deck. I rushed on board and asked for Captain Farragut. One of the sailors took me to the poop deck, where I found myself in the presence of a handsome officer, who stretched out his hand.

'Dr Pierre Aronnax?'

'Himself. Captain Farragut?'

'In person. Welcome aboard, Dr Aronnax. Your cabin is ready.'

I bowed and, leaving the captain to his work of getting under way, was shown to the designated cabin.

The *Abraham Lincoln* had been perfectly chosen and fitted out for its new task. It was a high-speed frigate, equipped with superheating apparatus allowing its steam pressure to attain seven atmospheres. At this pressure, the *Abraham Lincoln* typically reached 18.3 knots: a considerable speed but still insufficient to compete with the gigantic cetacean.

The accommodation of the frigate reflected its nautical function. I was very satisfied with my cabin, located at the stern and opening on to the officers' wardroom.

'We'll be comfortable here,' I said to Conseil.

'With all due respect, monsieur, as comfortable as a hermit-crab in a whelk's shell.'

I left Conseil to stow our trunks suitably, and went back up on deck to watch the preparations for weighing anchor.

Captain Farragut was just ordering the casting-off of the last ropes securing the *Abraham Lincoln* to the Brooklyn pier. A quarter of an hour's delay, less even, and the frigate would have left without me; and I would have missed out on that extraordinary, supernatural, implausible expedition, whose recounting may indeed find a few disbelievers.

Captain Farragut did not wish to waste a day, nor even an hour, before heading for the seas where the animal had just been reported. He sent for his engineer.

'Are we under pressure?'

'Aye-aye, sir.'

'Go 'head!'* cried Captain Farragut.

Hearing this order, transmitted to the machine-room by means of an air tube, the engineers activated the starting-up wheel. The steam hissed as it rushed through the half-open slide valves. The long horizontal pistons groaned and pushed the crank arms of the drive shaft. The propeller blades beat the waves with increasing speed as the *Abraham Lincoln* advanced majestically through a hundred ferry-boats and tenders[1] filled with a retinue of spectators.

The wharves of Brooklyn and the part of New York lining the East River were covered with bystanders. Three successive hoorays resounded from half a million chests. Thousands of handkerchiefs continued waving above the dense mass cheering the *Abraham Lincoln* until it reached the waters of the Hudson, at the tip of the elongated peninsula that forms New York City.

Then the frigate followed the splendid right bank of the river, the New Jersey shore crowded with villas, and passed between the forts, which saluted it with their largest cannons. The *Abraham Lincoln* responded by lowering and raising the American flag three times, with the 39 stars* resplendent on the tip of the mizzenmast. Then,

---

[1] Small steam-driven boats that serve the great steamships. [JV]

slowing down to take the buoys marking the channel which curves round the bay formed by Sandy Hook, it hugged the sandy shore, where thousands of spectators greeted it with more applause.

The escort of boats and tenders continued to follow the frigate, only leaving it when abeam of the lightship whose two beacons mark the entrance to New York Bay.

Three o'clock was striking. The pilot climbed down into his boat and boarded the small schooner waiting for him to leeward. The boilers were stoked up, the propeller beat the waves faster, and the frigate skirted the low, yellow coast of Long Island. At eight o'clock, having left the lights of Fire Island to the north-west, it was steaming at full speed over the dark waters of the Atlantic.

4

NED LAND

Captain Farragut was a fine sailor, and worthy of the frigate he commanded. He and his ship were one. He was its soul. He did not allow the slightest doubt about the cetacean to enter his mind, nor did he permit any discussion on board as to whether the animal existed. He believed in it as some good women believe in Leviathan,* through faith not reason. The monster existed; and he had taken an oath to rid the seas of it. He was like a Knight of Rhodes,* a Dieudonné of Gozo,* marching out to face the serpent laying waste to his island. Either Captain Farragut would kill the narwhal or the narwhal would kill Captain Farragut. There could be no middle course.

The officers shared the captain's views. You could hear them chatter and debate and argue and calculate the chances of an encounter as they scanned the vast stretches of ocean. Quite a few of them voluntarily stood watch, clambering up to the fore-topmast crosstrees, when under other circumstances they would have cursed the duty as a terrible chore. Every moment the sun spent describing its daily arc, the rigging was full of people unable to remain in one place on deck, like cats on hot bricks. And yet the *Abraham Lincoln*'s stem had not even started cutting the suspicious waters of the Pacific.

As for the ship's crew, they longed with all their hearts to meet the unicorn and so harpoon it, hoist it on board, and carve it up. They painstakingly scrutinized the sea. Captain Farragut had in fact promised $2,000 to the first person to spot the animal, whether cabin boy, able seaman, mate, or officer. So I leave to your imagination how much those on board the *Abraham Lincoln* used their eyes.

For my own part, I was as engrossed as the others, and would not have let anyone take my share of the daily watch. The frigate could have had a hundred reasons to be called the *Argus*.* The only exception was Conseil; he demonstrated indifference to the question absorbing us, thus constituting a slight 'damper' to the enthusiasm on board.

I previously mentioned that Captain Farragut had carefully armed his ship with everything needed to catch the enormous cetacean. A whaling ship could not have been better equipped. We possessed all known weapons, from the simple hand-harpoon, via a blunderbuss firing barbed arrows, to exploding bullets from a punt-gun. On the fo'c'sle stood the latest model of breech-loading cannon with a great thick barrel and narrow bore, identical to the one due to be exhibited at the 1867 Universal Exposition.* This valuable American-made weapon could send a 4-kilogram conical shot a mean distance of 16 kilometres with the greatest of ease.

Thus every means of destruction was at hand on the *Abraham Lincoln*. But there existed better than this. There was Ned Land,* the king of the harpooners.

Ned was a Canadian of almost unbelievable manual dexterity, unrivalled in his perilous profession. He possessed skill and composure, bravery and cunning to a remarkable degree, and it was an exceptionally devious whale or smart cachalot that could elude his harpoon.

Ned was about forty years old. He was burly, more than six feet tall, muscular, grave, silent, sometimes aggressive, and very bad-tempered when contradicted. He compelled attention through his appearance, especially the power of his gaze, which made his facial expression quite remarkable.

I believe that Captain Farragut had done well to engage this man. Because of his steadiness of eye and arm, he was worth the rest of the crew put together. I can only compare him to a powerful telescope combined with a cannon always ready to go off.

A Canadian is really a Frenchman, and however uncommunicative Ned Land seemed, I must admit that he developed a certain affection for me. My nationality attracted him no doubt. It was an opportunity for him to speak and for me to hear the old language of Rabelais,* still in use in some of the Canadian provinces. The harpooner's family came from the town of Quebec, and had already become a tribe of robust fishermen when that town belonged to France.

Gradually Ned came to enjoy chatting: I liked listening to his tales of adventure on the Arctic seas. He showed much natural poetry of expression in recounting his fishing exploits and battles. His stories had an epic form, and I imagined I was listening to a Canadian Homer* reciting some *Iliad* of the polar regions.

I am in fact describing this hardy companion as I now know him. We became old friends, united by an unshakeable friendship that was initiated and sealed by the most terrible shared experiences. Oh good Ned, how I long to live another hundred years just to be able to remember you for longer!

So what was Land's opinion concerning the marine monster? I must admit that he scarcely credited the unicorn theory, being the only man on board not to share the general conviction. He even avoided the subject when I tried to engage him on it.

On the lovely evening of 30 July, three weeks after our departure,* the frigate was about 30 miles to leeward of Cape Blanco on the coast of Patagonia. We had crossed the tropic of Capricorn, and the Strait of Magellan was scarcely 700 miles southwards. Within a week the *Abraham Lincoln* would be sailing over the waters of the Pacific.

Sitting on the poop deck, Ned and I were chatting about this and that while watching the mysterious ocean, whose depths are still hidden from human eyes.* I brought the conversation discreetly round to the subject of the giant unicorn, and explored the chances of success of our expedition. Then, noticing that Ned was letting me talk without saying a word, I pressed him more directly:

'But how is it, Ned, that you are so unconvinced of the existence of the cetacean we are pursuing? Have you any particular reason for being so sceptical?'

The harpooner looked at me for a few seconds without replying, struck his forehead with a gesture he often used, closed his eyes as if to collect his thoughts, and at last said:

'Perhaps I have, Dr Aronnax.'

'But, Ned, a man like you, a professional whaler, familiar with the great marine animals, who must easily be able to accept the idea of enormous whales—under these circumstances you ought to be the last person to harbour any doubts!'

'It's just there that you're wrong, monsieur. It's one thing for common folk to choose to believe in incredible comets crossing space or prehistoric monsters living inside the earth; but neither the astronomer nor the geologist accept such fantasies.* The same goes for the whaler. I've hunted hundreds of whales, harpooned scores, killed quite a few; but however strong and well-armed they were, not one of their tails or tusks could have pierced the side of a metal steamship.'

'But, Ned, there have been cases when a narwhal's tooth has pierced ships through and through!'

'Wooden ships perhaps,' replied the Canadian, 'although personally I've never seen it. But until I have proof to the contrary, I can't believe that a whale, cachalot, or sea-unicorn could manage such a thing.'

'Just listen to me, Ned . . .'

'No, sir, no. Anything you like except that. Perhaps a giant squid . . .?'

'Even less likely. The squid is only a mollusc; and its flesh is soft, as that very term implies. Even if it were 500 feet long, the squid wouldn't belong to the branch of vertebrates, and so remains perfectly harmless to ships like the *Scotia* or *Abraham Lincoln*. We must therefore relegate all feats of krakens and suchlike monsters to the realm of fable.'

'Then, sir,' said Ned in rather a mocking tone, 'as a naturalist, are you sticking to your opinion of a huge cetacean?'

'Yes, Ned, I repeat my view with a conviction based on the logic of facts. I believe in the existence of a large powerful mammal belonging to the vertebrates, like the whale, cachalot, or dolphin, and endowed with a tusk made of horn of very great penetrative power.'

'H'm,' said the harpooner, shaking his head like one refusing to be convinced.

'Just consider, my good Canadian, that if such an animal does exist, and lives a few miles below the surface of the ocean, it would have to have a body of unparalleled strength.'

'And why would it need such a powerful body?'

'Because it would require incredible strength to live so far down and resist the pressure.'*

'Really?' said Ned, looking at me and winking.

'Yes, and a few statistics can easily prove it.'

'Oh statistics! You can do anything you want with statistics!'

'In business, Ned, but not in mathematics. Please listen. Let us assume that atmospheric pressure is equivalent to the pressure of a column of water 32 feet high. In reality the column would be shorter, since it would be sea water, which is denser than fresh water. Well, Ned, when you dive, your body undergoes a pressure equal to 1 atmosphere for every 32 feet of water you go down, that is 1 kilogram for each square centimetre of its surface. It follows that this pressure would be 10 atmospheres at 320 feet, 100 atmospheres at 3,200 feet, and 1,000 atmospheres at 32,000 feet, or about 2½ leagues. In other words, if you could reach this depth, each square centimetre on your body would be undergoing a pressure of 1,000 kilograms. Now, my good Ned, do you know how many square centimetres you have on your body?'

'No idea, Dr Aronnax.'

'About 17,000.'

'As many as that?'

'And since atmospheric pressure is in fact slightly more than 1 kilogram per square centimetre, your 17,000 square centimetres are at this very moment undergoing a pressure of 17,568 kilograms.'

'Without me realizing?'

'Without your realizing. And the only reason you are not crushed is the air entering your body with equal force. The inward and outward pressures are in perfect equilibrium, they cancel each other out, and so you can bear them without discomfort. But it is not the same underwater.'

'Now I understand,' Ned replied, suddenly more attentive. 'Because the water is all round me, and isn't coming into my body.'

'Precisely, Ned. So at 32 feet you would be subject to a pressure of 17,568 kilograms; at 320 feet ten times that pressure, namely 175,680 kilograms; at 3,200 feet a hundred times, or 1,756,800 kilograms; and at 32,000 feet at least a thousand times, or 17,568,000 kilograms. In other words you would be as flat as if between the plates of a hydraulic press.'

'Amazing!' exclaimed Ned.

'So my good harpooner, if vertebrates several hundred metres long and of corresponding girth inhabit such depths, their surface area is millions of square centimetres and the pressure on their bodies must be estimated to be billions of kilograms. Calculate now what the strength of their skeletons and robustness of their bodies must be to withstand such pressures.'

'They must be made of 8-inch metal plate, like ironclads.'

'Exactly, Ned, and now think of the damage that such a mass would do if it hit the hull of a ship while moving at the speed of an express train.'

'Well . . . yes . . . perhaps,' said the Canadian, shaken by these figures but unwilling to concede.

'Are you convinced now?'

'You have convinced me of one thing, monsieur, which is that if such animals do live at the bottom of the seas, they must clearly be as strong as you say they are.'

'But if they do not exist, my obstinate harpooner, how can you possibly explain the accident to the *Scotia*?'

'Perhaps . . .' he began.

'Well go on!'

'. . . because it's not true,' he retorted, unwittingly echoing a celebrated riposte of Arago's.* But this reply simply proved the harpooner's obstinacy—nothing more. I pressed him no further on this occasion. The accident to the *Scotia* was undeniable. The hole existed to the extent that it had had to be stopped up, and I do not think that a hole's existence can be demonstrated any more conclusively. And as the incision did not get there on its own, and since it had not been produced by submarine rocks or weaponry, it must have been caused by the perforating tool of some animal.

Now in my view, and for the reasons already listed, this animal had to belong to the branch of vertebrates, class of mammalia, group of pisciforms, order of Cetaceae. As for the family—i.e. whale, cachalot, or dolphin—and genus and species, these could be determined later. To decide, we would have to dissect the unknown monster; to dissect it, catch it; to catch it, harpoon it, which was Ned Land's job; to harpoon it, see it, the ship's affair; and to see it, first encounter it—which was up to chance.

5

AT RANDOM

FOR a while the voyage of the *Abraham Lincoln* continued without any particular incident. Nevertheless, something did occur which served to demonstrate both Land's remarkable prowess and the confidence one could have in him.

On 30 June,* off the Falklands, the frigate communicated with some American whalers, who told us that they had had no contact with the narwhal. But the captain of one of the ships, the *Monroe*,* knew that Ned was on board the *Abraham Lincoln*, and asked for his help in hunting down a whale then in view. Captain Farragut wanted to see Ned Land in action, and therefore authorized him to go on board the *Monroe*. And luck so favoured the Canadian that he harpooned two whales for the price of one so to speak, striking one through the heart and capturing another after a chase of only minutes.

Decidedly, if ever the monster came to grips with Ned Land, my bet would not be on the monster.

The frigate sailed down the south-east coast of the Americas at a tremendous rate of knots. On 3 July we were at the mouth of the Strait of Magellan near Cape Virgins. But Captain Farragut didn't want to enter such a tortuous channel, and directed our course round Cape Horn instead.

The crew lent their unanimous support. After all, was it likely we would encounter the narwhal in such a narrow passage? A number of sailors declared that the monster couldn't get through, 'as it's too big to fit!'

At about 3 p.m. on 6 July, keeping fifteen miles to the south, the *Abraham Lincoln* rounded a solitary island, an isolated rock at the extreme tip of the American continent: Cape Horn as it was called by Dutch sailors after their native town. Our course now lay north-westwards; and next day the frigate's screws were finally beating the waves of the Pacific.

'Keep your eyes peeled,' the sailors kept saying to each other.

And they did keep them exceptionally peeled. There was not a moment's rest for eyes or for telescopes—both slightly dazzled, admittedly, by the prospect of the $2,000. The ocean was scanned day and night. Those with good night-vision had a 50 per cent better chance, and thus a very respectable prospect of winning the prize.

As for me, although largely immune to the lure of the money, I was one of the most watchful on board. Wasting only minutes on meals and a few hours on sleep, oblivious to the glare and wind, I rarely left the deck. Sometimes I leaned over the fo'c'sle rail but sometimes on the poop-rail, my greedy eyes devouring the cottony wake that whitened the ocean as far as the horizon. And how often I shared the officers' and men's emotions when some whale capriciously raised its blackish back above the surface! The frigate's deck would be crowded in an instant. The hatchways would throw up a torrent of officers and men. Panting for air, with restless eyes, all would watch the cetacean as it moved through the waves. I also looked, at the risk of wearing out my retinas and going blind—while Conseil, always phlegmatic, kept calmly repeating:

'If monsieur would be so good as to open his eyes a little less, monsieur would see much better.'

But the excitement was invariably unrequited. The *Abraham Lincoln* would change its course towards the animal in question, a mere whale or common cachalot, which soon disappeared amidst a volley of curses.

For the moment the weather remained favourable. The voyage was taking place in perfect conditions. It was meant to be the stormy season, for July in the southern latitudes corresponds to our January in Europe, but the sea remained calm and could be observed over vast distances.

Ned still displayed the most unwavering scepticism. Except on his watch, he pretended not to examine the sea, at least when there were no whales in view. Even though his perfect eyesight would have rendered great service, the stubborn Canadian spent eight out of twelve hours reading or sleeping in his cabin. A hundred times I reproached his detachment.

'Bah!' he would reply. 'There's nothing there, Dr Aronnax, and even if there was, what chance would we have of seeing it? We're wandering at random, aren't we? People have seen this invisible beast on the high seas of the Pacific, or so they say, and I accept that; but two months have gone by since then, and to judge from your narwhal's temperament, it doesn't like hanging around the same area. It can move at outrageous speeds. Now you know as well as me, Dr Aronnax, that nature doesn't do anything the wrong way round. So a naturally slow animal wouldn't have been given a speed that it didn't need. Therefore if the beast does exist, it'll be hundreds of miles away by now!'

I had no reply. We were evidently travelling blind. But how else could we proceed? Our chances of success were very slim. However, no one gave up hope, and there wasn't a sailor on board who would have laid odds against the narwhal making a new appearance.

We crossed the tropic of Capricorn at 105° W on 20 July, and on the 27th the equator at 110° W. Having taken its bearings, the frigate now set a more westerly course, heading into the middle of the Pacific. Captain Farragut thought, quite sensibly, that the monster would be most likely to frequent deeper waters. It would keep away from landmasses or islands, which it seemed reluctant to approach, 'no doubt because there wasn't enough water', as the boatswain opined. The frigate passed by the Tuamotus, the Marquesas, and Hawaii, crossed the tropic of Cancer at 132° E, and then sailed on towards the China seas.

We had finally reached the scene of the monster's latest antics. We lived for nothing else. Our hearts palpitated fearfully, laying the foundation for incurable aneurysms in the future. The entire ship's company suffered from a nervous over-excitement that is impossible to describe.

No one ate, no one slept. Twenty times a day an optical illusion or a mistake by some sailor perched on the yardarms gave rise to unbearable aches and pains, and this emotion, repeated twenty times, kept us in a state of permanent erythrism,* one too overwhelming not to produce a reaction sooner or later.

And the reaction did eventually come. For three months—three months when each day lasted a century—the *Abraham Lincoln* had been sailing across every sea in the South Pacific, running up when a whale was signalled, making abrupt turns, sailing first on one tack then on the other, stopping suddenly, reversing then going ahead—all in swift succession and in a manner designed to put the engine entirely out of joint. The ship did not leave a single point unexplored between the shore of Japan and the west coast of America. But there was nothing there, nothing except the vastness of the watery wilderness. No sign of a giant narwhal, nor of a submerged islet, shipwrecked hulk, or shifting reef, and no sign whatsoever of anything remotely supernatural.

Then the reaction set in. First came discouragement, which permeated minds and prepared the way for scepticism. A new mood arose, made up of three-tenths shame and seven-tenths anger. Everyone on board felt very foolish, and all the more annoyed because we had been taken in by a mirage. The mountains of arguments that had piled up for a year crumbled away immediately, and the only idea in everybody's head was to employ the hours for eating and sleeping, and so make up for all the time so stupidly lost.

With the fickleness of the human mind, we went from one extreme to the other. The keenest supporters of the enterprise inevitably became its most ardent detractors. The reaction came, starting from the depths, moving from the stokers' hold to the officers' watchroom; and had it not been for the uncommon obstinacy of Captain Farragut, the frigate's prow would certainly have headed straight back south again.

In fact this fruitless search could not go on any longer. The *Abraham Lincoln* could have no reason to reproach itself, having done its utmost to ensure success. Never had an American Navy crew shown more patience or energy, and the failure could not be blamed on anyone. There now remained no choice but to go home.

A representation to this effect was addressed to the captain. He stood firm. The sailors did not conceal their discontent, and the service deteriorated. I do not mean that there was actually a mutiny, but after a reasonable period of perseverance Captain Farragut asked for three more days, like Columbus before him.* If in that time the monster had still not appeared, the helmsman would receive orders to put about, and the *Abraham Lincoln* would head for the North Atlantic.

This promise was made on 2 November. Its immediate effect was to restore the crew's failing courage. The ocean was scanned with fresh zeal. Everyone wished to take that one last look wherein memory lies. Telescopes were feverishly employed. This was the final challenge hurled at the giant narwhal: he couldn't now refuse to reply to this taunt to show himself!

Two days went by. The *Abraham Lincoln* stayed on low pressure. The crew employed a thousand ways of catching the attention or stirring the apathy of the animal, should he happen to be passing by. Enormous quantities of bacon were trailed from the stern—to the great satisfaction of the sharks, I may add. While the frigate lay hove to, the boats rowed in all directions round it, not leaving a single spot of the ocean unexplored. But the evening of 4 November arrived without any elucidation of the submarine mystery.

The grace period was due to expire at noon the following day. After determining his position, Captain Farragut, faithful to his promise, would have to give orders to head south-east and abandon the northern Pacific.

The frigate was at 3° 15′ N, 136° 42′ E. The landmass of Japan lay less than 200 miles to leeward. Night was coming down. Eight bells had just rung out. Heavy clouds veiled the moon, now in its first quarter. The sea rose and fell calmly below the stern.

I was for'ard, leaning over the starboard rail. Conseil was beside me, staring ahead. The ship's crew, perched in the shrouds, were scanning the horizon, which was closing in as it got darker. The officers, equipped with night glasses, peered into the increasing gloom. The sombre sea would at times scintillate from the moonlight darting between the edges of the clouds. Then all luminous trace would be swallowed up again by the darkness.

Observing Conseil, I noticed that the good fellow was yielding ever so slightly to the general mood. Or at least I thought so. Perhaps, for the first time in his life, his nerves were tingling with a feeling of curiosity. 'Well, Conseil,' said I; 'here is our last chance to pocket the $2,000.'

'Monsieur must permit me to say that I have never counted on winning this sum; and the government of the Union might have promised $100,000 and been none the poorer.'

'You're right, Conseil. This has turned out to be a crazy business that we rushed into without aforethought. Consider how much time we've wasted! Worrying about nothing! We could have been back in France a full six months ago.'

'In monsieur's little apartment, in monsieur's museum. I would already have classified monsieur's fossils, and the babirusa would be settled in his cage in the Jardin des Plantes, attracting all the inquisitive people of Paris.'

'Exactly, Conseil, and no doubt they will all laugh at us.'

'Yes,' he said quietly, 'I do think they may laugh at monsieur. And may I add . . .?'

'You may.'

'Well, monsieur will only be getting what monsieur deserves.'

'Indeed!'

'When one has the honour of being a scholar like monsieur, one does not expose oneself . . .'

But Conseil was never to finish his compliment. A voice had just rung out through the surrounding silence. It was Ned Land's, shouting: 'Ahoy! The thing itself, to leeward on the weather beam!'

6

FULL STEAM AHEAD

AT this cry the whole crew ran towards the harpooner: captain, officers, mates, seamen, and cabin boys—even the engineers abandoned the engine-room, and the stokers the boilers. The order 'Stop her!' was heard, and now the frigate was gliding over the water under its own momentum.

It was very dark: however good the Canadian's eyes might be, I wondered exactly what he had seen and how he had been able to see it. My heart was pounding as if to burst.

But Ned Land had not been mistaken, and we all soon spotted the object he was pointing at.

Not far from the *Abraham Lincoln*, on the starboard quarter, the sea seemed to be illuminated from below. There could be no mistake, for this was no ordinary phosphorescence. Several fathoms below the surface, the monster gave forth a very strong, inexplicable light, as described in the reports of several captains. This fantastic irradiation must have been produced by some tremendously powerful illuminating agent. The luminous area on the surface formed a huge, highly elongated ellipse, whose centre was a burning, concentrated focus of unbearable intensity, but which gradually faded further from the centre.

'It's just a mass of phosphorescent organisms!' cried one of the officers.

'No, sir,' I replied with conviction. 'Neither the common piddock nor the salpa produces such a powerful light. This brilliance is essentially electric . . . In any case look, *look!* It's moving, moving forward—going back—coming straight at us!'

A cry rose from the frigate.

'Quiet!' shouted Captain Farragut. 'Put the helm up hard! Ship astern!'

The sailors rushed to the wheel; the engineers to the engine-room. The power was immediately reversed and the *Abraham Lincoln* paid off, describing a semicircle to port.

'Helm straight . . . go ahead!' cried Farragut.

As these orders were executed, the frigate moved swiftly away from the luminous centre.

I am wrong. The frigate *tried* to move away, but the supernatural animal closed in at twice our speed.

We could hardly breathe. Astonishment rather than fear kept us silent as if transfixed. The animal caught up with us with the greatest of ease. It swam round the frigate, which was making 14 knots, and bathed us in its electric beams like luminous dust. It then moved two or three miles off, leaving a phosphorescent trail, like the spirals of steam behind the locomotive of an express train. All of a sudden, from the dark limits of the horizon, the monster accelerated and rushed at the *Abraham Lincoln* at frightening speed, then stopped abruptly only 20 feet from the frigate's wales and extinguished its light—not by plunging beneath the surface, since the brilliance did not disappear gradually—but suddenly, as if the source of the brilliant discharge had instantly dried up! It then appeared on the other side, meaning it had either gone round or underneath. At every moment a collision seemed imminent: one which could easily be fatal to us.

I was puzzled by the frigate's behaviour. It was running away and not fighting. It was being hunted when it was meant to be the hunter—and I said as much to Captain Farragut. His normally impassive face betrayed an indefinable astonishment.

'Dr Aronnax,' he replied, 'I do not know what formidable creature I am dealing with—and I do not want to risk my ship needlessly in this darkness. In any case, how can one attack an unidentified object, or even defend oneself? Let's wait for daylight, when the tables will be turned.'

'So you have no doubts about the nature of the animal?'

'It's obviously a giant narwhal, but an electric one too.'

'Perhaps it is just as dangerous to approach as an electric eel or ray?'

'Quite possibly. And if it does have the ability to give an electric shock, then it will be the most terrible beast ever to have sprung from the Creator's hand. That is why, sir, I must remain on my guard.'

That night the entire crew stayed at action stations. Nobody thought of going to bed. Unable to outrun the creature, the *Abraham Lincoln* had first decreased its pace, and then stayed on easy steam. For its part, the narwhal lay rocking on the waves, just like the frigate: it seemed to have decided to remain at the scene of battle.

At about midnight, however, it disappeared, or rather 'went out' like an enormous glow-worm. Had it left? This was to be feared, rather than hoped for. But then at 12.53 a deafening hissing sound came, like the one produced by a head of water escaping with tremendous force.

Captain Farragut, Ned, and I were on the poop. We intently searched the deep darkness.

'Ned Land,' said the captain, 'have you often heard whales blowing?'

'Yes, sir, but never whales that pay $2,000 when you sight them.'

'You have indeed earned the prize. But tell me, is this the same noise cetaceans make when they eject water from their blowholes?'

'It's the same sound, sir, but much, much louder. I'm certain it's a whale astern. With your permission, sir, we'll have a word or two with him at first light.'

'If he is in a mood to listen, Master Land,' I said in a sceptical tone.

'If I get within four harpoons' distance,' riposted the Canadian, 'he'll have to listen!'

'But for you to get near must I give you a whaling-boat?' enquired the captain.

'Obviously, sir.'

'And in so doing, risk the lives of my men?'

'And mine too,' replied Land simply.

At about two in the morning, the light came back, just as bright but five miles to windward of the *Abraham Lincoln*. Despite the distance and the noise from the wind and waves, the formidable beating of the monster's tail could distinctly be heard, even its hoarse respiration. When the huge narwhal came to the surface to breathe, the air rushing into its lungs was just like the steam in the massive pistons of a 2,000-horsepower engine.

'H'm,' I thought, 'a whale with the horsepower of a whole regiment of cavalry must be a fine specimen!'

Everyone remained active until daybreak, getting ready for battle. The fishing tackle was laid out along the rails. The first mate ordered the loading not only of the blunderbusses that could throw a harpoon a distance of a mile but also of the long punt-guns for firing exploding bullets which are fatal to the most powerful of animals. Ned Land merely sharpened his harpoon, a terrible weapon in his hands.

At six o'clock dawn began to break, and with the first gleams, the narwhal's electric light went out. At seven the sun was high enough, but visibility was destroyed by a thick fog which the best glasses could not pierce. Hence considerable disappointment and exasperation.

I climbed the mizzenmast. A few officers were already perched around the masthead.

At eight o'clock the fog began to roll heavily over the waves, as its thick spirals dissipated. Our horizon gradually expanded as the mists cleared.

Ned's voice rang out, just like the day before.

'The thing in question, port astern!'

Everyone looked in the direction indicated.

About a mile and a half from the frigate, a long black body emerged about 3 feet above the waves. Its tail was beating violently and producing a considerable swell. Never had a tail hit the water with such force. An enormous wake of dazzling whiteness marked the course of the animal as it described a long curve.

The frigate approached the cetacean. I examined it as closely as I wished. The *Shannon* and *Helvetia*'s reports had slightly exaggerated its dimensions, for I estimated its length to be only 250 feet. As for its girth, this was difficult to evaluate, but the animal's dimensions appeared admirably in proportion.

While I was examining the phenomenal creature, two jets of water and vapour spurted from its blowholes and rose to a height of 120 feet—thus settling its method of respiration. I concluded once and for all that the animal belonged to the vertebrates, class of mammals, sub-class of monodelphians, group of pisciforms, order of cetaceans, family—but here I was unable to make up my mind. The order of Cetaceae comprises three families, whales, cachalots, and dolphins, with narwhals classified in the last category. Each family is in turn divided into several genera, each genus into species, and each species into varieties. I did not yet know the creature's variety, species, genus, or family, but I felt confident about being able to complete my classification with the help of Heaven and Captain Farragut.

The crew were waiting impatiently for orders. The captain observed the creature carefully, then called the chief engineer, who quickly ran up.

'Have you plenty of steam?'

'Aye-aye, sir.'

'Good. Fire up; and full steam ahead.'

Three cheers greeted this order. The time had come to fight. Soon the frigate's two funnels were belching forth torrents of black smoke and the engines were making the deck shudder and shake.

Propelled on by its powerful screw, the *Abraham Lincoln* headed for the animal. The creature allowed the frigate to get quite close, but then moved slightly away, keeping at the same distance but not bothering to dive.

This pursuit continued for about three-quarters of an hour without the frigate gaining three metres on the cetacean. It became obvious that if we carried on in this way we would never catch up.

Captain Farragut was angrily twisting the thick clump of hair sprouting from his chin.

'Land!'

The Canadian arrived.

'Well, Master Land,' said the captain, 'do you still think we should launch the boats?'

'No, sir; for the creature will not let you take him unless he wants you to.'

'So what should we do then?'

'Keep maximum pressure, sir. With your permission, I'll wait under the bowsprit, and if we get within distance I'll harpoon him.'

'Fine, Ned!'

And to the engineer: 'Go ahead faster!'

Ned Land took up his position. The furnaces were stoked, the propeller turned at 43 revolutions a minute, and the steam roared through the valves. The log was heaved, and showed the frigate's speed to be 18½ knots.

But the cursed animal was also moving at 18½ knots.

For another hour the frigate continued at this pace without gaining a metre. This was rather humiliating for one of the fastest vessels in the United States Navy. A profound anger overwhelmed the ship's crew. They swore at the monster, which did not, however, condescend to reply. Captain Farragut no longer twisted his goatee, he chewed it.

The engineer was summoned again.

'Are you at your absolute maximum pressure?'

'Yes, sir!'

'What pressure?'

'Six-and-a-half atmospheres.'

'Make it ten!'

This was truly an American order. It couldn't have been bettered in a Mississippi riverboat race, 'so as to leave the competition behind'.

'Conseil,' said I to my faithful servant standing nearby, 'do you realize that we may easily blow up?'

'Whatever monsieur says.'

But I had to admit I was glad we were giving it a go.

The steam-gauge rose. The furnaces overflowed with coal. The fans sent torrents of air on to the flames. The ship moved faster. The very steps of the masts shook, and the funnels seemed hardly big enough to let out the thick vortices of smoke.

The log was heaved again.

'Well, helmsman?' enquired the captain.

'Nineteen point three sir.'

'Stoke the fires higher.'

The engineer obeyed. The steam-gauge showed 10 atmospheres. But the narwhal had 'fired up' as well, for it was now also proceeding at 19.3 knots, without effort.

What a chase! I cannot describe the feelings that moved my whole being. Ned stood at the ready, harpoon in hand. Several times the animal allowed us to get nearer.

'We're gaining, we are!' cried the Canadian.

But just as he was preparing to strike, the cetacean would shoot ahead at a speed I cannot estimate at less than 30 knots. And even at the frigate's maximum speed, it played with us by going round us! Cries of fury came from every man's breast.

At noon we had got no further than at eight o'clock.

Captain Farragut decided to employ more direct methods.

'So', he said, 'the animal can move faster than the *Abraham Lincoln*. We will see if he can outrun a conical shell. Bosun, man the for'ard gun.'

The bow gun was immediately loaded and aimed. It went off, but the shot passed several feet above the cetacean, half a mile away.

'Somebody with a better aim!' shouted the captain. 'And there's $500 for the man who puts a shot into the infernal beast.'

An old gunner with a grey beard—I can still see him—came forward with a determined air and a steady eye. He pointed the gun and took careful aim. A loud detonation was heard amidst the crew's cheers.

The shot reached its target and hit the animal, but not at right angles: it glanced off its rounded flank, and fell into the sea two miles away.

'Humph!' cried the angry old gunner. 'The cursed thing is armoured in 6-inch iron plate!'

'Damnation!' shouted Captain Farragut.

The chase began again. The captain leaned towards me: 'I shall pursue that animal until my frigate blows up!'

'Good on you, you're right!'

Our only hope was that the creature would be more prone to fatigue than a steam-driven engine and would sooner or later exhaust itself. But no such luck. The hours passed and still the animal showed no sign of feeling weary.

I must say in support of the *Abraham Lincoln* that it fought with tireless determination. I estimated the distance it covered on that unfortunate 6 November* to be at least 300 miles. But eventually night fell and cloaked the blustery sea in its shadows. I imagined that our expedition was finished, that we had seen the last of the fantastic creature. But I was wrong.

At 10.50, roughly three miles to windward, the electric light appeared again, as clear and as bright as the night before.

The narwhal seemed to be motionless. Perhaps it felt tired after the day's exertions, and was sleeping in the swaying cradle of the billows? This was an opportunity Farragut decided to seize.

He gave a few orders. The frigate was put on easy steam, and proceeded cautiously so as not to wake its enemy. It is not unusual to meet whales fast asleep in mid-ocean, and they are sometimes attacked with success: Ned Land had frequently harpooned them in this way. He took up position under the bowsprit.

The frigate moved towards the animal and stopped its engines not far away, quietly drifting on under its momentum. No one dared breathe. A profound silence reigned on deck. We were now less than 100 feet from the bright centre, whose light began to blind us as we got closer.

I saw Land on the fo'c'sle below, holding the martingale in one hand and brandishing his terrible harpoon in the other. We were scarcely 20 feet from the motionless monster.

Suddenly Ned's arm moved violently, and the harpoon shot forward. I heard the sonorous blow as it hit the prey; it sounded as though it had come into contact with a hard substance.

The electric light went out abruptly. Two enormous columns of water* crashed over the frigate's deck, rushed fore and aft like a river, knocked the crew down, and broke the lashings on the spars.

There was an awesome impact and before I had time to hold on, I was thrown over the bulwark and into the sea.

7

AN UNKNOWN SPECIES OF WHALE*

ALTHOUGH I was surprised by my unexpected fall, I retained nonetheless a clear memory of my sensations.

At first I was plunged down to a depth of about 20 feet. I am a strong swimmer, although not claiming to be as good as Byron or Poe, who are masters;* and this nosedive did not cause me any panic. Two strong kicks took me back to the surface.

My first concern was to locate the frigate. Had the crew noticed my disappearance? Had the *Abraham Lincoln* put about? Was Captain Farragut launching a boat? Could I hope to be rescued?

It was very dark. I could see a black object disappearing in the east, its position lights dimmed by the distance. It was the frigate. I felt lost.

'Help! Help!' I shouted, swimming despairingly in the direction of the *Abraham Lincoln*.

My clothes got in the way. The water made them stick to my body, greatly hampering my movements. I was sinking; I was suffocating.

'Help!'

This was the last cry I uttered. My mouth filled with water. I fought as I sank into the depths.

Suddenly my clothes were seized by a strong hand. I felt myself being pulled roughly back up to the surface, and I heard—yes, heard—words in my ear: 'If monsieur would have the great kindness to lean on my shoulder, monsieur could swim more easily.'

I seized the arm of my faithful Conseil.

'Is it you?' I said. '*You!*'

'In person,' replied Conseil; 'at monsieur's orders.'

'The collision threw you into the sea at the same time?'

'Not at all; but I followed monsieur since I am in monsieur's service.'

The worthy fellow could see nothing extraordinary in that!

'And the frigate?'

'The frigate,' replied Conseil turning on his back; 'I think monsieur would do better not to rely on it.'

'What do you mean?'

'I mean that as I jumped overboard, I heard the helmsman shout "The screw and rudder are broken!" '

'Broken?'

'Yes, by the tusk of the monster. It was apparently the only damage to the *Abraham Lincoln*. But unfortunately for us, it can no longer steer.'

'Then we are lost!'

'Perhaps so,' replied Conseil calmly. 'But we still have some hours ahead of us, and a great many things may be accomplished in such a time.'

The imperturbable equanimity of Conseil gave me new strength. I swam more energetically; but I was hindered by the clothes sticking to me like lead weights, and found it very difficult to stay afloat. Conseil noticed this.

'Will monsieur permit me to make a slight incision?'

And sliding a naked blade into my clothes, he slit them from top to bottom with a quick slash. Then he smartly took them off, while I swam for us both.

I rendered him the same favour; and we continued to 'navigate' close together.

But the situation remained alarming. Our disappearance had perhaps not been noticed, and even if it had, the rudderless frigate could not come back for us against the wind. The boats were our only chance.

Conseil calmly reasoned out this idea, and made plans accordingly. What an amazing character! The phlegmatic fellow was behaving as if at home!

It was thus concluded that our only chance of being saved constituted being rescued by the frigate's dinghies and that we needed to arrange matters so as to wait for them as long as possible. I decided that we should divide our energies in order not to exhaust us both; and this was how we managed it. While one lay motionless on his back, with arms folded and legs extended, the other would swim and push him along. The role of tugboat was to last for only ten minutes, and by taking it in turn, we might be able to swim for several hours, possibly even until dawn.

It was only a small chance, but hope is firmly rooted in the human heart. Also, there were two of us. Although I tried to destroy all hope, indeed to fall into the deepest despair, I declare my inability to do so, however improbable this may seem.

The collision between the frigate and the cetacean had happened at about 11 p.m. I estimated eight hours' swimming before sunrise: a perfectly feasible operation if we took it in turns. The sea was smooth, and did not tire us greatly. Sometimes I tried to penetrate the thick darkness, broken only by the phosphorescence from our movements. I looked at the luminous wavelets breaking over my hand, with their gleaming surface covered with paler areas. It was as if we were swimming in a bath of mercury.

At about one o'clock I suddenly felt very tired. My limbs were seized by violent cramps. Conseil had to support me, and our survival now depended upon his unaided efforts. I soon heard the poor fellow panting. His breathing was coming short and hurried. I realized that he couldn't go on much longer.

'Let me go!' I cried. 'Leave me behind!'

'Abandon monsieur? Never! I intend to drown before he does.'

Just then the moon broke through the edge of a large cloud running eastwards before the wind. The surface of the sea shone with light. This generous radiance brought back our strength. I raised my head again. I looked round at every point on the horizon. I spotted the frigate. It was about 5 miles away—a black and scarcely identifiable point. And there was no boat!

I tried to cry out; although what was the point at such a distance? My swollen mouth refused to utter a single sound. Conseil could speak a little, and I heard him shouting several times:

'Help! Help!'

Temporarily ceasing our swimming, we listened out. Was that buzzing noise coming from congested blood pressure in my ear; or was it an answer to Conseil's cry?

'Did you hear that?' I murmured.

'Yes, yes!'

And Conseil sent another desperate cry into the air.

This time there could be no mistake. A human voice replied. Was it the voice of some other unfortunate abandoned in the midst of the ocean—some other victim of that collision? Or was it a boat from the frigate hailing us through the darkness?

Conseil made a supreme effort and, leaning on my shoulder while I resisted in a final paroxysm, he half rose out of the water before falling back exhausted.

'What did you see?'

'I saw,' he murmured, 'I saw—but let's not talk, let's keep our strength up!'

What had he seen? For some reason, the monster came back to my mind for the first time. But there was the voice. Gone are the days when Jonahs lived in the bellies of whales!*

Conseil paddled me forward once more. At times he raised his head to look ahead, and uttered a cry of acknowledgement, to which a voice replied, closer each time. I could scarcely hear. My strength was spent; my fingers no longer obeyed me; my hands could no longer keep me up; my mouth, convulsively opening, was filling with salt water; and my limbs were seized by cold. I raised my head one last time, and went under.

At that moment a hard body struck me. I clung to it. Then I felt someone pulling me upwards, bringing me back up to the surface, and with my chest collapsing, I fainted.

I must have come to very quickly thanks to the vigorous massage moving up and down my body. I half opened my eyes.

'Conseil!' I murmured.

'Did monsieur call?'

At the same time, in the last light of the moon going down towards the horizon, I caught sight of another face, not Conseil's, which I immediately recognized.

'Ned!' I exclaimed.

'In person, sir, looking for his prize money!'

'So you were thrown into the sea by the frigate's collision?'

'Yes,' he replied; 'but I was luckier than you were, and managed to set foot on a floating island straightaway.'

'An island?'

'Yes, or rather upon our giant narwhal . . .'

'Explain yourself, Ned.'

'Though I soon realized why my harpoon hadn't stuck in the creature's hide and why it was blunted.'

'But why, Ned, why?'

'Because this beast is made of steel plate!'

I now have to recover my composure, search my memory, and make sure my statements are entirely accurate.

The Canadian's last words produced a sea-change in my mind. I pulled myself up to the top of the half-sunken being or object on which we had taken refuge. I kicked it. It was certainly a hard body: impenetrable and not made of the yielding substance of which the larger marine mammals are made.

But this hard substance might be a bony carapace, like that of certain prehistoric animals; and I might be able to get away with classifying it amongst the amphibious reptiles such as the turtle or alligator.

But it was not to be! The blackish surface I was standing on was smooth and polished, and had no overlapping sections. It gave a metallic sound when struck and, incredible as it seems, I swear that it appeared to be made of riveted metal plates.

Doubt was no longer possible. It had to be admitted that the creature, the monster, the natural occurrence which had puzzled the entire scientific world and baffled and distressed the minds of seamen in both hemispheres, constituted a still greater marvel—a man-made phenomenon.

I would not have been nearly so astonished to find the most fabulous and mythological of creatures. That what is extraordinary could have come from the Creator is easy to believe. But to discover all of a sudden a mysterious human realization of the impossible, to find it before your very eyes, was enough to unhinge your mind.

Nevertheless there was no excuse for hesitation. Here we were sitting on the back of a species of submarine boat, in the shape of a massive steel fish, in so far as I could judge. Such was Ned's firm opinion. Conseil and I had no choice but to agree with him.

'But', said I, 'this contrivance must contain some sort of machinery for moving from place to place, as well as a crew to operate it?'

'It has to,' replied the Canadian; 'but all the same, I've been on this floating island for three hours, and it hasn't given a single sign of life.'

'The boat hasn't moved?'*

'No, Dr Aronnax; it's been rocked by the waves, but it hasn't budged.'

'We know for a fact that it can travel very fast. Now it needs an engine to produce this velocity, and an engineer to operate the engine, therefore I can conclude that we are saved.'

'H'm,' voiced Ned dubiously.

Just then, and as if to prove my point, a disturbance came from the stern of the strange vessel, evidently screw-driven, and it began to move. We scarcely had time to seize hold of the top part, nearly a metre out of the water.* Luckily the speed was not very great.

'As long as it goes over the waves, we're all right,' murmured Ned Land. 'But if it decides to dive, I wouldn't give two dollars for my hide!'

The Canadian might have made a still lower assessment. In any case we now needed to communicate with whatever beings were within the flanks of the machine. I searched on its surface for an opening: a hatch, or manhole to use a more technical term; but the lines of rivets solidly fixed along the joints of the iron plates were secure and regular.

Also the moon disappeared, leaving us in utter darkness. We would be forced to wait for daybreak to find a way of getting inside the submarine vessel.

Our survival thus depended on the caprice of the mysterious helmsmen piloting the machine: if they decided to dive, we were lost. But if they didn't, I was confident of being able to make contact with them. And indeed, if they didn't manufacture their air themselves, they had to come up to the surface sometimes to replenish their supply of breathable molecules. Hence the need for an aperture to open up the interior of the boat to fresh air.

We had given up all hope of being rescued by Captain Farragut. We were being carried westwards; I estimated that we were going at the relatively moderate speed of 12 knots. The screw beat the waves with mathematical regularity, but sometimes emerged and sent phosphorescent jets of water to a great height.

At about 4 a.m. the speed increased. We found it quite difficult to cope with the giddy pace, since the waves whipped into us. Fortunately Ned Land found a large ring set in the upper part of the iron back, and we managed to hold firmly on to it.

The long night finally came to an end. My imperfect memory cannot bring back all the impressions I felt. But one small point comes to mind. During some of the lulls in the wind and the waves, I fancied I could vaguely hear some sort of elusive harmony produced by distant chords. What then was the nature of this submarine navigation which the whole world was seeking in vain to understand? What kind of beings lived in this strange vessel? How did they move at such a prodigious rate?

Daylight appeared. The morning mist wrapped us in its folds, but was then torn asunder. I was about to make a careful survey of the hull, whose upper part formed a kind of horizontal platform, when I realized that it was slowly sinking.

'Hey! What the hell!' cried Ned, loudly stamping on the hull. 'Open up, I say, you pirates!'

But it was difficult to produce a sound while the screw was beating vigorously. Fortunately the sinking stopped.

Suddenly from inside the boat the sound came of bars being pushed back. A plate was raised; a man appeared, uttered a strange cry, and immediately vanished.

A few seconds later, eight strong fellows with expressionless faces silently came out and pulled us into their formidable machine.

8

MOBILIS IN MOBILI*

THIS action, so roughly executed, was carried out with lightning speed. My companions and I had no time to look around. I do not know what Ned and Conseil felt as they entered the floating prison, but for my part I must confess that a brief shudder chilled me to the bone. Who were we dealing with? Doubtless pirates of a new sort, using the seas for their own ends.

Scarcely was the small hatch closed than I was in complete darkness. Coming in from the daylight so suddenly, my eyes were blinded. I felt my bare feet on the rungs of an iron ladder. Land and Conseil, tightly held, followed. At the foot of the ladder a door opened, and immediately shut behind us with a loud clang.

We were alone. Where, I could not say—scarcely even imagine. Everything was black, but of such an absolute blackness that even after several minutes my eyes had not seen any of those uncertain scintillations that linger on, even on the darkest nights.

Ned Land was furious at such treatment and gave free vent to his indignation.

'What the devil!' he cried. 'Even the New Caledonians are more hospitable than these people. All we need now is for them to be cannibals.* I wouldn't be at all surprised; but I will not be eaten without protest!'

'Calm down, Ned, my friend, calm down,' Conseil said quietly. 'Don't get carried away too soon. We're not in the frying pan yet.'

'Frying pan no,' riposted Land, 'but we *are* in the oven. At any rate it's as dark. Luckily I've still got my Bowie-knife[1] on me, and I can see well enough to use it. The first of these bandits that lays a finger on me . . .'

'Don't get angry, Ned,' I said, 'and don't make our position worse by pointless violence. Maybe they can hear us.* Let's try instead to find out where we are.'

I advanced with arms outstretched. At five paces I reached a wall of riveted iron plates. Turning round, I bumped into a wooden table, surrounded by a few stools. The floor of this prison was covered with a thick matting of New Zealand flax that deadened the sound of our feet. The bare walls didn't seem to have any doors or windows. Conseil, who had been working his way round the opposite way, bumped into me, and we came back to the middle of the cabin, which seemed to be about 20 feet by 10. Even Ned, tall as he was, could not find out how high the ceiling was.

The situation did not change for half an hour, but then our eyes were abruptly exposed to a cruelly bright light. Our prison was now

---

[1] A broad-bladed knife that an American always carries with him. [JV]

filled with a luminous element of such brilliance that at first I could not bear it. From its whiteness and intensity I recognized the electric light which had produced the magnificent phosphorescence around the submarine vessel. After being forced to close my eyes, I opened them again and realized that the light came from a ground-glass half-globe in the ceiling of the chamber.

'At last we can see,' cried Ned Land, standing on the defensive, Bowie-knife in hand.

'Yes,' I replied, and risked an antithesis: 'although the situation is no less obscure.'

'If monsieur will only be patient,' said the impassive Conseil.

The sudden illumination of the cabin gave us the opportunity to examine it minutely. It contained nothing but the table and five stools. The door was invisible but clearly hermetically sealed, for no sound reached our ears. Everything seemed dead on board the vessel. I had no idea whether it was still moving over the surface of the ocean or plunging into the depths.

All the same, the lamp had not been lit without reason. I therefore hoped that the crew of the vessel would soon put in an appearance. When you wish to put people away for ever you do not illuminate their dungeon.

I was not mistaken; the sound came of bolts being released, the door opened, and two men came in.

One was rather short but with strong muscles; he had broad shoulders, robust arms and legs, a good head, thick black hair, a vigorous moustache, and alert piercing eyes: his whole body was stamped with that southern vivacity which distinguishes the people of Provence. Diderot* has correctly maintained that man's gestures are metaphoric, and this diminutive man was living proof. One had the impression that his talking would be full of prosopopoeia, metonymy, and hypallage.* But I was never in a position to discover whether this was the case, since he always spoke in my presence in an odd and utterly incomprehensible language.

The second stranger deserves a more detailed description. A pupil of Gratiolet or Engel would have read his physiognomy like a book.* I instantly recognized his dominant feature: self-confidence, for his head rose nobly from the curve of his shoulders and his dark eyes looked at you with a cool assurance. He was calm, since his skin, more pale than ruddy, indicated composure in the blood. Energy he possessed, as shown by the quick contraction of his eyebrow muscles. And courage also, since his deep breathing betrayed great vitality and expansiveness.

In line with the observations of the physiognomists, I should also say that this man was proud, that his steadfast, self-possessed look seemed to reflect lofty views, and that all this and the harmony of expression in the movements of his face and body revealed an indisputable openheartedness.

I felt 'involuntarily' reassured in his presence, which augured well for our interview.

This individual might have been thirty-five or fifty, I couldn't tell. He was tall; he had a broad forehead, straight nose, well-defined mouth, and magnificent teeth; his hands were long, thin, and eminently 'psychic', to use the word from palmistry:* that is, apt for a noble and passionate being. This man was certainly the most admirable specimen I had ever met. One particular detail: his eyes, set far apart, could capture nearly a quarter of the horizon.* This faculty—as I later realized—was accompanied by eyesight superior even to Land's. When this strange personage was looking intently at something, his brow knitted and his large eyelids closed round his pupils so as to limit his field of vision—and he *did* look. What a gaze! How he magnified distant objects, and how he penetrated your very soul! How he could pierce the liquid depths,* so obscure to our eyes, and how he could read to the bottom of the seas!

The two strangers wore sea-otter-fur caps, sealskin sea-boots, and clothes of a strange material that sat loosely, allowing them great freedom of movement.

The taller of the two—evidently the chief on board—studied us with great concentration but without a word. Then turning to his companion, he conversed with him in a tongue I could not understand. The language was ringing, harmonious, supple, with the vowels seeming to receive highly varied stresses.

The other replied with a movement of his head, adding two or three totally unintelligible words. Then he appeared to be questioning me personally with his regard.

I replied, in good French, that I did not know his language; but he did not appear to understand, and the situation became somewhat embarrassing.

'Monsieur should try to relate our story,' said Conseil. 'Perhaps the gentlemen would comprehend a few words.'

I then began the story of our adventures, distinctly pronouncing all the syllables and not omitting a single detail. I announced our names and positions: I properly presented Dr Aronnax, Conseil his manservant, and Master Ned, harpooner.

The individual with calm and gentle eyes listened quietly, even politely, with remarkable concentration. But his expression showed no sign he understood my story. When I had finished, he said not a word.

There still remained the resort of using English. Perhaps we would be able to make ourselves understood in that almost universal language. I knew some, and some German as well: enough to read fluently, but not to speak accurately. Here, however, we needed to be very clear.

'Go on,' I said to the harpooner; 'it's your turn, Master Land. Draw from your bag the best English ever spoken by an Anglo-Saxon, unlawfully keeping us prisoners and try to be more successful than I was.'

Ned needed no prompting, and repeated my tale. I followed fairly well, for the contents were similar, if the form was different. The Canadian, carried away by his character, spoke with great passion. He complained bitterly about being imprisoned, infringing natural law, asked what law was used to detain him in this way, invoked *habeas corpus*,* threatened to take to court those unlawfully incarcerating us, waved his arms, gesticulated, exclaimed, and finally, in a most expressive pantomime, communicated clearly that we were dying of hunger.

This was true as a matter of fact, although we had more or less forgotten.

To his tremendous surprise, the harpooner did not appear to be more intelligible than I had been. Not a muscle moved on our visitors' faces. It was evident that they knew neither the language of Arago nor that of Faraday.* I was very perplexed, having exhausted our philological resources to no avail; and did not know what to do next, when Conseil intervened:

'If monsieur will permit, I will tell the story in German.'

'What, you know German!'

'Like a Fleming,'* he replied, 'if monsieur has no objection.'

'None at all—quite the contrary. Go ahead, my lad.'

And Conseil calmly recounted our various adventures for the third time. But notwithstanding the narrator's excellent accent and elegantly turned phrases, German was no more successful than before.

At last, and as a final resort, I summoned everything I could from

my early studies, and ventured to relate our adventures in Latin.
Cicero* would have blocked his ears at such dog Latin, but I did make
it through to the end. With the same result, however.

Our last attempt having utterly failed, the two strangers exchanged
a few words in their incomprehensible idiom and then withdrew, not
even giving us one of those reassuring signs understood in every country in the world. The door closed behind them again.

'It's a disgrace!' cried Ned Land as he exploded for the twentieth
time. 'Why, we spoke to those crooks in French, English, German, and
Latin, and neither had the courtesy to reply!'

'Calm yourself, Ned,' I said to the fiery harpooner; 'getting angry
will not help.'

'But don't you realize,' persisted our irascible companion, 'that we
may easily starve to death in this iron cage?'

'Bah,' said Conseil philosophically, 'we can hold on for a long
time yet.'

'My friends,' I said, 'we must not despair. We have been in worse
situations. Do me the favour of waiting a while before forming an
opinion of the captain and crew of this vessel.'

'My opinion's already formed,' countered Ned. 'They're rogues.'

'All right, but from what country?'

'From the land of rogues.'

'My good Ned, that country is not yet clearly indicated on the
world map; I must confess that the nationality of the two strangers is
difficult to determine. That they are neither British nor French nor
German is all we can say. I am inclined to think that the captain and
his mate must have been born at the lower latitudes. There is a southern look about them; but their physical type does not allow me to
decide whether they are Spaniards, Turks, Arabs, or Indians. As for
their tongue, it is simply incomprehensible.'

'That is the drawback of not knowing every language,' commented
Conseil, 'and of not having a universal one.'

'Which would not help us at all!' said Ned Land. 'Don't you see
that those men have a language of their own, invented to annoy anyone who asks for something to eat? If you open your mouth, move
your jaws, and smack your lips and teeth, don't they know what you
mean in every country in the world, with room to spare? Wouldn't it
indicate "I am hungry; give me something to eat" in Quebec and the
Tuamotus, in Paris and the antipodes?'

'Oh?' said Conseil. 'There are some so stupid . . .'

The door opened as he was speaking. A steward[1] entered. He brought us clothing:* jackets and sea trousers of a material I could not identify. I quickly put them on, my companions following suit.

During this time the steward—dumb, and perhaps deaf as well—laid three places at table.

'This is significant', said Conseil, 'and even most promising!'

'Bah!' retorted the Canadian resentfully. 'What the devil do you expect to be able to eat here: turtle liver, fillet of shark, dogfish steak?'

'Wait and see,' replied Conseil.

The dishes, with silver covers, were placed harmoniously on the cloth, as we took our places. Decidedly we were dealing with civilized beings; and had it not been for the electric light flooding over us, I might have thought we were seated at the Adelphi Hotel in Liverpool or the Grand Hotel in Paris. I should mention the absence of wine and bread. The water was pure and fresh; but water it was, and so not to Ned's taste. Amongst the dishes served I recognized various kinds of fish, delicately prepared; but I could not come to an opinion on some of the dishes, albeit excellent, since I could not say whether they belonged to the animal or vegetable kingdom. The table service was elegant, and in perfect taste. Every knife, fork, spoon, plate, and utensil was inscribed with a letter surmounted by a curved motto, of which the following is an exact facsimile:

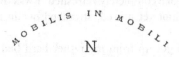

*Mobile in the mobile element!** The motto fitted the submarine vessel perfectly, provided that the Latin preposition 'in' was translated as 'in' rather than 'on'. The *N* was no doubt the initial of the enigmatic individual who commanded the depths of the ocean.

Ned and Conseil did not waste time on such cogitation. They had begun to eat, and I quickly followed them. I felt in fact reassured as to our fate, for it seemed clear that our hosts did not want us to die of starvation.

---

[1] An assistant on board a ship. [JV]

Everything must have an end in this world, however, even the hunger of those who have not eaten for fifteen hours. Our appetite satisfied, the need for sleep began to make itself imperiously felt: a natural reaction after the interminable night in which we had wrestled with death.*

'My goodness, I could do with a nap . . .' said Conseil.

'I'm off already,' from Land.

My companions lay down on the matting, and were soon sound asleep. For my part I yielded less easily to the urgent need for slumber. Too many thoughts crowded into my brain, too many unanswerable questions pressed upon me, too many impressions kept my eyes half open. Where were we? What strange force was carrying us away? I felt, or rather thought I felt, the machine sinking down to the furthest depths of the ocean. Fearful waking nightmares tormented me. I glimpsed a whole world of unknown creatures sheltering in mysterious refuges, with the submarine vessel as one of their congeners, living, moving, formidable like them. Then my brain settled down a little, my imagination dissolved into a vague somnolence, and I fell into a dull sleep.

9

NED LAND'S FITS OF ANGER

How long we slept I do not know, but it must have been a considerable period, for we awoke completely refreshed. I was the first to stir. My companions had not yet moved, stretched out in their corners like inert masses.

Scarcely had I got up from my rather hard bed, when I realized that my head was clear and my mind invigorated. I began to examine the cell attentively.

Its layout had not changed at all. The jail was still a jail, the prisoners still imprisoned. But the steward had cleared the table while we slept. There was no sign of any change in our situation and I seriously wondered whether our fate might be to live in this cell indefinitely.

This prospect was made more unpleasant by a great weight on my chest, although my brain was free of the obsessions of the day before. I could breathe only with difficulty. The heavy air was no longer sufficient for my lungs to function. Although the cell was very large, it was evident that we had consumed most of the oxygen in it. In an hour a man uses up the oxygen in 100 litres of air, and this air, filled with an almost identical quantity of carbon dioxide, becomes unbreathable.

It was therefore urgent for the air in our prison to be replenished, and presumably in the rest of the submarine craft as well.

This was a question that taxed my mind. How did the captain of such a floating habitation proceed? Did he obtain air by chemical means, using heat to free the oxygen contained in potassium chlorate, and absorbing the carbon dioxide with caustic potash? In that case he would still have to maintain contact with dry land to obtain the necessary chemicals. Did he store air in high-pressure tanks, and then decompress it as the crew needed? Possibly. Or, using a method that was much more natural, economical, and therefore probable, did he simply come up to the surface to breathe like a whale, and thus renew his supply of air for another twenty-four hours? Whatever the case, however he did it, it seemed sensible to act as soon as possible.

I was already needing to breathe more quickly to extract what little oxygen was left in the cell—when I was suddenly refreshed by a draught of pure air, full of a salty fragrance. It was a real sea breeze, invigorating and overflowing with iodine! I opened wide my mouth, and drenched my lungs with the fresh molecules. Meanwhile I was aware of a rocking or rolling motion that, although slight, was clearly perceptible. The boat, the metal monster, had obviously just come up to the surface to breathe, exactly as whales do. How the ship was ventilated was now perfectly clear.

When I had filled my lungs with the pure air, I looked for the method by which it had come in, the 'aerifery' which allowed this life-giving discharge to get to us; and I did not take long to discover it. Over the door was an opening through which the fresh air entered and renewed the air in our cell.

I had got thus far in my observation when Ned and Conseil woke up under the influence of the invigorating air, almost at the same time. After rubbing their eyes and stretching their arms, they were soon on their feet.

'Did monsieur sleep well?' enquired Conseil with his usual politeness.

'Like a log,' I replied. 'And you, Master Land?'

'Very soundly. But—it can't be true?—I seem to be breathing a sea breeze!'

A sailor couldn't be wrong, and I told the Canadian what had happened while he was asleep.

'That explains the roarings we heard when the so-called narwhal was near the *Abraham Lincoln*.'

'Quite so, Master Land, that was its breathing.'

'Dr Aronnax, I have no idea what time it is—unless it's dinner-time?'

'Dinner-time, my good harpooner? More likely breakfast, for it is certainly the day after yesterday.'

'Which would mean', said Conseil, 'that we had slept round the clock!'

'Indeed.'

'I won't argue,' said Ned Land. 'But I'd be glad to see the steward again, whether for dinner or breakfast.'

'Both,' said Conseil.

'Good point. We're entitled to two meals, and I can easily manage both.'

'Well, Ned, let's wait,' said I. 'These people are obviously not planning to let us die of starvation, as otherwise yesterday's meal would have been wasted.'

'Unless they wanted to fatten us up a bit.'

'Don't be stupid. We have not fallen into the hands of cannibals.'

'They might make an exception,' replied the Canadian in all seriousness. 'Maybe these people have been starved of fresh meat for ages? And in that case, three healthy and well-built individuals like monsieur, his manservant, and me . . .'

'Banish all such thoughts, Master Land, and above all do not use them as an excuse to get angry with our hosts. It would only make matters worse.'

'Anyway,' said Ned, 'I could eat a couple of horses. Dinner or breakfast, where is it?'

'We must fit in with the ship's routine,' I replied. 'I imagine that our appetites have run ahead of the chef's bell.'

'So we'll simply have to reset them to the correct time,' said Conseil calmly.

'That's just like you, my friend Conseil,' retorted the impetuous Canadian. 'You don't ever worry or fuss, you're always calm. You're the kind to give thanks for what you have yet to receive, and starve to death rather than complain!'

'But what would be the point?'

'The point would be to complain! That would already help. And if these pirates—I use the word advisedly, to avoid upsetting the professor who won't let us call them cannibals—if these pirates imagine that they're going to keep me prisoner in this suffocating cell without learning what swear words spice up my anger, then they're making a serious mistake. Look here, Dr Aronnax, and tell me straight out: how long do you think we'll be in this iron crate?'

'To tell the truth, I do not know any more than you, Land, my friend.'

'But what do you *think*?'

'I think that chance has made us privy to an important secret. Now if it is in the submarine crew's interest to keep the secret, and if this interest is more important than the lives of three men, then I believe we are in great danger. But if not, the monster that has swallowed us up will return us to the world of our fellow men at the first opportunity.'

'Unless it impresses us as crew,' said Conseil, 'and keeps us that way.'

'Until a frigate faster or cleverer than the *Abraham Lincoln* beats this den of thieves, and hangs us all from the yardarm.'

'A good point, Master Land,' said I, 'but it seems to me nobody has yet made us such a proposition. It is therefore pointless to discuss what to do in that case. I repeat, let's wait and make our decisions according to circumstances: let's do nothing, because there is nothing to be done.'

'No, sir,' retorted the harpooner, who would not give in; 'we must do something.'

'But what?'

'Escape!'

'To escape from jail is difficult enough on land, but to get out of a submarine prison appears quite impossible.'

'Now, Ned, my friend,' said Conseil, 'what do you say to monsieur's argument? I cannot believe that an American is ever at a loss for words.'

The harpooner, visibly put out, said nothing. Given the hand fate had dealt us, leaving was absolutely not on the cards. But a Canadian is half French, as Master Land soon showed.

'So, Dr Aronnax,' he said after a moment's consideration, 'don't you know what people do when they can't escape from prison?'

'No, my friend.'

'It's very simple: they get used to staying . . .'

'Yes indeed,' said Conseil, 'we are better off inside than above or below!'

'. . . after throwing out the jailers, turnkeys, and watchmen!'

'What, Ned, are you seriously contemplating taking over the vessel?'

'Very seriously.'

'Impossible!'

'Why? We may easily get the chance; and I don't see what should stop us taking it. If there are only about twenty men on board, how much chance do they stand against two Frenchmen and a Canadian?'

It was wiser to concur with such a view than to discuss it, so I merely said:

'Let's wait and see what events throw up. But until then please control your temper. We can only act by ruse, and you will not produce favourable opportunities by getting angry. So promise me you will take things as they come, without getting too annoyed.'

'I promise,' replied Ned, in a not very reassuring tone. 'I shall not say or do a single nasty thing, even if the table isn't served with the required punctuality.'

'I have your word, Ned.' Our conversation ended here, and we each began to think our own thoughts. For my part, I must confess that I had few illusions, despite the harpooner's pledge. I didn't believe in a favourable opportunity like Ned. To run such a tight submarine ship needed a large crew, and if push came to shove we would be overwhelmed. Besides we would need to be at liberty, which was not the case. I couldn't even see a way of escaping from this hermetically sealed cell of metal plates. And if the vessel's strange commander had any sort of secret to maintain—which was highly probable—he would not allow us to act freely on board. Might he not eliminate us by violent means, or one day cast us off on some remote piece of land? There was no way of telling. But all these conjectures appeared extremely plausible, and I thought that you had to be a harpooner to hope to escape again.

I understood, moreover, that Ned's thoughts were becoming gloomier as he considered matters. I heard oaths beginning to growl from the depths of his throat, and I could see his movements becoming threatening again. He got up and started to pace around like a wild beast in a cage, and to hit and kick the walls. As time went by, hunger began to seriously distress us, and this time the steward failed to appear. Our situation as castaways had been forgotten about for too long if they really did have good intentions towards us.

Ned Land, tormented by the gnawing pains of his capacious stomach, got more and more wound up; and I was afraid that there really would be an explosion if the crew arrived, whatever promises he had made.

For two more hours Ned's anger grew. He shouted and screamed, but in vain. The metal walls were deaf. I could not hear a single sound from the boat, which was as if dead. It was not moving, for I would have felt the trembling of the hull from the throbbing of the screw. It was probably plunged into the depths of the waters, far removed from the earth. The deathly silence felt terrifying.

As for our abandonment, our isolation in this cell, I dared not guess how long it might continue. The hopes I had entertained during our meeting with the commander faded by degrees. The kind expression of the person, the generosity of his physiognomy, the nobility of his bearing, all disappeared from my mind. I saw the enigmatic individual as essentially pitiless and cruel, as he had to be. I sensed him to be beyond the pale of humanity, insensible to feelings of pity, the remorseless enemy of his fellow beings, against whom he must have sworn an undying hatred!

But was this man simply going to let us die of hunger, locked up in a cramped prison, exposed to those terrible temptations that assail men under the influence of extreme hunger? This fearful thought took on terrible strength in my brain, and with my imagination at work, I felt myself becoming the prey of mad terror. Conseil remained quite calm. Ned was raging.

At this point in my thoughts a sound came outside, and footsteps resounded on the metal plates; the bolts shot back, the door opened, and the steward appeared.

Before I could block or prevent him, the Canadian had flung himself on to the wretch, thrown him to the ground, and gripped his throat. The steward was being strangled in a powerful grasp.

Conseil was already attempting to loosen the harpooner's deadly hold on his half-suffocated victim, and I was just about to help, when I was suddenly transfixed by these words:

'*Calmez-vous, maître Land, et vous, monsieur le professeur, veuillez m'écouter!*'*

10

THE MAN OF THE SEA

IT was the commander of the vessel.

Land got up quickly. The steward, almost strangled, staggered out on a sign from his master; but such was the captain's authority on board, that the man betrayed no indication of what was surely his resentment against the Canadian. Conseil was interested in spite of himself, and I, astonished: we awaited the denouement of the scene without speaking.

The commander, leaning on the corner of the table, his arms crossed, regarded us with very great attention. Was he hesitating before speaking, or did he regret addressing us in French? That might easily be the case. After a few moments' silence, which none of us dreamed of breaking: 'Gentlemen,' he said in a calm and penetrating voice, 'I can speak French, English, German, and Latin with equal ease. I would have been able to reply to you at our first meeting, but I wished to learn about you first and then reflect. Your fourfold account agreed in every particular, and assured me of your identity. I now know that fate has brought me Dr Pierre Aronnax, lecturer in natural history at the Museum of Paris, on an overseas scientific mission; Conseil, his man-servant; and Ned, a Canadian by birth, harpooner on the frigate *Abraham Lincoln* of the United States navy.'

I nodded to indicate my acquiescence. The captain had not asked me a question, so no reply was necessary. He expressed himself with perfect ease, without an accent. His sentences were well phrased, his words well chosen, his fluency remarkable. Nevertheless, I had the impression he was not French.

He continued as follows:

'You doubtless thought that I took a long time to pay you a second visit. This was because, once your identity had been established, I wished to consider carefully how to treat you. I hesitated for a long time. The most unfortunate circumstances have brought you into contact with a man who has broken with humanity. You have come to disturb my existence . . .'

'Unintentionally,' I put in.

'Indeed?' repeated the stranger, raising his voice. 'Was it unintentionally that the *Abraham Lincoln* searched for me on every ocean? Was it unintentionally that you embarked on that ship? Was it unintentionally that your shells ricocheted off the hull of my vessel? Was it unintentionally that Master Ned Land here struck me with his harpoon?'*

I perceived a controlled irritation in these words. But to all such recriminations I had a perfectly natural answer to give, and I gave it.

'Monsieur,' said I, 'you are not aware of the discussions about you which have taken place in Europe and America. You do not know that the various accidents you have caused by the collisions with your submarine machine have disturbed public opinion on both sides of the Atlantic. I spare you the countless hypotheses which have been erected to explain the inexplicable phenomenon of which you alone possessed the secret. But you must realize that in pursuing you even to the heart of the Pacific, the *Abraham Lincoln*'s crew were under the impression that they were pursuing some powerful marine monster, which it was necessary to rid the ocean of at any cost.'

A half smile parted the lips of the captain; then in a calmer voice:

'Dr Aronnax, dare you affirm that your frigate would not have followed and fired balls at a submarine vessel rather than a monster?'

This question caused me some embarrassment, for Captain Farragut would not have hesitated a single moment. He would have considered it his duty to destroy a device of that kind as much as a giant narwhal.

'So you appreciate, monsieur,' continued the stranger, 'that I have the right to treat you as enemies.'

I did not reply, and with good reason. What was the point of debating such a proposition, when force could vanquish the strongest of arguments?

'I hesitated for a long time,' repeated the captain. 'Nothing obliged me to offer you hospitality. Had I wished to part company with you, I would not have desired to meet again. I could have returned you to the platform of this ship on which you took refuge. I could have dived beneath the surface and forgotten that you ever existed. Did I not have this right?'

'Perhaps the right of a savage, but not that of a civilized person.'

'Dr Aronnax,' answered the captain sharply, 'I am not what you call a civilized person! I have broken with society for reasons which I alone have the right to appreciate. So I do not obey its rules, and I ask you never to invoke them in my presence again!'

This was clearly articulated. A flash of anger and disdain had lit up the stranger's eyes, and I caught a glimpse of a frightening past in his life. Not only had he placed himself outside humanity's laws, but he had made himself independent, free in the strictest sense of the word, out of all reach! Who would dare pursue him to the bottom of the seas, given that he could foil any attempts on the surface? What ship could resist a collision with his submarine monitor? What iron cladding, however thick, could resist an attack from his ram? No man alive could demand from him an account of his works. God, if he believed in Him, and his conscience, if he had one, were the only judges before whom he could appear.

These thoughts flashed through my mind, while the strange individual was silent, absorbed as if withdrawn into himself. I regarded him with an apprehension mixed with curiosity, in the same way as Oedipus must have looked at the Sphinx.*

After a fairly long silence the commander spoke again.

'So I hesitated, but I thought that my own interest might coincide with that natural pity* to which every human being has an intrinsic right. You will remain on board, since fate has cast the three of you here. You will be free, and in exchange for this freedom, admittedly quite limited in scope, I will impose only one condition. Your word of honour that you accept will suffice.'

'Pray continue, sir,' I said. 'I presume that it is a condition honourable men can accept.'

'Certainly, and it is as follows. It is possible that certain unforeseen situations may compel me to confine you to your cabins for a few hours, or days in some cases. As I never wish to have to use force, I expect passive obedience from you, even more than in other circumstances. In acting in this way, I remove all responsibility, I absolve you completely, for it will be my duty to ensure that you do not see what should not be seen. Will you accept this condition?'

So things happened on board that were strange, to say the least, and which were not fit to be witnessed by people who had not placed themselves outside social laws! Amongst the surprises that the future would hold for me, this was not to be the least.

'We accept,' I replied. 'But I request your permission to ask one question—only one.'

'Pray continue, sir.'

'You have said that we will be free on board?'

'Entirely.'

'I would like to enquire what you mean by such freedom.'

'I mean the freedom to come and go, and to study and observe all that takes place here, except in a few rare circumstances: in short, the same freedom my companions and I enjoy.'

It was clear that we were talking about different things.

'I beg your pardon,' I added, 'but that liberty is only the one granted every prisoner, to walk around his prison. That is not enough for us.'

'Well it must suffice, in any case.'

'What! You would have us renounce ever seeing our friends, relatives, or homelands again?'

'Yes, monsieur. But to give up the intolerable yoke of the dry land which men equate with freedom is perhaps not such a great sacrifice as you may imagine.'

'What an idea!' cried Ned Land. 'I will never give my word not to try and escape!'

'I am not asking for your word, Master Land,' the captain replied coldly.

'Monsieur,' I replied, carried away in spite of myself, 'you are taking advantage of us. This is cruelty.'

'No, monsieur, it is mercy. You are my prisoners after the battle. I am holding you when, with just a word, I could have you cast back to the depths of the ocean. You attacked me. You came and uncovered a secret that no man on earth must penetrate—the secret of my entire life. And you imagine that I am going to send you back to dry land, where nothing must be known about me? Never! By holding you, it is not you I am protecting, but myself.'

The captain's words indicated a resolve against which no argument could prevail.

'So,' I continued, 'you are merely giving us the choice between life and death?'

'Yes.'

'My friends,' I said, 'to such a question no reply is possible. But no promise binds us to the master of this ship.'*

'None, sir,' replied the stranger.

And in a gentler voice:

'Now, let me finish what I have to say. I know you, Dr Aronnax. You, if not your companions, will have little to complain about the destiny that has bound you to my fate. Amongst the books which make up my favourite reading you will find the work you published on the ocean deeps. I have often studied it. Your book went as far as earthbound science allowed. But you do not know everything, you still have things to see. So let me tell you that you will not regret the time spent on board my vessel. You are going to travel through a wonderland. Astonishment and stupefaction will probably be your normal state of mind. You will not easily become blasé about the sights continually offered to your eyes. I am going to make a new tour around the underwater world—who knows, perhaps the last?—and revisit everything I have studied in the depths I know so well; and you will be my study companion. Starting today, you will move in a new element, you will see what no one has ever seen (for my men and I no longer count); and our planet, thanks to me, will deliver up its last secrets.'

I cannot deny that these words of the captain's had a tremendous effect on me. He had touched me on my weak spot, and for a moment I forgot that the contemplation of such sublime things could not compensate for the loss of liberty. But in any case, I counted on the future to settle this important question. So I merely replied:

'Sir, if you have broken with humanity, I cannot believe that you have given up all human feeling. We are castaways, magnanimously taken on board, and we will not forget it. I recognize in full that if interest in science can override even the desire for freedom, what is promised thanks to our meeting will offer me personally a great deal of compensation.'

I thought the captain was going to offer me his hand to seal our treaty. He did nothing of the sort. I thought he should have.

'One last question . . .' I said, just as the unfathomable being seemed about to withdraw.

'I am listening.'

'How should I address you?'

'Monsieur,' replied the captain, 'I will merely be Captain Nemo for you;* and you and your companions will simply be for me the passengers of the *Nautilus*.'*

Captain Nemo called. A steward appeared. The captain gave him orders in that foreign tongue I could not place. Then, turning to Ned and Conseil:

'A meal is waiting for you in your cabin. Please follow this man.'

'I won't say no!' said the harpooner.

And Conseil and he finally left the cell they had been imprisoned in for more than thirty hours.

'And now, Dr Aronnax, our lunch is ready. Allow me to lead the way.'

'At your disposal, captain.'

I followed Captain Nemo, and immediately outside the door found myself in a sort of corridor lit by electricity, rather like the gangway on a ship. After about 10 metres, another door opened in front.

I entered a dining-room, furnished and decorated with austere taste. Tall oak dressers, full of ebony ornaments, rose at both ends of the room, and on their scallop-edged shelves sparkled fine china, porcelain, and glassware of an inestimable value. The plates in particular shone in the rays from the brilliant ceiling, whose glare was filtered and softened by fine paintings.

In the centre of the room stood a richly laid table. Captain Nemo indicated the place where I was to sit.

'Please be seated,' he said, 'and eat like one who must be dying of hunger.'

Lunch consisted of a number of dishes made of ingredients from the sea, as well as a few portions whose nature and origin I could not guess. I had to admit that they were good, with a peculiar flavour which I quickly got used to. All the different foodstuffs seemed rich in phosphorus and I decided that they had to come from the sea.

Captain Nemo was watching me. I did not say anything, but he read my thoughts and without prompting answered the questions I was dying to ask.

'Most of the dishes are unknown to you,' he said. 'But you can eat them without fear. They are good and nourishing. I gave up food from the land a long time ago and my health is none the worse for it. My crew, who are fit and well, eat the same dishes.'

'So all this food is produced by the sea?'

'Yes, the sea provides for all my needs. Sometimes I let out nets and draw them in full to breaking. Sometimes I go hunting in the midst of this element thought inaccessible to man, and pursue the game living in my underwater forests. My flocks, like those of Neptune's old shepherd,* graze without fear on the immense ocean plains. There I have a vast property which I alone farm and which is always replanted by the Creator of all things.'

I looked at Captain Nemo somewhat astonished and replied:

'I understand perfectly well, monsieur, that nets provide excellent fish for your table; I comprehend less well how you can pursue aquatic game in your underwater forests; but I entirely fail to grasp how any meat, however small the amount, can appear on your menu.'

'But I never touch the flesh of land animals.'

'Then what is this?' I said, pointing to a dish where a few scraps of fillet still remained.

'What you believe to be meat is simply turtle fillet, doctor. Here are also a few dolphin livers that you would take for pork stew. My chef is skilful, and excels at conserving these products of the ocean. Feel free to taste all these dishes. Here is a sea-slug conserve that a Malay would declare unrivalled anywhere in the world; this is a cream made from milk provided by whales' udders and sugar from the great wracks of the North Sea; and finally let me offer you some anemone jam which is the equal of the most delicious fruits.'

I tasted them, more out of curiosity than as a gourmet, while Captain Nemo enchanted me with his incredible ideas.

'But the sea, Dr Aronnax, this prodigious, inexhaustible wet-nurse doesn't just feed me, it also clothes me. The materials you are wearing are woven from the byssus of certain shellfish; they are dyed with the purple used by the ancients or else the fine violet shades that I extract from the Mediterranean sea hare. The perfumes you will find on the wash-stand in your cabin were produced by distilling marine plants. Your bed is made of the softest wracks in the ocean. Your pen will be made from whalebone, your ink from the liquid secreted by a cuttle-fish or squid.* Everything I use comes from the sea, as everything will one day return to it!'

'You love the sea, captain.'

'Yes, I do love it! The sea is everything. It covers seven-tenths of the terrestrial globe. Its breath is healthy and pure. It is a spacious wilderness where man is never alone, for he can feel life throbbing all around him. The sea is the environment for a prodigious, supernatural existence; it is pure movement and love; it is a living infinity, as one of your poets has put it.* And indeed, sir, nature is present there in her three kingdoms, animal, vegetable, and mineral. The animal kingdom is well represented by the four groups of zoophytes, three classes of articulates, five classes of molluscs, and three classes of vertebrates— mammals, reptiles, and countless legions of fish, which constitute an innumerable order of more than 13,000 species, of which only a tenth live in fresh water. The sea is nature's vast reserve. It was more or less through the sea that the globe began, and who knows if it will not end in the sea! Perfect peace abides there. The sea does not belong to despots. On its surface immoral rights can still be claimed, men can fight, devour each other, and commit all the earth's atrocities. But

30 feet below the surface their power ceases, their influence fades, their authority disappears. Ah, sir, live, live in the heart of the sea! Independence is possible only here! Here I recognize no master! Here I am free!'

Captain Nemo suddenly fell silent in the midst of the enthusiasm welling out of him. Had he allowed himself to get carried away beyond his usual reserve? Had he said too much? For a moment he paced agitatedly back and forth. Then he calmed down, his physiognomy took on its customary coldness, and he turned to me.

'Now, monsieur,' he said, 'if you wish to visit the *Nautilus*, I am at your disposal.'

11

THE *NAUTILUS*

CAPTAIN NEMO got up. I followed. Double doors opened at the back of the dining-room, and I discovered a room of the same size as the one I had just left.

It was a library.* Tall furniture, made of black rosewood and inset with brass, bore on its long shelves a large number of books with uniform bindings. The shelves followed the shape of the room, with vast settees below them, upholstered in brown leather and offering the most comfortable of curves. Light reading-desks, which could be moved around at will, provided support for books being read. In the centre stood a huge table covered with periodicals, including several newspapers that seemed already quite old. The harmonious setting was flooded with electric light from four frosted-glass globes recessed in the vaults of the ceiling. I looked with real admiration at this room, so judiciously arranged, and I could scarcely believe my eyes.

'Captain Nemo,' I said to my host, who had just stretched out on a sofa, 'this is a library that would do honour to more than one palace in the New and Old Worlds, and I am truly astonished when I think that it travels with you to the deepest parts of the ocean.'

'Where could one find more privacy or silence? Does your study in the Museum offer so complete a peace?'

'No, sir, and I must add that it is very thin in comparison with yours. You must have six or seven thousand volumes here . . .'

'Twelve thousand, Dr Aronnax. These are the only ties still connecting me to the land. The world ended for me the day my *Nautilus* dived beneath the water for the first time. That day I bought my last books, my last magazines, my last newspapers, and I would like to believe that humanity has thought or written nothing since then. These books, Dr Aronnax, are at your disposal and you can make free use of them.'*

I thanked Captain Nemo, and approached the shelves. Books abounded on science, on ethics, and on literature, written in every language, but I could not see a single work of political economy, which seemed totally prohibited on board. Strangely enough, none of the books were classified according to language; and this lack of system implied that the captain of the *Nautilus* had little trouble reading any of the volumes he might select.

Amongst the works, I noticed the masterpieces of the great modern and ancient artists, comprising everything that humanity has produced of greatest beauty in history, poetry, the novel, and science: from Homer to Victor Hugo, from Xenophon to Michelet, from Rabelais to Mme Sand.* But the focus of the library was more on science; books on mechanics, ballistics, hydrography, meteorology, geography, geology, etc. took up at least as much space as works on natural history, making me realize that they must form the captain's principal study. I saw there all of Humboldt and Arago, the works of Foucault, Henri Sainte-Claire Deville, Chasles, Milne-Edwards, Quatrefages, Tyndall, Faraday, Berthelot, Father Secchi, Petermann, Commander Maury, Agassiz,* etc., the reports of the Academy of Sciences, the bulletins of the various geographical societies, etc., and, in a prominent position, the two volumes which were perhaps the reason why Captain Nemo had given me a relatively warm welcome. Amongst the books of Joseph Bertrand, *Les Fondateurs de l'astronomie** even gave me a definite date: as I knew that it was published in 1865, I was able to conclude that the fitting out of the *Nautilus* did not date from after that.* Captain Nemo had accordingly begun his underwater existence not more than three years previously. I hoped, moreover, that still newer works would let me determine the date even more closely; but I had plenty of time to carry out such research, and did not wish to hold up the tour of the *Nautilus*'s wonders.

'Sir,' I said, 'thank you for making this library available to me. It contains treasures of science that I will put to good use.'

'This room is not just a library,' responded Captain Nemo, 'it is also a smoking-room.'

'A smoking-room? Do people smoke on board?'

'They do.'

'Then I must conclude that you have maintained relations with Havana.'

'Not at all. Please accept this cigar, Dr Aronnax, and although it does not come from Havana, you will appreciate it if you are a connoisseur.'

I took the cigar offered. The shape reminded me of a Havana cigar, but it looked as if made from gold leaf. I lit it using a small lighter on an elegant bronze stand, and inhaled the first mouthfuls with all the delight of a smoker who has not indulged for two days.

'It is excellent, but it is not tobacco.'

'Quite right; this tobacco does not come from Havana or the East. It is a sort of seaweed rich in nicotine that the sea provides me, rather sparingly in fact. Do you regret your Havanas, sir?'

'Captain, I shall disdain them from this day on.'

'Smoke then as much as you wish, and without wondering where the cigars came from. No state monopoly has licensed them; but I may presume they're none the worse for that?'

'On the contrary.'

While speaking, Captain Nemo opened the door opposite the one we had used to enter the library, and I passed into an enormous, magnificently lit salon.

It was a vast rectangle truncated at the corners, more than 10 metres long, 6 wide, and 5 high. A luminous ceiling decorated with delicate arabesques provided a clear but soft light for all the wonders gathered together in this museum. For it *was* a museum, within whose walls an intelligent and prodigal hand had assembled every treasure of nature and art—but in the artistic disorder typical of a painter's studio.

About thirty identically framed paintings by masters, alternating with dazzling coats-of-arms, hung on the walls, which were covered with tapestries of a severe design. I saw paintings of the very highest worth, most of which I had previously viewed in private European collections or exhibitions. The various schools of the old masters were represented by a Madonna by Raphael, a Virgin by Leonardo da Vinci, a nymph by Correggio, a woman by Titian, an Adoration by Veronese, an Assumption by Murillo, a portrait by Holbein, a monk by Velazquez, a martyr by Ribera, a country fair by Rubens, two Flemish landscapes by Teniers, three small genre paintings by Gerrit Dou, Metsu, and Paul Potter, canvases by Géricault and Prud'hon, and a few seascapes by Backhuysen and Vernet.* The works of modern art included paintings signed Delacroix, Ingres, Decamps, Troyon, Meissonier, Daubigny,* etc.; and standing on pedestals in the angles of this magnificent museum were a few outstanding marble figures and bronze statues, reproductions of the finest models of antiquity. The condition of stupefaction that the captain of the *Nautilus* had predicted was seeping into my mind.

'Dr Aronnax,' said this strange being, 'please excuse the informality with which I receive you as well as the untidiness of the room.'

'Sir,' I replied, 'without trying to discover who you are, may I possibly recognize in you an artist?'

'At best an amateur. I used to enjoy assembling the finer works created by man's hand. I was an avid collector, an untiring visitor of antique shops, and was able to pick up a few objects of value. These are my last memories of the world which is now dead for me. In my eyes, your modern artists are not to be distinguished from the ancients: they could be two or three thousand years old and I conflate them all in my mind. The great masters are ageless.'

'And these musicians?' I said, pointing to scores by Weber, Rossini, Mozart, Beethoven, Haydn, Meyerbeer, Herold, Wagner, Auber, Gounod,* and several others, scattered over a piano-organ* of a famous make filling one of the side panels of the salon.

'These musicians are contemporaries of Orpheus,* for chronological differences are obliterated in the memory of the deceased—and I am dead, sir, as dead as those of your friends resting six feet below ground!'

Captain Nemo fell silent and seemed lost in a deep reverie.* I considered him with emotion, silently analysing his strange features. Leaning on the corner of a precious mosaic table, he no longer saw me, he forgot I was there.

I respected this meditation, and continued to examine the curiosities adorning the salon.

Compared with the works of art, natural rarities took up a great deal of room. These were principally plants, shells, and other objects of the ocean, apparently Captain Nemo's own finds. In the centre of the salon the water of a fountain, lit by electricity, rose and fell into a basin made of a single *Tridacna*. This shell, from the largest of the acephalous molluscs, had a delicately festooned rim of a circumference of about six metres; it was therefore larger than the two fine *Tridacnae* given to François I* by the Republic of Venice, from which the Church of St Sulpice in Paris made gigantic baptismal fonts.

Around this fountain, in elegant display cabinets supported by copper stays, the most precious products of the sea ever to be made available to a naturalist's scrutiny were classified and labelled. One can imagine how happy the scientist in me felt.

The branch of the zoophytes offered very strange specimens from its two groups of polyps and echinoderms. In the first group, comprising mostly corals, appeared tubipores, fan-shaped gorgons, soft sponges from Syria, isises from the Moluccas, sea pens, an admirable virgularian from the seas off Norway, varied umbellulas, alcyonarians, and a whole series of the madrepores that my master Milne-Edwards has so judiciously classified into subdivisions. Amongst the latter I noticed adorable flabelliforms, Oculinidae from Reunion, Neptune's chariots from the Caribbean, some superb varieties of corals, and lastly all the kinds of curious polyparies that agglomerate to form whole islands and will one day constitute continents. Among the echinoderms with their remarkable spiny covering, the whole collection of individuals of this group was represented by starfish, sea stars, pentacrinoids, comatulids, astrophytons, sea urchins, holothurians, etc.

A highly strung conchologist would certainly have fainted at the many display cases classifying specimens from the branch of molluscs. There I saw a collection of inestimable value, which time does not allow me to describe in full. Amongst the various products, I will cite for the record only: the elegant royal hammer-shell of the Indian Ocean, with regular white spots standing vividly out from a red and brown background; a brightly coloured imperial spondylus, all bristling with spikes, a specimen rarely seen in the museums of Europe, and worth, I thought, about twenty thousand francs; a much-sought-after common hammer-shell from the seas of Australia; some exotic cockles from Senegal: fragile white shells with double valves, that a breath would have blown away like soap bubbles; several varieties of the watering-can shells off Java: sorts of chalky tubes edged with foliaceous folds, highly coveted by collectors; a whole series of top shells: some greenish-yellow ones found in the seas of America, some of a reddish-brown common in the waters off Australia, others remarkable for their complex shells from the Gulf of Mexico, yet other stellaria found in the Southern Seas, and finally the rarest of all, the magnificent spur-shell from New Zealand; then admirable sulphuret tellins, precious species of cytherea and venus-shells, the trellised solarium of the Tranquebar coasts, the turban shell veined with resplendent mother-of-pearl, the green parrot shell from the seas of China, the nearly unknown cone shell of the genus *Cenodulli*, all the varieties of cowries which serve as currency in India and Africa, the most precious shell in the East Indies, the Glory-of-the-Seas; and finally some periwinkles, delphiniums, screw shells, ianthines, ovules, volutes, olives, mitre shells, casques, murexes, whelks, harps, winkles, triton's shells, cerites, spindle-shells, wing shells, scorpion shells, limpets, hyales, and *Cleodora*: all delicate and fragile shells that science has baptized with its most charming names.

Set apart in special compartments lay pearl chaplets of the greatest beauty, picked out in fiery points by the electric light: pink pearls plucked from the marine pinna of the Red Sea, green pearls from the *Haliotis iris*, yellow ones, blue ones, black ones. These were the strange products of the varied molluscs from every ocean and of distinctive mussels from the northern rivers, and finally a few specimens of inestimable value distilled by the rarest of pearl oysters. A few of these pearls were bigger than a pigeon's egg. They were therefore worth more than the one that the traveller Tavernier* offered to the Shah of Persia for three million francs, and surpassed the pearl of the Imam of Muscat, which I had previously thought without rival anywhere in the world.

To ascribe a value to this collection was virtually impossible. Captain Nemo must have spent millions acquiring the different items,* and I was just wondering what source he might use to satisfy his collector's whims, when I was interrupted:

'You are examining my shells, sir. They may indeed interest a scientist; but for me they have an additional charm as I collected them all myself. There is not a sea on the surface of the globe that I have not searched.'

'Captain, I can understand the delight of strolling through such wealth. You are among those who have amassed their treasures by themselves. No museum in Europe possesses a comparable collection of marine products. But if I exhaust all my admiration here, there will be none left for the ship bearing them! I do not wish to penetrate secrets which are yours alone. However, I must confess that the *Nautilus*, the propulsive force it incorporates, the mechanism allowing it to be steered, the powerful agent which gives life to it—all this arouses my curiosity to the highest degree. I can see instruments hanging on the walls of the salon, with functions I am unaware of. May I possibly know . . .?'

'Dr Aronnax,' replied Captain Nemo, 'I have said that you are free on board my ship, and consequently no part of the *Nautilus* is forbidden. You can visit any section of it, and it will be a great pleasure for me to act as your guide.'

'I do not know how to thank you, captain, but I will not abuse your kindness. I will simply ask what these scientific instruments are for . . .'

'These same instruments are to be found in my bedroom, and it is there that I will have the pleasure of explaining their use to you. But first come and visit the cabin reserved for you. You must see how your domestic arrangements are to be taken care of on board the *Nautilus*.'

I followed Captain Nemo through one of the doors in the oblique angles of the salon, and into the ship's gangways. He took me for'ard and there I found not a cabin but an elegant bedroom, complete with a bed, dressing table, and various other pieces of furniture.

I could only thank my host.

'Your room is next to mine,' he said opening the door, 'and mine leads into the salon we have just left.'

I entered the captain's room. It had a severe, almost hermit-like appearance. A small iron bedstead, a work table, a few pieces of furniture for his toilet. Everything lit indirectly. No comfort. Only the barest of necessities.*

Captain Nemo indicated a chair.

'Please be seated.'

I sat down and he began to speak as follows:

12

ALL BY ELECTRICITY

'Dr Aronnax,' said Captain Nemo, pointing to the instruments hanging on the walls of his room, 'these are the instruments needed for sailing the *Nautilus*. Here, as in the salon, I have them always in view, telling me my position and exact direction in the heart of the ocean. Some of them you already know, such as the thermometer, which tells me the temperature inside the *Nautilus*; the barometer, which measures the weight of the air and hence forecasts changes in the weather; the hygrometer, which registers the amount of moisture in the air; the storm-glass, whose contents separate out and settle to herald the arrival of storms; the compass, which shows me the course to take; the sextant, which indicates my latitude by the height of the sun; the chronometers, which enable me to calculate my longitude; and lastly the telescopes, for day and night use, which I employ to examine every point of the horizon when the *Nautilus* is on the surface.'*

'These are the usual navigational equipment, and I am aware of their functions. But I can see others which must correspond to the special requirements of the *Nautilus*. Isn't that dial with the moving needle a pressure-gauge?'

'Yes indeed. It is in contact with the water outside, and by telling me the pressure, indicates what depth my vessel is at.'

'And are these a new kind of sounding instrument?'

'They're thermometric sounding devices registering the temperature at various depths.'

'And these other instruments whose purpose I cannot begin to guess?'

'Before going any further, Dr Aronnax, I must explain a few things. So please pay attention to what I have to say.'

Captain Nemo paused briefly and then continued:

'There is one agent which is powerful, responsive, easy to use, suitable for all kinds of work, and which reigns supreme on board. It does everything. It provides me with heat and light; it is the soul of my machines. That agent is electricity.'*

'Electricity!' I exclaimed, somewhat surprised.

'Yes indeed.'

'But, captain, the great speed you move at seems to have little to do with the power of electricity. Until now the dynamic capacity of electricity has remained very limited, only capable of producing small forces!'

'Dr Aronnax,' answered Captain Nemo, 'my electricity is not the commonly used sort, and that is all I wish to say on the matter.'

'I will not press the point, monsieur, but merely remain astonished at the outcome. A single question, however, which needs no answer if it seems indiscreet. The elements you use to produce this astonishing agent must be consumed quickly. Zinc, for example: how do you replace it since you no longer have any contact with land?'

'Your question will be answered. First let me tell you that there are zinc, iron, silver, and gold deposits on the bottom of the sea whose extraction would certainly be possible. But I decided to owe nothing to the metals of the earth and I simply derive the means to produce my electricity from the sea itself.'

'From the sea?'

'Yes, sir, and I had plenty of choices. For example, I could have established a circuit between wires sunk to different depths, and hence obtained electricity from the difference in temperature between them;* but I decided to employ a more practical method.'

'Which is?'

'You are aware of the composition of sea water. In 1,000 grams, 96.5 per cent is water and about 2.66 per cent sodium chloride, with small quantities of magnesium chloride, potassium chloride, magnesium bromide, magnesium sulphate, lime sulphate, and lime carbonate. You will see that sodium chloride is found in considerable proportions. Now, it is this sodium which I extract from sea water to give me my ingredients.'

'Sodium?'

'Yes. Mixed with mercury it forms an amalgam which replaces zinc in Bunsen* batteries. The mercury is never used up. Only the sodium is consumed, and the sea itself provides me with more. Also, sodium batteries must be considered to produce the most energy, for their electro-motive power is double that of zinc ones.'

'I fully understand the suitability of sodium in your present circumstances. It is to be found in the sea. So far so good. But it must still be produced, or rather extracted. How do you do this? Clearly you could use your batteries; but if I am not mistaken, the sodium utilized by the electrical apparatus would be greater than the quantity extracted. You would be consuming more than you were producing!'

'Consequently I do not use batteries for extraction, but simply the heat from coal.'

'Coal found underground?' I persisted.

'Let's say sea coal if you like.'

'And you are able to work underwater coalmines?'

'Dr Aronnax, you will see me doing so.* I will only ask for a little patience, since you have plenty of time to be patient. Just remember one thing. I owe everything to the sea: it produces electricity and electricity gives the *Nautilus* heat, light, and movement—in a word, life.'

'But not the air you breathe?'

'Oh, I could manufacture all the air I need for my consumption, but that would be pointless since I go back up to the surface whenever I wish. But even if electricity does not provide me with air for breathing, it does work the powerful pumps that store air in special tanks, thus allowing me, if necessary, to remain at the deepest levels as long as I wish.'

'Captain, I can only admire this. You have evidently discovered the real dynamic power of electricity that others will undoubtedly discover one day.'

'I do not know whether they will,' replied Captain Nemo rather coldly. 'But in any case, you are already familiar with the first application I have made of such an invaluable tool. It is this agent which gives us light more constantly than the sun could. Look at this clock: it is electric, and keeps time more accurately than the best chronometers. I have divided it into twenty-four hours, like Italian clocks, since for me there is neither night nor day, sun nor moon, but only the artificial light I take with me to the bottom of the seas. Look, it is now ten in the morning.'

'I see.'

'Another application of electricity: this dial before us serves to indicate the speed of the *Nautilus*. An electric circuit connects it to the screw log, and its needle shows me the actual speed of the engine. Look, at the moment we are moving at a moderate speed of 15 knots.'

'It's amazing, and I can see, captain, that you were right to use this agent which will one day replace wind, water, and steam.'*

'We haven't finished yet, Dr Aronnax,' said Captain Nemo getting up, 'and if you would like to follow me, we will visit the rear section of the *Nautilus*.'

I was already familiar with the entire forward section of the submarine craft, whose exact layout I give here, proceeding from the centre to the ram: the 5-metre dining-room, separated from the library by a sealed bulkhead preventing any water from penetrating; the 5-metre library; the 10-metre salon, separated from the captain's bedroom by a second watertight division; the bedroom itself, 5 metres long; mine, 2½ metres; and finally a 7½-metre air tank reaching to the bow. The total length was about 35 metres.* The bulkheads had doors in them that closed hermetically by means of rubber seals, and these allowed total safety on board should the *Nautilus* ever spring a leak.

I followed Captain Nemo through one of the gangways situated along the sides of the ship, and arrived at its centre. Here there was a sort of open shaft between two watertight compartments. An iron ladder, fixed firmly to the wall, led to the top of the stairwell.

I asked the captain what the ladder was for.

'It goes up to the dinghy.'

'What, you have a dinghy!' I exclaimed in astonishment.

'But of course. An excellent craft, light and unsinkable, which we use for excursions and fishing.'

'But presumably you have to go up to the surface, when you want to use the boat?'

'Not at all. The dinghy is fixed to the upper part of the *Nautilus*'s hull, in a purpose-built recess. It is completely decked over, absolutely watertight, and held in place by strong bolts. This ladder leads to a manhole in the *Nautilus*'s hull, which corresponds to a similar hole in the side of the dinghy. I enter the boat through this double opening. The hole on the *Nautilus* is then closed; I shut the one in the boat by means of a pressure screw; I release the bolts, and it rises to the surface at a prodigious speed. I open the cover on the deck, carefully fastened until then, hoist the mast and raise my sail or use my oars, and so move as I wish.'

'But how do you come back on board?'

'I don't, Dr Aronnax; it is the *Nautilus* that comes back.'

'Following your instructions?'

'Following my instructions. I am connected to it by an electric wire. I send a telegram, and that's that.'

'Indeed,' I said, intoxicated by these miracles; 'what could be simpler!'

Having gone past the well of the staircase leading up to the platform, I saw a cabin 2 metres long; in it Conseil and Ned, delighted with their meal, were busy wolfing it down. Soon a door opened on to the 3-metre kitchen situated between the huge storerooms.

All the cooking was done by electricity, even more powerful and obedient than gas. The wires under the cookers evenly distributed and maintained the heat over the platinum plates. The electricity also heated distillation devices which used evaporation to provide excellent drinking water. Near the kitchen opened a bathroom, comfortably laid out, with taps providing hot or cold water at will.

After the kitchen came the crew room, 5 metres long. But its door remained closed* and I could not see how it was arranged, which might have told me how many men were required to operate the *Nautilus*.

At the end was a fourth watertight division separating the crew room from the machine-room. A door opened, and I found myself in the chamber where Captain Nemo—certainly an engineer of the first order—had installed his machinery for propulsion.

The engine-room was brightly lit, and more than 20 metres long. It was divided into two parts. The first contained the equipment for generating the electricity, and the other the machinery for transmitting the movement to the propeller.

Right from the start I was surprised by the highly distinctive smell filling the room.

Captain Nemo noticed my reaction.

'There are a few gas discharges because sodium is being used; but they are only a slight inconvenience. In any case, we ventilate the ship in the open air every morning.'

While he was talking, I examined the machinery of the *Nautilus* with an interest easy to comprehend.

'You can see that I use Bunsen batteries rather than Ruhmkorff* ones. Ruhmkorff batteries would not produce the same output. Being massive and powerful, not so many Bunsen ones are needed, and I have found that they form a better choice. The electricity produced goes to the rear, where, via huge electromagnets, it acts on a special system of levers and gears which transmit their motion to the propeller shaft. The diameter of the propeller is 6 metres with a total pitch of 7½ metres, which can produce up to 120 revolutions per second.'*

'Giving . . .?'

'A speed of 50 knots.'*

There was still a mystery here, but I did not insist on trying to solve it. How could electricity possibly act with such power? Where did this almost unlimited force come from? Was it obtained from a new kind of coil of extremely high voltage? Could it come from the transmission being increased indefinitely through a system of unknown levers?[1] This was what I could not understand.

'Captain Nemo, I note the results and will not attempt to find an explanation for them. I saw the *Nautilus* manoeuvring near the *Abraham*

---

[1] In fact there is talk at the moment of a discovery of this sort in which a new set of levers produces considerable force. So has its inventor met Captain Nemo? [JV]

Lincoln, and I know what sort of speed we are talking about. But that is not everything. You need to know where you're going! And you need to be able to move right or left, up or down. How do you reach the great depths, where you must encounter an increasing resistance, amounting to hundreds of atmospheres? How do you come back up to the surface? And how do you stay in one particular place? Or am I being indiscreet by asking all these questions?'

'Not at all, sir,' replied the captain after a moment's hesitation, 'since you are never to leave this submarine vessel. Come into the salon. It is our real study and there you will learn all you wish to know about the *Nautilus*.'

13

A FEW FIGURES

A MOMENT later, we were sitting on a divan in the salon, smoking cigars. The captain laid before me a blueprint containing the floor plan, section, and elevation of the *Nautilus*. Then he began his description:

'The various dimensions of the ship you are on are as follows. It is a long cylinder with conical ends.* Its shape is quite close to that of a cigar, a design already adopted in London for several constructions of the same type. The cylinder measures exactly 70 metres from end to end, and its beam is 8 metres at its widest point. It is not, therefore, constructed on an exact ratio of ten to one like your high-speed steamships, but its lines are sufficiently long and its run extensive enough for the displaced water to escape easily and to provide no obstacle to headway.

'These two measurements allow you to calculate the surface area and volume of the *Nautilus*.* Its surface area is 1,011.45 square metres, its volume 1,507.2 cubic metres*—which is the same as saying that, when completely submerged, it displaces 1,500 cubic metres or weighs 1,500 tons.

'When I drew up the plans for this ship, designed as you know for submarine navigation, I wanted it to be nine-tenths submerged when in equilibrium in the water, with only a tenth above the surface. In other words, it had to displace nine-tenths of its volume, or 1,356.48 cubic metres, and so had to weigh 1,356.48 tons. This weight was to be the maximum when I constructed the ship to the above dimensions.

'The *Nautilus* has two hulls, one inside the other, joined by T-bars which give it very great strength. Thanks to this modular construction, it has the same resistance as a solid block. Its plating cannot give; it holds together by virtue of its construction and not through the tightness of the rivets; and its unified construction, thanks to the perfect assembly of the materials, allows it to defy the most violent seas.

'The two hulls are constructed from steel plate with a density 7.8 times that of water. The first hull is no less than 5 centimetres thick, and weighs 394.96 tons. The keel alone, which is 50 centimetres high by 25 centimetres wide, weighs 62 tons; and the total weight of the keel, the second hull, the engine, the ballast, the various fixtures and fittings, and the bulkheads and internal braces is 961.62 tons, which, when added to the 394.96, gives the required total of 1,356.48 tons. Am I clear?'

'Perfectly,' I replied.

'So when the *Nautilus* is floating in equilibrium, a tenth of it emerges from the water. Now if I have arranged tanks of a capacity equal to this one-tenth, in other words holding 150.72 tons, and if I fill the tanks with water, the boat will then weigh and consequently displace 1,507 tons, and will be completely submerged. And this is what happens in actual practice. The tanks are placed very near the sides of the lower part of the *Nautilus*. I open the taps, the tanks fill, and the boat sinks until it is just touching the surface of the water.'

'Fine, captain, but now we are approaching the real difficulty. I understand how you can be just touching the surface of the ocean. But when it dives, isn't your submarine craft going to encounter a pressure and consequently an upwards impulse of 1 atmosphere for each 30 feet of water it goes down, or about 1 kilogram per square centimetre?'

'Absolutely, sir.'

'So unless you fill the *Nautilus* entirely, I do not see how you can make it go down into the depths.'

'Dr Aronnax,' replied Captain Nemo, 'one must not confuse statics with dynamics, for that can lead to serious errors. Very little effort is required to reach the lower levels of the ocean, for bodies have a tendency to sink. Please follow my reasoning.'

'I am listening, captain.'

'When I wished to determine the increase in weight the *Nautilus* would require to dive, my only concern was the progressive reduction in volume that sea water experiences as it becomes deeper.'

'Clearly.'

'Now although water is not completely incompressible, it *is* very hard to compress. Indeed, according to the most recent calculations, the reduction is only 436/10,000,000ths per atmosphere of pressure, or for each 30 feet down. So if I wish to reach a depth of 1,000 metres, I need to take into account the reduction of volume due to a pressure equivalent to a column of water 1,000 metres high, that is at a pressure of 100 atmospheres.* This reduction will then be 436/100,000ths. I must therefore increase the weight so as to displace 1,513.77 tons instead of 1,507.2. The increase will consequently be only 6.57 tons.'

'Is that all?'

'Yes, Dr Aronnax, and the calculation can easily be checked. Now I have auxiliary tanks with a capacity of 100 tons. I can therefore descend to considerable depths. When I wish to come back up to the surface and stay there, all I have to do is expel the water by emptying all the tanks if I want the *Nautilus* to have a tenth of its total volume out of the water again.'

Given these figures, I had no objections to make against this reasoning: 'I accept your calculations, captain, and would appear foolish to contest them, since experience proves them daily. But I am now faced with one real difficulty . . .'

'Which is, sir?'

'When you are at a depth of 1,000 metres, the hull of the *Nautilus* undergoes a pressure of 100 atmospheres. If you wish at this moment to empty the auxiliary tanks so as to lighten your boat and head back up to the surface, the pumps will need to overcome a pressure of 100 atmospheres, i.e. 100 kilograms per square centimetre. Hence a power . . .'

'That only electricity can give,' interjected Captain Nemo. 'I repeat, sir, that the dynamic power of my machines is almost infinite. The pumps of the *Nautilus* have a prodigious strength, as you must have seen when the jets of water fell like a torrent on the *Abraham Lincoln*. In any case, I use the extra tanks only to go down to about 1,500 or 2,000 metres, in order to economize on my engines. When the desire takes me to visit the deeps of the ocean, perhaps two or three leagues down, I use methods that take longer but are just as reliable.'

'Namely, captain?'

'This leads me logically to explain how I steer the *Nautilus*.'

'I'm impatient to hear.'

'To direct the ship to starboard or to port, that is to steer it in the horizontal plane, I use an ordinary rudder with a long blade attached to the back of the stern post, operated by a wheel and tackle. But I can also make the *Nautilus* move in the vertical direction by means of two inclined planes attached to the vessel's sides at its centre of flotation. These planes can be set in any position, and they are operated from inside by means of powerful levers. If the planes are kept parallel to the vessel, it will move horizontally. If they are inclined, then, according to their angle and the thrust of the propeller, the *Nautilus* dives or climbs on a diagonal of my choosing. But if I want to come up to the surface more quickly, I force the propeller which, with the water pressure, makes the *Nautilus* rise like a hydrogen-filled balloon climbing swiftly through the air.'

'Bravo, captain!' I exclaimed. 'But how does the pilot follow the course that you tell him?'

'The pilot is housed in an enclosure protruding from the top of the *Nautilus*'s hull, with windows shaped like lenses.'

'Capable of resisting such pressures?'

'Yes. Although crystal is fragile when subject to blows, it generally offers considerable resistance. In experiments involving fishing with electric lights carried out in the heart of the northern seas in 1864, plates of glass only 7 millimetres thick were able to withstand a pressure of 16 atmospheres, while at the same time allowing the beams to pass through to dissipate the heat. Now the glass I use is never less than 21 centimetres thick at its centre, that is thirty times as thick.'

'All right, Captain Nemo, but to be able to see in the first place, there must be light to dispel the gloom, and I wonder how in the midst of the dark waters . . .'

'Behind the pilot-house is a powerful electric reflector, whose beam can illuminate the sea for half a mile.'

'Oh congratulations, captain, heartiest congratulations! Now I understand the phosphorescence from the supposed narwhal which so intrigued scientists! And while on the subject, could you possibly tell me whether the collision between the *Nautilus* and the *Scotia*, which caused such a stir, was the result of an accident?'

'A pure accident, sir. I was sailing 2 metres below the surface when the impact occurred. I saw in any case that no serious damage had been done.'

'None, sir. But as for your encounter with the *Abraham Lincoln* . . .?'

'Dr Aronnax, I am sorry this had to happen to one of the best ships of the fine American Navy, but I was being attacked and I had to defend myself! I did no more, all the same, than putting the frigate in such a condition that it could no longer do me any damage—it will not be difficult to repair at the nearest port.'

'Ah, captain,' I cried with conviction, 'your *Nautilus* is truly a magnificent ship!'

'Yes, sir,' responded Captain Nemo with genuine emotion, 'and I love it like the flesh of my flesh!* Now everything seems dangerous for one of your ships subject to the hazards of the ocean, for the first impression when *on* the sea is that of feeling the abyss below one, as the Dutchman Jansen* so well put it. But on board the submerged *Nautilus*, people can set their heart at ease. There is no change in the shape of the ship to worry about, for the double hull is as strong as iron; no rigging to be strained by rolling and pitching; no sails for the wind to carry off; no boilers for the steam to tear to pieces; no danger of fire, for this vessel is made of metal, not wood; no coal to run out, for it is powered by electricity; no collision to be feared, since it is the only craft to navigate these deep waters; and no storms to endure, since it is a few metres below the surface and hence in absolute tranquillity! Yes, it is the ultimate ship! And if the engineer has more confidence in his ship than its builder, and the builder more than the captain, you can understand with what entire confidence I entrusted myself to the *Nautilus*, since I am at one and the same time the captain, the builder, and the engineer!'

Captain Nemo was speaking with a captivating eloquence. The fire in his eyes and the passion in his gestures transformed him. He loved the ship like a father loves his child!

But one question, perhaps indiscreet, impulsively occurred to me, and I could not resist asking it.

'Are you an engineer then, Captain Nemo?'

'I am. I studied in London, Paris, and New York when I lived on dry land.'

'But how did you construct this superb *Nautilus* in secret?'

'Each of its components, Dr Aronnax, was sent to me from a different point on the globe via a forwarding address. Its keel was forged by Le Creusot, its propeller shaft by Penn and Co. of London, the iron plates for its hull by Laird's of Liverpool, and the propeller itself by Scott and Co. of Glasgow. Its tanks were constructed by Cail & Co. of Paris, its engine by Krupp of Prussia, its ram by the workshops at Motala in Sweden, its precision instruments by Hart Brothers of New York,* and so on; with each of the suppliers receiving my plans under a different name.'

'But', I countered, 'once these pieces had been manufactured, they still had to be assembled and adjusted?'

'I set up my workshops on a small desert island in mid-ocean. There with my workmen, that is my good companions whom I instructed and trained, I completed our *Nautilus*. Then once the work was over, fire destroyed any trace of our presence on the island, which I would have blown up had I been able.'

'So one can deduce that the cost of the ship was extremely high?'

'Dr Aronnax, an iron ship costs 1,125 francs per ton. Now the *Nautilus* displaces 1,500 tons. Its cost was therefore 1,687,500 francs,* about two million if you include the fitting out, or four or five million with the works of art and other collections it contains.'

'One last question, Captain Nemo.'

'Go on.'

'You must be very well off then?'

'Immeasurably, sir, and without undue difficulty I could pay off the ten billion francs of France's debts!'*

I stared at the peculiar person speaking like that. Was he abusing my credulity? Only time would tell.

14

THE BLACK RIVER

THE area of the terrestrial globe covered by water is estimated to be 383,255,800 square kilometres, or more than 38 million hectares.* This liquid mass occupies 2,250 million cubic miles and would form a sphere of 60 leagues diameter, whose weight would be three quad-rillion tons. To understand this number, it should be pointed out that a quadrillion is to a billion as a billion is to one, i.e. it is a billion

billion. This quantity is approximately equivalent to the water that all the rivers on earth would produce over forty thousand years.

In past geological eras, the period of fire was followed by the period of water. At first there was nothing but ocean. Then, in the Silurian Period, mountain tops began to appear, islands emerged and disappeared again in incomplete floods, then surfaced once more, next joined together and formed landmasses; and finally the land settled down in the geographical locations we are familiar with. The liquid was forced to give up 37,000,657 square miles to solid ground, that is 12,916,000,000 hectares.

The forms of the continents allow the sea to be divided into five main areas: the Arctic, the Antarctic, the Indian, the Atlantic, and the Pacific oceans.

The Pacific extends from north to south between the two polar circles, and west to east between Asia and America, comprising 145 degrees of longitude. It is the most tranquil of seas; its currents are broad and slow, its tides minimal, its rainfall abundant. Such was the first ocean that destiny had called me to crisscross, in the strangest of circumstances.

'If you wish, sir,' Captain Nemo said to me, 'we can determine our exact position and thus the starting-point of our voyage. It is quarter to twelve. I am going to return to the surface.'

The captain rang an electric bell three times. The pumps began to expel water from the tanks; the needle of the pressure-gauge showed the changing pressure and hence the upward movement of the *Nautilus*, but finally stabilized.

'We're there,' said the captain. I headed for the central staircase leading to the platform. I went up the metal steps, through the open hatch, and out on to the top of the *Nautilus*.

The platform was only 80 centimetres above the water. The bow and stern of the *Nautilus* were spindle-shaped, making it resemble a long cigar. I noticed that its metal plates overlapped slightly,* like the scales which cover the bodies of great land reptiles. I therefore understood full well how this boat had invariably been taken for a marine animal, in spite of the best telescopes.

Near the middle of the platform, the ship's boat formed a bulge where it was half recessed in the hull of the ship. Fore and aft were structures with angled sides, of moderate height, partially covered by thick glass lenses: one of them for the pilot who steered the *Nautilus*, the other for the powerful electric light to illuminate the route.

The sky was clear, the sea magnificent. The long vessel was hardly affected by the broad undulations of the ocean. A light easterly breeze ruffled the surface of the water. The horizon, free of mist, allowed perfect observation.

There was nothing in sight. Not a reef, not the tiniest of islands. The *Abraham Lincoln* had disappeared. An immense desert.

Captain Nemo, equipped with his sextant, was about to measure the height of the sun in order to calculate the latitude. He waited for the sun to move and touch the edge of the visible horizon as viewed through his sextant. While he watched not one muscle moved, and the instrument would not have been held steadier by a hand of marble.

'Twelve noon,' he said. 'Dr Aronnax, whenever you wish . . .?'

I scanned the slightly yellowish seas off the Japanese coast one last time, and went back down to the salon.

There the captain calculated his position by comparing the chronometer with the longitude and checking it against his previous observations of the hour angles. Then he said to me:

'Dr Aronnax, we are at 137° 15′ W . . .'

'Of which meridian?' I asked quickly, hoping the captain's reply might indicate his nationality.

'I have various chronometers, set respectively to the Paris, Greenwich, and Washington meridians. But, in your honour, I will use the Paris one.'

This reply taught me nothing.* I bowed, and the captain continued: 'Longitude 137° 15′ west of the Paris meridian, and latitude 30° 7′ N, that is about 300 miles from the coast of Japan. Today is 8 November, it is twelve o'clock, and our voyage of underwater exploration begins at this precise moment.'

'God be with us!'

'And now, Dr Aronnax,' added the captain, 'I will leave you to your studies. I have set an east-north-easterly course at 50 metres' depth. Here are large-scale maps where you can follow our movements. The salon is at your disposal, and with your permission I will now retire.'

Captain Nemo bowed. I remained alone, absorbed in my thoughts. They all focused on the master of the *Nautilus*. Would I ever know from what nation this strange man hailed, who boasted of belonging to none? Who had produced the hatred he had sworn for the whole of humanity, the hatred which might perhaps seek terrible vengeances? Was he one of those unrecognized scholars, one of those geniuses 'who had been hurt' to use Conseil's expression, a modern Galileo; or was he one of those scientists like the American Maury, whose career was ruined by a political revolution?* I could not yet say. He had received me coolly but courteously, as a person thrown on board his ship by chance, a person whose life he held in his hands. The only thing was that he had not taken the hand I had held out to him. He had not offered me his.

For a whole hour I remained plunged in these reflections, seeking to pierce the mystery which so intrigued me. Then my eye happened on the vast planisphere spread out over the table, and I placed my finger on the exact point of intersection of our observed lines of longitude and latitude.

The sea has rivers like dry land. These are distinctive currents, recognizable by their temperature and colour, the most noteworthy being known as the Gulf Stream. Science has determined the direction of five main currents on the globe: one in the North and one in the South Atlantic, one in the North and one in the South Pacific, and a fifth in the southern Indian Ocean. It is even probable that a sixth current used to exist in the northern Indian Ocean, when the Caspian and Aral Seas were connected to the great lakes of Asia to form a single expanse of water.

Now, one of the currents flowed past the point on the planisphere where we were: the Kuro-Shio of the Japanese, the Black River, which leaves the Bay of Bengal where it is heated by the vertical rays of the tropical sun, then negotiates the Strait of Malacca, works its way up the coast of Asia and round to the North Pacific as far as the Aleutian Islands. It carries with it trunks of camphor trees and other indigenous products, and the pure indigo of its warm water contrasts with the ocean waves. It was this current that the *Nautilus* was going to cross. I followed it with my eyes until it vanished in the immensity of the Pacific, feeling myself being carried along with it, when Ned Land and Conseil appeared at the door of the salon.

My two good companions stood stock still as if turned to stone by the marvels displayed before them.

'Where are we?' the Canadian kept exclaiming. 'In the Quebec Museum?'

'If monsieur pleases, it looks more like the Hôtel du Sommerard!'*

'My friends,' I answered, motioning them to come in, 'you are in neither Canada nor France, but on board the *Nautilus*, 50 metres below sea level.'

'If monsieur says so, it must be true,' replied Conseil, 'but to be frank, this room is enough to astonish even a Fleming like me.'

'Be astonished, my friend, and look, since there is work to be done by a classifier of your talent.'

I had no need to encourage Conseil. The good fellow, leaning over the display cases, was already murmuring words in the naturalists' language: class of Gastropods, family Buccinidae, genus cowrie, species *Cypraea madagascariensis*, etc.

During this time Land, who was not much of a conchologist, was asking about my discussion with Captain Nemo. Had I found out who he was, where he was from, where he was going, how deep he was going to take us—in sum, a thousand questions which I had no time to reply to.

I told him what I knew, or rather everything I did not know, and asked in turn what he had seen or heard.

'Seen nothing, heard nothing! I haven't even seen the crew of this boat. Are they also electric, do you think?'

'Electric?'

'You would certainly think so. But, Dr Aronnax,' asked Ned, who tended to follow a single line of thought, 'can't you tell me how many men there are on board? Ten, twenty, fifty, or a hundred?'

'I cannot say, Master Land. In any case, believe me, give up for the moment any idea of taking over the *Nautilus* and escaping. This boat is a masterpiece of modern technology, and I would regret not seeing it! Many would gladly accept the situation we are now in, if only to be able to stroll through its wonders. So please remain calm, and try to observe what is going on around us.'

'Observe!' exclaimed the harpooner. 'But we can't see anything, we will never see anything from this metal prison! We are moving and sailing blind . . .'

Just as Ned Land pronounced these last words, it went dark, completely and utterly dark. The luminous ceiling went out so quickly that my eyes were hurt by the change, just as if the opposite had happened and it had gone from total darkness to bright light.

We remained silent and motionless, not knowing what surprise was in store for us, whether pleasant or unpleasant. We heard a sliding noise. It sounded as though panels on the sides of the *Nautilus* were being opened or closed.

'This is the end of days!' said Ned Land.

'Order of the hydromedusas!' murmured Conseil.

But suddenly light appeared on both walls of the salon, coming in through two oval openings. The water was now brightly lit by electricity. Two crystal-clear panes separated us from the sea. I trembled at first at the thought that these fragile partitions might break, but strong copper fastenings secured them, giving them almost infinite resistance.

The sea was distinctly visible over a radius of a mile around the *Nautilus*. And what a sight! What pen could ever describe it? Who could ever depict the effects of light on those transparent strata, or the gradations of its slow fading away into the upper and lower regions of the ocean!

The diaphanous quality of the sea is famed. It is known to be clearer than fresh water, for the mineral and organic substances it holds in suspension actually increase its transparency. In certain parts of the West Indies, the sandy seabed can be seen with surprising clarity through 145 metres of water. Sunlight can indeed penetrate as deep as 300 metres. But in the environment the *Nautilus* was moving through, the electric brilliance was produced within the heart of the sea itself. It was no longer illuminated water, but liquid light.

If we accept Ehrenberg's* hypothesis, which proposes that the submarine depths are illuminated by phosphorescence, nature has certainly reserved one of her most spectacular sights for the inhabitants of the sea, as I could now judge from the thousand effects of the light. On each side I had a window on the unexplored abysses. The darkness in the salon made the light outside seem all the brighter, and we watched as if this pure crystal were the window of some enormous aquarium.

The *Nautilus* gave the impression of being motionless. The reason was that we lacked all point of reference. Sometimes, however, the lines of water, cut by its prow, shot past our eyes at tremendous speed.

In a state of wonder, we propped ourselves up before the display windows. None of us had yet broken our flabbergasted silence, when Conseil said:

'You wanted to see, Ned, my friend, well now you *can* see!'

'Amazing, amazing!' said the Canadian, overwhelmingly captivated, having forgotten all about his anger and ideas of escape. 'You'd go to the ends of the earth to see such a fantastic sight!'

'Ah!' I cried. 'Now I understand this man! He has built a world of his own which reveals its most astonishing wonders only to him!'

'But where are all the fish?' asked the Canadian. 'I can't see a single one!'

'Why should you worry, my dear Ned,' replied Conseil, 'since you do not know anything about them?'

'Me? I'm a fisherman!'

And a discussion ensued between the two friends, for both knew about fish, but each in a very different way.

As is well known, fish form the fourth and last class of the primary division of vertebrates. They have quite correctly been defined as 'vertebrates with double circulation, coldblooded, breathing through gills and designed for life underwater'.* There are two distinct series: bony fish, whose spinal columns are comprised of bone vertebrae, and cartilaginous fish, with spines made of cartilaginous vertebrae.

The Canadian was perhaps aware of this distinction, but Conseil knew it more thoroughly, and now that he had made friends with Ned, he could not admit that he was any less knowledgeable. So he said:

'Ned, my friend, you are a slayer of fish, a highly skilled fisherman. You have caught a large number of these fascinating creatures, but I bet that you do not know how they are classified.'

'Yes I do,' seriously replied the harpooner. 'They are classified as fish that can be eaten and fish that can't!'

'That is a glutton's distinction. But tell me whether you know the difference between bony fish and cartilaginous fish?'

'Perhaps I do, Conseil.'

'And the subdivisions of the two main classes?'

'Not a clue,' said the Canadian.

'Well, Ned, my friend, listen and remember! The bony fish are divided into six orders. *Primo*, the acanthopterygians, whose upper jaw is complete and movable, and whose gills have the form of combs. This order contains fifteen families, or three-quarters of all known fish. Type: the common perch.'

'Quite tasty,' replied Ned.

'*Secundo*,' continued Conseil, 'the abdominals, which have ventral fins under the abdomen and behind the pectorals but not attached to the shoulder bones—an order which contains the majority of freshwater fish. Types: the carp and the pike.'

'Pouah!' cried the Canadian with some disdain. 'Freshwater fish!'

'*Tertio*,' said Conseil, 'the subbrachials, whose ventral fins are attached below the pectorals and directly suspended from the shoulder bones.

This order contains four families. Types: plaice, dab, turbot, brill, sole, etc.'

'Excellent, excellent!' exclaimed the harpooner, who only liked to consider fish from the comestible point of view.

'*Quarto*,' resumed Conseil, not at all put out, 'the apodals with elongated bodies, absence of ventral fins, and a thick and frequently sticky skin—an order which consists of only one family. Types: the eel and electric eel.'

'Pathetic, pathetic!'

'*Quinto*, the lophobranchiates, which have complete jaws, moving freely, but whose gills are formed of small crests arranged in pairs along the branchial arches. This order consists of only one family. Types: the sea-horses and the pegasus dragons.'

'Rubbish, rubbish!'

'*Sexto* and finally,' said Conseil, 'the plectognaths, whose jawbone is attached firmly to the side of the intermaxillary forming the jaw, and whose palatine arch meshes with the cranium via sutures, thus rendering it immobile—an order which does not have genuine ventral fins and which is made up of two families. Types: the tetrodons and the sunfish.'

'Not worth spoiling the pot with!'

'Do you understand, Ned, my friend?'

'Not a single word. But carry on, it's all very interesting.'

'As for the cartilaginous fish,' Conseil continued imperturbably, 'they only contain three orders.'

'So much the better.'

'*Primo*, the cyclostomes, whose jaws are fused into a movable ring, and whose gills lead to numerous apertures—an order consisting of only one family. Type: the lamprey.'

'An acquired taste.'

'*Secundo*, the Selachii, with gills similar to those of the cyclostomes, but whose lower jaw is movable. This order, the biggest in the class, comprises two families. Types: the rays and the sharks.'

'What?' cried Ned. 'Rays and sharks in the same order? Well, my friend, in the rays' interest, I don't recommend you put them in the same tank together!'

'*Tertio*, the sturionians, whose gills, as is normal, open into a single slit fitted with gill covers—an order which contains four genera. Type: the sturgeon.'

'Ah, my friend Conseil, you've kept the best for the end—in my view anyway. And is that it?'

'Yes, my good Ned; and notice that when one knows all this, one still knows nothing, for families are subdivided into genera, sub-genera, species, varieties . . .'

'Well, my friend,' said the harpooner, leaning on the glass panel, 'we've certainly got lots of varieties passing.'

'Yes, so many fish! It is as if one was in an aquarium!'

'Hardly,' I said, 'for an aquarium is just a prison, and these fish are as free as the birds of the air.'

'Well, my good Conseil, name them, go on, name them!'

'I am unable to! That's my master's department.'

And indeed the worthy boy, although a fanatical classifier, was not a naturalist, and I do not know whether he would have distinguished a tuna from a bonito. He was, in short, the opposite of the Canadian, who named all fish without hesitation. 'A triggerfish,' I said.

'A Chinese triggerfish,' responded Ned Land.

'Genus *Balistes*, family of Sclerodermi, order of plectognaths,' murmured Conseil.

Decidedly Ned and Conseil would have made a brilliant naturalist between the two of them.

The Canadian was not mistaken. A school of triggerfish, with squashed bodies and coarse-grained skin, armed with stings on their dorsal fins, were playing around the *Nautilus* while moving the four rows of spines that bristled on either side of their tails. Nothing could be more attractive than their skin, grey on top and white underneath with golden patches glittering in the dark undertow of the waves. Amongst them some rays undulated, like tablecloths flapping in the wind, and I noticed to my great joy that they included the Chinese ray, yellowish on top, a delicate pink on its stomach, and with three stings behind its eyes; a rare species, and even uncertain in Lacépède's time, who saw it only in Japanese sketches.

For two hours, a whole armada of marine creatures escorted the *Nautilus*. During their games and their leaps, their competitions of beauty, colour, and speed, I distinguished the green wrasse, the Barbary mullet marked with two black stripes, the elytrous goby with rounded caudal fins, which is white with violet blotches on its back, the Japanese scombroid, the admirable mackerel of these seas, with a blue body and silver head, and brilliant azuries whose very name renders otiose any description, striped sparids with fins dressed up in blue and yellow, sparids with bends sinister picked out in black stripes on their caudal fins, zonifer sparids elegantly corseted in their six belts, *Aulostomus*, genuine snipefish or oystercatchers some of which reached one metre, Japanese newts, *Echidnae muraenae*, six-foot-long serpents with small bright eyes and huge mouths bristling with teeth, and so on.

Our admiration still knew no bounds. Our exclamations never ceased. Ned named the fish while Conseil classified. I was in ecstasy at the vitality of their appearance and the beauty of their silhouettes. I had never before had the chance to observe living creatures that could move freely in their natural element.

I will not cite all the varieties that passed before our dazzled eyes, an entire collection from the seas of Japan and China. These fish rushed up, more numerous than the birds of the air, undoubtedly drawn by the dazzling electric light.

Suddenly the light came on in the salon. The metal panels closed again. The enchanting vision disappeared. But I continued to dream for a long time, until my eyes chanced upon the instruments on the walls. The compass showed the direction still to be north-north-east, the pressure-gauge five atmospheres, corresponding to a depth of 50 metres, and the electric log a speed of 15 knots.

I expected to see Captain Nemo. But he didn't show himself. The clock read 5 p.m.

Ned and Conseil returned to their cabin. I too went back to my room. My dinner was already there. It consisted of turtle soup made from the most delicate hawksbills, a red mullet with slightly flaky white flesh, whose separately prepared liver made a delicious dish, and fillets of emperor fish, whose flavour I found superior to salmon.

I spent the evening reading, writing, and thinking. Then, with my eyelids drooping, I stretched out on my sea-wrack bed and fell into a deep sleep, while the *Nautilus* glided through the swift current of the Black River.

15

A LETTER OF INVITATION

THE following day, 9 November, I woke up after a sleep of twelve hours. Conseil came in as usual to find out 'how monsieur had slept' and to offer his services. He had left his friend the Canadian slumbering like one who had never done anything else.

I let the good fellow chatter on as he wished, without bothering to reply much. I was preoccupied by Captain Nemo's absence from the viewing session the evening before, and hoped to be able to see him again today.

Soon I had put on my byssus clothes. Once or twice Conseil commented on this material. I told him it was made from the glossy silky threads which attach fan mussels to rocks, these being a variety of shell plentiful on the Mediterranean shores. It was formerly used to make fine materials like stockings and gloves, being very soft and warm. The crew of the *Nautilus* could therefore clothe themselves economically without needing cotton plants, sheep, or silkworms from dry land.

Once dressed I went into the salon. It was deserted.

I plunged into studying the treasures of conchology assembled in the display cabinets. I also moved through vast herbariums filled with the rarest marine plants, which maintained their admirable colours despite being dried. Among these precious hydrophytes, I noticed whorled *Cladostephi*, peacock's tails, caulerpas with vine leaves, graniferous *Callithamna*, delicate ceramiums in scarlet hues, fan-shaped agars, acetabulums like the caps of very short mushrooms, classified for a long time among the zoophytes, and finally a whole series of kelps.

The whole day went by without the honour of a visit from Captain Nemo. The panels of the salon did not open. Perhaps we were not meant to become too blasé about such beautiful things.

The *Nautilus* maintained an east-north-easterly course, its speed 12 knots, its depth between 50 and 60 metres.

The next day, 10 November, the same abandonment, the same solitude. I saw nobody from the crew. Ned and Conseil spent most of the day with me. They too were astonished at the captain's baffling absence. Was the strange man ill? Was he preparing to change his plans for us?

In any case, as Conseil pointed out, we enjoyed total freedom. We were exquisitely and copiously fed. Our host kept his side of the bargain. We had no grounds for complaint, and in any case the strangeness of our situation provided us with such fabulous compensation that we did not yet have the right to criticize it.

It was that day that I began a diary of our adventures, which has allowed me to recount them with the most scrupulous accuracy; as a curious detail, I wrote my journal on paper made from sea-wrack.

Early on the morning of 11 November the fresh air coursing through the *Nautilus* told me we had gone back up to the surface to replenish our supply of oxygen. I headed for the central staircase, and went up on to the platform.

It was six o'clock. I found the sky overcast, the sea grey but calm. Hardly any swell. Would Captain Nemo put in an appearance? I was hoping to meet him here. But I found only the pilot, enclosed in his glass dome. Sitting on the bulge caused by the dinghy, I breathed in the salt air with great pleasure.

The mist began to dissipate in the rays of the sun. The sun itself emerged from the eastern horizon. The sea caught fire under its regard like a trail of powder. The clouds, scattered over the heights, took on all sorts of bright colours, with subtle shades and plenty of 'mares' tails'[1] promising wind for the whole day.

But what difference did the wind make to the *Nautilus*, undaunted by storms?

I was admiring the cheerful sunrise, so joyful and so vivifying, when I heard somebody else coming up to the platform.

I was preparing to greet Captain Nemo, but it was his first officer who appeared—I had already seen him on the captain's first visit. He came forward on the platform, but did not seem to notice my presence. A powerful telescope at his eye, he studied every point of the horizon with extreme care. Then, having completed his examination, he went up to the hatch and pronounced the sentence consisting of the following words. I can remember it, as it was repeated every morning in identical circumstances. It ran as follows:

'Nautron respoc lorni virch.'*

What it meant, I could not say.

Having pronounced these words, the first officer went below again. I imagined that the *Nautilus* was going to continue its underwater

---

[1] Little white clouds, light and with serrated edges. [JV]

navigation. So I went back down the hatch staircase, along the gang-way, and returned to my room.

Five days went by like this, without any change to the situation. Each morning I went up on to the platform. The same sentence was pronounced by the same individual. Captain Nemo did not appear.

I had concluded that I would never see him again, when, on 16 November, going back into my room with Ned and Conseil, I found a note addressed to me on the table.

I opened it impatiently. It was written in clear bold handwriting, a little Gothic-looking and reminiscent of German script.

The letter was couched in these terms:

16 November 1867

Dr Aronnax
On board the *Nautilus*

Captain Nemo invites Dr Aronnax on a hunting party to visit his forests of Crespo Island tomorrow morning. He hopes that nothing will prevent Dr Aronnax from attending, and he would be pleased if his companions could join him.

Captain Nemo
Commander of the *Nautilus*

'Hunting!' cried Ned.

'In the forests of Crespo Island!' added Conseil.

'So that individual does sometimes visit dry land?' asked Ned Land.

'That seems clearly stated,' I said rereading the letter.

'Well we've got to accept,' answered the Canadian. 'Once on land, we can decide what to do. In any case, I wouldn't say no to a few helpings of fresh venison.'

Without trying to make sense of the discrepancy between Captain Nemo's manifest horror for the land and his invitation to go hunting in forests, I merely replied:

'Let's first of all see what Crespo Island is.'

I consulted the planisphere, and at latitude 32° 40′ N and longitude 167° 50′ W I found a tiny island charted by Captain Crespo in 1801, that the old Spanish maps called Roca de la Plata, meaning 'Silver Rock'.* We were therefore about 1,800 miles from where we had started, and the *Nautilus* had changed direction a little and was now heading south-east.

I showed my companions the tiny rock lost in the heart of the Northern Pacific.

'If Captain Nemo sometimes goes ashore,' I said, 'at least he chooses islands that are utterly deserted.'

Ned Land bobbed his head without replying, and Conseil and he left the room. After supper, served to me by a silent and impassive steward, I went to bed, not without a slight feeling of worry.

When I woke up the following day, 17 November, I realized that the *Nautilus* was not moving at all. I quickly got dressed and went into the salon.

Captain Nemo was there. He had been waiting for me, and got up, greeted me, and asked if it would be agreeable to accompany him.

As he made no reference to his absence over the last week, I did not mention it, and simply replied that my companions and I were ready to join him.

'But', I added, 'I will take the liberty of asking one question.'

'Ask, Dr Aronnax, and if I can answer it, I will.'

'Well, captain, how does it arise that you own forests on Crespo Island, you who have broken all contact with the land?'

'Sir, the forests I own need neither light nor heat from the sun. No lions, tigers, panthers, or any other quadrupeds live there. I am the only person to know them. They grow for me alone. They are not terrestrial forests, but underwater ones.'

'Underwater ones!' I exclaimed.

'Yes, Dr Aronnax.'

'And you're offering to take me there?'

'Quite.'

'On foot?'

'Without even getting our feet wet.'

'Whilst hunting?'

'Whilst hunting.'

'With guns?'

'With guns.'

I looked at the captain of the *Nautilus* with an expression that was not at all flattering for him.

'His brain must have gone,' I thought. 'He has had a fit which has lasted a week, and which is still continuing. What a pity! I liked him better when he was peculiar rather than insane!'

This thought could clearly be read on my face, but Captain Nemo simply invited me to follow him, which I did like a man resigned to anything.

We arrived in the dining-room, where breakfast was already served. 'Dr Aronnax, please be so good as to share my breakfast without further formality. We can talk while we eat. I promised you a walk in a forest, but I did not promise to take you to a restaurant. So please eat your breakfast knowing that your dinner will probably be very late.'

I did justice to the meal. It was made up of various fish and slices of sea slug, which is an excellent zoophyte, accompanied by very appetizing seaweeds such as *Porphyra laciniata* and *Laurencia pinnatifida*. We had perfectly clear water to drink, to which, following the captain's example, I added a few drops of an alcoholic beverage extracted from the seaweed known as waterleaf, as is customary in Kamchatka.

At first Captain Nemo ate without a word. Then he said:

'When I suggested that you accompany me to the forests of Crespo, you thought I was contradicting myself. When I informed you that they were underwater forests, you thought I was mad. Sir, you should never judge men too hastily.'

'But, captain, I assure you . . .'

'Please listen to me, and you will see if you should accuse me of madness or inconsistency.'

'I'm listening.'

'Sir, you know as well as I do that man can live underwater provided he takes with him a supply of air for breathing. While carrying out works underwater, the workman wears watertight clothing and his head is enclosed in a metal capsule which receives air from the outside by means of force pumps and inflow valves.'

'Diving suits.'

'Indeed, but in such conditions man is not free. He is tied to the pump which provides the air through a rubber tube, a real chain riveting him to the land; and if we were bound to the *Nautilus* in such a way we would not go very far.'

'But how can one escape this constraint?'

'By using the Rouquayrol-Denayrouze apparatus,* first developed by two of your compatriots, and which I have improved for my own use: it will allow you to meet new physiological conditions without your organs suffering in any way. It is comprised of a tank made of thick metal in which I store air at a pressure of 50 atmospheres. The tank is fastened to one's back by means of straps, like a soldier's knapsack. Its upper part is a closed container where air is kept in by a one-way mechanism, and can escape only at normal pressure. In the

Rouquayrol apparatus, as normally used, two rubber pipes emerge from the container and lead to a type of round mouthpiece enclosing the user's mouth and nose; one pipe is used as an inlet for the air for breathing, the other for the escape of the used air, with one's tongue moving between the two tubes as one breathes in and out. But since I undergo considerable pressure at the bottom of the sea, I have had to enclose my head in a copper sphere, like those of diving suits, with the tubes for breathing in and out leading to this sphere.'

'Fine, Captain Nemo, but the air you take with you must get used up quickly and as soon as the oxygen goes below 15 per cent, it becomes unbreathable.'

'Quite right, Dr Aronnax. But as I mentioned, the *Nautilus*'s pumps allow me to store it at considerable pressure and so the tank can provide breathable air for up to nine or ten hours.'

'I have no further objection. I will simply ask you, captain: how do you manage to light your way on the ocean floor?'

'With the Ruhmkorff device,* Dr Aronnax. Whereas the first apparatus is carried on one's back, this one is carried on the belt. It has a Bunsen battery which I activate, not with potassium dichromate but with sodium. An induction coil absorbs the electricity produced and directs it to a lantern of a special kind. In this lantern is a glass coil which contains slight traces of carbon dioxide. When the apparatus is operating, the gas is luminous, providing a continuous whitish light. Thus equipped, I can breathe and I can see.'

'Captain Nemo, you provide such overwhelming answers to all my objections that I no longer dare to doubt. However, although forced to accept the Rouquayrol and Ruhmkorff devices, I must reserve my position regarding the gun you plan to give me.'

'But the gun does not work with powder,' said the captain.

'So it is an air gun?'

'Yes. How do you think I can manufacture powder on board my ship, since I have neither saltpetre, nor sulphur, nor charcoal?'

'But in any case,' I persisted, 'in order to be able to fire it underwater, in a medium 855 times as dense as air, you need to overcome considerable resistance.'

'That is no problem. There exist certain guns, following Fulton's design and improved by the Britons Phipps Coles and Burley, the Frenchman Furcy, and the Italian Landi,* which are equipped with a special closing device and so can fire underwater. But I repeat: not having access to powder, I substituted compressed air, abundantly available from the *Nautilus*'s pumps.'

'But the air must get used up quickly?'

'Yes, but do I not have my Rouquayrol tank which can provide more as needed? All that is required is a suitable valve. In any case, Dr Aronnax, you will see for yourself that one does not use much air or ammunition for underwater hunting.'

'Nevertheless, in semi-darkness, immersed in this liquid which is much denser than air, shots can surely not carry very far and can rarely be fatal?'

'On the contrary, sir. With this gun every shot is lethal: as soon as an animal is hit, however slightly, it falls down as if struck by lightning.'

'But I don't understand!'

'Because this gun does not fire ordinary bullets but small glass capsules, invented by the Austrian chemist Leinebrock,* of which I have considerable supplies. These glass capsules, covered with steel casings and weighted with lead balls, are exactly like miniature Leyden jars,* into which electricity has been forced at a very high voltage. They discharge at the slightest impact, and however powerful the animal, it falls down dead. I will add that these capsules are of just .4 calibre, and that a fully loaded gun can contain up to ten of them.'

'I have no more objections,' I replied getting up from the table, 'and all I can do is take my gun. Wherever you go, I will follow.'

Captain Nemo took me towards the stern of the *Nautilus*, and as I passed Ned and Conseil's cabin, I called to my two companions who immediately came and joined us.

We arrived at a compartment situated on the flank near the engine-room. This was where we were to put on our excursion clothing.

16

AN EXCURSION OVER THE PLAINS

THIS compartment was both the arsenal and the cloakroom of the *Nautilus*. A dozen diving suits were hanging on the walls, ready for the excursionists.

When he saw them, Ned was visibly reluctant to put one on.

'But, my good Ned,' I told him, 'the forests of Crespo Island are actually underwater forests!'

'Oh!' said the disappointed harpooner as his dreams of fresh meat evaporated. 'What about you, Dr Aronnax, are you going to put one of those contraptions on?'

'We need to, Master Ned.'

'You can do as you wish, sir,' replied the harpooner, shrugging his shoulders. 'But I'm not going to put one on unless I'm forced to.'

'Nobody is forcing you, Master Ned,' said Captain Nemo.

'And is Conseil going to take the risk?' enquired Ned.

'I follow wherever monsieur goes.'

At a sign from the captain, two of the crewmen came and helped us put on the heavy watertight suits, made of seamless rubber and designed to withstand considerable pressure. They were like coats of armour that were both elastic and strong. Each suit consisted of trousers and jacket. The trousers ended in thick boots with heavy lead soles. The material of the jacket was kept in position by strips of copper which shielded the chest and protected it from the water pressure, allowing the lungs to work freely; its sleeves finished in supple gloves which allowed one's hands free movement.

It will be seen that these much-improved diving suits were a far cry from the items of shapeless clothing invented and extolled in the eighteenth century, like the cork breastplates, the life-vests, the sea clothing, the buoys, etc.

Captain Nemo, one of his companions—a Hercules, who looked stupendously strong—Conseil, and I had soon put on our diving suits. All we had to do now was place the metallic spheres on our heads. But before doing this, I asked the captain if I could examine the guns we would be using.

One of the *Nautilus*'s crewmen gave me a simple rifle with a relatively large butt made of hollowed-out steel plate. The butt served as a tank for the compressed air: a valve, operated by a trigger, allowed the air to escape into the metal tube. A container for the projectiles, hollowed out in the butt, held about twenty electric bullets* which a spring automatically placed in the barrel of the gun. As soon as one shot had been fired, another was ready to go off.

'Captain Nemo, this weapon is flawless and easy to use. Now all I wish is to try it out. But how are we going to get to the ocean floor?'

'Dr Aronnax, the *Nautilus* is already resting on the bottom, 10 metres down, and we merely have to leave.'

'But how do we get out?'

'You will soon see.'

Captain Nemo put his head into his spherical helmet. Conseil and I did likewise, not before the Canadian had given us a mocking 'Happy hunting!' The top of our clothing had a collar of copper, incorporating a thread on to which the metal helmet could be screwed. Three apertures, covered in thick glass, meant we could see in any direction just by turning our heads inside the spheres. The Rouquayrol apparatuses began to work as soon as they had been placed on our backs, and I was able to breathe quite easily. With a Ruhmkorff lamp attached to my belt and gun in hand, I was ready. But to be honest, imprisoned in the heavy clothing and pinned to the deck by my lead soles, I wouldn't have been able to take a single step.

However, this difficulty had been foreseen, for I could feel myself being propelled into a small room next to the cloakroom. My companions, similarly conveyed, followed behind. I heard a door fitted with a seal closing behind us, and then we were in complete darkness.

After a moment, a loud hissing sound reached my ears. Cold started rising from my feet to my chest. Using a tap inside the ship, water had obviously been let in from the outside and was now completely filling the room. A second door then opened in the side of the *Nautilus*. A faint light came through. Moments later our feet were treading the ocean floor.

And now, how can I possibly record the impression made on me by this excursion under the waters? Words are inadequate to convey such wonders! When even the artist's brush is incapable of portraying the unique effects of the liquid element, how could a pen begin to render them?

Captain Nemo was walking ahead, his companion a few steps behind us. Conseil and I stayed close together, as if we could talk through our metal shells. I no longer felt the weight of my clothing, my shoes, my air tank, nor the weight of the thick sphere in which my head was shaken round like an almond in its shell. All these objects, with water on every side, lost a weight equal to the liquid displaced, and I felt very comfortable, thanks to the physical law discovered by Archimedes. I was no longer an inert object but could move quite freely.

The light astonished me with its power of penetration, for it lit up the ground as far as 30 feet from the surface. The sunlight easily penetrated the aqueous substance but its colours dissolved. I could see objects 100 metres away quite clearly. Beyond that, the depths were tinted in fine shades of ultramarine, becoming bluer in the distance and fading into a sort of nebulous darkness. The water all round me was in effect a sort of air, denser than the terrestrial atmosphere but almost as clear. I could see the calm surface of the sea above my head.

We were walking over fine smooth sand, not rippled like beaches that retain the waves' imprint. This dazzling carpet reflected the sunlight with surprising intensity, almost like a mirror. Hence a pervasive dazzle that filled the liquid molecules. Will I be believed if I say that at a depth of 30 feet, I could see as clearly as in the open air?

For quarter of an hour I walked over the glowing sand, strewn with the impalpable dust of shells. Although the hull of the *Nautilus*, silhouetted like a long reef, slowly disappeared, when night fell in the depth of the waters, its searchlight would send out rays of perfect brilliance to help us find our way back on board. This will be difficult to understand for anyone who has only seen those whitish, clear-cut beams on land. There the dust filling the air gives the rays the appearance of a luminous mist; but on the sea's surface, and under it, the electric shafts are transmitted with incomparable purity.

We moved over a sandy plain which seemed so vast as to be limitless. I was using my hands to push aside the liquid curtains which then closed up again behind me, and my footprints were being quickly erased by the water pressure.

Soon I could make out the shapes of a few objects, hazy in the distance. I observed a magnificent foreground of rocks, carpeted with the finest zoophytes, and I was immediately struck by an effect peculiar to this environment.

It was ten in the morning. The sun's rays struck the surface of the waves at an oblique angle, and the light was decomposed by the refraction as if passing through a prism. It fell on the flowers, rocks, plantlets, shells, and polyps, and shaded their edges with the seven colours of the solar spectrum. It was a marvel, a feast for the eyes, this interweaving of coloured tones, a true kaleidoscope of green, yellow, orange, violet, indigo, and blue, the complete contents of a crazy colourist's palette! Oh, why could I not tell Conseil the vivid sensations intoxicating my brain and vie with him in admiring exclamations!

Why was I not able to convey my thoughts in that sign language used by Captain Nemo and his companion! For lack of better, I talked to myself, I shouted out in the copper vessel on my head, perhaps using up more air in vain words than I should have.

On seeing this splendid spectacle, Conseil had stopped, as had I. Clearly the good chap, in the presence of these representatives of zoophytes and molluscs, was classifying, constantly classifying. Polyps and *Echinodermata* lay in profusion on the ground. The varied *Isidae*, the *Cornularia* which lived in isolation, the clumps of virgin oculini-dae formerly called 'white coral', the fungus coral bristling like mushrooms, and the anemones adhering by their muscular discs—all constituted a flowerbed, spangled with porpoids and their involucres of blue-tinged tentacles, with starfish studded in the sand, with ver-rucous astrophytons, a fine lace embroidered by naiads' hands and whose garlands swung in the slight undulations as we passed. I was unhappy at crushing under my feet the brilliant specimens of molluscs strewn in their thousands, the concentric combshells, the hammer-shells, the donaxes, veritable jumping shells, the top-shells, the red helmets, the angel-wing strombs, the aplysias, and so many other products of the inexhaustible ocean. But we could not stop, and headed on, whilst above our heads sailed the schools of Portuguese men-of-war trailing their ultramarine tentacles, jellyfish whose opaline or deli-cate rose umbrellas festooned with sky-blue strakes shielded us from the sunlight, and pelagic panopea, which would have sprinkled our path with phosphorescent gleams, had it been dark!

I glimpsed all these marvels within a quarter of a mile, scarcely stopping as I followed Captain Nemo, waving me on. Soon the ground changed. The sandy plain was replaced by a layer of sticky mud that the Americans call 'ooze', composed exclusively of siliceous and lime-stone shells. Then we passed through a field of pelagic seaweed plants growing vigorously, not yet torn away by the water. These lawns of fine-woven material felt soft underfoot and could be compared to the silkiest rugs made by man's hand.

But just as the vegetation stretched before our feet, our heads were also catered for. A trellis of marine plants, from the exuberant family of algae of more than two thousand known species, crisscrossed the surface of the water. I could see long floating ribbons of sea-wracks, some globular and some tubular: there were *Laurencia*, *Cladostephi* with slender foliage, and water leaves like cactus fans. I noticed that the green plants kept closer to the surface, whilst the red ones were at medium depth, leaving the black or brown water-plants the task of forming the gardens and flowerbeds of the furthermost depths of the ocean.

These seaweeds are truly one of the miracles of creation, one of the marvels of the world's flora. This family produces both the smallest and the biggest vegetation on the globe. For if forty thousand of these imperceptible plantlets have been counted in 5 square millimetres, wracks have also been found whose length exceeds 500 metres.

We had left the *Nautilus* about an hour and a half before. It was nearly midday. I realized this from the vertical sunlight, no longer refracted. The magical colours were slowly disappearing, and the emerald and sapphire nuances faded from our firmament. We were walking with a regular step that resonated on the ground with astonishing intensity. The slightest sounds were transmitted at a speed to which the ear is not accustomed on dry land. The reason being that water is a better conductor of sound than air, and transmits it four times as quickly.

Soon the ground went down more steeply. The light took on a uniform colour. We had reached a depth of 100 metres, and were now at a pressure of 10 atmospheres. But my diving suit had been designed in such a way that I was not affected at all. I merely felt a certain stiffness in my fingers, and even this discomfort quickly disappeared. As for the fatigue that should have resulted from a two-hour excursion kitted out in such an unfamiliar way, it was non-existent. Helped by the water, I was moving with surprising ease.

Even at 300 feet, I could still see the sunlight, if faintly. Its intense brilliance had given way to a reddish twilight intermediate between day and night. But we could still see well enough to find our way, and did not yet need to switch on our Ruhmkorff lamps.

Suddenly Captain Nemo stopped. He waited for me to catch up, and pointed to some dark masses against the shadows not far away.

'These must be the forests of Crespo Island,' I thought. I was not mistaken.

17

AN UNDERWATER FOREST

WE had finally reached the edge of the forest, doubtless one of the most beautiful in Captain Nemo's immense dominion. He considered it his own, claiming the same rights as the first men in the first days of the world. In any case, who could dispute his possession of the underwater property? What braver pioneer could come, axe in hand, to cut down the dark brushwood?

The forest was made of huge tree-like plants, and as soon as we went under their vast arches, our eyes were struck by the forms of their branches, remarkable shapes I had never seen before.

None of the grasses carpeting the ground, none of the branches sprouting on the shrubs crept or drooped, and none stretched out horizontally. All rose towards the surface. There was not a single filament, not a single blade, however thin, which did not stand up as straight as iron stalks. The wracks and the creepers grew in rigid perpendicular lines determined by the density of the element that had given them birth. The plants were motionless, but when I shifted them with my hand, they immediately moved back to their original positions. It was the realm of the vertical.

I soon got used to this bizarre arrangement and to the semi-darkness enveloping us. The ground of the forest was strewn with sharp rocks, difficult to avoid. The underwater flora seemed relatively complete, even richer perhaps than in a tropical or Arctic zone, where there is less variety. For a while, however, I involuntarily mixed up the kingdoms, taking zoophytes for hydrophytes, animals for plants. And who wouldn't have made such a mistake? Flora and fauna were so close in this submarine world!

I noticed that all the products of the vegetable kingdom were only lightly attached to the ground. Devoid of roots, indifferent to the fixed points they were tied to, whether sand, shells, tests, or pebbles, they merely needed them as a point of contact, not for life. These plants were self-propagating, and the essence of their existence was in the water that bore and nourished them. Most of them did not produce leaves but lamellas of fantastic shapes, although limited to a narrow range of colours: only pink, crimson, green, olive, fawn, and brown. I again saw, but this time not dried like the specimens in the *Nautilus*,

Padinae pavoni in fans seeming to implore the breeze, scarlet rose-tangles, laminaria extending their edible young shoots, threadlike flexuous *Nereocystis* opening out to reach a height of 15 metres, clumps of acetabulums with stems growing from the top, and many other pelagic plants, all without flowers. 'A strange aberration,' one witty naturalist* has said, 'where the animal kingdom flowers and the vegetable kingdom does not!'

Between the various shrubs as big as trees in the temperate zones, or else under their humid shade, grew genuine bushes with living flowers, hedges of zoophytes on which bloomed meandrine corals crisscrossed with meandering furrows, yellowish *Caryophylli* with diaphanous tentacles, cespitose clumps of zoantharians, and, to complete the illusion, fish flies flying from branch to branch like a swarm of humming birds, while yellow *Lepisanthes*, with bristling jaws and sharp scales, dactylopterous and Monocanthidean, rose from under our feet, like a flock of snipe.

At about one o'clock Captain Nemo gave the signal to halt. For my part I was quite pleased, as we stretched out under a bower of aralias, whose long thin blades stood up like arrows.

I found this rest period delightful. The only thing missing was the charm of conversation. But it was impossible to speak, impossible to reply. I merely brought my big copper head close to Conseil's. I could see the worthy man's eyes shining with pleasure, and to show his satisfaction he moved about within his carapace in the most comical way imaginable.

After our four-hour march, I was astonished not to feel ravenous. Why my stomach behaved like this, I cannot say. But in contrast, I felt an uncontrollable desire to sleep, as happens with all divers. My eyes quickly closed behind the thick glass, and I fell into an irresistible slumber that until then only the movement of walking had been able to fight. I was in fact imitating Captain Nemo and his burly companion who were already stretched out in the crystal limpidity, fast asleep.

How long I was out I could not calculate; but when I woke again, the sun seemed to be already going down towards the horizon. Captain Nemo had already got up, and I was just stretching when a startling sight brought me suddenly to my feet.

A few paces away, a monstrous sea spider, 3 feet tall, was looking at me with its shifty eyes, ready to throw itself on me. Although my diving suit was thick enough to protect me from the animal's stings,

I could not prevent a shudder of horror. Conseil and the sailor from the *Nautilus* woke up just then. Captain Nemo pointed out the hideous crustacean to his companion, and the animal was immediately knocked down with a blow from his rifle butt: I saw the monster's dreadful legs twisting in terrible convulsions.

This encounter made me realize that other, more redoubtable animals surely haunted these dark depths, and that my diving suit would not protect me from their attacks. I hadn't thought of it until then, but decided to keep a watchful eye open. I imagined in any case that this halt was as far as our excursion would go; but I was mistaken for, instead of returning to the *Nautilus*, Captain Nemo continued on his daring venture.

The ground was still descending, its slope getting steeper and leading us into greater depths. It must have been about three o'clock when we reached a narrow gully between high vertical walls, at about 150 metres' depth. Thanks to the quality of our equipment, we had gone 90 metres further than the limit nature seemed to have imposed on man's underwater expeditions.

I say 150 metres, although no instrument allowed me to calculate the depth. But I did know that even in the clearest seas the sunlight could penetrate no further. It was at this precise point that the darkness became intense. Nothing could be seen at ten paces. I was therefore groping my way along when I suddenly saw a bright white light. Captain Nemo had just switched on his electric lamp. His companion did likewise. Conseil and I followed their example. By turning a screw, I established contact between the coil and the glass spiral, and the sea, lit up by our four lanterns, was illuminated for 25 metres around.

Captain Nemo continued to force his way into the dark depths of the forest whose shrubs were growing scarcer and scarcer. I noticed that vegetable life was disappearing faster than animal life. The pelagic plants were already forsaking the ground which had become arid, although an enormous number of animals could still be seen— zoophytes, articulates, molluscs, and fish.

While walking, I was thinking that the light from our Ruhmkorff lamps would automatically attract the inhabitants of these dark levels.

But if they did come nearer, they still kept at a distance that frustrated the huntsmen. Several times I saw Captain Nemo stopping and aiming his gun; then, after a moment's observation, he would get up again and resume walking.

Finally, at about four o'clock, our stunning expedition came to an end. A splendid rock wall of imposing height rose up in front: a jumble of gigantic blocks, an enormous cliff of granite, with dark grottoes leading into it but no practicable way up. This was the underwater coast of Crespo Island. This was land.

The captain abruptly stopped. His signal brought us to a halt, for however much I wanted to go beyond the wall, I too had to stop. Here Captain Nemo's realm finished. He did not wish to leave it. Beyond lay that portion of the globe where he would never again set foot.

We started back. Captain Nemo had taken the lead of our little troop once more, finding his way along without the slightest hesitation. I thought I could see that we were not following the same path back to the *Nautilus*. The new route, very steep and thus very difficult, brought us quickly up towards the surface. However, this return to the upper strata was not so sudden that decompression occurred too quickly, for this would have caused grave disorders to our bodies, producing those internal injuries so fatal to divers. Very soon daylight came back and grew stronger, and since the sun was already low on the horizon, the refraction again gave many objects a spectral ring.

At ten metres' depth we were walking through a swarm of small fish of every sort, more plentiful than the birds of the air, and more lively; but no aquatic game worth a gun-shot had yet appeared before our eyes.

All of a sudden, I saw the captain swiftly aiming his weapon and following an object moving amongst the shrubbery. The shot went off, I heard a faint hissing sound, and an animal fell stricken a few paces away.

It was a magnificent sea otter, an *Enhydra*, the only quadruped that is exclusively marine. The five-foot otter was surely very valuable. Its skin, rich brown on top and silver underneath, was one of those admirable furs that are so sought after on the Russian and Chinese markets; the fineness and sheen of its coat meant it was worth at least two thousand francs. I admired this strange mammal with its rotund head and short ears, round eyes, white whiskers like a cat's, webbed and clawed feet, and bushy tail. This precious carnivore, tracked and hunted down by fishermen, is becoming extremely rare, and it has taken refuge principally in the northern Pacific, where its species will probably soon become extinct.*

Captain Nemo's companion came and picked up the animal and loaded it on his shoulder, as we set off again.

For an hour the plain of sand stretched out before our feet. It often rose to less than two metres from the surface. I could then see our image clearly reflected upside down: above us appeared an identical troop, reproducing all our movements and gestures, identical in every point except they were marching with heads inverted and feet in the air.

Another effect to be noted. This was the passage of thick clouds which formed and disappeared very quickly; but on reflection, I realized that these so-called clouds were due merely to variations in the height of the long waves; and I also noticed the foaming white horses produced on the surface by the breaking crests. I was even able to follow the shadows of large birds passing over our heads as they lightly skimmed the surface.

It was then that I witnessed one of the finest shots ever to play on the heart-strings of a hunter. A sizeable bird with a large wingspan, clearly visible, was gliding towards us. Captain Nemo's companion aimed and shot at it when it was only a few metres above the waves. The animal fell down dead, and dropped within reach of the skilful hunter, who picked it up. It was an albatross of the finest class, an admirable specimen of those pelagic birds.

Our progress had not been interrupted by this incident. For two hours we followed sandy plains alternating with seaweed-strewn prairies, very difficult to negotiate. I could indeed hardly take another step, when I noticed a vague glimmer breaking the watery darkness about half a mile off. It was the *Nautilus*'s searchlight. Within twenty minutes we would be on board, able to breathe as I wished, for I felt that the air from my tank was no longer rich enough in oxygen. But I hadn't reckoned on an encounter which slightly postponed our arrival.

I had remained about twenty paces behind, when suddenly I saw Captain Nemo coming back towards me. With his strong hand he pushed me down, whilst his companion did the same to Conseil. I did not know what to make of this brusque attack, but felt reassured when I realized that the captain was lying down near me and remaining motionless.

I was stretched out on the ground in the shelter of a seaweed bush when, raising my head, I noticed huge shapes moving noisily past, giving out phosphorescent gleams.

My blood froze in my veins! I had recognized the formidable sharks threatening us. It was a pair of blue sharks, terrible beasts with enormous tails and dull glassy eyes, which secrete a phosphorescent substance through holes near their muzzles. Monstrous fireflies* that can chew an entire man in their iron jaws! I was not aware whether Conseil was busy classifying them, but I know that for my part, I scarcely studied their silver bellies and menacing mouths bristling with teeth from a scientific point of view, but more as a potential prey than as a naturalist.

Very fortunately, these voracious animals cannot see very well. They passed by without noticing us, brushing past us with their brownish fins; and as if by a miracle we escaped this threat, certainly more dangerous than an encounter with a tiger in the heart of the jungle.

Half an hour later, guided by the electric beam, we reached the *Nautilus*. The outside door was still open, and Captain Nemo closed it as soon as we were back in the first compartment. Then he pressed a button. I could hear the pumps working inside the ship, felt the water going down around me, and in a few moments the compartment was entirely empty. The inside door was opened, and we moved into the cloakroom.

There our diving suits were taken off, not without difficulty; and totally exhausted, faint from lack of food and sleep, I returned to my room—in a state of complete wonder at this extraordinary excursion over the ocean floor.

18

FOUR THOUSAND LEAGUES UNDER THE PACIFIC

THE following morning, 18 November, I had completely recovered from my fatigue of the day before. I went up on the platform just as the *Nautilus*'s first officer was enunciating his daily phrase. The idea then came to me that it referred to the state of the sea, and in particular that it meant 'we have nothing in sight'.

The ocean was indeed deserted. Not a sail to be seen. The heights of Crespo Island had vanished overnight. The sea absorbed all the colours of the spectrum except blue, which it reflected in every direction, and so took on an admirable shade of indigo. A wavering rainbow with broad bands appeared frequently above the rolling waves.

I was admiring the magnificent vision when Captain Nemo emerged.

He did not seem to notice me, and began a series of astronomical observations. Then, his work over, he went to lean on the searchlight casing and gazed abstractedly at the surface of the ocean.

Meanwhile about twenty of the *Nautilus*'s sailors, all strong, strapping men, had arrived on the platform. They had come to pull in the nets, left to drag overnight. They clearly belonged to different nations, although the European type could be discerned in all of them. I recognized what were clearly Irish, French, a few Slavs, a Greek, and a Cretan.* These men were sparing of words, and used amongst themselves only that bizarre language whose origin I could not begin to guess. As a result I had to give up any hope of asking questions.

The nets were pulled on board. These were trawls like those used on the Normandy coasts, huge pouches kept half-open by a floating yard and a chain threaded through the lower meshes. The pouches, dragged along by their metal gantries, swept the bottom of the ocean and gathered in all its produce as they moved. That day, they brought in some strange specimens of these fishing waters: angler fish whose comic movements have given them the name of histrions, black Commerson's fish with antennae, undulating triggerfish with thin red stripes, expanding-tetrodons with an extremely subtle venom, a few olive-hued lampreys, pipefish covered in silvery scales, trichiures whose electric power is equal to that of the electric eel and ray, scaly notopterids with brown transversal stripes, greenish cod, several varieties of gobies, etc.; and finally a few fish of greater size, a metre-long scad with a large head, a few fine bonito mackerel bedecked in blue and silver, and three magnificent tuna whose speed had not saved them from the trawl.

I estimated that this operation was netting nearly half a ton of fish. It was a good catch, but not unexpected. The nets had been dragging for several hours and had captured a whole aquatic world in their stranded prison. We were guaranteed indefinite supplies of food of excellent quality, thanks to the *Nautilus*'s speed and the attraction of its electric light.

These diverse products of the sea were straightaway lowered through the hatch towards the storerooms, some to be eaten fresh and others preserved.

Once the fishing was over and the air supplies renewed, I thought that the *Nautilus* would continue its underwater journey. I was getting ready to return to my room, when Captain Nemo turned and said without preamble:

'Look at this ocean, Dr Aronnax, is it not endowed with an authentic life of its own? Does it not have its angers and its moments of tenderness? Yesterday it went to sleep just like us, and now it is waking up again after a peaceful night!'

Neither good-day nor good morning! Wouldn't one have thought that this strange character was continuing a conversation from before?

'Look,' he added; 'it is awakening in the sun's caresses! It is again going to live its usual life! How captivating it is to study this organism's full cycle! It has its pulse and arteries and it has its contractions, and I entirely agree with the scientist Maury, who discovered a genuine circulation in it exactly like the blood in animals.'

It was evident that Captain Nemo was not expecting a reply, and it seemed pointless to offer responses of 'clearly', 'yes, definitely', and 'you're quite right'. He was speaking mainly to himself, leaving a long gap after each sentence. He was thinking out loud.

'Yes,' he said, 'the ocean has a real circulation, and to start it off, the Creator of all things merely had to increase the caloric,* salt, and animalculae in it. The caloric produces different densities, which then create currents and counter-currents. Evaporation is negligible in the polar regions but very swift in the tropical zones, and so produces a permanent interchange between the tropical and polar waters. I have also been able to detect currents going from top to bottom and back up again, which truly form the ocean's respiration. I have observed molecules of salt water heating up on the surface, descending towards the depths, reaching their maximum density at -2°, then cooling further, becoming lighter and starting to move back up again. You will see the consequences of this phenomenon at the Poles,* and you will understand why, through this law of far-sighted nature, ice can form only on the surface of the waters!'

While Captain Nemo was finishing his sentence, I said to myself: 'The Pole! Does this intrepid individual claim he can take us there?'

The captain had meanwhile fallen silent and was examining the element he so completely, so unceasingly studied. Then continuing:

'There are large quantities of salt dissolved in the sea, Dr Aronnax, and if you were to take it all out, you would have a mass of 4½ million cubic leagues which, if spread over the whole globe, would form a layer more than 10 metres thick.* And do not think that the salt might only be there due to a caprice of nature. No; it makes sea water less subject to evaporation, and so prevents the winds from carrying off too much water vapour, which would then fall as rain and swamp the temperate zones. A huge role, a role as stabilizer of the globe's overall economy!'

Captain Nemo fell silent, then straightened up and took a few steps across the platform, before finally coming back towards me.

'As for the infusoria,' he continued, 'those billions of animalculae, their role is no less important. The tiniest drop contains millions of them, and eight hundred thousand are required to make one milligram. They absorb the sea salt, they assimilate the solid component from the water, they build the corals and the madrepores, and so are the real builders of the limestone landmasses! And then the drop of water, deprived of its mineral sustenance, becomes lighter, rises to the surface, absorbs salts left there by evaporation, grows heavier, descends again, and brings back down new material for the animalculae to absorb. Hence a double current, rising and falling, and constant movement, continuous life! Life more intense than on land, more exuberant, more immeasurable, blossoming in every part of the ocean, a deadly habitat for man, it has been said, a life-giving element for the myriads of animals—and for me!'

When Captain Nemo spoke in this way, he was transformed and he produced in me an extraordinary emotion.

'Here is real life!' he added. 'And I could imagine founding cities in the sea, clusters of submerged dwellings, which, like the *Nautilus*, would come up each morning to breathe on the surface of the oceans, free towns if ever any were, independent cities! And yet, who knows if some tyrant . . .'

Captain Nemo interrupted his sentence with a fierce gesture. Then, addressing me directly, as if to chase away some unhappy thought:

'Dr Aronnax,' he asked, 'do you know what the depth of the ocean is?'

'All I know, captain, is what the main soundings have taught us.'

'Could you please cite them, so that I may corroborate them as necessary?'

'Here are the few I can remember. If I am not mistaken, the average depth of the North Atlantic has been found to be 8,200 metres, and the Mediterranean, 2,500 metres. The deepest soundings were made in the South Atlantic, near the 35th parallel, and gave 12,000, 14,091, and 15,149 metres.* In sum, it has been estimated that if all the water in the oceans were to be levelled off, its average depth would be about seven kilometres.'

'Very well, Dr Aronnax,' replied Captain Nemo. 'I hope we can show you better than that. As for the average depth of this part of the Pacific, I can tell you that it is only 4,000 metres.'

Upon which, Captain Nemo headed for the hatch and disappeared down the ladder. I followed him into the salon. The propeller promptly started revolving, and the log soon indicated a speed of 20 knots.

In the days and weeks that followed, Captain Nemo was very sparing with his visits. I saw him only at rare intervals. His first officer took regular bearings, which I found marked on the map, enabling me to follow the *Nautilus*'s exact course.

Conseil and Land spent long hours with me. Conseil had related the wonders of our excursion to his friend, and the Canadian regretted not coming. But I hoped there would be further opportunities to visit the oceanic forests later.

Almost every day, the panels in the salon were opened for a few hours. Our eyes never grew tired of penetrating the mysteries of the underwater world.

The overall direction of the *Nautilus* was south-easterly, and it stayed at a depth of 100 to 150 metres. One day, however, through some mysterious caprice, it used its inclined planes to dive at an angle and reached water 2,000 metres down. The thermometer indicated a temperature of 4.25° C, which, at this depth, seems common to all latitudes.

At 3 a.m. on 26 November, the *Nautilus* cut the tropic of Cancer at longitude 172°. On the 27th it passed within sight of the archipelago of Hawaii, where Captain Cook* met his fate on 14 February 1779. We had then covered 4,860 leagues from our starting-point. When I went out that morning, I sighted Hawaii two miles to leeward, the biggest of the seven islands forming the group. I could clearly make out the fields on its seaboard, the various mountain chains running parallel to the coast, and the volcanoes, dominated by Mauna Kea rising 5,000 metres above sea level.* Amongst other specimens of these areas, the nets brought in pavonated fans, which are compacted polyps of a gracious form peculiar to this part of the ocean.

The *Nautilus* continued on its south-easterly course. It crossed the equator at longitude 142° on 1 December, and on the 4th, after a swift and uneventful navigation, we sighted the Marquesas. Three miles away, at 8° 57′ S, 139° 32′ W, I perceived Cape Martin on Nuku Hiva, the main island in this group belonging to France. But I saw only the forested mountains standing up above the skyline, for Captain Nemo did not like approaching the land. There the nets brought in fine specimens: dolphin fish with pale blue fins and golden tails, whose flesh is unequalled anywhere, *Hologymnosi* which have virtually no scales but an exquisite taste, *Ostorhinchi* with their bony jaws, and yellowish frigate mackerel which are just as good as bonito—all fish worthy of being classified in the ship's galley.

Having quit these charming islands protected by the French flag, the *Nautilus* covered approximately 2,000 miles from 4 to 11 December. This navigation was noteworthy for an encounter with an enormous troop of calamar, strange molluscs closely related to the cuttlefish. French fishermen classify them as squid; and they belong to the class of cephalopods and family of dibranchiates, which also includes the cuttlefish and the argonaut. These calamar were studied particularly keenly by the naturalists of classical times, and they provided numerous metaphors for the orators of the Agora, plus an excellent dish for the tables of the rich, if we are to believe Athenaeus, a Greek doctor who lived before Galen.*

It was on the night of 9–10 December that the *Nautilus* encountered this army of molluscs of highly nocturnal habits. There were millions of them. They were migrating from the temperate to the warmer zones, following the paths of the herrings and sardines. Through the thick crystal windows, we watched them swimming backwards extremely fast by means of propulsion tubes as they chased the fish and molluscs: eating the little ones, being eaten by the big ones, and waving in indescribable confusion the ten legs that nature has implanted on their heads, like a head-dress of inflatable snakes. Despite its speed, the *Nautilus* sailed through this massive army of creatures for several hours, and its nets brought in countless numbers, amongst which I recognized the nine species d'Orbigny* has classified as inhabiting the Pacific Ocean.

It can be seen that the ocean provided its most wondrous sights during this crossing, incessantly and beyond all reckoning. It varied them indefinitely. The sea changed its backdrop and its scenery for our pleasure, and we were called on to contemplate the Creator's works in the midst of the liquid element, but also to penetrate the ocean's most terrible mysteries.

On 11 December I was reading in the salon. Ned Land and Conseil were observing the luminous waters through the half-open panels. The

Nautilus was motionless. With tanks full, it lay at a depth of 1,000 metres, a sparsely inhabited region of the oceans, where only larger fish put in an occasional appearance.

The book I was reading was a charming one by Jean Macé* called *Les Serviteurs de l'estomac*, and I was savouring its sagacious lessons, when Conseil interjected.

'Would monsieur please come here for a moment?' he said in an unusual tone.

'What is it, Conseil?'

'Something monsieur should see.'

I got up, went to lean against the glass, and gazed.

In the bright electric light, an enormous blackish object was suspended motionless in the midst of the waters. I observed it attentively, trying to identify the gigantic cetacean. But a sudden thought crossed my mind.

'A ship!' I exclaimed.

'Yes,' replied Ned Land, 'a crippled ship that went straight down!'

He was quite right. It was a ship with cut shrouds still hanging from their plates. Its hull seemed to be in good condition, and it could not have been wrecked for more than a few hours. The stumps of three masts, chopped two feet above the deck, showed that the waterlogged ship must have sacrificed its masts. But it must have keeled sideways and filled up with water: it was still listing to port. A sad sight, this carcass lost beneath the waves; but sadder still, the sight of the deck where a few bodies still lay, made fast with ropes. I counted four—all men, with one of them still standing at the helm—then a woman half emerging through the deadlight in the poop, holding a child with both arms. She was young. I was able to make out her features, brilliantly illuminated by the *Nautilus*'s lights and not yet decomposed by the water. In a supreme effort, she had raised the child above her head, a poor little creature whose arms still clasped the neck of its mother! The forms of the four sailors were frightening, twisted as they were in convulsive movements, making a final attempt to tear themselves from the ropes tying them to the ship. Only the helmsman, calmer, face clear and serious, greying hair stuck to forehead, hand tightly seizing the wheel, appeared to be still steering the wrecked three-master through the ocean depths.*

What a scene! We stood silent, our hearts pounding, at the sight of this shipwreck captured in mid-act, photographed as it were at its ultimate moment! And already I could see huge sharks advancing, their eyes ablaze, drawn by the lure of human flesh!

The *Nautilus* had been manoeuvring around the submerged ship. For a brief moment I could read the board on its stern:

'The *Florida*, Sunderland.'*

19

VANIKORO

THIS terrible sight inaugurated a series of maritime disasters that the *Nautilus* was to encounter on its route. From the time it started moving through more-frequented seas, we often sighted sunken hulls, completely rotten and hanging in the water, or, deeper, cannons, cannonballs, anchors, chains, and a thousand other iron objects being devoured by rust.

However, always borne on by the *Nautilus*, where we effectively lived in seclusion, we sighted the Tuamotu Archipelago on 11 December.* This was Bougainville's* former Dangerous Archipelago, extending across 500 leagues from east-south-east to west-north-west, between 13° 30′ and 23° 50′ S, and 125° 30′ and 151° 30′ W, from Ducie Island to Matahiva. The archipelago covers an area of 370 square leagues, and includes about sixty island groups, amongst which can be noted the Gambier Islands, on which France has imposed its protectorate. These islands are coral-producing. A slow but steady ascent, due to the work of the polyps, will one day join them all up. The new island will later attach itself to the neighbouring archipelagos, and a fifth continent will extend from New Zealand and New Caledonia all the way to the Marquesas.

The day I expounded this theory to Captain Nemo, he coldly replied: 'It is not new lands that the earth needs, but new men!'

The chances of its navigation had brought the *Nautilus* towards Reao, discovered in 1822 by Captain Bellingshausen of the *Mirny*,* and one of the most curious of the group. I was thus able to study the system of madrepores which built up the islands in this ocean.

Madrepores must not be confused with corals, for they are covered in a limestone crust; the changes in their structure led M. Milne-Edwards, my illustrious mentor, to classify them in five categories.

The billions of tiny animalculae which secrete this polypary live inside their cells. The limestone they deposit creates rocks, reefs, islets, and islands. Sometimes they form a circular ring, or lagoon, round a small inland lake, with gaps communicating with the open sea. Sometimes they produce barrier reefs like those off the coasts of New Caledonia and many of the islands of the Tuamotus. In other cases, like Réunion and Mauritius, they form fringed reefs with high straight walls, where the ocean drops off very steeply.

While we worked our way along the shores of Reao at a distance of only a few cables, I admired the gigantic task completed by these microscopic workers. The walls were mainly the work of the madrepores known as millepores, porites, astrea, and meandrines. These polyps develop particularly in the rough waters near the surface, and consequently they start their foundations at the top, which then gradually sink down together with the remains of the secretions holding them together. Such at least is the theory of Mr Darwin,* who explains in this way the formation of atolls—a better theory, in my view, than positing that the madrepores build on the summits of volcanoes or mountains submerged a few feet below sea level.

I was able to observe these strange walls very closely, for directly beside them our sound gave 300 metres' depth, and our electric flux made this brilliant limestone sparkle.

Replying to Conseil, who had asked how long these colossal barriers took to grow, I astonished him greatly when I told him that scientists had calculated their growth as an eighth of an inch per century.

'So to produce these walls, it must have taken . . .?'

'A hundred and ninety-two thousand years,* my good Conseil, thus uncommonly lengthening the biblical days. In any case the formation of coal—that is the mineralization of forests swamped by floods—required an even greater period. But I will add that the "days" of the Bible are simply eras and not the time between two sunrises for, according to the Bible itself, the sun does not date from the first day of creation.'

When the *Nautilus* came back to the surface, I could make out the whole of Reao, a low and wooded island. Its madreporian rocks had clearly been fertilized by storms and cyclones. One day a seed, carried by a hurricane from neighbouring land, fell on the limestone strata, covered with vegetable humus from the decomposed remains of fish and marine plants. A coconut, pushed by the waves, arrived on the new coast. The seed took root. The tree grew bigger and captured the water vapour. A stream was born. Vegetation began to grow. A few animalculae, worms, and insects came ashore on tree-trunks brought over from other islands by the wind. Turtles came to lay their eggs. Birds nested in the young trees. In this way animal life developed and, drawn by the greenness and fertility, man appeared. Thus were formed these islands, the gigantic work of microscopic animals.

Towards evening, Reao melted into the distance and the *Nautilus* changed course noticeably. After cutting the tropic of Capricorn on the 135th degree of longitude, it headed west-north-west, across the Tropics. Although the summer sun was generous with rays, we did not suffer from the heat, for at 30 to 40 metres down the temperature never rose beyond 10° or 12°.

On 15 December we passed to the west of the captivating archipelago of the Society Islands, including gracious Tahiti, the queen of the Pacific. In the morning I saw the tall summits of this island a few miles to leeward. Its waters provided the ship's tables with excellent fish: mackerel, bonitos, albacores, and varieties of a sea snake called muraenophis.

The *Nautilus* had now covered 8,100 miles. The log indicated 9,720 miles when it passed through the archipelago of Tonga—the final resting-place for the crews of the *Argo*, the *Port-au-Prince*, and the *Duke of Portland*—and Samoa, where Captain de Langle, La Pérouse's friend, was killed.* Then the Fijian archipelago was sighted, where the savages massacred Captain Bureau from Nantes, the commander of the *Aimable Josephine*, as well as sailors from the *Union*.

This archipelago, which extends 100 leagues north to south and 90 east to west, lies between 6° and 2° S and 174° and 179° W. It consists of a number of islands, islets, and reefs, notable amongst which are the islands of Viti Levu, Vanua Levu, and Kadavu.

It was Tasman who discovered the group in 1643, the same year that Torricelli* invented the barometer and Louis XIV ascended the throne. I leave to the reader to decide which of these events was the most useful to mankind. Next came Cook in 1774, d'Entrecasteaux in 1793, and finally Dumont d'Urville* resolved the geographical chaos of this archipelago in 1827. The *Nautilus* approached Vaileka Bay, where terrible adventures befell Captain Dillon, the first man to throw light on the mystery of La Pérouse's shipwreck.*

The bay was dredged several times, and provided us with excellent oysters in profusion. We ate immoderately, opening them at the table itself following Seneca's precept.* These molluscs belonged to the species known as *Ostrea lamellosa*, very common in Corsica. The bed at Vaileka was clearly very large; without multiple causes of destruction, the molluscs would end up filling the bays they live in, since as many as two million eggs have been found inside a single individual.

If on this occasion Master Ned had no reason to regret his gluttony, it was because the oyster is the only food which never causes indigestion. No less than sixteen dozen of these acephalous molluscs are needed to provide the 315 grams of nitrogen-based food necessary for the daily sustenance of a single man.

On 25 December the *Nautilus* was sailing through the archipelago of Vanuatu, which Quiros* discovered in 1606, Bougainville explored in 1768, and which Cook named the New Hebrides in 1773. The group is made up of nine main islands, forming a strip 120 leagues long from north-north-west to south-south-east, between 15° and 2° S, and 164° and 168° E. We passed quite close to the island of Aru; when we carried out our noon-day observations, it appeared as a mass of green forest surmounted by a very high peak.

It was Christmas Day, and it seemed to me that Land was sorely missing the Anglo-Saxon Christmas, the big family festival which the Protestants are fanatical about.

I hadn't seen Captain Nemo for about a week, when on the morning of the 27th he came into the salon, again just like a man who has left you five minutes before. I was busy tracing the route of the *Nautilus* on the planisphere. The captain approached, put a finger on a point on the map, and said a single word:

'Vanikoro.'*

The name was magical. It was the name of the small islands where La Pérouse's vessels were wrecked. I stood up quickly.

'The *Nautilus* is taking us to Vanikoro?'

'Yes indeed.'

'And I will be able to visit those famous islands where the *Boussole* and the *Astrolabe* came to grief?'

'If that is your wish, monsieur.'

'When will we be in Vanikoro?'

'We are there now.'

With Captain Nemo following, I went up on to the platform and my eyes avidly scoured the horizon.

To the north-east emerged two volcanic islands of unequal size, surrounded by a coral reef some 40 miles in circumference. We were near the island of Vanikoro itself, to which Dumont d'Urville gave the name of Île de la Recherche, and more precisely, at the little haven of Vanu, situated at 16° 4′ S, 164° 32′ E. The island was covered with green vegetation, from the beach to the peaks of the interior, dominated by the 476-fathom Mount Kapogo.

Once the *Nautilus* had slipped through a narrow pass in the outer ring of rocks, it was protected from the breakers, in waters of 30 to 40 fathoms. Under the verdant shade of the mangroves, I spotted a few savages who showed extreme surprise at our approach. And did they not see some formidable cetacean in this long blackish body, advancing almost submerged, apt to strike fear in their hearts?

Captain Nemo asked me what I knew about La Pérouse's shipwreck.

'Only what everyone knows, captain.'

'And could you please tell me what everyone knows?' he asked in a slightly ironic tone.

'Certainly.'

I recounted what Dumont d'Urville had concluded in his last research, of which the following is a very brief summary:

In 1785 La Pérouse and his first officer Captain de Langle were sent by Louis XVI to circumnavigate the globe. They sailed off on the corvettes the *Boussole* and the *Astrolabe*—but never came back.

In 1791, the French government, understandably concerned about the fate of the two corvettes, armed two cargo ships, the *Recherche* and the *Espérance*,* which left Brest on 28 September under the command of Bruni d'Entrecasteaux. Two months later, it was stated in the declaration of a certain Bowen, captain of the *Albemarle*, that debris from wrecked ships had been seen on the coasts of New Georgia Island.* But d'Entrecasteaux, not aware of this information—which was slightly suspect in any case—headed for the Admiralty Islands, indicated as where La Pérouse was shipwrecked in a report by Captain Hunter.*

His searches were in vain. The *Esperance* and the *Recherche* even went right past Vanikoro without stopping, and this voyage was generally ill-starred, for d'Entrecasteaux lost his life, as did two of his officers and several sailors.

It was an old Pacific hand, Captain Dillon, who was the first to find incontrovertible traces of the shipwrecked men. On 15 May 1826 his

ship, the *St Patrick*, passed near the island of Tikopia in Vanuatu.*
There a lascar accosted him in a dugout canoe and sold him a silver
sword-handle with characters engraved on it with a burin. This individual claimed that six years before, while staying on Vanikoro, he had
seen two Europeans who had come from ships that had run aground
on the island's reefs many years before.

Dillon conjectured that these were La Pérouse's ships, whose disappearance had agitated the whole world. He tried to sail to Vanikoro,
where his informant said numerous remains from the shipwreck were
still to be found, but was prevented by the winds and currents.

Dillon went back to Calcutta. There he was able to interest the Royal
Asiatic Society and the East India Company in his discovery. A ship,
which he baptized the *Research*, was put at his disposal, and he left
again on 23 January 1827, with a French agent on board.

Having put into port at several points of the Pacific, the *Research*
anchored off Vanikoro on 7 July 1827, in the harbour of Vanu where
the *Nautilus* was now floating.

There he collected numerous remains from the shipwreck: metal
implements, anchors, strops from pulleys, swivel guns, an 18-pound
cannonball, the remains of astronomical instruments, a piece of taff-
rail, and a bronze bell with the inscription, '*Bazin m'a fait*', the hall-
mark of the foundry of Brest Arsenal in about 1785. Doubt was no
longer possible.

Dillon remained on the spot of the tragedy gathering extra information until October. Then he left Vanikoro, headed for New Zealand,
anchored in Calcutta on 7 April 1828, and finally returned to France,
where he was very warmly received by Charles X.

But meanwhile Dumont d'Urville, not aware of the results of
Dillon's work, had already left to seek the shipwreck elsewhere. The
reason was that a whaling vessel had reported that medals and a St
Louis cross had been found in the hands of savages in the Louisiades
and New Caledonia.

Dumont d'Urville and his *Astrolabe** had therefore put to sea,
anchoring at Hobart two months after Dillon left Vanikoro. There he
learned of Dillon's findings, and also that a certain James Hobbs, first
officer of the *Union* of Calcutta, had landed on an island at 8° 18′ S,
156° 30′ E and noticed iron bars and some red material being used by
the natives of those shores.

Dumont d'Urville was quite perplexed, not knowing whether to believe such tales reported by rather unreliable newspapers; so in the end he decided to pursue Dillon's traces instead.

On 10 February 1828 the *Astrolabe* arrived at Tikopia, took as guide and interpreter a deserter living on the island, headed for Vanikoro, sighted it on 12 February, skirted its reefs until the 14th, and finally on the 20th anchored within the barrier, in the harbour of Vanu.

On the 23rd several officers travelled round the island, and brought back a few scraps of wreckage. The natives, adopting a system of denials and red herrings, refused to take them to the place where the accident happened. Such suspicious behaviour implied that they had mistreated the shipwrecked men and, indeed, they seemed afraid that Dumont d'Urville had come to revenge La Pérouse and his unfortunate companions.

However, on the 26th, won over by presents and realizing that they had no reprisals to fear, they led the first officer, M. Jacquinot,* to the scene of the shipwreck.

At three or four fathoms deep, between the reefs of Pacu and Vanu, lay anchors, cannons, and iron and lead bars covered with limestone sediment. The dinghy and whaling-boat of the *Astrolabe* were sent to the spot and with considerable effort, the crew were able to raise an 1,800-pound anchor, a cast-iron eight-pound cannon, a lead bar, and two copper swivel guns. Questioning the natives, Dumont d'Urville learned that La Pérouse had lost his two ships on the reefs of the island, had built a smaller vessel, but had finally foundered a second time. Where? No one knew.

The captain of the *Astrolabe* then built a memorial to the celebrated navigator and his companions under a clump of mangrove trees. It was a simple square pyramid on a coral base, built without any iron-work that might tempt the natives' light fingers.

Dumont d'Urville wanted to leave; but his crew were greatly weakened by the fevers of these unhealthy shores and, very ill himself, he was unable to sail until 17 March.

Meanwhile the French government, fearing that Dumont d'Urville was unaware of Dillon's work, had sent a corvette stationed on the west coast of America to Vanikoro. The *Bayonnaise*, commanded by Le Goarant de Tromelin,* anchored off Vanikoro a few months after the *Astrolabe* had left, found no new evidence, but observed that the savages had respected the memorial to La Pérouse.

That was the essence of the tale I recounted to Captain Nemo.

'So', he said, 'no one yet knows the last resting place of the third vessel constructed by the shipwrecked sailors on the island of Vanikoro?'

'No one knows.'

Captain Nemo said nothing, but motioned to follow him into the salon. The *Nautilus* sank a few metres below the waves and the panels opened.

I rushed towards the window, and saw a coral reef covered with fungus coral, Siphulina, halcyons, and *Caryophylli*. Through the myriads of charming fish, rainbow wrasses, Glyphisidon, pempheridae, Diacope, and soldierfish, I recognized pieces of wreckage that the grappling hooks had been unable to lift. There were iron stirrups, anchors, cannons, cannonballs, part of a capstan, a prow—all objects from the wrecked ships, now carpeted with living flowers.

And whilst I was contemplating this sad wreckage, Captain Nemo said in a grave voice:

'Captain La Pérouse left with his ships the *Boussole* and *Astrolabe* on 7 December 1785. He anchored first at Botany Bay, then visited Tonga and New Caledonia, headed for Santa Cruz, and put in at Nomuka in the Haapai group. Then his ships arrived at the unknown reefs of Vanikoro. The *Boussole* was sailing in front, and hit the southern coast.

The *Astrolabe* came to its help but also grounded. The first ship was destroyed almost immediately. Stranded to leeward, the second survived for a few days. The natives gave a relatively warm welcome to the shipwrecked sailors; and they settled on the island to build a smaller vessel from the remains of the larger ones. A few sailors voluntarily remained on Vanikoro. The others, weak and ill, left with La Pérouse. They headed for the Solomon Islands and perished with all hands on the western coast of the main island of that group, between Capes Deception and Satisfaction.'*

'But how do you know?' I exclaimed.

'This is what I found at the site of that last shipwreck.'

Captain Nemo showed me a tin box stamped with the arms of France, utterly corroded by salt water. As he opened it, I saw a bundle of papers, yellowed but still legible.

These were the instructions from the Minister for the Navy to Captain La Pérouse, with marginal annotations by Louis XVI!

'Ah, what a fine death for a sailor!' said Captain Nemo. 'A coral tomb provides a peaceful resting-place and may Heaven grant none other to my companions and me!'

20

TORRES STRAIT

During the night of 27–8 December the *Nautilus* left the shores of Vanikoro at extraordinary speed. It headed south-west and within three days covered the 750 leagues from La Pérouse Island* to the south-eastern tip of New Guinea.

Very early on 1 January 1868, Conseil joined me on the platform.

'With monsieur's permission,' said the good fellow, 'I would like to wish him a Happy New Year.'

'What, Conseil, exactly as if I were in Paris in my office at the Jardin des Plantes? But I accept your wishes with thanks. I only ask what you mean by "a Happy New Year" in our present circumstances? Will this year bring an end to our imprisonment, or will it see our strange voyage continue?'

'To be frank,' answered Conseil, 'I do not really know how to reply to monsieur. There can be no doubt that we are witnessing strange things and that in two months we have not had time to become bored. The latest marvel is always the most astonishing and if this progression continues, I do not know how it will all end. My view is that we will never again have such an opportunity.'

'Never again, Conseil.'

'In addition, Mr Nemo lives up to his Latin name, and does not bother us any more than if he did not exist.'

'As you say, Conseil.'

'I believe, therefore, if monsieur pleases, that a happy new year would be one which allowed us to see everything.'

'Everything, Conseil? That might be a very long year. But what does Ned Land think?'

'Ned thinks exactly the opposite. He is a positive spirit with an imperious stomach. Looking at fish and constantly eating them is not enough for him. The lack of wine, bread, and meat does not suit a pure Anglo-Saxon accustomed to steaks, and who appreciates his glass of brandy or gin!'

'For my part, Conseil, that is not what torments me, and I'm managing very well with the diet on board.'

'So am I. I therefore wish to stay as much as Master Land wishes to escape. So if the new year is good for him, it will be bad for me, and vice versa. There will always be someone satisfied. In conclusion, I wish for monsieur whatever pleases monsieur.'

'Thank you, Conseil. I merely ask if you can put off the question of presents, and replace them for the moment with a good handshake. That is all I have on me.'

'Monsieur has never been so generous.'

And the good fellow left me.

On 2 January we had covered 11,340 miles, or 5,250 leagues, from our starting-point in the Sea of Japan. Before the *Nautilus*'s prow stretched the perilous shores of the Coral Sea, off the north-eastern coast of Australia. Our boat kept a few miles from the dangerous reef* where Cook's ships almost sank on 10 June 1770. His own ship hit a rock, and the only reason it did not go down was that a piece of coral broke off in the collision and stayed wedged in the hole in the hull.

I very much wanted to visit this 360-league-long reef, against which a permanently squally sea breaks with terrible intensity, like rolls of thunder. But the inclined planes of the *Nautilus* took us down to a great depth and I could no longer see anything of the high coral walls. I had to be content with the various specimens of fish brought up by our nets. I noted, amongst others, albacores, sorts of scombroid as large as tunas, with bluish flanks and transversal stripes which disappear when it dies. Schools of these fish accompanied us and provided our table with a very delicate flesh. We also caught a large number of 5-centimetre green-and-gold sparids with the taste of sea bream, and some flying pirapeda, genuine submarine swallows, which on dark nights streak their phosphorescent gleams through both the airs and the waters. Among the molluscs and zoophytes in the meshes of the dragnet, I found various species of alcyonarians, sea urchins, hammer-shells, spur-shells, solariums, cerites, and hyales. The flora were represented by lovely floating seaweed: oarweed and *Macrocystis* soaked in mucilage sweating through their pores, and amongst which I collected an admirable *Nemastoma gelinarioides*, for placing with the natural curiosities of the ship's museum.

Two days after crossing the Coral Sea, on 4 January, we sighted the coast of New Guinea. At this juncture Captain Nemo told me he intended to enter the Indian Ocean via Torres Strait. He provided no other information. Ned was happy that this route was leading us closer to the seas of Europe.

Torres Strait is considered dangerous because of the reefs with which it abounds, but also because of the savage inhabitants of its coasts. It separates Australia from the main island of New Guinea, also known as Papua.

New Guinea is 400 leagues long by 130 wide, with an area of 40,000 square leagues. It lies between 0° 19′ and 10° 2′ S and 128° 23′ and 146° 15′ E. At noon when the first officer was determining the elevation of the sun, I noticed the Arfak Mountains, rising in terraces and culminating in sharp peaks.

The island was discovered by the Portuguese Francisco Serrao in 1511, and successively visited by: Don Jorge de Meneses in 1526, Grijalva in 1527, the Spaniard General Alvaro de Saavedra in 1528, Inigo Ortiz de Retes in 1545, the Dutchman Schouten in 1616, Nicholas Struyck in 1753; by Tasman, Dampier, Funnell, Carteret, Edwards, Bougainville, Cook, Forrest, and McCluer; and by d'Entrecasteaux in 1792, Duperrey in 1823, and Dumont d'Urville in 1827.* According to M. de Rienzi, 'It is where the dark-skinned peoples who occupy the entire Malay archipelago originally came from'; and I had no doubt that the hazards of our navigation would bring me face to face with the redoubtable Andamanese.*

The *Nautilus* was thus heading for the entrance of the most dangerous strait on the globe, the one that the boldest captains hardly dare enter, the strait that Luis Vaez de Torres* braved when he came back from the Pacific to this part of Melanesia, and where in 1840 Dumont d'Urville's grounded corvettes came close to going down with all hands. The *Nautilus*, impervious to all the sea's dangers, was itself going to make acquaintance with the coral reefs.

Torres Strait is about 34 leagues wide, but is obstructed by an uncountable number of islands, islets, breakers, and rocks, making it virtually impossible to navigate. Consequently, to go through, Captain Nemo took every possible precaution. The *Nautilus* remained on the surface, advancing at moderate speed. Like a whale's tail, its screw sluggishly beat the waves.

Profiting from the situation, my two companions and I had taken up position on the still-deserted platform. In front of us rose the pilot-house and, unless I am gravely mistaken, Captain Nemo must have been there as well, steering the *Nautilus* himself.

Before my eyes were the excellent maps of Torres Strait charted and drawn by the hydrographic engineer Vincendon-Dumoulin and Ensign (now Admiral) Coupvent-Desbois,* who were Dumont d'Urville's officers on his last voyage of circumnavigation. Together with Captain King's,* these are the maps that make best sense of the confusion of the narrow passage, and I examined them with the closest attention.

Around the *Nautilus* the sea boiled furiously. The current, running from south-east to north-west at a rate of 2.5 knots, was breaking over the coral tips that emerged here and there.

'A bad sea!' said Ned.

'Very bad,' I answered, 'and not at all suited to a vessel like the *Nautilus*.'

'That damned captain', continued the Canadian, 'must be very sure of his route, because I can see coral clusters that would shred his hull into a thousand pieces if it just grazed them!'

The situation was indeed highly dangerous but the *Nautilus* slid as if by enchantment through the furious reefs. It was not following the exact route of the *Astrolabe* and the *Zélée*, so fatal to Dumont d'Urville. It headed further north, hugged Murray Island, and then came back south-westwards heading for the Cumberland Passage. I thought it was going to enter this passage, when it headed north-west again, moving towards Toud Island and the Bad Channel* through a large number of badly charted islands and islets.

I was already wondering whether Captain Nemo, reckless to the point of madness, intended to engage his ship in the pass where Dumont d'Urville's two corvettes had hit, when he changed direction for the second time, cut due west, and headed for Gueboroar Island.*

It was 3 p.m. The current was slowing; it was almost high tide. The *Nautilus* approached the island, with its remarkable coast of pandanuses, that I can still see today. We were following the shoreline at a distance of less than two miles.

Suddenly I was knocked over. The *Nautilus* had hit a reef; it remained motionless, listing slightly to port.

When I got up I saw that Captain Nemo and his first officer were on the platform. They studied the position of the ship, exchanging a few words in their incomprehensible idiom.

The situation was as follows. Gueboroar Island was visible two miles to starboard, its coastline stretching round from the north to the west like an enormous arm. To the south and east a few heads of coral were visible, already uncovered by the ebbing tide. We had gone aground at high tide in a sea where the tides are not large, an unfortunate circumstance for the chances of refloating the *Nautilus*. So solidly constructed was the ship, however, that its hull was not damaged in any way. But if it could neither sink nor be holed, it ran a high risk of remaining stuck on the reefs indefinitely, in which case Captain Nemo's submarine vessel was done for.

These thoughts were running through my mind when the captain, as usual cool and collected and in control of himself, came up, appearing neither upset nor annoyed.

'An accident?' I asked.

'No, an incident.'

'But an incident which may oblige you to dwell once more on the very land you have fled!'

Captain Nemo gave me a very strange look and made a negative gesture. This told me quite clearly that nothing could ever force him to set foot again on terra firma. Then:

'Dr Aronnax, the *Nautilus* is far from finished: it will still carry you through the ocean's wonders. Our voyage is only just beginning, and I do not wish to deprive myself so quickly of the honour of your company.'

'However, Captain Nemo,' I said, ignoring the irony of his words, 'the *Nautilus* has run aground at high tide. The tides are not very great in the Pacific and if you cannot lighten the *Nautilus*, which seems probable, I do not see how it can be refloated.'

'The tides are not great in the Pacific, as you say. But in Torres Strait there is still 1½ metres between high and low tide. Today is 4 January and in five days' time the moon will be full. So I would be very surprised if that kindly satellite did not raise the mass of water sufficiently to grant a favour that I wish to owe only to her.'

Upon which, Captain Nemo went back inside the *Nautilus* followed by his first officer. As for the vessel, it was no longer moving and remained as inert as if the coral polyps had already fixed it in their indestructible cement.

'Well, sir?' said Ned Land, who came over after the captain had left.

'Well, my good Ned, we shall calmly wait for high tide on the 9th, since it appears that the moon will be kind enough to refloat us.'

'Just like that?'

'Just like that.'

'And the captain is not going to drop his anchors, attach his engine to the chains, and try his utmost to haul us off?'

'No need, because of the tide,' said Conseil.

The Canadian looked at him, then shrugged his shoulders. This was the sailor in him talking.

'Monsieur,' he said, 'you can believe me when I tell you that this piece of iron will never sail under or over the seas again. It's just worth its weight in scrap, so I think the time's come to take our leave of Captain Nemo.'

'My good Ned,' I replied, 'unlike you I have not given up hope for the valiant *Nautilus*: in five days' time we will see what the Pacific tides can do. In any case thinking of escape would be appropriate off the coast of England or the South of France, but the shores of New Guinea are different. We will have plenty of time to take such extreme measures if the *Nautilus* is unable to get free, which I would consider to be a serious situation.'

'But can't we at least have a feel of this solid ground? It's an island. On the island are trees. Under the trees, land animals, bearers of chops and steaks which I would very much like to sink my teeth into.'

'Here my friend Ned is right,' said Conseil; 'I share his opinion. Could monsieur not ask his friend, Captain Nemo, to put us ashore, if only so that we can remain accustomed to setting foot on the solider parts of the planet?'

'I can ask him but he will refuse.'

'Monsieur should take that risk,' said Conseil; 'so that we know where we stand.'

To my great surprise, Captain Nemo gave his permission, and did so with a great deal of grace and alacrity, without even extracting my promise to return on board. But an escape via New Guinea would have been highly dangerous, and I would not have advised Ned Land to try it. It was better to be a prisoner on board the *Nautilus* than to fall into the hands of the Papuan natives.

The dinghy would be put at our disposal the following morning. I did not try to find out if Captain Nemo was going to accompany us. I even felt sure that no crewman would be provided, and that Ned would have sole responsibility for managing the boat. The island was at most two miles away, and it would be mere play for the Canadian to steer the light boat between the lines of reefs, so fatal for larger vessels.

The following day, 5 January, the dinghy, with its cover off, was taken out of its recess on the platform and launched into the sea. Two men were enough to perform this operation. The oars were in the boat and all we had to do now was to get in.

At eight o'clock we left the *Nautilus*, armed with guns and axes. The sea was calm. A light breeze was blowing from the land. Conseil and I rowed vigorously while Ned steered us through the narrow channels between the breakers. The boat was easy to handle and moved quickly.

Ned Land could hardly contain his joy. He was a prisoner escaped from jail, and he scarcely thought that he had to go back inside again.

'Meat!' he kept repeating. 'We're going to eat meat, and what meat: real game! Not bread, I tell you! I can't say that fish is exactly bad, but you can have too much of a good thing, and a piece of fresh venison grilled on glowing coals will make a nice change from our usual fare.'

'Glutton,' replied Conseil, 'you are making my mouth water!'

'We still need to find out', I said, 'if the forests contain game and if the game is not sizeable enough to hunt the hunter.'

'Well,' said the Canadian, whose teeth seemed as sharp as daggers, 'I'll eat tiger—sirloin of tiger—if there are no other four-legged animals on the island.'

'My friend Ned is worrying me,' said Conseil.

'The first animal with four legs and no feathers, or two legs and feathers,* of whatever kind, will be greeted by my bullet.'

'So!' I replied. 'We're going to see hot-headed Master Land again!'

'Have no fear, Dr Aronnax, and row as hard as you can. I'll only need twenty-five minutes to offer you a tasty dish.'

At half past eight, the *Nautilus*'s boat had successfully negotiated the coral reef around Gueboroar and smoothly landed on a sandy beach.

21

A FEW DAYS ON LAND

SETTING foot on land again made quite an impression on me. Ned Land tested the ground with his foot as if to take possession of it. All the same, it was only two months that we had been what Captain Nemo called 'the passengers of the *Nautilus*': in reality the prisoners of its commander.

Within a minute or two we were a gun-shot away from the shore.

The ground was almost entirely madreporian but some of the beds of the dried-up streams, strewn with pieces of granite, showed that the island had been formed in the primordial era. The horizon was entirely hidden behind a curtain of beautiful forest. The enormous trees, some reaching a height of 200 feet, were linked with garlands of creepers, true natural hammocks swaying in the light breeze. There were mimosas, banyans, casuarinas, teak, hibiscuses, pandanuses, and palm-trees, all mixed up in profusion; and in the shade of their verdant vault, at the feet of their gigantic trunks, grew orchids, leguminous plants, and ferns.

But without heeding any of these fine specimens of Papuan flora, the Canadian was combining serious business with pleasure. He spotted a coconut tree, knocked a few of its nuts down, and broke them open; we drank their milk and ate their flesh with a satisfaction that protested against the normal fare on board the *Nautilus*.

'Excellent!' pronounced Ned.

'Exquisite!' retorted Conseil.

'And I don't suppose', said the Canadian, 'that your Nemo could object to us bringing a cargo of coconuts back on board?'

'I'm sure not,' I replied, 'but he won't want any!'

'His loss,' said Conseil.

'And our gain. All the more for us.'

'Just a moment, Master Land,' I said as the harpooner began to attack another tree. 'Coconuts are all very well but before filling the boat up with them, it would be as well to see whether the island produces some other substance just as useful. Fresh vegetables would be most welcome on board.'

'Monsieur is right,' said Conseil, 'and I propose we divide our boat into three sections, one for fruit, one for vegetables, and one for meat, of which I have not seen the slightest trace so far.'

'You should never give up, Conseil,' replied the Canadian.

'Let's continue on our way,' I said, 'but with eyes peeled. Even if the island might appear uninhabited, it perhaps contains individuals whose taste in game is less selective than ours.'

'Hey, hey!' voiced Land, with a meaningful move of his jaws.

'Ned!' said Conseil.

'Heck,' riposted the Canadian, 'I'm beginning to realize what cannibalism's all about!'

'Ned, Ned, what are you saying?' said Conseil. 'You a cannibal? Then

I will never be safe since I share your cabin! Am I to wake up one day half-devoured?'

'Dear Conseil, I like you a great deal, but not enough to eat you unless I really have to.'

'I am not so sure,' said Conseil. 'But let's get on with the hunting for we urgently need to shoot some game to satisfy this cannibal, or else one of these mornings monsieur will find only bits and pieces of his manservant to attend to him.'

During this exchange, we had begun to penetrate the dark vaults of the forest, and for two hours we crisscrossed it in every direction.

We were very fortunate in our search for edible vegetables, and one of the most useful products of the Tropics was to provide us with precious food lacking on board.

I am referring to the breadfruit tree, in great supply on Gueboroar Island; I noticed mainly the seedless variety called *rima* in Malay.*

It is different from other trees in having a straight trunk, 40 feet long. Its top, which is gracefully rounded and formed of large, multi-lobed leaves, enables a naturalist to identify it as that same *Artocarpus* which has been so profitably introduced to the Mascarene Islands. Large round fruit stood out from the mass of greenery, 10 centimetres across and with hexagonal protuberances. They provide a valuable example of the plants which nature has bestowed on regions lacking wheat, and though not requiring any cultivation, provide fruit eight months of the year.

Ned Land was well acquainted with this fruit. He had already eaten it on previous voyages, and knew how to prepare the edible part. Seeing it excited his desire so much that he was unable to hold on any longer.

'Sir, I'll die if I don't taste some of the inside of this breadfruit!'

'Go ahead, Ned, my friend, you can taste to your heart's delight. We're here to try things out, so feel free.'

'It won't take long,' said the Canadian.

Using a lens he lit a fire with some deadwood, which soon began crackling cheerfully. Meanwhile Conseil and I were choosing the best fruit from the *Artocarpus*. Some were not ripe enough, with their thick skin revealing a white pulp, not very fibrous. A large number of others, sticky and yellowish, were just waiting to be plucked.

The fruit did not have any stones. Conseil carried about a dozen back to Ned, who cut thick slices and put them on the hot coals, repeating all the while:

'You'll soon see, sir, how good it is!'

'Especially when you haven't had any for a long time!' said Conseil.

'It's no longer bread, it's delicate pastry. Have you ever had any, sir?'

'No, Ned.'

'Well, get ready to taste something out of this world! If it doesn't knock you out, I'm not the king of the harpooners!'

After a while the side of the fruit on the fire had turned completely black. Inside was a sort of dry white paste, or soft crumb, which tasted like artichoke.

It must be admitted that it was very good, and I ate with great pleasure.

'Unfortunately', I said, 'this paste can't be kept fresh, and so there seems little point in stocking up on board.'

'What are you saying!' cried Ned. 'You're speaking as a naturalist, but I'm going to act as a baker. Conseil, gather lots of these bread-fruit, and we'll pick them up again on our way back.'

'But how will you prepare them?' I asked.

'By using the pulp to make a fermented paste which will keep indefinitely. When I want some, I'll just cook it in the kitchen, and you will find it excellent despite a slightly acidic taste.'

'So, Master Ned, I can see that this bread is perfect . . .'

'No, sir, it still needs a few fresh fruit or, failing that, vegetables.'

'Well then, let's go and look for some.'

Once our bread harvest was over, we set off to complete this earthly meal.

Our search was not in vain, for by about midday we had gathered a generous supply of bananas. These delicious products of the tropical zone ripen the whole year round, and the Malays, who call them *pisang*, eat them uncooked. Along with the bananas we collected enormous, very strong-tasting jackfruit, delicious mangoes, and pineapples of an incredible size. All this took a long time, but we had no reason to regret it.

Conseil was still observing Ned. The harpooner was walking ahead and as he worked his way through the forest, he was completing his provisions by collecting fine fruit with a sure hand.

'So now you have everything you wish, Ned, my friend?'

'H'm.'

'You can't still be complaining?'

'All this fruit doesn't really make up a dinner. It's the end of the meal, the pudding. But what about the soup and the main course?'

'Indeed,' I said. 'Ned promised us chops, which now seem unlikely to materialize.'

'Sir, not only has the hunting not finished, but it hasn't even started yet. Patience! We'll certainly end up meeting some sort of animal with either feathers or hair, if not here, then somewhere else . . .'

'And if not today, then tomorrow,' added Conseil, 'for we should not wander too far. I even suggest returning to the boat.'

'What, already!'

'We have to be back by nightfall,' I said.

'So what time is it?'

'At least two o'clock,' replied Conseil.

'How time flies on dry land!' exclaimed Master Ned Land with a sigh of regret.

'Off we go!' said Conseil.

So back we went through the forest, completing our harvest by raiding the palm cabbage trees, whose palms need to be taken from the tops of the trees, and gathering some small beans, that I recognized to be what the Malays call *abrou*, as well as some yams of superior quality.

We were loaded down by the time we got back to the boat. Ned, however, still did not find his supplies sufficient, although luck was to favour him. Just as he was getting back in he spotted a few 25- or 30-foot trees belonging to the palm-tree family. This variety, as precious as the *Artocarpus*, is considered one of the most useful products in the Malay archipelago.

They were sago palms, which grow wild, similar to the mulberry in that they reproduce from their own offspring and their own seeds.

Land knew what to do. He took his axe, chopped with great vigour, and soon felled two or three sago palms: they were fully grown, as could be seen from the white powder speckling their leaves.

I watched him more as a naturalist than a starving man. He cut a strip of bark 1 inch thick from each trunk and revealed a network of long fibres forming inextricable knots, gummed together with a sort of sticky flour. This flour was sago, an edible substance that forms the principal diet of the Melanesians.

For the moment Ned merely chopped the trunks up, as if making wood for burning: he thus postponed the job of extracting the flour, sifting it through cloth to separate out the fibrous parts, evaporating the liquid in the sun, and putting it in moulds to set.

We finally pushed off at five o'clock, laden down with our booty, and half an hour later drew up alongside the *Nautilus*. No one appeared. The enormous metal cylinder lay as if deserted. Once the provisions were loaded, I went down to my room. I found my dinner ready. I ate, then went to bed.

The next day, 6 January, nothing had changed on board. No sound, no sign of life. The dinghy remained alongside where we had left it. We decided to go back to Gueboroar Island. Ned Land wanted to visit another part of the forest, hoping to have better luck hunting than the day before.

At dawn we were already on our way. The boat was carried along by the ebb-tide, and we reached the island very quickly.

We got out and followed Ned Land, preferring to trust to his instinct, although his long legs nearly left us behind.

He headed west along the coast, then forded a few streams, before reaching a plateau surrounded by splendid forests. A few kingfishers were stalking along the water-courses, but it was impossible to get near them. Their caution told me that these birds knew what to expect from bipeds like us, and I deduced that if the island was not actually inhabited, it was at least regularly visited.

Having crossed a rich plain, we arrived at the edge of a little wood brightened by the song and flight of a large number of birds.

'They're still only birds,' said Conseil.

'But some are edible.'

'On the contrary, dear Ned, I can see they're nothing but parrots.'

'My dear Conseil,' he solemnly intoned, 'the parrot is the pheasant of those who have nothing else to eat.'

'And I will add', I said, 'that when properly prepared, the bird is worth sticking your fork into.'

And indeed, beneath the thick foliage, a large number of parrots were swooping from branch to branch, merely awaiting more education to learn a human tongue. For the moment they cackled together in the company of multicoloured parakeets and grave cockatoos apparently pondering some philosophical problem. All the while, brilliant red lories flew past like pieces of bunting carried off on the breeze, amongst noisy flights of calaos, papua birds decorated in the finest shades of azure, and a whole assortment of delightful but generally inedible birds.

However, a bird particular to those regions and one which has never lived beyond the limits of the islands around Papua and Aru was missing from this collection, although chance was to allow me to admire one before long.

Having crossed a wood, we found a plain covered with bushes. Soon I saw some magnificent birds taking wing. The way their long feathers were arranged meant they had to head into the wind to do so. Their undulating flight, the grace of their aerial curves, and the iridescence of their colours allured and charmed one's eyes. I had no difficulty identifying them:

'Birds of paradise!'

'Order of Passeriformes, section of clystomores,' replied Conseil.

'Family of partridges?'

'I do not think so, Master Land. I am, nevertheless, counting on your skill to secure one of these charming products of the Tropics.'

'I'll have a go, sir, though I'm handier with a harpoon than a gun.'

The Malays, who trade a large number of these birds with the Chinese, have various methods for catching them that we could not employ. Sometimes they set snares at the tops of tall trees where the birds of paradise like to live. Sometimes they capture them with a strong glue which immobilizes them. Sometimes they even poison the springs where the birds habitually drink. As for us, we were reduced to firing at them in flight, which left little chance of hitting them; and indeed we wasted much of our ammunition in vain.

By about eleven o'clock we had reached the foothills of the mountains in the centre of the island, and had still bagged nothing. Hunger spurred us on. The hunters in us had relied on the results of our own skill, generally a mistake. But very fortunately Conseil killed two birds with one stone, to his great surprise, and thus ensured lunch. He shot a white pigeon and a wood pigeon, which were quickly plucked, spitted, and grilled over a roaring deadwood fire. While these strange animals were cooking, Ned prepared some *Artocarpus*. Then the two pigeons were devoured down to the bones, and declared excellent. The nutmeg which they gorge themselves on endows their flesh with a delicious flavour.

'It's like chicken raised on truffles,' said Conseil.

'And now, Ned, what else do you need?'

'Some game with four legs, doctor,' he replied. 'All these pigeons and so on are only hors-d'oeuvres and nibbles! I won't be satisfied until I've killed an animal with chops on it!'

'Nor me, Ned, until I catch a bird of paradise.'

'Let's continue then,' said Conseil, 'but heading back towards the coast. We are in the foothills of the mountains and it would appear sensible to return to the forest region.'

This seemed a good idea and was duly adopted. After an hour's walk we had reached a real forest of sago palms. A few harmless snakes fled from under our feet. Birds of paradise escaped as we approached, and I was truly giving up catching any, when Conseil, who was ahead, suddenly bent down, gave a shout of triumph, and came back carrying a magnificent specimen.

'Congratulations!' I exclaimed.

'Monsieur is too kind.'

'But no, my good fellow, a master-stroke. To capture one of these birds alive, using bare hands!'

'If monsieur will study it closely he will see that my merit is not so great.'

'But why, Conseil?'

'Because this bird is as drunk as a lord.'

'Drunk?'

'Yes, monsieur, tipsy from the nutmeg it was eating under the nutmeg tree where I caught it. See, Ned, the terrible effects of intemperance.'

'My God! Considering how much gin I've had in the last two months, one can hardly talk.'

I examined the strange bird. Conseil was quite right. The bird of paradise was drunk on the heady juice, totally incapacitated. It could not fly, it could hardly walk; but this didn't bother me, and I let it stew in its own nutmeg.

The bird belonged to the most beautiful of the eight species that have been observed in New Guinea and the neighbouring islands. It was the great emerald bird of paradise, one of the rarest.* It was a foot long. Its head seemed relatively small, with tiny eyes near the beak. But it had a wonderful collection of tints, with a yellow beak, brown feet and claws, hazel wings with purple tips, a pale yellow head and back of neck, an emerald throat, and a rich brown stomach and breast. Two horned and downy frenums rose above its tail, with feathers that were very light and long and amazingly fine, and these completed the display of that marvellous bird, poetically called 'the bird of the sun' by the natives.

I would have very much liked to take this superb bird of paradise back to Paris, and donate it to the Jardin des Plantes, which does not have a single living specimen.

'Is it that rare then?' asked the Canadian, in the tone of a hunter who hardly appreciates game from an aesthetic point of view.

'Very rare, my friend, and above all very difficult to capture alive; even dead these birds are the subject of an important trade. As a result, the natives have ingeniously reconstructed them, just as pearls or diamonds are fabricated.'

'What!' exclaimed Conseil. 'They make fake birds of paradise?'

'Yes, Conseil.'

'And does sir know how they go about it?'

'He does. During the easterly monsoon season the birds of paradise shed their magnificent tail feathers, which the naturalists call subalary. These are gathered by the bird-fakers, and carefully stitched on to some poor parakeet which has previously been mutilated. Then they dye the stitching and varnish the bird, before sending the product of their singular industry to the museums and collectors of Europe.'

'Well,' said Ned, 'shame about the bird, but at least the feathers are all right, so unless you actually want to eat the creature, I don't see the problem.'

But if my desires were satisfied by catching this bird of paradise, the Canadian hunter's were not. Fortunately, at about two o'clock, Ned shot a magnificent wild boar that the natives call *babi hutan*. The animal thus provided us with real quadruped meat, and was warmly welcomed. Land appeared very proud of his shot. The pig, struck by the electric bullet, had fallen stone-dead.

The Canadian skinned and carefully gutted it, having extracted half a dozen chops to provide a grill for the evening meal. Then the hunting started again, soon to be marked by further exploits from Ned and Conseil.

The two friends had beaten around the bushes, and thus set off a herd of kangaroos, who hopped off on their supple legs. But these animals did not flee fast enough to escape an electric capsule in full flight.

'Ah, sir!' cried Ned Land, beginning to be affected by hunting mania. 'What excellent game, especially when braised; what supplies for the *Nautilus*! Two, three, five on the ground, and when I think that we can guzzle all this meat ourselves and those idiots on board won't have a single scrap!'

I believe that carried away by his enthusiasm, the Canadian would have massacred the whole herd, at least if he had not spent so much time talking. But he contented himself with a dozen of these fascinating marsupials, which, as Conseil pointed out, form the first order of the aplacental mammals.

They were quite small, belonging to a species of 'rabbit kangaroos' which normally live in the hollows of trees,* and can move very quickly. But if their size is not great, they do provide the best meat.

We were very pleased with the results of our hunting. A happy Ned suggested coming back the following day to this enchanted isle, which he wished to clear of all its edible quadrupeds; but events were to prove otherwise.

At six in the evening, we got back to the beach. Our boat was at its usual spot on the shore. Two miles out, the *Nautilus* emerged from the waves like a long reef.

Without further ado Ned got down to the serious business of cooking dinner. He knew his stuff. *Babi hutan* chops, grilled over the coals, were soon filling the air with a delicious aroma.

But I realize that I have become exactly like the Canadian. Here I am in ecstasy about freshly grilled pork! May I be forgiven, for the same reason I excused Master Land.

In the end the dinner was very good indeed. Two wood pigeons completed our extraordinary menu. The sago paste, some breadfruit from the *Artocarpus*, a few mangoes, half a dozen pineapples, and the fermented milk from selected coconuts made our happiness complete. I even believe that the lucidity of my worthy companions' brains left something to be desired.

'What about not going back to the *Nautilus* tonight?' said Conseil.

'What about never going back?' Ned Land rejoined.

Just then a stone fell at our feet, interrupting the harpooner's train of thought.

22

CAPTAIN NEMO'S LIGHTNING

WE looked in the direction of the forest without getting up, my hand suspended half-way to my mouth, although Land's reached its destination.

'Stones do not fall from the sky,' said Conseil; 'unless they are meteorites.'

A second stone, of carefully rounded shape, took a savoury wood pigeon's leg from Conseil's hand and lent support to his observation.

The three of us rose to our feet, guns to shoulders. We were ready for any attack.

'Is it monkeys?' exclaimed Ned.

'More or less,' said Conseil; 'savages.'

'To the boat!' I said, heading for the water.

It was indeed necessary to beat a retreat, since about twenty natives armed with bows and slings appeared on the edge of a thicket blocking the horizon less than a hundred paces to the right.

Our boat was on the shore, ten fathoms away.

The savages approached, without running but making the most hostile gestures. Stones and arrows rained down.

Ned Land did not want to give up his provisions and in spite of the danger closing in, he picked up his pig with one hand, and kangaroos in the other, before fleeing at a rate of knots.

Seconds later we were on shore. Dropping the provisions and guns into the boat, pushing it out to sea, and starting the two oars going took only an instant. We had not gone any distance at all when a hundred savages, shouting and gesticulating, came waist-deep into the water. I watched to see if their arrival would bring anyone from the *Nautilus* on to the platform, but in vain. Lying in the distance, the enormous machine remained absolutely deserted.

Twenty minutes later we climbed on board. The hatches remained open. We made the boat fast and went inside.

I went down to the salon, where music was playing. Captain Nemo was bent over his organ, deep in musical ecstasy.

'Captain?'

He did not hear.

'Captain!' I repeated, touching him.

He shivered, and turned round.

'Ah, it's you, doctor?' he said. 'Well, how was your hunting? Did you gather any interesting plant specimens?'

'Yes, captain,' I replied. 'But unfortunately we also brought back a pack of bipeds, whose proximity worries me somewhat.'

'What sort of bipeds?'

'Savages.'

'Savages!' retorted Captain Nemo in a sarcastic tone. 'And you're surprised, Dr Aronnax, that when you set foot on one of the lands of this globe, you find savages? Where are there not savages, and are those that you call savages any worse than the others?'*

'But, captain . . .'

'For my part, sir, I have encountered them everywhere.'

'But', I replied, 'if you don't want to have them on board the *Nautilus* you should take some precautions.'

'Calm yourself, sir, there is nothing to worry about.'

'But there are a lot of natives.'

'How many did you see?'

'At least a hundred.'

'Dr Aronnax,' replied Captain Nemo, whose hands had gone back to the keyboard, 'even if all the natives in New Guinea were assembled on the beach, the *Nautilus* would still have nothing to fear from their attack.'

The captain's fingers then ran over the instrument; I noticed that he only used the black keys, giving his melodies an essentially Scottish tonality. Soon he had forgotten I was there, and was deep in a reverie that I did not try to interrupt.

I went back to the platform. Night had already fallen, for at these latitudes the sun goes down quickly and there is no dusk. I could make out Gueboroar Island only vaguely now. But a large number of fires on the beach showed that the natives had not yet decided to leave.

I remained alone for several hours, sometimes musing about the natives, but without really being afraid of them. The captain's imperturbable confidence had won me over, and sometimes forgetting all about them and admiring the splendour of the tropical night, my memory flew back to France, following the stars in the sky which would shine over it in a few hours' time. The moon was radiant amid the constellations of the zenith. My thoughts then returned to this faithful and obliging satellite, which would come back to the same spot the day after tomorrow to raise the waves and pluck the *Nautilus* from its coral bed. At about midnight, seeing that everything was quiet on the darkened waters and beneath the trees on shore, I returned to my cabin and fell into a deep sleep.

The night went by without incident. The Papuans undoubtedly felt frightened at the mere view of the monster lying grounded in the bay, for its open hatches would have granted them easy access to the *Nautilus*.

At 6 a.m. on 8 January, I went back up to the platform. The shadows were lifting. Through the disappearing mists the island revealed its beaches and then its peaks.

The natives were still there, but more than the day before—perhaps five or six hundred. Some of them had taken advantage of the low tide to come forward on the coral heads to very near the *Nautilus*. I could easily make them out. They were true Papuans, men of athletic build and fine stock, with broad high foreheads, large noses, not flattened, and white teeth. Their woolly hair, dyed red, contrasted with their bodies, as black and shiny as Nubians'. Their earlobes were cut and stretched, with bone beads hanging from them. These savages were generally naked. Amongst them I noticed a few women, clothed from the haunches to the knees with real grass skirts, held up by belts made of plants. Some of the chiefs had adorned their necks with crescents and necklaces of red and white glass beads. Nearly all of them were armed with bows, arrows, and shields, and carried on their shoulders a sort of net containing those rounded stones that they throw accurately with their slings.

One of the chieftains closest to the *Nautilus* was studying it with great attention. This was clearly a *mado* of high rank, for he was dressed in plaited banana leaves, finely worked on the edges and picked out in dazzling colours.

I could easily have shot this native, within close range, but I believed it better to wait for real hostile behaviour. When dealing with savages, it is better for Europeans to riposte, rather than attack first.

During the entire low tide the natives prowled near the *Nautilus*, but without making a great commotion. I heard them frequently repeating the word *assai*, and I understood from their gestures that they were inviting me to come ashore, an invitation I felt it better to decline.

So the dinghy did not leave the vessel that day, to the great displeasure of Master Land, unable to complete his provisions. The talented Canadian used the time to prepare the meat and flour he had brought back from Gueboroar. As for the savages, they went ashore again at about eleven in the morning, as soon as the tops of the coral began to disappear under the rising tide. But I could see that there were even more of them collecting on the beach. They had probably come from the neighbouring islands, or from New Guinea itself. I had not, however, noticed a single native dugout.

Having nothing better to do, I thought I would dredge these fine clear waters, where there could be seen a profusion of shells, zoophytes, and open-sea plants. This was in any case the last day the *Nautilus* would spend on these shores, that is if it floated at high tide the following day as Captain Nemo had promised.

I therefore called for Conseil, who brought me a small, light dredge, more or less like those used for collecting oysters.

'What about the savages?' asked Conseil. 'If monsieur pleases, they do not seem to me to be very ill-intentioned after all.'

'They *are* cannibals, my good fellow.'

'One can be a cannibal and a good man,' replied Conseil, 'just as one can be a glutton and honest. One does not exclude the other.'

'All right, Conseil, I concede that they are honest cannibals, and that they eat their prisoners honourably. However, I do not wish to be devoured, even honestly, so will remain on my guard, for the captain of the *Nautilus* does not seem to be taking any precautions. And now to work.'

For a couple of hours we worked hard at our fishing, but without bringing in anything rare. The dredge filled with Midas's ears, harp shells, *Melaniae*, but also the finest hammer-shells I had ever seen. We also took some sea slugs, pearl oysters, and a dozen small turtles, which were set aside for the pantry.

But at the moment I least expected it, I found a marvel, or rather I should say, a very rarely encountered natural deformity. Conseil had just used the dredge, and his net was coming up laden with various quite ordinary shells, when all of a sudden he saw me quickly plunge my arm into the net, pull a shell out, and give a conchologist's whoop, the most piercing cry the human throat is capable of.

'Is monsieur all right?' asked Conseil, startled. 'Has monsieur been bitten?'

'No, my good fellow, but I would have willingly given a finger for my discovery.'

'What discovery?'

'This shell,' I said, showing the reason for my triumph.

'But it's simply a porphyry olive shell, of the genus *Oliva*, order of pectinibranchiates, class of gastropods, branch of molluscs . . .'

'Yes, yes, Conseil, but instead of turning clockwise, this olive goes from left to right!'

'It can't do!'

'It can and it does, my good fellow, it's a left-handed shell!'

'A left-handed shell?' repeated Conseil, his heart beating madly.

'Just look at its convolution!'

'Ah, monsieur can believe me,' said Conseil, taking the precious shell in his trembling hands, 'never have I experienced such emotion before.'

And there was good reason to be excited. As naturalists have pointed out, right-handedness is a law of nature. In their movements of translation and rotation, stars and their satellites move from right to left. Man uses his right hand more than his left, and consequently his instruments and his machines, his staircases, locks, watch-springs, etc., are all designed to be used in the same direction. Now nature has generally followed this law in the winding of her shells. They are all right-handed, with rare exceptions; and when by chance their convolution is left-handed, collectors pay their weight in gold.*

Conseil and I remained plunged in contemplation of our treasure, and I had promised myself to enrich the Museum with it, when an ill-fated stone, projected by one of the natives, arrived and broke the precious object in Conseil's hand.

I uttered a cry of despair. Conseil threw himself on his gun, and took aim at a savage raising his sling about ten metres away. I tried to stop him but the shot went off and broke the bracelet of amulets on the native's arm.

'Conseil,' I shouted. 'Conseil!'

'What, did monsieur not see that it was the cannibal's fault?'

'But a shell is not worth a man's life!'

'Oh, the rogue! I would have preferred if he had broken my shoulder.'

Conseil was sincere, although I could not share his opinion. However, the situation had changed in the last few moments without our noticing. About twenty dugout canoes had surrounded the *Nautilus*. These boats, hollowed out of tree-trunks, were long, narrow, and quite fast: they kept their balance by means of two bamboo outriggers floating on the surface. They had skilful half-naked paddlers in them, and it was not without trepidation that I saw them advancing.

It was evident that these Papuans had already had dealings with Europeans, and were familiar with their ships. But what could they possibly make of this long iron cylinder stretched out in the bay with neither masts nor funnels? Nothing good, for they had kept a respectful distance at first. But seeing it motionless, they slowly regained confidence, and were now trying to familiarize themselves. Now it was precisely this familiarity which needed to be prevented. Our guns, lacking detonations, could merely make a moderate impression on these indigenous people, who only respect noisy devices. Lightning without claps of thunder would frighten people little, although the danger is in the lightning not the sound.

Suddenly the canoes came nearer and a cloud of arrows rained down on the *Nautilus*.

'Good heavens, it's hailing,' said Conseil, 'and perhaps with poisoned hail!'

'We'd better go and tell Captain Nemo,' I said, disappearing through the hatch.

I went into the salon. No one was there. I ventured to knock on the door of the captain's bedroom.

I heard a 'Come in' and entered, finding Captain Nemo plunged in calculations filled with x's and algebraic signs.

'Am I disturbing you?' I said out of politeness.

'A little, Dr Aronnax,' replied the captain; 'but I assume you must have a serious reason to wish to see me.'

'Very serious. We are surrounded by native canoes, and will certainly be attacked by several hundred savages within minutes.'

'I see,' said Captain Nemo calmly; 'they have come with their canoes?'

'Yes, they have.'

'Well, all that is needed is to close the hatches.'

'Precisely, and I came to say . . .'

'Nothing could be simpler,' said Captain Nemo.

He pressed an electric button to transmit an order to the crew room. 'It is now taken care of,' he said after a pause, 'the dinghy is secured and the hatches closed. You are not afraid, I hope, that these gentlemen might pierce the walls that your frigate's shells could not dent?'

'No, captain, but there is still a danger.'

'Yes?'

'Tomorrow at the same time, we will need to open the hatches again to replenish the air inside the *Nautilus*.'

'That is true, since our vessel breathes like the cetaceans.'

'And if the Papuans are on the platform at that moment, I am unable to see how you can prevent them coming in.'

'So, sir, you think they will venture on board?'

'I'm certain of it.'

'Well, doctor, let them. I can see no reason to prevent them. These Papuans are poor wretches after all, and I do not want my visit to Gueboroar Island to cost the life of a single one of such unfortunates!'

I was going to withdraw at that point, but Captain Nemo detained me and invited me to sit near. He asked with interest about our land excursions and hunting, but did not seem to understand the need for meat that drove the Canadian. The conversation then touched on various other subjects, and Captain Nemo showed himself most kind, although not any more communicative.

Amongst other things, we got to talking about the *Nautilus*'s situation, aground at precisely the same spot where Dumont d'Urville got into great difficulty. On this subject:

'D'Urville was one of your great sailors, one of your most intelligent navigators! He was France's Captain Cook. Unfortunate savant! To have braved the ice-floes of the South Pole, the corals of the South Seas, the cannibals of the Pacific, only to perish miserably in a train accident! If this tireless man was able to reflect in his final moments, imagine what his last thoughts must have been.'

Speaking in this way Captain Nemo seemed moved, and his emotion was, I thought, to his credit.

Then, map in hand, we retraced what the French navigator had achieved: his voyages of circumnavigation; his two attempts to reach the South Pole, leading to the discovery of Adélie Land and Louis-Philippe Land; and finally his hydrographical surveys of the main islands of the South Pacific.

'What your d'Urville did on the surface of the seas,' Captain Nemo said, 'I have done in the interior of the oceans, but more easily, more completely than he could. The *Astrolabe* and the *Zélée*, always pushed hither and thither by hurricanes, could not equal the *Nautilus*, a peaceful base for study, truly at ease in the heart of the waters!'

'There is one point of resemblance, however, between Dumont d'Urville's corvettes and the *Nautilus*.'

'Which one, sir?'

'It is that the *Nautilus* has run aground like them!'

'The *Nautilus* is not aground!' Captain Nemo coldly replied. 'The *Nautilus* is designed to rest on the seabed; and I do not have to undertake the demanding work and manoeuvres that d'Urville had to perform to refloat his corvettes. The *Astrolabe* and *Zélée* nearly perished, but my *Nautilus* is in no danger. At the said hour tomorrow, the tide will lift it calmly up, to continue its navigation through the seas.'

'Captain,' I said, 'I do not doubt . . .'

'Tomorrow,' Captain Nemo added as he got up, 'at 2.40 p.m., the *Nautilus* will float and leave Torres Strait unharmed.'

Having pronounced these words in a slightly sharp tone, Captain Nemo bowed slightly. This was to take leave of me, and so I went back to my room.

There I found Conseil, keen to know the outcome of my conversation with the captain.

'My good fellow, when I implied that his *Nautilus* was in danger from the Papuan natives, the captain replied very ironically. So I only have one thing to say to you: have confidence in him and go to sleep without worrying unduly.'

'Monsieur has no need of my services?'

'No, my friend. What is Ned Land doing?'

'With all due respect, monsieur,' replied Conseil, 'my friend Ned is making a kangaroo pie that will be an absolute wonder.'

I remained alone and went to bed, but slept quite badly. I could hear the savages, who were stamping about on the platform uttering deafening cries. But the night wore on without the crew abandoning its usual inertia. They were no more worried by the presence of these cannibals than the soldiers inside a strong fort by ants running over their battlements.

I got up at 6 a.m. The hatches had not been opened, and so the air inside had not been renewed. But the tanks, designed to cope with any eventuality, were functioning properly, pumping a few cubic metres of oxygen into the thin atmosphere of the *Nautilus*.

I worked in my room until midday but without seeing Captain Nemo for a single moment. Apparently no preparations for leaving were being made on board.

I waited a while longer, then went into the salon. The clock read half past two. In ten minutes the sea would have reached its maximum height, and if Captain Nemo had not made a rash promise, the *Nautilus* would immediately be freed. If not, many months would pass before it could leave its coral bed.

Soon a few preliminary vibrations could be felt in the hull of the vessel. I could hear its plates grinding against the hard limestone of the coral underneath.

At 2.35, Captain Nemo appeared in the salon.

'We're about to leave,' he said.

'Ah!' I said.

'I have given the order to open the hatches.'*

'But what about the Papuans?'

'The Papuans?' replied Captain Nemo, shrugging his shoulders slightly.

'Won't they come inside the *Nautilus*?'

'But how?'

'By coming down the hatches that you are opening.'

'Dr Aronnax,' he calmly replied, 'it is not that easy to enter the hatches of the *Nautilus*, even when open.'

I stared at the captain.

'You do not understand?'

'No, not at all.'

'Well, come and you will see.'

I headed for the central stairwell. There, Ned and Conseil, puzzled and fascinated, were watching a few of the crewmen opening the hatches, whilst cries of anger and blood-curdling howls could be heard outside.

The hatch covers opened outwards. Twenty horrible faces appeared. But the first of these natives to put his hand on the handrail of the stairs* was thrown backwards by some invisible force and ran off, uttering awful cries and making exaggerated leaps.

Ten of his companions did likewise. Ten suffered the same fate.*

Conseil was in ecstasy. Land, carried away by his violent instincts, rushed on to the staircase, but the moment he touched the handrail, he too was thrown back.

'My God!' he cried. 'I've been struck by lightning!'

This explained everything. It was no longer a handrail, but a metal conductor fully charged with electricity from the vessel and culminating in the platform. Whoever touched it received a powerful shock, and this shock would have been fatal if the captain had put the entire current from his apparatus into the conductor! Between his assailants and him, Nemo had extended an electric circuit that none could cross with impunity.*

The terrified Papuans had meanwhile retreated, crazed with terror. Half laughing, we massaged and consoled poor Ned, swearing like a madman.

Just then the *Nautilus,* raised by the last ripples of the tide, left its coral bed at that precise fortieth minute predicted by the captain. Its screw started beating the waters with majestic slowness. Its speed gradually increased, and sailing safe and sound on the ocean's surface, it left behind the dangerous passes of Torres Strait.*

23

*ÆGRI SOMNIA**

THE next day, 10 January, the *Nautilus* continued its progress underwater, but at a remarkable speed that I cannot estimate as less than 35 knots. The speed of its screw was such that I could not follow its revolutions, let alone count them.*

When I thought that the marvellous electrical agent not only gave movement, heat, and light, but also protected the *Nautilus* from external attacks, transforming it into a holy ark* which no desecrator could transgress without being smitten by lightning, my admiration knew no limits; and this went from being directed to the machine back to the engineer who had built it.

We were heading due west, and on 11 January we rounded Cape Wessel, which lies at longitude 135° and latitude 10° N, forming the eastern point of the Gulf of Carpentaria. There were still quite a number of reefs, but now more spread out and pinpointed on the chart with great precision. The *Nautilus* thus easily avoided the breakers of Money Reef to port and Victoria Reefs to starboard, situated at longitude 130° on the 10th parallel which we were following without deviation.

On 13 January Captain Nemo, having arrived in the Timor Sea, sighted the island of the same name at longitude 122°. With an area of 1,625 square leagues, this island is governed by rajahs. These princes profess to be sons of crocodiles, that is, issued from the highest origin to which human beings can lay claim. Accordingly, these scaly ancestors abound in the island's rivers, and are the subject of a particular veneration. They are protected, they are spoilt, they are adulated, they are nourished, they are offered young maidens as fodder—and cursed be the foreigner who lays a hand on the sacred lizards.*

But the *Nautilus* did not have to deal with these ugly animals. Timor was visible for a mere moment at noon, while the first officer was determining our position. In the same way, I caught only a glimpse of the little island of Roti, part of the same group, whose women have a firmly established reputation for beauty on the Malaysian markets.

Starting from that point, the direction of the *Nautilus*, which of course could go where it wished, switched to the south-west. It headed for the Indian Ocean. Where were Captain Nemo's caprices going to take us? Would he head back to the coasts of Asia? Would he approach the shores of Europe? Such decisions seemed highly unlikely on the part of a man who fled from inhabited lands. Would he go then even further south? Would he round the Cape of Good Hope, then Cape Horn, and head for the South Pole? Would he finally come back to the waters of the Pacific, where his *Nautilus* could find easy and independent seafaring? Time would tell.

Having passed the last attempts of the solid element to withstand the liquid element, namely the reefs of Cartier, Hibernia, Seringapatam, and Scott, we were far from all land on 14 January. The speed of the *Nautilus* had dropped markedly, and it was moving very capriciously, sometimes navigating underwater, sometimes floating on the surface.

During this stretch of the voyage, Captain Nemo carried out interesting experiments on the temperature of the water at different depths. Ordinarily, these measurements are obtained using quite complicated instruments, whose results are dubious at best, either thermometric sounds whose glasses often break under the water pressure or devices based on the change in the resistance of metal to electric currents. The results obtained in this way cannot be properly verified. In contrast, Captain Nemo was going to measure the temperatures of the sea depths using his own observations, for his thermometer, in direct contact with the various parts of the water, gave him the temperatures immediately and reliably.

By filling its tanks or descending obliquely with its planes inclined, the *Nautilus* successively reached depths of 3,000, 4,000, 5,000, 7,000, 9,000, and 10,000 metres. The final conclusion of the experiments was that the sea enjoyed a constant temperature of $4\frac{1}{2}°$ at a depth of 1,000 metres, whatever the latitude.

I followed these experiments with inordinate interest. Captain Nemo showed a true passion for them. I often wondered why he made these observations. Was it to benefit his fellow beings? This seemed improbable, for sooner or later his studies were destined to perish with him in some unknown sea. Unless he was intending the results of his experiments for me. But that would mean he accepted that my strange voyage might come to an end, and this end I could not yet envision.

Whatever the reasons, Captain Nemo also told me of the various figures he had obtained, which established the relative densities of water in the main seas of the globe. From this information I drew a personal lesson which had nothing to do with science.

It was on the morning of 15 January. The captain, with whom I was strolling on the platform, asked me if I knew what the different densities of the oceans were. I replied that I did not, and that science lacked rigorous observations on the subject.

'I have carried out such observations, and I can vouch for their accuracy.'

'Yes,' I replied. 'But the *Nautilus* is a world apart and its scientists' secrets do not reach dry land.'

'You are quite right, sir,' he said after a moment's silence. 'It is a world apart, as foreign to terra firma as the planets accompanying this globe round the sun, and we will never benefit from the studies of Saturn's or Jupiter's scientists. However, since chance has linked our two lives, I can communicate the results of my observations to you.'

'I am all ears, captain.'

'As you know, sea water is denser than fresh, but not uniformly. If I take the density of fresh water as 1.000, I find 1.028 for the waters of the Atlantic, 1.026 for the Pacific, 1.030 for the Mediterranean . . .'

'Aha!' I thought. 'So he does venture into the Mediterranean.'

'. . . 1.018 for the Ionian Sea,* and 1.029 for the Adriatic.'

Decidedly the *Nautilus* did not avoid the frequented waters of Europe, and I deduced from this that it would bring us back towards more civilized lands, perhaps quite soon. I thought that Ned Land would be pleased to hear the news.

For a few days our time was spent entirely on all sorts of experiments concerning the salt content of water at different depths, its electric charge, colour, and clearness; and in all these circumstances Captain Nemo displayed an ingenuity which was equal only to his good disposition towards me. Then I did not see him again for a few days, and remained as though quarantined on board his ship.

On 16 January, the *Nautilus* seemed to fall asleep only a few metres below the surface of the waves. Its electrical machines were no longer operating, and its motionless screw meant it wandered at the whim of the currents. I supposed that the crew must be busy with internal repairs, made necessary by the vigour of the mechanical movements of the engine.

My companions and I were then witness to a strange scene. The panels of the salon were open, and as the searchlight of the *Nautilus* was not on, a dim darkness reigned amidst the waters. The stormy sky, covered with thick clouds, gave only the top parts of the ocean an insufficient light.

I observed the state of the sea in conditions where the largest fish appeared merely as faintly sketched shadows, when the *Nautilus* was suddenly bathed in full light. At first I thought the searchlight had been switched on and that it was projecting its electric brilliance through the liquid mass. I was wrong, as I realized at a glance.

The *Nautilus* was floating in a phosphorescent stratum, which was becoming dazzling in this darkness. The light was produced by myriads of glowing animalculae, whose brightness increased as they slid over the metallic hull. I then noticed sparks in these luminous waters, as if produced by streams of molten lead in a fiery furnace or metallic bodies heated to red or white heat; as a result of the contrast, certain radiant parts appeared as shadows in this burning situation, from which, however, all shades should logically have been banished. For this was no longer the even illumination of our normal lighting! A very unusual vigour and movement were present. This light felt as if alive.

There was indeed an infinite agglomeration of pelagic infusoria and miliary noctilucents, globules of diaphanous jelly with threadlike tentacles, of which 25,000 have been counted in 30 cubic centimetres of water. Their light was further increased by the distinctive gleams of jellyfish, starfish, *Aurelia*, piddocks, and other phosphorescent zoophytes, steeped in the fertilizer from organic materials decomposed by the sea, and perhaps also in mucus secreted by fish.

For several hours the *Nautilus* floated amongst these brilliant billows, with our admiration growing when we saw large marine animals playing there like salamanders. In the midst of that fire which did not burn, I saw swift, elegant porpoises, the tireless clowns of the seas, as well as three-metre sail-fish, the intelligent forecasters of hurricanes, whose formidable swords sometimes struck the window of the salon. Small fish also appeared, a variety of triggerfish, jumping scombroids, wolf-unicorns, and a hundred others, streaking the luminous atmosphere as they swam.

The dazzling sight was an enchantment. Perhaps the effect of the phenomenon was being increased by some state of the atmosphere? Did perhaps a storm rage above the surface of the waves? But at a few metres' depth the *Nautilus* did not feel any fury as it swayed peacefully in the midst of the tranquil waters.

We continued on our way, constantly charmed by some new marvel. Conseil observed and classified the zoophytes, articulates, molluscs, and fish. The days went by quickly, and I no longer counted them. As was his wont, Ned attempted to vary the diet on board. Like true snails, we had got used to our shells—I maintain that it is very easy to be a perfect snail.

This existence seemed easy and natural to us, and we could no longer imagine a different life on the terrestrial globe—when an event occurred to remind us of the strangeness of our situation.

On 18 January, the *Nautilus* was at longitude 105° and latitude 15° S. The weather was threatening, the sea hard and squally. There blew a strong easterly wind. The barometer, which had been falling for several days, announced an approaching battle of the elements.

I went up to the platform while the first officer was taking his measurements of the hour angles. I waited for the sentence to be pronounced, following the daily custom, but that day it was replaced by another phrase, no less incomprehensible. I saw Captain Nemo appear almost immediately and his eye, equipped with a telescope, focus on the horizon.

For a minute or so the captain remained motionless, concentrating on the point captured in his field of vision. Then he lowered his telescope and exchanged about ten words with his first officer. The latter seemed to be in the sway of an emotion that he was trying in vain to control. Captain Nemo, more master of himself, remained cool. He seemed in any case to be raising objections, to which the first officer was replying with formal assurances. At least that is what I understood from the difference in their tones and gestures.

As for myself, I had carefully scrutinized the direction in question, but without spotting anything. The sky and the water melted together in a horizontal line of perfect clarity.

Captain Nemo had started walking from one end of the platform to the other, without looking at me, perhaps without seeing me. His pace was assured, but less regular than usual. He stopped sometimes and examined the sea, arms crossed on chest. What could he be looking for in that immense space? The *Nautilus* was lying a few hundred miles from the nearest coast!

The first officer had picked up his telescope again, and was obstinately scouring the horizon, coming and going, stamping his feet, his nervous agitation in contrast to the commander's calm.

In any case the mystery was inevitably going to be solved; for after a while, on an order from Captain Nemo, the engine increased its propulsive power and the screw turned faster.

Now the first officer again drew his chief's attention to something. The captain stopped pacing, and directed his telescope at the point indicated. He examined it for a long time. For my part, fascinated, I went down to the salon to fetch the excellent telescope I normally used. Then, leaning on the framework of the searchlight projecting near the front of the platform,* I prepared to study the whole line of sea and sky.

But my eye had not yet been applied to the glass, when the instrument was suddenly torn from my hands.

I turned round. Captain Nemo was before me, but I hardly recognized him. His face was transfigured. His eyes, burning with a dark fire, stood out under a frowning brow. His teeth were half bared. His stiff body, clenched fists, and head hunched on his shoulders betrayed the violent hatred filling his whole being. He did not move. My telescope, dropping from his hand, rolled at his feet.

Had I inadvertently provoked this angry attitude? Did this bewildering individual imagine that I had surprised some secret forbidden to the guests of the *Nautilus*? No! I was not the object of the hatred, for he was not looking at me: his eyes remained implacably fixed on the invisible point of the horizon.*

At long last, Captain Nemo regained his self-control. His face, which had been so deeply altered, recovered its usual calm. He said a few words in the foreign tongue to his first officer, and then he turned to me.

'Dr Aronnax,' he said, in rather an imperious tone, 'I want you to observe one of the engagements which bind you to me.'

'Yes, captain?'

'You must allow your companions and you to be locked up, until such time as I consider it appropriate to restore your liberty.'

'You are the master,' I replied, gaping at him, 'but may I ask you a question?'

'You may not, sir.'

I could no longer question this, but merely obey, since any resistance would have been impossible.

I went down to the cabin Ned and Conseil occupied, and told them of the captain's decision. I leave it to the imagination how the news was greeted by the Canadian. But in any case there was no time for further explanation. Four crewmen were waiting at the door, and they led us to the cell where we had spent our first night on board.

Ned Land tried to protest, but the only reply was the door closing in his face.

'Could monsieur tell me what this means?' enquired Conseil.

I told my companions what had happened. They were as astonished as I was, and understood as little.

I fell into a deep reflection; the strange apprehension on Captain Nemo's face would not leave my mind. I felt incapable of putting two logical ideas together, and was losing myself in the most absurd hypotheses, when my concentration was interrupted by these words from Land:

'Look, lunch is served.'

The table was indeed ready. It was clear that Captain Nemo had arranged it at the same time as increasing the speed of the *Nautilus*.

'Would monsieur allow me to make a suggestion?'

'Yes, my good fellow.'

'Well, monsieur should have lunch. It would only be sensible, because we do not know what might happen later.'

'You're right, Conseil.'

'Unfortunately', said Ned, 'we've only been given the normal menu on board.'

'Dear Ned,' said Conseil, 'what would you have said had there been no food at all?'

This reasoning cut short the harpooner's complaints.

We sat down. The meal was rather quiet. I did not eat much. Conseil 'forced himself' through prudence, and Ned Land did not waste a mouthful, whatever his feelings. Then, lunch finished, each of us rested in his corner.

Suddenly, the luminous globe went out, leaving the cell in total darkness. Ned Land soon went to sleep, and Conseil also allowed himself to fall into a heavy slumber, which astonished me. I was wondering what had caused his imperious need for sleep, when I felt my own brain being permeated by a thick torpor. My eyes, which I tried to keep open, kept closing despite my best efforts. I was prey to unhappy hallucinations. Sleeping tablets had clearly been added to the food we had eaten. Prison was not enough to hide Captain Nemo's activities from us, he also needed to employ sleep!

I heard the hatches closing. The rocking of the sea, which caused a slight rolling movement, stopped. Had the *Nautilus* left the surface? Had it gone back down into the motionless depths?

I tried to resist drowsiness. It was impossible. My breathing grew weaker. I felt a mortal cold numbing my arms and legs, as heavy as if paralysed. My eyelids, like leaden skull-caps, fell over my eyes. I could not raise them again. An unhealthy sleep, full of nightmares, took hold of my entire being. Then the visions disappeared, and left me completely prostrate.

24

THE CORAL KINGDOM

THE following day I woke up with a remarkably clear head. To my great surprise I was in my room. My companions had undoubtedly also been put back in their cabin, without them realizing any more than myself. Their ignorance of what had happened during the night would equal mine, and I could only count on chances in the future to solve the mystery.

Next I thought about leaving the room. Was I free once again or still a prisoner? Entirely free. I opened the door, and went along the corridors, heading up the central stairwell. The hatches, closed the day before, were now open again. I arrived on the platform.

Ned and Conseil were waiting for me. I asked them a few questions. They knew nothing, having fallen into a deep sleep which left them with no recollection, and had been very surprised to find themselves in their cabin.

As for the *Nautilus*, it seemed as peaceful and mysterious to us as ever. It was moving over the surface of the waves at moderate speed. Nothing seemed changed on board.

Land examined the sea with his penetrating eyes. It was deserted. The Canadian could see nothing new on the horizon. Neither sails nor land. A westerly breeze was noisily blowing, and long waves, dishevelled by the wind, were making the vessel roll quite noticeably.

Once it had replenished its air, the *Nautilus* remained at an average depth of 15 metres, from where it could come quickly up again. Most unusually, this latter action was carried out several times on 19 January.* The first officer went up to the platform on each occasion, and the accustomed phrase rang out through the ship.

As for Captain Nemo, he did not appear. Of those serving on board, I only saw the impassive steward, who served me with his usual precision and silence.

At about two o'clock I was busy sorting through my notes in the salon, when the captain opened the door and appeared. I greeted him. He gave me an almost imperceptible nod, without saying a word. I went back to my work, hoping he would perhaps provide an explanation of the events of the previous night. He did nothing of the sort. I gazed at him. His red eyes looked unrefreshed by sleep, his face tired; it expressed a deep sadness, a real distress. He walked to and fro, then sat down then got up again. He took a book at random, but put it down immediately. He consulted his instruments without taking his usual notes, and seemed unable to remain on one spot for a single moment.

Finally he came up to me, and asked:

'Monsieur, are you a doctor?'

I expected this question so little that I looked at him for a while without replying.

'Are you a doctor?' he repeated. 'Several of your colleagues studied medicine: Gratiolet, Moquin-Tandon,* and others.'

'Yes, I'm a doctor and a former hospital intern. I practised for several years before joining the Museum.'

'Good.'

My reply had evidently satisfied Captain Nemo, but not knowing the point of the conversation, I waited for further questions, thus retaining the option of replying according to circumstances.

'Dr Aronnax, would you consent to treating one of my men?'

'One of your men is ill?'

'Yes.'

'I am ready.'

'Please come this way.'

I will admit that my heart was pounding. For some reason, I could see a connection between this illness of a crewman and the events of the day before, and the mystery absorbed me at least as much as the sick man himself.

Captain Nemo took me to the stern of the *Nautilus,* and invited me to enter a cabin situated near the crew room.

On a bed lay a man of about forty years, with an energetic face, a typical Anglo-Saxon.

I leaned over him. He was not only ill, but wounded. His head, resting on two pillows, was swathed in blood-stained dressings. I removed the bandages: the injured man, staring with wide eyes, allowed me without uttering a single complaint.

The wound was horrible. The cranium had been shattered by a blunt instrument, the brain lay exposed, and the cerebral matter had undergone a deep abrasion. Blood clots had formed in the diffluent matter, which had turned maroon. There had been both contusion and concussion of the brain. The man's breathing was laboured, and a few spasms worked the muscles of his face. The cerebral phlegmasia was complete, and had produced a paralysis of sensation and movement.

I took the wounded man's pulse. It was intermittent. The extremities of the body were already becoming cold, and I could see that death was approaching, without it appearing possible to slow it down. Having seen to the poor man's wounds, I reapplied the dressings to his head; and turned to Captain Nemo.

'How did he get his wound?'

'What difference does it make!' the captain evasively replied. Then: 'A jolt from the *Nautilus* broke one of the levers of the engine, which struck this man.* What is your diagnosis of his condition?'

I hesitated to give my view.

'You can speak freely. This man does not understand French.'

I looked at the wounded man one more time, and said: 'He will be dead within two hours.'

'Can nothing save him?'

'Nothing.'

Captain Nemo's hand tightened, and a few tears slipped from his eyes, which I had not believed capable of weeping.

For a few moments longer, I examined the dying man, as his life slowly ebbed away. He got paler and paler in the electric light bathing his deathbed. I looked at his intelligent head, furrowed with premature wrinkles, which unhappiness, perhaps poverty, had hollowed out long before. I wanted to guess the secret of his life from the last words to escape his lips.

'You can retire now, Dr Aronnax,' said Captain Nemo.

I left the captain in the dying man's cabin and went back to my room, greatly moved by the scene. The whole day I was disturbed by sinister forebodings. That night I slept badly and, between my frequently interrupted dreams, I thought I could hear distant sighs and something like a funereal plain-chant. Was this the prayer for the dead,* murmured in that language I could not understand?

The following morning I went back on deck. Captain Nemo was already there. As soon as he saw me, he came up.

'Dr Aronnax, would you like to go on an underwater excursion today?'

'With my companions?'

'If they wish.'

'They are at your disposal, captain.'

'Please put on your diving suits then.'

There was no discussion of the dying or dead man. I rejoined Ned Land and Conseil and told them of Captain Nemo's invitation. Conseil quickly accepted, and this time the Canadian willingly agreed to accompany us.

It was eight in the morning. At 8.30 we were fitted out for our second excursion, equipped with lighting and breathing apparatus. The two doors opened one after the other, and accompanied by Captain Nemo, who was followed by about ten crewmen, we set foot on solid ground where the *Nautilus* was resting at a depth of 10 metres.

A slight slope led to an uneven floor at about 15 fathoms. The bottom looked completely different from the one I had visited on my first excursion under the Pacific Ocean. Here there lay no fine sand, no underwater prairie, no pelagic forest. I instantly recognized the marvellous region which Captain Nemo was presenting to us that day. It was the coral kingdom.*

In the branch of the zoophytes, and in the class of the alcyonarians, one can observe the order of Gorgonacea, which includes the three groups of Gorgon heads, isidia, and corallines. It is to this latter group that coral belongs, a strange substance which has been classified in turn in the mineral, vegetable, and animal kingdoms. A medication for the ancients, a jewel for the moderns, it was only in 1694 that the Marseillais Peyssonnel* definitively placed it in the animal kingdom.

Coral is a collection of animalculae amalgamated on a polypary of stony and brittle nature. These polyps have a unique begetter which produces them by means of budding; they have their own existence while at the same time participating in communal life. They thus live a sort of natural socialism. I was aware of the latest studies carried out on this strange zoophyte, which becomes mineralized while arborizing, as the apposite terms of the naturalists would have it; and nothing could be of greater interest for me than to visit one of the petrified forests that nature has planted on the ocean floor.

The Ruhmkorff lamps were switched on and we followed a coral reef which was still being formed and which would, with the help of time, close off one day this portion of the Indian Ocean. The path was lined with labyrinthine bushes formed from the intermingling of small shrubs, covered with little starred flowers with white petals. But these arborescences fixed to the rocks on the ground were the opposite of plants on dry land, for all grew downwards.

The light produced a thousand charming effects playing through the brightly coloured branches. I thought I could see the membranous and cylindrical tubes trembling in the movement of the water. I was tempted to gather their fresh corollas, adorned with delicate tentacles: some of them had just bloomed, while others, which were hardly born, had small fish with swift fins grazing past them like flocks of birds. But if my hand approached these living flowers, these sensitive mimosae pudicae, the alert was immediately given throughout the colony. The white corollas moved back into their red sheaths, the flowers went out before my eyes, and the bush changed into a block of stony nipples.

Chance had placed me in the presence of the most valuable examples of this zoophyte. The coral was of similar quality to that collected on the Mediterranean coasts of France, Italy, and North Africa. Its brilliant shades justified its poetic names of 'blood flower' and 'foam of blood', the names the trade gives to its finest products. Coral sells at up to five hundred francs a kilogram, and the watery depths at this spot protected a fortune from all the coral fishermen in the world. This precious matter, often mixed with other polyparies, formed compact inextricable groups called 'macciotta', on which I noticed some admirable specimens of pink coral.

But soon the bushes grew smaller and the arborescences larger. True petrified woods and the long aisles of a fantastic architecture opened before our feet. Captain Nemo headed into a dark gallery, whose gentle slope led us to a depth of 100 metres. The light from our coils sometimes produced magical effects, clinging to the asperities of these natural arches and to pendentives hanging like chandeliers, where it picked out points of fire. Between the coral shrubs I noticed other polyps just as remarkable, mellites and irises with articulated ramifications, then tufts of corallines, some green and some red: real wracks encrusted in their limestone salts, that the naturalists, after long debate, have definitively placed in the vegetable kingdom. But as one thinker has remarked,* 'Perhaps this is the real point where life dimly rises from a sleep of stone, without yet cutting itself off from that rude starting-point.'

After two hours' march, we had finally reached a depth of about 300 metres, the furthest point where coral begins to form. But here there were no longer isolated bushes or modest copses of low trees. This was an enormous forest, with great mineral vegetation and enormous petrified trees linked together by garlands of elegant Plumularia, those sea creepers, all adorned with tones and glints. We passed freely under their high branches, lost in the shadow of the waves, whilst at our feet the tubipores, the meandrines, the astrea, the mushroom corals, and the caryophyllenes formed a flowery carpet strewn with dazzling gems.

Oh, what indescribable visions! Why could we not communicate our feelings? Why were we imprisoned behind these glass and metal masks? Why were words to each other not possible? Why could we not live the life of the fish populating the liquid element, or even that of amphibians who can move for long hours through the twin realms of land and water as the mood takes them?

Captain Nemo had stopped. My companions and I came to a halt, and when I turned round I saw that his men had formed a semicircle around their leader. Looking closer, I noticed that four of them were carrying a long object on their shoulders.

We were now standing at the centre of a vast clearing, surrounded by the soaring arborescences of the underwater forest. Our lamps projected a sort of dusky light over the space, inordinately lengthening the shadows on the ground. On the edge of the clearing, the darkness became immense, containing only the tiny sparks thrown up by the sharp edges of the coral.

Ned and Conseil were beside me. As we looked I understood that I was going to assist at a strange scene. When I examined the ground, I realized that it was swollen by slight extumescences encrusted with chalk deposits, laid out with a regularity that betrayed the hand of man.

In the midst of the clearing, on a pedestal of rocks roughly piled up, stood a coral cross, extending its long arms as if made of petrified blood.

On a sign from Captain Nemo, one of the men came forward, untied a pick from his belt, and began to dig a hole a few feet from the cross.

Suddenly everything became clear! The clearing was a cemetery,* the hole a grave, the long object the body of the man who had died during the night! Captain Nemo and his men had come to bury their companion in this communal resting place on the bed of the inaccessible ocean!

Never was my mind inflamed to such a point! Never was my brain invaded by more excited ideas! I did not want to see what my eyes could see!

Meanwhile the grave was slowly being dug out. From time to time the fish would flee their disturbed sanctuary. I could hear the iron pick resounding on the chalky ground, sometimes producing sparks when it hit some flint lost at the bottom of the waters. The hole got longer and wider, and soon it was deep enough to admit the body.

The bearers approached. The body, wrapped in a cloth of white byssus, was lowered into the watery grave. Captain Nemo, arms crossed on chest, and all the friends of that man who had loved them, knelt in an attitude of prayer. My two companions and I had devoutly lowered our heads.

The grave was then covered with the debris torn from the ground, forming a slight swelling.

When it was done, Captain Nemo and his men stood up. Approaching the grave, all knelt down again, and all stretched out their hands in a final farewell.

Then the funeral procession headed back to the *Nautilus*, passing once more under the arches of the forest, through the coppices, along the coral bushes, constantly climbing.

Finally the lights on board appeared. Their luminous trail guided us towards the *Nautilus*. At one o'clock we were back again.

As soon as I had changed my clothes, I went back up on the platform, and in the grip of a terrible obsession of ideas, I went to sit beside the searchlight.

Captain Nemo joined me. I got up and asked him:

'So this man died during the night, as I expected?'

'Yes, Dr Aronnax.'

'And he is now resting beside his companions in that coral cemetery?'

'Yes, forgotten by all, but not by us! We dig the graves and the polyps have the task of sealing the dead there for eternity!'

And in a sudden movement, hiding his face in clenched fists, the captain tried in vain to suppress a sob. Then he added:

'It is our cemetery there, tranquil, hundreds of feet below the surface of the waves.'*

'At least your dead slumber in peace, captain, out of the reach of sharks.'

'Yes,' Captain Nemo replied gravely, 'sharks and men!'

PART TWO*

1

THE INDIAN OCEAN

HERE begins the second part of this voyage under the seas.* The first one ended with that moving scene in the coral cemetery, which left such a deep impression on me. So was Captain Nemo's life spent completely in the bosom of the immense ocean, where everything, even his tomb, lay ready in the furthermost chasms? There, not a single sea creature would come to trouble the final sleep of the inhabitants of the *Nautilus*, friends welded to each other in death as they were in life! 'Not a single man, either!' the captain had added.

Always the same defiance of human society, wild and implacable.*

For my part, I was no longer content with the hypothesis that satisfied Conseil. The worthy fellow persisted in seeing in the captain of the *Nautilus* merely one of those unrecognized scientists, who return humanity's indifference with mistrust. For him he was still a misunderstood genius, weary of the disappointments of the earth, who had had to take sanctuary in that inaccessible environment where he could give free play to his instincts. But in my view this theory explained only one of Captain Nemo's sides.

The mystery of the previous night, when we had been enchained in slumber and in prison; the captain's violent safeguard of tearing from my eye the telescope I was preparing to use to scour the horizon; that man's fatal wound, caused by an inexplicable collision involving the *Nautilus*: everything pushed me in a new direction. No, Captain Nemo was not content merely to flee from mankind! His formidable machinery served not only his passion for freedom, but perhaps the pursuit of some terrible but unknown sort of revenge.*

For the moment nothing is clear to me; I can only glimpse gleams in the dark, and must limit myself to writing, so to speak, at the dictation of events.*

But in any case nothing binds us to Captain Nemo. He knows that escape is impossible from the *Nautilus*. We are not even prisoners on our parole. No word of honour holds us back. We are merely captives, prisoners disguised by being called guests, in a semblance of courtesy. However, Ned Land has not given up hope of regaining his liberty. It is clear that he will take the first opportunity chance offers him. I will undoubtedly do the same, and yet it will be a wrench to carry away with me what the captain's generosity has let us guess of the mysteries of the *Nautilus.* For is this man, all things considered, to be hated or admired? Is he the predator or the prey? Also, to be truthful, before leaving him for ever, I would like to complete this tour of the submarine world whose beginnings have been so magnificent. I would like to study the wonders strewn under the seas of the globe in their entirety! I would like to finish seeing what no man has yet seen, even if I have to pay with my life for this insatiable need to know! What have I discovered to date? Nothing, or almost nothing, since we have covered only 6,000 leagues of the Pacific!

However, I know full well that the *Nautilus* is approaching inhabited shores, and that if some chance of escaping is offered, it would be cruel to sacrifice my companions for my passion for the unknown. I will have to follow, perhaps even guide them. But will such an opportunity ever arise? Forcibly deprived of his free will, the human being longs for such an opportunity, but the scientist, the enquiring mind, fears it.

At noon on that day, 21 January 1868, the first officer came to take the height of the sun. I went up on top, lit a cigar, and followed the operation. It seemed clear that this man could not understand French, for I made observations out loud several times which would have drawn some involuntary sign of attention if he had understood them, but he remained mute and impassive.*

Whilst the officer was carrying out his observations with the sextant, one of the *Nautilus*'s sailors—the vigorous man who had accompanied us to Crespo Island on our first underwater excursion—came to clean the glass of the searchlight. I studied the workings of the apparatus, whose power was multiplied a hundred times by rounded lenses like those on lighthouses, and which served to direct the light in a particular direction. The electric lamp was set up in such a way as to provide the maximum power of illumination. Thus its light was produced in a vacuum, which ensured it was both uniform and intense. The vacuum also economized on the graphite points generating the luminous arc. In these conditions they hardly ever wore out—an important saving for Captain Nemo, who would not have been easily able to renew his supply.

While the *Nautilus* prepared to continue its underwater travel, I went back down to the salon. The hatches closed again and we set sail due west.

We were ploughing the waves of the Indian Ocean, a vast liquid plain covering 550 million hectares, with waters so transparent that anyone looking down from the surface feels dizzy. The *Nautilus* was generally sailing at between 100 and 200 metres' depth. This carried on for a few days. To anyone but I, with my immense love for the sea, the hours would surely have seemed long and monotonous, but the time was fully occupied by daily excursions to the platform, where I got new strength from the invigorating ocean air, viewing the rich waters through the salon's windows, reading the books in the library, and writing my memoirs, the sum of which did not leave a moment for fatigue or boredom.

The health of all of us remained in a very satisfactory state. The diet on board suited us perfectly, and personally, I could easily have managed without the variety that Ned spent his efforts on producing, through a spirit of protest. Even colds were not frequent in this constant temperature. In any case, there was a supply of the stony coral dendrophyllia on board, known in the South of France as sea fennel, which provided an excellent cough pastille in the form of its polyps' melting flesh.

For a few days we saw many aquatic birds, palmipeds and seagulls of various sorts. Some were adroitly killed and when prepared in a certain way provided a very acceptable water-game. Amongst the great long-flight birds, winging at a considerable distance from all land and resting on the waves from the fatigues of flight, I spotted some magnificent albatrosses with discordant cries like donkeys' braying, birds belonging to the family of longipennates. The representatives of the family of totipalmates included swift frigate birds which fished deftly on the surface, and large numbers of boatswain birds or tropic-birds, including ones that were as large as pigeons, with red ribbing and white plumage shaded in varieties of pink, bringing out the black of their wings.

The *Nautilus*'s nets brought in several kinds of turtle of the hawksbill genus, with curved shells that are much appreciated. These reptiles are good at diving, for they can stay underwater for a long time by closing the fleshy valves where their nasal tubes emerge. When caught, some of the hawksbills were still sleeping in their shells, safe from marine animals. The flesh of these turtles was generally second-rate, but their eggs produced a dish fit for kings.

As for the fish, they never failed to fill us with admiration as we surprised them in their secret aquatic life through the open panels. I observed several species that I had not had the opportunity to study until then.

I will cite principally ostracions, peculiar to the Red Sea, Indian Ocean, and the tropical oceans off the coasts of America. These fish resemble tortoises, armadillos, sea urchins, and crustaceans in being protected by an armour which is neither cretaceous nor lapideous, but actual bone. Its armour is solid and is triangular or quadrangular. Amongst the triangular ones, I noted some that were 5 centimetres long, with a health-giving flesh of an exquisite flavour, and brown tails and yellow fins; I recommend their acclimatization even in fresh water, to which a certain number of salt-water fish easily become accustomed. I will also cite the quadrangular ostracions with four large tubercules mounted on their backs; speckled ostracions with white points on their lower bodies, which can be domesticated like birds; trigonals fitted with spurs formed by the extension of their bony hides, whose bizarre groaning has given them the nickname of 'sea pigs'; and dromedaries with large conical humps and flesh that is tough and leathery.

I again pick out from the daily notes kept by Master Conseil two fish of the genus tetrodon peculiar to these seas: seven-inch Electridae eels of the brightest colours and bandtail puffers with red backs and white breasts and with three highly distinctive longitudinal rows of filaments. Next, from other genera: tail-less oviforms looking like black-brown eggs covered in white stripes; porcupine-fish, veritable sea porcupines armed with stings and able to swell up to form a ball bristling with darts; the seahorses found in all oceans; flying pegasi with long snouts and very long pectoral fins arranged in the form of wings, thus allowing them, if not to fly, at least to spring into the air; longtail sea-moths whose tails are covered with many scaly rings; macrognathic fish with long jaws, fine 25-centimetre fish shining in the most pleasant colours; pale Callionymidae with rough heads; thousands of jumping blennies with black stripes and long pectoral fins gliding over the surface at tremendous speeds; delicious veliferous fish able to hoist their fins as if unfurling sails to catch favourable winds; splendid specimens of *Kurtus* on which nature has lavished yellow, azure, silver, and gold; trichoptera whose wings are formed of filaments; *Cottus* always soiled with silt and which produce a swishing sound; gurnards whose livers are considered poisonous; *Bodiani* with moving eye-flaps; and finally snipefish with long tubular snouts, the veritable fly-catchers of the ocean, armed with guns not designed by any Chassepot or Remington,* but which kill insects by simply hitting them with a drop of water.

In the 89th genus of fish classified by Lacépède, belonging to the second sub-class of osseous fish characterized by a gill cover and a bronchial membrane, I noticed the scorpion fish, whose head has stings on it and which has only one dorsal fin: according to the subgenus, these creatures are either devoid of small scales or covered in them. The latter subgenus provided us with specimens of didactyls 30 to 40 centimetres long, with yellow stripes and fantastic-looking heads. As for the former, it offered several specimens of that bizarre fish fittingly nicknamed the 'sea toad', a fish with a big head, sometimes hollowed out with deep sinuses, sometimes swollen with protuberances; it bristles with spurs and is studded with tubercules; it has hideous irregular horns; its body and tail are covered with calluses; its stings produce dangerous injuries; and it is vile and repugnant.

From 21 to 23 January, every twenty-four hours the *Nautilus* covered 250 leagues, or 540 miles, averaging 22 knots. If the diverse varieties of fish could be identified as they went past, this was because they were attracted by the electric light and tried to travel with us; most were left behind by the speed and quickly fell back; some, however, managed to keep up with the *Nautilus* for a while.

On the morning of the 24th, at latitude 12° 5′ S and longitude 94° 33′ E, we sighted Keeling Island, a madreporian upheaval covered in magnificent coconut trees, visited by Mr Darwin and Captain Fitzroy.* The *Nautilus* followed the coasts of this desert island close in. Its dredges brought in numerous specimens of polyps and echinoderms, as well as curious tests from the branch of molluscs. A few precious examples of the species of delphinium added to Captain Nemo's treasures, to which I joined a punctiferous astrea, a sort of parasitic polypary often attached to a shell.

Soon Keeling Island disappeared below the horizon, and sail was set for the north-west and the tip of the Indian subcontinent.

'Civilized lands,' Land said to me that day. 'Better than those islands of Papua, where there are more savages than deer! In India, Dr Aronnax, there are roads, railways, and British, French, and Indian towns. You can't go five miles without meeting a compatriot. Hey, isn't this the time to take our leave from Captain Nemo?'

'No, Ned, no,' I answered in a very determined tone. 'Let it run, as you sailors say. The *Nautilus* is getting closer to the inhabited land-masses. It is heading for Europe, so let it take us there. Once we are back in our own seas, we can see about what we should do. In any case, I don't suppose that Captain Nemo will let us go hunting on the Malabar or Coromandel Coasts as he did in the forests of New Guinea.'

'Well, sir! Can't you try without his permission?'

I did not reply. I didn't want to talk about it. Deep down, I longed to see through to the end the events brought about by destiny, the one that had cast me on board the *Nautilus*.

From Keeling Island onwards, our speed usually reduced. It was more changeable and often took us down to great depths. Several times we used the inclined planes, placed at an angle to the waterline by means of internal levers. In this way we descended two or three kilo-metres, but without ever probing the distant bottoms of the Indian Ocean, that sounds of 13,000 metres have not been able to reach. As for the temperature of the lower strata, the thermometer still invariably indicated $+4°$.* I observed only that the water of the upper strata was always colder when above shallows than on the open sea.

On 25 January the ocean was totally deserted, and the *Nautilus* spent the day on the surface, beating the waters with its powerful screw and making them spurt up to a great height. In these conditions, how could it not have been mistaken for a gigantic cetacean? I spent three-quarters of the time on the platform. I gazed at the sea. Nothing in view except, westerly at about 4 p.m., a long steamer, heading on the opposite tack. Its masts were visible for a while, but it could not sight the *Nautilus*, too flat and too low in the water. I decided that the steamer had to belong to the Peninsular and Oriental Line, which goes from the island of Ceylon to Sydney, putting in at King George Sound and Melbourne.

At five o'clock, before that swift dusk which links day to night in the tropical zones, Conseil and I were marvelling at a strange spectacle.

There is one charming animal whose encounter is a promise of good fortune, according to the ancients. Aristotle, Athenaeus, Pliny, and Oppian* studied its habits and exhausted on it the entire poetics of the Greek and Italian scholars. They called it *Nautilus* or *Pompylius*.

But modern science has not endorsed their terminology, and the mollusc is now known as the argonaut.

Anyone consulting the worthy Conseil would have learned that the branch of molluscs is divided into five classes; that the first class, the cephalopods, whose members are sometimes exposed and sometimes testaceous, consists of two families, the *Dibranchia* and the *Tetrabranchia*; that these two families are distinguished by the number of their gills; that the *Dibranchia* has three genera, the argonaut, the calamar, and the cuttlefish; and that the *Tetrabranchia* only has one, the nautilus. If, following this nomenclature, a rebel spirit confused the argonaut, which is 'acetabuliform', that is equipped with suckers, with the nautilus, which is 'tentaculated' or endowed with tentacles, he would have no excuse for his mistake.

It was a school of these argonauts that were travelling over the surface of the ocean. We could count several hundred. They belonged to the species of tuberculous argonauts, unique to the seas round India.

The gracious molluscs were using their propulsive tubes to move backwards using their tubes to expel the water they had taken in. Of their eight tentacles, six were long and thin and floating on the water, and two were rounded into palmate shapes raised for the wind like light sails.* I could easily see their spiral wavy shell, accurately compared by Cuvier to an elegant launch. A true vessel in fact. It transports the animal which has secreted it, but is no longer attached.

'Although the argonaut is free to leave its shell,' I said to Conseil, 'it never does.'*

'Just like Captain Nemo,' he judiciously replied. 'Which is why he should have called his ship the *Argonaut*.'*

For another hour the *Nautilus* floated in the midst of this school of molluscs. Then some mysterious fright took hold of them all of a sudden. As if on a signal, all the sails were abruptly brought down, the arms brought in, the bodies contracted; the shells changed their centre of gravity and turned over, and the whole fleet disappeared under the waves. It happened instantaneously, and never did ships of a squadron manoeuvre with more precision.

Night fell abruptly at this moment, as, hardly lifted by the breeze, the waves stretched peacefully out under the wales of the *Nautilus*.

The following day, 26 January, we cut the equator at the 82nd meridian, and returned to the northern hemisphere.

During the day, a formidable pack of sharks formed a procession around us. Terrible animals, which abound in these seas, making them highly dangerous. They were *Heterodontus portusjacksoni* with brown backs and whitish stomachs, armed with eleven rows of teeth, eyed sharks whose necks are marked with a large black spot surrounded by white, resembling an eye, and Isabella sharks with round muzzles and dotted with dark points. Often these powerful animals would throw themselves against the salon window with somewhat worrying force. Ned Land was no longer master of himself. He wanted to go back up to the surface and harpoon these monsters, especially certain dogfish sharks with jaws full of teeth laid out like a mosaic and great 5-metre striped sharks which provoked him with remarkable persistence. But soon the *Nautilus* would increase its speed and easily leave the fastest of these sharks behind.

On 27 January, at the opening of the vast Bay of Bengal, we encountered dead bodies floating on the surface on several occasions, a dreadful sight! These were the dead from Indian towns, washed down the Ganges and into the open sea, and which the vultures, the only gravediggers of the country, had not finished eating. But there was no shortage of sharks to help them in their funereal work.

At seven in the evening, the half-submerged *Nautilus* was sailing through a milky sea. As far as the eye could see, the ocean looked as if it had changed to milk. Was it the effect of the moon's rays? Hardly, since the moon was scarcely two days old and still hidden below the horizon, in the rays of the sun. The whole sky, although lit up by the scintillations of the stars, seemed black in contrast with the whiteness of the waters.

Conseil could hardly believe his eyes, and asked me the reason for this remarkable phenomenon. Fortunately I was in a position to reply.

'It is what is called a sea of milk,' I told him, 'a vast expanse of white billows, often seen on the coasts of Amboina and the waters around.'

'But could monsieur inform me what produces such an effect, for I do not imagine that the water has actually changed to milk!'

'No, my good fellow, this whiteness which so surprises you is due merely to the presence of myriads of tiny infusoria creatures, types of tiny glow-worms of a gelatinous translucent appearance, the thickness of a hair, no longer than a fifth of a millimetre. Some of these creatures join together over a distance of several leagues.'

'Several leagues!'

'Yes, my good fellow, and do not try to calculate the number of such infusoria. You would not get far, for navigators have apparently sailed on these seas of milk for more than 40 miles.'

I do not know if Conseil followed my recommendation, but he seemed plunged into deep thought, no doubt trying to calculate how many fifths of a millimetre there are in 40 miles square. As for me, I continued to observe the phenomenon. For several hours, the *Nautilus*'s prow cut the whitish waves, and I noticed that it floated soundlessly over the silky water, as if gliding over those foamy expanses that are sometimes produced in bays by the collision of currents and counter-currents.

At about midnight the sea suddenly resumed its normal colour, but behind us, as far as the eye could see, the sky reflected the whiteness of the waves for a long time as if filled with the dim gleams of an aurora borealis.

2

A NEW INVITATION FROM CAPTAIN NEMO

At noon on 28 February,* when the *Nautilus* surfaced at latitude 9° 4′ N, it was in view of some land lying eight miles to the west. My eye was drawn to a range of mountains about 2,000 feet high, forming very wild shapes. Our position taken, I went back to the salon, and when it had been plotted on the map, I realized that we were in the environs of the island of Ceylon, that pearl hanging from the ear-lobe of the Indian subcontinent.

I went into the library to look for a book about the island, the most fertile on the globe. I found a volume by H. C. Sirr, entitled *Ceylon and the Cingalese.** Returning to the salon, I first noted the coordinates of Ceylon, which antiquity called by so many different names. It lies between 5° 55′ and 9° 49′ N and 79° 42′ and 82° 4′ E of the Greenwich meridian, its length is 275 miles, its maximum width 150 miles, its circumference 900 miles, and it covers 24,448 square miles, making it slightly smaller than Ireland.

Captain Nemo and his first officer appeared.

The captain glanced at the map, then turning to me:

'The island of Ceylon,' he said. 'A realm famous for pearl fishing. Would it suit you, doctor, to visit one of the fishing grounds?'

'Most certainly, captain.'

'Good, it's easy to arrange. But if we can see the fishery, we won't be able to see the fishermen. The season has not started yet. No matter. I will give orders to head for the Gulf of Mannar, which we will reach tonight.'

The captain said a few words to his first officer, who immediately went out. Soon the *Nautilus* returned to the liquid element, the pressure-gauge indicating a depth of 30 feet.

With the map in front of my eyes, I looked for the Gulf of Mannar. I found it on the 9th parallel, on the north-west coast of Ceylon. It was formed by a strip of land stretching out from the little island of Mannar. To reach the bay, we needed to work our way up the western coast of Ceylon.

'Dr Aronnax,' Captain Nemo continued, 'pearls are fished in the Bay of Bengal in the Indian Ocean and in the seas of China and Japan, of South America, of the Gulf of Panama, and of the Gulf of California; but it is Ceylon that has the best catches. We are undoubtedly arriving a little early. The fishermen only assemble in the Gulf of Mannar in the month of March, when their three hundred boats work for thirty days on the lucrative exploitation of the sea's treasures. Each boat has ten oarsmen and ten divers. The divers work in two groups, which work alternately, going down to a depth of 12 metres by means of a heavy stone held between their feet and connected to the boat by a rope.'

'So this primitive method is still in use?'

'It is,' said Captain Nemo, 'although the fisheries belong to the hardest-working people in the world, the British, to whom they were given by the Treaty of Amiens in 1802.'*

'It seems to me nevertheless that the diving suit, as you employ it, would be very useful in such an operation.'

'Indeed, since the poor divers cannot remain underwater for long. The Briton Percival,* in his journey to Ceylon, speaks of a "Kaffir" who spent five minutes without coming back up. But this appears hardly credible to me. I know that some divers can stay as much as 57 seconds and very good ones, 87;* however, these are rare, and when these unfortunates come back on board, their noses and ears are dripping water tinted with blood. I believe that on average the divers can manage thirty seconds, during which they rush to cram into a little net all the pearl oysters they can tear off; but generally these divers do not live to a ripe old age: their sight diminishes; ulcerations break out on their eyes; sores form on their bodies; and often they have strokes at the bottom of the sea.'

'Yes, a sad profession which serves only to satisfy a few caprices. But tell me, captain, how many oysters can a boat collect in a day?'

'About forty to fifty thousand. It is even said that the British government carried out diving on its own account in 1814, and that its divers brought back seventy-six million oysters in twenty days' work.'

'Are these divers at least paid enough?'

'Scarcely. In Panama they earn only a dollar a week. Most of them just get one sol per pearl-bearing oyster, and how many they bring back with none inside!'

'A sol for the poor who make their masters rich! It's odious.'

'So, doctor, you and your companions will visit Mannar Bank, and if by chance some early diver is already there, we will see him at work.'

'Agreed, captain.'

'Incidentally, Dr Aronnax, you're not afraid of sharks?'

'Sharks!' I exclaimed.

The question appeared senseless, or worse.

'Well?' said Captain Nemo.

'I must admit, captain, that I am not yet familiar with this sort of fish.'

'We are, and with time you will get used to them. Besides, we will be armed, and as we follow our route perhaps we can bag a few. It's interesting work. So, Dr Aronnax, until tomorrow, first thing.'

Having said that in a casual tone, Captain Nemo left the salon.

If you are invited to hunt bears in the mountains of Switzerland, you would say: 'Fine! Tomorrow we are going bear hunting.' If you are invited to hunt lions on the plains of the Atlas Mountains or tigers in the jungles of India, you would say: 'Oh, apparently we are going to try and bag a few tigers or lions!' But if you were invited to go hunting sharks in their natural element, you would perhaps request a few moments for reflection before accepting.

As for me, I passed a hand over my forehead, where a few drops of cold sweat were standing out.

'Let's reflect with due caution,' I said to myself. 'Hunting for otters in the underwater forests as we did at Crespo Island is all right. But running around the ocean floor, when you are more or less certain to bump into sharks, is another kettle of fish! I know full well that in certain places, the Andaman Isles for example, the dark-skinned natives do not think twice about attacking sharks, dagger in one hand and noose in the other. But I also know that many of those who face the dreadful beasts don't come back alive! In any case I'm not a native, and even if I were, I do believe that some slight hesitation on my part would not be out of place.'

So there I was, dreaming of sharks, in a reverie of vast jaws, armed with multiple rows of teeth and capable of cutting a man in two. I already felt the pain around my middle section. Also, I could not digest the casual way in which the captain had made the deplorable invitation! Would one not have put it that way if we were going to track some inoffensive fox through the woods?

'Well!' I thought. 'Conseil will never want to come, and that will let me off going with the captain.'

As for Ned, I must admit that I did not feel as confident of his judgement. Dangers, however great, always held an attraction for his aggressive nature.

I started reading Sirr's book again, but was turning the pages automatically.* Between the lines I could see jaws that gaped frighteningly.

Just then Conseil and the Canadian came in, with peaceful, even happy demeanours. They did not know what was waiting for them.

'You know what, sir?' Ned Land said to me. 'Your Captain Nemo—cursed be his name!—has just made a very nice suggestion.'

'Ah,' I said, 'you know . . .'

'If monsieur pleases,' said Conseil, 'the captain of the *Nautilus* has invited us to visit the magnificent pearl fisheries of Ceylon tomorrow in monsieur's company. He did it in highly cordial terms, and behaved like a thorough gentleman.'

'He didn't say anything else?'

'Nothing, sir,' replied the Canadian. 'Except that he had spoken to you about this little excursion.'

'Just so, and did he give you any details about . . .'

'None. You'll be coming with us, I suppose?'

'Me . . .? I imagine so. I can see that you're looking forward to it, Master Land.'

'Yes' it sounds interesting, very interesting.'

'Dangerous, perhaps!' I added in an appealing tone.

'Dangerous?' replied Land. 'A mere excursion to an oyster bed?'

Captain Nemo had clearly not judged it useful to intimate the idea of sharks to my companions. As for me, I was looking at them with unfocused eyes, as if they were already missing a limb or two. Should I warn them? Undoubtedly, but I didn't know how to go about it.

'Monsieur,' Conseil said, 'would monsieur like to give us some details of pearl fishing?'

'About the work itself, or the incidents . . .'

'The fishing,' replied the Canadian. 'Before venturing on to territory, it's useful to have some information about it.'

'Well, be seated, my friends, and I'll tell you everything that the Briton Sirr has just told me.'

Ned and Conseil sat on the settee, and the Canadian started by asking:

'Sir, what is a pearl?'

'My good Ned, for the poet the pearl is a tear from the sea; for the East Asians it is a solidified dewdrop; for ladies it is a jewel of elongated form, of a hyalin lustre, made of mother-of-pearl, that they wear on their finger, ear, or neck; for the chemist it is a mixture of lime, phosphate, and carbonate with a little gelatine; and finally, for the naturalist it is merely an unhealthy secretion in certain bivalves by the organ that produces mother-of-pearl.'

'Branch of molluscs, class of acephalics, order of testaceans.'

'Precisely, Professor Conseil. Now amongst these testaceans, pearls are produced by the earshell, iris, turban, *Tridacna*, and marine pinna, in a word by all those that secrete mother-of-pearl, the blue, bluish, violet, or white substance lining their valves.'

'Mussels as well?' asked the Canadian.

'Yes, the mussels of certain rivers in Scotland, Wales, Ireland, Saxony, Bohemia, and France.'

'Well, we'll pay attention to them in future,' Ned replied.

'But', I continued, 'the mollusc which secretes pearls par excellence is the pearl-bearing oyster, the *Meleagrina margaritifera*, that precious shellfish. The pearl is merely a mother-of-pearl accretion that takes on a globular shape. Either it adheres to the shell of the oyster, or it encrusts itself in the creature's folds. On the valves, the pearl is firmly attached; on the flesh, it floats free. But its core is always a small hard body, either a sterile ovule or a grain of sand, around which the mother-of-pearl is deposited over several years in thin concentric layers.'

'Can several pearls be found in a single oyster?' asked Conseil.

'Yes, my good fellow, there are certain pearl oysters that are a true jewel-case. An oyster has even been cited, although I permit myself to doubt this, which contained no less than 150 sharks.'

'A hundred and fifty sharks!' exclaimed Ned.

'Did I say sharks!' I said quickly. 'I mean 150 pearls. Sharks would make no sense.'

'Indeed,' said Conseil. 'But will monsieur now tell us how the pearls are extracted?'

'There are several methods. When the pearls adhere to the valves, the fishermen sometimes tear them off with pliers. But more frequently, the pearl oysters are laid out on mats of esparto grass spread across the shore. They die in the open air, and after ten days are at the appropriate level of decay. They are plunged into vast tanks of sea water, and opened and washed. This is the beginning of the two stages of the gutters' work. First they separate the pieces of mother-of-pearl, known in the trade as "true silver", "bastard white", or "bastard black", and pack them in boxes of 125 to 150 kilograms. Then they remove the parenchyma from the oyster and boil and sieve it, so as to separate out even the smallest pearls.'

'Does the price of pearls vary according to their size?' asked Conseil.

'Not only their size, but also their shape, their "water", or colour, and their "orient", or iridescent and variegated lustre which lends such charm to their appearance. The finest pearls form separately in the tissue of the mollusc; called virgin pearls or paragons, they are white, often opaque, but sometimes of an opaline transparency, and most commonly spherical or piriform. When spherical they are made into bracelets; piriform, drop-earrings and are sold individually, being the most precious. The other pearls adhere to the oyster's shell and, being less regular, are sold by weight. Lastly, the small pearls known as seed pearls are classified as low grade; they are also sold by weight and serve in particular for embroidery on church vestments.'

'But this work of separating the pearls according to size must be long and tedious?' asked the Canadian.

'No, my friend. The work is carried out by means of eleven sieves or colanders containing variable numbers of holes. The pearls that remain in the colanders containing twenty to twenty-four holes are of the first order. Those caught by the sieves with a hundred to eight hundred holes are of the second order. Sieves with nine hundred to a thousand holes produce the seed pearls.'

'Ingenious,' said Conseil, 'and now I understand how the grading is carried out. But can monsieur tell us how much the work on the pearl-oyster beds brings in?'

'According to Sirr's book,' I replied, 'the pearl fisheries of Ceylon are leased for the sum of three million sharks per year.'

'Francs!' said Conseil.

'Yes, francs. Three million francs, but apparently these pearl fisheries no longer bring in what they used to. The same holds true of the American ones, which produced four million francs in the reign of Charles V of France* but at present, only two-thirds of that. In sum, the total turnover from pearls can be evaluated at nine million francs.'

'But', asked Conseil, 'are some pearls not celebrated for having been sold at a very high price?'

'Yes, my good fellow. It is said that Caesar gave Servilia a pearl estimated to be worth about 120,000 francs of our money.'*

'I have even heard it told', said the Canadian, 'of a certain lady in ancient times who drank pearls in vinegar.'

'Cleopatra,' said Conseil.

'I bet it tasted bad.'

'Awful, Ned, my friend,' replied Conseil; 'but at one-and-a-half million francs, a small glass of vinegar is highly priced.'

'I'm sorry I didn't marry that lady,' said the Canadian, moving his arm in a disturbing way.

'Ned Land, the husband of Cleopatra!'* exclaimed Conseil.

'But I needed to get married, Conseil,' the Canadian replied seriously, 'and it wasn't my fault if it didn't actually work out. I even bought a necklace of pearls for Kat Tender, my fiancée, who then married somebody else. Well, that necklace only cost me a dollar and a half, and yet—Dr Aronnax should believe me—the pearls in it would have been caught by the colander with twenty holes.'

'My good Ned,' I said with a laugh, 'those were artificial pearls, mere globules of glass coated on the inside with essence of orient.'

'Oh, that essence of orient', replied the Canadian, 'must cost a great deal.'

'Almost nothing! It is merely the silvery substance from the scales of a fish called bleak, collected underwater and preserved in ammonia. It has no value.'

'Perhaps that's why Kat Tender married someone else,' philosophically replied Master Land.

'But', I said, 'to come back to pearls of great value, I do not think that a king ever possessed one superior to Captain Nemo's.'

'This one?' said Conseil, pointing to a magnificent jewel displayed in a case.

'Yes, I believe I can assign it a value of two million . . .'

'Francs!' Conseil said quickly.

'Yes, two million francs, and it undoubtedly cost the captain only the effort of picking it up.'

'Hey!' cried Ned Land. 'Maybe we'll find another one on our excursion tomorrow!'

'Bah!' said Conseil.

'And why not?'

'What would be the point of millions of francs on board the *Nautilus*?'

'On board there would be none,' said Ned, 'but elsewhere . . .'

'Oh, elsewhere!' said Conseil, shaking his head.

'In fact', I said, 'Master Land is right. If ever we bring a pearl worth several million back to Europe or America, it would lend both great authenticity and a great price to the story of our adventures.'

'Right,' said the Canadian.

'But', said Conseil, who always came back to the instructive side of things, 'is pearl fishing dangerous?'

'No,' I said quickly, 'especially if you take certain precautions.'

'What are the risks in that profession?' said Land. 'Swallowing a few mouthfuls of water!'

'As you say, Ned. Incidentally,' I said, trying to adopt Captain Nemo's casual tone, 'are you afraid of sharks, my good Ned?'

'Me?' said the Canadian. 'As a professional harpooner, I'm paid to laugh at them.'

'It is not a question of catching them with a swivel hook, hoisting them up on deck, cutting their tails off with axes, opening up their stomachs, tearing out their hearts, and throwing them back into the sea!'

'Then, we're . . .?'

'Yes, precisely.'

'In the water?'

'In the water.'

'What the hell, with a good harpoon! You know, sir, these sharks are poorly designed creatures. They have to turn on to their stomach to bite you, and during that time . . .'

Ned Land had a way of saying the word *bite* that made cold shivers run down your spine.

'Well, and you, Conseil, what do you think of these sharks?'

'Me?' said Conseil. 'I will be frank with monsieur.'

'Here we go,' I thought.

'If monsieur can face such sharks,' said Conseil, 'I do not see why his faithful manservant should not face them with him.'

3

A PEARL WORTH TEN MILLION

NIGHT fell. I went to bed, and slept rather badly. Sharks played an important part in my dreams, and I found it both very appropriate and very inappropriate that etymology derives the French word for shark, *requin*, from the word *requiem*.*

I was woken at four in the morning by the steward that Captain Nemo had put at my personal service. I got up quickly, dressed, and went into the salon.

Captain Nemo was waiting.

'Are you ready, Dr Aronnax?'

'I am.'

'Then please follow me.'

'And my companions, captain?'

'They have been informed, and are waiting for us.'

'Shouldn't we put on diving suits?'

'Not yet. I haven't brought the *Nautilus* too close to the shore, and we are still some distance from Mannar Bank; but I have prepared the dinghy to take us to the exact spot for the diving, which will save us a long journey. The diving equipment is in the dinghy, and we can put it on when we actually begin our submarine exploration.'

Captain Nemo led the way to the central staircase leading up to the platform. There we found Ned and Conseil, delighted at the prospect of a 'holiday outing'. Five sailors from the *Nautilus*, oars at the ready, were waiting, moored alongside.

The night was still dark. Patches of cloud covered the sky, revealing only the occasional star. I looked towards the land, but could see only an uncertain line masking three-quarters of the horizon between the south-west and the north-west. Having worked its way up the western coast of Ceylon during the night, the *Nautilus* was now to the west of the bay, or rather of the gulf formed by Ceylon itself and Mannar Island. There, beneath the dark waters, lay the bank of pearl oysters, an inexhaustible source of pearls, over 20 miles in length.

Captain Nemo, Conseil, Ned, and I took our places in the stern of the small boat. The coxswain took the tiller, his four companions leaned over the oars, the painter was cast away, and we pushed off.

The boat headed southwards. The oarsmen did not hurry. I noticed that while they pulled strongly, their strokes came at ten-second intervals, following the method generally used in national navies. As the boat coasted between strokes, droplets pattered down on the dark waves like globules of molten lead. A slight swell, rolling in from the open sea, made the boat rock slightly, and the crests of a few waves lapped at the bow.

We were silent. What was Captain Nemo thinking? Perhaps about the land he was approaching, too near for his taste—unlike the Canadian, for whom it seemed still too far. As for Conseil, he was a mere spectator.

At about half past five the first tints on the horizon showed the outline of the coast more clearly. It appeared to be somewhat flat on the eastern side, but undulating towards the south. We were still five miles away, and the coast blended into the misty waters. Between us and the shore the sea was deserted. Not a single diver or boat. A profound solitude reigned over the pearl-fishers' meeting place. As Captain Nemo had said, we were arriving in these waters a month early.

At six o'clock the day broke with the abruptness characteristic of the Tropics, which have no dawn or dusk. The sun's rays pierced the shoal of clouds piled up on the eastern horizon, as the radiant orb climbed swiftly.

I could now see the land distinctly, with a few trees scattered here and there.

The boat approached Mannar Island, whose rounded shape loomed to the south. Captain Nemo had risen from his seat, and was gazing over the sea.

At a sign from him the anchor was dropped, but the chain hardly ran, for just there was one of the highest points of the bed of pearl oysters and the depth was no more than a metre. The boat swung round following the ebb-tide heading back out to sea.

'We're there, Dr Aronnax,' said Captain Nemo. 'You can see that the bay is sheltered. In a month's time, large numbers of boats will gather here, and the divers will boldly embark on their search. The bay is marvellously shaped for this kind of fishing. It is protected from strong winds, and the sea is never very high: highly favourable conditions for the divers' work. We will now put on our diving suits, and begin our excursion.'

I made no reply and, staring all the time at the suspect sea, was helped into my heavy suit by the sailors. Captain Nemo and my two companions also put on theirs. None of the men from the *Nautilus* were to accompany us on this latest excursion.

We were soon enclosed in rubber garments up to our necks, with air equipment fastened on with shoulder straps. There was no sign of the Ruhmkorff lighting devices. Before placing my head in the copper helmet I mentioned this to the captain.

'They would be useless, as we shall not be descending to any great depth, and the sun will be enough to light our path. Besides, it would not be a good idea to carry an electric lamp in these waters. The light might accidentally attract some of the dangerous local inhabitants.'

As Captain Nemo spoke, I turned to Ned Land and Conseil. These two friends had already put their heads into the metal spheres, and could neither hear nor talk.

I had one last question for the captain.

'Our weapons?' I said. 'What about our guns?'

'Guns?' he said. 'What for? Do your mountaineers not attack bears dagger in hand? And is steel not safer than lead? Here is a faithful blade. Pass it through your waist and let's go.'

I looked at my companions. They were armed like us and Ned was also brandishing an enormous harpoon which he had placed in the boat before we left the *Nautilus*.

Following the captain's example, I allowed the heavy copper sphere to be set on my head, and the air tanks immediately began to operate.

A moment later, the sailors let us gently down into the water one after another, and we set foot on fine sand at a depth of about five feet. Captain Nemo made a sign to us. We followed him, descended a gentle slope, and disappeared under the waves.

The ideas which had obsessed me now vanished. I became astonishingly calm. The ease with which I was able to move increased my confidence, and the unusual sights all round me captured my imagination.

The sun was already producing enough light underwater. The smallest objects could be seen. After ten minutes' walk, we were about fifteen feet below the surface, and the ground became more or less level.

At our step, like flocks of snipe in a marsh, there rose flights of strange fish, of the genus *Monoptera*, whose only fin is the tail-fin. I recognized the moray eel, a real snake about 80 centimetres long with a pale stomach, which might easily have been taken for a conger eel, but for the gold lines on its sides. Amongst the stromatas, whose bodies are flattened and oval-shaped, I observed parus with brilliant colours and scythe-like dorsal fins, edible fish which, dried and marinated, make an excellent dish called *karawade*; I also saw tranquebars belonging to the *Aspidophoroides*, whose bodies are covered with eight lengthwise sections of scaly armour.

The light grew stronger as the sun rose progressively higher. The ground gradually changed. The fine sand was replaced by a veritable causeway of round stones carpeted in molluscs and zoophytes. Amongst the specimens of these two branches, I noticed *Placuna* with thin unequal valves, an ostracod characteristic of the Red Sea and Indian Ocean, some orange Lucinae with orbicular shells, subulate terebra, some Persian murexes which provided the *Nautilus* with an excellent dye, some 15-centimetre horned murexes which stood up in the waves like hands trying to grasp hold of you, cornigerous *Turbinella* all bristling with spikes, ianthine ligules, *Anatinella*, edible shellfish consumed in Northern India, slightly luminous pelagic panopea, and lastly some beautiful flabelliform oculinidae, magnificent fans which form some of the richest branching structures in these seas.

In the midst of these living plants, beneath these bowers of hydrophytes, ran awkward legions of articulates, chiefly the *Ranina dentata*, whose carapace forms a slightly rounded triangle, birguses particular to these shores, and horrible parthenopes, of repugnant appearance. A no less hideous animal, one that I encountered several times, was the enormous crab observed by Mr Darwin, on which nature has bestowed the instinct and strength required to live off coconuts.* It climbs trees on beaches, knocks down the coconuts, making them fall and crack, and then prises them open with its powerful pincers.

Here beneath the transparent waves this crab scampered with inimitable agility, while green turtles, of the same species that frequent the Malabar Coast, moved slowly between the rocks strewn here and there.

At about seven we finally reached the beds on which the millions of pearl oysters reproduced. These valuable molluscs adhered to the rocks, being strongly attached by a brown byssus which stopped them moving. In this respect, the oyster is inferior to the lowly mussel, which nature has given some powers of locomotion.

The pearl oyster, *Meleagrina* or 'mother-of-pearl', whose valves are more or less equal in size, has a rounded shell with thick walls, very rough on the outside. Some of the shells were laminated and grooved with greenish bands running from the top. These belonged to young oysters. Others, with rough black surfaces, ten years old or more, were as much as six inches across.

Captain Nemo pointed to the prodigious stockpile of pearl oysters, and I understood that the supply was inexhaustible, for nature's creative power is beyond man's destructive bent. Land, faithful to his instinct, hastened to fill the net carried on his side with the finest oysters he could find.

But we could not tarry. We had to follow the captain, who seemed to be following paths known to him alone. The ground was rising appreciably, and sometimes, when I held my arm up, it rose above the surface of the water. But then the level of the beds would capriciously descend again. We often rounded high rocks worn into pyramid shapes. In their gloomy fissures enormous crustaceans, standing on their long limbs like war-machines, looked at us with fixed eyes, while beneath our feet crawled myriapods, glycera, *Aricia*, and annelids, stretching out their exaggerated antennae and groping tentacles.

A huge grotto now opened before us, excavated from a picturesque pile of rocks covered with tall ribands of submarine flora. At first sight the grotto looked very dark indeed. The sun's rays seemed to gradually go out in it. Its vague transparency became nothing but drowned light.

Captain Nemo entered. We followed him. My eyes soon got used to the gloom. I realized that the springings of the arches were capriciously elaborate, supported by natural pillars standing firmly on broad granite bases like the heavy columns of Tuscan architecture. Why was our guide leading us into this submarine crypt? I was to find out before long.

Having descended quite a steep decline, our feet were treading the bottom of a kind of circular pit. Here Captain Nemo stopped and pointed out something I had not yet noticed.

It was an oyster of the most extraordinary size, a gigantic *Tridacna*: a font able to hold an entire lake of holy water, a basin whose breadth was more than two metres and therefore larger than the one in the *Nautilus*'s salon.

I approached the phenomenal mollusc.* It was fixed by its byssus to a granite slab, and there on its own it grew in the calm waters of the grotto. I estimated the weight of the *Tridacna* to be 600 pounds. Now an oyster like this would contain about 30 pounds of flesh, and one would need the stomach of a Gargantua to swallow a few dozen of them.

The captain was aware of the bivalve's existence. It was obviously not the first time he had come here, and at first I thought that he had brought us only to demonstrate this natural curiosity. I was mistaken. Captain Nemo had the specific motive of checking the *Tridacna*'s condition.

The two valves of the mollusc were half open. The captain went over and thrust his dagger between the two halves so as to prevent the shell shutting again. He then used his hand to raise the membranous tissue with fringed edges which formed the covering of the creature.

There, between the foliate folds, I saw a loose pearl the size of a small coconut. Its globular shape, its perfect transparency, its splendid water stamped it as a jewel of inestimable value. Carried away by curiosity, I stretched out my hand to hold it, to weigh it, to feel it. But the captain stopped me, shook his head, withdrew his dagger with a swift movement, and let the shell suddenly close.

I then understood Captain Nemo's purpose. By leaving the pearl entombed in the *Tridacna*'s protection, he allowed it to grow imperceptibly. With each year the mollusc's secretion added new concentric rings.

The captain alone knew of the grotto where this admirable fruit of nature was 'ripening'; he alone was raising it, so to speak, in order to enrich his inestimable museum one day. Perhaps, after the fashion of the Chinese and Indians, he had even brought the pearl into being by placing a piece of glass or metal in the folds of the mollusc, which by degrees the nacreous substance covered. In any case, comparing this pearl to those I already knew, and to those which gleamed in the captain's collection, I estimated its value to be at least ten million francs. It was more a magnificent natural curiosity than a luxurious jewel, for I am unaware of any ladies' ears capable of bearing it.

Our visit to the extravagant *Tridacna* was over. Captain Nemo left the grotto, and we returned to the oyster beds, to the clear waters not yet disturbed by the divers' work.

We walked separately, just like strollers, each of us stopping or wandering, following our fancy. For my part I no longer worried about the dangers that my imagination had so ridiculously exaggerated. The bottom was rising noticeably, and my head soon rose above the surface as I stood in 3 feet of water. Conseil drew near me and, sticking his large capsule close to mine, said a friendly hello with his eyes. But this high ground only lasted a few metres and soon we were back in our element. I believe I now have the right to call it that!

Ten minutes later, Captain Nemo suddenly stopped. I thought he was going to go back the way he had come. No—he gestured to us to crouch beside him, at the bottom of a large hollow. He pointed towards a particular spot in the liquid mass, and I stared at it.

About 6 metres away a shadow appeared and fell over the ground. The worrying idea of sharks crossed my mind. But I was wrong and, once more, we were not dealing with ocean monsters.

It was a man—a living man, an Indian, a black—a poor devil of a diver no doubt, who had come to glean some pickings before the main harvest. I saw the keel of his boat moored some feet above his head. He dived and surfaced repeatedly. A stone cut in the shape of a sugar loaf held between his feet helped him sink more quickly, while a rope secured him to the boat. That was his only equipment. As he reached the bottom at about 15 feet, he fell to his knees and filled his net with pearl oysters, collected at random. He then surfaced, emptied the bag, pulled up the stone, and started his operation again, each time taking only thirty seconds.

The diver did not see us. We were hidden by the shadow of a rock. And besides, how could this poor Indian imagine that beings like himself were underwater, watching his every movement, not losing a single detail of his fishing?

He dived and rose again many times. He only brought up about ten oysters each time, for he was obliged to tear some away from the bed they were attached to with their byssuses. And how many of the oysters had no pearls, although he was risking his life for them!

I watched with great concentration. His movements were regular, and for half an hour no danger seemed to threaten. I was getting used to watching this absorbing fishing, when suddenly, as the Indian was kneeling on the ground, I saw him make a sign of terror, stand up, and spring towards the surface.

I understood his terror. a gigantic shadow had appeared above the unfortunate diver. It was a large shark, swimming diagonally: eyes flaming and jaws wide open!

I was petrified with horror, unable to move.

The voracious fish, with a strong movement of its fins, accelerated towards the Indian. He threw himself aside, avoiding the shark's open jaws, but not the stroke of its tail, for he received a blow on his chest which laid him out on the ground.

This scene had taken only a few seconds. The shark came to attack again and, turning on its back, was about to cut the Indian in two, when Captain Nemo jumped up. Dagger in hand, he moved straight at the monster, ready for a hand-to-hand fight.

The shark noticed this new adversary just as it was about to swallow the unfortunate diver. Turning on its belly, it went for the captain.

I can still see Captain Nemo's stance. Coiled up on himself, he waited for the attack of the formidable shark with wonderful self-possession; when it rushed at him, the captain jumped aside with amazing agility, avoiding the impact and plunging his dagger into the brute's belly. But it was not over yet. A terrible battle ensued.

The shark had 'roared', so to speak. The blood poured from its wounds in torrents. The sea had turned red, and I could see nothing through this opaque medium.

Nothing until, as it cleared away, I caught sight of the brave captain hanging on to the shark's fin and stabbing again and again at its stomach, unable, however, to place a mortal blow to the centre of the heart. In its struggle the shark beat the water with fury, and the turbulence almost made me fall over.

I wanted to go to the captain's assistance. But I was frozen with horror, and could not move.

I looked on with a haggard eye. I saw the varying phases of the combat. The captain fell to the ground, overturned by the enormous mass weighing down on him. The shark's jaws opened inordinately, like industrial shears, and would have made an end of the captain, had Ned, as quick as thought, not thrust himself upon the shark, harpoon in hand, and driven the terrible weapon into its side.

The water was filled with masses of blood. It shook as the shark beat it with indescribable fury. But Ned Land had struck home. It was the monster's last gasp. Pierced to the heart, it thrashed out its life in terrifying spasms, as the impact knocked Conseil down.

Ned Land had meanwhile freed the captain. On his feet and unharmed, Nemo rushed up to the Indian, quickly cut the cord which fastened the stone, took him in his arms, and then ascended to the surface using a vigorous kick.

We all followed, and moments later, miraculously preserved from death, we reached the diver's boat.

Captain Nemo's first care was to restore the unfortunate to life. I was afraid he might not succeed. But the chances were good, for the poor man's submersion had not lasted long, although the blow from the shark's tail could easily have been fatal.

Fortunately, after vigorous rubbing from Conseil and the captain, I saw the diver gradually regaining consciousness. He opened his eyes. How surprised he must have been to find four great copper heads leaning over him!

And still greater must have been his surprise when Captain Nemo took a string of pearls from a pocket in his clothing, and placed them in his hand. This magnificent generosity from the man of the seas was accepted by the poor Sinhalese with trembling hands. His startled eyes showed that he did not know to what superhuman being he owed his fortune and his life.

At a sign from the captain we returned to the oyster beds, retraced our steps, and reached the anchor of the *Nautilus*'s boat. Once aboard, we removed the heavy copper carapaces with the sailors' assistance.

Captain Nemo's first words were addressed to the Canadian.

'Thank you, Master Land.'

'For services rendered,' said Ned. 'I owed you that one.'

A wan smile flitted across the captain's features, and that was all.

'To the *Nautilus*!' he cried.

The boat flew over the waves. A few minutes later we saw the floating body of the shark.

From the black markings on the ends of its fins, I recognized the terrible melanopterus of the Indian Ocean, belonging to the species of sharks in the strict sense. It was more than 25 feet long; and its enormous mouth took up a third of its body. It was an adult, as could be seen from the six rows of teeth in its upper jaw, arranged in the shape of an isosceles triangle.

Conseil regarded it entirely from a scientific point of view, and I am sure he classified it, not incorrectly, amongst the cartilaginous animals—order of chondropterygians with fixed gills, family of selachians, genus sharks.

While I was looking at the inert mass, a dozen of its voracious relatives suddenly appeared around the boat; without worrying about us, they threw themselves upon the corpse and fought for the pieces.

At half past nine we were back on board the *Nautilus*.

I began to reflect upon the incidents of our excursion to Mannar Bank. Two considerations inevitably followed. One was the outstanding bravery of Captain Nemo; the other, his devotion to a fellow creature, a representative of the human race that he shunned under the seas. Whatever he might say, this strange man had not yet totally succeeded in killing his heart.

When I said as much to him he replied, with some little emotion:

'That Indian, doctor, is the inhabitant of an oppressed country. I am his compatriot, and shall remain so to my very last breath!'

4

THE RED SEA

ON 29 January the island of Ceylon disappeared below the horizon, and the *Nautilus*, moving at 20 knots, slid into the labyrinth of channels separating the Maldives from the Laccadives. It even came close to Kiltan Island, a land of madreporian origin discovered in 1499 by Vasco da Gama,* and one of the nineteen main islands of the Laccadive archipelago, situated between 10° and 14° 30′ S and 69° and 50° 72′ E.

We had now covered 16,220 miles, or 7,500 leagues, since our starting-point in the seas of Japan.

When the *Nautilus* surfaced the next day, 30 January, there was no land in sight. It was moving north-north-westwards in the direction of the Gulf of Oman, which is hollowed out between Arabia and the Indian subcontinent and serves as an outlet for the Persian Gulf.

This was obviously a cul-de-sac, without any way out. So where was Captain Nemo taking us? I had no idea. My ignorance did not satisfy the Canadian, who asked me where we were heading.

'We are heading, Master Ned, where the captain's whims take us.'

'His whims won't take us anywhere. The Persian Gulf has no exit; so if we go in, we'll be heading back out again in double-quick time.'

'Well then, we will just head back, and if the *Nautilus* wishes to visit the Red Sea after the Persian Gulf, the strait of Bab el Mandeb will always be there to give us a way through.'

'As you well know,' replied Ned, 'the Red Sea is just as closed as the Gulf, since the isthmus of Suez has not been cut through yet. And even if it had been, a mysterious boat like ours couldn't venture into its canals with their regularly spaced lock gates. So the Red Sea is still not the route to take us back to Europe.'

'Which is why I didn't say we were going back to Europe.'

'So what do you imagine?'

'I imagine that after visiting the strange shores of Arabia and Egypt, the *Nautilus* will work its way back down the Indian Ocean, perhaps through the Mozambique Channel or past the Mascarene Islands, and hence reach the Cape of Good Hope.'

'And once at the Cape of Good Hope?' asked the Canadian with remarkable insistence.

'Well, we will enter the Atlantic, which is still unknown to us. Ah Ned, my friend, are you already tired of our journey under the seas? Are you already blasé at this constantly changing spectacle of submarine wonders? For my part, I would be most upset to come to the end of this voyage which so few have had the chance to make.'

'But don't you realize, Dr Aronnax, that we've been imprisoned in the *Nautilus* for almost three months?'

'No, Ned, I didn't know, nor do I want to know, and I count neither the days nor the hours.'

'So what is the conclusion to all this?'

'The conclusion will come in its own good time. In any case, we can't do anything about it, so there is no point in discussing it. If you came and told me, "A chance of escape is available to us", I would talk it over with you, my good Ned. But such is not the case, and to be frank, I do not believe that Captain Nemo ever ventures into the seas of Europe.'

Through this short dialogue it will be seen that I had been reincarnated in the skin of the captain and had become a real *Nautilus* fanatic.

As for Ned, he concluded the conversation with a soliloquy: 'All that is good and fine, but as far as I'm concerned, when you're not relaxed you just don't enjoy it any more.'

For four days, until 3 February, the *Nautilus* visited the Gulf of Oman at various speeds and depths. It seemed to be moving at random, as if hesitating about the route to follow, but it never went further than the tropic of Cancer.

As we left this sea, we briefly sighted Muscat, the largest town in Oman. I admired its strange appearance, with its pale houses and forts standing out from the black rocks all around. I noticed the round domes of its mosques, the elegant tips of its minarets, its fresh, green terraces. But this was just a vision, and soon the *Nautilus* plunged again under the dark waves of those shores.

It followed the Arabian coasts of Mahrah and Hadramaut at a distance of six miles, parallel to the undulating line of the mountains, relieved by a few ancient ruins. On 5 February we finally entered the Gulf of Aden, a funnel into the bottleneck of Bab el Mandeb that pours Indian waters into the Red Sea.

On 6 February the *Nautilus* was floating in sight of Aden, which is perched on a promontory with a narrow neck connecting it to the mainland. It forms an unassailable Gibraltar, whose fortifications the British have rebuilt since seizing them in 1839. I caught sight of the octagonal minarets of this town, which was once the richest and biggest trading entrepot on the coast, according to the historian Idrisi.*

I firmly believed that, having reached this point, Captain Nemo would turn round; but to my great surprise, he did not.

The following day, 7 February, we entered the strait of Bab el Mandeb, which means 'Gate of Tears' in Arabic. Twenty miles wide, it is a mere 52 kilometres long, and the *Nautilus* took hardly an hour to cover it at full speed. I saw nothing, not even the island of Perim which the British government has used to strengthen the position of Aden. There were too many British and French steamers serving routes between Suez and Bombay, Calcutta, Melbourne, Reunion, and Mauritius through this narrow passage for the *Nautilus* to attempt to show itself. So it remained prudently submerged.

Finally, at midday, we were ploughing the waves of the Red Sea.

That celebrated lake of biblical tradition is hardly refreshed by rainwater, has no major river flowing into it, is constantly being reduced by evaporation, and loses a liquid layer 1½ metres deep each year. The Red Sea is a remarkable gulf which would probably dry up entirely, if it were closed like a lake; it is worse off in this respect than its neighbours the Caspian or the Dead Sea, whose levels have only lowered to the point where their evaporation is equal to the sum of waters running into their basins.

The Red Sea is 2,600 kilometres long and 240 kilometres wide on average. At the time of the Ptolemies and the Roman emperors it was the main commercial artery in the world, and the cutting of the isthmus will restore this classical importance, one which the railways of Suez have already brought back in part.*

I did not even try to understand the whim that had led Captain Nemo to bring us into this gulf. Rather I unreservedly approved the *Nautilus*'s entering it. It went at moderate speed, sometimes staying on the surface, at others diving to avoid a ship, so I was able to observe both the depths and the surface of this remarkable sea.

During the early hours of 8 February Mocha appeared to us, a town now in ruins, with walls that crumble at the mere sound of cannons and which is shaded here and there by green date trees. Formerly a major city, it has public markets, twenty-six mosques, and a three-kilometre-long city wall defended by fourteen forts.

Next the *Nautilus* drew close to the African shore where the sea is quite deep, and the water as clear as crystal. Through the open panels we could contemplate wonderful shrubs of dazzling corals and huge slabs of rock covered in a splendid green fur of seaweeds and wracks. What indescribable sights, and what variety of places and scenery where the reefs and volcanic islands drop away off the Libyan coast! But where the arborescences appeared in all their glory was near the eastern shores, which the *Nautilus* wasted no time in heading for. Off the coasts of Tihama, not only did the displays of zoophytes flourish below sea level, but they also formed picturesque intertwinings unwinding 60 feet over its surface; the latter more capricious but less highly coloured than the former, which used the water's vitality to maintain their freshness.

How many charmed hours I spent in this way at the window of the salon! How many new specimens of submarine flora and fauna I admired in the bright light of our electric lamp! I saw umbrella-shaped fungus coral, blue-grey sea anemones including *Thalassianthus aster*, horizontal tubipores like flutes that waited only for the breath of the god Pan; shells particular to this sea, which settle in the madreporian excavations and whose bases are formed of short spirals; and finally a thousand specimens of a polypary that I had not yet observed, the common sponge.

The class of Porifera, the first of the group of polyps, was created for precisely this strange product, of such obvious usefulness. The sponge is not a vegetable, as a few naturalists still believe, but an animal of the lowest order, a polypary which is below coral. Its animal nature cannot be doubted, and one cannot support the ancients who considered it a being intermediate between the plants and animals. I must say, however, that naturalists are not in agreement on how the sponge is organized. For some it is a polypary, and for others, such as M. Milne-Edwards, it is an isolated and unique individual.

The class of Porifera contains about three hundred species, which are encountered in a large number of seas and even certain rivers, where they have been described as 'fluviatile'. But their preferred waters are the Mediterranean, the Greek Islands, and the coasts of Syria and the Red Sea. There the fine soft sponges, which can fetch up to a hundred and fifty francs apiece, reproduce and grow: the golden sponge of Syria, the hard sponge of Barbary, etc. But since I could not hope to study these zoophytes in the ports of the eastern Mediterranean, from which we were separated by the uncrossable isthmus of Suez, I was content to observe them in the waters of the Red Sea.

I called Conseil to my side, while the *Nautilus*, at an average depth of 8 or 9 metres, slowly skimmed over the beautiful rocks on the eastern coastline.

There grew sponges of all forms: pediculate, foliaceous, globular, and digitate. They aptly deserved their names of baskets, chalices, bulrushes, elkhorns, lions' feet, peacocks' tails, and Neptune's gloves, given them by fishermen, who are more poetic than scientific. Little dribbles of water, after carrying life into each cell, were constantly being squeezed out by their fibrous material, covered with a sticky, semi-fluid substance. This substance disappears after the death of the polypary and putrefies while giving off ammonia. Nothing then remains apart from the hard or gelatinous fibres making up the domestic sponge, which takes on a reddish tint and is used for various purposes, according to its degree of elasticity, permeability, and resistance to maceration.

These polyparies stuck to the rocks, to the shells of molluscs, and even to the stalks of hydrophytes. They filled the smallest gaps, some spreading out and others standing up or hanging down like coral growths. I informed Conseil that sponges were collected in two ways, either by net or by hand. The latter method, requiring the use of divers, is preferable,* for it leaves the polypary undamaged and so guarantees a much higher price.

The other zoophytes proliferating near the poriferans consisted mainly of jellyfish of a very elegant species; molluscs were represented by varieties of squid which d'Orbigny says are found only in the Red Sea; and reptiles by *virgata* turtles belonging to the genus of *Chelones*, which provided us with a healthy and delicate dish.

As for fish, they were numerous and often remarkable. The following were brought in most frequently by the nets of the *Nautilus*: rays, amongst them lymma with oval bodies of a dull red colour and irregular blue spots, recognizable from their twin serrated stings; Forsskal's stingrays with silvery backs; whip-tailed stingrays with dotted tails; bockats, huge two-metre-long cloaks undulating through the water; totally toothless aodons, which are a sort of cartilaginous fish closely related to the shark; dromedary *Ostracea*, whose hump ends in a curved sting a foot and a half long; ophidians, which are actually moray eels with silver tails, blue backs, and brown pectorals bordered in grey; fiatolae, species of stromateids zigzagged with narrow golden strips and decked out in the three colours of France; 40-centimetre-long gourami blennies; superb scads with seven transversal bands of a fine black tint, blue and yellow fins, and gold and silver scales; snooks; oriflamme mullets with yellow heads; parrot fish, wrasses, triggerfish, gobies, etc., and a thousand other fish found in the oceans we had already visited.

On 9 February the *Nautilus* was floating on the broadest part of the Red Sea, between Suakin on the west coast and Al Qunfudhah on the east, where it is 190 miles wide.

At noon that day, once our position had been taken, Captain Nemo came up on the platform after me. I promised myself not to let him go down again without at least sounding him out on his plans for the future. He came up as soon as he spotted me, graciously offered me a cigar, and said:

'Well, monsieur, does the Red Sea please you? Have you seen enough of the wonders it contains, fish and zoophytes, its beds of sponges and the forests of corals? Have you seen the towns dotted along its shores?'

'Yes, captain, and the *Nautilus* lent itself marvellously to all this study. Ah, what an intelligent boat it is!'

'Yes, intelligent, audacious, and invulnerable! It fears neither the terrifying storms of the Red Sea, nor its currents, nor even its reefs.'

'This sea is indeed one of the worst, and if I am not mistaken, had an atrocious reputation in ancient times.'

'Yes indeed, Dr Aronnax. The Greek and Latin historians never speak well of it, and Strabo* says that it is particularly difficult in the Etesian winds and the rainy season. The Arab Idrisi, who calls it the Gulf of Colzoum, recounts that ships perished in great numbers on its sandbanks and that nobody ventured to navigate it at night. It is, he claims, a sea subject to terrible hurricanes, dotted with inhospitable islands, and "has nothing good" either in its depths or on its surface. The same views were held by Arrian, Agatharchidas, and Artemidorus.'*

'It is easy to see that these historians never sailed on the *Nautilus*.'

'Indeed,' the captain replied smiling, 'but in this respect, the moderns are little further advanced than the ancients. Many centuries were needed to discover the mechanical power of steam! Who knows whether a second *Nautilus* will appear in the next hundred years! Progress is slow, Dr Aronnax.'

'Agreed. Your ship is a century ahead of its time, or perhaps several. What a shame that such a secret must die with its inventor!'

Captain Nemo did not reply. After a moment's silence:

'You were speaking of the ancient historians' views on the dangers of navigating the Red Sea?'

'Yes, but were their fears not exaggerated?'

'Yes and no,' replied the captain, who seemed to be an expert on all aspects of 'his' Red Sea. 'What no longer poses a problem for a modern ship, well rigged, solidly constructed, master of its direction thanks to obedient steam, offered all sorts of dangers to the vessels of the ancients. One must try to imagine those early navigators venturing out on boats that were made of planks held together by ropes made of palm leaves, caulked with powdered resin, and waterproofed with tallow from dogfish. They didn't even have instruments to determine their direction, and so sailed by dead reckoning in the midst of currents they hardly knew. In those conditions, shipwrecks were necessarily common. But in our time, the steamers plying between Suez and the South Seas no longer have anything to fear from the angers of this gulf, in spite of the contrary monsoons. Their captains and passengers do not prepare for departure with propitiary sacrifices, and, once back, they no longer adorn themselves with garlands and golden strips before going to thank the gods in their neighbourhood temples.'

'Admittedly,' I said, 'and steam seems to have killed the skill of observation in sailors. But captain, since you appear to have specially studied this sea, can you tell me where the name comes from?'

'There are many explanations for it. Would you like to hear the ideas of a fourteenth-century chronicler?'*

'Certainly.'

'This joker claimed that it got its name from the crossing by the Israelites, when the pharaoh perished in the waves that closed up again on Moses' command:

> To miraculously portend
> The dark sea encardin'd
> And made them decree
> Call it then the Red Sea.'

'A poet's explanation, Captain Nemo, but insufficient to convince me. I would like to ask your personal opinion.'

'Here it is then. In my view, Dr Aronnax, the Red Sea's name should be seen as a translation of the Hebrew word "Edom",* the name the ancients gave it because of the peculiar colour of its waters.'

'Until now, however, I have only seen waves which were clear, without any particular colour.'

'No doubt, but when we head for the end of the Gulf, you will notice their remarkable appearance. I remember seeing the bay of El-Tor entirely red, like a sea of blood.'

'And you attribute this colour to the presence of microscopic algae?'

'Quite right. There is a viscous purple matter produced by those sickly-looking plantlets known as *Trichodesma*, of which forty thousand are contained in a square millimetre. Perhaps you will observe some at El-Tor.'

'So, Captain Nemo, this is not the first time you have travelled through the Red Sea on the *Nautilus*?'

'No, monsieur.'

'Then, since you were speaking of the Crossing of the Red Sea and the drowning of the Egyptians, I would like to ask if you have found underwater traces of that great historic event?'

'No, and for a very good reason.'

'Namely?'

'That the spot where Moses crossed with all his people is so full of sand nowadays that camels can hardly bathe their legs there. My *Nautilus* would clearly not have enough water for it.'

'And this place . . .?'

'It's situated a little above Suez, in the arm of the sea that formed a deep estuary when the Red Sea stretched as far as the Bitter Lakes. Now whether their crossing was miraculous or not, the Jews did pass through that place on the way to the Promised Land, and the pharaoh's army did perish on that exact spot. I deduce that excavations in its sands would uncover a great quantity of arms and tools of Egyptian origin.'

'Yes indeed,' I replied, 'and for the archaeologists' sake one must hope that such excavations will be carried out sooner or later, when new towns are built on this isthmus after the Suez Canal is opened. A canal which is totally useless for a ship like the *Nautilus*!'

'Undoubtedly, but useful for the world at large. The ancients understood full well the importance to their commercial affairs of creating a link between the Red Sea and Mediterranean; still they did not dream of digging a direct canal, but used the Nile as an intermediary instead. The canal connecting the Nile to the Red Sea was very probably begun under Sesostris, if tradition is to be believed. What is certain is that in 615 BC, Necho* initiated work on a canal drawing water from the Nile and going across the plains of Egypt opposite Arabia. This canal took four days to navigate, and was wide enough for two triremes to pass abreast. It was continued by Darius, son of Hystaspes, and probably finished by Ptolemy II.* Strabo saw it being used by ships; but the lack of gradient between its starting-point near Bubastis and the Red Sea meant that it was only navigable a few months of the year. This canal served trade until the century of the Antonines; then it was abandoned, silted up with sand, but was later restored on the orders of Caliph Umar.* But in 761 or 762 it was filled in once and for all by Caliph al-Mansur to prevent food reaching Mohammed ben Abdallah, who had rebelled against him.* During his expedition to Egypt, your General Bonaparte* rediscovered the traces of these works in the desert of Suez; but he was caught out by the tide, and almost died a few hours before reaching Hazeroth, the very place where Moses had camped 3,300 years before.'*

'Well, captain, what the ancients did not dare undertake, namely a link to connect two seas and reduce the distance from Cadiz to the

Indies by 9,000 kilometres, M. de Lesseps* has done, and very shortly he will have made Africa into an enormous island.'

'Yes, Dr Aronnax, and you can justifiably be proud of your compatriot. He does more honour to his nation than the greatest of sea-captains! Like so many others, he began with obstacles and disappointments, but has triumphed because he has the necessary willpower. And it is sad to think that his works, which should have been international, enough to render illustrious an entire reign, succeeded in the end only through the energy of a single man. So all honour to M. de Lesseps!'

'Yes, all honour to this great citizen,' I replied, astonished by the intensity with which Captain Nemo had spoken.

'Unfortunately', he continued, 'I cannot take you through the Suez Canal, but you will be able to catch a glimpse of the long breakwaters of Port Said the day after tomorrow, when we are in the Mediterranean.'

'In the Mediterranean!' I exclaimed.

'Yes, monsieur. Are you surprised?'

'What astonishes me is to think we will be there the day after tomorrow.'

'Really?'

'Yes, captain, although I ought not to be amazed by anything since arriving on board your ship!'

'But why the surprise?'

'Because of the frightful speed you will have to sail the *Nautilus* at in order to reach the Mediterranean the day after tomorrow, having circled Africa and the Cape of Good Hope!'

'But who says it is going to circle Africa, Dr Aronnax? Who said anything about rounding the Cape of Good Hope?'

'Nevertheless, unless the *Nautilus* can cross the isthmus by sailing over dry land . . .'

'Or under, Dr Aronnax.'

'Under?'

'Yes,' Captain Nemo replied calmly. 'A long time ago nature made beneath that stretch of land what men are making today on its surface.'

'What, there is a passage!'

'Yes, an underground passage that I have called the Arabian Tunnel. It begins under Suez and finishes in the Bay of Pelusium.'

'But isn't the isthmus formed of moving sand?'

'Down to a certain depth. But at 50 metres there is only immovable bedrock.'

'And did you discover this passage by chance?' I asked, more and more surprised.

'By luck and reasoning, but more reasoning than luck.'

'I am listening, captain, but my ears won't believe what they can hear.'

'Ah, monsieur! *Aures habent et non audient** is of every age. Not only does this passage exist, but I have been through it several times. Without it, I wouldn't have ventured into this Red Sea cul-de-sac today.'

'Would it be indiscreet to enquire how you discovered the tunnel?'

'Monsieur,' answered the captain, 'there can be no secrets between people who are never to part.'

I did not react to the implication but waited for Captain Nemo's story.

'It was the simple reasoning of a naturalist that led me to discover the passage which I alone know about. I had noticed that in the Red Sea and the Mediterranean there are a number of fish of absolutely identical species: ophidians, fiatola, rainbow wrasses, perches, horse-mackerel, and flying fish. Given this fact, I wondered if there might not be some link between the two. If it did exist, the underground current had to go from the Red Sea to the Mediterranean because of the difference in the levels. So I caught a large number of fish near Suez, put copper rings on their tails, and threw them back in the water. A few months later, I caught a few of my specimens on the coast of Syria, still with their identification rings. That is how I demonstrated the link between the two seas. I looked for it with my *Nautilus*, found it, ventured in, and before long, monsieur, you too will have passed through my Arabian Tunnel!'

5

ARABIAN TUNNEL

THAT same day, I told Conseil and Ned the part of the conversation which directly concerned them. When I informed them that within two days we would be in the waters of the Mediterranean, Conseil clapped his hands but the Canadian simply shrugged his shoulders.

'An underwater tunnel,' he cried, 'a link between two seas! Who ever heard of such a thing?'

'Ned, my friend,' replied Conseil, 'had you ever heard of the *Nautilus?* No. But it does exist. So do not shrug your shoulders so lightly, and do not reject things just because you have never heard of them.'

'We shall see!' retorted Land, shaking his head. 'After all, I would be only too pleased to believe in the captain's passage, and may God grant us that it does lead into the Mediterranean.'

That same evening, at 21° 30′ N, the *Nautilus* neared the Arabian coast, sailing on the surface. I spotted Jeddah, the trading post for Egypt, Syria, Turkey, and India. I could quite clearly make out groups of buildings, ships tied up alongside the quays, and other ships whose draught forced them to anchor in the roads. The sun was quite low on the horizon and struck the houses of the town full on, bringing out their whiteness. Further out, a few reed and wooden huts indicated the Bedouin quarter.

Soon Jeddah faded into the shades of evening, and the *Nautilus* dived back down through the slightly phosphorescent water.

The following day, 10 February, several ships appeared, sailing on the opposite tack from us. The *Nautilus* resumed its submarine navigation; but at noon the sea was deserted when we took our bearings, so it remained on its flotation line.

Accompanied by Ned and Conseil, I went to sit on the platform. The coast to the east was a bare outcrop totally blurred by the misty haze.

Leaning on the side of the dinghy, we were chatting about one thing and another, when Ned Land pointed out to sea, and said:

'Can you see something there, Dr Aronnax?'

'No, Ned, but I haven't got your eyes, you know.'

'Look carefully,' said Ned, 'there, off the starboard bow, at about the same height as the searchlight. Can you see something moving?'

'Yes,' I said after careful observation. 'I can make out something like a long black fish's body on the surface.'

'Another *Nautilus?*' said Conseil.

'No,' answered the Canadian; 'unless I am gravely mistaken, it's some sort of marine animal.'

'Are there whales in the Red Sea?' asked Conseil.

'Yes, my good man,' I replied, 'they are sometimes encountered.'

'It isn't a whale,' said Ned, not taking his eyes off the object. 'Whales and I are old friends, and I wouldn't make a mistake about the way they move.'

'Let's wait,' said Conseil. 'The *Nautilus* is heading in that direction, and it won't be long before we know what we're up against.'

The blackish object was soon only a mile away. It resembled a large reef stranded in the open sea. What was it? I was still unable to say for sure.

'Ah! It's moving! It's diving!' cried Ned Land. 'Good Heavens! What can it be? It hasn't got a forked tail like a baleen or sperm whale and its fins look like foreshortened limbs.'

'But then . . .' I said.

'Hey,' said the Canadian, 'it's on its back now, raising its breasts in the air!'

'It's a mermaid!' exclaimed Conseil. 'An authentic mermaid, with all due respect to monsieur.'

Conseil's term put me on the right track, and I realized that the animal belonged to the order of marine creatures which legend has made into mermaids, half women, half fish.

'No,' I said to him, 'it is not a mermaid, but a strange creature which has almost disappeared from the Red Sea. It is a dugong.'*

'Order of sirenians, group of pisciforms, sub-class monodelphians, class of mammals, branch of vertebrates,' replied Conseil.

And when Conseil had spoken, nothing more could be said.

Ned Land was still staring. His eyes burned with cupidity at the sight of the animal. His hand seemed ready for the harpoon. He looked as though he was just waiting for the moment to throw himself into the sea and attack the animal in its element.

'Oh, monsieur!' he said in a voice trembling with emotion. 'I have never killed one of *those*.'

The whole harpooner was encapsulated in that one word.

Just then, Captain Nemo appeared on the platform and noticed the dugong. He understood the feelings of the Canadian, and addressing him directly:

'If you were holding a harpoon, Master Land, wouldn't you be itching to use it?'

'Quite right, sir.'

'And wouldn't you like to follow your trade of fisherman for a day, and add this cetacean to your tally?'

'Very much.'

'Well, you can try!'

'Thank you, sir,' Ned replied, his eyes blazing.

'Just one thing,' added the captain, 'I warn you not to miss the animal, for your own sake.'

'Is it dangerous to attack the dugong?' I asked, in spite of the Canadian's shrug.

'Yes, sometimes. The animal comes back on its attackers and capsizes their boat. But with Master Land, there should be no fear. His eye is quick, his arm is sure. I am only saying he shouldn't miss the dugong because it is considered fine game, and I know that Master Land appreciates the finest cuts.'

'Oh,' said the Canadian, 'so that animal takes pleasure in providing fine fare as well, does it?'

'Yes, Master Land, its flesh is real meat. It is held in very high esteem, reserved for the tables of princes throughout Malaysia. This excellent animal is so fiercely hunted that, just like its congener, the manatee, it is becoming rarer and rarer.'

'And so, captain,' Conseil said seriously, 'if by chance this were the last of its race, would it not be better to spare it—in the interests of science?'

'Perhaps,' responded the Canadian; 'but in the interests of the table, it is better to hunt it.'

'So go ahead, Master Land,' replied Captain Nemo.

Just then seven crewmen, as silent and impassive as always, climbed up to the platform. One was carrying a harpoon and line like those used by whalers. The boat's cover was removed, and it was taken from its recess and launched. Six oarsmen took their places on the seats as the coxswain held the tiller. Ned, Conseil, and I sat at the back.

'Aren't you coming, captain?' I asked.

'No, monsieur, but I wish you good hunting.'

The boat shoved off and, carried on by its six oars, headed quickly towards the dugong, floating at a distance of two miles.

Once we were a few cables from the cetacean, the oars were slowed, silently entering the quiet waters. Ned Land, harpoon in hand, went and stood at the front of the boat. The whaling harpoon is normally attached to a very long rope which unwinds quickly when the wounded animal drags it off. But here the rope was only about ten fathoms long, and its end was fastened to a small keg which would float to indicate the underwater position of the dugong.

I had got up and could distinctly see the Canadian's adversary. The dugong, also called the halicore, closely resembled a manatee. Its long, broad body ended in a greatly elongated caudal fin, and its side-fins in genuine fingers. The difference with the manatee was that its upper jaw was armed with two long, pointed teeth, which formed splayed tusks.*

The dugong Ned Land was getting ready to attack was of colossal dimension, more than seven metres in length. It was not moving and seemed to be sleeping on the surface, making it easier to capture.

The boat carefully approached to within three fathoms of the animal. The oars remained suspended in their rowlocks. I half got up. Ned, his body leaning back a little, was brandishing his harpoon with an experienced hand.

Suddenly, there came a hissing sound and the dugong disappeared. The harpoon, thrown with some strength, had undoubtedly struck only water.

'Hell!' exclaimed the furious Canadian. 'I missed!'

'No,' I said, 'the animal is wounded—look at the blood—but your weapon did not lodge in its body.'

'My harpoon, my harpoon!' cried Ned Land.

The sailors started rowing again, as the coxswain steered the boat towards the floating keg. Once the harpoon had been fished out of the water, the boat started pursuing the animal again.

The dugong came back up to the surface to breathe from time to time. Its wound had not unduly weakened it, for it was proceeding at great speed. The boat, rowed by strong arms, was flying along. Several times we got to within a few fathoms, but just as the Canadian got ready to strike, the dugong would suddenly dive, and so escape.

One can imagine the anger filling the impatient Ned Land. He hurled the most vivid swear words in the English language at the unfortunate creature. For my part, I went no further than annoyance at seeing the dugong foil all our tricks.

We had pursued it without stopping for an hour, and I was beginning to believe that it would prove very difficult to catch, when the animal had the unfortunate idea of revenge, which it was to regret. It came back at the boat to attack in its turn.

This trick was not lost on the Canadian.

'Careful!' he said.

The coxswain said a few words in his strange language, undoubtedly warning his men to stay on their guard.

The dugong, now only 20 feet from the boat, stopped and brusquely sniffed the air with its huge nostrils, not at the end but on the top of its snout. Then, gathering momentum, it threw itself at us.

The boat could not avoid the collision; half capsized, it took on board one or two tons of water that needed to be bailed; but thanks to the coxswain's skill, it was hit at an angle rather than side on, and so did not turn over. Ned held tightly on to the prow and stabbed his harpoon at the gigantic animal; with its teeth enmeshed in the gunwales, it lifted the boat out of the water like a lion seizing a deer. We were thrown on top of one another, and I really do not know how the adventure would have finished, if the Canadian had not continued relentlessly attacking the animal, finally striking it to the heart.

I heard the grinding of teeth on metal as the dugong vanished, taking the harpoon with it. But soon the keg came back up, and moments later the body of the animal appeared, lying on its back. The boat went alongside, and started towing the dugong back to the *Nautilus*.

Heavy lifting gear was needed to hoist the dugong on to the platform. It weighed 5,000 kilograms. The animal was cut up before the Canadian's eyes, who considered it essential to follow every detail of the operation. That same day, the steward served me a few slices of the flesh for dinner, skilfully prepared by the ship's cook. I found it excellent, superior even to veal, if not to beef.

The next day, 11 February, the *Nautilus*'s pantry was further enhanced with delicate game. A flock of sea-swallows settled down on the *Nautilus*. They were of a species of *Sterna nilotica* peculiar to Egypt, with black beaks, grey speckled heads, eyes surrounded with white dots, greyish backs, wings, and tails, white stomachs and throats, and red feet. We also caught a few dozen Nile ducks, wild birds with a gamey taste, whose necks and crowns are white flecked with black.

The *Nautilus*'s speed was moderate. It ambled along, so to speak. I noticed that the water of the Red Sea was becoming less and less salty as we approached Suez.

At about five in the evening, we sighted the cape of Ras Muhammad to the north. It is this cape which forms the tip of Arabia Petraea, between the Gulf of Suez and the Gulf of Aqaba.

The *Nautilus* entered the Strait of Jubal, which leads to the Gulf of

Suez. I distinctly noticed a high mountain, above Ras Muhammad and between the two gulfs. This was Mount Horeb, the Sinai on whose summit Moses saw God face to face,* and which one imagines constantly crowned with lightning.

At six o'clock, the *Nautilus*, at times on the surface and at others submerged, passed El-Tor, at the end of a bay whose waters seemed dyed red, as remarked by Captain Nemo. Night fell in a heavy silence, broken only occasionally by the cry of a pelican or a few night birds, the crash of surf hitting rocks, or the far-off groaning of a steamer beating the water of the gulf with its noisy blades.

From eight to nine o'clock the *Nautilus* remained a few metres underwater. According to my calculations, we were very close to Suez. Through the salon's panels, I could see the rocky floor brightly illuminated by our electric light. It seemed that the strait was getting narrower and narrower.

At quarter past nine the boat had surfaced, and I went up on the platform. Very impatient to pass through Captain Nemo's tunnel, I felt quite restless, and wished to breathe the fresh night air.

Amongst the shadows, I soon noticed a pale light half discoloured by the mist, shining about a mile away.

'A floating beacon,' somebody said close by.

I turned round and saw the captain.

'The buoy of Suez,' he continued. 'It will not be long before we enter the tunnel's mouth.'

'It can't be easy to get in?'

'No, monsieur. So it is my custom to direct the operation myself from the pilot-house. And now if you wish to go below, Dr Aronnax, the *Nautilus* is about to dive, and will only surface again at the other end of the Arabian Tunnel.'

I followed Captain Nemo. The hatch closed, the water tanks filled, and the vessel dived about ten metres.

Just as I was getting ready to return to my room, the captain stopped me.

'Dr Aronnax,' he said, 'would you like to accompany me to the pilothouse?'

'I did not dare ask.'

'Please do come. You will see everything that can be seen of this channel which is both underground and underwater.'

Captain Nemo led me towards the central staircase. When half-way up, he opened a door, followed the upper gangways, and arrived at the pilot-house, which, as the reader knows, emerged near the end of the platform.

It was a cabin measuring 6 feet square, basically similar to those occupied by helmsmen of Mississippi or Hudson steamboats.* In the middle was a vertical wheel which engaged the rudder-chains running to the aft of the *Nautilus*. Four glass-lens portholes in the walls of the cabin allowed the pilot to see in all directions.

The cabin was dark, but my eyes soon got accustomed, and I noticed the pilot, a vigorous man, his hands resting on the spokes of the wheel. The sea outside was bright in the searchlight, beaming out from the other end of the platform, behind the cabin.

'And now', said Captain Nemo, 'let's look for the way through.'

Electric wires ran from the pilot-house to the engine-room, enabling the captain to control both the direction and speed of his *Nautilus*. He pressed a metal button, and immediately the propeller slowed down markedly.

In silence I examined the high, sheer wall we were now running along, which formed the unshakeable foundation of the sandy massif of the coast. For an hour we followed it at a distance of only a few metres. Captain Nemo did not take his eyes off the two concentric circles of the suspended compass. With a single movement, the pilot was constantly changing the direction of the *Nautilus*.

I had taken up a position at the port window, and could see magnificent substructures of corals, plus zoophytes, algae, and crustaceans waving their enormous legs as they stretched out of the holes in the rocks.

At quarter past ten, Captain Nemo took the wheel himself. A wide tunnel, black and deep, opened up in front of us. The *Nautilus* plunged boldly into it. An unusual churning sound could be heard along its sides. This was the water of the Red Sea rushing towards the Mediterranean because of the slope of the tunnel. The *Nautilus* followed the torrent, quick as an arrow in spite of the efforts of the engine to slow it down by means of the propeller, thrown into reverse.

On the narrow walls of the passage, I could no longer see anything but dazzling streaks, straight lines, fiery furrows traced by the speed and the electric light. My heart was beating wildly, as I compressed it with my hand.

At 10.35 Captain Nemo left the wheel and, turning to me, said:

'The Mediterranean.'

The *Nautilus*, carried on by the torrent, had crossed the Isthmus of Suez in less than twenty minutes.

6

THE GREEK ISLANDS

THE following day, 12 February, the *Nautilus* surfaced at daybreak. I rushed on to the platform. Three miles to the south the vague silhouette of Pelusium was outlined. A river had carried us from one sea to another. But this tunnel, although easy to descend, had to be impossible to ascend.

At about seven o'clock, Ned and Conseil joined me. The inseparable companions had slept peacefully, without worrying about the *Nautilus*'s feat.

'Well, monsieur the naturalist,' asked the Canadian in a slightly bantering tone, 'and what about the Mediterranean?'

'We're floating on its surface, Ned, my friend.'

'What!' said Conseil. 'During the night?'

'Yes, this very night we crossed that uncrossable isthmus in a matter of minutes.'

'I don't believe a word of it.'

'Well you had better, Master Land,' I said. 'That low rounded coast to the south is the Egyptian coast.'

'Try the other one,' retorted the obstinate Canadian.

'But if monsieur says so,' Conseil told him, 'we have to believe monsieur.'

'Moreover, Ned, Captain Nemo did me the honours of his tunnel, and I was beside him in the pilot-house when he himself steered the *Nautilus* through that narrow passage.'

'Do you hear, Ned?' said Conseil.

'And since you have such good eyes,' I added, 'you can see the jetties at Port Said stretching out to sea.'

The Canadian looked carefully.

'Actually,' he said, 'you are quite right, monsieur, and your captain is a great man. We're in the Mediterranean. Good. Let's now chat about our business, please, but where nobody can hear us.'

I could see what the Canadian was driving at. In any case, I thought it better to talk if he wanted to, so all three of us went and sat near the searchlight, where we were less exposed to the wet spray from the waves.

'Now, Ned, we are listening,' I said. 'What is on your mind?'

'What I have to tell you is very simple. We're now in Europe, and before Captain Nemo's whims drag us to the ends of the polar seas or back to the South Seas, I would like to leave the *Nautilus*.'

I will admit that this discussion with the Canadian worried me. I did not wish to fetter the freedom of my companions in any way, but nevertheless felt no desire to leave Captain Nemo. Thanks to him, thanks to his vessel, I was furthering my underwater studies each day, I was rewriting my book about the submarine depths in the very midst of that element. Would I ever again have such an opportunity to observe the wonders of the ocean? No, never! So I could not get used to the idea of abandoning the *Nautilus* before our cycle of investigation was finished.

'Ned, my friend,' I said, 'please tell me frankly. Are you bored here? Do you regret the fate that placed you in Captain Nemo's hands?'

The Canadian remained silent for a moment. Then, crossing his arms:

'Frankly,' he said, 'I don't regret this voyage under the seas. I will be pleased to have done it; but in order for me to have done it, it must be over. That's how I see it.'

'It *will* be over, Ned.'

'Where and when?'

'Where, I don't know. When, I cannot say; or rather I imagine it will end when these oceans have nothing to teach us. Everything that starts must have an end in this world.'

'I agree with monsieur,' replied Conseil; 'it is very likely that, having covered all the oceans of the globe, Captain Nemo will let the three of us go.'

'Go!' cried the Canadian. 'He'll have a go at us, don't you mean?'

'Let's not exaggerate, Master Land,' I said. 'We have nothing to fear from the captain, but I do not share Conseil's ideas either. We are masters of the *Nautilus*'s secrets, and I have little hope that the captain will resign himself to giving us our freedom and revealing them to the whole world.'

'But then what do you hope for?' asked the Canadian.

'That circumstances will arise that we can—that we must—profit from, whether in six months' time or tomorrow.'

'Yeah!' said Ned Land. 'And where will we be in six months, do you think, monsieur the naturalist?'

'Perhaps here, perhaps in China. As you know, the *Nautilus* moves quickly. It crosses the oceans as swallows cross the air, or expresses the continents. It has no fear of busy seas. Who can say if it won't head right now for the coast of France, Britain, or America, where an escape could be attempted as easily as here?'

'Dr Aronnax,' retorted the Canadian, 'your arguments are fundamentally flawed. You're speaking in the future: "We will be here! We may be there!" But I am speaking in the present: "We are here, and we must seize the opportunity."'

Land's logic was hemming me in; and I felt on very shaky ground. I no longer knew what argument to put forward in my favour.

'Monsieur,' he continued, 'let us suppose, by some remote chance, that Captain Nemo offered you freedom this very day, now. Would you accept?'

'I'm not sure.'

'And if he added that the offer he was making today would never be repeated, would you accept?'

I did not answer.

'And what does my friend Conseil think?' enquired Ned.

The worthy fellow calmly replied:

'Your friend Conseil has nothing to say. He is totally disinterested in this question. Like his master, like my friend Ned, he is not married. Neither wife, nor parents, nor children are waiting for him back at home. He is in monsieur's service, he agrees with monsieur, he speaks in unison with monsieur, and, to his great regret, he should not be counted on to form a majority. There are only two people here: monsieur on the one hand and Ned on the other. Having said that, his friend Conseil is listening, and would be glad to keep the score.'

I couldn't help smiling to see Conseil annihilate his personality so completely. Deep down, the Canadian had to be delighted not to have him as adversary.

'So, monsieur,' said Ned Land, 'since Conseil doesn't exist, let's discuss this between the two of us. I have spoken, you have listened. What is your reply?'

It was clearly necessary to come to a conclusion, and I hated subterfuges.

'Ned, my friend,' I said, 'here is my reply. You are quite right, and my arguments cannot prevail against yours. We cannot count on Captain Nemo's good will. Elementary self-interest prevents him from setting us free. Conversely, self-interest requires that we profit from the first opportunity to leave the *Nautilus*.'

'Good, Dr Aronnax, wisely spoken.'

'But', I said, 'I have one point to make, only one. The opportunity must be a real one. Our first attempt to escape must succeed; because if it fails, we will not have another, and Captain Nemo will never forgive us.'

'All that is good,' replied the Canadian. 'But your remark applies to any attempt to escape, whether in two years' or two days' time. So the conclusion remains the same: if a favourable occasion arises, we must seize it.'

'Agreed. And now will you tell me, Ned, what you mean by a favourable occasion?'

'One which would bring the *Nautilus* close to a European coast on a dark night.'

'And would you try to escape by swimming?'

'Yes, if we were close enough to shore, and if the vessel was on the surface. No, if we were far away and the ship was underwater.'

'And in that case?'

'In that case, I would try to use the ship's dinghy. I know how it works. We could get inside, remove the bolts, and head back up to the surface, without even the pilot, who is for'ard, noticing our escape.'

'Well, Ned. Look out for this opportunity; but do not forget that one failure will ruin us.'

'I will not forget, monsieur.'

'And now, Ned, would you like to know exactly what I think of your plan?'

'I do, Dr Aronnax.'

'Well, I think—I do not say I hope—I think that this favourable opportunity may not arise.'

'Why?'

'Because Captain Nemo cannot hide from himself that we have not given up hope of regaining our liberty, and will remain on his guard, above all in the seas around Europe and in sight of the coast.'

'I agree with monsieur,' said Conseil.

'We shall see,' replied Ned Land, who was resolutely shaking his head.

'And now, Ned,' I added, 'let's stop there. Not another word on all this. The day that you are ready, you will tell us and we will follow you. I put myself completely in your hands.'

Our conversation, which was later to have such grave consequences, finished there. I must say now that circumstances seemed to confirm my view, to the Canadian's great despair. Did Captain Nemo not trust us in these busy seas, or did he merely wish to hide from the many ships of all nations ploughing the Mediterranean? I do not know, but most often he kept submerged and away from the coast. Either the *Nautilus* came up with only the pilot-house showing, or it went down to great depths—for between the Greek Islands and Asia Minor we could not find the bottom at 2,000 metres.

Accordingly I did not sight the island of Karpathos, one of the Sporades. But Captain Nemo quoted to me this verse of Virgil about it, putting his finger on a point on the planisphere:

> *Est in Carpathio Neptuni gurgite vates*
> *Caeruleus Proteus . . .* *

This was, indeed, the antique sojourn of Proteus, the ancient shepherd of Neptune's flocks, who kept watch over this island between Rhodes and Crete, now called Scarpanto. But I only saw its granite foundations through the window of the salon.

The next day, 14 February,* I resolved to devote a few hours to studying the fish of the archipelago; but for some reason the panels remained tightly closed. Plotting the direction of the *Nautilus*, I realized that it was heading for Candia, as Crete was formerly known. When I embarked on the *Abraham Lincoln*, the whole island had just rebelled against Turkish despotism. But what had become of the insurrection since then, I had absolutely no idea.* And it was not Captain Nemo, cut off from any communication with dry land, who could have told me.

I accordingly made no allusion to this event when, that evening, I found myself alone with the captain in the salon. In any case, he looked taciturn and preoccupied. Then, unlike his usual habit, he had the two panels of the salon opened, and going from one to the other, attentively observed the water outside. With what aim? I could not guess, and for my part I spent the time studying the fish swimming before my eyes.

Amongst others, I noticed those aphid gobies cited by Aristotle, vulgarly known as 'sea slugs', which are especially encountered in the salt water around the Nile Delta. Near them meandered some half-phosphorescent sea bream, a type of sparid which the Egyptians considered sacred: their arrival in the waters of the river, whose fertile overflowing they heralded, was celebrated in religious ceremonies. I noticed also some *Cheilini* 30 centimetres long, bony fish with transparent scales whose pale skin is marked with red spots; they are great devourers of marine vegetation, which gives them an exquisite taste. Accordingly these *Cheilini* were very much sought after by the gourmets of ancient Rome, and their entrails, cooked with milt from moray eels, peacock brain, and flamingo tongues, made up that divine dish which delighted Vitellius.*

Another inhabitant of these seas caught my attention and brought back all my memories of antiquity. This was the remora, which travels attached to the bellies of sharks. According to the ancients, this small fish, attached to the keel of a ship, could stop it moving, and one of them held back Mark Antony's vessel at the Battle of Actium, in this way helping Augustus to victory.* On such things hang the destinies of nations! I also observed admirable *Anthias* from the family of Lutjanidae, fish sacred to the Greeks who attributed to them the power of expelling marine monsters from the waters they frequented; their name means 'flowers', which they justified with their shimmering colours, their reds going from scarlet to pale pink to the brilliance of rubies, and their fleeting, glistening hues seeming to moisten their dorsal fins. My eyes could not tear themselves away from the wonders of the sea—but were suddenly struck by an unexpected sight.

In the water a man appeared, a diver carrying a leather pouch on his belt. It was not a body abandoned to the waves. It was a living person, swimming with a vigorous stroke, disappearing sometimes to go up and breathe on the surface, and diving down again immediately.

I turned to Captain Nemo, and exclaimed in an emotional voice:

'A man, someone shipwrecked! We must save him at all costs!'

The captain did not reply, but went and leaned against the window.

The man had come close and, with his face pressed against the panel, was looking at us.

To my great stupefaction, Captain Nemo made a sign. The diver replied using his hand, immediately headed back up to the surface, and did not appear again.

'Don't worry,' the captain said. 'That was Nicolas, from Cape Matapan, nicknamed the "Pesce".* He is well known all over the Cyclades. A keen diver! The water is his element, and he lives here more than on land, constantly going from one island to another, as far as Crete.'

'So you know him, captain?'

'And why not, Dr Aronnax?'

Having said that, Captain Nemo walked up to a cabinet placed near the port side of the salon. Near it I saw a trunk reinforced with iron bands; it had a copper plate bearing on it the monogram of the *Nautilus* and its motto *Mobilis in mobili*.

Without worrying about my presence, the captain opened the cabinet, a kind of safe containing a large number of bars.

They were gold bars. Where had this precious metal come from, representing as it did an enormous sum of money?* How had the captain accumulated this gold, and what was he planning to do with it?

I did not say a word, but simply looked. Captain Nemo took the bars one by one and methodically arranged them in the trunk which he completely filled up. I estimated that it contained more than 1,000 kilograms of gold, that is nearly five million francs' worth.

The trunk was securely closed, and the captain wrote an address on its lid, using characters that looked like modern Greek.*

Then Captain Nemo pressed the button connected by wires to the crew room. Four men appeared, and with some effort they hauled the trunk out of the salon. Then I heard them moving it up the metal stairs using a hoist.

Suddenly Captain Nemo turned to me:

'You were saying, monsieur?'

'Nothing, captain.'

'Then, monsieur, you will allow me to say goodnight.'

And with this Captain Nemo left the salon.

I returned to my room highly intrigued, as can be imagined. I tried in vain to sleep. I endeavoured to find a connection between the appearance of the diver and the trunk full of gold. Soon I felt from the pitching and rolling that the *Nautilus* was leaving the lower strata of the water to come back up to the surface.

Then I heard the sound of feet on the platform. I understood that the dinghy was being taken out and launched. It struck the side of the *Nautilus*, and then all sounds ceased.

Two hours later, the same sounds and the same comings and goings. The boat was hoisted on board, then fitted into its recess, and the *Nautilus* dived under the waves once more.

The millions had been transported to their destination. To what part of the land? Who had Captain Nemo sent them to?

The following day, I recounted the night's events to Conseil and the Canadian, my curiosity aroused to the highest possible degree. My companions were no less surprised than I.

'But where does he get it all?' asked Land.

To that, we had no answer. I went back to the salon after lunch, and set to work. Until five o'clock I wrote up my notes.* Suddenly—was it due to some personal indisposition?—I felt extremely hot, and had to take my byssus jacket off. This was incomprehensible, for we were not at high latitudes,* and in any case the *Nautilus*, submerged, should not have suffered from any rise in temperature. I looked at the pressure-gauge. It marked a depth of 60 feet, which heat from the atmosphere could not have reached.

I continued my work, but the temperature rose to the point of becoming unbearable.

Might there be a fire on board? I wondered.

I was just going to leave the salon, when Captain Nemo came in. He went to the thermometer, examined it, and turned to me:

'Forty-two degrees.'

'I had noticed, captain, and if this heat increases a little more, we won't be able to bear it.'

'Oh, monsieur, this heat will only increase if we want it to.'

'So you can vary it as you wish?'

'No, but I can move away from the source producing it.'

'It is coming from the outside then?'

'Yes. We are floating in a stream of boiling water.'

'You're joking!'

'Look.'

The panels opened, and I saw that the sea was entirely white around the *Nautilus*. A smoky sulphurous vapour was curling through the current which was bubbling like water in a boiler. I leaned my hand on one of the windows, but the heat was so intense I had to withdraw it.

'But where are we?'

'Near the island of Santorini, monsieur. To be precise, in the channel separating Nea Kameni from Palea Kameni. I wanted to show you the interesting sight of a submarine eruption.'

'I thought these new islands had finished forming.'

'Nothing is ever finished in the vicinity of volcanoes,' he replied, 'and the globe is still worked by underground fires. According to Cassiodorus* and Pliny, as early as the year 19 of our era a new island, Thira the divine, appeared on the same spot where these small islands were recently formed. Then it disappeared under the waves, to appear again in 69, only to plunge down once more. From then until the modern era, the plutonic work ceased. But on 3 February 1866 a new piece of land, which was named George Island, emerged in the midst of sulphurous vapours near Nea Kameni and united with it on 6 February. A week later, on the 13th, Aphroessa Island appeared, leaving a channel of 10 metres between it and Nea Kameni. I was in these seas when it happened, and could observe each of the phases. Aphroessa Island measured 300 feet across by 30 feet high. It was composed of black vitreous lavas mixed with feldspathic fragments. Finally, on 10 March a small island called Reka appeared* near Nea Kameni, and since then these three little pieces of land have joined together, and now form a single island.'

'And the channel where we are now . . . ?' I asked.

'Here,' replied Captain Nemo, showing me a map of the Greek islands. 'You can see that I have traced the new lands on it.'

'But will this channel fill up one day?'

'Possibly, Dr Aronnax, for eight islets of lava have sprung up opposite St Nicholas Port on Palea Kameni since 1866. It is therefore evident that Nea and Palea will join up relatively soon. In the middle of the Pacific, it is the infusoria that form the landmasses, but here it is eruptive phenomena. Look, monsieur, look at the work going on under the waves.'

I went back to the window. The *Nautilus* was no longer moving. The heat was becoming intolerable. Previously white, the sea was now becoming red, due to the presence of an iron salt. In spite of the hermetically closed salon, an unbearable sulphurous smell was being given off, and I noticed scarlet flames whose vividness killed the brightness of the electricity.

I was dripping with perspiration, stifling, I felt I was going to cook. Yes, in truth, I felt myself cooking!

'We cannot remain in this boiling water any longer!' I cried.

'No, it would not be prudent,' replied an impassive Nemo.

An order was given. The *Nautilus* went about and headed away from this furnace that it could not defy with impunity. Quarter of an hour later, we were breathing on the surface again.

The thought then occurred to me that if Ned had chosen these shores to carry out our escape, we would not have come out alive from this sea of fire.

The next day, 16 February, we left the basin between Rhodes and Alexandria, which has depths of 3,000 metres. The *Nautilus* passed Cerigo, rounded Cape Matapan, and left the Greek Islands.

7

THE MEDITERRANEAN IN FORTY-EIGHT HOURS

THE blue sea par excellence, the 'Great Sea' of the Hebrews, 'the Sea' of the Greeks, the *mare nostrum* of the Romans.* Bordered by orange trees, aloes, cacti, maritime pines, embalmed in the perfume of myrtle trees, framed by severe mountains, saturated with a pure, transparent air, but constantly worked by the fires of the earth—the Mediterranean is a veritable battlefield where Neptune and Pluto* still fight for world domination. It is there, says Michelet, on its shores and in its waters that man bathes in one of the globe's most invigorating climates.

But however beautiful, I was only able to catch a fleeting glimpse of this basin of 2 million square kilometres. And nor was Captain Nemo's personal knowledge made available to me, for that enigmatic character did not appear once during our high-speed trajectory. I estimate the distance the *Nautilus* covered under the waves of this sea to be about 600 leagues, and it finished the voyage in forty-eight hours. Having left the shores of Greece on the morning of 16 February, we had passed through the Strait of Gibraltar by sunrise on the 18th.

It was clear to me that the Mediterranean displeased Captain Nemo, pressed in as it was by the lands he wished to flee. Its waves and breezes brought back too many memories, perhaps too many regrets. Here he no longer had that freedom of movement, that manoeuvrability which the other seas afforded, and his *Nautilus* felt cramped between the narrow shores of Africa and Europe.

Accordingly our speed was 25 knots, that is 12 leagues of 4 kilometres per hour. It goes without saying that Ned Land had to give up his escape plans, to his great annoyance. He could not use the dinghy while being transported at a speed of 12 or 13 metres a second. To have left the *Nautilus* would have been like jumping off a train moving at the same speed, a dangerous action if ever there was one. In addition, our vessel only surfaced in order to renew its supply of air at night, steering using the compass and information from the logline.

As a result I saw of the Mediterranean's depths merely what the traveller on an express glimpses of countryside passing before his eyes: far-off horizons, and not the close-ups which go past in a flash. However, Conseil and I were able to observe some Mediterranean fish whose powerful fins kept them alongside the *Nautilus* for a few seconds. We remained on the lookout at the windows of the salon, and our notes allow me to summarize the ichthyology of that sea in a few words.

Of the various fish living there, I saw some and glimpsed others, and many were whisked away from my eyes by the speeding *Nautilus*. Please permit me then to classify them according to this eccentric method. It will better depict my swift observation.

Amidst the waters, brightly lit by the electric beams, snaked past some of those metre-long lampreys common to almost every climate. Oxyrhynchous creatures, kinds of five-foot-wide rays with white stomachs and ash-grey spotted backs, appeared like huge shawls carried off by the currents. Other rays passed so quickly that I could not tell whether they deserved the title of eagle given them by the Greeks, or the epithets of rat, toad, and bat which modern fishermen give them. Dogfish sharks, twelve feet long and particularly feared by divers, raced each other. Eight-foot marine foxes, blessed with a very fine sense of smell, appeared like great blue shadows. Dorados of the genus *Sparus*, some measuring up to 1.3 metres, paraded in their circular-banded silver and azure clothing, contrasting with the dark colours of their fins. These are fish devoted to Venus, with eyes highlighted by golden eyebrows: a precious species, at home in fresh and salt water, living in the rivers, lakes, and oceans of all climates, adapting to every temperature. Their race goes back to the early geological periods of the earth and has kept all its beauty from the first days.

Travelling long distances, magnificent sturgeons of nine or ten metres struck the glass of the panels with their powerful tails and showed their bluish backs with small brown spots; they resembled sharks though they are not so powerful and are encountered in all seas; in the springtime they like to ascend the great rivers, fighting the currents of the Volga, Danube, Po, Rhine, Loire, and Oder. They live off herring, mackerel, salmon, and gadid; although they belong to the cartilaginous class they are delicate, are eaten fresh, dried, marinated, or salted, and were formerly carried in triumph to the table of Lucullus.*

But of the various Mediterranean denizens, those that I could observe the most usefully when the *Nautilus* approached the surface belonged to the sixty-third genus of bony fish. These were scombrid tuna, with blue-black backs, silver stomachs, and dorsal combs radiating golden gleams. They have the reputation of following moving ships, seeking their cool shadows under the fire of the tropical sky; and they lived up to their reputation, escorting the *Nautilus* as they accompanied the ships of La Pérouse in times past. For long hours, they raced our vessel. I never grew tired of admiring animals so well designed for speed, with their little heads, their streamlined, slender bodies, in certain cases longer than 3 metres, their pectorals of remarkable strength, and their forked caudal fins. They swam in a triangular formation, like certain flocks of birds whose speed they matched, prompting the ancients to say that geometry and strategy were known to them. And yet they do not escape the pursuit of the Provençaux, who appreciate them as much as the inhabitants of Italy and the Sea of Marmara, for these precious animals throw themselves by the thousand into the nets of Marseilles, there to perish blindly and silently.

I will cite, from memory, the Mediterranean fish that Conseil or I merely glimpsed. There were whitish fierasfers-knifefish passing like imperceptible vapours; conger *Muraenae*, three- or four-metre serpents, bright in their green, blue, and yellow shades; three-foot-long cod-hakes, whose livers make a delicacy; taenia-bandfish floating like fine seaweed; gurnards that the poets call lyre-fish, and sailors whistler-fish, whose snouts are adorned with two triangular serrated blades that reproduce ancient Homer's instrument; swallow-gurnards swimming with the speed of the bird whose name they have taken; grouper-soldierfish with red heads and dorsal fins adorned with filaments; shad decorated with black, grey, brown, blue, yellow, and green spots, and which respond to the silvery sound of bells; splendid turbots, the pheasants of the sea, diamond-shaped with yellowish fins, dotted with brown, and whose upper left part is usually marbled brown and yellow; and finally admirable shoals of grey mullet, veritable oceanic birds of paradise for which the Romans paid up to ten thousand sesterces each, and which they killed on their tables, so as to follow with cruel eyes the colour-changes from the cinnabar red of life to the pallid white of death.

And if I was not able to observe the *miraleti*, the triggerfish, the tetrodons, the sea-horses, the jewel-fish, the trumpetfish, the blennies, the surmullets, the wrasses, the smelts, the flying fish, the anchovies, the bream, the bogues, the orfes, nor any of the main representatives of the order of pleuronectes, namely the dab, flounders, plaice, soles, and flatfish common to the Atlantic and the Mediterranean, the blame should be placed on the dizzying speed of the *Nautilus* through these rich waters.

As for marine mammals, near the opening of the Adriatic I believe I recognized two or three sperm whales of the genus *Physeter* with dorsal fins, a few dolphins of the genus *Globicephala* particular to the Mediterranean with foreheads adorned with small light lines, and a dozen seals with white stomachs and black coats, known as Mediterranean monk seals and which perfectly resemble 3-metre-long Dominicans.

For his part, Conseil thinks he saw a six-foot-wide turtle adorned with three lengthwise ridges. I regret not seeing this reptile, for I thought I recognized the leatherback from the description Conseil gave me—quite a rare species. For my part, I only noticed a few loggerhead turtles with their long carapaces.

As regards the zoophytes, for a few moments I was able to appreciate a beautiful orange *Galeola* which attached itself to the window of the port panel; it formed a long fine filament, spreading into infinite branches and terminating in the finest lace ever spun by the rivals of Arachne.* Unfortunately, I was not able to catch this splendid specimen, and perhaps no other Mediterranean zoophytes would have shown themselves if, on the evening of the 16th, the *Nautilus* had not markedly slowed down. This is what happened.

We were passing between Sicily and Tunisia. In the confined space between Cape Bon and the Strait of Messina, the sea-floor rises very suddenly. A ridge is located there covered in only 17 metres of water, whilst on either side the depth is 170 metres. Accordingly the *Nautilus* had to manoeuvre carefully in order to avoid the submarine barrier.

I showed Conseil this long reef on the map of the Mediterranean.

'With due respect, monsieur,' observed Conseil, 'it is like an isthmus connecting Europe and Africa.'

'Yes, my good fellow,' I replied, 'it blocks the whole of the Strait of Libya, and Smyth's soundings prove that the two continents were formerly connected between Capes Bon and Farina.'*

'I can easily believe it.'

'I will add that a similar barrier exists between Gibraltar and Ceuta, and completely closed the Mediterranean in earlier geological periods.'

'So what if one day a volcanic thrust were to lift the two barriers out of the waves!'

'It is hardly probable, Conseil.'

'But, if monsieur would allow me to finish, if this did happen, it would be quite annoying for M. de Lesseps, working so hard to cut his isthmus!'

'I agree, but I repeat that this phenomenon will not happen. The strength of the underground forces is constantly diminishing. Volcanoes, so numerous in the first days of the world, are gradually dying; their internal heat is reducing, for the temperature of the earth's lower strata is lessening by a perceptible amount each century—and our globe will be the worse for it, since this heat is life.'

'However, the sun . . .'

'The sun is insufficient, Conseil. Can it restore heat to a dead body?'

'I do not know about that.'

'Well, my friend, the earth will one day be a cold corpse. It will become uninhabitable and consequently uninhabited like the moon, which lost its vital heat a long time ago.'

'In how many centuries?' asked Conseil.

'In some hundreds of thousands of years, my good man.'

'Well then, we still have time to finish our voyage, provided, that is, Ned does not meddle with things!'

And Conseil, reassured, returned to his study of the shallows that the *Nautilus* was closely skimming over at moderate speed.

On that rocky and volcanic ground flourished a whole living flora of sponges, holothurians, hyalin Cydippes adorned with reddish tendrils giving off a slight phosphorescence, beroes, popularly known as sea cucumbers, bathing in the shimmerings of the solar spectrum, metre-wide itinerant comatulids whose purple tint reddened the waters, arborescent sea spiders of the greatest beauty, pavonaceous plants with long stalks, a large number of edible sea urchins of various species, and finally green sea anemones with brown discs on greyish trunks which disappeared amongst the olive-coloured hair of their tentacles.

Conseil worked hard at observing the molluscs and the articulates, and although the nomenclature is a little arid, I do not wish to upset the good fellow by omitting his personal observations.

In the branch of molluscs, he cites numerous pectiniform scallops, asses-foot thorny oysters piled up on each other, triangular donaxes, tridentate hyalinae with yellow fins and transparent shells, orange pleurobranchiates, which are eggs with greenish dots or stippling, aplysias sometimes known as sea hares, small dolabriforms, plump Accrata, umbrella shells specific to the Mediterranean, earshells whose shells produced a much-sought-after mother-of-pearl, flammulated scallops, beaked cockles that the Languedocians are said to prefer to oysters, the clam that is so dear to the Marseillais, fat white double clams, some of the kinds of clams so abundant on the coasts of North America and so quickly snapped up in New York, opercular pectens with varied colours, date mussels hiding in their holes and whose peppery taste I greatly appreciated, furrowed heart cockles with bulging sides to their ventricose shells, *cynthiae* bristling with scarlet tubers, *carinariae* with curved points like delicate gondolas, crowned ferules, atlantas with spiral shells, grey tethys with white spots and fringed mantilla, eoliths like little slugs, cavolinids crawling on their backs, *Auriculae* including the forget-me-not *Auricula* in its oval shell, timid angel fish, periwinkles, ianthines, cineraria, *petricola*, Lamellariidae, cabochons, pandoridae, etc.

As for the articulates, Conseil's notes very accurately put them into six classes, of which three belong to the marine world. These are the crustaceans, cirripeds, and annelids.

The crustaceans are further divided into nine orders, of which the first includes the decapods—that is creatures with heads and thoraxes usually welded together, mouth mechanisms composed of several pairs of jaws, and four, five, or six pairs of thoracic and ambulatory limbs. Conseil had followed the method of our master Milne-Edwards, who divides the decapods into three sections: the Brachyura, the Macrura, and the Anomura. The names are somewhat barbaric, but accurate and useful. Amongst the Brachyura, Conseil cites the

Amathia whose foreheads have two large divergent lumps, the scorpion *Inachus* crabs, which for some strange reason symbolized wisdom for the Greeks, amber massenes, amber spinimanes which had probably strayed into this reef since they normally live at great depths, *Xanthidae*, *Pilumnus*, rhombuses, granular *Calappa*—very easy to digest, according to Conseil—toothless *Corystes*, *Ebalia*, cymopolias, woolly dorippes, etc. Amongst the Macrura—subdivided into five families: the armour-plated, the fossorials, the Astacidae, the prawns, and the Ocypodidae—Conseil cites common crayfish, the flesh of the female being very highly valued, scyllarian bears or sea cicadas, riparian decapods, and all sorts of other edible species; but he does not mention the subdivision of the Astacidae containing the lobsters, for the crayfish are the only lobsters found in the Mediterranean. Finally amongst the Anomura, he saw some common drocinas sheltering in some of those abandoned shells they take over, Homolidae with spiny foreheads, hermit crabs, hairy porcelain crabs, and so on.

Here, however, the work of Conseil stopped. There had been no time to conclude the class of shellfish by examining the Stomapoda, the Amphipoda, the homopods, the isopods, the Trilobita, the Branchiopoda, the Ostracoda, and the Entomostraca. Also, to end the study of the marine articulates properly, he should have cited the class of cirropods which contains the cyclops, and the arguluses, as well as the class of annelids that he would automatically have divided into the tubicolous and the dorsibranchiates. But the *Nautilus* had got past the shallow bottom of the Sicilian Channel, and resumed its normal speed in the deeper waters. Hence no more molluscs, no more articulates, no more zoophytes. Just a few large fish passing like shadows.

During the night of 16 to 17 February we entered the second Mediterranean basin, whose greatest depths reach 3,000 metres. Under the thrust of its propeller and sliding down on its inclined planes, the *Nautilus* plunged to the furthest parts of that sea.

There, although lacking in natural wonders, the mass of waters offered my eyes many moving and terrible scenes. We were crossing that part of the Mediterranean which is so rich in wrecks. From the Algerian coast to the shores of Provence, how many ships have been wrecked, how many vessels lost! The Mediterranean is a mere lake compared to the vast liquid plains of the Pacific, but it is a capricious lake with changeable waves, today propitious and caressing for the frail tartan floating between the twin ultramarine of water and sky, tomorrow in a rage, tormented, dislocated by winds, beating the strongest ships with its short waves and so breaking them with hurried blows.

In this swift excursion through the lower strata, how many wrecks I spotted lying on the sea-floor, some already coated by coral, others covered only with a layer of rust; together with anchors, cannons, cannonballs, iron fittings, propeller blades, pieces of machinery, broken cylinders, stoved-in boilers; and finally in midwater, hulls floating suspended, some of them still upright and others upside down.

Some had perished in collisions, others by hitting a granite reef. I saw ships that had sunk straight down, with their masts erect and their sails stiffened by the water. They looked as if anchored in an enormous open roadstead, waiting for the moment to depart. When the *Nautilus* passed amongst them and enveloped them with its electric beams it seemed these ships were going to greet it with their colours and send their registration numbers! But no, nothing but silence and death on the field of such disasters!

I observed that the Mediterranean floor became more crowded with sinister wrecks as the *Nautilus* approached the Strait of Gibraltar. As the coasts of Africa and Europe drew closer, encounters in this narrow space were more frequent. I saw numerous iron carinas, fantastic ruins of steamers, some keeling over, others upright like fierce animals. One of the boats presented a terrifying sight, with its sides open, funnel bent, and only the frames of its paddlewheels remaining, its helm separated from the stern post but still attached by an iron chain, and the rear nameboard eaten away by marine salt! How many lives broken by these shipwrecks! How many victims carried down beneath the waves! Had some sailor on board survived to tell the tale of the terrifying disaster, or did the waves still keep the secret of the accident? I do not know why the thought came to me that this boat lying buried under the sea could be the *Atlas*, which had disappeared with all hands twenty years before,* never to be heard of again! Ah, what a sinister history could be written from the Mediterranean floor, that vast bone cemetery, where so many treasures have been lost, where so many men have found death! Meanwhile the *Nautilus*, fleet and indifferent, was moving through the ruins on full propeller. On 18 February, at about three in the morning, it arrived at the entrance to the Strait of Gibraltar.*

There are two currents here: an upper current, known for a long time, which brings the waters from the ocean into the Mediterranean basin; and a lower counter-current, whose existence has been demonstrated by hypothesis. The sum of the waters of the Mediterranean, constantly increased by the current from the Atlantic and the rivers flowing into it, should raise its level each year, for the rate of evaporation is insufficient to re-establish equilibrium. But nothing of the sort occurs, and so the existence has had to be posited of a lower current pouring the surplus through the Strait of Gibraltar into the Atlantic basin.

True indeed. It was this counter-current that the *Nautilus* was using to sail quickly through the narrow pass. For a moment I was able to glimpse the admirable ruins of the temple of Hercules, sunk, according to Pliny and Avienus,* together with the low island on which it stood, and then a few minutes later we were floating on the waves of the Atlantic.

8

VIGO BAY

THE Atlantic! that vast area of water covering 25 million square miles, 9,000 miles long by 2,700 miles wide on average. An important sea, almost unknown to the ancients except perhaps to the Carthaginians, those Dutchmen of antiquity, who travelled down the west coast of Europe and Africa looking for trade. An ocean whose parallel winding shores form an immense circumference channelling the world's largest rivers: the St Lawrence, the Mississippi, the Amazon, the Plata, the Orinoco, the Niger, the Senegal, the Elbe, the Loire, and the Rhine, bringing in waters from the most civilized countries and the most savage! A magnificent plain, continuously ploughed by ships of all nations, protected by the flags of the whole world, and terminating in those two terrible points so feared by sailors, Cape Horn and the Cape of Good Hope!

The *Nautilus* was slicing the waters with its ram, having covered nearly 10,000 leagues in three-and-a-half months, a distance longer than two lines of longitude. Where would we go next, and what lay in store for us?

Having left the Strait of Gibraltar, the *Nautilus* made for the open sea. As it had surfaced we could once again enjoy our daily promenade on the platform.

I immediately went up, accompanied by Ned Land and Conseil. Cape St Vincent, the south-western point of the Iberian Peninsula, appeared indistinctly 12 miles away. A southerly wind was blowing strongly. The sea was agitated and heaving, and was imparting a strong rolling motion to the *Nautilus*. It was almost impossible to stand up on the platform, continuously slammed by the huge sea. We went down again after drawing a few mouthfuls of air.

I returned to my room. Conseil went to his cabin; but the Canadian, looking rather preoccupied, came with me. Our swift journey through the Mediterranean had not allowed him to execute his plans and he did not hide his disappointment.

Once the door of my room was closed, he sat down and looked at me in silence.

'Ned, my friend,' I said to him, 'I understand how you feel, but there is nothing you could have done. It would have been madness to leave from the *Nautilus* moving as it was.'

Land did not reply. His pursed lips and frowning brow showed the violent obsession of a fixed idea at work in him.

'Look, we don't need to give up yet. We're moving up the coast of Portugal. Not far off are France and Britain where we could easily find refuge. Ah! if the *Nautilus* had sailed south after the Strait of Gibraltar, if it had carried us off into regions where there is no land, I would share your worries too. But we now know that Captain Nemo is not fleeing civilized seas, and I believe that in a few days you will be able to act with some degree of safety.'

Ned stared at me even more fixedly than before, and finally loosened his lips enough to say:

'It's for tonight.'

I stood up quickly. I admit I was not prepared for this. I would have liked to reply to the Canadian, but words failed me.

'We agreed to wait for an opportunity,' continued Ned Land. 'We now have that opportunity: this evening, while we are a few miles off the Spanish coast. The night will be dark with the wind blowing from the open sea. I have your word, Dr Aronnax, and I am counting on you.'

As I still did not utter a word, the Canadian got up, came up to me, and said:

'Tonight at nine o'clock. I have told Conseil. At that time Captain Nemo will be shut in his room, probably asleep. Neither the engineers nor the crewmen will be able to see us. Conseil and I will head for the central staircase. You, Dr Aronnax, will remain in the library a few feet from us, waiting for my signal. The oars, the mast, and the sail are in the dinghy. I've even managed to put in a few supplies. I've got hold of an adjustable spanner to undo the bolts holding the dinghy to the *Nautilus*'s hull. So everything's ready. See you tonight.'

'The sea is quite rough.'

'Admittedly,' replied the Canadian, 'but we have to risk that. Freedom is worth paying for. In any case, it's a tough boat so a few miles with a following wind will not be much of a problem. Who knows if by tomorrow the submarine won't be 100 leagues out to sea? So let's rely on luck, and by ten or eleven o'clock we'll either be on dry land or dead. So in God we trust, and till tonight!'

The Canadian withdrew, leaving me dumbfounded. I had imagined that, given the right circumstances, I would have time to think and discuss the situation. My opinionated companion did not allow me this. But in any case what could I have said to him? Ned Land was 100 per cent right. It was a reasonable chance, and he was making the most of it. Could I now go back on my word and take responsibility for risking my companions' futures for completely selfish reasons? Might Captain Nemo not carry us off tomorrow into the open seas far from any land?

At this point, a loud hissing sound told me that the tanks were being filled; and the *Nautilus* dived under the waves of the Atlantic.

I remained in my room. I wished to avoid the captain so that he could not see the emotion overwhelming me. So it was a sad day I spent, between my wish to regain freedom and my regret at saying goodbye to the marvellous *Nautilus* and leaving my underwater studies unfinished! To quit this ocean, 'my Atlantic' as I liked to call it, without observing her every stratum and without uncovering her secrets, as the Indian and Pacific oceans had been revealed to me! My novel was falling from my hand half-way through,* my dream was interrupted at the vital moment! What terrible hours I spent, now seeing myself safe on land with my companions, now wishing, despite my rational side, that some unforeseen circumstance would prevent Ned's plans from unfolding.

Twice I went into the salon. I wanted to consult the compass. I wanted to see whether or not the *Nautilus* was really taking us towards the coast. The *Nautilus* was still in Portuguese waters. It was heading northwards following the coastline.

So I had to come to terms with my situation and get ready for an escape. My luggage was not heavy. My notes, nothing else.

As for Captain Nemo, I wondered what he would think of our escape, what anxiety, what anguish it might cause him, and what he would do if our plans got out or if we did not succeed! Doubtless I had no reason to complain. Indeed, never had hospitality been more open than his. But I could not be accused of ingratitude for leaving him. No oath tied us to him: he counted only on the force of circumstances, and not on our word, to bind us to his company for ever. Moreover, all our attempts were justified because of his freely admitted claim to keep us prisoner on board his ship in perpetuity.*

I hadn't seen the captain since our visit to Santorini Island. Would chance make me meet him before our departure? I wanted and feared it at one and the same time. I listened out for him pacing in the room next to mine. No sound reached my ears. His bedroom was probably empty.

I wondered if this strange character was even still on board. Since that night when the dinghy had left the *Nautilus* on a mysterious errand, my ideas about him had changed a little. I believed that whatever Captain Nemo said, he must maintain relations of some sort with dry land. Did he ever leave the *Nautilus*? Entire weeks had often gone by without my seeing him at all. What did he do during this time? Whilst I had believed him to be in the grip of spells of misanthropy, could he not have been far away carrying out some secret mission of which I had no inkling?

All these ideas and a thousand others assailed me at the same time. Room for conjecture had to be infinite in the strange situation where we found ourselves. I felt an unbearable malaise. That day of waiting seemed to go on for ever. The hours chimed too slowly for my impatience.

Dinner was served in my room as usual. I ate badly as I was so preoccupied. I left the table at seven o'clock. A hundred and twenty minutes—I was counting them—still stretched out before I was to meet Land. My agitation grew twice as great. My pulse started throbbing violently. I was unable to stay in one place. I paced up and down, hoping to calm my troubled mind by moving around. The idea of perishing in our bold enterprise was the least of my worries; my heart beat much more wildly at the thought of our plan being discovered before we had left the *Nautilus*, of being taken to an angry Captain Nemo or, worse, one saddened by my abandonment.

I wished to see the salon one last time. I went along the gangway to that museum where I had spent so many agreeable and useful hours. I looked at all the riches, all the treasures, as if on the eve of an eternal exile, a departure without any hope of return. I was going to renounce for ever the wonders of nature and masterpieces of art amongst which I had been living for so long. I would have liked to examine the waters of the Atlantic through the windows of the salon; but the panels were tightly closed and a cloak of metal separated me from that still-unfamiliar ocean.

While working my way round the salon, I arrived at the door in the triangular section which opened on to the captain's bedroom. To my great surprise, it was slightly ajar. I involuntarily stepped back. If Captain Nemo was in his room, he might see me. Hearing no sound, however, I went closer. The room was empty. I pushed the door. I stepped inside. The same severe atmosphere, monk-like.

My attention was caught by a few etchings on the walls that I had not noticed on my first visit. They were portraits of those great men of history whose lives were entirely devoted to a grandiose human idea: Kosciusko, the hero who fell with the cry *Finis Poloniae*, Botsaris, the Leonidas of modern Greece, O'Connell, the defender of Ireland, Washington, the founder of the American Union, Manin, the Italian patriot, Lincoln, who fell shot by a supporter of slavery, and finally John Brown,* that martyr to the freeing of the black race, hanging from his gallows, as so terribly depicted by Victor Hugo.

What link existed between these heroic souls and the soul of Captain Nemo? Could I finally solve the mystery of his existence from this collection of portraits? Was he a champion of downtrodden peoples, a liberator of enslaved races? Had he taken part in the recent political and social upheavals that had marked the century? Had he been one of the heroes of that terrible American Civil War, that frightful but for ever glorious battle . . .?

Suddenly the clock struck eight. The first blow of the hammer tore me from my dreams. I trembled as if an invisible eye had penetrated my innermost thoughts, and rushed out of the room.

There my eyes stopped at the compass. We were still heading north.

The logline indicated a moderate speed, the pressure-gauge a depth of about 60 feet. Circumstances were favouring the Canadian's plans.

I returned to my room. I dressed warmly in sea-boots, sea-otter cap, and byssus jacket lined with sealskin. I was ready. I waited. Only the shuddering vibrations of the propeller broke the deep silence reigning on board. I listened out, ears wide open. Would some ruckus suddenly tell me that Ned Land had been caught in his preparations for escape? A deadly fear took hold of me. I tried in vain to calm my nerves.

At a few minutes to nine, I put my ear against the captain's door. No sound. I left my room and went back to the salon: it was deserted and plunged into semi-darkness.

I opened the door communicating with the library. The same lack of light, the same solitude. I went and stood near the door opening on to the well of the central staircase. I waited for Ned's signal.

The vibrations of the propeller decreased noticeably, and then stopped altogether. Why the change in the *Nautilus*'s speed? Whether this halt helped or hindered Ned Land's plans, I could not say.

The silence was now broken only by the beating of my heart.

Suddenly I felt a bump. I realized that the *Nautilus* had come to rest on the ocean floor. My nervousness grew much worse. There was still no sign of the Canadian's signal. I wanted to go and find Land and urge him to put off his attempt. I was convinced there had been some change in the conditions of our navigation.

At this point, the door of the main salon opened, and Captain Nemo appeared. He noticed me, and without further preamble:

'Ah, monsieur,' he said in a pleasant tone, 'I was looking for you. Do you know your history of Spain?'

Even if I had known the history of my own country off by heart, I would not have been able to quote a single detail of it under the circumstances, my mind troubled and my head empty.

'Well?' said Captain Nemo. 'Did you hear my question? Do you know the history of Spain?'

'Not at all well,' I replied.

'That's scientists for you, they don't know their history. Do sit down', he added, 'and I will relate a strange historical episode.'

The captain stretched out on a sofa and, mechanically, I took a place in the shadows near him.

'Monsieur,' he said to me, 'please listen carefully. This story will appeal to you as it answers a question that you have doubtless never been able to resolve.'

'I am listening, captain,' I said, not knowing quite where my interlocutor was heading, and wondering whether this incident had any connection with our ideas of escape.

'If you will permit,' said Captain Nemo, 'we will go back to 1702. You surely know that at that period your king Louis XIV, believing that a mere gesture from a potentate could make the Pyrenees disappear into the ground, had imposed his grandson, the Duke of Anjou,* on the Spanish throne. This prince, who reigned more or less badly under the name of Philip V, had to deal with strong external opposition.

'In fact, the previous year the royal houses of Holland, Austria, and England had signed a treaty of alliance at the Hague with the aim of removing the crown of Spain from Philip V and placing it on the head of an archduke, whom these countries prematurely called Charles III.

'Spain was obliged to resist this coalition. But she had practically no soldiers or sailors. However, she had plenty of money provided that her galleons, loaded with gold and silver from America, could enter her ports. Now in late 1702, Spain was expecting a rich convoy that France was escorting with a fleet of twenty-three vessels commanded by Admiral de Château-Renaud,* for the navies of the coalition were patrolling the Atlantic together.

'The convoy was to head for Cadiz, but the admiral learned that the English fleet was cruising nearby, and resolved to head for a French port instead.

'The Spanish captains of the convoy protested at the decision. They wanted to be accompanied to a Spanish port, and if it could not be Cadiz, then it had to be Vigo Bay on the north-west coast of Spain, not blockaded at the time.

'Admiral de Chateau-Renaud was weak enough to accept these demands, and the galleons entered Vigo Bay.

'Unfortunately this bay formed an open roadstead which could not be defended. It was therefore necessary to unload the galleons quickly before the coalition fleet arrived: there would have been enough time for the disembarkation, if an unhappy question of rivalry had not suddenly arisen.

'Can you see how the events fit together?' Captain Nemo asked me.

'Perfectly,' I said, still not knowing the reason this history lesson was being given.

'I'll continue then. This is what happened. The merchants of Cadiz had the right to receive all merchandise coming from the New World. Unloading the gold bars from the galleons in Vigo port would have gone against their rights. They therefore complained to Madrid, and persuaded the weak Philip V that the convoy should remain sequestered in the roadstead of Vigo without unloading, until the enemy fleets had gone away again.

'Now while this decision was being taken, the English vessels arrived in Vigo Bay,* on 22 October 1702. Although outnumbered, Admiral de Chateau-Renaud fought courageously. But when he saw that the convoy's riches were going to fall into the enemy's hands, he burned and scuppered the galleons and so sank them with their enormous treasure.'

Captain Nemo had stopped. I admit that I still could not see how his story concerned me.

'Well?' I asked.

'Well, Dr Aronnax, we are in Vigo Bay, and you are now in a position to penetrate its mysteries.'

The captain got up and asked me to follow him. I had had time to recover and did as he requested. The salon was dark, but the water sparkled through the clear windows. I looked.

Around the *Nautilus*, for a distance of half a mile, the waters appeared impregnated with electric light. The sandy bottom was clear and clean. Some of the crewmen in diving suits were busy salvaging half-rotten barrels and gaping trunks in the midst of still-blackened wrecks. From these trunks and barrels escaped gold and silver bars, as well as cascades of pieces-of-eight and jewellery. The sand was strewn with them. Then, laden with their precious booty, the men were coming back to the *Nautilus*, depositing their burdens, and going back to continue their inexhaustible harvest of gold and silver.

I understood. This was the scene of the battle of 22 October 1702. The galleons loaded for the Spanish government had sunk at this very spot. Captain Nemo came here whenever he needed to load up with the millions with which he ballasted his *Nautilus*. It was for him, and him alone, that America had given up its precious metals. He was the direct and only inheritor of the treasures taken from the Incas and others defeated by Hernando Cortez!*

'Did you know, monsieur,' he asked, smiling, 'that the sea contained so many riches?'

'I knew that there are estimated to be 2 million tons of silver held in suspension in the water.'

'Doubtless, but the cost of extracting them would be greater than the profit. Here, in contrast, all I have to do is pick up what others have lost, not only in Vigo Bay but also at a thousand other ship-wrecks noted on my submarine charts. Do you understand now why I am a multimillionaire?'

'Yes indeed, captain. Allow me, however, to tell you that in putting Vigo Bay to use, you are merely anticipating the work of a rival company.'*

'Which one?'

'A company which has received the right from the Spanish govern-ment to search for sunken galleons. The shareholders are attracted by a potentially enormous profit, for the value of these riches has been estimated to be five hundred million francs.'

'Five hundred million!' responded Captain Nemo. 'There used to be, but not any more.'

'So I gather. Accordingly, informing the shareholders would be a kind gesture. But who knows how the news would be received? What gamblers usually regret the most is losing not their money but their mad hopes. In the end, I pity them less than the thousands of wretches who could have benefited from so many riches if properly distributed, whilst now they will not be of any use to them at all!'

No sooner had I formulated this regret, than I felt it must have hurt Captain Nemo.

'Not be of any use!' he replied animatedly. 'What makes you believe, monsieur, that these riches must be considered wasted if I collect them? Do you think that it is for my own benefit that I take the trouble to gather such treasures? Who told you that I do not put them to good use? Do you think I am unaware there are suffering beings and oppressed races on this planet, wretches to be helped and victims to be avenged? Don't you understand . . .?'

Captain Nemo stopped with these last words, perhaps regretting hav-ing said too much. But I *had* understood. Whatever the reasons that had made him seek independence under the seas, he had above all remained a human being! He still felt the sufferings of humanity, and his great generosity extended to subjugated peoples as well as individuals!

I realized then for whom Captain Nemo's millions were destined, when the *Nautilus* was sailing through the waters of rebellious Crete!

9

A LOST WORLD

THE following morning, 19 February, the Canadian came into my room. I was expecting his visit. He looked very disappointed.

'Well, monsieur?' he said to me.

'Well, Ned, luck was against us yesterday.'

'Yes, that damned captain had to stop at the exact moment we were going to escape from his boat!'

'Yes, Ned, he was dealing with his banker.'

'His banker!'

'Or rather his bank. By which I mean this ocean where his riches are safer than in the storerooms of a state.'

I then recounted the incidents of the day before, in the secret hope of bringing Ned round to the idea of not leaving the captain; but the only effect of my tale was that Ned expressed strong regrets at being unable to visit the site of the Battle of Vigo Bay.

'But in fact', he said, 'it's not over yet. It's just a harpoon-throw that went wide! We'll win next time, even tonight if need be . . .'

'In what direction is the *Nautilus* heading?'

'No idea,' Ned replied.

'Well, at noon we will see the position being taken.'

The Canadian went to rejoin Conseil. Once dressed, I made for the salon. The compass was not reassuring. The *Nautilus* was heading south-south-west. We were leaving Europe behind.

I waited impatiently for our position to be marked on the map. At about half past eleven the tanks emptied and the vessel surfaced. I rushed on to the platform. Ned was already there.

No land in sight. Nothing but the immense sea. Just a few sails on the horizon, doubtless some of those which seek favourable winds as far out as Cape Sao Roque to be able to round the Cape of Good Hope. The sky was overcast. A squall was coming on.

In a rage, Ned tried to pierce the misty horizon. He still hoped that behind all the murk stretched the landfall he so eagerly sought.

At noon the sun came out for a moment. The first officer profited from the bright spell to shoot the sun. Then, with the sea getting stormier, we went below again and the hatch was closed once more.

An hour later I consulted the map and saw that the position of the

Nautilus was indicated as 33° 22′ N, 16° 17′ W, that is 150 leagues from the nearest coast.* There was no way of even dreaming of an escape and I leave to the reader's imagination how angry the Canadian was when I told him our situation.

For my part, I was not too disappointed. It felt as though a weight bearing down on me had lifted, and I was able to resume my daily studies with relative calm.

At about eleven in the evening I received a totally unexpected visit from Captain Nemo. With a great deal of grace, he asked me if I felt tired from staying up the night before. I replied in the negative.

'Then, Dr Aronnax, may I suggest a strange excursion?'

'Pray continue, captain.'

'You have visited the submarine depths only in the daytime and in sunlight. Might it interest you to visit them on a dark night?'

'Yes indeed.'

'The excursion will be tiring, I warn you. We will need to march for a long time and climb a mountain. And the paths are not very well looked after.'

'What you say only increases my curiosity. I am ready when you are.'

'Please come, monsieur; we will put on our diving suits.'

When I got to the changing-room, I saw that neither my companions nor any of the crewmen were going to accompany us. Captain Nemo had not even mentioned the possibility of taking Ned or Conseil.

We had soon put on our equipment. On our backs were tanks filled with plenty of air, but the electric lamps had not been prepared. I mentioned this to the captain.

'They would not be of any use to us,' he replied.

I thought I had misheard but could not repeat my question, for his head had already disappeared into its metallic container. I finished my preparations. I felt a reinforced stave being placed in my hand, and a few minutes later, after the usual procedure, we were walking on the floor of the Atlantic at a depth of 300 metres.

It was nearly twelve. The waters were very dark, but Captain Nemo pointed out a distant reddish point like a protracted gleam, glowing about two miles from the *Nautilus*. What this fire was, what materials fed it, how and why it was maintained in the liquid element, I could not have said. In any case it lit our path, albeit dimly; I soon got used to the peculiar gloom, and understood why the Ruhmkorff device would not have helped in these conditions.

Captain Nemo and I walked close together, heading directly for the light he had indicated. The smooth ground climbed imperceptibly. We were taking long strides, helping ourselves along with our sticks; but progress was slow, for our feet sank into the mud mixed with seaweed and dotted with flat stones.

While walking, I heard a sort of sizzling sound above my head. The noise sometimes got much louder and became a continuous crackling. I soon understood the reason. It was rain, pattering violently down on the surface. Instinctively the thought came to me that I was going to get wet! Being rained on underwater: I couldn't help laughing at the strange idea! But to tell the truth, in the thick clothing of the diving suit I no longer had any sensation of being underwater, merely of being in an atmosphere slightly denser than on land.

After half an hour the ground became rocky. Jellyfish, microscopic crustaceans, and pennatulaceous creatures lit it up slightly with their phosphorescent gleams. I caught glimpses of piles of stones, sometimes covered by millions of zoophytes and thickets of seaweed. My feet often slid on the sticky carpet of kelp, and without my solid stave I would have fallen down more than once. Turning round, I could see the whitish searchlight of the *Nautilus* growing paler in the distance.

The stone piles I have just mentioned were laid out on the ocean floor with a certain regularity that I could not explain. I noticed gigantic furrows vanishing into the distant darkness and could not begin to guess how long they were. Other peculiarities also appeared which I could not understand. It seemed to me that my lead soles were heavily crushing a bed of bones which cracked with dry sounds. What was this vast plain I was crossing? I would have liked to ask the captain, but I still could not understand the sign language he used to communicate with his companions while on their submarine excursions.

Meanwhile the reddish glow which had been guiding us grew and soon inflamed the whole horizon. The existence underwater of this light intrigued me tremendously. Was I witnessing some outflow of electricity? Was I heading for some natural phenomenon that was still unknown to land scientists? Or even—for the thought did cross my mind—did man perhaps have a part in this blaze? Was some hand fanning the fire? Would I meet companions or friends of Captain Nemo in these deep strata, living as strange an existence as his, to whom he was paying a visit? Would I find a whole colony of exiles weary of the miseries of the earth, who had sought independence on the bottom of the ocean—and found it? All these crazy, impossible ideas haunted me. In this frame of mind, overstimulated by the new wonders from the bottom of the sea constantly passing before my eyes, I would not have been surprised to encounter one of those cities in the sea that Captain Nemo had dreamed of!

Our path grew brighter and brighter. A whitening glow radiated from the summit of a mountain of about 800 feet. But it was only a secondary image produced in the prism of those strata of water. The source of this inexplicable light, the focus, was located on the far side of the mountain.

Captain Nemo moved forward without hesitation through the stony mazes furrowing the bed of the Atlantic. He knew this dark route. Doubtless he had often walked it, and could not get lost. I followed him with perfect confidence. He appeared to me as some ocean spirit. While he was walking in front, I admired his tall build silhouetted in black against the luminous backdrop of the horizon.

It was now one in the morning. We had arrived at the first slopes of the mountain. But to start climbing them, we had to venture on to difficult paths leading through a huge thicket.

Yes, a thicket of dead trees, without leaves and without sap, trees mineralized by the water, dominated here and there by gigantic pines. It was like a seam of coal still standing, holding on to the sunken soil with its roots. Its branches, like fine cut-outs of black paper, stood out clearly against the ceiling of the waters. The reader should imagine a Hartz forest clinging to the sides of the mountain, but a submerged forest. The paths were blocked by seaweed and wracks, amongst which teemed a whole world of crustaceans. I went on climbing the rocks, stepping over fallen trunks, breaking the sea creepers which swung from tree to tree, frightening away the fish which flew from branch to branch. Carried away, I no longer felt tired. I followed my guide, who maintained his pace.

What a sight! How can I depict it! How can I paint the image of the woods and rocks in the liquid milieu, their dark and savage overhangs, their surfaces coloured by the red tones of this light increased by the refractive capacity of the water? We clambered over boulders which collapsed in great masses, avalanching with heavy groans. To the right and left gaped dark tunnels whose ends could not be made out.

Huge clearings looked as though they had been made by man, and I wondered if some submarine inhabitant were not suddenly going to appear.

But Captain Nemo kept on climbing. I did not want to lose touch and so boldly followed him.* My stick proved very useful. Stumbling would have been dangerous on these narrow paths cut into the sides of chasms; but I walked with a firm tread and without the intoxication of vertigo. Sometimes I jumped over a crevasse of a depth to make me recoil on land glaciers; sometimes I ventured on to wobbling tree-trunks thrown across one abyss after another, not looking under my feet, my eyes simply admiring the savage sights all round. Monumental rocks appeared, leaning on their irregularly cut bases, seeming to defy the laws of equilibrium. Between their stony knees, trees sprouted like jets under formidable pressure, and held up the same rocks that gave them root. Natural towers and broad rock faces, cut sheer like fortified walls, leaned at an angle that the laws of gravity would not have allowed on dry land.

I could certainly feel the difference made by the great density of the water when I scaled the inclines of impracticable slopes, despite my heavy clothing, copper head, and metal soles, when I climbed with the agility of a wild goat or chamois!

As I speak of this underwater expedition, I fully realize how unbelievable it all sounds! I am the recorder of things which may sound impossible but which are real and incontestable. I did not dream them. I felt and I saw them.

Two hours after leaving the *Nautilus* we crossed the tree-line; the mountain peak towered 100 feet above our heads, its dazzling radiation projecting a shadow on the slope below. A few petrified shrubs ran here and there in grimacing zigzags. Fish rose as one before our feet like birds surprised in tall grass. The rocky massif was hollowed out with impenetrable burrows, deep caverns, and pits at the bottom of which I could hear frightening things moving about. I blanched when I spotted an enormous antenna blocking my route, or terrifying claws clattering shut in the darkness of a cavity! Thousands of luminous points shone in the darkness. They were the eyes of huge crustaceans lurking in their dens, of gigantic lobsters standing to attention like halberdiers and waving their legs with metallic clanks, of titanic crabs set like cannon on their mounts, and of awe-inspiring squid* twisting their tentacles into a living brush of snakes.

What was this outrageous world where I still felt such an outsider? These articulates for whom the rocks seemed like a second carapace— to which order did they belong? Where had nature developed the secret of their brutish life, and for how many centuries had they been living in these furthermost recesses of the ocean?

But I could not stop. Captain Nemo, familiar with these terrifying animals, was no longer paying attention to them. We had arrived at a first plateau, where further surprises awaited me. Here picturesque ruins stood up, bearing the marks of man's hand and not those of the Creator.* They were vast accumulations, massed piles of stones where one could make out the vague forms of castles and temples, carpeted with a world of flowering zoophytes and over which, instead of ivy, seaweed and algae formed a thick vegetable cloak.

But what was this land sunk by cataclysms? Who had laid out these rocks and stones like the dolmens of prehistoric times? Where was I—to what place had Captain Nemo chosen to bring me?

I would have liked to ask him. Not able to, I stopped him. I seized hold of his arm. But he shook his head and pointed to the last summit of the mountain, seeming to say to me:

'Come on! Further! Come with me!'*

I followed him in a last surge, and a few minutes later had reached the summit, about ten metres above the rest of the rocky massif.

I looked in the direction we had just come from. The mountain rose only about 700 or 800 feet above the plain; but on the other side there was twice this drop to the bottom of the Atlantic. My eyes wandered into the distance, encompassing a vast space dazzlingly lit by the burning light. The mountain was a volcano. Fifty feet below the peak, in a rain of stones and volcanic slag, a large crater was vomiting torrents of lava, which spread out in a cascade of fire through the water. Like an enormous torch, the volcano lit up the plain below to the furthest points of the horizon.

I have said that the submarine crater was throwing out lava, not flames. Flames need oxygen from the air, and cannot be produced underwater; but flows of lava, which already contain their own incandescence, can be heated to white-hot, acting successfully against the liquid element and vaporizing it on contact. Quick-flowing currents carried away all the resulting half-dissolved gases as the lava torrents slid to the bottom of the mountain, like the ejecta of Vesuvius in another Torre del Greco.*

Right there in front of my eyes—ruined, broken, collapsed—appeared a city destroyed, its roofs fallen, its temples flattened, its arches broken, its columns lying on the ground, but with the solid proportions from a type of Tuscan architecture still discernible. Further on lay a few remains of a gigantic aqueduct; here, the silted bulge of an acropolis, with the floating forms of a Parthenon; there a few traces of a quayside, as if some antique port had once sheltered the merchant vessels and war triremes on the shores of a long-lost ocean; further still, long lines of crumbling walls and broad deserted streets: a whole Pompeii sunk beneath the waters,* that Captain Nemo was bringing back to life before my very eyes!

Where was I? Where? I wanted to know at any cost, I wanted to speak, I wanted to tear off the copper sphere imprisoning my head.

But Captain Nemo came close and stopped me with a sign. Then, picking up a chalky piece of stone, he approached a rock of black basalt and wrote a single word:

ATLANTIS

What a flash crossed my mind! Atlantis, that ancient Meropis of Theopompus, the Atlantis of Plato, the continent denied by Origen, Porphyry, Iamblichus, d'Anville, Malte-Brun, and Humboldt, who all classified its disappearance as a legendary tale, but accepted by Posidonius, Pliny, Ammianus Marcellinus, Tertullian, Engel, Scherer, Tournefort, Buffon, and d'Avezac;* it was there in front of my eyes, still bearing the irrefutable signs of the catastrophe that had struck it! So this was the sunken region that had existed outside Europe, Asia, and Libya and beyond the pillars of Hercules, the land of the powerful Atlanteans* against whom ancient Greece had fought its first wars!

The historian who recorded the main events of those heroic times was Plato himself. His dialogues of *Timaeus* and *Critias* were, so to speak, dictated under the inspiration of Solon, poet and legislator.*

One day, Solon was talking with a few wise old men from Sais, a town already 800 years old,* as shown by the annals engraved on the sacred walls of its temples. One of these old men recounted the story of another town a thousand years more ancient. This first Athenian city, nine hundred centuries old, had been invaded and partly destroyed by the Atlanteans. The Atlanteans, he said, occupied an immense continent greater than Africa and Asia combined and covering an area between the twelfth and the fortieth degrees north. Their domination stretched as far as Egypt. They wished to extend it even to Greece, but had had to retreat before the indomitable resistance of the Hellenes. The centuries went by. A cataclysm struck in the shape of floods and earthquakes. A night and a day were sufficient to destroy Atlantis, whose highest summits still emerge at Madeira, the Azores, the Canary Islands, and the Cape Verde Islands.

These were the historic memories that Captain Nemo's inscription brought to life in my mind. Led by the strangest of destinies, I was treading one of the mountains of that continent, my hands were touching ruins hundreds of thousands of years old, contemporary with the early geological periods! I was walking on the same spot where the coevals of the first man had walked! I was crushing under my heavy soles skeletons of animals from those fabulous times, which the now mineralized trees formerly covered with their shade!

Oh, why did I not have enough time? I longed to climb down the steep slopes of this mountain, cover every point of this immense continent which had doubtless connected Africa and America, and visit the great cities from before the Flood. There in front of my eyes, perhaps, stretched Machimos the warlike and Eusebia the holy,* whose gigantic inhabitants lived entire centuries and were strong enough to pile up these blocks which still resisted the movements of the water. One day, perhaps, some eruptive phenomenon would bring these sunken ruins back up to the surface! Submarine volcanoes have often been recorded in this portion of the ocean, and ships have frequently felt extraordinary earthquakes while passing over the tormented deeps. Some vessels have registered dull sounds signalling turmoil between the elements in the deep; others have gathered volcanic cinders sent up from the sea. All this ground, as far as the equator, is still worked by plutonic forces. And who knows if in some far-off period, the summits of fire-breathing mountains will not one day be built up by the volcanic ejecta and successive strata of lava, and appear at the surface of the Atlantic!

While I was dreaming in this way, wishing to engrave in my memory every detail of this grandiose landscape, Captain Nemo, leaning on a mossy stele, remained motionless as if turned to stone in a silent ecstasy. Was he dreaming of the lost generations, was he asking them the secret of human destiny? Was it here that this strange being came to commune with history, to relive ancient life—he who wanted nothing to do with modern times? What I would have given then to know his thoughts, to share them, to understand them!

We remained at this place for an entire hour, contemplating the vast plain in the bright light from the lava which sometimes took on a surprising intensity. At times the interior boiling sent quick shivers through the crust of the mountain. Deep sounds, transmitted clearly in the liquid environment, reverberated with majestic amplitude.

The moon suddenly appeared for a moment through the mass of waters, sending a few pale rays down to the sunken continent. It was only a gleam, but produced an indescribable effect. The captain got up, looked on the huge plain one last time, then signalled to me to follow him.

We quickly descended the mountain. Once past the mineral forest, I saw the *Nautilus*'s searchlight shining like a star. The captain marched straight ahead; and we were back on board by the time the first tints of dawn came and whitened the surface of the ocean.

10

UNDERWATER COALMINES

THE next day, 20 February, I woke up very late. The fatigue of the night had extended my sleep until eleven o'clock. I got up quickly. I was keen to know what direction the *Nautilus* was heading in. The instruments showed me that it was still sailing southwards at a speed of 20 knots and a depth of 100 metres.

Conseil came in. I recounted our nocturnal excursion to him; since the panels were open, he could still glimpse part of the submerged continent.

The *Nautilus* was skimming only ten metres from the floor of the Atlantean plain. It was flying like a balloon carried over the terrestrial prairies by the wind; but it would be more truthful to say that being in the salon was just like being in the compartment of an express train. The foreground before our eyes was made up of rocks cut into fantastic shapes and forests of trees that had changed from vegetable to animal, their motionless silhouettes grimacing under the waves. We saw masses of stones covered with carpets of axidias and anemones and bristling with long vertical hydrophytes, followed by blocks of strangely twisted lava bearing witness to the fury of the plutonic eruptions.

While these bizarre objects shone in our electric light, I narrated the history of the Atlantean inhabitants to Conseil, which, in a purely imaginary vein, inspired Bailly* to write so many charming pages. I told him about the wars of those heroic peoples. I discussed the question of Atlantis from a believer's point of view. But Conseil seemed distracted, and hardly listened to me; his indifference concerning historical questions was soon explained.

Numbers of fish were drawing his eyes; when the fish passed, Conseil was carried off into the depths of classification, and left the real world. This being the case, my only choice was to follow him and to pursue again our ichthyological studies.

In fact, the fish of the Atlantic were not much different from those we had observed until now. There were rays of gigantic dimensions, five metres long and with great muscular power that allows them to fly over the waves, plus sharks of various species. These included: a 15-foot glaucous shark with sharp triangular teeth whose transparency made it nearly invisible in the water, some brown sagrees, and some spine sharks shaped like prisms and reinforced with tubercular skin; as well as some sturgeons similar to their congeners in the Mediterranean and yellowish-brown 1½-foot pipefish with small grey fins but without teeth or tongues, swimming past like thin, lithe snakes.

Amongst the osseous fish, Conseil noted some blackish *Makairae*, 3 metres long and with a piercing sword in their upper jaws, some brightly coloured stingfish, known in Aristotle's time as sea dragons and very dangerous to touch because of the stings in their dorsals, then some dolphinfish with brown backs striped with blue lines framed in golden edging, some lovely sea bream, some moonfish, like discs with azure reflections which when illuminated by the sunlight above seemed to form silver patches, and finally some 8-metre xiphoid swordfish moving in packs and equipped with yellowish fins shaped like scythes and six-foot-long scimitars: these were intrepid animals, but herbivore rather than piscivore and, like well-trained husbands, obeyed the slightest signal from their females.

But while observing the diverse specimens of the marine fauna, I continued to examine the wide plains of Atlantis. Sometimes capricious changes in the ground forced the *Nautilus* to slow down, and it slid with the skill of a cetacean through the narrow bottlenecks of the hills. If the labyrinth became inextricable, then the machine would rise like a balloon, go over the obstacle, and continue its swift progress a few metres above the seabed. A memorable and engrossing journey recalling the manoeuvres of an aerostatic flight, with the difference being that the *Nautilus* entirely obeyed its pilot's hand.

At about four in the afternoon the terrain, generally composed of thick mud mixed with mineralized branches, began to change: it became rockier and seemed strewn with conglomerates and basaltic tuffs, with a few sprinklings of lava and sulphurous obsidian. I thought that a mountain region would soon interrupt the broad plains and, indeed, during some of the *Nautilus*'s manoeuvres, I caught a glimpse of the southern horizon blocked by a high wall apparently closing the way out. Its top part was clearly above water level. This had to be a large landmass or at the very least an island, perhaps one of the islands of the Canaries or Cape Verde. Since the position had not been taken—on purpose perhaps—I did not know where we were.* But in any case such a wall seemed to mark the end of Atlantis, of which we had actually only covered a tiny part.

Night did not interrupt my observations. I remained alone, Conseil having gone back to his cabin. The *Nautilus* slowed down and cruised over the confused shapes on the sea-floor, sometimes pushing down past them as if it wished to land there, sometimes capriciously surfacing. I caught glimpses then of a few bright constellations through the crystal of the waters, and particularly five or six stars which trail behind Orion's tail.

I would have stayed at my glass for a long time yet, admiring the beauties of the sea and the sky, but the panels suddenly closed. At this moment the *Nautilus* had just arrived at the high vertical wall. How it would manoeuvre I could not guess. I went back to my room. The *Nautilus* was no longer moving. I fell asleep with the firm intention of waking up after a few hours.

But the following day it was eight o'clock before I returned to the living-room. I looked at the pressure-gauge. It told me that the *Nautilus* was afloat on the surface. I could also hear footsteps on the platform. But there was no rolling to indicate the waves.

I headed up to the hatch. It was open. But instead of the daylight I expected, I found myself in total darkness. Where were we? Had I made a mistake? Was it still night? No, not a star shone, and the night is never of such absolute blackness!

I did not know what to think, when a voice said:

'Is that you, Dr Aronnax?'

'Ah! Captain Nemo,' I replied; 'where are we?'

'Underground, monsieur.'

'Underground! And the *Nautilus* is still afloat?'

'It is still afloat.'

'But I don't understand?'

'Wait a moment. Our searchlight is going to be switched on, and if you like clear situations, you'll be pleased.'

I stepped on to the platform and waited. The darkness was so complete that I could not see Captain Nemo at all. However, looking at the zenith exactly over my head, I thought I could detect an indeterminate gleam, like faint daylight through a circular aperture. But the searchlight suddenly came on, and its brilliance washed away the vague light.

For a moment my eyes were blinded by the dazzling electric jet, but then I looked again. The *Nautilus* was stationary. It was floating beside a shore converted to a quayside. The sea bearing it formed a lake imprisoned in a circle of walls measuring two miles in diameter, or about six miles right round. The water level—as indicated by the pressure-gauge—had to be the same as the outside level, for there necessarily existed some means of communication between the lake and the ocean. The high walls were inclined at their bases, but then converged to form a vault like an immense upside-down funnel 500 or 600 metres high. At the summit was the circular orifice where I had detected the pale gleam, evidently coming from the sun.

Before examining the internal shape of the enormous cavern more attentively, and deciding if it was the work of nature or man, I went straight up to Captain Nemo.

'Where are we?' I said.

'In the very centre of an extinct volcano, a volcano invaded by the sea following some convulsion of the earth. While you were sleeping the *Nautilus* entered this lagoon via a natural channel ten metres below the surface of the ocean. This is its home port, its safe haven: convenient, secret, and sheltered from the wind in every direction! Find me a harbour on the coasts of your landmasses or islands which is as good as this refuge, guaranteed to be safe from the fury of hurricanes!'

'You're certainly safe here, Captain Nemo. Who could ever reach you at the centre of a volcano? But didn't I notice an opening at the top?'

'Yes, the crater; formerly filled with lava, steam, and flames, it now gives passage to this invigorating air we are breathing.'

'So what is this volcanic mountain then?'

'It forms one of the many small islands dotting the sea. A mere obstacle for other ships, but for us an enormous cavern. Chance led me to discover it, and so served me well.'*

'But couldn't someone enter the mouth of the crater?'

'Not any more than I could climb up there. For about 100 feet the internal slopes of this mountain are scalable but above that the walls overhang, and are no longer climbable.'

'I can see, captain, that nature serves you everywhere and on all occasions. You are safe and sound on this lake, and nobody but you can visit its waters. But what is the point of this refuge? The *Nautilus* does not need a port.'

'No, doctor, but it does need electricity to move, batteries to produce its electricity, sodium to feed its batteries, coal to make its sodium, and mines to furnish its coal. And just here, the sea covers entire forests swallowed up in earlier geological times: now mineralized and turned into coal, this seam I own is inexhaustible.'

'So your men work as miners, captain?'

'Precisely. The mine extends under the waves like those of Newcastle.* Dressed in their diving suits, pick and pickaxe in hand, my men descend here to extract the coal, with the result that I do not require any from the mines on land. When I burn it to manufacture sodium, the smoke escaping from the crater gives the mountain the appearance of an active volcano.'

'And will we see your companions at work?'

'No, at least not this time, I am in a hurry to continue our tour of the underwater world. I am merely going to draw from the sodium reserves I have already accumulated here. When we have loaded them on board, which will take just a day, we will continue our voyage. So if you wish to explore this cavern and go round the lagoon, please make use of this time, Dr Aronnax.'

I thanked the captain, and went in search of my two companions who had not yet left their cabin. I invited them to follow me without telling them where we were.

They went up on to the platform. Conseil, who was astonished at nothing, considered it natural to wake up under a mountain after going to sleep under the waves. But Ned Land's only idea was to search and see if the cavern had some way out.

After finishing breakfast at about ten o'clock, we climbed down to the shore.

'Here we are on dry land once more,' said Conseil.

'I do not call this "dry land",' replied the Canadian. 'And in any case, we are not on but under it.'

Between the foot of the mountain wall and the water of the lake stretched a sandy shore measuring 500 feet at its widest point. Following this shore, it was perfectly possible to go round the lake. But the base of the high wall itself was made up of fractured ground, on which lay volcanic blocks and enormous pumice stones in picturesque disorder. All these disaggregated masses, which subterranean fires had left with a polished glaze, scintillated as the electricity from the searchlight flowed over them. The mica dust on the shore, kicked up by our feet, flew into the air in sparkling clouds.

The ground rose noticeably as it left the sand flats, and we soon arrived at long winding slopes, acting for us as mountain paths on which to climb little by little. But we needed to walk carefully over the conglomerates that no cement held together, as our feet slipped on the vitreous trachytes made of feldspar and quartz crystals.

The volcanic origin of this enormous pit was visible everywhere. I pointed it out to my companions.

'Can you imagine what this funnel must have been like when it was filling with boiling lava, when the level of the incandescent liquid reached the mouth of the mountain, like cast iron up the walls of a blast furnace?'

'I can imagine it perfectly,' replied Conseil. 'But will monsieur tell me why the great foundryman interrupted his work, and how it comes about that the oven has been replaced by the quiet waters of a lake?'

'Very probably because of the same convulsion that produced the underwater passage that let the *Nautilus* through. The waves of the Atlantic must have rushed inside the mountain. There was presumably a terrifying battle between the two elements, which ended to Neptune's advantage. But many centuries have passed since then, and the submerged volcano has now become a peaceful grotto.'

'Very well,' said Ned Land, 'I accept that explanation. But from our point of view, I'm sorry that the passage Dr Aronnax is talking about wasn't produced above sea level.'

'But, Ned, my friend,' said Conseil, 'if the passage hadn't been underwater, the *Nautilus* wouldn't have been able to come through!'

'And I would add, Master Land, that the water wouldn't have rushed under the mountain and the volcano would have remained a volcano. So your regrets are perhaps misplaced.'

Our climb continued. The incline grew steeper and steeper and narrower and narrower. Sometimes it was interrupted by crevasses which we had to cross. Overhangs needed to be worked around. We slid on our knees, we crept on our bellies. But with Conseil's skill and the Canadian's strength, we overcame all obstacles.

About 100 feet up the terrain changed, but did not become any easier going. The conglomerates and trachytes gave way to black basalt, stretching out in strata full of blistered bulges; the conglomerates formed regular prisms lined up like a row of columns supporting the springs of an enormous vault, thus constituting an admirable example of natural architecture. Between the basalt sections snaked long torrents of solidified lava encrusted with bituminous spokes; at places wide carpets of sulphur stretched out. A more powerful light came in through the high crater, and washed a vague light over all these volcanic ejecta, entombed for ever in the heart of an extinct mountain.

But our climb was interrupted by insurmountable obstacles at a height of approximately 250 feet. The interior arch moulding changed into an overhang and our climb had to follow a circular route. At this height, the vegetable kingdom began to struggle for dominance with the mineral. A few shrubs and even trees emerged from the cracks in the rock face. I recognized some euphorbia oozing their caustic sap. Heliotropes were not living up to their name since the sunlight never reached them, and sadly displayed their bunches of flowers with half-faded colours and perfumes. Here and there, a few chrysanthemums grew timidly at the feet of aloes with long, sad, ill leaves. But between the lava flows I spotted some small violets, still slightly fragranced, and I must admit I breathed in their scent with great delight. Perfume is the soul of the flower, but the flowers of the sea, the splendid hydrophytes, have no souls!

We had arrived at the foot of a clump of robust dragon trees, pushing the rocks aside with their muscular roots, when Ned suddenly exclaimed:

'Ah, monsieur, a hive!'

'A hive!' I repeated, making a gesture of incredulity.

'Yes, a hive,' repeated the Canadian, 'with bees buzzing around.'

I went up to it and was forced to admit that it was true. Around a hole in the trunk of a dragon tree were several thousand of those ingenious insects, so common throughout the Canary Islands, where their products are so much sought after.

Quite naturally, the Canadian wished to make a provision of honey, and it would have been ill grace for me to oppose him. A quantity of dry leaves mixed with sulphur were lit using the spark from Ned's tinder-box lighter, and he began to smoke out the bees. The buzzing ceased little by little, before the eviscerated hive gave up several pounds of fragrant honey. Land filled his haversack with it.

'When I mix this honey with the breadfruit dough,' he said, 'I'll be able to cook you a delicious cake.'

'*Parbleu!*' said Conseil. 'Gingerbread?'

'A good idea,' I said. 'But let's continue our interesting walk.'

At bends in our path, the whole lake appeared before us. The searchlight lit up every part of its tranquil surface, not marred by a single ripple. The *Nautilus* remained perfectly still. The crewmen were moving briskly about the platform and the shore—black shadows neatly silhouetted in the luminous atmosphere.

We had reached the highest part of the first level of rocks holding up the vault. I realized that the bees were not the only representatives of the animal kingdom in the volcano. Birds of prey were gliding and turning here and there in the shadows, all descending from their nests perched on points of rock. There were sparrowhawks with white stomachs and screeching kestrels. Crashing down the slopes came fine fat bustards, carried down on their swift long legs. I will let the reader imagine if the Canadian's appetite was whetted by the sight of this savoury game, and whether he regretted not having a gun. He tried replacing shot with stones and, after several unsuccessful attempts, managed to wound one of the magnificent birds. To say that he risked his life twenty times trying to catch it is the simple truth, but he managed well enough, for the bustard eventually joined the honeycomb in his bag.

We had to climb down towards the shore again, for the crest was becoming impassable. Above us, the gaping crater appeared like the wide opening of a well. From where we were the sky could be made out quite clearly; I could see dishevelled clouds running before the west wind, leaving their misty shreds behind on the summit of the mountain. They must have been at a low altitude, for the volcano did not rise more than 800 feet above sea level.

Half an hour after the Canadian's final exploit, we got back to the enclosed shore. Here the flora was represented by broad carpets of samphire, a small umbelliferous plant very good for preserving and making jam, and which is also called saxifrage, glasswort, and sea fennel. Conseil gathered a few bunches. As for the fauna, this consisted of thousands of crustaceans of all sorts: lobsters, spider-crabs, palaemons, mysis, arachnids, *Galathea*, and a prodigious number of shells, including cowries, murexes, and limpets.

A magnificent cavern opened out at this point. My companions and I took pleasure in stretching ourselves out on its fine sand. Fire had polished its glazed and sparkling walls, all sprinkled with dust from the mica. Ned Land tested the walls, trying to find out how thick they were. I could not stop myself smiling. The conversation then turned to his perpetual plans for escape, and I thought I could give him some hope, without committing myself too much: namely that Captain Nemo had only come down south to renew his supply of sodium. I therefore hoped he would now head for the coasts of Europe or America, and thus allow the Canadian to try again with greater success this time.

We had been stretched out in this charming cavern for about an hour. The conversation, lively at the beginning, was now languishing. a certain drowsiness took hold of us. As I could see no reason to resist sleep, I let myself fall into a deep slumber. I dreamed—one does not choose one's dreams—that my life was reduced to the vegetable life of a simple mollusc. The cavern seemed to form the double valve of my shell . . .

All of a sudden, I was woken by Conseil's voice.

'Danger! Look out!' shouted the good fellow.

'What's the matter?' I asked, half rising.

'There's water coming in!'

I got up. The sea was rushing into our shelter like a river, and, since we were decidedly not molluscs, we needed to move.

A few moments later, we were in safety above the cavern.

'So what's happening?' asked Conseil. 'Some new phenomenon?'

'No, my friends,' I replied, 'it's the tide, only the tide which almost caught us out, just like Walter Scott's hero!* The ocean is rising outside and through a completely natural law of equilibrium, the level of the lake is also rising. We've got out of it with half a bath. Let's go and change in the *Nautilus*.'

Three-quarters of an hour later, we had finished our circular tour and returned on board. The crew were finishing loading the supply of sodium, and the *Nautilus* could have left immediately.

However, Captain Nemo did not issue any instructions. Did he want to wait for night and leave his submarine passage under the cover of secrecy? Possibly.

Whatever the reason, the following day the *Nautilus* had left its home port and was sailing a few metres below the waves of the Atlantic, on the high seas far from any land.

11

THE SARGASSO SEA

THE direction of the *Nautilus* had not changed, so any hope of returning to European waters had to be put aside for the moment. Captain Nemo maintained a southerly course. Where was he taking us? I dared not think.

That day, the *Nautilus* crossed a remarkable region of the Atlantic Ocean. Everyone is aware of the existence of that great current of warm water known as the Gulf Stream. After leaving the Florida Strait, it heads towards Spitsbergen. But before reaching the Gulf of Mexico at about 44° N, the current divides into two. The larger branch heads for the coasts of Ireland and Norway, whilst the second heads south starting from a point opposite the Azores; then, striking the African coast and describing an extended oval, it heads back towards the West Indies once more.

Now the warm water of this second branch—which is more like a necklace than a branch—surrounds that portion of the ocean which is cold, peaceful, and motionless and is called the Sargasso Sea.* A true lake in the middle of the Atlantic, which the waters of the great current take no less than three years to go round.

The Sargasso Sea, to be precise, covers the whole submerged area of Atlantis. Some authors have even claimed that the numerous grasses with which it is strewn are torn from the plains of the submerged continent. It is more probable, however, that the grasses, seaweeds, and wracks are taken from the shores of Europe and America and carried into this area by the Gulf Stream. This was one of the reasons that led Columbus to suppose a new world existed. When the ships of the bold searcher arrived in the Sargasso Sea, they had problems sailing through the grasses which stopped their progress, to the great alarm of his crews, and they wasted three long weeks crossing them.

Such was the region that the *Nautilus* was now visiting. It was nothing less than a prairie, a tightly knit carpet of seaweeds, fucus natans, and bladder-wracks, so thick and compact that the prow of a vessel could barely tear through it. Captain Nemo did not wish to engage his screw in this grassy mass, and so kept a few metres below the surface of the waves.

The name Sargasso comes from the Spanish *sargazo** meaning 'sea-wrack'. This sea-wrack, floating varec, or gulfweed, is the main constituent of the immense bed. According to the scientist Maury, author of *The Physical Geography of the Globe*,* such hydrophytes gather in this peaceful basin of the Atlantic:

The explanation that can be given for this, he says, seems to result from an experiment everyone is familiar with. 'If bits of cork or chaff, or any floating substance, be put into a basin, and a circular motion be given to the water, all the light substances will be found crowding together near the centre of the pool, where there is the least motion. Just such a basin is the Atlantic Ocean to the Gulf Stream, and the Sargasso Sea is the centre of the whirl.'

I share Maury's opinion, and have been able to study the phenomenon in that special environment which ships rarely enter. Above us floated bodies of every origin, piled up amongst the brownish grasses: tree-trunks torn from the Andes or the Rocky Mountains and carried down by the Amazon or the Mississippi, and numerous wrecks, either the remains of keels or hulls or stove-in sections so weighed down by shells and barnacles that they could no longer float on the surface. There is another idea of Maury's which will be proved one day: that this matter, accumulated for centuries, will mineralize in the action of the water and come to form inexhaustible coalmines. A precious reserve that farsighted nature is laying down for the time when man has exhausted the mines on dry land.

In the midst of this inextricable fabric of grasses and fucus, I noticed charming star-shaped alcyonarians in pink colours, sea anemones that let their long tresses of tentacles drag in the current, green, red, and blue jellyfish, and especially the great rhizostomes described by Cuvier, with bluish umbrellas edged with violet frills.

The whole of 22 February was spent in the Sargasso Sea, where fish find abundant food among the marine plants and crustaceans. The next day, the ocean's appearance was back to normal.

From that moment on, for the eighteen days from 23 February to 12 March, the *Nautilus* kept to the North Atlantic, carrying us on at a constant speed of 100 leagues every twenty-four hours. Captain Nemo evidently wished to finish his submarine programme, and there was no doubt in my mind that he was planning to head back to the South Seas of the Pacific after rounding Cape Horn.

Ned had therefore been right to worry. In these wide seas, bereft of islands, we could not try to leave the vessel. Nor was there any way of opposing Captain Nemo's wishes. The only choice was to submit; but what we were unable to obtain using brute strength or ruse, I liked to think we could obtain by means of persuasion. Once the voyage was over, might Captain Nemo not agree to give us back our freedom if we swore never to reveal his existence? An oath of honour which we would have kept. But we needed to discuss this delicate question with the captain as soon as possible. Would I receive a warm reception if I asked for this freedom? Had he not declared, at the beginning and in formal fashion, that the secret surrounding his life demanded that we be kept imprisoned on board the *Nautilus* for ever? Would my silence over the last four months not appear to be tacit acceptance of the situation? Wouldn't raising the subject again cause suspicion which could hinder our plans if some favourable circumstance arose later? I weighed up all these questions, turned them over in my mind, and raised them with Conseil, but he remained just as undecided as I. The upshot was that, although not easily discouraged, I could see the chances of ever meeting my fellows again diminishing with each day, especially now that Captain Nemo was heading boldly towards the South Atlantic!

During the eighteen days I mentioned above, no particular incident marked our voyage. I saw little of the captain. He was working. In the library I often found books he had left open, mainly books on natural history. My work on the submarine depths had been read by him, and the margin was covered with notes, sometimes contradicting my theories and systems. But the captain satisfied himself with improving my work in this way, and it was rare for him to discuss it directly with me. Sometimes I heard the melancholy sounds of his organ, which he played with great expression, but only at night, in the midst of the most secret darkness, while the *Nautilus* was sleeping in the ocean wilderness.

During this part of the voyage, we sailed for entire days on the surface.

The ocean was virtually empty—just a few sailing ships, with cargo for the Indies, heading for the Cape of Good Hope. One day we were pursued by boats from a whaling ship which undoubtedly took us for an enormous whale of great value. But Captain Nemo did not wish to have these good men waste their time and effort, so he ended the chase by diving underwater. This incident seemed to greatly interest Ned Land. I believe I am quite right to say that the Canadian was sorry our cetacean could not be killed by the fishermen's harpoons.

The fish observed by Conseil and myself during this period differed little from those we had studied at other latitudes. They were mainly specimens from that terrible genus of cartilaginous fish, divided into three sub-genera and no less than thirty-two species: five-metre gallooned sharks, with squashed heads that are wider than their bodies, curved tail-fins, and backs bearing seven large black lengthwise stripes; and seven-gill sharks, cinder-grey with seven branchial openings and a single dorsal fin at approximately the middle of the body.

Large dogfish also passed, voracious fish if ever there were any. One cannot lend credence to fishermen's tales, but this is what they say. In one has been found a buffalo head and an entire calf; in another, two tuna fish and a uniformed sailor; in another, a soldier with his sword; and in a fourth, a horse and its rider.* All this, to be frank, is not necessarily gospel truth. But as not one of these animals allowed itself to be caught in the *Nautilus*'s nets, I was not able to check exactly how voracious they are.

Elegant and playful schools of dolphins accompanied us for entire days. They went around in groups of five or six, hunting in packs like wolves in the countryside. They are no less voracious than the dogfish, so that I can believe a certain gentleman from Copenhagen,* who claims to have taken thirteen porpoises and fifteen seals from the stomach of one dolphin. It was, admittedly, an orca, belonging to the biggest known species, that sometimes exceed 24 feet. This family of Delphinidae includes ten genera, and those that I saw belonged to the genus of *Delphinorhynchi*, remarkable for their extremely narrow snouts, four times as long as their heads. Their bodies, three metres long and black on top, were coloured pinkish-white underneath with very occasional small dots.

I will also cite strange specimens amongst these seas of fish from the order of acanthopterygians and family of sciaenoids. A few authors—more poets than naturalists—have claimed that these fish sing harmoniously, and that their assembled voices form a concert that a choir of human voices could never equal. I am sure this is true, but to my regret, these sciaenas did not serenade us as we passed.

And finally, Conseil classified a great number of flying fish. Nothing was more engrossing than to watch the dolphins hunting them with ingenious skill. Whatever the range of their flight, whatever trajectory they described, even jumping right over the *Nautilus*, the unfortunate fish always found the mouth of a dolphin open to receive them. They were either pirapeda or red gurnards, and during the night their luminous mouths traced fiery tracks through the air that plunged into the dark waters like shooting stars.

Until 13 March, we continued on our course without change. That day, the *Nautilus* engaged in an experiment with soundings that interested me tremendously.

We had then covered 13,000 leagues since our starting-point in the open seas of the Pacific. Our position had been taken as 45° 37′ S, 37° 53′ W. These were the same waters where Captain Denham of the *Herald** had dropped 14,000 metres of sound without finding the bottom. There also, Lieutenant Parker of the American frigate *Congress** was unable to reach the submarine floor at 15,140 metres.

Captain Nemo resolved to take the *Nautilus* to the greatest possible depth in order to investigate the different soundings. I got ready to note all the results of the experiment. The panels of the salon were opened and operations began for reaching those prodigious deeps.

It can easily be seen that diving by merely filling the tanks was out of the question. They would not have been able to increase the specific weight of the *Nautilus* sufficiently. But in any case, to have come up again, it would have been necessary to expel this water, and the pumps would not have been powerful enough to overcome the external pressure at those great depths.

Captain Nemo decided to head for the ocean floor by following a sufficiently oblique path, using his lateral planes placed at an angle of 45° to the *Nautilus*'s waterline. The propeller was also set at maximum speed, and its four blades soon began to thrash the water with indescribable violence.

Under this powerful impulse, the hull of the *Nautilus* trembled like a vibrating cord as it cut steadily into the waters. The captain and I, at our station in the salon, followed the swiftly descending needle of the pressure-gauge. Soon the inhabitable zone where most fish live had been left behind. Whilst there are some fish which can only live on the surface of the seas or rivers, there are a few which can survive at quite great depths. Amongst them, I observed the hexanchus, a sort of dogfish equipped with six respiratory slits, the telescope-fish with enormous eyes, the armoured gurnard with grey thoracic and black pectoral fins, with its plastron protected by light red bony plates, and finally a sort of grenadier, living at 1,200 metres and supporting a pressure of 120 atmospheres.

I asked Captain Nemo if he had observed fish at still greater depths.

'Fish?' he replied. 'Rarely. But do tell me: in the present state of science, what has been deduced, what do people really know?'

'The following, captain. It is known that when going towards the greatest depths of the ocean, vegetable life disappears more quickly than animal life. It is known that at points where animate life-forms are still encountered, there no longer lives a single hydrophyte. It is known that scallops and oysters live 2,000 metres down, and that McClintock, the hero of the polar seas,* drew a living starfish from a depth of 2,500 metres. It is known that the crew of the Royal Navy's *Bull-Dog* fished an asteria at 2,620 fathoms, or more than a league down. So, Captain Nemo, how can you tell me that nothing is known?'

'I cannot, monsieur,' he replied, 'I would not be so impolite. However, I would like to ask how you explain that these creatures can live at such depths?'

'I can give two explanations. First of all, the vertical currents caused by the differences in salt concentration and density of the water produce a movement which suffices to maintain a rudimentary life of crinoids and asterias.'

'Absolutely,' said the captain.

'And secondly, if oxygen is the basis of life, it is known that the quantity of oxygen dissolved in sea water actually increases with depth, since the pressure of the lowest depths helps to compress it.'

'Ah, that *is* known?' replied Captain Nemo, in a slightly surprised tone. 'Well, monsieur, people are quite right to assume that, because it is the truth. I would add that the swimming bladders of fish contain more nitrogen than oxygen when they are caught on the surface, but more oxygen than nitrogen when they are drawn from the great depths; which confirms your system. But let us continue our observations.'

My eyes turned to the pressure-gauge. It indicated a depth of 6,000 metres. We had been diving for an hour. The *Nautilus*, thanks to its inclined planes, was still descending. The deserted waters were beautifully transparent, of an indescribable clarity. An hour later, we were at 13,000 metres—approximately 3½ leagues—and the bottom of the ocean was still nowhere in sight.

However, at 14,000 metres I noticed some dark peaks emerging from the waters, but these summits could belong to mountains as high as Mont Blanc or the Himalayas, higher even, for the depth of the chasms remained impossible to estimate.

The *Nautilus* descended lower still, in spite of the tremendous pressure it was undergoing. I could feel the plates trembling where their bolts were fixed; bars were bending; bulkheads were groaning; the windows in the salon seemed to be bending under the pressure of the water. And this robust machine would undoubtedly have given way if, as its captain had said, it had not been able to resist like a solid block.

Skimming over the slopes of these rocks lost under the waters, I noticed a few remaining shells, together with some serpula and living spirorbises, plus a few starfish.

But soon these last representatives of animal life had disappeared and below three leagues* the *Nautilus* left behind the limits of submarine life, just as a balloon rises in the air above aerial zones where breathing is possible. We reached a depth of 16,000 metres—four leagues—and the sides of the *Nautilus* were at this moment supporting a pressure of 1,600 atmospheres, that is 1,600 kilograms for every square centimetre of its surface!

'It's incredible!' I cried. 'To roam these deep regions where man has never ventured! Look, captain, look at the magnificent rocks, the uninhabited grottoes, the last areas of the globe where life is no longer possible! Can it be that all we will have to take back up with us are the memories of these yet-unseen sights?'

'Would it please you', Captain Nemo asked, 'to take back more than memories?'

'What do you mean?'

'I mean that nothing would be easier than to make a photographic record of this submarine region!'

I had not had time to express my surprise at this new suggestion, when, following a sign from Captain Nemo, a camera was brought into the salon. The electrically illuminated liquid element distributed a perfectly even light through the wide-open panels. No shadow, no distortion from this artificial light. The sun could not have been more suited to tasks of this kind. The *Nautilus* was kept motionless by the thrust of its propeller working against its angled planes. The camera was aimed at the scene on the ocean floor, and within a few seconds we had obtained a very clear negative.

I attach the photographic print. One can see: primordial rocks which have never known the light of day; the inferior granites which form the powerful bedrock of the globe; deep grottoes hollowed out in the rocky masses; profiles of an incomparable clarity whose extremities are picked out in black, as if by certain Flemish artists; then, beyond, a horizon of mountains, a superb undulating line which forms the background to the scene. I simply cannot describe this collection of resplendent rocks: polished black, without moss, without marks, in oddly cloven shapes, firmly anchored on the carpet of sand, sparkling in the beams of electric light.

Once Captain Nemo had finished the operation, he said to me:

'Let's go back up again, monsieur. We must not abuse this situation or expose the *Nautilus* to such pressures for too long.'

'Let's go up then,' I replied.

'Please hold on.'

Before I had had time to understand why the captain had given me this advice, I was thrown on to the carpet.

With its propeller engaged on a signal from the captain and its planes now at the vertical, the *Nautilus*, carried like a balloon into the air, rose at a staggering speed. It raced through the waters. All details were blurred. In four minutes it covered the 4 leagues to the surface, emerged noisily like a flying fish, and fell back again, sending a wash soaring to a prodigious height.

12

BALEEN AND SPERM WHALES*

DURING the night of 13 to 14 March, the *Nautilus* continued on its route southwards. I thought that once at Cape Horn it would set sail for the west, in order to head for the seas of the Pacific and thus complete its journey around the world. It did nothing of the sort, and continued to head down towards the southern polar regions. Where did the *Nautilus* mean to go? To the Pole? That was crazy. I began to believe that Ned was right to fear the captain's recklessness.

The Canadian had not spoken to me for a long time about his plans to escape. He had become noticeably less communicative, almost silent. I could see how the long imprisonment was weighing down on him. I could feel how much anger was building up inside him. When he met the captain, his eyes would light up with a dark fire, and I always feared that his violent nature would lead to some extreme action.

That day, 14 March, he came with Conseil to find me in my room. I asked them the reason for their visit.

'A simple question to ask you, monsieur,' the Canadian said.

'Speak, Ned.'

'How many men do you think there are on board the *Nautilus*?'

'I cannot say, my friend.'

'It seems to me', he continued, 'that it would not require a very large crew to run the *Nautilus*.'

'Just so, at present, ten men at most would be enough to operate things.'

'Exactly, why would there be more?'

'Why?' I repeated.

I stared at Land, whose plans were easy to guess.

'Because', I continued, 'if I follow my hunch and if I have properly understood the captain's life, the *Nautilus* is not only a ship, it must also be a place of refuge for those, like its captain, who have broken all ties with the land.'

'Perhaps,' said Conseil. 'But the *Nautilus* can only contain a finite number of men, and could monsieur not estimate what the maximum might be?'

'How could I do that, Conseil?'

'Through calculation. Given that monsieur knows the capacity of the ship, and consequently the quantity of air it contains; knowing also how much each man consumes in breathing; comparing these figures with the *Nautilus*'s need to surface every twenty-four hours . . .'

Conseil's sentence did not seem to have an end, but I could see what he was getting at.

'I understand, but though that calculation is easy to make, I can only reach a very approximate figure.'

'It doesn't matter,' said Ned insistently.

'Here are the figures, then,' I replied. 'In an hour each man exhausts the oxygen in 100 litres of air, or in twenty-four hours the oxygen in 2,400 litres. We need, therefore, to find out how many times 2,400 litres goes into the air in the *Nautilus*.'

'Precisely,' said Conseil.

'Now', I continued, 'since the capacity of the *Nautilus* is 1,500 tons, and a ton is 1,000 litres, the *Nautilus* contains 1.5 million litres of air, which, divided by 2,400 . . .'

I quickly wrote down some calculations.

'. . . gives 625, which means that the air in the *Nautilus* could easily be sufficient for 625 men for twenty-four hours.'

'Six hundred and twenty-five!' exclaimed Ned.

'But take it from me that including passengers and sailors, as well as officers, we do not make up a tenth of that figure.'

'Still too many for three men!' murmured Conseil.

'So, my poor Ned, I can only advise patience.'

'More than patience,' replied Conseil; 'resignation.'

Conseil had indeed picked the appropriate term.

'But on the other hand,' he said, 'Captain Nemo cannot head south for ever. He will have to stop at some point, even if it's only at the ice-cap! He will then have to head towards more civilized seas! Then will be the time to execute Ned Land's plans.'

The Canadian shook his head, wiped his forehead with the back of his hand, and went out without another word.

'If I may be allowed to make an observation,' said Conseil, 'poor Ned is thinking about all the things he cannot have. Everything casts him back to his former life. Everything appears jaded to him, because everything is restricted. His past memories oppress him, and he is sore at heart. We need to understand. What can he do here? Nothing. He is not a scientist like monsieur, and so is not able to take the same interest as us in the incredible things in the sea all around. He would risk everything to go to a tavern in his home country!'

It seemed clear that the monotony on board was unbearable to the Canadian, accustomed as he was to a free and active life. There were few things he could take any interest in. However, that day something happened to remind him of his glory days as a harpooner.

At about eleven in the morning, being on the surface, the *Nautilus* fell in with a school of whales. An encounter which did not surprise me, for I knew that these animals, under outrageous pressure from hunting, have taken refuge in the higher latitudes.

The role played by the whale in the marine world and its influence on geographical discoveries have been considerable. The whale encouraged the Basques to follow it, then lured on the Asturians of north-west Spain, the British, and the Dutch, inured them to the dangers of the ocean, and took them from one end of the earth to the other. Whales like to frequent the Arctic and Antarctic oceans. Ancient legends even claim that these cetaceans led fishermen to a mere seven leagues from the North Pole. If the tale is false now, it will be true one day, for it will probably be while hunting a whale in the Arctic or Antarctic that men will reach those virgin points of the globe.

We were sitting on the platform in a calm sea. The equivalent of October gave us fine autumn days in those latitudes. It was the Canadian—never mistaken—who reported a whale on the eastern horizon. Looking carefully, one could see its blackish back rising and falling above the waves, about 5 miles from the *Nautilus*.

'Ah!' cried Ned Land. 'If I was on board a whaling ship, here is an encounter that would please me. It's a huge one. Look how high its blowholes are sending columns of air and vapour! Damn! Why do I have to be chained to this piece of old iron!'

'What, Ned! Have you not yet got over your old ideas of harpooning?'

'Can a whaler ever forget his former trade? Can you ever get tired of the feelings of the hunt?'

'Have you never been whaling in these seas, Ned?'

'Never, monsieur. Just the Arctic seas, and the Bering Strait as often as the Davis Strait.'

'Then you still haven't seen an Antarctic whale. It is the right whale that you have hunted until now, which never ventures into the warm waters around the equator.'

'Ah, monsieur, what are you trying to tell me?' replied the Canadian in an incredulous tone.

'I am telling you the facts.'

'You can't be! As I stand here, in '65, that's two-and-a-half years ago, I boarded the body of a whale near Greenland which still had the stamped harpoon of a Bering whaling ship in its side. Now I ask you, how could the animal have come and got itself killed east of America, since that was where it was caught, after being wounded west of America, unless it rounded either Cape Horn or the Cape of Good Hope and then crossed the equator?'

'I agree with Ned, my friend,' said Conseil, 'and await monsieur's reply.'

'Monsieur will reply by saying, my good friend, that each species of whale is particular to certain seas that it never leaves. And if one of these animals went from the Bering Strait to the Davis Strait, it must be because there is a passage from one to the other, round either the American or Asian coast.'

'Do we have to believe you?' asked the Canadian, winking.

'We have to believe monsieur,' said Conseil.

'So, since I have never been whaling in these waters, I don't know which whales live here?'

'That's what I told you, Ned.'

'All the more reason for getting acquainted with them,' replied Conseil.

'Look, look!' cried the Canadian, emotion in his voice. 'It's getting nearer! It's coming at us! It's provoking me! It knows I can't do anything about it.'

Ned was stamping his foot. His hand was trembling as if holding an imaginary harpoon.

'These cetaceans, are they as big as those of the Arctic seas?'

'More or less, Ned.'

'Because I have seen some big ones, monsieur. Whales up to 100 feet long! I've even been told that the *culammak* and the *umgullick* of the Aleutians sometimes exceed 150 feet.'

'That seems exaggerated to me,' I replied. 'Those animals are only rorquals with dorsal fins, and like sperm whales, they are generally smaller than the right whale.'

'Ah!' exclaimed the Canadian, whose eyes did not leave the ocean. 'It's getting nearer, it's coming within reach!'

Then, continuing his conversation:

'You speak of the sperm whale as a small animal! But gigantic sperm whales have been sighted. They are intelligent creatures. Some of them, it is said, cover themselves with seaweed and wracks. They are taken for small islands. People camp on them, they settle in and make fires . . .'

'They build houses,' said Conseil.

'Yes, joker,' replied Ned. 'Then one fine day the animal dives, and takes all its inhabitants to the bottom of the seas.'

'Like in the voyages of Sinbad the Sailor,'* I replied with a laugh. 'Ah! Master Land, you seem to like extraordinary stories! How wonderful your sperm whales are! I hope you don't really believe in them?'

'Mr Naturalist,' replied the Canadian seriously, 'you have to be able to believe anything once whales are involved. Look how this one moves! Look how it swerves! It has been claimed that these animals can travel round the world in a fortnight.'

'I don't disagree.'

'But what you certainly don't know, Dr Aronnax, is that at the beginning of the world, whales could move still quicker.'

'Ah really, Ned! And why is that?'

'Because at that time their tails moved sideways like fish, that is they were vertical, and struck the water from left to right. But the Creator realized that they could move too quickly and so He twisted their tails, and since then they have beaten the waves from top to bottom and cannot move so fast.'

'Well, Ned,' I said, adopting one of the Canadian's expressions, 'do we have to believe you?'

'Not too much,' he replied, 'and not more than if I told you there are whales 300 feet long weighing 50 tons.'*

'That's quite a lot to believe,' I said. 'However, it must be agreed that certain cetaceans grow to a considerable size, since it is said they can provide up to 120 barrels of oil.'

'That I've seen,' said the Canadian.

'I can easily credit it, Ned, as I can believe that certain whales are the size of a hundred elephants. Think of the effect produced by such a mass travelling at full speed!'

'Is it true', asked Conseil, 'that they can sink ships?'

'Ships, I don't think so,' I replied. 'But it has been recounted that in 1820, in these same South Seas, a whale threw itself at the *Essex* and made it move backwards at a speed of four metres per second. Water came in aft, and the *Essex* sank almost immediately.'*

Ned looked at me sarcastically.

'For my part,' he said, 'I have been hit by a whale's tail—in my boat, I mean. My companions and I were thrown to a height of six metres. But compared to monsieur's whale, mine was only a baby.'

'Do such animals live a long time?' asked Conseil.

'A thousand years,' replied the Canadian without hesitation.

'And how do you know, Ned?'

'Because people say so.'

'And why do people say so?'

'Because they know.'

'No, Ned, they do not know, they've worked it out. And here is the reasoning on which they base their arguments. Four hundred years ago, when fishermen first hunted whales, the animals were bigger than those caught today. It was therefore quite logically deduced that the smaller size of present-day whales is because they have not had time to reach their full size. This is what led Buffon to conclude that these cetaceans could—indeed had to—live a thousand years. Do you understand?'

Land did not understand. He was no longer listening. The whale was still approaching. He devoured it with his eyes.

'Ah!' he cried. 'It's not just one whale, it's ten, it's twenty—an entire school! And not to be able to do anything! To be here with my hands and feet tied!'

'But, Ned, my friend,' said Conseil, 'why not go and ask Captain Nemo for permission . . .?'

Conseil had not finished, before Ned Land had galloped down the hatch and was running off in search of the captain. A moment later, both men appeared on the platform.

Captain Nemo observed the school of cetaceans playing on the water a mile from the *Nautilus*.

'They're Antarctic whales,' he said. 'There are enough here to make the fortune of a whole fleet of whalers.'

'Well, monsieur!' asked the Canadian. 'Would it be all right to hunt them, if only to keep my hand in as harpooner?'

'What would be the point? Hunting simply to destroy! We have no use for whale oil on board.'

'Nevertheless, monsieur,' persisted the Canadian, 'in the Red Sea you authorized us to chase a dugong!'

'We needed fresh meat for my crew. Here, it would be killing for killing's sake. I realize that it is one of man's privileges, but I cannot condone these murderous pastimes. By destroying the Antarctic whale like the right whale, inoffensive and good creatures as they are, your fellows commit a damnable action, Master Land. They have already emptied the whole of Baffin Bay, and will eventually destroy a class of useful animals. So leave the unfortunate whales in peace. They already have enough problems with their natural enemies,* the sperm whales, the swordfish, and the sawfish, without you interfering.'

I leave to your imagination the expression on the Canadian's face during this moral lesson. To reason with a hunter like this was to waste one's words. Ned looked at Captain Nemo and evidently did not understand what he was trying to say. Nevertheless the captain was right. The barbaric and unthinking relentlessness of the hunters will one day eliminate the last whale from the ocean.

Ned whistled *Yankee Doodle* between his teeth,* thrust his hands into his pockets, and turned his back on us.

Meanwhile Captain Nemo was observing the school of cetaceans, and addressing me:

'I was right to claim that, even without man, whales have enough natural enemies. These ones are going to have a battle to fight before long. Can you see those moving dark points eight miles to leeward, Dr Aronnax?'

'Yes, captain.'

'They are sperm whales, terrifying animals that I have sometimes encountered in schools of two or three hundred! In their case, it is right to exterminate such cruel and malevolent animals.'

At these words the Canadian quickly turned round.

'Well, captain,' I said, 'there is still time in the interests of the Antarctic whales themselves . . .'

'No point in taking the risk, monsieur. The *Nautilus* will suffice to head off the sperm whales. It is armed with a steel ram, which is easily worth Master Land's harpoon, I think.'

The Canadian did not bother to conceal his shrugs. Bodily attacking cetaceans with a ram! Who had ever heard of such a thing?

'You'll see, Dr Aronnax,' said Captain Nemo. 'We will show you some hunting you have not yet experienced. No pity for the ferocious cetaceans. They are only mouth and teeth!'

Mouth and teeth! There was no better way to depict the macro-cephalous creature, which sometimes exceeds 25 metres in length. The enormous head of this cetacean occupies about a third of its body. Better armed than the baleen whale, whose upper jaw is equipped only with bony plates, it has twenty-five huge teeth:* 20 centimetres long, cylindrical but with conical ends, weighing two pounds each. In the great cavities formed by the cartilage on the upper part of the enormous head are found 300 or 400 kilograms of that precious oil called spermaceti. The sperm whale is a disgraceful animal, more tadpole than fish, as Frédol remarks. It is poorly constructed, being a failure, so to speak, in the whole left-hand part of its framework, and hardly seeing except through its right eye.

Meanwhile the monstrous school was still approaching. They had spotted the baleen whales, and were getting ready to attack them. One could predict in advance that the sperm whales would win, not only because they are better built for attack and their adversaries are inoffensive, but also because they can remain underwater longer without having to come up to breathe.

It was time to go to the baleen whales' help. The *Nautilus* dived under the water. Conseil, Ned, and I took our places at the windows in the salon. Captain Nemo went to join the pilot, so as to manoeuvre his vessel, transformed into a destructive engine. Soon I could feel the throb of the propeller accelerating and our speed increasing.

The battle between the sperm whales and the whales had already begun when the *Nautilus* arrived. It manoeuvred in such a way as to split the school of macrocephalous creatures in two. At first they appeared undisturbed at the sight of the new monster joining the battle, but soon they had to pay attention to its attacks.

What a battle! Ned Land himself quickly became enthusiastic, and ended up clapping. In the captain's hands, the *Nautilus* had become a formidable harpoon. It threw itself at the fleshy masses, cutting right through the animals, leaving behind two flailing halves. The *Nautilus* was insensible to the frightening blows from the tails striking its sides. Nor did our vessel heed the impacts from its own efforts. Once one sperm whale had been killed, it chased after the next one, or turned on the spot so as to find its new prey: manoeuvring back and forth under the direction of the helm, diving when a cetacean plunged into the depths, coming back up when it surfaced, smashing into it head-on or obliquely, cutting or tearing, striking from every direction and at any speed, skewering with the terrifying ram.

What a blood-letting! What a commotion on the surface of the waves! What high-pitched whistlings and distinctive bellowings came from the frightened animals. Their tails produced great surges through the ordinarily peaceful waters.

This Homeric massacre, from which the sperm whales could not escape, continued for an hour. Several times, ten or twelve together tried to crush the *Nautilus* between their bodies. Through the windows we could see their enormous jaws paved with teeth and their formidable eyes. Land, no longer master of himself, threatened and swore at them. We could feel them seizing hold of our vessel like dogs gripping a young boar's ears in undergrowth. But the *Nautilus*, increasing the power of its propeller, would carry them off, drag them down, or take them up to the surface, unaffected by their enormous weight or powerful embrace.

Finally the number of sperm whales began to reduce. The waves became calm once more. I could feel that we were moving up towards the surface. The hatch was opened, and we rushed on to the platform.

The sea was covered with mutilated bodies. A huge explosion could not have divided these fleshy masses or torn them to pieces with more violence. We were floating amongst gigantic bodies: bluish-backed, white-bellied, completely covered with enormous protuberances. A few frightened sperm whales were still fleeing on the horizon. The waves were dyed red for a distance of several miles; the *Nautilus* was floating on a sea of blood.

Captain Nemo joined us.

'Well, Master Land?'

'Well, monsieur,' replied the Canadian, whose enthusiasm had diminished; 'it was a terrible sight indeed. But I am not a butcher, I am a hunter, and this was just butchers' work.'

'It was a massacre of evil animals,' said the captain, 'and the *Nautilus* is not a butcher's knife.'

'I prefer my harpoon.'

'To each his weapon,' replied the captain, staring at Ned.

I was afraid that Ned would allow himself to get carried away into some violent act, which would have had deplorable consequences. But his anger was distracted by the view of a baleen whale alongside which the *Nautilus* was drawing.

The animal had not been able to escape the sperm whales' teeth. I recognized the Antarctic whale, with a flattened, entirely black head. Anatomically, it is distinguished from the right whale and the North-Caper by its seven cervical vertebrae being joined, and it also has two ribs more than its relatives. The unfortunate cetacean, lying on its side, its stomach perforated with bites, was dead. At the end of its mutilated fin still hung a small baby whale it had not been able to save from the massacre. Its open mouth allowed the water in and out, which murmured like a backwash through its bony plates.

Captain Nemo had brought the *Nautilus* near the whale's body. Two of his men climbed on its flank, and I saw with astonishment that they were drawing from its breasts all the milk contained in them, that is two or three barrelfuls.

The captain offered me a cup of the still-warm milk. I could not stop myself showing repugnance at this brew. He assured me that the milk was excellent, and no different from cows' milk.

I tasted it, and agreed with him. It was in fact a useful reserve for us, since this milk, in the form of salted butter or cheese, would bring pleasant variety to our ordinary fare.

From that day on, I noticed with anxiety that Ned Land's attitude towards Captain Nemo deteriorated steadily. I resolved to keep as close an eye as possible on the Canadian's behaviour.

13

THE ICE-CAP

THE *Nautilus* had continued its imperturbable route southwards. It was tracing the 50th meridian at considerable speed. Did the *Nautilus* wish to reach the Pole? I hardly thought so, because all attempts so far had failed to get to that point of the globe. In any case it was already late in the season, since 13 March in the Antarctic corresponds to 13 September in the Arctic, and ushers in the period of the equinox.

On 14 March I noticed pieces of ice floating at 55° S, mere pallid debris 20 to 25 feet long, forming reefs over which the sea broke. The *Nautilus* stayed on the surface. Ned Land, having already been whaling in the Arctic seas, was familiar with the spectacle of icebergs. Conseil and I admired them for the first time.

Hanging in the air above the southern horizon stretched a dazzling white strip. The British whalers have named it 'ice-blink'. However thick the clouds are, it can always be seen. It indicates the presence of pack-ice or an ice-shelf.

Larger blocks whose lustre changed depending on the caprices of the haze did in fact soon appear. Some of the masses were streaked with green veins, as if by undulating copper sulphate. Touched as they were with bright limestone reflections, they would have been sufficient to construct a whole town of marble. Others were like enormous amethysts, allowing the light to penetrate and deflecting the sun's rays from the thousand facets of their crystals.

The further south we went, the more floating islands there were, and the larger they got. Polar birds nested on them in their thousands. There were petrels, black and white gulls, and shearwaters, all deafening us with their cries. Some of them took the *Nautilus* for the body of a whale, came and rested on it, and pecked at it with resounding metal taps.

During this navigation through the ice, Captain Nemo often stayed on the platform. He carefully scanned those lonely seas. I could see his calm regard sometimes becoming more intense. Was he saying to himself that in these polar seas, forbidden to man, he was at home, master of the uncrossable spaces? Perhaps. But he did not speak. He remained motionless, only interrupting his dreaming when his instinct for action took over again. Then, steering his *Nautilus* with consummate skill, he would carefully avoid collision with the hulking masses, which occasionally measured several miles long by a height of between 70 and 80 metres. Often the horizon would appear entirely closed. At the 60th degree of latitude, indeed, all passes had vanished. But Captain Nemo studied the situation, and soon found some narrow opening through which he audaciously slipped, although knowing full well that it would close up again behind him.

In this way the *Nautilus*, guided by his skilful hand, passed through all the ice, which is classified by its form or size with a precision which enchanted Conseil: icebergs, literally meaning mountains; icefields, meaning unified, limitless areas; drift-ice, also called floating ice; and pack-ice, meaning broken pieces and called 'patches' when the pieces are round and 'streams' when they are longer.*

It was quite cold. Exposed to the outside air, the thermometer read two or three degrees below zero. But we were warmly dressed in furs from seals or marine bears. The interior of the *Nautilus*, constantly heated by its electrical devices, defied the most intense cold. In any case, it would have only had to dive a few metres below the waters to find a more bearable temperature.

Two months earlier we would have enjoyed permanent daylight at this latitude, but three- or four-hour nights were already falling, and later six months of shadow would be thrown over these circumpolar regions.

On 15 March we passed the latitude of the South Shetlands and South Orkney. The captain told me that numerous herds of seals had formerly lived on these islands, but British and American whalers had massacred adults and pregnant females in a destructive rage, leaving behind them, in place of vivacious life, the silence of death.

On 16 March, at about eight in the morning, the *Nautilus*, which was following the 55th meridian,* cut the Antarctic Circle. Ice surrounded us in all directions, closing the horizon. Nevertheless, Captain Nemo moved from pass to pass, always heading south.

'But where is he going?' I asked.

'Straight ahead,' replied Conseil. 'But he will stop when he has to.'

'I wouldn't swear to it!'

And to be frank, I have to admit that this adventurous expedition rather pleased me. I cannot express how much the beauty of these new regions entranced me. The ice took on fantastic perspectives. Here it seemed to form an oriental town with its countless minarets and mosques, there a city that had collapsed, thrown down by an earthquake. Views were constantly varied by the oblique sunlight, or became lost in the grey mists of snowy dawns. From every side, explosions, landslides, and great inversions of icebergs changed the background, like the countryside in a diorama.

If the *Nautilus* happened to be submerged when these equilibriums broke, the sound would be transmitted underwater with frightening intensity, and the falling masses would create horrendous turbulence deep in the ocean. The *Nautilus* would then pitch and roll like a ship abandoned to the fury of the elements.

Often I could see no way out, and thought that we were definitely taken prisoner; but with his instinct guiding him, using the slightest sign, Captain Nemo would discover new passes. By observing the thin threads of bluish water streaking the icefields, he never faltered. I was convinced that he had already ventured into the Antarctic Ocean with the *Nautilus*.

However, on 16 March the ice completely blocked our route. It was not yet a single ice-cap, but many vast icefields stuck together by the cold. Such an obstacle could not stop Captain Nemo, and he threw himself at it with awesome violence. The *Nautilus* penetrated the crumbling mass like a wedge, breaking it up with terrifying cracking noises. It was the antique ram, but propelled by infinite power. Pieces of ice were thrown high into the air and fell back around us like hail. Our vessel was opening itself a channel using its own momentum. Sometimes, carried on by inertia, it mounted the icefield and crushed it under its weight; sometimes, when caught fast from underneath, it would split the icefield in two merely by rolling and producing a large crack.

During these few days, violent squalls sometimes hailed down on us. When there were thick fogs we could not see each other from one end of the platform to the other, and the wind brusquely jumped around all the points of the compass. The snow would build up in layers so hard that they had to be broken up with a pick. At a temperature of just −5° all the external parts of the *Nautilus* became covered in ice. Rigging could not possibly have functioned, for the falls would have been blocked in the grooves of the pulleys. A vessel without sails, driven by an electric motor and without the need for coal, was the only one able to face such high latitudes.

In these conditions the barometer generally stayed very low. It even fell to 73.5 degrees.* Compass readings no longer meant very much. The maddened needles marked contradictory directions as they approached the Southern Magnetic Pole, which should not be confused with the Geographic Pole. According to Hansteen,* the Magnetic Pole is actually situated at about 70° S, 130° E and according to Duperrey's observations, at 135° E and 70° 30′ S. Hence repeated observations had to be made using the compasses at different places on the ship and then take their average. But often we relied on dead reckoning to calculate the route covered, a relatively unsatisfactory method in the sinuous passes, with their constantly changing landmarks.

Finally, on 18 March,* after twenty unsuccessful assaults, the *Nautilus* found itself blocked once and for all. It was no longer a question of streams, patches, or icefields, but an interminable and motionless barrier formed of mountains melded together.

'The ice-cap!' the Canadian said.

I understood that for Ned, like all the navigators who had preceded us, this was an insuperable obstacle. Since the sun appeared for a moment at about midday, Captain Nemo was able to obtain a relatively precise observation which gave our position as 51° 30′ W and 67° 39′ S. We had already reached an advanced point of the Antarctic.

Before our eyes there was no longer any sign of sea or of any liquid. A vast tormented plain stretched beyond the ram of the *Nautilus*, tangled, confused blocks, with all the capricious chaos that characterizes the surface of a river well before the ice starts to break up, but hugely magnified. Sharp peaks like slender needles rose here and there to a height of 200 feet; and a succession of cliffs, cut sheer and shaded in greyish tints, formed vast mirrors reflecting the few rays of sunlight, half drowned in the mist. Over this desolate nature loomed a savage silence, hardly broken by the petrels' and shearwaters' beating wings. Everything was frozen, even sound.

The *Nautilus* was accordingly forced to halt its adventurous route through the fields of ice.

'Monsieur,' Land said to me that day, 'if your captain goes further . . .'

'Well?'

'Then he will be a master among men.'

'Why, Ned?'

'Because nobody can cross the ice-cap. Your captain is powerful, but hell, he is not as powerful as nature, and you always have to stop when she has laid down her limits.'

'Right, Ned; and yet I would like to know what lies behind that icefield! Nothing annoys me more than a wall!'

'Monsieur is right,' said Conseil. 'Walls were invented to annoy scientists. There shouldn't be any walls.'

'Hey!' said the Canadian. 'Everybody knows what's behind the icefield.'

'And that is?' I said.

'Ice, and yet more ice!'

'You seem certain of the fact, Ned,' I replied, 'but I personally am not so sure. That is why I would like to go and see for myself.'

'Well, please give up the idea. You have reached the ice-cap: that is already enough, and neither you, your Captain Nemo, nor his *Nautilus* will go any further. Whether he wants to or not, we will eventually have to head back north, towards the realm of honest folk.'

I must admit that Ned Land was right, and until ships are made to navigate over icefields, they will have to stop in front of them.

The *Nautilus* was effectively immobilized, despite all its efforts, and despite the powerful methods used to break up the ice. Normally, anyone who can go no further is quite satisfied to turn round and go back; but here going back was as impossible as going forward, for the passes had closed up again behind us, and indeed if our vessel remained stationary it would not take long to be totally blocked. This is in fact what happened at about two in the afternoon, with the young ice forming on the sides with astonishing speed. I must say that Captain Nemo's behaviour appeared highly imprudent.

I was on the platform. The captain, who had been observing the situation for a while, said:

'Well, monsieur, what do you think?'

'I think that we are caught, captain.'

'Caught! And what do you mean by that?'

'I mean that we can go neither forwards nor backwards, nor in any other direction. This is, I believe, what people mean by "caught", at least in inhabited lands.'

'So, Dr Aronnax, you think the *Nautilus* will not be able to free itself?'

'With difficulty, captain, for the season is already too advanced for you to count on the ice breaking up.'

'Ah, monsieur,' replied Captain Nemo in a sarcastic tone, 'you'll always be the same! You only see snags and obstacles! I can personally tell you that not only will the *Nautilus* free itself, but it will go still further!'

'Still further south?' I asked, looking at the captain.

'Yes, monsieur, to the Pole.'

'To the Pole!' I cried, unable to hide my incredulity.

'Yes!' the captain replied coldly. 'To the South Pole, to that unknown point where the meridians of the globe meet. You know that I can do what I wish with the *Nautilus*.'*

Yes, I knew he could. I also knew that this man was bold to the point of madness! Only the deluded mind of a madman could contemplate overcoming the obstacles around the South Pole, even less accessible than the North Pole, itself still not reached by the bravest navigators!

It suddenly occurred to me to ask Captain Nemo if he had already been to the Pole, sullied by the foot of man.

'No, monsieur, we will discover it together. Where others have failed, I will not. Never have I taken my *Nautilus* so far into the southern seas; but I repeat, it will go still further.'

'I want to believe you, captain,' I said in a sarcastic tone. 'I do believe you! Let's go forward! There are no obstacles for us! Let us break the ice-cap! Let's blow it up, and if it resists, give the *Nautilus* wings so that it can pass over!'

'Over?' calmly replied Captain Nemo. 'Not over, but under.'

'Under!'

A sudden revelation had just filled my mind. I had finally understood the captain's project. The marvellous capabilities of the *Nautilus* were going to serve it once again in this superhuman endeavour!

'I can see that we are beginning to understand each other,' the captain said to me, half smiling. 'You can already glimpse the feasibility— I would say the chance of a successful conclusion—of such an attempt. What is impossible for an ordinary ship is child's play for the *Nautilus*.* If there is a landmass at the Pole, the *Nautilus* will stop at that landmass. But if the Pole is open sea, the *Nautilus* will go to the Pole itself!'

'Exactly,' I said, carried away by the captain's reasoning; 'if the surface of the sea is frozen, its lower layers will be free, by that providential law which places the maximum density of sea water at a temperature above freezing. And if I am not mistaken, isn't the ratio of the underwater part of the icefield to the part above the water four to one?'*

'Approximately, monsieur. For each foot that icebergs stand up above sea level, they have three below. Now since these mountains of ice do not exceed a height of 100 metres, they go no more than 300 into the water. Now what are 300 metres to the *Nautilus*?'

'Nothing, monsieur.'

'It can even seek the uniform temperature of the marine waters at a greater depth, and there we can defy with impunity the thirty or forty degrees of cold on the surface.'

'Absolutely, monsieur, perfectly!' I cried, getting excited.

'The only difficulty', continued Captain Nemo, 'will be to remain several days underwater without replenishing our reserves of air.'

'Is that all?' I replied. 'The *Nautilus* has vast tanks, we can fill them up and they will provide us with all the oxygen we need.'

'Well thought out, Dr Aronnax,' the captain replied smiling. 'But not wishing to be accused of temerity, I am submitting all my objections to you in advance.'

'You still have some?'

'Only one more. If there is a sea at the South Pole, it is possible that this sea is entirely frozen, and consequently that we will not be able to surface.'

'All right, monsieur, but have you forgotten that the *Nautilus* is armed with a redoubtable ram, which could break up these icefields if we launched it diagonally against them?'

'Well, monsieur, we are producing ideas today!'

'In any case, captain,' I added, getting more and more enthusiastic, 'what will stop us finding an open sea at the South Pole just like the North Pole? The actual Poles and the Magnetic Poles of the earth are not found at the same spot in either hemisphere, and until proof to the contrary, it has to be assumed that there is either a continent or an ocean free of ice at these two points of the globe.'

'I agree, Dr Aronnax,' replied Captain Nemo. 'I will only observe that after producing so many objections to my plan, you are now overwhelming me with arguments in its favour.'

Captain Nemo was right. I had got to the point of overtaking him in audacity. It was I who was carrying him off to the Pole! I was moving ahead of him. I was leaving him behind . . . But no, poor fool! Captain Nemo knew much better than you the pros and cons of the question, and was enjoying seeing you indulging in fantastic reveries!

He did not waste a moment. On a signal, the first officer appeared. The two men quickly spoke in their incomprehensible language, and either the first officer had been told about it before, or he saw no problem in carrying out the plan, for he showed no surprise at all.

However impassible, his impassiveness failed to match Conseil's when I announced to the worthy fellow that we were heading for the South Pole. An 'As monsieur pleases' was all that greeted my news, and I had to be content with that. As for Ned, if ever shoulders were shrugged, the Canadian's were.

'Can't you see?' he said. 'I pity you, and your Captain Nemo!'

'But we are going to the Pole, Master Ned.'

'Possibly, but we shan't be coming back!'

And Ned Land returned to his cabin, 'so as not to do something stupid', he said as he left.

Meanwhile the preparations for the audacious attempt had begun. The *Nautilus*'s powerful pumps were forcing air into the tanks, storing it at high pressure. At about four o'clock Captain Nemo announced that the platform hatches were going to close. I cast a final look at the thick ice-cap we were going to go under. The weather was clear, the atmosphere pure, the cold very keen at −12° C. But the wind had dropped, and the temperature did not seem too intolerable.

About ten men armed with pickaxes climbed on to the sides of the *Nautilus*, broke the ice around the hull, and freed it. The operation did not take long, for the young ice was still thin. We all went inside. The tanks were filled up as usual using water kept free at the flotation line. Soon the *Nautilus* dived.

I sat in the salon with Conseil. Through the open window we watched the depths of the Southern Ocean. The thermometer was rising. The needle of the pressure-gauge oscillated.

At about 300 metres, and as Captain Nemo had predicted, we were moving below the undulating lower surface of the ice-cap, as the *Nautilus* dived further. It reached a depth of 800 metres. The temperature of the water, −12° on the surface, was now only −11°. Two degrees already gained.* It goes without saying that the temperature of the *Nautilus*, raised by its heating devices, stayed at a much higher level. All these operations were carried out with extraordinary precision.

'We'll get through, if monsieur has no objection,' said Conseil.

'I'm counting on it!' I replied in a tone of deepest conviction.

In this unobstructed sea, the *Nautilus* had taken a route going directly towards the Pole, not deviating from the 52nd meridian. From 67° 30′ to 90°, 22.5° remained to be covered, that is a little more than 500 leagues. The *Nautilus* maintained a moderate speed of 26 knots, the velocity of an express train. If it continued in the same way, forty hours would be enough to reach the Pole.

For part of the night, the novelty of the situation kept Conseil and me at the window of the salon. The sea was illuminated by the electric radiation of the searchlight, but seemed deserted. Fish did not live in the imprisoned waters. They only made their way through from the Antarctic Ocean to the open sea at the Pole. Our progress was swift. We could feel this from the tremblings of the long steel hull.

At about two o'clock, I went to take a few hours' rest. Conseil did the same. Going through the gangways, I did not meet Captain Nemo. I supposed that he had stayed in the pilot-house.

At five in the morning the next day, 19 March,* I took up my position again in the salon. The electric log told me that the *Nautilus* had slowed down. It was moving towards the surface, but carefully, slowly emptying its tanks.

My heart was beating. Were we going to come out and find the free polar air once more?

No. A jolt told me that the *Nautilus* had hit the lower surface of the ice-cap, still very thick to judge from the dullness of the impact. We had 'touched', to employ the marine expression, but in the other direction and at a depth of 1,000 feet: there were 2,000 feet of ice above us, of which 1,000 emerged. The ice-cap thus reached a greater height than we had noted at its perimeter. Not a very reassuring fact.

During the day the *Nautilus* tried the experiment again several times, and each time it came up against the ice forming a ceiling above. On occasion the *Nautilus* encountered ice at 900 metres, which implied 1,200 metres' thickness of which 200 rose above the surface of the ocean.* This was twice its height at the spot where the *Nautilus* had dived under the waves.

I carefully noted the various depths of the ice encountered, and thus obtained a submarine profile of the range jutting down into the waters.

By evening there was no change in our situation. The ice was 400 to 500 metres deep. Definitely a reduction, but what a thickness still lay between us and the surface!

It was eight o'clock. According to the daily custom, the air should already have been renewed inside the *Nautilus* four hours before. However, I did not suffer too much, although Captain Nemo had not yet called for extra oxygen from the tanks.

My sleep was troubled that night. Hope and fear besieged me in turn. I got up several times. The *Nautilus*'s probes continued. At about three o'clock, I noted that we had touched the lower surface of the ice-cap at only 50 metres' depth. A hundred and fifty feet separated us from the surface. The ice-cap was gradually becoming an isolated icefield. The mountain was changing into a plain.

My eyes no longer left the pressure-gauge. We were moving continuously upwards, at an angle, with the resplendent ice sparkling in the electric rays all the while. The ice-cap was getting thinner, both above and below. It was reducing mile after mile.

Finally at six in the morning on that memorable day of 19 March, the door of the salon opened. Captain Nemo appeared.

'The open sea!' he said.

14

THE SOUTH POLE

I RUSHED on to the platform. Yes, the open sea! Just a few scattered ice-floes and floating icebergs. In the distance, a large sea; in the air, a world of birds; and myriads of fish in the water, which varied from deep blue to olive green according to the depth. The thermometer marked 3°. In relative terms, this was like a spring trapped behind the icefield, whose distant masses stood out on the northern horizon.

'Are we at the Pole?' I asked the captain, my heart beating wildly.

'I cannot tell. We will determine our position at noon.'

'But will the sun appear through the mists?' I asked, staring at the beige sky.

'However briefly it appears, it will be enough for me.'

Ten miles to the south of the *Nautilus*, a solitary island rose to a height of 200 metres. We sailed towards it, but carefully, for the sea could be strewn with reefs.

An hour later we arrived. Two hours after that we had finished going round the island. It measured four or five miles in circumference. A narrow channel separated it from a considerable expanse of land, a continent perhaps, whose limits we were not able to gauge. The existence of dry land seemed to confirm Maury's hypothesis. The ingenious American noticed that between the South Pole and the 60th parallel, the sea is covered with floating ice blocks of enormous dimensions, rarely encountered in the North Atlantic. From this fact he drew the conclusion that the Antarctic Circle encompasses considerable land, since icebergs cannot form in the open sea but only on coasts. According to his calculations, the blocks of ice surrounding the South Pole form a huge ice-cap, whose width must reach 4,000 kilometres.

Fearing a collision, the *Nautilus* had stopped three cables from the shore, which was dominated by a superb rocky massif. The boat was launched. The captain, two of his men carrying instruments, and Conseil and I embarked. It was ten in the morning. I had not seen Ned Land. Without doubt the Canadian was not ready to concede defeat as regards the South Pole.

A few oar-strokes took the boat to the sand, where it ran aground. Just as Conseil was about to jump ashore, I held him back.

'Monsieur,' I said to Captain Nemo, 'the honour of being the first to set foot belongs to you.'

'Indeed, monsieur,' replied the captain, 'it will bring me great joy to be the first man to leave footprints on this polar ground.'

Having said that, he jumped lightly on to the sand. A strong emotion caused his heart to beat faster. He climbed a rock forming an overhang at the end of a little promontory, and there, with arms crossed, eyes gleaming, motionless and silent, he seemed to take possession of the southern regions.* After five minutes spent in this trance, he turned towards us again.

'When you wish, monsieur,' he shouted to me.

I disembarked, followed by Conseil, leaving the two crewmen in the boat.

The ground appeared to be a coloured tuff that spread into the distance, as if made of ground brick. It was covered in scoriae, lava flows, and pumice stones. One could not mistake its volcanic origin. At places, a few slight exhalations produced a sulphurous smell, witness to still-active interior fires. Nevertheless, having climbed a high escarpment, I could not see any volcanoes within a radius of several miles. It is well known that James Ross* found the craters of Erebus and Terror in full activity in these Antarctic lands at the 167th meridian and 77° 32′ S.

The vegetation of this desolate landmass seemed extremely limited. A few lichens of the species *Usnea melanoxantha* covered the black quartzose rocks. The meagre flora of the region was entirely composed of microscopic plantlets called rudimentary diatoms, forms of cells fitted between two quartzose shells, together with long purple and crimson wracks attached to little swimming bladders which the swell threw on to the coast.

The shore was dotted with molluscs: little mussels, limpets, smooth heart-shaped cockles, and especially clios with oval-shaped membranous bodies and heads made up of two round lobes. I could also see myriads of three-centimetre southern clios of which a whale swallows a whole world with each mouthful. These charming pteropods, true sea butterflies, gave life to the open water near the shore.

Amongst other zoophytes appearing on the shallows were a few coral arborescences, which James Ross reports as living in the Antarctic seas as deep as 1,000 metres, small dead man's fingers belonging to the species *Procellaria pelagica*, a large number of *Asterias* peculiar to these climes, and some starfish dotting the ground.

But in contrast life was over-abundant in the air. Thousands of birds of varied species flew and fluttered, deafening us with their cries. Others covered the rocks, watching us pass without fear and crowding familiarly under our feet. These birds were penguins: although clumsy and heavy on land, they are quite agile and supple in the water, where they have sometimes been confused with the fleet bonito. They produced raucous cries, and formed numerous assemblies; sober in gesture, but with much clamour.

Amongst the birds, I noticed sheathbills belonging to the family of waders, as big as pigeons: white, with short conical beaks, and eyes surrounded by red circles. Conseil stocked up with them, for they make a pleasant dish when properly prepared. Sooty albatrosses, with a wing-span of four metres, passed through the air; gigantic petrels with curved wings, including some lammergeiers, which are great devourers of seals, and are appropriately called the vultures of the sea; chequered gulls, like little ducks with the tops of their bodies coloured black and white; and finally a whole series of petrels, some of them verging on white with wings edged in brown, others blue and peculiar to the Antarctic seas. These petrels are 'so oily', as I said to Conseil, 'that the inhabitants of the Faroe Islands merely add a wick before lighting them'.

'If they are so oleaginous,' replied Conseil, 'they would indeed make perfect lamps! The only thing one could ask is for nature herself to provide them with the wick!'

After about half a mile, the ground was completely covered with penguin 'nests', which are burrows for laying eggs, and from which numerous birds were emerging. Later on, Captain Nemo had a few hundred hunted down, for their black flesh is highly edible. They produce a braying noise like a donkey's. These creatures are the size of a goose, their bodies slate-coloured turning white below and with ruffs of lemon piping, and they allowed themselves to be stoned to death without trying to escape.

Meanwhile the mist was not lifting, and at eleven o'clock the sun had still not appeared. Its absence continued to worry me. Without it, no observation was possible. How then could we determine whether or not we had reached the Pole?

When I rejoined Captain Nemo, I found him silently leaning against a slab of rock and looking at the sky. He seemed impatient and upset. But what could he do? This audacious and energetic man did not command the sun as he did the sea.

Midday arrived without the sun showing itself for a single moment. It was not even possible to deduce where it was behind the curtain of cloud. And soon the cloud began to snow.

'Tomorrow,' the captain said simply, and we went back to the *Nautilus* through the gusty eddies.

During our absence the nets had been spread, and I studied with interest the fish that had been hauled on board. The Antarctic seas serve as refuge for a very great number of migrators, which flee the storms of the less elevated zones only to fall into the mouths of porpoises and seals. I noticed a few 10-centimetre southern bullheads, off-white cartilaginous animals, covered with pale stripes and armed with spicules; and then some three-foot Antarctic chimaeras with very long silvery-white bodies and smooth skins, round heads, backs with three fins, and snouts ending in trunks which curve back round towards their mouths. I tasted their flesh, but found it insipid, although Conseil appreciated it greatly.

The blizzard continued the next day. It was impossible to remain on the platform. From the salon, where I recorded the incidents of our excursion to the polar landmass, I heard the cries of the petrels and albatrosses piercing the storm. The *Nautilus* moved away and headed about 10 miles south along the coast, through the half-light produced by the sun skimming above the edge of the horizon.

The following day, 20 March,* the snow had stopped. The cold was a little worse, with the thermometer marking +2°. The fog lifted, and I hoped that we could make our observation today.

Since Captain Nemo had not yet appeared, the boat took Conseil and me to land. The ground was still volcanic in nature. Everywhere were traces of lava, scoriae, and basalt, although I was not able to locate the crater that had vomited them out. Here as before, myriads of birds gave life to the polar continent. But they shared this empire with vast herds of marine mammals, looking at us with their soft eyes. There were seals of various species, some stretched out on the shore, some lying on ice-floes, others climbing out of the sea or returning to it. They did not flee at our approach, never having had dealings with man, and I calculated that altogether there were enough to provision several hundred ships.

'Heavens,' said Conseil, 'what a good job Ned didn't come with us!'

'Why, Conseil?'

'Because the mad hunter would have killed everything.'

'That is going a little far, but I do believe we wouldn't have been able to stop our friend harpooning a few of these magnificent cetaceans. And that would have upset Captain Nemo, for he never spills the blood of innocent creatures without good reason.'

'He is right.'

'Certainly, Conseil. But tell me, have you classified these superb specimens of marine fauna?'

'Monsieur knows full well that I have not had much practice. Monsieur needs to tell me the names of the animals first.'

'These are seals and walruses.'

'Genera of the family of pinnipeds,' hastened to say my learned Conseil, 'order of carnivores, group of unguiculates, sub-class of monodelphians, class of mammals, branch of vertebrates.'

'Good,' I replied. 'But these genera of seals and walruses also divide into species, and if I am not mistaken we will soon have an opportunity to observe them more closely. So let's take a walk.'

It was eight in the morning. There were still four hours to fill until the sun could usefully be observed. I headed towards a vast bay that cut into the granite cliff of the coast.

As far as the eye could see, the ground and ice-floes were covered with marine mammals, and I involuntarily looked for old Proteus, the mythological shepherd who watches over Neptune's enormous flocks. Seals were particularly numerous. The males and females formed distinct groups, the father watching over his family, the mother suckling her babes, while some stronger juveniles were testing their independence a few feet away. When these mammals wanted to move they produced little jumps, contracting their bodies and helping themselves clumsily along with their imperfect fins, which form real forearms in their congeners, the manatees. I must say that in their natural element these animals swim admirably, with their flexible spines, narrow pelvises, short, close-knit coats, and webbed feet. When resting on the shore, they adopt extremely graceful attitudes. Accordingly, when the ancients observed their soft faces, charming poses, and deep, expressive, velvet eyes that the most beautiful woman would not be able to surpass, they poeticized them in their own way, changing the males into tritons* and the females into sirens.

I pointed out to Conseil the considerable development of the cerebral lobes in these intelligent cetaceans.* No mammal except man has richer brain matter. Accordingly, seals are suited to receiving a degree of education. They are easily domesticated, and like certain other naturalists, I believe that if properly trained they could be of great service as fishing dogs.

Most were sleeping on the rocks or the sand. Amongst the seals in the strict sense, that is without external ears—differing in this respect from the otaries whose ears protrude—I observed several varieties of the three-metre-long *Stenorhincus*. They had white hair, bulldog heads, and ten teeth in their jaw: four incisors at the top, four at the bottom, and two great canines standing out in the form of a fleur-de-lis. Between them slid a few sea elephants, a kind of seal with a short mobile trunk: the giant of the species has a girth of 20 feet and a length of 10 metres. They did not move as we approached.

'Are these animals not dangerous?' asked Conseil.

'Not unless attacked. When seals defend their young, their fury is terrifying, and it is not uncommon for them to smash fishermen's boats to pieces.'

'They have the right to.'

'Perhaps so.'

Two miles further on, we had to stop at the headland which protected the bay from the south wind. This promontory fell sheer into the sea and its foot was foaming with swell. Beyond it could be heard some formidable roaring noises, like those made by a herd of ruminants.

'But', said Conseil, 'is it a bulls' concert?'

'No,' I said; 'walruses.'

'Are they fighting?'

'Fighting or playing.'

'With respect, we should go and see them.'

'Of course.'

And there we were, clambering over the black rocks, with the ground sometimes collapsing unexpectedly, working our way over stones made very treacherous by the ice. I slipped more than once, doing my back no good. Conseil, more cautious or more solidly built, never raised an eyebrow, but would simply say as he picked me up:

'If monsieur would be so good as to spread his weight more, monsieur would maintain his equilibrium better.'

Once at the top of the cape, I could see a vast white plain covered with walruses. They were playing together; the cries were of joy, not anger. Walruses resemble seals as regards the shape of their bodies and the way their limbs are attached, but have no canines or incisors in their lower jaws; and their upper canines form tusks 80 centimetres long and 33 centimetres in circumference where they join the body. These teeth are very much sought after, being made of compact ivory without ridges, harder than elephants' and less prone to yellowing. As a result, walruses are excessively hunted, and will soon be destroyed down to the last, since the hunters indiscriminately massacre the pregnant females and their young, destroying in fact more than four thousand of them each year.

Passing by these strange animals, I examined them at my leisure, for they did not bother to move. Their skin was thick and rough, fawn shading into red, and their coat short and sparse. Some of them were as much as four metres long. Calmer and less fearful than their northern congeners, they did not appoint sentinels to keep watch over the surroundings of their camp.

After examining the city of walruses, I thought of turning back. It was eleven o'clock, and if Captain Nemo encountered favourable conditions to make an observation, I wanted to be present when he did. However, I had little hope that the sun would show itself that day. Crushed clouds lying on the horizon hid it from our eyes. It was as if that jealous star did not wish human beings to take observations at this unreachable point of the globe.

All the same, I decided to go back to the *Nautilus*. We followed a narrow track along the summit of the cliff. By half past eleven we were back on the landing strip. The boat had come ashore with the captain. I saw him standing on a block of basalt. His instruments lay near him and his eyes were fixed on the northern horizon, above which the sun was describing its flattened path.

I stood near him and waited in silence. Noon arrived: just like the day before, the sun did not appear.

Such was fate. We had still not made our observation. If we were not able to do so the next day, we would have to give up trying to measure our position.

It was 20 March. Tomorrow, the 21st, was the equinox, and if one ignored the refraction, the sun would vanish under the horizon for six months. With its disappearance the long polar night would begin. At the September equinox the sun had emerged from the northern horizon, rising in flattened spirals until 21 December. From that date, the summer solstice of these Antarctic regions, it had begun to decline once more; and tomorrow it was to send out its last rays.

I told Captain Nemo of my thoughts and fears.

'You are quite right, Dr Aronnax. If I cannot observe the height of the sun tomorrow, I will not be able to do so for another six months. But because the hazards of my navigation have brought me to these seas by 21 March, my position will be easy to take if the sun does show itself at midday tomorrow.'

'But why, captain?'

'Now, when the celestial orb describes such flat spirals, it is difficult to measure its exact height above the horizon, and our instruments are prone to serious errors . . .'

'How will you proceed then?'

'I will just use my chronometer,' he said. 'If tomorrow, 21 March at noon, taking account of refraction, the sun's disc is exactly cut by the northern horizon, then I am at the South Pole.'

'Just so. Nevertheless, your affirmation cannot be mathematically rigorous because the equinox does not necessarily fall at noon.'

'Yes, monsieur, but the error will be less than 100 metres,* and that's all we need. Till tomorrow then.'

Captain Nemo returned on board. Conseil and I stayed until five o'clock, working our way up and down the beach, observing and studying. I did not find any unusual objects except a penguin's egg of remarkable size, which a collector would have paid more than a thousand francs for. Its cream colour and stripes and its characters like hieroglyphics made it a rare curio. I put it into Conseil's hands, and the careful fellow, sure-footed and holding it like precious porcelain from China,* got it back to the *Nautilus* in one piece.

There I deposited the rare egg behind one of the panes in the museum. I dined with gusto on an excellent piece of seal liver, which reminded me of pork. And then I went to bed, having invoked like a Hindu the favours of the radiant star.

The next day, 21 March, I went up on the platform as early as five o'clock. I found Captain Nemo already there.

'The weather is slightly clearer,' he said. 'I have high hopes. After breakfast, we'll head for land to choose an observation point.'

Having agreed this matter, I went back in to look for Ned Land. I suggested he come with me, but the obdurate Canadian refused, and I could see full well that his taciturnity and bad mood were worsening by the day. But really, under the circumstances, I did not regret his stubbornness. There were too many seals on shore, and I didn't want to lead the unreflecting huntsman into temptation.

After breakfast, I headed for land again. The *Nautilus* had moved a few miles further on overnight. It was now floating on the open sea a good league from the coast, which was dominated by a sharp peak 400 or 500 metres high. Captain Nemo and I were in the boat with two crewmen, along with the instruments: a chronometer, a telescope, and a barometer.

As we headed for land, I saw a large number of whales from the three species particular to the southern seas: the right whale, as the British call it, without a dorsal fin; the humpback or rorqual, with a wrinkled stomach and huge white fins, which do not form wings despite its French name, *baleinoptere*; and the finback, yellowish-brown in colour and the quickest of the three. This powerful animal can make itself heard at great distances when it sends columns of air and vapour up to considerable heights, turning into misty whorls. These various mammals were playing in schools in the peaceful waters, and I realized that this basin of the South Pole now served as a refuge for the cetaceans, too fiercely hunted by mankind.

I also saw long off-white funicles of salps, a type of clustered mollusc, as well as jellyfish of great size rocking on the waves.

We reached land at nine o'clock. The sky was brightening as the clouds fled southwards.* Mists rose from the cold surface of the water. Captain Nemo headed for the peak, which he undoubtedly intended to be his observatory. It was hard going on the sharp lavas and pumice stones, through an atmosphere often filled with sulphurous air from the exhalations. For a man unused to walking on shore, the captain climbed the steepest slopes with a suppleness and agility that I could not equal and which a hunter of mountain goats would have envied.

It took us two hours to reach the summit, half made of porphyry and half basalt. From there, our eyes took in a vast sea, whose culmination towards the north coincided with the bottom of the sky. At our feet, dazzling fields of whiteness. Above our heads, pale blue, clear of mist. To the north, the sun's disc, a ball of fire, already trimmed by the sharp edge of the horizon. From the heart of the waters, hundreds of liquid jets falling in magnificent showers. In the distance, the *Nautilus* like a slumbering cetacean. Behind us, to the south and east, an immense land, a chaotic jumble of rocks and ice, whose limits could not be seen.

Upon arriving at the peak itself, Captain Nemo carefully noted the height using the barometer, for he had to take account of it in his observation.

At quarter to twelve the golden disc of the sun, at present seen only by refraction, appeared and bestowed its last rays on this lonely continent, on these seas that man had never sailed.

Using a reticule telescope which used a mirror to correct the refraction, Captain Nemo observed the heavenly body as it slowly sank beneath the skyline, following a very oblique course. I was holding the chronometer.* My heart was beating wildly. If the disappearance of the sun's semicircle coincided with noon on the chronometer, we were at the Pole.

'Midday!' I exclaimed.

'The South Pole,' Captain Nemo announced in a grave voice, as he handed me the telescope showing the celestial orb cut in two equal portions by the horizon.

I watched the last rays crowning the peak as the shadows gradually climbed the slopes.

Just then, Captain Nemo put his hand on my shoulder and said:

'Monsieur, in 1600 the Dutchman Gherritz,* carried off by currents and storms, reached 64° S and discovered the South Shetlands. On 17 January 1773, the illustrious Cook, following the 38th meridian, arrived at 67° 30′ S, and on 30 January 1774, reached 71° 15′ S on the 109th meridian. In 1819, the Russian Bellingshausen found himself on the 69th parallel, and in 1821, on the 66th at 111° W. In 1820, the Briton Bransfield was stopped at the 65th degree. The same year, the American Morrell, whose tales are doubtful, discovered an open sea at 70° 14′ S while working his way along the 42nd meridian. In 1825, the Briton Powell was not able to go further than the 62nd degree. That same year, a mere sealer, the Briton Weddell, went as far as 72° 14′ S on the 35th meridian, and as far as 74° 15′ on the 36th. In 1829, the Briton Foster, captain of the *Chanticleer*, took possession of the Antarctic continent at 63° 26′ S, 66° 26′ W. On 1 February 1831, the Briton Biscoe discovered Enderby Land at 68° 50′ S, Adelaide Island at 67° S on 5 February 1832, and Graham Land at 64° 45′ S on 21 February. In 1838, the Frenchman Dumont d'Urville, halted by the ice-cap at 62° 57′ S, took note of Louis-Philippe Land; on 21 January 1840, in a new push south, he named Adélie Land at 66° 30′, and a week later, Clarie Coast at 64° 40′. In 1838 the Briton Wilkes advanced to the 69th parallel on the 100th meridian. In 1839, the

Briton Balleny* discovered Sabrina Coast, on the limit of the Antarctic
Circle. Finally, on 12 January 1842 the Briton James Ross, captain of
the ships the *Erebus* and the *Terror*, reached 70° 56′ S, 171° 7′ E, and
discovered Victoria Land; on the 23rd of the same month, he noted the
74th parallel, the furthest point reached until then; on the 27th he was
at 76° 8′, on the 28th, 77° 32′, on 2 February, 78° 4′, and in 1842, he
came back to the 71st degree, which he was not able to surpass. Well,
on this 21st day of March 1868, I, Captain Nemo, have attained the
South Pole and the 90th degree, and I take possession of this part of
the globe, now comprising one-sixth of all the discovered continents.'

'In whose name, captain?'

'In my own, monsieur!'

And saying this, Captain Nemo unfurled a black flag, carrying
a golden 'N' quartered on its bunting.* Then turning to the sun,
whose last rays were licking the sea at the horizon:

'Farewell, sun!' he exclaimed. 'Vanish, O bright orb. Take your
sleep under this open sea, and let a night of six months cloak my new
realm* in its shades!'

15

ACCIDENT OR INCIDENT?

THE following day, 22 March, preparations for departure began at
six in the morning. The last gleams of dusk were melting into the
night. There was a piercing cold. The constellations shone with surprising intensity. At the zenith sparkled the beautiful Southern Cross,
the North Star of the Antarctic.

The thermometer marked −12° and when the wind freshened, it
produced a sharp biting sensation. The ice-floes were multiplying
on the open sea. The ocean was beginning to freeze in all directions.
Numerous translucent black patches spreading over its surface showed
that young ice was soon going to form. Clearly the southern basin,
frozen for six months each winter, was totally inaccessible during that
season. What did the whales do during that time? Undoubtedly they
swam under the ice-cap to look for more hospitable seas. The seals and
the walruses, used to living in the harshest climates, remained on the
iced-over waters. These animals possess an instinct for digging holes

in the icefields and keeping them permanently open, in order to come and breathe. When the birds, chased away by the cold, have emigrated north, these marine mammals remain the sole masters of the Antarctic.

Meanwhile the water tanks had been filled, and the *Nautilus* was slowly sinking. At a depth of 1,000 feet, it stopped. Its propeller began to beat the water, and it moved directly northwards at a speed of 15 knots. By evening it was already floating under the immense frozen carapace of the ice-cap.

The panels of the salon had been closed as a safety measure, for the *Nautilus*'s hull might collide with some sunken block. Accordingly I spent the day putting my notes in order. My mind was completely filled with my memories of the Pole. We had reached that inaccessible point without fatigue, without danger, as if our floating compartment had run along the tracks of a railway. And now our return was under way. Would it hold similar surprises for me? I thought it would, so inexhaustible are the submarine wonders! During the five-and-a-half months that fate had kept us on board, we had covered 14,000 leagues, a distance longer than the terrestrial equator. How many interesting or terrifying incidents had marked our voyage: hunting in the forests of Crespo, running aground in Torres Strait, the coral cemetery, fishing in Ceylon, the Arabian Tunnel, the fires of Santorini, the riches of Vigo Bay, Atlantis, and the South Pole! During the night, all these memories flitted from dream to dream, and would not let my mind drift into sleep for a single moment.

At three o'clock, I was fully woken by a violent jolt. I sat up on my bed and was listening out in the darkness, when I was suddenly thrown into the middle of the room. The *Nautilus* was now listing badly, having clearly run aground.

I felt my way along the walls, and dragged myself through the gangways as far as the salon, still lit by the luminous ceiling. The furniture had fallen over. Fortunately the display cabinets, with their feet solidly fixed, had not moved. As the perpendicular was displaced, the starboard paintings were pressed hard against the wall coverings while the lower edges of the port ones hung a foot in the air. The *Nautilus* was listing to starboard and lay completely motionless.

From inside I could hear sounds of feet and confused voices. But Captain Nemo did not appear. Just when I was about to leave the salon, Ned Land and Conseil came in.

'What's happened?' I immediately asked them.

'I was just coming to ask monsieur,' replied Conseil.

'Hell!' cried the Canadian, 'I know! The *Nautilus* has hit ground, and judging from the angle we're listing at, I don't think we'll get out of this one like we did in Torres Strait.'

'But has it at least gone back up to the surface?'

'We don't know,' replied Conseil.

'It's easy to find out.'

I consulted the pressure-gauge. To my great surprise it indicated a depth of 360 metres.

'What does that mean?' I exclaimed.

'We must ask Captain Nemo,' said Conseil.

'But where can we find him?' asked Ned.*

'Follow me,' I said.

We left the salon. In the library, not a soul. On the central staircase and in the crew room, no one. I supposed that Captain Nemo had to be stationed in the pilot-house. It was best to wait. The three of us came back to the salon.

I will skip over the Canadian's complaints. He had sufficient reason to explode. I let him vent his spleen as much as he wished, without replying.

We had been in this situation for twenty minutes, trying to detect the slightest sound from the interior of the *Nautilus*, when Captain Nemo came in. He did not seem to see us. His face, usually so impassive, revealed a certain anxiety. He silently studied the compass and pressure-gauge, and came and put his finger on a point of the planisphere, in the part showing the southern seas.

I did not want to interrupt. But when he turned to me a moment later, I echoed an expression he had used in Torres Strait:

'An incident, captain?'

'No, monsieur, an accident this time.'

'Serious?'

'Perhaps.'

'Is there immediate danger?'

'No.'

'Has the *Nautilus* run aground?'

'Yes.'

'And how did we run aground?'

'From a quirk of nature, not from human error. There were no operational failures. However, we cannot resist the effects of equilibrium. One can disdain human laws, but not resist natural ones.'

Captain Nemo had chosen an odd moment to indulge in such philosophical reflections. His answer left me totally in the dark.

'May I know, monsieur, what caused the accident?'

'An enormous block of ice, an entire mountain, overturned. When icebergs are undermined at the bottom by warmer waters or by repeated collisions, their centre of gravity rises. They invert, they turn upside down. That is what happened here. One such block turned over, colliding with the *Nautilus* sailing beneath it. The iceberg rose under its hull and picked it up with irresistible force, and has now brought the *Nautilus* up to lighter strata, where it is at present lying on its side.'

'But can't we free the *Nautilus* by emptying its tanks to restore its equilibrium?'

'That is what is going on at present, monsieur. You can hear the pumps working. Look at the needle of the pressure-gauge. It indicates that the *Nautilus* is rising but the block of ice is also moving with it, and unless something stops it rising, our situation will not change.'

The *Nautilus* was indeed still listing the same amount to starboard. It would undoubtedly return to upright when the block came to a stop. But when it did, who knew if it wouldn't be due to hitting the main body of the icefield, and being frighteningly crushed between two icy surfaces?

I was thinking about the various repercussions of the situation. Captain Nemo did not take his eyes off the pressure-gauge. Since the collapse of the iceberg the *Nautilus* had climbed approximately 150 feet, but was still lying at the same angle.

Suddenly we felt a slight movement in the hull. The *Nautilus* was shifting slightly back to upright. The objects hanging in the salon began to move perceptibly towards their normal position. The walls were approaching the vertical. Nobody spoke. With our hearts pumping, we could see, we could feel equilibrium returning. The floor was becoming horizontal under our feet again. Ten minutes went by.

'Finally we are straight again!' I exclaimed.

'Yes,' said Captain Nemo, heading for the door.

'But will we float?'

'The tanks,' he replied, 'still contain water; so once they are empty, the *Nautilus* will inevitably rise to the surface again.'

The captain went out, and I quickly realized that he had ordered the *Nautilus*'s ascent to be stopped. It would soon have hit the icefield from below, so it was better to remain where we were.

'That was a close shave!' said Conseil.

'Yes; we might have been crushed between huge blocks of ice, or at least imprisoned. And then, not able to renew our air . . . Yes, a close shave!'

'If it's really over,' murmured Ned.

I did not wish to start a pointless debate with the Canadian, and so did not reply. In any case the panels opened at that moment, and light surged in through the window.

We were underwater, as I have said, but a dazzling wall of ice rose at a distance of 10 metres on each side of the *Nautilus*. Above and below, a continuation of the same wall. Above, because the lower surface of the ice-cap arched over us like an enormous vault. Below, because the upturned block had slid little by little, and had found two points of contact on the side walls, which maintained it in position. The *Nautilus* was imprisoned in a veritable tunnel of ice about 20 metres wide and filled with calm water. It was therefore easy for it to get out, either backwards or forwards, before continuing freely on its way under the ice-cap, albeit a few hundred metres further down.

The luminous ceiling had been switched off, and yet the salon was scintillating in intense light. The reason was the powerful illumination from the walls of ice, violently throwing back the searchlight's beams. I cannot depict the impact of the voltaic rays on these great, capriciously carved blocks, with each angle, each corner, each facet radiating a different effect, according to the nature of the veins running through it.

A glittering mine of gems, especially sapphires, crisscrossing their blue rays with shafts of emerald green. Here and there opaline shades of infinite subtlety ran through the shining points like fiery diamonds, unbearably dazzling the eye. The power of the searchlight was multiplied a hundred times, like that of a lamp through the lenses of a lighthouse of the first order.

'How beautiful it is! How beautiful!' exclaimed Conseil.

'Yes,' I said, 'it's a wonderful sight. Isn't it, Ned?'

'Hell yes,' riposted Land. 'It's superb! I hate to have to agree. We've never seen anything like it. But this vision may cost us dear. To be frank, I think that we're seeing things here that God wanted to hide from man's eyes.'

Ned was right. It was too beautiful. Suddenly a cry from Conseil made me turn round.

'What is it?'

'Monsieur should close his eyes! Monsieur should not look.'

As he spoke, Conseil vigorously rubbed his eyelids.

'What's the matter, my lad?'

'I am dazzled, blinded!'

My eyes turned involuntarily towards the window, but I was not able to bear the fire that consumed them.

I understood what had happened. The *Nautilus* had started moving very quickly. All the discreet reflections from the walls of ice had then changed into flashing rays. The fire from these myriads of diamonds joined together. The *Nautilus,* carried on by its propeller, was sailing through a sheath of lightning.

The panels of the salon closed. We put our hands over our eyes, still inundated with those circular gleams that float in front of your retina when sunlight has struck it too violently. It took quite a while before our eyes recovered.

Finally we lowered our hands.

'Goodness, I would never have believed it,' said Conseil.

'And I still don't!' replied the Canadian.

'When we are back on land, and take for granted so many of these brilliant works of nature,' added Conseil, 'what will we think of the grey landmasses and the paltry works of art man has crafted! No, the inhabited world is no longer fit for us!'

Such words in the mouth of an impassive Fleming showed what level of turmoil our enthusiasm had reached. But the Canadian threw cold water on it as usual.

'The inhabited world,' he repeated, shaking his head. 'Calm down, Conseil, my friend, you'll never see it again!'

It was five in the morning. Just then, a jolt reverberated from the front of the *Nautilus.* I understood that its ram had hit a wall of ice. This had to be an accident—the underwater tunnel, strewn with odd blocks, did not make for easy navigation. I thought that Captain Nemo would now adjust his route and work his way round the obstacle by following the outside of the tunnel. In any case, the forward motion would not be stopped. However, against my expectation, the *Nautilus* began moving backwards very fast.

'Have we changed direction?' said Conseil.

'Yes,' I replied, 'the tunnel must have no way out at this end.'

'But then . . .?'

'Then the consequence is quite simple. We head back and we leave by the southern exit. That's all.'

Speaking like this, I wished to appear more confident than I really was. The backwards movement of the *Nautilus* increased, and proceeding on reverse propeller, it carried us along at tremendous speed.

'This will slow us down,' said Ned.

'What difference do a few hours more or less make, provided we get out?'

'Yes,' said Ned, '*provided* we do get out.'

I spent a while walking around the salon and the library. My companions remained seated without saying a word. I soon threw myself on to a sofa, and picked up a book, which my eyes began mechanically scanning.

Quarter of an hour later, Conseil came up to me and said:

'Is monsieur reading something interesting?'

'Very interesting,' I replied.

'I agree. Monsieur is reading his own book.'

'My own book?'

I was indeed holding *The Ocean Deeps*. I had had no idea I was doing this. I closed the volume and continued my pacing. Ned and Conseil got up to go to bed.

'Please remain, my friends,' I said, restraining them, 'let's stay together until we have got out of this cul-de-sac.'

'As monsieur pleases,' replied Conseil.

A few hours went by. I often looked at the instruments on the salon walls. The pressure-gauge indicated that the *Nautilus* was staying at a constant depth of 300 metres, the compass, that it was still heading south, and the logline, that it was moving at 20 knots, a very high speed in such an enclosed space. But Captain Nemo knew that no speed could be too great, that minutes were in this case worth centuries.

At 8.25 we felt a second jolt, at the back this time. I turned pale. My companions had come close. I had taken Conseil's hand. We questioned each other with our eyes, more directly than if our thoughts had been expressed in words.

The captain entered the salon. I went up to him.

'So the route is blocked to the south?'

'Yes, monsieur. When the iceberg overturned, it closed every way out.'

'Then we're trapped?'

'Yes, we are.'

16

NOT ENOUGH AIR

So all around the *Nautilus*, above and below, was an impenetrable wall of ice. We were prisoners of the ice-cap. The Canadian struck the table with his tremendous fist. Conseil remained silent. I looked at the captain. His face had resumed its customary impassiveness. He had pensively crossed his arms. The *Nautilus* was no longer moving.

Then the captain spoke again:

'Messieurs,' he said in a calm voice, 'there are two ways of dying in our present circumstances.'

The incomprehensible character resembled a professor of mathematics carrying out a demonstration for his students.

'The first is to die through being crushed. The second is to die of asphyxiation. I do not mention the possibility of dying from hunger, for the provisions of the *Nautilus* will certainly last longer than we will. Let us therefore consider our chances of being crushed and of being asphyxiated.'

'As for asphyxiation, captain,' I replied, 'there is little danger because our tanks are full.'

'True,' said Captain Nemo, 'but they will only provide us with two days of air. We have been underwater for thirty-six hours, and already the heavy atmosphere of the *Nautilus* needs replenishing. In forty-eight hours' time our reserves will also be exhausted.'

'Well, captain, let's make sure we are safe within forty-eight hours!'

'We will at least try cutting through the wall surrounding us,' he replied.

'In which direction?' I asked.

'Soundings will tell us. I am going to ground the *Nautilus* on the lower surface, and using their diving suits my men will attack the iceberg at its thinnest wall.'

'Can we open the panels of the salon?'

'Certainly. We are not moving.'

Captain Nemo went out. Soon hissing sounds told me that water was being let into the tanks. The *Nautilus* slowly sank and came to rest on the icy floor at a barometric reading of 350 metres, the depth of the lower surface of ice.

'My friends,' I said, 'our situation is serious, but I am counting on your courage and energy.'

'Monsieur, I will not bother you with my reproaches at this stage. I am ready to do anything for our collective safety.'

'Good, Ned,' I said, stretching out my hand to him.

'I'll add that I'm as good with a pickaxe as a harpoon, and so am at the captain's service if I can be of any use.'

'He will not refuse your help. Come, Ned.'

I took him to the room where the crew of the *Nautilus* were putting on their diving suits. I told the captain of Ned's offer, which he accepted. The Canadian put on his sea clothing, and was soon as ready as his work companions. Each man carried a Rouquayrol apparatus on his back, to which the tanks had added a large amount of pure air. A considerable but necessary borrowing from the *Nautilus*'s reserves. As for the Ruhmkorff lamps, they were useless in waters fully illuminated by electric beams.

When Ned was ready I went back to the salon, where the windows were already uncovered, and took up position with Conseil to study the water around the *Nautilus*.

A few moments later, we saw a dozen crewmen stepping out on to the floor of ice, Ned Land amongst them, identifiable by his size. Captain Nemo was also there.

Before proceeding to hollow out the walls, he had soundings made in order to ensure the work would proceed in the right direction. Long sounds were inserted into the side walls, but after 50 metres they were still blocked by the thick ice. It was useless to attack the top surface because this was the ice-cap itself, stretching more than 400 metres above us. Finally Captain Nemo had the lower surface sounded. There 10 metres of wall separated us from the water. We needed to cut a piece of solid ice 30 feet thick and of the same surface area as the flotation line of the *Nautilus*. This meant cutting out about 6,500 cubic metres so as to make a hole through which we could reach the water below the ice-cap.

The work began immediately, executed with unyielding single-mindedness. Instead of digging around the *Nautilus*, which would have been more difficult, Captain Nemo had a massive trench outlined 8 metres from its port quarter. Then his men simultaneously pierced several points on its outer limit. Soon pickaxes were vigorously attacking the dense material, bringing large blocks out of the ice.

Through a strange effect of specific gravity, the blocks were lighter than water, and flew up, so to speak, to the vault of the tunnel, which grew thicker at the top by the same amount it reduced at the bottom. But this hardly mattered, given that the floor was getting progressively thinner.

After two hours of hard work, Ned returned exhausted. He and his companions were replaced by new hands, whom Conseil and I joined. The first officer of the *Nautilus* directed us.

The water seemed extraordinarily cold, but I soon warmed up using the pickaxe. My movements felt very free, although produced at a pressure of 30 atmospheres.

When I returned after two hours of work to take some food and rest, I found a notable difference between the pure air that the Rouquayrol apparatus had been giving me and the atmosphere of the *Nautilus*, already full of carbon dioxide. The air had not been renewed for forty-eight hours, and its life-giving qualities were considerably reduced. Also, in a period of twelve hours we had only removed a slab of ice a metre thick from the designated area, that is about 600 cubic metres. Assuming the same amount of work was executed every twelve hours, we still needed five nights and four days to finish.

'Five nights and four days,' I said to my companions, 'and we only have two days of air left in the tanks.'

'Not to mention', replied Ned, 'that even if we get out of this damned prison, we'll still be under the ice-cap without being able to reach the open air.'

It was true. Who could calculate the minimum time needed for our final deliverance? Would we not be smothered and asphyxiated before the *Nautilus* got back up to the surface? Was the *Nautilus* destined to perish in this icy tomb with all those it contained? Such a prospect seemed terrifying, but everyone had clearly faced up to it and was determined to do his duty until the end.

As I expected, a new layer 1 metre thick was removed from the enormous hole during the night. But when I put my diving suit on again in the morning, and entered the liquid element at a temperature of −6° or −7°, I noticed the side wall was getting gradually closer. The water furthest from the trench was not being warmed by the work of the men or the action of their tools and so was prone to freezing. In the presence of this new and imminent danger, what were our chances of survival—how could we prevent the solidification of the liquid, which might crush the sides of the *Nautilus* like glass?

I did not inform my two companions of this new danger. What was the point of running the risk of damping their ardour for the difficult work of saving us? But when I came back on board, I mentioned the serious complication to Captain Nemo.

'I know,' he said in that calm tone which the worst situations could not alter. 'It is an additional danger, but I can see no way of stopping it. The only chance of survival is to work more quickly than the solidification process. We need to finish first, that's all.'

Finish first! But I suppose I should have been used to such forms of expression.

For several hours that day I wielded the pickaxe with considerable obduracy. The work maintained my morale. In any case, to labour was to leave the *Nautilus* and to breathe the pure air supplied by the apparatus straight from the tanks. It was to leave an atmosphere which was impoverished and vitiated.

In the evening the trench was a metre deeper. When I returned on board, I was almost suffocated by the carbon dioxide filling the air. Ah, why did we not have some chemical means to eliminate this noxious gas? There was plenty of oxygen, for all this water contained huge quantities of the element, and decomposing it with our powerful batteries would have given us access to the life-giver. I had indeed thought of this, but what was the point, since the carbon dioxide we breathed out permeated every part of the ship? To absorb it, we would have needed containers of caustic potash, constantly shaken. But we had none on board, and nothing could replace it.

That evening, Captain Nemo had to open the taps of his tanks and send a few columns of pure air into the interior of the *Nautilus*. If he had not done so we would not have woken up again.

The next day, 26 March, I continued my miner's work and began on the fifth metre. The sides and ceiling of the ice-cap were getting visibly thicker. It was evident that they would join up before the *Nautilus* was able to free itself. Despair took hold of me for a moment. My pickaxe came near to falling from my hands. What was the point of digging if I was to suffocate to death, crushed by this water turning to stone, a torture that even the ferocity of savages could not have invented? It was as if I lay between the formidable jaws of a monster, ones inexorably snapping shut.

Just then Captain Nemo, directing the work and himself labouring, passed near me. I touched him with my glove, and showed him the walls of our prison. The port wall was now less than four metres from the *Nautilus*'s hull.

The captain understood, and signalled that I should follow him. We went back on board. Once my diving suit was off, I followed him into the salon.

'Dr Aronnax,' he said to me, 'we need to employ desperate measures, or else we are going to be sealed in this frozen water as if in concrete.'

'Yes, but what should we do?'

'Ah, if only my *Nautilus* were strong enough to bear this pressure without crumpling!'

'Well?' I asked, not really understanding his idea.

'Don't you understand that the freezing of the water would actually help us? Can you not see that the solidifying process would crack the walls of ice imprisoning us, as it cracks hard stones when they freeze! Can you not appreciate that it would then be an agent of survival rather than one of destruction!'

'Yes, captain, perhaps. But whatever resistance to being crushed the *Nautilus* has, it will not be able to bear such an awesome pressure, and would end up as flat as a pancake.'

'I know, monsieur. So we must not rely on help from nature, but only ourselves. We must prevent the solidification, or at least slow it down. Not only are the sides closing in, but there remain only 10 feet of water fore and aft of the *Nautilus*. The freezing is gaining on us in all directions.'

'How much time will the air from the tanks allow us to breathe on board?'

The captain looked me squarely in the face.

'The tanks will be empty the day after tomorrow!'

I was covered in a cold sweat, and yet how could I be surprised by his reply? The *Nautilus* had dived under the open seas of the Pole on 22 March. It was now the 26th. We had been living on the reserves for four days, and what breathable air remained needed to be given to the workers. As I write these things, my impressions are still so vivid that my whole body is stricken with involuntary terror and the air feels as if it is being tugged from my lungs!

However, Captain Nemo was reflecting, silent and motionless. An idea was clearly going through his mind, but he seemed to be rejecting it. He was responding to himself in the negative. At last, words escaped his lips:

'Boiling water,' he murmured.

'Boiling water!'

'Yes. We are enclosed in a relatively confined space. Would sending jets of boiling water continuously from the *Nautilus*'s pumps not raise the general temperature and so slow down the freezing?'

'We must try,' I said resolutely.

'Let's try then.'

The temperature outside read −7°. Captain Nemo took me to the kitchens, where vast distillation machinery produced drinking water by means of evaporation. It was now filled with water, then all the energy from the electric batteries was sent through the liquid in the coils. In a few minutes the water reached 100°. While it was sent to the pumps, an equivalent amount of fresh water was introduced. The heat developed by the batteries was such that, merely by going through this equipment, cold water drawn from the sea arrived boiling at the pumping machinery.

Three hours after the pumping began, the thermometer showed −6° outside. We had gained one degree. Two hours later, the thermometer read −4°.

'We're going to win,' I told the captain, having followed the progress of this operation and accompanying it with numerous comments.

'Perhaps,' he replied. 'We're not going to be crushed. We only have asphyxiation to worry about.'

Overnight the temperature of the water went up to −1°. The pumping could not make it rise any further. But since sea water freezes only at −2°, I finally stopped worrying about the dangers of solidification.

The following day, 27 March, six metres of ice had been torn from the hole. There remained only four metres to go. This was still forty-eight hours of work. The air could not be renewed inside the *Nautilus*. Accordingly, the day got gradually worse and worse.

An unbearable heaviness came over me. At about three in the afternoon, the feeling of anguish grew devastatingly. Yawns dislocated my jaws. My lungs worked fast as they searched for the combustive gas indispensable for breathing, now more and more rarefied. A mortal torpor took hold of me. I was stretched out feeling very weak, almost unconscious. My good Conseil, undergoing the same symptoms, suffering the same suffering, refused to leave me. He took my hand, he encouraged me, and I kept hearing him murmur:

'Ah, if only I could refrain from breathing in order to leave more air for monsieur!'

Tears came to my eyes when I heard him speak like this.

If the situation inside was intolerable for all of us, with what haste, with what joy we would put on our diving suits to take our turn to work! The pickaxes rang out on the frozen floor. Arms grew tired, hands blistered, but who cared about fatigue and pain! The vital air was entering our lungs! We were breathing, really breathing!

And yet no one prolonged his work underwater beyond the specified time. Once the task was over, each entrusted to his gasping companion the tank which would pour life into him. Captain Nemo showed the example, submitting first to this severe discipline. Once the time had come, he gave his apparatus to another and returned to the ship's vitiated atmosphere, always calm, without a moment of weakness, without a murmur.

That day, the work was carried out with still more vigour. Only two metres remained to be removed from the area. Only two metres separated us from the open sea, but the tanks were almost empty. The little which remained had to be kept for the workers. Not a single atom for the *Nautilus*!

When I returned on board, I half suffocated. What a night! I cannot depict it. Such suffering cannot be described. The next day my breathing was oppressed. I had headaches combined with stupefying dizziness, which made a drunkard of me. My companions experienced the same symptoms. A few crewmen were on their last legs.

That day, the sixth of our imprisonment,* Captain Nemo found the pick and pickaxe too slow, and resolved to assault the layer of ice still separating us from the liquid element. This man had kept his sang-froid and energy. He overcame his physical ills with moral force. He thought, he took himself in hand, he acted.

On his orders, the vessel was eased, that is, removed from its frozen resting place by slightly changing its specific weight. While floating it was hauled until it was over the massive trench shaped like its flotation line. Then its water tanks were opened slightly, it sank down again, and fitted into the hole.

The whole crew returned on board, and the double communication doors were closed. The *Nautilus* rested on the ice layer, less than a metre thick, pierced in a thousand places by bore holes.

The tanks' taps were then opened wide, and 100 cubic metres of water rushed into them, increasing the weight of the *Nautilus* by 100,000 kilograms.

We waited, we listened, forgetting our suffering, still hoping. We were gambling our lives on a last attempt.

In spite of the roaring sounds filling my head, I soon felt tremblings under the *Nautilus*'s hull. It shifted. The ice cracked with a bizarre sound like paper tearing and the *Nautilus* dropped down.

'We are going through!' Conseil murmured in my ear.

I was not able to reply. I grabbed his hand. I pressed it in the throes of an involuntary convulsion.

Suddenly, carried away by its massive overload, the *Nautilus* sank like a cannonball dropped in water—it fell as if in a vacuum. The whole electric force was then sent into the pumps, which immediately began to expel water from the tanks.

After a few minutes our fall stopped. Soon the pressure-gauge even indicated upward movement. The propeller, working at full speed, made the metal hull tremble down to the very bolts, and carried us off northwards.

But how long would this race under the ice-cap take before we reached the open sea? Another day? I would be dead by then.

Half stretched out on a sofa in the library, I was suffocating. My face was purple, my lips blue, my faculties suspended. I could no longer see, I could no longer hear. All idea of time had vanished from my mind. My muscles would not contract.

I could not count the hours that went by in this way, but I was aware that death-throes were coming on. I realized that I was on the point of perishing.

Suddenly I came to. A few mouthfuls of air had reached my lungs. Had we made it back up to the surface? Had we got through the icefield?

No! It was Ned and Conseil, my two good friends, depriving themselves to save me. A few atoms of air still remained at the bottom of a device. Instead of breathing it themselves, they had kept it for me; while themselves suffocating, they poured life into me drop by drop! I tried to push back the device. But they held my hands, and for a few moments I breathed in with voluptuousness.

My eyes turned to the clock. It was eleven in the morning. It must have been 28 March. The *Nautilus* was slicing through the water at a speed of 40 knots.

Where was Captain Nemo? Had he succumbed? Were his companions dead with him?

The pressure-gauge indicated that we were only 20 feet from the surface. A mere sheet of ice separated us from the free air. Could we not break it?

In any case, the *Nautilus* was going to try. I could feel it manoeuvring into an oblique position, lowering its stern and lifting its prow. Introducing some water had been enough to break the equilibrium. Then, pushed on by its powerful propeller, it thrust up into the icefield like a formidable ram. It was breaking it up piece by piece, the *Nautilus* was withdrawing, then again launching itself at full speed against the field. The ice began to perforate, and carrying through in a supreme lunge, it threw itself on to the icy surface, which it crushed under its weight.

The hatch was opened, or rather torn off, as pure air poured into every part of the *Nautilus*.

17

FROM CAPE HORN TO THE AMAZON

How I reached the platform I cannot say. Perhaps the Canadian dragged me there. But I was breathing, I was gulping down the invigorating sea air. Beside me, my two companions were drunk on the fresh air. Wretches who are deprived of food for too long must not throw themselves thoughtlessly on the first food they find. But we had no need to ration ourselves. We could breathe in great lungfuls of atmosphere, and the wind itself suffused us with its voluptuous intoxication!

'Ah,' said Conseil, 'how good oxygen is! Monsieur need not hold back from breathing it in. There is plenty for everyone.'

As for Ned, he was not speaking but had his mouth gaping to an extent that would have frightened a shark. And what powerful breathing! The Canadian was 'drawing' like a roaring stove.

Our strength soon came back, and when I looked round I realized that we were alone on the platform. No crew member, not even Captain Nemo. The strange sailors of the *Nautilus* satisfied themselves with the air circulating inside. Not one had come for refreshment in the open air.

The first words I said were words of thanks to my two companions. Ned and Conseil had saved my life in the last hours of that long death agony. My wholesale gratitude was not too much to give for such devotion.

'All right, monsieur!' Ned Land replied. 'Why go on about it? What did we have to do with it? Nothing. It was just a matter of arithmetic. Your life was worth more than ours, so we had to save you.'

'No, Ned,' I replied, 'it was not worth more, nobody is better than a man who is generous and good, and you are both of these!'

'All right, all right!' said the Canadian, embarrassed.

'And you, my good Conseil, also suffered tremendously.'

'Not too much, to tell the truth, monsieur. A few mouthfuls of air would not have gone astray, but I believe I would have got used to the situation. In any case, I saw monsieur fainting, and that did not give me the least desire to inhale. It took, as they say, my breath . . .'

Embarrassed to have launched himself into such a cliché, Conseil did not finish.

'My friends,' I said, greatly moved, 'we are bound to each other for life, and I am for ever in your debt.'

'Which I will draw on.'

'Eh?' said Conseil.

'Yes,' continued Land, 'I will call on the right to take you with me when I leave this infernal *Nautilus*.'

'Come to mention it,' said Conseil, 'are we heading in the right direction?'

'Yes,' I replied, 'since we are moving towards the sun, and the sun is in the north here.'

'Agreed,' said Ned. 'But we still need to know whether we're heading for the Pacific or the Atlantic, that is, for empty or for crowded seas.'

I could not reply, fearing that Captain Nemo was in fact taking us back to that vast ocean which washes the coasts of both Asia and America. He would thus complete his submarine journey round the world, and return to the seas where the *Nautilus* found the most independence. But if we were going back to the Pacific, far from friendly shores, what would become of Ned Land's plans?

This important point would be settled before long. The *Nautilus* was moving quickly. The polar circle was soon crossed, and sail set for Cape Horn. We were off the tip of America at seven in the evening of 31 March.

All our suffering was long forgotten. The memory of our icy imprisonment was fast fading from our minds. We only thought of the future. Captain Nemo did not appear either in the salon or on the platform. The position as measured by the first officer and plotted each day on the planisphere allowed me to follow the exact route of the *Nautilus*. And to my great satisfaction it became evident that evening that we were heading back north via the Atlantic.

I informed Ned and Conseil of the results of my deductions.

'Good news,' replied the Canadian, 'but where exactly is the *Nautilus* going?'

'I cannot say, Ned.'

'Does the captain now wish to conquer the North Pole having done the South Pole, and return to the Pacific via the famous Northwest Passage?'

'We must not try to dissuade him even if he does wish to do that,' replied Conseil.

'Well, we'll part company from him before then!'

'In any case,' added Conseil, 'Captain Nemo is a remarkable man, and we will not regret having known him.'

'Above all when we've left!' retorted Ned.

The following day, 1 April, when the *Nautilus* surfaced a few minutes before noon, we sighted a coast to the west. This was Tierra del Fuego, so called by the first navigators because they saw large amounts of smoke rising from the native huts. Tierra del Fuego forms a vast collection of islands more than 80 leagues in length by 30 leagues in width, between 53° and 56° S and 67° 50′ and 77° 14′ W. The coast seemed low, but high mountains rose in the distance. I even thought I glimpsed Mount Sarmiento, 2,070 metres above sea level. This is a block of schist in the shape of a pyramid with a very sharp summit, and whether it is covered in mists or is free of vapour 'forecasts good or bad weather', as Ned Land told me.

'A wonderful barometer, my friend.'

'Yes, monsieur, a natural barometer which has always been accurate when I've sailed the passes of the Strait of Magellan.'

Just then the peak appeared, clearly etched against the background of the sky: in other words, a portent of good weather.

Diving again, the *Nautilus* approached the coast and followed it for a few miles. Through the salon windows I could see long creepers and gigantic wracks, those *pyrifera* kelps of which the open sea at the Pole had contained a few specimens. With their shiny, viscous filaments, they measured up to 300 metres long. Veritable cables, thicker than a thumb and very strong, they often serve as ships' mooring ropes. Another plant, a sort of kelp, with 4-foot leaves covered in coral accretions, carpeted the depths. It served as a nest and as food for myriads of crustaceans and molluscs such as crabs and cuttlefish. Seals and otters enjoyed splendid meals there, combining fish with marine vegetables, a bit like the British do.

The *Nautilus* moved at great speed over the rich, luxuriant bottoms. In the evening it approached the Falkland Islands, whose rough summits I spotted the next day. The sea was not very deep. I accordingly thought, with good reason, that the two main islands, surrounded by a large number of smaller islands, were formerly part of the 'Magellanic Lands'. The Falklands were probably discovered by the celebrated John Davis,* who gave them the name of Davis Southern Islands. Later Richard Hawkins* called them Maidenland. At the beginning of the eighteenth century they were named the Malouines by fishermen from Saint-Malo, and finally the Falklands by the British, to whom they belong today.

On these shores, our nets brought in fine specimens of seaweed, and particularly a certain wrack with roots laden with mussels that are the best in the world. Dozens of geese and ducks rained down on to the platform, and soon took their places in the sculleries. As regards fish, I particularly observed bony ones belonging to the goby genus, and above all 20-centimetre double-spotted gobies, completely covered in white and yellow spots.

I also admired numerous jellyfish, particularly the most beautiful of the type, the *Chrysaora*, peculiar to the seas off the Falklands. Sometimes they formed very smooth hemispherical parasols with reddish-brown stripes, culminating in twelve regularly shaped scallops. Sometimes they constituted upside-down waste-paper baskets, from which grew broad, gracious leaves and long red twigs. They swam by, waving their four foliaceous arms and allowing their sumptuous head of tentacles to drift behind. I would have liked to keep a few specimens of these delicate zoophytes; but they are only clouds, shadows, appearances, which melt and evaporate once outside their native environment.

When the last hills of the Falklands had disappeared below the horizon, the *Nautilus* dived to between 20 and 25 metres and started following the American coast. Captain Nemo did not appear.

Until 3 April, sometimes below and sometimes on the surface, we did not leave the shores of Patagonia. The *Nautilus* passed the broad estuary of the mouth of the Rio de la Plata, and on 4 April was 50 miles off Uruguay. Its direction was still northerly as it followed the long curves of South America. We had now done 16,000 leagues since embarking in the seas of Japan.

At eleven in the morning we crossed the tropic of Capricorn on the 37th meridian, and passed Cape Frio in the distance. To Ned's great annoyance, Captain Nemo obviously disliked the neighbourhood of these populated coasts of Brazil, for he moved at dizzying speed. Not even the quickest of fish or birds could keep up with us, and observing the natural curiosities of these seas was no longer possible.

This speed was maintained for several days, and in the evening of 9 April we sighted the easternmost point of South America, Cape São Roque.* But then the *Nautilus* moved offshore again, and went to seek greater depths in a sunken valley between this cape and Sierra Leone on the African coast. The valley divides off the West Indies, and finishes in the north in an enormous depression 9,000 metres deep. At that point, the geological cross-section of the ocean forms a cliff 6,000 metres high, cut sheer as far as the Lesser Antilles, and, together with a similar wall off Cape Verde, encloses the whole of the sunken continent of Atlantis. The floor of this enormous valley is broken up by a few mountains which contribute to the picturesque views of the submarine depths. I speak about such matters on the basis of the hand-drawn maps in the *Nautilus*'s library. Maps evidently produced by Captain Nemo, based on his personal observations.

For two days we visited the deep deserted waters using the inclined planes on the *Nautilus* to make long diagonal descents, thus reaching any required depth. But on 11 April we suddenly resurfaced, and sighted land again near the opening of the Amazon, a vast estuary delivering so much water that it desalinates the sea for a distance of several leagues.

We crossed the equator. Twenty miles to the west stood the Guyanas, a French possession* where we could easily have found refuge. But a strong wind was blowing up, and the furious waves would not have allowed a mere dinghy to confront them. Land undoubtedly understood this, for he did not say anything. For my part, I made no reference to his escape plans, because I did not wish to encourage an attempt which would inevitably have failed.

I easily filled the time with interesting studies. On 11 and 12 April the *Nautilus* did not leave the surface and its trawl brought in a miraculous draught of zoophytes, fish, and reptiles.

Some zoophytes had been swept up by the chains of the dragnets. These were, for the most part, lovely *Phyllactis* belonging to the family of the actinias, and amongst other species the *Phyllactis protexta*: a native of this part of the ocean with a small cylindrical trunk, vertical lines, speckled with red points, and crowned with a spectacular burgeoning of tentacles. As for the molluscs, they consisted of products I had already observed: screw shells, porphyry olives with regular crisscrossing lines and red patches standing vividly out on a fleshy background, some fantastic scorpio shells like petrified scorpions, translucent hyales, argonauts, highly edible cuttlefish, and certain species of squid that the naturalists of antiquity classified amongst flying fish and which serve mostly as bait for cod fishing.

Amongst the fish of these waters that I had not yet had the opportunity to study, I noted a number of other species. Amongst the cartilaginous fish featured pike lampreys, sorts of 15-inch eels with greenish heads, violet fins, bluish-grey backs, brown and silver bellies dotted with bright patches, and bands of gold round the irises in their eyes: strange animals that the current of the Amazon must have carried down to the sea, for they live in fresh water; there were also tubercular rays with pointed snouts and long slender tails, armed with long toothed stings; small, one-metre sharks with grey milky skin and several rows of teeth curving backwards, commonly known as hammerheads; vespertilian Lophiidae, sorts of reddish isosceles triangles half a metre long, with pectorals connected to fleshy extensions giving them the look of bats and with horny appendixes near their nostrils that have given them the popular name of sea-unicorns; and finally two species of triggerfish, the *curassavicus* whose dotted flanks shine with a vivid golden colour and the light-purple *capriscus* with iridescent nuances like a pigeon's throat.

I will finish this very precise nomenclature, albeit slightly dry, with the series of bony fish that I observed: ramblers from the *Apteronotus* genus, which have a beautiful black body and a very blunt snout as white as snow, and are equipped with a very long and very slender fleshy thong; prickly *Odontognathas*, 30-centimetre-long sardines resplendent in a bright silvery brilliance; *Scomberesox saurus* with two anal fins; two-metre-long butterfly blennies in dark hues that are taken using burning torches, with plump firm white flesh, which when fresh taste like eel and, when dried, smoked salmon; half-red wrasses clothed in scales only as far as the base of their dorsal and anal fins; *chrysoptera* on which gold and silver mix their brilliance with ruby and topaz; golden-tail sparids whose flesh is extremely delicate and whose phosphorescence gives them away in the heart of the water; bogue sparids with fine tongues and orange hues; *Sciaena umbra* with golden tail-fins; specimens of *Acanthurus nigricans*; four-eyed fish from Surinam, etc.

This 'etcetera' will not prevent me from quoting yet another fish Conseil will remember for a long while, and with good reason.

One of our nets had brought in a type of very flat ray which, without its tail, would have formed a perfect circle and which weighed about 20 kilograms. It was white underneath and verging on red on top, with large, round, deep-blue spots surrounded by black. Its very smooth skin ended in a bilobate fin. Stranded on the platform, it was struggling convulsively to turn itself over, and making so many attempts that a last somersault was about to carry it back into the sea. But Conseil, who was keen on his fish, threw himself on to it and took hold of it in both hands before I could stop him. He was on his back immediately, his legs in the air and half of his body paralysed, crying:

'Ah, my master, my master! Help me.'

This was the first time the poor fellow hadn't addressed me in the third person.

The Canadian and I picked him up. We rubbed him down with all our might, and when he was himself again, this persistent classifier murmured in a trembling voice:

'Cartilaginous class, order of chondropterygians with fixed gills, suborder of selachians, family of rays, genus of torpedoes!'

'Yes, my friend,' I replied, 'it was a torpedo that put you in this deplorable state.'

'Ah, monsieur, believe me,' replied Conseil, 'I will take revenge on the animal!'

'But how?'

'By eating it.'

Which he did that very evening, but only out of vengeance, for to tell the truth it was very tough.

The unfortunate Conseil had been attacked by a torpedo of the most dangerous species, the *cumana*. In a conducting environment like water, this bizarre animal shocks fish at several metres' distance, such is the power of its electric organ, whose two main surfaces cover as much as 27 square feet.

The following day, 12 April, the *Nautilus* approached the Dutch coast near the mouth of the Maroni. There several groups of manatees lived in families. These manatees, like the dugong and Steller's sea cow, belong to the order of sirenians. Six or seven metres long, these fine animals, peaceful and inoffensive, must have weighed at least 4,000 kilograms.* I told Ned Land and Conseil that far-seeing nature had given such mammals an important role. Like the seals, they graze on the submarine prairies and thus destroy the accumulated grass which obstructs the mouths of tropical rivers.

'And do you know', I added, 'what happened when men almost entirely destroyed such beneficial species? Decaying grass poisoned the air, and the contaminated air produced yellow fever which is destroying these admirable countries. Poisonous vegetation has proliferated in the warm seas, and the damage has spread irresistibly from the mouth of the Rio de la Plata to Florida!

'And if Toussenel* is to be believed, this plague is nothing beside that which will strike our descendants when the seas are emptied of whales and seals. Crowded with squid, jellyfish, and calamar, they will become huge centres of infection because their waters will no longer have the vast stomachs that God mandated to scour the surface of the seas.'

However, although not disdaining these theories, the crew of the *Nautilus* took half-a-dozen manatees. The aim was to supply the ship's kitchens with an excellent flesh, better than beef or veal. The hunting was not interesting. The manatees let themselves be struck without defending themselves. Several tons of meat were taken on board for drying.

That same day, a remarkably conducted exercise in these seas so full of game increased the reserves of the *Nautilus* still further. The trawl nets had brought in a certain number of fish whose heads ended in oval plates with fleshy edges. They were echeneids, of the third family of subbrachial malacopterygians. Their flattened disc is made of transversal mobile cartilaginous laminae, which the animal can use to produce a vacuum, allowing it to adhere to objects like a sucker.

The strata I had observed in the Mediterranean were also home to this species, but the ones here were *Echeneis osteochir*, particular to this sea. Each one that our sailors caught was placed in a pail of water.

The fishing over, the *Nautilus* approached the coast. A number of turtles were sleeping on the surface. It would have been difficult to catch the precious reptiles, for the slightest sound rouses them and their solid carapace resists harpoons. But the echeneids were to perform the capture with extraordinary sureness and precision. The creatures were to act as living bait, a method which would have delighted any angler.

The men of the *Nautilus* fixed rings to the tails of these fish that were wide enough not to get in the way of their movements, and the rings were attached to long cords, tied at the other end to the side.

The echeneids were thrown into the sea, and immediately did their job by sticking to the plastrons of the turtles. So tenacious were they that they would have been torn to pieces rather than let go. They were hauled on board, together with the turtles to which they adhered.

We thus took several loggerheads a metre wide and weighing 200 kilograms. Their carapaces were covered with great flat corneas which were thin, transparent, and brown with white and yellow dots; and this made them very precious. In addition they were excellent from the point of view of comestibility, just like exquisite-tasting green turtles.

This fishing terminated our sojourn on the shores around the Amazon, and after nightfall the *Nautilus* headed out for the open sea once more.

18

SQUID

For several days the *Nautilus* kept well away from the American coast. It clearly did not wish to tarry in the Gulf of Mexico or the Caribbean. Nevertheless, its keel would have had plenty of water, for the average depth of these seas is 1,800 metres; but probably the waters dotted with islands and crisscrossed by steamers did not suit Captain Nemo.

On 16 April we sighted Martinique and Guadeloupe at a distance of about 30 miles. I caught a brief glimpse of their high peaks.

The Canadian was counting on implementing his plans in the Gulf, either by reaching a piece of land or by hailing one of the numerous boats which worked their way along the shores of the islands; and so he was very disappointed. Escape would have been practicable if Ned had managed to get hold of the boat without the captain knowing. But we could not even dream of doing so in mid-ocean.

Ned, Conseil, and I had quite a long conversation on the subject. We had been prisoners on board the *Nautilus* for six months. We had travelled 17,000 leagues and, as Ned pointed out, there was no reason to expect any change. He therefore made a suggestion I was not expecting: I should categorically ask Captain Nemo if he planned to keep us on board the vessel indefinitely.

Such a course of action did not appeal to me. In my view, it couldn't possibly succeed. We couldn't count on the captain of the *Nautilus*, only on ourselves, completely and exclusively. Also, for some time the captain had become more sombre, withdrawn, and anti-social. He seemed to be avoiding me, as I met him only at rare intervals. Formerly, he had enjoyed explaining the underwater wonders to me; but now he left me to my studies and no longer came into the salon.

What change had come over him? What was he reacting to? I had done nothing with which to reproach myself. Perhaps our very presence on board weighed on him? But in any case, he was certainly not the sort of person to give us back our freedom.

I therefore asked Ned to give me more time to think about the question. If his suggestion failed, it could wreck his plans by rekindling the captain's suspicions, and make our situation very difficult. In addition, I had no arguments to offer concerning the state of our health. With the exception of the difficulties under the ice of the South Pole, Ned, Conseil, and I had never been in better health. The wholesome food, healthy atmosphere, regularity in our lives, and uniformity of temperature simply did not allow illnesses to gain a foothold. I could understand how a life like this would suit a man who had no regrets about leaving life on shore, a Captain Nemo who was at home here, who went where he wished, and who pursued goals that were mysterious to others and known only to himself; but as for the three of us, we had not been made to break with humanity. For my part, I did not wish my intriguing and original studies to be buried with me. I was now in a position to write the real book of the sea, and I wanted this book to appear sooner rather than later.

Through the open panel, ten metres below the surface of the West Indian waters, how many interesting specimens I could observe and record in my daily notes! Amongst other zoophytes, there were the

Portuguese men-of-war known as *Physalia pelagica*, which are thick oval-shaped bladders with a pearly sheen, spreading their membranes out to be blown in the wind and letting their blue tentacles float like threads of silk, charming jellyfish to look at but authentic nettles to the touch for they secrete a corrosive liquid. Amongst the articulates there were 1½-metre-long annelids, with pink trunks and 1,700 propulsive organs, which snaked through the water, passing through all the colours of the rainbow as they swam by. In the branch of the fish there were enormous cartilaginous mobula rays, 10 feet long and 600 pounds in weight, with triangular pectoral fins, a slight swelling in the middle of the back, and fixed eyes on the edge of the front of the head; floating like wrecked ships, they sometimes adhered to our window like dark shutters. There were American triggerfish for which nature had mixed only white and black paint, long, fleshy, feathered gobies with yellow fins and prominent jaws, and 1.6-metre scombroids of the species of albacores with short sharp teeth and a fine covering of scales. Then red mullets appeared in clouds, covered from head to tail in golden stripes and waving their glorious fins; they are true masterpieces of jewellery that were formerly offered to Diana,* particularly sought out by rich Romans and the subject of the proverb: 'Those that catch them don't eat them!' Finally golden *Pomacanthus* passed before our eyes, decked out in emerald strips and clothed in velvet and silk, like lords out of Veronese's paintings; sea bream from the Sparidae family fled using their swift thoracic fins; 15-inch clupeids produced an aura of phosphorescent gleams; grey mullets threshed the water with their large fleshy tails; red coregonids seemed to scythe the sea with their sharp pectoral fins; and silvery selenes justified their name by rising on the horizon of the waters with milky gleams like so many moons.

How many other amazing specimens I would have observed, if the *Nautilus* hadn't gradually moved down towards the lower strata! Its inclined planes carried it to depths of 2,000 then 3,500 metres. The animal life now consisted only of crinoids, starfish, charming medusa-head pentacrinites whose straight stems supported small calyxes, top-shells, bloody dentalia, and fissurella, coastal molluscs of great size.

On 20 April we had come back up to an average depth of 1,500 metres. The closest land was the Bahamas, spread like cobblestones over the surface of the waters. High submarine cliffs rose, vertical walls of roughly hewn blocks resting on wide bases, with black holes opening up between them whose bottoms our electric rays could not penetrate.

The rocks were carpeted with huge grasses, giant laminarias, and enormous wracks: a true espalier of hydrophytes worthy of a world of Titans.

From this colossal flora, Conseil, Ned, and I naturally turned to listing the gigantic animals of the sea. The former were evidently destined to be the food of the latter. However, through the windows of the *Nautilus*, almost motionless, I could not yet see anything clinging to the long plant filaments except the principal articulates of the division of Brachyuras: decapods with long limbs, purple crabs, and *Clio* peculiar to the seas of the West Indies.

It was about eleven o'clock when Ned Land drew my attention to a formidable swarming moving through the large expanses of seaweed.

'Well,' I said, 'these are real squids' caves, and I wouldn't be surprised to see a few monsters here!'

'What?' said Conseil. 'Calamar, mere calamar of the class of cephalopods?'

'No,' I said, 'giant squid. But my friend Land is undoubtedly mistaken, for I can't see anything.'

'What a shame,' replied Conseil. 'I long to come face to face with one of those squid I have heard about so often, which can drag ships down to the bottom of the sea. Those beasts are called Krak . . .'

'Cracks . . .' interjected the Canadian.

'Krakens,' continued Conseil, ignoring his companion's joke.

'I will never be able to believe', said Land, 'in the existence of such animals.'

'Why ever not? We ended up believing in monsieur's narwhal.'

'We were wrong, Conseil.'

'Undoubtedly, but others still believe in it.'

'Probably, Conseil, but for my part I have resolved to admit the existence of such monsters only after I have dissected them with my own hand.'

'So', Conseil asked, 'monsieur does not believe in giant squid?'

'Hey, who the hell has ever believed in them?' cried the Canadian.

'Many people, Ned, my friend.'

'Not fishermen. Scientists perhaps!'

'With respect, Ned: fishermen and scientists.'

'But as I stand here,' said Conseil in the most serious tone, 'I can perfectly remember seeing a large ship being dragged under the waves by the arms of a cephalopod.'

'You have seen that?' asked the Canadian.

'Yes, Ned.'

'With your own eyes?'

'With my own eyes.'

'Where, please?'

'At Saint-Malo,' Conseil replied imperturbably.

'In the port?' Ned asked sarcastically.

'No, in a church.'

'In a church!'

'Yes, Ned, my friend. It was a painting of the said squid!'*

'So!' said Ned Land, bursting out laughing. 'Mr Conseil has been leading me on!'

'Actually, he is right,' I said. 'I have heard of the painting, but its subject is taken from legend, and you know what use legends are in natural history!* When people start talking about monsters, their imaginations can easily go off at a tangent. Not only has it been claimed that these squid can drag down ships, but a certain Olaus Magnus speaks of a mile-long cephalopod,* which seemed more like an island than an animal. It is also said that one day the Bishop of Nidaros erected an altar on an immense rock. Once his mass was over, the rock started moving and returned to the sea.* The rock was a squid.'

'And that's all?' asked the Canadian.

'No,' I replied. 'Another bishop, Pontoppidan of Bergen, speaks of a squid on which a whole regiment of cavalry could manoeuvre!'

'They didn't mess around, those bishops of olden days!' Ned remarked.

'Finally, the naturalists of antiquity cite monsters whose jaws resembled bays, and which were too big to get through the Strait of Gibraltar!'

'You don't say!'

'But what truth is there in all those tales?' asked Conseil.

'None, my friends, at least none amongst the parts which go beyond the limits of plausibility and become fable or legend. However, if no foundation is needed for the imagination of storytellers, some sort of pretext is. It cannot be denied that there are very big squid and calamar, even if they are smaller than whales. Aristotle observed the dimensions of a squid five cubits long, that is 3.1 metres. Our fishermen frequently see specimens longer than 1.8 metres. The museums of Trieste and Montpellier contain skeletons of squid that are two metres long. What is more, the naturalists have calculated that an animal only six feet in length would have 27-foot tentacles, which is more than enough to make for a formidable monster.'

'And are they still caught nowadays?' asked the Canadian.

'If they are not captured, at least sailors still see them. One of my friends, Captain Paul Bos of Le Havre,* has often told me that he encountered one such colossal monster in the Indian Ocean. And the most astonishing thing happened only a few years ago, in 1861, an event which no longer allows the existence of these gigantic animals to be denied.'

'Go on,' said Ned Land.

'Thank you. In 1861, north-east of Tenerife, at the approximate latitude where we are now, the crew of the sloop *Alecton* sighted an enormous squid swimming in its wake. Captain Bouyer* closed on the animal and attacked it with harpoons and guns, but without great success, for bullets and harpoons passed through the soft flesh like unset jelly. After several attempts, the crew finally managed to put a slip knot round the mollusc's body. The knot slid as far as the tail-fins and stopped there. They then tried to haul the monster on board, but it was so heavy that the rope pulled the tail off, and, deprived of this adornment, it disappeared under the water.'

'Finally we have a fact.'

'An indisputable fact, my good Ned. That was why it was proposed to call it "Bouyer's squid".'

'And how long was it?' he asked.

'Did it not measure about six metres?' said Conseil, standing at the window and examining the holes in the cliff.

'Precisely,' I replied.

'Was its head not crowned with eight tentacles, which waved in the water like a nest of serpents?'

'Absolutely.'

'Were its eyes not extremely prominent and large?'

'Yes, Conseil.'

'And was its mouth not a real parrot's beak, a formidable one at that?'

'Indeed.'

'Well, if monsieur pleases,' calmly replied Conseil, 'if that isn't Bouyer's squid, then it must at least be one of its brethren.'

I gaped at him. Ned rushed to the window.

'What a frightening beast!' he exclaimed.

I looked in turn, and could not hide a movement of repulsion. Before my eyes flapped a horrible monster, worthy of appearing in any teratological legend.

It was a squid of colossal dimension, eight metres in length. It moved backwards at extreme velocity as it headed towards the *Nautilus*. It was staring with its enormous fixed eyes of a sea-green hue. Not only were its eight arms, or rather legs, implanted on its head, thus giving these animals the name of cephalopods, but were twice as big as its body and writhing like the Furies' hair. We could distinctly see the 250 suckers in the form of hemispherical capsules on the insides of the tentacles. Sometimes these suckers were placed on the salon's windows and stuck there. The monster's mouth—a horny beak like a parrot's—was opening and closing vertically. Its tongue emerged oscillating from this pair of shears, and was also made of a horny substance, itself equipped with several rows of sharp teeth. What a freak of nature: a bird's beak on a mollusc! Its body, cylindrical but swollen in the middle, formed a fleshy mass that had to weigh 20 to 25 tons.* Its colour changed in quick succession according to the animal's irritation, and went progressively from pale grey to reddish-brown.

What was the mollusc annoyed at? Undoubtedly the *Nautilus*, more formidable than itself, and on which its sucking arms and mandibles could not find a real grip. And yet what monsters these squid were, with what vitality the Creator had endowed them, and what vigour their movements had, since they possessed three hearts!

Chance had brought us to this squid, and I did not wish to waste the opportunity of closely studying such a specimen of the cephalopod. I overcame the horror its appearance caused me, picked up a pencil, and began to draw it.

'Perhaps it is the same one the *Alecton* saw,' said Conseil.

'It can't be,' replied the Canadian, 'since the other one lost its tail and this one still has it.'

'Not necessarily,' I replied. 'The arms and tails of these animals form again by "redintegration", and in seven years the squid's tail has undoubtedly had the time to grow back.'

'In any case,' replied Ned, 'if it's not this one, it's perhaps one of those!'

Other squid were indeed appearing at the starboard window. I counted seven of them. They formed a procession accompanying the *Nautilus*, and I could hear the grinding of their beaks on the metal hull. We had plenty on our plate.

I continued my work. These monsters stayed in our wake with such precision that they seemed motionless, and I could have traced them directly on to the window pane. We were in fact moving at moderate speed.

Suddenly the *Nautilus* stopped. The jolt made its whole framework tremble.

'Have we hit something?' I asked.

'If we have,' replied the Canadian, 'then we've moved off again.'

The *Nautilus* was undoubtedly floating freely, but was no longer advancing. Its propeller blades were not cutting the waves. A minute passed before Captain Nemo, followed by his first officer, came into the salon.

I had not seen him for some time. He looked sombre. Without speaking, perhaps not even seeing us, he approached the panel, looked at the squid, and said a few words to the first officer. His first officer went out.

Soon the panels closed again. The ceiling lit up. I approached the captain.

'A curious collection of squid,' I said, in the detached tone a visitor would use at the window of an aquarium.

'True,' he replied, 'and we are going to fight them hand to hand.'

I looked at the captain. I thought I had misheard.

'Hand to hand?' I repeated.

'Yes, monsieur. The propeller has stopped. I think that the corneous mandibles of one of the squid have got caught in the blades, preventing us from moving.'

'And what are you going to do?'

'Surface, and massacre all the vermin.'

'A difficult task.'

'Electric bullets are indeed powerless against this soft flesh, for they do not find enough resistance to explode. But we will attack them with axes.'

'And with harpoons, monsieur,' said the Canadian, 'if you will accept my help.'

'I accept, Master Land.'

'We're right behind you,' I said as Captain Nemo headed for the central staircase.

About ten men armed with boarding axes were standing ready for an attack. Conseil and I picked up two as well. Land seized a harpoon.

The *Nautilus* had meanwhile surfaced. One of the sailors, standing on the top steps, was loosening the bolts of the hatch. But the bolts were hardly free, when the hatch suddenly shot open, clearly yanked up by the suckers on the arm of a squid.

Immediately one of those long arms slid like a snake into the opening as twenty others waved above. With a single axe blow, Captain Nemo severed the formidable tentacle, which then slid down the stairs, writhing.

While we were all rushing in a group up towards the platform, two other arms, lashing through the air, landed on the sailor in front of Captain Nemo—and carried him off with irresistible force.

Captain Nemo exclaimed and rushed outside. We followed him with utmost speed.

What a scene! The poor man, seized by the tentacle and glued to its suckers, was being waved back and forth in the air at the whim of the enormous trunk. He was groaning as he suffocated, and he shouted: '*À moi! À moi!*' These words in French flabbergasted me. So I had a compatriot on board, perhaps several! I will hear his heart-breaking appeal in my head until the end of my days.

The unfortunate man was lost. Who could possibly have wrested him from that powerful embrace? However, Captain Nemo rushed at the squid, and with a single axe blow chopped off another arm. His first officer was angrily fighting other monsters crawling over the sides of the *Nautilus*. The crew were attacking them with their axes. The Canadian, Conseil, and I were plunging our weapons into the fleshy masses. A strong smell of musk filled the atmosphere. It was horrible.

For a moment I thought that the poor man enlaced by the squid could be saved from its powerful suction. Seven arms out of eight had been severed. The last one, brandishing its victim like a quill, remained twisting in the air. But just as Captain Nemo and his first officer were rushing at the animal, it gave out a spurt of blackish liquid, secreted from a bursa in its abdomen.* We were blinded. By the time the cloud had cleared, the squid had vanished, carrying with it my unfortunate compatriot.*

Then our rage boiled over against the monsters. We were no longer in control of ourselves. Ten or twelve squid had invaded the platform or sides of the *Nautilus*. We were sliding around in the midst of the truncated serpents, tossing about on the platform in waves of blood and black ink. It was as if the viscous tentacles were coming back to life again like Hydra's heads. Ned Land's harpoons plunged repeatedly into the glaucous eyes of the squid, destroying some with each blow. But my brave companion was abruptly knocked down by the tentacles of a monster he could not avoid.

God! My heart leapt with revulsion and horror! The formidable squid's beak gaped open before Ned. The poor man was about to be cut in two. I rushed to help him. But Captain Nemo was there first and his axe disappeared between the two enormous jaws. Miraculously saved, the Canadian got up and drove his harpoon right through the triple heart of the squid.

'For services rendered!' Captain Nemo said.

Ned bowed in silence.

The battle had lasted a mere quarter of an hour. The vanquished monsters, mutilated and fatally wounded, finally retreated and disappeared under the waves.

Captain Nemo, red* with blood, motionless near the searchlight, examined the sea which had swallowed up one of his companions, as large tears flowed from his eyes.

19

THE GULF STREAM

NONE of us will ever forget that terrible scene of 20 April. I wrote about it under the impression of powerful emotions. Since then, I have re-examined the narrative and read it to Conseil and Ned. They found it factually correct, but too pallid. To paint such a canvas would take the pen of the most illustrious of our poets, the author of *The Toilers of the Sea*.*

I said that Captain Nemo wept as he regarded the waves. His grief was immense. This was the second companion he had lost since we had arrived on board, and what an end! This friend had been crushed, suffocated, and broken by the formidable arms of the squid, then ground in its iron jaws, and so could not rest with his companions in the peaceful waters of the coral cemetery!

As for me, it was the cry of despair the wretch uttered in the heart of the battle which had torn at my heart. The poor Frenchman had forgotten his conventional language and had gone back to speaking the tongue of his country and his mother to issue his ultimate appeal. Amongst the crew of the *Nautilus*, bound to Captain Nemo body and soul, like him fleeing contact with humanity, I had a compatriot! Was he the only one representing France in this mysterious association, clearly composed of individuals of different nationalities? This was yet another of the unanswerable questions constantly surfacing in my mind.

Captain Nemo went back to his room, and I did not see him for some time.* But how evidently sad, desperate, and irresolute he was, if I can judge the state of his soul from our ship, which reflected his every mood! The *Nautilus* no longer maintained a fixed course. It came, it went, it drifted like a plaything of the waves. Its propeller had been freed, and yet was hardly used. The *Nautilus* was sailing at random, unable to tear itself away from the scene of its great battle, the sea which had swallowed up one of its own!

Ten days went by in this way. It was only on 1 May that the *Nautilus* again set a clear course for the north, after sighting the Bahamas at the opening of the Bahama Channel. We were following the current of the sea's largest river, with its own banks, its own fish, and its own temperature. I refer to the Gulf Stream.

It is indeed a river, flowing freely through the heart of the Atlantic, but without mixing with the surrounding water. It is a salt river, saltier than the adjoining sea. Its average depth is 3,000 feet, and width, 60 miles. At places it moves at a speed of 4 kilometres an hour. The unchanging volume of its water is larger than all the rivers of the globe combined.

The true source of the Gulf Stream, discovered by Commander Maury, its starting-point so to speak, is the Bay of Biscay. There its pale water, still cool, begins to collect. It heads southwards, heads along equatorial Africa, warms its water in the rays of the tropics, crosses the Atlantic, reaches Cape São Roque on the Brazilian coast, and then splits into two branches, with one heading off to renew itself in the warm molecules of the Antilles. Then the Gulf Stream begins its role as moderator, for it is charged with re-establishing the equilibrium between temperatures and with mixing the waters of the tropics with the northern waters. Greatly heated in the Gulf of Mexico, it heads north along the American coast, reaches as far as Nova Scotia, changes direction under the impact of the cold current from the Davis Strait, and heads back out to sea. Following a line of latitude, a loxodromic track, it splits in two at about the 43rd degree, with one branch, helped on by the north-east trade wind, returning to the Bay of Biscay and the Azores, and the other, having slightly warmed the shores of Ireland and Norway, heading past Spitsbergen, where it falls to 4° and forms the open sea of the Pole.*

It was on this oceanic river that the *Nautilus* was sailing. When it leaves the Bahama Channel, which is over 14 leagues wide and 350 metres deep, the Gulf Stream moves at 8 kilometres an hour, but this speed decreases constantly as it heads north. Indeed, we have to hope that this regularity is maintained; for if its speed and direction were ever to change, as some believe is happening already, the climate of Europe will undergo changes of an unforeseeable scope.

At about midday I was on the platform with Conseil. I explained the peculiarities of the Gulf Stream. When my description was over, I asked him to put his hand in the current. Conseil obeyed, and was astonished to feel a sensation of neither cold nor warmth.

'This is because the water of the Gulf Stream is at almost blood-temperature when it leaves the Gulf of Mexico. The Gulf Stream is a huge reservoir of heat, allowing the coasts of Europe to cloak themselves in permanent foliage, and if Maury can be believed, the heat from this current would provide enough calorific value to maintain in fusion a river of molten iron as big as the Amazon or the Missouri.'

At this point the Gulf Stream was moving at 2.25 metres a second. Its current is so distinct that its water clearly stands out from the cold water of the sea around. Darker and with a greater concentration of saline matter, its pure indigo contrasts markedly with the green water around it. Such indeed is the clearness of the line of demarcation, that off the Carolinas the *Nautilus* visibly had its ram in the Gulf Stream, while its propeller was still beating the ocean.

This current held a whole universe of living beings within it. The argonauts, so common in the Mediterranean, sailed here in numerous schools. Amongst the cartilaginous fish, the most remarkable were the rays, whose slender tails made up about a third of their bodies, in vast rhomboids 25 feet long. We also saw some small, metre-long sharks, with big heads, short rounded snouts, several rows of pointed teeth, and bodies apparently covered in scales.

Amongst the bony fish, I noted some dusky wrasses particular to these seas; *Sparus sinagris* with irises shining like fires; metre-long sciaenas with large jaws bristling with tiny teeth, and which produce a slight cry; specimens of the *Acanthurus nigricans* mentioned above; blue dolphinfish picked out in gold and silver; parrot fish, true oceanic rainbows competing in colour with the most beautiful birds of the Tropics; naked blennies with triangular heads; bluish rhombuses without scales; batrachoidids with a crossways yellow strip representing a Greek 't'; swarms of small *Gobiosoma bosc* covered in brown blotches; lungfish with silvery heads and yellow tails; various examples of salmonids; mullets with slender waists and dazzling soft lustres, fish which Lacépède dedicated to his good lady wife;* and finally a beautiful fish, the *Eques americanus* decorated with all the orders and bedecked with every ribbon, which frequents the shores of that great nation where ribbons and orders are so little valued.

I will add that during the night, the phosphorescent water of the Gulf Stream competed with the electric beam from our searchlight, especially in the stormy weather that frequently assailed us.

On 8 May we were still off Cape Hatteras, with North Carolina to our left. The width of the Gulf Stream is 75 miles here, and its depth, 210 metres. The *Nautilus* continued to wander at will. It was as if no lookout existed on board. I will admit that an escape would have been possible in these circumstances. Everywhere were populated shores offering easy refuge. The sea was crisscrossed by numerous steamers between New York or Boston and the Gulf of Mexico, and traversed day and night by the little schooners plying between various points on the American coast. We could hope to be picked up. It was in sum a perfect opportunity, despite the 30 miles between the *Nautilus* and the shore of the Union.

But an unfortunate circumstance scuppered the Canadian's plans. The weather was very bad. We were approaching waters where frequent storms blew, the home of waterspouts and cyclones generated by none other than the Gulf Stream. To confront an often raging sea in a frail boat was to face certain death. Even Ned Land agreed. So he reined in his terrible homesickness, that only escape could cure.

'Monsieur,' he said that day, 'it's got to finish. I have to know what's what. Your Nemo is steering clear of land and heading north, but I tell you I have already had enough of the South Pole, and am not going with him to the North Pole.'

'What can we do, Ned, since escape is impossible for the moment?'

'I come back to my original idea. The captain needs to be confronted. You said nothing when we were in your home seas. I wish to speak now that we are in mine. When I think that in a few days' time the *Nautilus* is going to be off Nova Scotia, that a large bay opens out there near Newfoundland, and that the St Lawrence empties into that same bay! When I think that the St Lawrence is my own river, the river of my home town, Quebec; when I think of all this, I get very angry. My hair stands on end. Look, monsieur, I would prefer to throw myself into the sea! I can't stay here! I'm suffocating!'

The Canadian was clearly at the end of his tether. His energetic personality could not get used to our extended imprisonment. His physiognomy changed from day to day. His personality was getting gloomier and gloomier. I knew how much he was suffering for I too was feeling homesick. It was nearly seven months since our last news from land. In addition, Captain Nemo's isolation, his taciturnity, and especially his changed mood since the battle with the squid—all this made things appear in a different light to me. I no longer felt the same enthusiasm as at the beginning. One had to be a Fleming like Conseil to accept an environment designed for whales and sea creatures. Truly, if this good fellow had had gills instead of lungs, I think he would have made a very good fish.

'Well, monsieur?' Land asked again, seeing that I was not going to reply.

'Well, Ned, would you like me to ask Captain Nemo what his intentions are?'

'Yes, monsieur.'

'Even though he has already told us?'

'Yes, I wish to be doubly certain. Say it's from me, from me alone if you wish.'

'But I rarely meet him. He even seems to be avoiding me.'

'All the more reason for going and finding him.'

'I'll ask him then.'

'When?' said the Canadian insistently.

'When I next meet him.'

'Dr Aronnax, do you want me to go and see him myself?'

'No, let me do it. Tomorrow . . .'

'Today.'

'All right. I will see him today,' I replied to Ned, who would certainly have ruined everything had he acted on his own.

I remained alone; having decided to put our case, I resolved to get it over with immediately. I like things that have been done more than things still to do.

I returned to my room. From there I could hear steps in Captain Nemo's. The opportunity of seeing him had to be seized. I knocked on his door. There was no reply. I knocked again, then turned the knob. The door opened.

I went in. The captain was there. Bent over his desk, he had not heard me. Determined not to leave until I had spoken to him, I went up to him. He raised his head, frowned brusquely, and said to me in an abrupt tone:

'You here! What do you want?'

'To speak to you, captain.'

'But I am busy, monsieur, I am working. Will you not give me the same freedom to remain alone that I give you?'

This reception was hardly encouraging. But I was determined to hear him out so I could respond to everything he said.

'Monsieur,' I said coldly, 'I have to speak to you of a matter which will suffer no delay.'

'Which matter, monsieur?' he replied sarcastically. 'Have you made some discovery which has slipped my attention? Has the sea yielded some new secrets?'

We were still a long way off the point. Before I could reply, he showed me a manuscript open on his desk, and said to me in a graver tone:

'This, Dr Aronnax, is written in several languages. It contains a summary of my studies on the sea, and God willing, it will not perish with me. This manuscript, signed with my name and also containing the story of my life, will be enclosed in a small floating container.* The last survivor from among us on board the *Nautilus* will cast the container into the sea, and it will go wherever the waves carry it.'

The name of this man! His story written by himself! Would his mystery be unveiled one day? But at this moment,* I only saw what he said as a way of broaching my subject.

'Captain,' I replied, 'I can only approve your intentions. The results of your studies must not be lost. But the means you employ seem slightly crude to me. Who knows where the wind will send the container, into whose hands it will fall? Why don't you or one of your men . . .?'

'Never, monsieur!' said the captain, sharply interrupting me.

'But my companions and I would be prepared to keep this manuscript secret, and if you gave us back our freedom . . .'

'Your freedom!' repeated Captain Nemo, getting up.

'Yes, monsieur, and it is this subject that I wished to speak to you about. We have been on board your vessel for seven months, and I wish to ask you today, in my name and my companions', if it is your intention to keep us here for ever.'

'Dr Aronnax,' said Captain Nemo, 'I will answer you today as I answered you seven months ago: he who enters the *Nautilus* is destined never to leave it again.'

'But you are inflicting slavery on us!'

'Give it whatever name you wish.'

'But wherever you go, the slave retains his right to regain freedom! And no holds are barred in how he attempts to do so!'

'Who is depriving you of that right?' replied Captain Nemo. 'Have I ever thought of binding you with oaths?'

The captain was staring at me, his arms crossed.

'Monsieur,' I said to him, 'covering this same ground a second time would be neither to your taste nor to mine. So since this subject has been broached, let us make sure we close it. I repeat, I am not the only one concerned. For me, study is a support, a powerful diversion, a fascination, a passion which can help me forget everything. Like you, I can live unknown and obscure in the fragile hope of some day leaving the results of my work to the future, in a risky container entrusted to the winds and waves of chance. In short, I admire and happily follow you in your role, part of which I can understand. But there are other aspects of your life I have caught glimpses of, which remain shrouded in confusion and mystery, and in which my companions and I have no part. Even on the occasions when our hearts have gone out to you, moved by some of your pain or acts of genius or courage, we have had to hide all signs of the sympathy that comes from the sight of what is fine and good, whether displayed by friend or enemy. Well, it is this feeling that we are foreign to everything that concerns you which makes our position untenable. An impossible one even for me, but doubly impossible for Ned. Every human being, by the very fact of being human, is worthy of respect. Have you ever asked yourself what plans of vengeance could be engendered by the love of freedom and hatred of slavery in a nature like the Canadian's, what he could think or do . . .?'

I fell silent. Captain Nemo got up.

'Ned Land can think or do as he wishes. What difference does it make to me? It was not I who sought out his company. It is not for my own pleasure that I keep him on board my vessel! As for you, Dr Aronnax, you are amongst those who can understand anything, even silence. I have nothing more to say to you. May this first time that you have raised this subject be also the last; I will not even be able to listen to you a second time.'*

I withdrew. Starting from that day, our relationship was very tense. I relayed the conversation to my two companions.

'We now know', said Ned, 'that there is nothing to be expected from this man. The *Nautilus* is approaching Long Island. We will try to escape, whatever the weather.'

But the sky was becoming more and more threatening. Signs of a hurricane were approaching. The air was turning pale white, even milky. The fine sheaves of cirrus on the horizon were being replaced by strata of cumulonimbus. Other low-lying clouds were quickly fleeing. The sea roughened as it rolled in in long swells. The birds disappeared, with the exception of the petrels, which revel in storms. The barometer was dropping significantly, showing an exceptional amount of moisture in the air. The contents of the storm-glass were decomposing due to the electricity filling the air. A battle of the elements was nigh.

The storm broke on 18 May,* when the *Nautilus* was off Long Island and a few miles from the passes into New York. I am able to describe this battle of the elements, because Captain Nemo felt an inexplicable caprice and decided to brave it on the surface, instead of fleeing to the depths of the sea.

The wind was blowing from the south-west, first as a near gale, namely 15 metres a second, and then increasing to 25 at about three in the afternoon. In other words, a tempest had blown up.

Captain Nemo, unshakeable in the blasts, had taken up position on the platform. He had made himself fast at the waist, so as to resist the huge wash of the waves. I had hoisted myself up and attached myself as well, dividing my admiration between the storm and the peerless man defying it.

The raging sea was swept by large shreds of clouds that dipped into the waves. I could no longer see any of those small intermediate waves that form at the bottom of big troughs. Nothing but long fuliginous undulations, whose crests were so firm that they did not break. Aroused by each other, they grew taller. Now lying on its side, now erect like a mast, the *Nautilus* was pitching and rolling frighteningly.

At about five o'clock, a torrential rain fell, but did not damp down the wind or sea. A hurricane unleashed itself at a speed of 45 metres a second, that is nearly 40 leagues an hour. In such conditions it tears tiles from roofs and smashes them into doors, breaks iron grilles, and bodily moves 24-calibre cannon. And yet even in the midst of the storm the *Nautilus* bore out the words of a wise engineer: 'There is no well-constructed hull that cannot withstand the sea!' This was not a fixed rock, that the waves would have demolished, but a mobile and obedient steel cylinder, without rigging or masts, and so able to resist the fury without suffering any damage.

I carefully examined the unbridled waves. They measured up to 15 metres high by 150 to 175 metres long, and their speed was 15 metres a second, or half that of the wind. Their volume and power increased with the depth of the water. I understood then the function of the waves, capturing air and sending it down to the bottom of the sea, including life-giving oxygen. It has been calculated that their pressure reaches the enormous figure of 3,000 kilograms per square foot of the surface they batter. It was waves like this which moved a block in the Hebrides weighing 42 tons. It was they that, having flattened part of Tokyo in the Japanese storm of 23 December 1854,* went and broke on the shores of America the very same day, having crossed at 700 kilometres an hour.

The intensity of the tempest increased as dusk fell. The barometer dropped to 710 millimetres, as happened during a cyclone in 1860 on Réunion. As the day ended, I saw a large ship passing on the horizon, struggling a great deal. It lay to at low steam in order to remain head-on to the wind. It was clearly from one of the lines between New York and Liverpool or Le Havre. It soon disappeared into the darkness.

At ten o'clock the sky appeared to be on fire. The air was sundered by powerful flashes of lightning. I could not stand the light, but Captain Nemo contemplated them face on, as if drawing the soul of the storm into him. A terrifying noise filled the air, a complex sound composed of the roar of crushed waves, moans from the wind, and peals of thunder. The wind turned to all points of the compass, as the cyclone, which had started from the east, went back there after turning through north, west, and south, having rotated the opposite way from the storms of the southern hemisphere.

Ah, the Gulf Stream! It fully justified its name of Ruler of Storms! It is the Gulf Stream which creates these frightening cyclones from the temperature difference between the air strata and its own currents.

The drops had become a fiery rain. The tiny points of water had changed into exploding crests. It was exactly as if Captain Nemo, desiring a death worthy of him, was endeavouring to be struck by lightning. In a terrible movement of pitching, the *Nautilus* erected its steel ram into the air like the point of a lightning conductor, and I could see long sparks spurting from it.

Exhausted, no strength left, I crawled to the hatch on my stomach. I opened it, and climbed back down again to the salon. The storm was now reaching its maximum. It was impossible to stand up inside the *Nautilus.*

Captain Nemo came in about midnight. I could hear the tanks filling gradually as the submarine gently sank below the surface of the waves.

Through the open windows of the salon, I could see great frightened fish, passing like ghosts through the fiery waters. A few were struck by lightning in front of my eyes.

The *Nautilus* was still going down. I thought that it would find calm water at a depth of 15 metres. But the upper strata were being shaken too violently. It needed to seek repose at 50 metres into the bowels of the sea.

But what calm there, what silence, what peace! Who could have thought that a terrifying hurricane was being unleashed at that moment on the surface of the same ocean?

20

47° 24´ N, 17° 28´ W

AFTER this storm we were pushed eastwards. All hope disappeared of escaping to the landfalls of New York or the St Lawrence. Poor Ned, desperate, shut himself away like Captain Nemo. Conseil and I never left each other's company.

I have said that the *Nautilus* headed east. More precisely, I should have said north-east. For several days it wandered, now beneath the surface, now on top amongst those fogs that are so feared by navigators. They are mainly caused by ice melting, which produces a very high degree of humidity in the atmosphere. How many ships have been lost in these waters when just about to sight the glimmering lights on shore! How many wrecks due to these opaque blankets! How many impacts on reefs whose undertow was hidden by the noise of the wind! How many collisions between ships, in spite of their position lights and the warnings of their whistles and alarm bells!

As a result, the floor of the sea resembled a battle-scene, where there still lay all the vanquished of the ocean: some old and already encrusted, others young and reflecting the light from our searchlight on their copper fittings and hulls. Amongst them, how many vessels lost with all hands and their communities of immigrants, on the dangerous spots, notorious in the accident statistics, of Cape Race, St Paul Island, the Strait of Belle Isle, and the St Lawrence estuary! And in just the last few years, how many victims have been added to those funereal annals by the Royal Mail, Inman, and Montreal lines! How many ships: the *Solway*, the *Isis*, the *Parramatta*, the *Hungarian*, the *Canadian*, the *Anglo-Saxon*, the *Humboldt*, and the *United States*, all wrecked; the *Arctic* and the *Lyonnais*, sunk in a collision; and the *President*, the *Pacific*, and the *City of Glasgow*,* all vanished, cause unknown: sombre debris, amongst which the *Nautilus* navigated as though inspecting the dead!

On 15 May we were near the southern tip of the Bank of Newfoundland. This bank is the product of considerable amounts of marine alluvium, an accumulation of organic waste brought either from the equator by the current of the Gulf Stream or from the North Pole by the counter-current of cold water running down the American coast. Erratic blocks of disintegrating ice were piled up on one another, and a vast bone cemetery of billions of dead fish, molluscs, and zoophytes had built up.

The sea is not very deep at the Bank of Newfoundland, a few hundred fathoms at most. But to the south, a deep depression suddenly drops, a 3,000-metre hole. There the Gulf Stream grows wider and its current spreads out. But in losing speed and temperature, it becomes a sea.

Amongst the fish that the *Nautilus* frightened as it passed, I will cite the metre-long cyclopteroid with a black back and orange stomach, providing an example of conjugal fidelity rarely followed by its congeners, a huge Forsskal's stingray, a sort of emerald moray eel which has an excellent taste, big-eyed wolf-fish whose heads resemble dogs', blennies viviparous like snakes, 20-centimetre dusky frill gobies or black gudgeons, and *Macrura* with long tails and shining with a silvery glitter: fast-moving fish that had ventured far from the hyperborean seas.

The nets also brought in a fish that is daring, audacious, energetic, muscly, and armed with spines on its head and spurs on its fins, a real two- or three-metre scorpion, the relentless enemy of the blennies, gadids, and salmon: this was the *Cottus* of the southern seas, with a brown tuberculous body and red fins. The fishermen of the *Nautilus* found it difficult to take hold of this animal, which uses the shape of its opercula to protect its respiratory organs from the drying effect of the atmosphere and so can live some time out of water.

I will cite—for the record—naked blennies, which are small fish that accompany ships in the northern seas, oxyrhynchous whitebait found only in the northern Atlantic, and scorpion fish; and so I reach the gadids, principally from the species of cod, which I surprised in their favourite waters on that inexhaustible Bank of Newfoundland.

These cod can be said to be mountain fish, for Newfoundland is really a submarine mountain. While the *Nautilus* opened up a route through their crowded battalions, Conseil could not refrain from making an observation:

'Are those cod?' he said. 'But I thought that cod were flat like dab or sole?'

'Fool!' I exclaimed. 'Cod are only flat at the grocer's, where they are slit open and spread out. But in the water, they are spindle-shaped like mullet, and perfectly adapted for swimming.'

'I can well believe it, monsieur,' replied Conseil. 'What a swarm, what an ant-heap!'

'Well, my friend, there would be more without their enemies, namely scorpion fish and men! Do you know how many eggs have been found in a single female?'

'Let's not be stingy. Five hundred thousand.'

'Eleven million, my friend.'

'Eleven million! I will never believe it until I have counted them myself.'

'Count them, Conseil. But it would be quicker if you believed me. In any case, the French, British, Americans, Danes, and Norwegians catch cod by the thousand. They are consumed in tremendous quantities, and without the astonishing fecundity of these fish, the seas would soon be emptied of them. In Britain and America alone, 5,000 ships with 75,000 men work at cod fishing. Each ship brings back 40,000 fish on average, which makes a total of 25 million.* On the coasts of Norway, the same again.'

'Well, I will trust monsieur, and not count them.'

'Pardon?'

'The eleven million eggs. But I will simply make a remark.'

'Yes?'

'That all the eggs hatched by four cod would be sufficient to feed Britain, America, and Norway.'

While we were skimming over the bottom of the Bank of Newfoundland, I could easily see the hundreds of long lines, each with two hundred hooks, deployed by each boat. The lines, dragged along using small clips, were stopped from sinking by cross-hatched cords fixed to cork buoys. The *Nautilus* had to manoeuvre carefully through this submarine network.

But in any case we did not remain long in these busy waters. The *Nautilus* moved up to the 42nd degree of latitude. This was off St John's, Newfoundland, and the port of Heart's Content, where the transatlantic cable ends.

Instead of continuing northwards, the *Nautilus* headed east, as if wanting to follow the telegraphic plateau on which the cable rests, and whose relief has been mapped out with extreme precision by large numbers of soundings.

It was on 17 May, approximately 500 miles from Heart's Content and at a depth of 2,800 metres, that I first spotted the cable lying on the ground. I had not warned Conseil, and at first he took it for a gigantic sea serpent, and was about to classify it according to his usual method. But I soon enlightened the worthy fellow, and to make up for his disappointment, told him various details of the laying of the cable.

The first one was laid in 1857–8; but it stopped working after transmitting about four hundred telegrams. In 1863 the engineers constructed a new cable, measuring 3,400 kilometres and weighing 4,500 tons, and loaded it on to the *Great Eastern*. This attempt also failed.

On 25 May the *Nautilus* was at 3,836 metres depth, at the precise spot where the first break happened that halted the enterprise. It occurred 638 miles from the coast of Ireland. It was realized at two o'clock one afternoon that communication with Europe had been interrupted. The electricians on board decided to cut the cable before bringing it up again, and by eleven o'clock they had brought up the damaged parts. A join and splice were made; and then the cable was let down again. But a few days later it broke once more and could not be retrieved from the depths.

The Americans were not discouraged. The audacious Cyrus Field,* the promoter of the enterprise, who was risking his entire fortune, launched a new subscription. It was immediately snapped up. Another cable was installed taking greater precautions. The cluster of conducting wires was insulated in a sheath of gutta-percha, but also protected by a coating of textile matter, in turn enclosed in a metal casing. The *Great Eastern* sailed off again on 13 July 1866.

This time the operation worked well. However, one incident did occur. Several times while unrolling the cable, the electricians noticed that nails had recently been driven into it so as to damage its core. Captain Anderson* and his officers and engineers held a meeting, discussed the problem, and put up notices saying that if the guilty party were found, he would be thrown into the sea without further notice. From that moment on, the criminal acts ceased.

On 23 July the *Great Eastern* was only 800 kilometres off Newfoundland, when the news of the armistice between Prussia and Austria after Sadowa* was telegraphed to it from Ireland. On the 27th it sighted Heart's Content through the fog. The enterprise had succeeded, and in its first telegram, young America sent old Europe wise words which are so rarely understood: 'Glory to God in the highest, and on earth peace, good will to men.'*

I did not expect to find the electric cable in the same state as when it came out of the workshops. The long serpent, covered with the remains of shells and bristling with foraminifers, was indeed encrusted in a stony coat, thus protecting it from the perforators of molluscs. It rested calmly, sheltered from the movements of the sea, at a pressure suitable for the transmission of the electric spark, which goes from America to Europe in 0.32 seconds. The life of this cable will undoubtedly be infinite, for it has been observed that its gutta-percha covering actually improves the longer it stays in salt water.

In addition, this plateau is very well chosen, and the cable is never submerged so deep that it could break. The *Nautilus* followed it to its lowest point at 4,431 metres, where it was still lying without undue stretching. Then we approached the spot where the 1863 accident happened.

The ocean floor formed a valley 120 kilometres wide: Mont Blanc could have been put in it without emerging from the surface of the water. This valley is enclosed to the east by a vertical wall 2,000 metres high. We arrived there on 28 May; the *Nautilus* was only 150 kilometres from Ireland.

Was Captain Nemo going to head north, so that he could land in the British Isles? No; to my great surprise, he went back down south again, heading for the seas of Europe. While we were working our way around the Emerald Isle, I briefly glimpsed Cape Clear and Fastnet lighthouse,* which provides light for thousands of ships from Glasgow and Liverpool.

An important question then arose in my mind. Would the *Nautilus* dare to venture into the English Channel? Ned Land had reappeared once we had come close to land, and never stopped asking me. How could I answer? Captain Nemo remained invisible. Having let the Canadian catch a glimpse of the shores of America, was he now going to show me the coasts of France?

The *Nautilus* was still heading south. On 30 May it came within sight of Land's End, and passed between that extreme point of England and the Scilly Isles, on the starboard side.

If it wanted to go into the Channel, it would have to cut sharply to the east. It did not do so.

During the whole of 31 May the *Nautilus* described a series of circles on the surface, greatly intriguing me. It seemed to be looking for a spot it had difficulty in finding. At noon, Captain Nemo came to measure the position himself. He did not speak to me. He seemed more sombre than ever. What could be making him so unhappy? Was it being so close to European shores? Did he have memories of his abandoned homeland? In that case, what did he experience—remorse or regret? For a long time such thoughts filled my mind, and I had a hunch that chance would shortly betray the captain's secrets.*

The following day, 1 June, the *Nautilus* performed the same manoeuvres. It was clear that it was trying to identify a precise point in the ocean. As on the day before, Captain Nemo came to take the height of the sun. The sea was fine, the sky pure. Eight miles to the east, a large steam-driven ship stood out on the line of the horizon. No flag was visible on its gaff and I could not identify its nationality.

A few moments before the sun passed the meridian, Captain Nemo took his sextant and made extremely precise observations. The absolute stillness of the water facilitated the operation, since the *Nautilus* lay motionless, neither pitching nor rolling.

I was on the platform. When he had taken our bearings, the captain said only these words:

'It is here!'

He went back down through the hatch. Had he seen the vessel, which now changed direction and seemed to be coming nearer? I cannot say.

I went back to the salon. The hatch was closed, and I could hear the hissing of water in the tanks. The *Nautilus* began to sink—straight down, for its propeller was not operating and so did not affect its movement.

A few minutes later, it stopped at a depth of 833 metres, and came to rest on the seabed.

The salon's luminous ceiling went out, the panels opened, and through the windows I could see the ocean brightly lit up by the searchlight for half a mile around.

I looked to port, but saw nothing but the immensity of the calm water.

On the seabed to starboard appeared a large extumescence which drew my attention. It resembled ruins buried under a coating of whitish shells like a cloak of snow. When I examined the shape more carefully, I thought I recognized the thickened forms of a demasted vessel, which must have sunk bow first. The wreck certainly dated from a long time before. Its hull must have spent many years on the ocean floor to be so encrusted with limestone from the water.

What was this ship? Why had the *Nautilus* come to visit its tomb? Was it not some shipwreck that had sunk the vessel?

I did not know what to think, when near me I heard Captain Nemo saying in a slow voice:

'Formerly this ship was called the *Marseillais*. It carried seventy-four cannons and was launched in 1762. On 13 August 1778, commanded by La Poype-Vertrieux, it fought bravely against the *Preston*. On 4 July 1779, it took part in the capture of Grenada with the fleet of Admiral d'Estaing. On 5 September 1781, it participated in the fighting in Chesapeake Bay with the Count of Grasse. In 1794, the French Republic gave the ship a new name. On 16 April of the same year, it joined the fleet of Villaret de Joyeuse in Brest, charged with escorting a convoy of wheat from America under the command of Admiral Van Stabel.* On 11 and 12 *Prairial* of the year II, this fleet encountered British vessels. Monsieur, it is today 13 *Prairial*, 1 June 1868. Seventy-four years ago to the day, on this same spot of 47° 24′ N, 17° 28′ W, this ship lost two of its three masts in a heroic battle; it had taken on water and a third of its crew were out of action. It preferred to scuttle itself with its 356 crew rather than surrender.* Nailing its flag to the poop, it disappeared under the waves with the cry "Long live the Republic!"'

'The *Vengeur*!* I exclaimed.

'Yes, monsieur.* The *Vengeur*! A fine name!* said Captain Nemo, crossing his arms.

21

A MASSACRE

THE way he spoke, the unexpectedness of the scene, the recounting of the tale of the patriotic ship, and the vehemence with which this strange individual had pronounced the final words about the *Vengeur*, leaving me in no doubt about his meaning: everything combined to make a deep impression on me. My eyes no longer left the captain. Arm stretched out to sea, he was studying the glorious wreck* with glowing eyes. Perhaps I would never know who he was, where he came from, where he was going, but I could see the man more and more distinctly from the scientist. It was not common misanthropy that had enclosed Captain Nemo and his companions in the flanks of the *Nautilus*, but a monstrous or sublime hatred that time could not diminish.*

Was this hatred still seeking revenge? The future would soon show me.

Meanwhile the *Nautilus* was moving slowly up to the surface, and I could see the blurred form of the *Vengeur* disappearing little by little. Soon a slight rolling told me that we were floating in the open air.

Just then a dull explosion sounded. I looked at the captain. He did not move.

'Captain?' I said.

He made no reply.

I left him and went up to the platform. Conseil and the Canadian were already there.

'Where did that explosion come from?'

'A cannon being fired,' Ned replied.

I looked in the direction of the ship I had seen. It had got closer and was clearly sailing at full steam. It was now six miles away.

'What sort of vessel is it, Ned?'

'From its rigging and its low masts, I would bet that it's a warship. I hope it comes at us and sinks us if need be, our damned *Nautilus*!'

'Ned, my friend,' replied Conseil, 'what harm can it do to the *Nautilus*? Will it come and attack underwater? Will it shell the bottom of the seas?'

'Tell me, Ned,' I said, 'can you see the nationality of the vessel?'

The Canadian compressed his brow, lowered his eyelids, screwed up the corners of his eyes, and stared for a few moments at the ship with all the power of his vision.

'No, monsieur, I can't see what nation it belongs to. Its flag is not hoisted. But I can tell that it's a warship, for there's a long pennant at the end of the mainmast.'

For quarter of an hour we continued to observe the ship as it steamed towards us. I could not accept, however, that it had recognized the *Nautilus* at such a distance, still less that it knew what this submarine machine was.

Soon the Canadian announced to me that the vessel was a great warship with a ram: an armour-plated double-decker.* Thick black smoke was pouring from its two funnels. Its furled sails could not be distinguished from the yard line. Its gaff bore no flag. The distance still prevented the colours of its pennant from being identifiable, for they hung down in a thin ribbon.

It was coming nearer quickly. If Captain Nemo allowed it to approach, we stood a chance of being saved.

'Monsieur, if this ship passes within a mile, I'm going to jump into the sea, and I urge you to do the same.'

I did not reply to the Canadian's suggestion, but continued watching the ship as it got larger. Whether British, French, American, or

Russian, it was certain that it would pick us up, if only we could reach it.

'Monsieur should be so kind as to remember', interjected Conseil, 'that we have some experience of swimming. He can entrust me with the task of towing him to the ship, if it suits him to follow Ned, my friend.'

I was going to reply, when white smoke spurted from the stern of the warship. A few seconds later, the water was disturbed by the impact of a heavy body, splashing the stern of the *Nautilus*. Shortly afterwards, an explosion struck my ear.

'What! Are they firing at us?' I cried.

'Good for them,' murmured Ned.

'So they are not taking us for shipwrecked people clinging to a wreck!'

'With respect, monsieur . . . oh!' said Conseil, shaking off the water that a new shell had splashed on him. 'With respect, monsieur, they have seen a narwhal and are firing their cannon at the narwhal.'

'But they must see full well', I expostulated, 'that they are dealing with people!'

'Perhaps for that very reason!' said Land staring at me.

A sudden revolution took place in my mind. The existence of the so-called monster must have been cleared up. When the Canadian struck it with his harpoon during the encounter with the *Abraham Lincoln*, Captain Farragut must have realized that the narwhal was a submarine boat, more dangerous than any supernatural cetacean.

Yes, that had to be the case, and this terrible machine of destruction was evidently being pursued over every ocean!

It would indeed be awful if Captain Nemo was using the *Nautilus* for the sake of revenge, as now seemed plain. During that night in the middle of the Indian Ocean when he had us locked up in the cell, had he not attacked some ship?* That man buried in the coral cemetery, had he not been a victim of a collision that the *Nautilus* had caused? Yes, I repeat, it had to be that. Part of Captain Nemo's mysterious life had been unveiled, and if his identity was still not clear, at least the coalition of nations against him were no longer pursuing a fantastic being, but a man who had sworn implacable hatred against them!

All this formidable past appeared before my eyes. Instead of encountering friends on the approaching ship, we could only find merciless enemies.

Meanwhile the shells were increasing around us. Some of them hit the surface of the sea, bounced off, and covered considerable distances. But none touched the *Nautilus*.

The armour-plated ship was no more than three miles away now. In spite of the violent cannon attack, Captain Nemo did not appear on the platform, and yet if one of those conical projectiles had struck the hull of the *Nautilus* head on, it would have been fatal.

The Canadian then said:

'Monsieur, we must try everything to get out of this situation we're in. Let's make signals! Heck! Perhaps they'll realize that we're honest men!'

Ned Land took out his handkerchief and began to wave it in the air. But he had hardly raised it when, despite his tremendous strength, he was floored by an iron hand and thrown to the deck.*

'Wretch!' exclaimed the captain. 'Do you want me to nail your miserable carcass to the ram of the *Nautilus* when it is launched at that ship!'

Captain Nemo, terrible to hear, was yet more terrifying to behold. His face had grown pale: his heart must have undergone spasms and stopped beating for a moment. His pupils were severely contracted. His mouth no longer spoke, it roared. With his body bent forward, he was twisting the Canadian's shoulders in his hands.

Then, letting go and turning again to the warship, whose shells were raining down around him:

'Ah, you know who I am, ship of an accursed nation!'* he declaimed in a powerful voice. 'As for me, I do not need your colours to identify you! Look, I am going to show you mine!'

And Captain Nemo unfurled a black flag at the front of the platform, identical to the one he had planted on the South Pole.

At that moment, a shell obliquely struck the hull of the *Nautilus*, but without making a hole, ricocheted near the captain, and finished up in the sea.

Captain Nemo shrugged his shoulders. Then, addressing me:

'Go inside,' he said curtly. 'Go inside, you and your companions.'

'Monsieur!' I cried. 'Are you going to attack this ship?'

'I am going to sink it.'

'You are not!'

'I am,' he coldly replied. 'Do not take it on yourself to judge me, monsieur. Fate is showing you what you should not have seen. The attack has come* and the response will be terrible. Go back down.'

'What ship is this?'

'You do not know? Well, so much the better! Its nationality will remain a secret for you. *Go down.*'*

The Canadian, Conseil, and I could only obey. About fifteen sailors from the *Nautilus* stood around the captain, staring with implacable hatred at this ship bearing down on them. The same thought of revenge was clearly filling each of their souls.

I went back in, just as another projectile grazed the *Nautilus*'s hull. I could hear the captain exclaiming:

'Strike, crazy ship! Waste your useless shells. You shall not escape from the *Nautilus*'s ram. But it is not on this spot that you shall perish! I do not want your carcass to sully the remains of the *Vengeur*!

I went back to my room. The captain and his first officer remained on the platform. The propeller started up. The *Nautilus* moved away at speed, and was soon out of reach of the vessel's shells. But the pursuit continued, with Captain Nemo content merely to maintain his distance.

At about four in the afternoon, unable to contain the impatience and worry devouring me, I returned to the central staircase. The hatch was open. I ventured out. The captain was still agitatedly pacing up and down. He was looking at the ship, five or six miles to leeward. He was moving back and forth like a wild animal, as he allowed himself to be pursued, drawing it eastwards. However, he did not attack. Perhaps he was still hesitating?

I tried one last time to intervene, but I had hardly addressed Captain Nemo before he imposed silence on me.

'I am the law, I am the justice!'* he said. 'I am the oppressed, and they are the oppressor! It is because of them that everything I loved, cherished, venerated—country, wife, children, parents—perished as I watched!* Everything I hate is there! Keep quiet!'

I cast a last glance at the warship, which was straining at full steam. Then I rejoined Ned and Conseil.

'We're going to escape!' I cried.

'Well,' said Ned, 'what ship is it?'

'I don't know, but whatever it is, it will be sunk before nightfall.* It would be better to perish with it than be involved in reprisals, whose fairness we cannot judge.'

'That is also my opinion,' Ned coldly replied. 'Let's wait for darkness.'

Night fell. A deep silence reigned on board. The compass showed that the *Nautilus* had not changed direction. I could hear the beating as its propeller struck the waves with a quick rhythm. It remained on the surface and the slight rolling took it now to one side, now to the other.

My companions and I resolved to attempt an escape as soon as the vessel was close enough for us to make ourselves heard or seen, for it was three days to the full moon, and the light was bright. Once on board the ship, if we could not prevent it being attacked, at least we would have tried everything that circumstances allowed. Several times I thought that the *Nautilus* was getting ready for an assault, but it would merely let its adversary come closer, and then shortly afterwards accelerate away again.

Part of the night went by without incident. We watched out for a chance to act. We said little, for we were too much on edge. Ned would have liked to throw himself into the sea. I forced him to wait. I thought the *Nautilus* would surely attack the double-decker on the surface of the waves, and it would then be not only possible but easy to escape.*

At three in the morning, feeling rather worried, I went back up to the platform. Captain Nemo was still there. He stood at the front near his flag, which a light breeze unfurled above his head. His eyes no longer left the vessel. His extraordinarily intense gaze seemed to be attracting it, beguiling it, dragging it in more surely than if he had winched it!

The moon was at its zenith. Jupiter was rising in the east. In the midst of this peaceful nature, sky and sea vied in serenity, and the water offered the moon the most beautiful mirror that had ever reflected it.

But when I thought of the deep calm of the elements, compared to all the angers growing in the flanks of the imperceptible *Nautilus*, I felt my whole being quake.

The vessel remained two miles from us. It had come closer, moving towards that phosphorescent light which indicated the *Nautilus*'s presence. I could see its green and red position lights and its white navigation light on the main foresail stay. A vague glow lit up its rigging, and showed that the boiler was being pushed to the very limit. Sheaves of sparks and cinders of burning coal escaped its funnels, producing stars in the air.

I remained until 6 a.m., without Captain Nemo seeming to have noticed me. The vessel stayed a mile and a half away, and as soon as the first gleams of dawn began to appear, it started firing its cannons again. The time could not be far off when the *Nautilus* would start attacking its adversary, and my companions and I would leave once and for all this man that I dared not judge.

I was getting ready to go below and tell them, when the first officer came out. Several sailors were with him. Captain Nemo did not see them, or perhaps did not wish to. Preparations were being made to the *Nautilus* as if for action stations. They were very simple. The jack-stay forming the handrail around the platform was lowered. The domes for the searchlight and the pilot-house slid into the hull so as to form a unified line with it.* The surface of the long metal cigar no longer offered a single point to interfere with its operation.

I went back down to the salon. The *Nautilus* was still on the surface. A few morning gleams were slipping into the liquid strata. As some of the waves rolled on, the windows were lit up by the red of the rising sun. That terrible day of 2 June was just beginning.

At five o'clock the log told me that the *Nautilus* was slowing.* I realized that it was allowing itself to be approached.* The explosions were getting louder. The shells were ploughing into the surrounding water, moving through it with a strange hissing sound.

'My friends,' I said, 'the time has come. Let's shake hands and God be with us!'

Ned Land was determined, Conseil calm, and I on edge, hardly able to control my nerves.

We went into the library. Just as I opened the door giving on to the well of the central staircase, I heard the hatch slam shut.

The Canadian rushed towards the steps, but I held him back. A familiar hissing sound told me that water was flooding into the tanks. Within seconds, the *Nautilus* had sunk a few metres below the surface.

I understood then what was happening. It was too late to do anything. The *Nautilus* was not planning to strike the impenetrable armour of the double-decker, but the section below its flotation line, where a metal sheath no longer protected the planking.

We were prisoners once more—forced witnesses to the sinister drama being prepared. In any case, we hardly had time to think. Taking refuge in my room, we looked at each other without a single word. A profound stupor had invaded my brain. My mind had stopped working. I found myself in that uncomfortable state of wait-ing for a frightening explosion. I waited and listened, my sense of hearing the only part of me alive!

Meanwhile the speed of the *Nautilus* had noticeably increased as it gathered momentum. Its hull trembled.

Suddenly, I gave a cry. A jolt had occurred, but a relatively slight one. I could feel the strength of penetration of the steel ram. I could hear scraping noises. The *Nautilus*, carried on by its propulsive force, was passing clean through the vessel,* like a sailmaker's needle through canvas!

I could no longer keep still. Maddened, bewildered, I rushed out of my room and into the salon.

Captain Nemo stood there. Silent, sombre, implacable, he was watching the port window.

An enormous object was sinking into the water; and, so as to follow every detail of its death-throes, the *Nautilus* was descending into the abyss with it. Ten metres away, I could see a hull torn open, water rushing in with the sound of thunder, then the twin ranks of cannons and bulwarks. The deck was covered with black shadows, all moving.

The water was rising. The wretches rushed up the rigging, clung on to the masts, twisted under the waters. It was a human ant-heap caught out by the invasion of a sea.

Paralysed, stiff with anguish, hair standing on end, eyes unnaturally wide, hardly able to breathe, without air, without voice, I was watch-ing too! An irresistible attraction glued me to the glass.

The enormous vessel slowly sank. The *Nautilus* followed it, watch-ing for its slightest movements. Suddenly, an explosion occurred. The pressure made the decks* of the vessel fly off, as if fire had broken out in its magazine. The thrust of the water was such that the *Nautilus* was pushed aside.

Now the unhappy ship sank more quickly. Its crow's nests, laden with victims, went down, next its crosstrees, bending under the weight of the clusters of men, and finally the tip of its mainmast. Then the sombre mass disappeared, and with it the crew of human forms, carried down in a formidable undertow . . .

I turned to Captain Nemo. That terrible lawgiver, that archangel of hatred, was watching still. When everything was finished, Captain Nemo headed for the door of his room, opened it, and went in. My eyes followed him.

On the far wall, below the pictures of his heroes, I saw the portrait of a woman, still young, with two small children. Captain Nemo looked at them for a few moments, stretched out his arms to them, and knelt down sobbing.*

22

CAPTAIN NEMO'S LAST WORDS

THE panels had closed again over this frightening vision, but the light had not been switched on again in the salon. Inside the *Nautilus* there reigned only darkness and silence. It was leaving that place of destruction, 100 feet beneath the water, at prodigious speed. In what direction was it heading? North or south? Where was this man fleeing after his terrible reprisal?

I had returned to my room where Ned and Conseil were silently waiting. I felt an invincible horror for Captain Nemo. Whatever he had suffered at the hands of men, he did not have the right to inflict punishment in this way. He had made me the witness to his acts of revenge, if not the accomplice. That was already too much.

At eleven o'clock the electric light came on again. I went into the salon. It was deserted. I consulted the various instruments. The *Nautilus* was fleeing north at a speed of 25 knots, sometimes on the surface of the water, sometimes 30 feet below.

Our bearings having been marked on the map, I realized that we were passing near the mouth of the English Channel, and that our movement was taking us towards the Arctic seas at unsurpassed speed.*

I could barely identify the quickly passing long-nosed sharks, hammerheads, or spotted dogfish of these waters; nor the great eagle rays, the clouds of sea-horses like knights in chess sets, the eels wiggling like firework squibs, the armies of crabs fleeing obliquely while crossing their pincers over their shells, nor finally the schools of porpoise racing the *Nautilus*. I did not even think of observing, studying, or classifying them.

By evening, we had covered 200 leagues of the Atlantic. Shadows fell, and the sea was cloaked in darkness; but then the moon rose.*

I went back to my room. I could not sleep. I was assailed by nightmares. The terrifying scene of destruction was repeating over and over in my mind.

Starting from that day, who could have said where the *Nautilus* took us through that basin of the North Atlantic? Always at a speed that could not be guessed! Always through the Arctic fogs. Did it put in at the tip of Spitsbergen, or on the shores of Novaya Zemlya? Did it go through those unknown waters, the White Sea, the Kara Sea, the Gulf of Ob, the Lyakhov Islands, or along the unexplored shores of the Asian coast? I could not say. Days and hours went by without me being able to calculate them. The time of the clocks on board had been suspended.* As in the polar regions, it was as if day and night no longer followed their regular course. I felt myself carried off to the realm of the extra-natural, where Poe's overworked imagination moved at ease. At each moment I expected to see, like the fabulous Gordon Pym, 'a shrouded human figure, very far larger in its proportions than any dweller among men, thrown across the cataract which defends the approaches to the Pole'!*

I estimate—but am perhaps mistaken—that this wild movement of the *Nautilus* continued on for two or three weeks; and I do not know how long it would have lasted had it not been for the catastrophe that terminated our voyage. Of Captain Nemo there was no longer any sign. Nor of his first officer. Not one crew member appeared for a single moment.* The *Nautilus* navigated almost permanently underwater. When it went up again to replenish its air, the hatches opened and closed automatically.* The position was no longer plotted on the planisphere. I had no idea where we were.

I must also say that the Canadian was at the end of his patience and tether, and no longer left his cabin. Conseil could no longer drag a single word out of him, and feared that he might kill himself in a fit of madness or devastating homesickness. He devotedly watched over him every second of the day.

It will be understood that in such circumstances the situation was no longer tenable.*

One morning—what date I cannot say*—I had started dozing in the first few hours of the day. An uncomfortable and unhealthy doze. When I awoke, I found Land leaning over me and saying in a low voice:

'We're going to escape!'

I sat up.

'When?'

'Tonight. All surveillance appears to have vanished from the *Nautilus*. There seems to be a total stupor on board. Will you be ready?'

'I will. But where are we?'

'In sight of some land that I glimpsed through the fog this morning, 20 miles east.'

'What land?'

'Not the foggiest, but whatever country it is, we will find shelter there.'*

'Yes, Ned! We will try to escape tonight, even if the sea does swallow us up!'

'The sea is stormy, the wind strong, but covering 20 miles in the *Nautilus*'s boat doesn't frighten me. I have been able to put some food in, plus a few bottles of water, without the crew realizing.'*

'I will follow you.'

'In any case, if I'm caught, I'll fight back, I'll give up my life.'

'We'll die together, Ned, my friend.'

I was ready for anything. The Canadian left me. I went out on to the platform, although I could scarcely stand up due to the shaking from the waves. The sky was threatening, but since there lay land behind that fog, we had to try to escape. We could not wait a day or even an hour.*

I went back to the salon, fearing and at the same time longing to meet Captain Nemo, wanting and not wanting to see him. What could I say to him? Would I be able to hide the involuntary horror he inspired in me? No, better not to come face to face with him! Better to forget him! And yet!

How this day dragged on, the last I was ever to spend on board the *Nautilus*! I remained alone. Ned and Conseil avoided speaking to me for fear of giving themselves away.

At six o'clock I dined, but did not feel hungry. In spite of my distaste, I forced myself to eat, wishing to maintain my strength.

At half past six, Ned Land came into my room:

'We won't see each other again before we go. At ten o'clock, the moon won't be up yet. The darkness will help us. Come to the boat. Conseil and I'll be waiting for you there.'

Then the Canadian went out without giving time for a reply.

I wished to know the *Nautilus*'s direction. I made for the salon. We were heading north-north-east at frightening speed and 50 metres' depth.

I made a final inspection of the wonders of nature and treasures of art amassed in the museum, at this unrivalled collection destined to perish one day at the bottom of the seas, together with the man who had assembled it. I wanted to engrave one last memory in my mind. I remained an hour thus, bathed in the emanations from the luminous ceiling, reviewing the resplendent treasures behind the panes. Then I returned to my room.

I put on strong sea clothing. I gathered my notes together, and tied them with great care to my body. My heart was beating violently. I could not reduce its throbbing. My trouble and unease would certainly have given me away before Captain Nemo.

What was he doing at this moment? I listened at the door of his room. I heard footsteps, telling me Captain Nemo was there. He had not gone to bed.* With each step I thought he would appear and ask me why I wished to escape. Feelings of alarm kept gripping me. My imagination magnified them. The impression became so strong that I wondered if it would not be better to march into the captain's room, look him in the face, and defy him with my attitude and my eyes!

These were the promptings of a madman. Fortunately I held back, and went back to stretch out on my bed so as to reduce the agitation in my body. My nerves calmed down a little, but in a swift vision of my overexcited brain I relived my whole life on board, all the happy and unhappy incidents that had marked the *Nautilus* following my disappearance from the *Abraham Lincoln*: underwater hunting, the Torres Strait, the savages of Papua, running aground, the coral cemetery, the route under Suez, the island of Santorini, the Cretan diver, Vigo Bay, Atlantis, the ice-cap, the South Pole, imprisonment in the ice, the battle with the squid, the storm on the Gulf Stream, the *Vengeur*, and that terrible scene of the sinking of the vessel with all hands. All these events passed before my eyes like minor scenes taking place on the backdrop of a stage. Then against this strange setting Captain Nemo grew out of all proportion. His character was accentuated and took on superhuman dimensions. He was no longer a fellow human, but a marine being, a spirit of the seas.

It was half past nine. I took my head in my hands to stop it exploding. I closed my eyes. I no longer wanted to think. Still half an hour to wait! Half an hour of a nightmare that might send me mad!

Suddenly I heard distant chords from the organ, the sad harmony of an indefinable melody, the veritable complaint of a soul yearning to break all ties with earth. I listened with all my senses, hardly breathing, plunged like Captain Nemo into musical ecstasies that carried him beyond the limits of this world.

Then a new thought terrified me. Captain Nemo had obviously left his room. He was in that salon I had to cross to escape. There I would meet him one last time. He would see me, perhaps even speak! A sign from him could destroy me, a single word chain me to his ship!

Meanwhile ten o'clock was about to strike. The time had come to leave my room and join my companions.

There was no time to hesitate, even were Captain Nemo to surge up before me. I carefully opened my door. And yet it seemed that as it moved on its hinges, it made a frightening sound. Perhaps the sound existed only in my imagination! I crawled forward through the dark gangways of the *Nautilus*, stopping after each step to compress the beatings of my heart.

I arrived at the angled door to the salon. I slowly opened it. The room was plunged in deep darkness. The chords of the organ were still faintly echoing. Captain Nemo was there. He did not see me. I think that even in full light he would not have noticed me, so much did his ecstasy absorb him.

I dragged myself across the carpet, avoiding the slightest contact whose sound might have betrayed my presence. It took me five minutes to reach the far door leading into the library.

I was going to open it, when a sigh from Captain Nemo nailed me to the spot. I realized that he was getting up. I even caught sight of him, for a few rays from the lights in the library were filtering as far as the salon. He came towards me, his arms crossed, silently gliding rather than walking, like a ghost. His oppressed breast heaved with sobbings, and I heard him murmuring. The closing words reached my ear:

'God almighty! Enough! Enough!'*

Was it an admission of remorse, escaping thus from the conscience of this man . . .?

Bewildered, I rushed into the library. I climbed the central staircase, followed the upper gangway, and reached the boat. I went through the opening which had already afforded access to my two companions.

'Let's go! Let's go!' I cried.

'Straightaway,' replied the Canadian.

The opening in the metal skin of the *Nautilus* was closed and bolted using an adjustable spanner Ned had brought with him. The cover of the boat itself was then put in place, and the Canadian began to undo the bolts still attaching us to the submarine vessel.

Suddenly a sound could be heard inside. Voices were sharply answering each other. What was it? Had our escape been discovered? I could feel Ned Land sliding a knife into my hand.

'Yes,' I murmured, 'we are ready to die!'

The Canadian had stopped his work. But one word, repeated many times, a terrifying word, told me the reason for the agitation spreading through the *Nautilus*. It was not us the crew were upset with.

They were exclaiming 'Maelstrom! Maelstrom!'*

The Maelstrom! Could a more frightening word reach our ears in a more desperate situation? Were we off the Norwegian coast, in its dangerous waters? Was the *Nautilus* being sucked down into that vortex at the very moment our boat prepared to cast off?

It is known that, at the greatest flow, the waters caught between Vaeroy and the Lofoten Islands* move with irresistible violence. They form a whirlpool from which no ship has ever been able to escape.* Monstrous waves rush in from all points of the horizon. They form a funnel fittingly called the 'navel of the ocean',* with a power of attraction stretching over a distance of 15 kilometres. Not only are ships sucked in, but also whales and even polar bears from the Arctic.

It was here that the *Nautilus* had involuntarily—or perhaps not—been engaged by its captain.* It was describing a spiral whose radius was decreasing all the time. The boat, still attached, was being transported with it at a dizzying speed. I could feel it. I was experiencing the turning feeling caused by a rotation that goes on for too long. We were in a state of terror! Terror of the highest degree! Our blood was no longer circulating, our nervous systems had closed down. We were covered in cold sweat, as if on a deathbed. What a noise all round our frail boat! What moanings echoed from miles around! What a din from the waters smashed on the sharp rocks of the bottom, where the hardest bodies break up, where tree-trunks wear themselves out, where they produce a 'fur of hair', as the Norwegian expression has it!*

What a situation! We were being shaken frightfully. The *Nautilus* was fighting like a human being. Its steel muscles were cracking. Sometimes it stood up, and us with it.*

'We need to hold on', said Ned, 'and screw the bolts back on. If we stay with the *Nautilus*, we can still get out alive . . .!'*

He had not finished speaking, when a cracking noise resounded. The bolts gave way; and the dinghy was torn from its recess and launched into the midst of the whirlpool like a stone from a sling.

My head struck an iron spar, and the forceful impact knocked me unconscious.

23

CONCLUSION

THIS is the conclusion of our journey under the seas. What happened that night, how the boat escaped from the formidable undertow of the Maelstrom, how Ned, Conseil, and I emerged from the deep, I cannot say. But when I came to, I was lying in the hut of a Lofoten Islands fisherman. My two companions were safe and sound beside me, squeezing my hands. We embraced warmly.*

For the moment, we cannot think of returning to France.* There are not many means of transport between the north and south of Norway. I am therefore forced to wait for the steamship which makes the fortnightly run to North Cape.

So it is here, in the midst of the good people who saved us, that I am revising the tale of these adventures.* It is scrupulously accurate. Not a single fact has been omitted, not the slightest detail exaggerated. It is the faithful narration of an incredible expedition through an element inaccessible to man, although progress will open it up one day.

Will I be believed? I do not know, but it is not all that important. What I can proclaim now is my right to speak of the seas under which I covered 20,000 leagues in less than ten months; and to speak of that submarine journey around the world, which has revealed so many of the wonders of the Mediterranean and Red seas and of the Pacific, Indian, Atlantic, Arctic, and Antarctic oceans!

But what became of the *Nautilus*?* Did it resist the embrace of the Maelstrom? Is Captain Nemo still alive?* Is he continuing his terrifying reprisals under the ocean, or did he stop with his last massacre? Will the waves one day wash up the manuscript containing the story of his whole life?* Will I finally discover his name? Will the nationality of the sunken vessel tell us Captain Nemo's own nationality?

I hope so. I also hope that his powerful vessel overcame the sea's most terrifying deep and that the *Nautilus* survived where so many ships have perished!* If that is the case, if Captain Nemo does still inhabit his adopted oceanic homeland, may hatred die down in that wild heart! May the contemplation of so many wonders quench his desire for revenge! May the lawgiver disappear and the scientist continue his peaceful exploration of the seas! If his destiny is strange, it is also sublime. Do I not understand it myself? Have I not lived ten months of that extranatural existence?

So, to that question which the Book of Ecclesiastes posed six thousand years ago, 'Hast thou walked in the search of the depth?',* two men, amongst all men, now have the right to reply. Captain Nemo and I.*

APPENDIX 1

INCEPTION

IN a letter to Verne dated 25 July 1865 the writer George Sand suggested that he should write an under-sea novel. Verne may have written an outline in August 1866, but stopped work until 1868 to finish the *Illustrated Geography of France and its Colonies*.

The novel often changed title: *Journey under the Waters*, *Twenty Thousand Leagues under the Waters*, *Twenty-Five Thousand Leagues under the Waters*, *Twenty-Five Thousand Leagues under the Seas*, and *Twenty Thousand Leagues under the Oceans*. The definitive title may have been Hetzel's idea.

Two manuscript versions ('MS1' and 'MS2') are known to exist of *Twenty Thousand Leagues*, both written in 1868–9 and now kept in the French National Library, with an online version freely available.[1] MS1 I (i.e. vol. 1, dating from the second quarter of 1868) corresponds to chapters 11 onwards of Part One, and MS1 II (first and second quarters of 1869) to Part Two. MS2 I (third quarter 1868), headed 'Twenty Thousand Leagues under the Oceans', and MS2 II (third and fourth quarters of 1868) again correspond to the two parts of the book.

In MS1, chapters I 12 and 13 form a single unit; and 14–16, only two chapters. Some of the titles are different: 'The Coalmines of Tenerife' instead of the published 'Underwater Coalmines' (II 10), 'An Attack' for 'A Massacre' (II 21), and 'Maelstrom' for 'Captain Nemo's Last Words' (II 22).

The second document, used to prepare the proofs, is more legible than the first, but contains, naturally, much less unpublished text. These vital documents, apparently in Verne's hand, remain almost completely unknown. Scores of exegetes have pored over the intensive, sometimes bad-tempered, epistolary exchanges with the publisher about the closing chapters. But the manuscripts, which constitute the primary evidence of most of the changes, have scarcely been read since the 1860s: apart from my own publications, only one article, written forty years ago, has been published.[2]

---

[1] A letter written by Verne's son, Michel, to Prince Roland Bonaparte in 1906 says that the manuscripts being sent to him 'seem' to include a third version of Part Two, although no trace of this has been found. C.-N. Martin states that Verne gave another manuscript to the Comte de Paris in 1878, but this has never been confirmed. In addition, to facilitate Hetzel's revision work, a Mme Lachaise recopied the second volume of Verne's fair copy [8 June 1869].

[2] As noted above, Destombes's study of 1975 (see Select Bibliography), which is excellent, examines only short sections of the manuscripts and the transcriptions contain a few mistakes.

It should be noted immediately that these earlier drafts of the novel are often classic Verne, sometimes preferable to the familiar version, so that one can regret many of the alterations—and suspect that they were introduced on Hetzel's initiative. Indeed the publisher's involvement is shown by the many partly-erased pencil marks and comments in the margins of MS2, usually beside changes in the text: some are even initialled 'H'. On occasion Verne retraces the pencil amendments in ink, meaning that it is Hetzel's contribution which is published.[3]

In a few pages, these precious documents cannot be explored in any great detail. The notes at the end of the volume cite some of the important variants in the successive versions of the book. Here, a few significant facets and themes will be studied, looking specifically at how *Twenty Thousand Leagues* could have been—was—different from the published version.

In both manuscripts, we see a different Nemo, more independent and more intransigent. In addition to being an engineer, naturalist, writer, and freedom-fighter, 'Juan Nemo'—perhaps an allusion to his Hispanic pride or grandiloquence or his anti-Don Juan lifestyle—is a composer. The music he prefers to 'all the ancient and modern' is his own: a striking image of a solipsistic artist short-circuited by his isolation. The incongruous Christian element in the published text is generally absent, including Nemo's cry of 'God almighty!' When scores of Papuans invade his ship, the captain simply electrocutes them, without remorse.

The sentence uttered every day by the crew is at this stage 'Nautron *restoll loni* virch', even harder to decrypt. The location of Nemo's home port, which Verne takes pains to hide, is given away as near 'Tenerife'. There is an allusion to Walter Scott; and a debt to Alexandre Dumas *fils*, Verne's friend, mentor, and collaborator, is also acknowledged.

MS2 contains a different agreement between Nemo and Aronnax concerning life on board: it has three conditions rather than one and makes the passengers 'prisoners' rather than 'guests', with the doctor formally undertaking never to escape. But in a final dialogue, Aronnax throws in Nemo's face his moral right to leave, who throws back: well, go then!

Whereas in the closing words of the published work Aronnax suggests that the captain should change his ways ('may hatred die down in that wild heart', etc.), in the first manuscript he is resoundingly praised as 'impregnable' and as 'the man of the waters, in his final homeland. The free man!'

In the Margin

As in Verne's other drafts, the margin of MS1 contains a treasure trove of information about the inception of the novel and the author's

---

[3] Additional information about the manuscripts of *20T* can be found in my *Jules Verne inédit*.

private, even intimate life, as well as Hetzel's and Verne's doodles and drawings.

Beside the main text appears an intriguing note: 'photographic prints so as to see using a magnifying lens. See savages Robinson' (I 22 fo. 56).[4] Although examining photographs with a magnifying glass could in theory be used to identify the ships harassing Nemo, in practice the idea does not appear in any version of *Twenty Thousand Leagues*. Nevertheless, scrutinizing a print in search of clues will be crucial in *The Mysterious Island* (1874)—making this apparently the first reference to the manuscript which will evolve into that novel.

Also in the margin of MS1, there appears a list of chapters, written in June or July 1868, a unique summary amongst the well-known *Extraordinary Voyages*. It begins with the title of a chapter already written, before setting out half of the chapters still to be composed:

1918 Torres Str. | 19 A Few Days on Land | 20 Universal Thunder | 21 The Indian Ocean | 22 A Pearl Worth 10 million | 23 Œgri [*sic*] Somnia | 24 The Coral World | | Volume 2 | 1 The Red Sea | 2 Santorini | 3 Lighthouse | 4 Mediterranean (I 19 fo. 43).[5]

The book does not contain a description of a 'lighthouse' in the Mediterranean—is this perhaps that of Alexandria, the last of the Seven Wonders of the World, whose underwater remains were discovered in the eighteenth century? Moreover, given that '4 Mediterranean' will become '7 | The Mediterranean in ~~24~~48 Hours' (MS1 II 7 fo. 27), it is possible that Verne, while aiming for a second volume of twenty-four chapters, planned to write about four more chapters set in European waters than were actually published.

The order is also surprising. In this summary, chapter '22 A Pearl Worth 10 million', set off the coast of Ceylon, is placed before '24 The Coral World', whereas in the manuscript text itself (II 3 fo. 8) and in the published book, it will be placed three chapters *after* 'The Coral Cemetery'[6] (MS1 I 22 fo. 57). In other words, chapters '23 Œgri Somnia' and '24 The Coral World' were planned at this early stage to take place between Ceylon and the Red Sea—waters that were partly French, and formed a cul-de-sac in 1868-9, just before the Suez Canal was opened. These two chapters are largely devoid of geographical clues—facilitating the transfer—but in the

---

[4] References to the manuscripts appear in this form (volume 1, chapter 22, page 56, following Verne's chapter and page numbering); in the Explanatory Notes, such references are generally omitted.

[5] I would like to thank the French National Library for its kind permission to publish extracts from documents in its possession.

[6] The innocuous title 'The Coral World' in the summary seems to correspond to 'The Coral Cemetery', which describes the underwater burial.

following drafts they will take place much further east, somewhere between Ceylon and Australia. They relate, crucially, the surreptitious drugging of Aronnax and the violent episode that leads to the death of a crew member and his underwater burial beneath the coral. The change in the order of episodes may have come in sum from a wish to locate these mysterious events in waters dominated by the British.

The draft manuscript also has about fifteen brief annotations in the margin, which reveal unsuspected sources for the novel—and the care with which it was documented. For example, opposite a description of a seabed of flowers, as if 'strewn with diamonds, emeralds, and other gems. | We were struck with admiration, with astonishment' (I 24 fo. 60), the margin reads: 'Grat. 49, 51'. There follow three blank lines, which in the second manuscript will be filled with a development of the feelings of admiration and astonishment. It can be easily checked that such references, opposite passages describing strong emotions, are citing *De la physionomie et des mouvements d'expression* (Hetzel, 1865), by physiognomist Louis-Pierre Gratiolet: his page 49 describes the physiological reactions to beauty, page 51, those produced by astonishment.

Other sources explicitly indicated in MS1 are the *Revue géographique* and the *Bulletin* of the French Geographical Society. Another series of references consists of a single character, invariably '2', 'R.', or 'Z', followed by two or three digits. For example, the Gulf of Aden is subject to a 'current of 8^2 in May. Dict. 2 406', information not used in later drafts.[7] A search shows that this entry refers to *Dictionnaire français illustré et encyclopédie universelle* (1847), edited by Dupiney de Vorepierre and Jean-François-Marie de Marcoux; and that in all such cases the page references and information are scrupulously accurate. Again, 'R. 82', opposite a passage about American clams, refers to *Le Fond de la mer* (The Bottom of the Sea), by Léon Renard (Hetzel, 1868).[8] Similarly, the notes in the margin beginning with 'Z.' refer, as can easily be verified, to *Le Monde sous-marin* (The Submarine World—Hetzel, September 1868), by Frédéric Zurcher and Élie Margollé.[9]

---

[7] The others are: between the Red Sea and the Mediterranean, 'only 80 centim. of difference. Dict. 2.407'; for information about the Mediterranean, 'dict. 2 407'; about the Atlantic, 'dict. 2 406'; about the Sargasso Sea, 'which gave Columbus idea for the new world. dict. 2 406'; and citing the water temperature in degrees, '4.17. Dict. 2 406'.

[8] In addition, Renard shares with Verne such ideas as underwater fishing, byssus clothing, Conseil's submarine, and Fulton's *Nautilus*.

[9] Zurcher and Margollé also contains such familiar elements as currents, the Maelstrom, the sounding of great depths, aquariums, atolls, Atlantis, and various species of fish. Verne wrote to his editor: 'the identical chapters of the books of MM. Renard and Margollé are the history of the submarine cable [and] the history of submarine boats' (30 April [1868]).

Climax

In the published book we have little information about the submarine's final route towards the Arctic, a frustrating gap since Verne was deeply attached to the waters in question. He visited the British Isles at least fourteen times and sailed along the north coast of France at every opportunity. Having gone round the world, the writer heads for the English Channel, but creates a geographical vacuum at the very spot where he is composing his masterpiece.

Fortunately both manuscripts conserve passages that disappeared before publication, of significance because they constitute the only descriptions of France in Verne's first thirty novels. In one, Nemo and Aronnax explore the Channel floor; in another, the narrator conjures up medieval visions from the dark cliffs near Le Havre. In a delightful seascape, finally, the *Nautilus* communes with a happy dawn of sunny tranquillity somewhere near Belgium.[10] While the pace of the chapter has to be maintained, we can still regret this fine vision of a peaceful European sea:

The sky was white, the air calm. Not a breath of wind. On the sea, slight regular ripples created intersecting diamond shapes. The sun picked them out in sparkling points. The water, like liquid emerald, heaved in broad billows that the *Nautilus* did not even feel. In the quivering haze, a few distant fishing boats and two or three luggers with flaccid sails faded indistinctly away. The smoke from a steamer traced a motionless cloud on the backdrop of the sky (II 22).

In the first manuscript, Nemo ardently supports the ship *Le Vengeur du peuple* (*The Avenger of the People*), a core element of the 'Republican legend', now reposing in a 'grand heroic tomb' (MS1 II 21 fo. 80). Such features are evidently a defence of the downtrodden and the values of the French Revolution. However, they disappeared in the reworking of the novel under the direction of Hetzel, who did not allow Verne to touch on even slightly controversial matters.

In MS2, before Nemo's final counter-attack, his exchange with Aronnax is franker and less courteous. The captain gives a self-justification which is similar but not identical to the published version: 'Do you know who you are imploring? A man expelled from his country, tyrannically exiled, far from his wife, far from his children, whom the suffering killed . . . For the last time, keep quiet!'[11]

Then, after the submarine has passed through the ship, a horror-stricken but fascinated Aronnax observes the underwater death-throes. The manuscript again contains more melodrama: 'There, a poor little cabin boy, as if enchained in the pale flame, twisted in a last convulsion'. Whereas the book

[10] MS1 marks this scene as 'a few miles from low landmasses which had to be those of Holland, scarcely shaded through the warm vapours of the horizon' (II 22).

[11] These sentences, together with those in the next two extracts, are struck through.

version refers to Nemo's 'terrible reprisal', both manuscripts call it his 'bloody execution'.

The antepenultimate chapter's closing words are also different, with aggression the dominant emotion:

. . . his eye shining, fixed to one side, his teeth uncovered under his raised lip, his body stiff, his fingers clenched, his head hunched in his shoulders. A veritable statue of hatred, such as he had already appeared to my eyes in the seas of India.[12]

In the correspondence, Verne promises that he will delete: 'the horror that Nemo inspires in Aronnax at the end, and remove that appearance of hatred which Nemo has on seeing the ship being sunk, and will not even make him assist at this sinking' [29? April 1869]. In other words, his concession merely involves the epiphenomena of what the doctor observes and feels about Nemo, rather than the captain's actions themselves. Nor does he entirely honour his undertaking, for, although Aronnax is not present at the attack and the cabin boy's convulsions are sacrificed, the good doctor does devour every gruesome detail of the ship's descent.

Much of the published closing battle seems in fact to have been Verne's fourth attempt to depict a menacing warship.

The first volume of the first manuscript contains an unknown scene in the Torres Strait, the second half of which is highly significant. Aronnax, Ned, and Conseil distinguish a 'three-master' in the distance, not displaying any flag, but which they recognize. Nemo is beside himself with rage:

For half an hour more we remained watching in silence. Soon the ship appeared in full view and was easy to recognize as armour-plated, probably of the French Solférino type. But as for its nationality, we could not judge at this distance, for no flag fluttered at its gaff; but a thin pennant, whose colours we could not distinguish, hung down from the truck of its mainmast.

'And you cannot identify, Ned, whether it is British, Russian, French, Italian, or American' [*sic*]

'No, Dr Oyonnax, the colours of its pennant blend in with the sun's rays, so I can't recognize anything.'

But as for him, Captain Nemo seemed to have recognized the ship; for a sort of muffled cry sprang from his breast; his foot struck the metal of the platform, and his right arm made a violent gesture, like a threat.

I looked at Nemo. He was no longer the same man; he was transformed. I would not have recognized him (I 21 fo. 56).

If part of this scene seems familiar, it is because the end of the last paragraph will be reused by Verne, first of all in the climax of the draft

---

[12] This description constitutes another of those copied from Gratiolet, as shown by the entry in the margin, 'hatred. Grat. 369'.

manuscript, where Nemo again tangles with a warship (perhaps the same as in the Torres Strait?). Although the text is slightly changed, the key words are retained, especially: 'a great warship with a ram, of the Solférino type, an armour-plated double-decker' (MS1 II 21 fo. 78). Then, in the second volume of the second manuscript, Verne again writes the same description of the vessel: 'a great warship, with a ram, an armour-plated double-decker of the Solférino type' (MS2 II 21 fo. 119). Even in the published book, the wording survives, except for the term 'three-master' and the identification of the class: 'a great warship with a ram: an armour-plated double-decker' (II 21).

The terminology common to the three descriptions thus includes 'of the Solférino type'. Not only was this class indeed constructed in France, but the only vessels built—the *Magenta* and the *Solférino*—also constituted the capital ships of the French Imperial Navy.

Although the novelist maintains in his letters that any identification has been eliminated, the class of this name was instantly recognizable due to its almost rectangular shape. In any case, the *Magenta* and *Solférino* were the only ships in the world to have two rows of guns on two decks, three main-masts, armour-plating, and a ram. In short, and despite Aronnax's question,[13] such a characterization could only be applied to two vessels worldwide, both of French construction and nationality.

If the ship is French, what nationality would Nemo be? As we saw in the Introduction, one possibility is that the captain shares the same nationality, even if, in the versions of the novel revised by the publisher, Verne feels obliged to remove most of the signs of a Gallic origin. Captain Nemo, exiled from his homeland, would then be viscerally opposed to the regime in place since 1848, that of Napoleon III.

The Correspondence

It is worth at this stage re-examining the nationality question in a chrono-logical perspective, but now following the correspondence from the period when Hetzel started reading the contentious second volume.

As we have seen, Nemo's national origin is central, since it seems to be linked to his violent interactions with the ships he meets. The published book, however, leaves the reader rather confused because, while distribut-ing clues about the involvement of different nations, it does not explain the reason for the final attack by the warship and for Nemo's riposte.

Before publication, the two nationalities in question underwent repeated revisions, invariably instigated by the publisher. Around 1866 Verne seems to have wanted Nemo, without discernible nationality, to be opposed to all

[13] His question may seem ingenuous, but such ships could conceivably have been sold by France to other navies during his eight-month stay on the *Nautilus*.

nations, to all men—an idea he calls the 'best'.[14] The second position has caused barrels of ink to flow. In the letters to Hetzel, the novelist repeatedly asserts his clear preference for the captain to have been a Polish patriot who opposes the Russians, and whose wife is murdered, daughters raped, and country wiped off the map. However, the publisher effectively vetoed the idea—for fear of offending the Russian government and losing the corresponding market.

In a third, relatively brief stage, the captain is called 'Juan Nemo' and his home base is explicitly in the Canary Islands. Some of his characteristics, such as his proud demeanour, do seem to conform to Spanish stereotypes.

In the final stage, which lasts over the extensive period of the revision of the second manuscript and the preparation of proofs, Hetzel subjects Verne's novel to a barrage of suggestions and instructions. For the seven months from March 1869, in particular, when the novel had already started coming out, Hetzel rejected the closing chapters. He claimed that the captain's attacks were intolerably violent and morally unacceptable—and he refused passages that implied a particular nationality for the warship that attacks Nemo.

Verne tries first to circumvent the problem, using gentle persuasion:

If Nemo had been a Pole *whose wife died under the scourge and children perished in Siberia*, and . . . had found himself faced with a Russian ship . . . everybody would admit his revenge . . . [8 May 1869]

Less good, there was the battle of the outlaw against those who had made him an outlaw, a Pole against Russia. That was *forthright*. We rejected it for purely commercial reasons.

But if it's now just a battle by Nemo against a chimerical enemy as mysterious as him, it's not a duel between two individuals any more.[15] It singularly diminishes the whole thing. (15 May 1869)

In the face of Hetzel's insistence, Verne details why the proposed changes are unacceptable. His words convey the depth of Hetzel's misunderstanding of the captain and the whole book, the scope of the changes, the extent of his indignation, and the strength of his logic:

I can see full well that you're picturing a very different fellow from mine . . . all I need to do is to justify the captain's terrible action in terms of the provocation he undergoes. Nemo doesn't run after ships to sink them, he responds to attacks. Nowhere, whatever your letter says, have I made him a man who kills for killing's sake. He has a generous nature and his feelings are sometimes

[14] 15 May 1869. It is true that, in an earlier letter [29 April 1869], Verne says that the Polish Nemo was the 'first idea'.

[15] It is not clear who the second 'individual' could be, but presumably from a country with an authoritarian leader; Napoleon III is one possibility.

brought into play in the environment he moves in. His hatred of humanity is sufficiently explained by what he has suffered, both he and his family.

I refuse to write the letter for you concerning Captain Nemo; if I cannot explain his hatred, either I will stay silent about the reason for the hero's hatred and life, his nationality, etc. or, if necessary, I will change the ending. [11? June 1869]

Reading the correspondence, of which the above is only a small selection, one must side with the author, 'tortured', as he says, by Hetzel's blind obstinacy. The publisher falls into the elementary trap of judging the captain's violent actions without looking at the reasons behind them. The quick-fix changes, made for basely 'commercial reasons', do seem wrongheaded.

In the end, however, Verne is forced to take on board most of the alien ideas. He does manage to subvert some of them, so subtly as to have taken in most readers, and indeed critics. But the final effect on Nemo's agenda and the meaning of the novel is to make both less convincing. The captain is not allowed to be explicitly French, or Polish, or any nationality at all. His rebellion cannot strike openly at any governmental authority, only *all* the great powers, with a mishmash of evasive hints at Confederate, Russian, British, French, Italian, and even Turkish ships. It is a sad result for Verne's greatest hero.

Verne may have had the last word, though. As we saw above, an inescapable identification of the warship that Nemo sinks, even in the published version, remains that it is French, by construction and by flag.

Conclusion

Twenty Thousand Leagues, which forms such an important part of the modern imagination, cannot be fully understood without assessing the original ideas from which it grew (or retreated?). It is to be hoped that the extensive manuscript material which has recently come to light, a small part of which has been presented here, can be made available to English-speaking readers.

It is clear that a significant part of the modifications introduced by Hetzel are to be regretted. The first conception is sometimes superior, in personal, political, even literary and philosophical vision. Admittedly, the style and the surface features of the manuscripts are very far from being uniformly better than in the following versions.

At best, the changes, on occasion making the text repetitive, ambiguous, or deceptive, are ingeniously reintegrated into the complex conceptual core of the novel. At worst, they are introduced without reference to the surrounding text, the change of tone and perspective betraying their alien origin.

Knowing the harrowing cuts made in the other novels, with the additional evidence of the correspondence, and aware as we now are of the extensive unpublished text, we can no longer accept the known version of *20T* as either representing Verne's real wishes or the work that is necessarily the most coherent or the most accurate.

But it is not clear what Verne would have done without Hetzel's changes. Trying to produce an edition of the novel to restore the author's intentions would be difficult, if only because of the knock-on effects of putting the deleted passages back in and because of the palimpsest effect, wherein each new draft melds into the previous one, like layers of paint.

However, even if we did not wish to remove the 'Hetzelized' version from the bookshops, nothing would prevent the parallel publication of *Journey under the Waters* as a work in its own right. Less famous novels are available in competing versions. Why not for the only French author of truly global renown?

APPENDIX 2

SOURCES

AMONGST the notable literary sources for *Twenty Thousand Leagues* are the Bible, Victor Hugo, Walter Scott, *Moby-Dick*,[1] and three works by Poe.

As we saw in Appendix 1, Verne himself cites four sources, chapter and verse, in the margin of the first manuscript, although his borrowing is more extensive than these acknowledged instances: Gratiolet, Renard, Vorepierre and Marcoux, and Zurcher and Margollé (see Select Bibliography).

The idea of situating a work underwater was by no means original. Among the titles on submarines published before 1870 were: Captain Mérobert (pseudonym of Clément-Jules Briois), *Voyage au fond de la mer* (1845); Léon Sonrel, *Le Fond de la mer* (1868); Henri de La Blanchère, *Voyage au fond de la mer* (1868); and Aristide Roger, *Les Aventures extraordinaires du savant Trinitus*.[2]

---

[1] *20T* contains a considerable density of biblical reference, including: Leviathan, Edom, the unicorn, the 'archangel of hatred', the 'days' of Genesis being 'eras', Jonah (Jonah 1: 17), the 'draught of the fishes' (Luke 5: 9), the ark (Genesis 6–7), the crossing of the Red Sea (Exodus 14: 21–31), the 'fiery furnace' (Daniel 3: 6), 'they have ears and do not hear' (Mark 8: 18), the 'fire which did not burn' ('the bush burned with fire, and the bush [was] not consumed', Exodus 3: 2), and the final 'hast thou walked in the search of the depth?'

Moby-Dick; or, the Whale (1850) by Herman Melville presents Captain Ahab's obsession for vengeance on the whale that took off his leg, culminating in his death and the sinking of his ship. A substantial extract from the novel was published in translation in Émile Forgues, *Gens de Bohème* (Hetzel, 1862), pp. 211–65; the novel was (partially) translated into French only in 1941, and Verne could not read English. In his 1962 article, Ray Bradbury finds important parallels between *Moby-Dick* and *20T*; certainly, they share a considerable number of ideas, although mostly not in Forgues, meaning no transmission route has been demonstrated. We find in Melville: Ecclesiastes, Leviathan, Seneca, Cleopatra, Dampier, Darwin, Maury, Agassiz, Albermarle, the Maelstrom, the Battle of Actium, the sea of milk, cannibalism, the *Argo*, the narwhal as a 'sea-unicorn', various shells, the rewarding of the first sailor to sight the monster, the deliberate drawing down on to the ship of an electrical storm, 'the great kraken of Bishop Pontoppodan [*sic*]'; a giant squid with 'innumerable long arms radiating from its centre, and curling and twisting like a nest of anacondas, as if blindly to catch at any hapless object within reach'; and 'Aristotle; Pliny . . . Linnaeus . . . Lacépède . . . Cuvier [and] John Hunter'—all ideas which appear in Verne's volume, together with many of Melville's localities. Ahab's vessel goes down in the trench off eastern Japan—where Verne's emerges. Both endings feature revenge and a whirlpool which swallows up the vessel, a short epilogue citing the Book of Job, and a closing reference to the sea, respectively 'five' and 'six thousand years ago'.

[2] Published in *Le Petit Journal* (May 1867 to January 1868); Roger was the pseudonym of Jules Rengade. There are a number of similarities with *20T*: a journal is written on

Another book by Zurcher and Margollé, *Histoire de la navigation* (Hetzel, 1867) was also a source for Verne, who cites it in a letter [27 October 1867].[3] The first attested occurrence of the phrase 'twenty thousand leagues' occurs in this book (p. 328), concerning Cook's circumnavigation of 1772–5; and so may have contributed to Hetzel and Verne's final choice of title.

The other non-fiction Verne consulted must have included: Louis Figuier, *Articulés, poissons, reptiles et zoophytes, mollusques* (n. d.) and Henri de La Blanchère, *La Pêche et les poissons* (1868).

Amongst the sources listed in the Select Bibliography, Frédol, *The World of the Sea*, shares a great deal of botanical and zoological vocabulary with Verne. The novelist acknowledges a debt to Jules Michelet's *The Sea*, once in the published book (I 7), but twice more in the manuscripts. He borrows extensively from *The Physical Geography of the Sea*, by the ocean-ographer Matthew Fontaine Maury,[4] especially as regards the ocean currents. He also obtained much information from *The Mysteries of the Ocean* by Arthur Mangin.[5] However, although citing Maury and Mangin in the novel, Verne does not acknowledge *Transoceanic Steam Navigation*, by engineer Eugène Flachat (1802–73), a work consulted for many of the details on ships

board and the *Éclair*, an electric submarine with portholes, goes around the world. The story also contains: a tunnel, a submarine forest and volcano, divers, the Antarctic and Sargasso seas, a narwhal, sperm whales, a combat with sea monsters, asphyxiation, and the final sinking of the submarine on rocks.

In a letter published on 1 November 1867, while admitting the 'analogy of subject between the two books', Verne claimed to have 'momentarily abandoned' the drafting of his own book: by this misleading claim, at a stage when composition had probably not begun, he must have been seeking to prevent suspicion of unfair borrowing.

[3] Mention should also be made of Élie Margollé, *Les Phénomènes de la mer* (Dubuisson, 1862), as a possible minor source.

[4] A selection of information shared with Maury includes: the references to Wilkes, Ehrenberg, Humboldt, Faraday, King, Fitzroy, Franklin, Parker, Denham, Dumont d'Urville, and Ross; 'ooze', the expansion undergone by freezing water, the proof of the Northwest Passage by finding whales impaled with stamped harpoons, the inability of right whales to pass the warm waters of the equator, British miles, burials at sea, messages-in-bottles, sounding techniques, and the transatlantic cable over the 'telegraphic plateau'; life on the seabed, the calm and the pressure in the deeps, jellyfish as nettles, the sea of milk, luminescence, salinity, animalculae, and the nautilus shell; the idea of driftwood from the Mississippi (not tree-trunks from the Missouri, as Verne implausibly claims), the difference in level between the Red Sea and the Mediterranean, the Sargasso Sea, the Gulf Stream, the Black Stream, the large Antarctic landmass needed to produce the icebergs, and many of the localities.

[5] Mangin published regularly in *Le Magasin pittoresque* and *Le Musée des familles*. Nearly all the information about the dugong (II 5) is taken from him, including the vocabulary of 'sirenian', 'siren', and 'half women, half fish', as well as the statistics and the comparison of its flesh with beef and veal. Many other paragraphs in *20T* are derived from Mangin, including perhaps those about sea monsters. Even Aronnax's title, *The Mysteries of the Ocean Deeps*, may show its influence.

and marine companies at the beginning of the novel. *Zoophytes and molluscs* by Louis Figuier seems to provide information about the seabed, some of the names of fish, and at least twenty technical terms. Bernard-Germain Lacépède, *Natural History of Fish* (1793–1803), provides a large proportion of the fish names.[6]

Figuier, Flachat, Lacépède, Mangin, Michelet, and Zurcher and Margollé could be found in Verne's library in pre-1870 editions. In Nemo's library, the only documentary sources admitted to are the popularizers Agassiz, Maury, and Michelet (the latter ranked amongst the non-scientists).

Submarine Navigation

Verne's ideas on submarines were not original. Many manned vessels had dived before 1868. (Details appeared in the 1998 World's Classics edition, pp. 382–4). Even *Nautile* and *Nautilus* were used as names for diving-bells and submarines, as Verne himself pointed out in a letter to his editor (13 November 1894). The novelist had already set the opening chapter of *Captain Hatteras* on a (conventional) ship moored in Liverpool docks and called the *Nautilus*.

As early as 1861 Verne himself had created a submersible that prefigures the *Nautilus* in some ways. The climax of his short story 'San Carlos' involves customs boats pursuing a vessel which is completely watertight thanks to a 'spacious' internal metal hull; it carries a whole world of clothing, 'hams, butter, fine wines, oil, tobacco, madder, soap, and metals'. The boat is kept submerged at a constant depth by means of 'forward and rear sections filled with air'. When finally surrounded by his pursuers, the eponymous hero and his companions simply 'open a valve in the bottom, and so escape by sinking to a depth of ten fathoms'. Additional similarities to *20T* are the Spanish hero, his outlaw condition, and his predilection for duty-free cigars and volcanoes.

An article under Jules Verne's name, entitled 'Future of the Submarine', appeared in *Popular Mechanics* in June 1904. It says 'I am not in any way the inventor of submarine navigation, and reference will show that many years . . . before . . . the Italians were at work upon submarine war vessels, and other nations were busied with them too'.

---

[6] A possible influence on *20T* was the catalogue of the exhibition of the Muséum d'Histoire Naturelle of Le Havre, published as *Les Merveilles de l'aquarium de l'exposition du Havre* (1868); Verne probably visited the exhibition in June 1868.

EXPLANATORY NOTES

5 *Cuvier . . . Quatrefages*: naturalists, specializing in ichthyology, amongst Verne's sources, often via intermediaries. *Cuvier*: Georges (1769–1832), a founder of comparative anatomy and palaeontology, and the creationist author of *De l'histoire naturelle des cétacés* (1804) and *Histoire naturelle des poissons* (1828–48), from which more than a third of Verne's fish names are drawn, but with the adjectives added. *Lacépède*: Bernard-Germain de (1756–1825), a disciple of Buffon, author of *Histoire naturelle des poissons* (1793–1803) and *Histoire des cétacés* (1804). *Duméril*: Henri-André (1812–70), doctor and author, or perhaps his father André-Marie-Constant (1774–1860), specialists in reptiles. *Quatrefages*: Jean-Louis-Armand de Quatrefages de Bréau (1810–92), naturalist and anthropologist, author of *Histoire de l'homme* (1867). He appears in the prehistoric section added to the 1867 edition of *Journey to the Centre of the Earth*. Quatrefages sent Verne a signed copy of this work ('Remembrance of the author'); who wrote back on 6 February 1868 to announce the underwater novel for that September.

6 *the Calcutta and Burmah Steam Navigation Company . . . five miles east of the Australian coastline*: (Verne: 'the Calcutta and Burnach'—this short-hand is adopted for quotations across most or all of the original editions, although it was sometimes Hetzel who introduced the errors), founded in 1856, it became the British India Steam Navigation Company in 1869. MS2 has a more logical '500 miles'. The ships mentioned in this chapter are authentic, unlike the encounters.

two columns of water: MS2 has the water rising only '50 feet' into the air; at the time whales were believed to have two nostrils.

the 'Cristóbal Colon' of the West India and Pacific Steamship Company: (1854), 1,100 tons (Flachat, p. 174—for further information about this author, see Appendix 2: Sources). This company was founded in 1838; 'West India' was part of the Caribbean.

the Helvetia of the French Line and the Shannon of the Royal Mail: the French Line (1861), or Compagnie Générale Transatlantique. However, a *Helvetia* (1864), of 3,319 tons and 350 horsepower (HP), belonged to the British National Steam Navigation Company (1863); the *Shannon* (1859), an iron paddleboat of 900 HP (Flachat, pp. 86 and 88); the *Royal Mail* (1840), or British and North American Royal Mail Steam Packet Company, or Cunard Line.

the culammak and the umgullick: (1871 edition: '*Kulammak*' here, and, later: '*Hullamock . . . Umgallick*' (I 12); MS2 here: 'Hullamack'). Although this information about the two species of whales appears in Arthur Mangin, *Les Mystères de l'océan* (1863, 1864—p. 330), Mangin seems to have borrowed it from the *Dictionnaire illustré* (see Appendix 2: Sources), which in turn cites the German naturalist Peter Simon Pallas (1741–1811).

6 *the Pereire . . . the Lord Clyde*: (Verne: 'Iseman'; *Magasin d'éducation et de récréation* (henceforth: *MÉR*): 'Inman'), the *Pereire*, 800 HP, propeller-driven; the *Etna*: 2,120 tons, 450 HP; the *Inman* line, or Liverpool and Philadelphia Steamship Company (1850), founded by William Inman (1825–81). Verne saw the 1,000-HP *Lord Clyde*, subject to rolling, on 20 or 21 March 1867, apparently at Birkenhead.

7 *the white whale, that awe-inspiring 'Moby Dick' . . . to the enormous kraken*: (*MÉR*: 'Maby Dick'; MS2: 'Maoby Dick'), probable allusion to *Moby-Dick; or, the Whale* (1850), by Herman Melville (1819–91). A possible source reads: 'Maby Dick' (Mangin, p. 297). Verne's *The Yarns of Jean-Marie Cabidoulin* (1901) echoes Mangin: 'the great white whale of the Greenland coast, the famous Moby Dick, which the Scottish whalers hunted for more than two centuries, without managing to reach it, for the good reason that they had never seen it' (ch. 4). But before Mangin and Melville, there was Mocha Dick—whose name fitted his appearance—living in the South Pacific at the turn of the century. The water column of this white whale was exceptionally continuous and perpendicular. The animal swam in convoy with ships, but like the *Nautilus*, Nemo and Ahab, turned ferocious if attacked. Mocha Dick influenced Poe's *The Adventures of Arthur Gordon Pym* (1838, French translation by Baudelaire, 1858), which in turn inspired not only *Moby-Dick* but also *20T. kraken*: sea monsters that lived off the coast of Norway and crushed ships with their tentacles, possibly based on giant squid (which can grow up to 50 feet and weigh 2 tons). *Cabidoulin* prominently features kraken (with some of its monsters curiously resembling . . . the *Nautilus*).

Aristotle . . . Egede: published works on sea monsters. Aristotle: (384–322 BC), philosopher and author of 'Auscultationes mirabiles', about Atlantis, and a *History of Animals* containing a biological classification which includes cephalopods and squid. *Pliny*: the Elder, Gaius Plinius Secundus (23–79); author of a *Natural History*, including whales covering four acres and a 700-pound 'polyp' which climbed over a fence in Spain. *Bishop Pontoppidan*: Erik Pontoppidan (1698–1764), bishop of Bergen, theologian, and author of a *Natural History of Norway* (1752). He describes a monster 'a mile and a half in circumference . . . like a number of small islands', with arms reaching out of the sea, a strong smell, and a discharge of muddy fluid. *Paul Egede*: (Verne: 'Heggede') (1708–89), Danish-Norwegian missionary and specialist in Greenlandic, author of *Eftererretninger Om Grønland* (1789), which describes a monster 'as tall as a mainmast . . . [with] a long pointed snout . . . great broad paws'.

Harrington . . . the old Constitutionnel: what George Henry Harrington and 20 others sighted about 10 miles from St Helena on 12 or 13 December 1857, a 200-foot serpent-like creature with a wrinkled crest, was recorded in a formal report to the Admiralty; *the 'Castilian'*: (Verne: '*Castillan*'), about 1,100 tons, described in *Cabidoulin* (ch. 4); *the old 'Constitutionnel'*: a liberal newspaper (1815–1914) which serialized George Sand, Eugène Sue, and Dumas *père*, and was suppressed and revived five times. Verne is 'de-metaphorizing' the cliché for any dubious story, 'the sea serpent of the *Constitutionnel*'.

the Geographical Institute of Brazil . . . Petermanns Mitteilungen: the Geographical and Historical Institute (1838). *The Berlin Royal Academy of Sciences*: founded in 1700; *the British Association*: for the Progress of Science (1831); *the Smithsonian Institution*: centre for scientific research (1846), financed by the bequest of James Smithson (1765–1829); *the Indian Archipelago*: *Journal of the Indian Archipelago* [East Indies, modern Indonesia] *and Eastern Asia* (1847–63). *Abbé Moigno's 'Cosmos'*: François-Napoléon Moigno (1804–84), mathematician and former Jesuit, who edited *Le Cosmos* from 1852 to 1862, when it was renamed *Les Mondes*; *Petermanns Mitteilungen*: (Verne: 'Petermann's *Mittheilungen*') or *Petermanns geographische Mitteilungen* (1860–1915), founded by the cartographer and geographer, August Petermann (1822–78).

punning on a saying of Linnaeus's . . . 'nature does not proceed by the lips of bounders': Carolus Linnaeus (1707–78), Swedish botanist who devised the binomial method of animal and plant classification based on evolutionary relationships, and who believed in kraken; *'nature does not proceed by the lips of bounders'*: 'la nature ne fait pas de sots', a pun on 'la nature ne fait pas de sauts' ('Nature does not proceed by leaps and bounds'—Linnaeus's *Philosophia Botanica* (1751), sec. 77), an expression that has become proverbial since Aristotle and is visible in the alchemists, Leibniz's *New Essays on Human Understanding* (1765, IV, 16), Mangin, Frédol, and Figuier. It was often quoted by Darwin to support his evolutionary thesis.

a much-feared satirical newspaper . . . like Hippolytus: MS2: 'an article in the *Figaro*', showing that Verne's acerbic comments are directed at the French press. The *Figaro* is a conservative newspaper (1826–present); the author in question may be the acerbic journalist, Henri Rochefort (1831–1913); *like Hippolytus*: Hippolytus was the son of Theseus in Greek mythology. Theseus calls on Poseidon, the god of the sea, who sends a sea monster to frighten Hippolytus's horses, causing him to be dragged to his death. Racine writes: 'Hippolytus . . . lunges at the monster, and with a spear . . . makes a large wound in his side' (*Phèdre*, Act V, scene 6). Verne's mixed metaphor ingeniously reverses the monster and Hippolytus's roles; but it is also an allusion to Hippolyte de Villemessant (1810–79), editor-in-chief of the *Figaro* from 1854. His message is that the journalist is being too bold.

8 *the Moravian of the Montreal Ocean Company was sailing at 27° 30′ N, 72° 15′ W*: the *Moravian* (1864), 2,246 tons, 400 HP; *the Montreal Ocean Steamship Company*: founded in 1854. MS2 has 'the *Lafayette* of the French Line, responsible for the postal service between Saint-Nazaire and Veracruz', and adds, 'Its laden displacement was 5,800 tons'. It was forgotten to

change the coordinates: a ship coming from Canada would not sail at 27° 30′ N.

8 *dry dock*: MS2 adds 'of Saint-Nazaire'. The deletion of the French references is due to Hetzel's sensitivity about anything that might be deemed remotely controversial.

Cunard: Sir Samuel (1787–1865), Canadian founder of the British and North American Royal Mail Steam Packet Company (1840), officially renamed the Cunard Line in 1878.

In 1853 . . . the Great Eastern: in fact the date only applies to the first ship; *the 'Arabia'*: Cunard's last wooden paddleship (1853); *the 'Persia'*: one of his first iron ships (1856); *the 'China'*: (which Phileas Fogg narrowly misses in New York), launched in 1862; *the 'Scotia'*: (1861), his last paddleship, which held the transatlantic record until 1869, at 8 days 22 hours; *the 'Java'*: built in 1865; *the 'Russia'*: (MS2: 'the *Prussia*'), built in 1867; *the 'Great Eastern'*: Verne saw Brunel's ship (then called the *Leviathan*) under construction in Greenwich in September 1859. By far the largest ship in the world, it was equipped with a single screw propeller, paddlewheels, and a full set of sails. In 1867 it was chartered to carry passengers to the Paris Universal Exposition; Verne was on board for both legs of the voyage (14 March–30 April 1867), describing it in a letter to Hetzel ([9 April 1867]—references in this abbreviated form indicate the letters of Verne and Hetzel, square brackets meaning interpolated dates) as 'an eighth wonder of the world', and, at great length, in the semi-fictional *A Floating City* (1871), whose title refers to the ship. Verne's unpublished manuscript, 'Carnet de voyage en Amérique', notes every detail of the voyage.

In addition, in 1867 Verne wrote an untitled two-page fragment of a novel or short story, which begins 'A Briton of great distinction . . .'. It contains the names of most of Cunard's ships mentioned in *20T*, together with similar remarks about their regularity and punctuality, derived from Flachat (pp. 90 and 117).

9 *Captain Anderson*: this dynamic fictional figure is presumably based on the forceful real-life Captain Anderson of the *Great Eastern* described in Part Two (ch. 20).

300 miles off Cape Clear: this position does not correspond to the coordinates above.

10 *an isosceles triangle*: this hole is very strange, since not motivated; Nemo's only depicted attack, much later in the novel, is launched horizontally towards a much lower point on the vessel. The ram, located half-way up the *Nautilus*, cannot climb to a depth of less than four metres—unless launched obliquely. Is it merely a coincidence that the hole proposed by Hetzel in the fabric of the balloon in *The Mysterious Island* is also triangular? (The idea is rejected by Verne, who emphasizes its uselessness and implausibility (for details, see my *Jules Verne inédit*, ch. 14).)

Bureau Veritas: 1828–present, rival to the *International Lloyd's Register*.

part-time lecturer: Aronnax is an occasional teacher ('professeur sup-pléant'), and not a professor, as has been the usual translation to date.

11 *doubting Thomases . . . in the Scotia's side*: reference to 'Except I . . . put my finger into the print of the nails, and thrust my hand into [the resurrected Jesus's] side, I will not believe' (John 20: 25).

'submarine' vessel: ('bateau "sous-marin"'), the first use of 'submarine' as a noun meaning 'vessel' was about in the 1890s in both French and English.

chassepot rifles . . . underwater rams: contemporary armaments: breech-loading rifles, improved by gunsmith Antoine Chassepot (1833–1905), used in the French armed forces from 1866. In a letter of 'Monday, 30 [December 1867]', highly critical of Napoleon III and the Empire, Verne writes: '. . . chassepots the only reasoning, a war in perspective . . . for 1848! [*sic*]'; Verne's 'floating mines' ('torpilles') may mean stationary ones, not 'torpedoes' in the modern sense; the term 'underwater rams' was first used about the *Merrimack* (cf. following note); Verne's 'béliers sous-marins' is unattested: it denotes male sheep!

12 *Monitor*: the *Monitor* (1861–2) and the *Virginia* (ex-*Merrimack*, 1855–62) fought the first battle between ironclads, in the American Civil War. The *Monitor*'s turret allowed its cannon to fire in different directions. In general, a 'monitor' was a heavily armoured warship with a flat deck and watertight hatches, operating nearly submerged. On 20 or 21 March 1867, Verne saw an 'ironclad' at Laird's of Birkenhead, the company that made the metal plates for the *Nautilus* (I 13).

New York Herald . . . the honourable Pierre Aronnax: the *New York Herald* (1835), perhaps the best-selling newspaper worldwide, was run in 1868 by James Gordon Bennett Jr; in 1866 it had sent Stanley in search of Livingstone. The epithet 'honourable' is normally reserved for elected officials or government delegates; Pierre was the name of Jules Verne's father.

'Aronnax' was not attested before 1869: the hard 'ax' is also visible in 'Axel', the hero of *Journey to the Centre of the Earth*. The illustration of Aronnax in the French edition, with arms folded, was based on a photograph of Verne himself. In MS1 his name is 'Oyonnax'; and in MS2, it is written 'Arronax' or 'Arronnax', except on the first occurrence—'Aronnax'—which may have caused this unconventional form to be retained. Oyonnax is a village in the Ain, near Lyon, cited for its peat in Verne's *Geography of France*.

12 or 15 miles below the surface: in I 20 the maximum depth is implied to be about 15 or 16 kilometres.

13 *a Giant Narwhal*: Verne constructs his mystery by mixing legend (the unicorn's horn, often brought back to Europe, was the narwhal's) and exaggeration (the maximum size of the narwhal, which lives only near the Arctic, is about 16 feet).

14 *that sea which never changes, unlike the terrestrial core which is almost continually being modified*: Verne delights in inverting opposites, in describing the sea in terrestrial terms and vice versa.

14 *The Shipping & Mercantile Gazette and Lloyd's List, the Paquebot, and
    the Revue maritime et coloniale*: (Verne: '*Shipping and Mercantile Gazette
    and Lloyd's*'), respectively: 1836–1916; 'Journal of Navigation and Sea
    Voyages', 1866–July 1869; and an official publication, 1861–present.

    Captain Farragut: the name must come from David G. Farragut (1801–70),
    the forceful Unionist admiral who said 'Damn the torpedoes—full speed
    ahead!' (1864); he visited France in 1867.

15 *on 3 July, it was learned that a steamer of the San Francisco–Shanghai line*:
    this date in 1867 marks the beginning of the main chronology, which will
    continue until a date fifteen or twenty days after 2 June 1868 (II 21). The
    novel opened with the encounters with the mysterious object, on 20 and
    23 July 1866, followed by the debate lasting six months, then new encounters
    on 5 March and 13 April 1867.

    MS2 and the 18mo edition of 1900 (henceforth: '1900') have the date as
    '2 July'. The *MÉR* edition and 1900, but not MS2, have 'the *Tampico*,
    a steamer': in *From the Earth to the Moon*, the *Tampico* is an 'aviso of the
    Federal Navy' (ch. 13).

    Fifth Avenue Hotel: Verne stayed there on 9–10 and 15–16 April 1867
    (*A Floating City*, ch. 34 and 39). Other American autobiographical details
    shared with *20T* include the *Great Eastern*, the hotel lift, the 20-franc cab
    ride to the 'pier' (in English), the Hudson, the East River, Broadway,
    Brooklyn, Sandy Hook, Napoleon, Agassiz, and George Sand.

    J. B. Hobson: a J. B. Hobson occurs in the records of the American Bible
    Society in 1860–1 and Yale University in 1865. In 1867 the Navy Secretary
    was Gideon Welles.

    the Northwest Passage: linking the Atlantic to the Pacific, discovered in the
    1840s, navigated at the end of the century.

16 *Conseil*: this surname may be taken from Jacques-François Conseil (born
    in 1814), who tested a three-ton ellipsoid submarine at Le Tréport and on
    the Seine in Paris in 1858–9. It had a hatch, a viewing chamber, automatic
    aeration valves, a screw, and diving fins, as recorded in his pamphlet
    entitled *Bateau de sauvetage, dit 'Pilote'* (1863).

17 *archaeotheria . . . chaeropotami*: extinct mammals. *Archaeotheria*: (Verne:
    'les archiotherium') huge warthog-like animals (N. America); *hyracothe-
    ria*: or *Eohippi*: genus of very small horse, found in Wyoming and Utah;
    oreodons: genus intermediate between pig, deer, and camel that lived near
    the Rockies; *chaeropotami*: genus close to hyracotherium.

    monsieur's live babirusa: why is Aronnax travelling with a wild pig found
    only in the East Indies? (The word 'live' is omitted in some editions.)

18 *The hotel lift*: the lift in the Fifth Avenue Hotel, installed in 1859, was
    innovative, being raised and lowered by a vertical screw.

19 '*Go 'head!*': naval form of the command (some Hetzel editions 'correct' it
    to 'Go ahead!').

the 39 stars: the American flag had 37 stars in 1867, reaching 39 only in 1889.

20 *Leviathan*: a monstrous sea creature in the Old Testament, later identified with the whale, described as 'piercing', 'crooked', and a 'sea-dragon' (Isaiah 27: 1; cf. Job 41: 1 and Psalms 104: 26).

Knight of Rhodes: a member of a military religious order, expelled from the Holy Land in about 1291, which settled in Rhodes in 1309 or 1310, then in Malta in 1530.

Dieudonné of Gozo: (d. 1353), a Provençal squire, a knight of Rhodes (1346–53), or member, more precisely Grand Master, of the Order of the Hospitallers of St John of Jerusalem; it was in about 1342 that he is reputed to have delivered Rhodes from a dragon.

21 *the Argus*: Argus was a giant with a hundred eyes, allowing him to keep watch while asleep, hence a watchful person.

due to be exhibited at the 1867 Universal Exposition: from 1 April to 3 November, on the Champ-de-Mars, with 52,000 exhibits and several million visitors. Aronnax is speaking in July 1867, when the Universal Exposition had already opened. Verne went to it, probably in June, and may have seen such important inspirations as: the Rouquayrol–Denayrouze diving apparatus, which won a gold medal for its innovative accessories, including a portable air tank; clothing made from byssus; and a giant aquarium with 800 fish, which gave visitors the impression of strolling on the seabed. He could also have seen Samuel Hallett's American submarine *Nautilus* (1857), with its riveted sheet-metal and magnifying panes; and section and complete models of Siméon Bourgeois and Charles-Marie Brun's *Plongeur*, an 80-HP submarine tested in Rochefort in 1863 and relaunched in 1867. It measured a slender 6 × 42 metres, weighed 410 tons, had a flat deck, a recessed lifeboat, a spur, inclined planes, and observation windows, and used compressed air for breathing and to expel the water from its ballast tanks.

Ned Land: he has an English surname common in Nova Scotia, and an English first name; he is Québécois, celebrates Christmas like a Protestant (I 19), and is simultaneously 'Anglo-Saxon' (I 7), 'half-French' (I 11), and 'American' (I 9). He served in the United States Navy; he swears in both languages, but his culture is largely French, as his ancestors seem to be.

Rabelais: François (*c.*1494–1553), author of *Gargantua* (1532) and *Pantagruel* (1534), present in Nemo's library.

22 *Homer*: writer (late 8th century BC), included in Nemo's library, author of the *Iliad* and the *Odyssey*.

three weeks after our departure: in fact closer to four weeks.

whose depths are still hidden from human eyes: the present tense implies that even at the end of the story, no one will have seen the depths.

23 *incredible . . . such fantasies*: Verne is ironic at the expense of his own *Journey to the Centre of the Earth* (1864, 1867).

23 *resist the pressure*: it is now known that certain primitive organisms live in the deepest parts of the ocean.

25 *unwittingly echoing a celebrated riposte of Arago's*: François Arago (1786–1853), astronomer, physicist, and politician. The answer 'Maybe because it isn't true' is attributed to Plutarch in his *Astronomie populaire* (vol. 3 (1856), book 15, ch. 24, p. 510), on the subject of links between the moon and mental perturbations.

On 30 June: they were off Patagonia on 30 July. This '30 June' and the following '3 July' and '6 July' should be in about the second week of August.

26 *the Monroe*: the name is perhaps taken from the *James Monroe*, an Antarctic exploration vessel of the 1820s.

28 *in a state of permanent erythrism*: erythrism is the 'abnormal sensitivity of an organ to stimulation'!

29 *three more days, like Columbus before him*: Christopher (1451–1506), the first to cross the Atlantic in the modern era; his request was made on 10 October 1492, two days before sighting land.

36 *that unfortunate 6 November*: in fact the 5th; this date marks the end of a four-month pursuit.

37 *Two enormous columns of water*: why does the submarine eject them? The tanks are normally emptied by 'injection' into the surrounding water (II 16); although the propeller sends water to a great height (II 1), this is unlikely to be as 'two . . . columns'; is the object trying to imitate a whale?

AN UNKNOWN SPECIES OF WHALE: the title in the second manuscript is the ironic 'A Whale Made of Galvanized Metal'.

Byron or Poe, who are masters: the present tense is unusual (some editions have 'were'). George Gordon Byron (1788–1824), militant Hellenist and Romantic author of the poems *Childe Harold* (1812–18), *The Corsair* (1814), and *Don Juan* (1819); he swam the Hellespont (now the Dardanelles) in 1810. The American Edgar Allan Poe (1809–49) claimed to have swum from Richmond to Warwick in 1823, although the current was four kilometres an hour.

40 *in the bellies of whales*: 'Jonah was in the belly of the whale three days and three nights' (Jonah 1: 17).

42 *'The boat hasn't moved?'*: if Conseil and Aronnax fell into the sea at the same spot as Land, and have been swimming for three hours, why do they finish up in the same place?

nearly a metre out of the water: if its height is eight metres and a tenth of its cylindrical form emerges (by volume, I 13), the *Nautilus* would come out of the water about twice as much—unless carrying a heavy cargo or ballast. In any case, the waves generated by the prow would cover the platform.

43 *MOBILIS IN MOBILI*: in Latin 'Mobilis' means 'nimble, mobile, lively; shifting, varying, changeable; inconstant, or fickle'; 'Mobilis in mobili' can be translated as 'Mobile in the mobile element' or 'Changing within change'.

Given that '*Mobili*' is here a substantivized adjective, both '*Mobile*' and '*Mobili*' may be considered correct. However, it was clearly intended to amend all instances of '*Mobile*', the original form in the proofs and some of the early editions, although this was only partially successful in the 1871 edition, for the monogram itself continued to read '*Mobile*'.

44 *New Caledonians . . . cannibals*: allusion to the eating of French people shipwrecked there in 1850.

Maybe they can hear us: the captain does seem to be able to read Aronnax and Ned's minds, and his entrances do have uncanny timing. In the closing chapters Aronnax remarks: 'Ned and Conseil avoided speaking to me for fear of giving themselves away.' Is there a secret listening device on board?

45 *Diderot*: Denis (1713–84), novelist, philosopher, main contributor and editor of the *Encyclopédie* (1751–72), and author of *Letter on the Deaf and Mute* (1751), which contains the words, 'the language of gestures is metaphorical' (I, p. 356), a phrase borrowed by Gratiolet (see note on this same page): 'Notice incidentally how much the language of gestures is metaphorical' (p. 41).

prosopopoeia, metonymy, and hypallage: classical figures of speech. In prosopopoeia, an imaginary or absent person is represented as speaking or acting; in metonymy, an idea replaces a related one, as in 'bottle' for 'strong drink'; in hypallage, the relation between two words is reversed, as in 'her beauty's face'.

A pupil of Gratiolet or Engel would have read his physiognomy like a book: Dr Pierre-Louis Gratiolet (1815–65), anatomist, naturalist, and author of *De la physiognomie et des mouvements d'expression* (1865), a work referenced twice in the margin of the first manuscript of *20T*. Probably the author Johann Jacob Engel (1741–1802).

46 *his hands . . . palmistry*: pseudo-science, associated with Stanislas d'Arpentigny (1791–1861), author of *La Chirognomie* (1843) and *La Science de la main* (c.1854), who presented Verne to Dumas *fils* in 1849; Dumas became his faithful friend and literary collaborator, and introduced him in turn to his father. Of d'Arpentigny's seven categories, the most sought after was the 'psychic hand', qualified in Verne's play, *Eleven-Day Siege* (1854–60) as 'Which must marvellously serve the conceptions of a superior intelligence' (Act II, scene 8).

nearly a quarter of the horizon: surely a slip; in the second manuscript, Verne explains that his eyes, following Gratiolet (p. 16), 'opened almost at the ends of the transversal diameter of his head, the parallelism of the scalar axes being partly destroyed and the man being largely able to see at an oblique angle, and thus take in half of the horizon at the same time'.

Nemo does not have a beard, and indeed MS2 describes him as clean-shaven; however, the illustrations in the Hetzel editions show him with a full beard and moustache.

46 *how he penetrated your very soul! How he could pierce the liquid depths*: as if
    anticipating Freudian ideas of the subconscious, Verne is equating seeing
    into the deeps of the mind and the sea.

47 *invoked habeas corpus*: the legal language in these two paragraphs reflects
    Verne's training as a barrister. 'Natural law' (*jus gentium*), ancestor of
    human rights, meant the minimum rights granted to foreigners; *habeas
    corpus* (1679) proscribes arbitrary detention.

    Faraday: Michael (1791–1867), physicist and chemist; inventor of the law
    and the cage that bear his name.

    Fleming: we will never find out whether Conseil hails from French Flanders
    or from Belgium.

48 *Cicero*: Marcus Tullius Cicero (106–43 BC), politician, orator, and author.

49 *He brought us clothing*: Aronnax omits that he and Conseil have been
    virtually naked since their swim.

    Mobile in the mobile element: the source is probably Flachat: 'An engineer
    had taken for coat-of-arms a rock beaten by the waves with this motto:
    immobilis in mobile; another more observant engineer chose a light skiff
    yielding to the agitation of the waves, with this motto: *mobilis in mobile*'
    (vol. 1, p. 117). The first engineer quoted by Flachat is Henri Sébastien
    Dupuy de Bordes (1702–76), whose coat-of-arms represents a rock, with
    a naked siren on it, and whose motto reads '*immobilis in mobili*'. The
    expressions '*immobilis in mobile/mobili*' and '*mobilis in mobili*' date back at
    least to the seventeenth century; the less correct form '*Mobilis in mobile*',
    on the other hand, is hardly attested before Flachat.

50 *a natural reaction . . . wrestled with death*: misleading remark, like the one
    about the steward's deafness. Later Nemo occasionally drugs his passen-
    gers: in the present case, to be able to respond unobserved, albeit with
    some delay, to the American ship's aggression?

55 *'Calmez-vous . . . veuillez m'écouter!'*: 'Calm down, Master Land, and you,
    Dr Aronnax, kindly listen to me!'

57 *Was it unintentionally that Master Ned Land here struck me with his harpoon?*:
    the captain's use of 'me' (some editions have 'it') shows his passionate
    identification with the vessel—and his antipathy for Ned.

58 *in the same way as Oedipus must have looked at the Sphinx*: the winged Sphinx
    proposed a riddle to travellers, killing them if they answered incorrectly;
    but when Oedipus solved the riddle, the Sphinx killed herself instead.

    natural pity: concept visible in Rousseau and Buffon.

59 *But no promise binds us to the master of this ship*: the captain's 'condition' is
    that of 'passive obedience' in being 'confine[d] . . . to cabins', which Aronnax
    accepts on behalf of the three men. The 'question' concerning the 'choice
    between life and death' seems to be simply whether they accept to live in
    the submarine, rather than go back overboard; to which, as Aronnax says,
    'no reply is possible' (or indeed given). In sum a promise *has* been made

('passive obedience'), but not a promise to stay. Nemo later says: 'I want you to observe one of the engagements which bind you to me.' But he is mistakenly using a plural; he has them locked up in the same cell as before, not in their cabins; and he seems to be abusing the ambiguity of Aronnax (at least) being 'bound' to the captain: bound by his promise or unable to leave?

The explanation of the three discrepancies is to be found in MS2: '"You are therefore my guests, I do not say my prisoners . . . I will impose ~~only three conditions~~ . . . their sole aim is to safeguard the mystery of my existence. | . . . "First, you will never seek to know who I used to be, nor who I am, what I used to do nor what I am doing, why I chose to live in these conditions nor why I still live in them. As for the events which take place on my ship and which you will witness, I leave them to your appreciation and do not ask you to keep them secret. You will be able to repeat what you have seen, heard, or understood, if ever you return to your fellows . . . Secondly," he continued, "you will never try to leave my ship without my authorization . . . I alone will judge the circumstances in which we will come to separate . . . you will patiently wait for the time to be ripe to take up again that unbearable yoke of the land that men call freedom. Do you accept?" | "We accept," I replied . . . this second condition explicitly made us prisoners on our parole.'

At this stage, Nemo imposes two extra conditions on his 'guests': secrecy and not attempting to return to their 'fellows' (as if the submariners were no longer 'terrestrials'), in return for which he holds out the possibility of releasing them one day. These ideas will exercise Aronnax's mind over the coming months, with frequent echoes of Nemo's deleted speech (e.g. 'We are not even prisoners on our parole'). Some of Aronnax's musings about Nemo, and even the terrible anguish he feels on leaving, may make more sense after reading the manuscript passage.

60 *I will merely be Captain Nemo for you*: in much of MS1 I, the commandant is 'Captain x', and he is often called 'the stranger' or 'the unknown man'; he is 'Juan Nemo' in I 16, and thereafter 'Captain Nemo' or baldly 'Nemo'. 'Juan Nemo' would make 'Nemo' a surname (cf. Conseil's 'Mr Nemo').

'Nemo' on its own has the advantage of concealing any nationality, and may be an allusion to many sources. First, Nemo, 'no one', is the name Ulysses takes on meeting Polyphemus the Cyclops, in the *Odyssey* in Latin. This alias allows the use of the ambiguity in 'Nemo/No one is killing me' to mislead him.

Nemo is, secondly, the assumed name of the dead opium addict at the beginning of Dickens's *Bleak House* (1853). The form also occurs in 'Nemo me impune lacessit' ('No one assails me with impunity'), the emblem of the Scots Guards and of Scotland, surely seen by Verne on his formative visit; it is quoted in Poe's 'The Cask of Amontillado' (1846).

The illustration of Nemo, described by Verne as 'the most energetic imaginable', is based on Colonel Jean-Baptiste Charras (1810–65), a former junior war minister, a friend of Hetzel's, and author of *Histoire de la*

Campagne de 1815: Waterloo (1857). He was banished from France from 1852 until his death.

60 *the Nautilus*: its form, *nauti-* plus a masculine ending, combines scientific and mythological resonances, and is Latin and so non-localized. A nautilus (< Latin < Greek 'sailor') is a cephalopod mollusc of the genus *Nautilus*, especially the *N. pompilius* found in the Indian and Pacific oceans. It has a spiral, mother-of-pearl-lined shell with air-filled chambers that regulate ascent and descent, plus grasping tentacles surrounding a sharp beak. The symbolism is in the self-sufficiency and security of the shell and the dual mode of locomotion—paddling and sailing.

61 *Neptune's old shepherd*: Neptune was the Roman god of the sea, corresponding to Poseidon for the Greeks; his shepherd was Proteus, a minor god and herdsman of the flocks of the sea, with the power to take on many shapes.

62 *Your pen will be made from whalebone, your ink from the liquid secreted by a cuttlefish or squid*: Aronnax has not indicated any plan to write on board. However, he starts a diary a few days later (I 15); this basic form will give rise to the rewriting of his published book on the submarine depths (II 6), and hence to the 'real book of the sea' (II 18), somewhere between documentary and autobiography. *a cuttlefish or squid*: the vocabulary of 'byssus . . . aplesias . . . sea-wrack . . . cuttlefish or squid' is visible in *La Mer* (1861) by Jules Michelet, as is the mistaken idea of sperm whales attacking baleen whales (II 12). In his preface to the Livre de poche *20T*, Chelebourg says the same source also provides: coral as 'the real point where life dimly rises from a sleep of stone, without yet cutting itself off from that rude starting-point'; whale sightings proving the existence of the Northwest and Northeast Passages; some of the details of Atlantis; the sea of milk, the Black River, the open sea at the South Pole, animalculae, madrepores as makers of worlds, 'blood flower' coral, and submarine forests; the Mediterranean as 'one of the globe's most invigorating climates'; the harpooner as bold hero confronting monstrous whales on a fragile skiff; the (incorrect) idea of the killer squid; giant crustaceans wearing armour; volcanoes as more active in the early geological periods (II 2, I 4, III 4, II 3, II 5, II 4, II 4, IV 2, III 1, III 1, II 10).

a living infinity, as one of your poets has put it: MS2 reads, 'as your illustrious Michelet said'.

63 *It was a library*: MS1: 'It was a library and smoking-room.' The plan of the *Nautilus* is as follows: air tank (length 7.5 metres), Aronnax's room (2.5 m), Nemo's room (5 m), these two presumably slightly raised so as to fit into the conical end, salon (10 m), library (5 m), dining room (5 m); Conseil and Ned's room (2 m), kitchen (3 m), bathroom (including no doubt the toilet), stairwell, storerooms, cloakroom, and the room the wounded man is put in (dimensions unknown), cell (6 m), crew room (5 m); perhaps a separate electricity room, and finally the engine room (20 m for the last two together). Although the 'service' rooms in the centre-rear of the

submarine must be on either side of the central corridor, and therefore not cumulative, the specified interior dimensions alone give a total of 71 m (compared with 70 m as the total length of the vessel, I 11). There is also an upper level, of which we know very little.

64 *free use of them*: MS1 adds: 'for the whole time that circumstances force me to keep you in this prison'.

Homer . . . Sand: writers. *Xenophon*: (430?–355? BC), historian, philosopher, and author of the *Anabasis*, which contains the quotation 'The sea! The sea!' (IV, ch. 7), central to Verne's 'Edom' (1910). *Victor Hugo*: (1802–85), poet, dramatist, and author of *The Hunchback of Notre Dame* (1831), *Les Misérables* (1862), and *The Toilers of the Sea* (1866—so not in the ship's library); lived in exile (1852–70). Hugo is the author, with Poe, Scott, and Dumas, who perhaps most influenced the young Verne. *Michelet*: Jules (1798–1874), Romantic historian, associate of Hetzel, opponent of Napoleon III, and author of *Histoire de la France* (1833–67) and *La Mer* (1861). *Mme Sand*: George, pseudonym of Amandine-Aurore-Lucie Dupin Dudevant (1804–76), novelist and playwright; on 25 July 1865 she wrote to Verne: 'I hope that you will soon take us into the depths of the sea and that you will have your characters travel in those divers' machines which your scientific knowledge and imagination will permit themselves to improve', a probable inspiration for *20T* that Verne recorded in an interview with Brisson in 1897.

Despite the phrase, 'everything that humanity has produced of greatest beauty in history, poetry, the novel', Hugo and Sand are the only nine-teenth-century novelists or poets mentioned in *20T*: both figured amongst Hetzel's best-sellers; and Michelet also had regular contacts with the publisher. Verne's lists are instead scientists, painters, and musicians.

MS2 adds '~~from Aeschylus to Dumas *fils*~~'. Aeschylus (525–456 BC) wrote accounts of an eruption of Etna and *The Persians* (472 BC), about Athens' naval victory over Persia. Concerning Alexandre Dumas (1824–95), the novelist and playwright of *La Dame aux camélias* (1848, 1852), Verne told Sherard in 1893: 'the friend to whom I owe the deepest debt of grati-tude and affection is Alexandre Dumas the younger . . . We became chums almost at once . . . he was my first protector . . . we wrote together a play called *Pailles rompues* [1849] . . . and a comedy . . . entitled *Onze jours de siège* [1850].' MS1 has '. . . of greatest beauty, ~~from the Holy Scriptures~~'.

Humboldt . . . Agassiz: scientists. *Humboldt*: Alexander (Baron von) (1769–1859), naturalist, statesman, and explorer; he wrote about Atlantis in *Kosmos* and *Examen critique de l'histoire et de la géographie du nouveau continent* (1836) (I, p. 167). *Foucault*: Léon (1819–68), physicist, invented the gyro-scope and studied refraction in water. *Henri Sainte-Claire Deville*: (1818–81), chemist and educator, studied the thermal disassociation of compounds and aluminium. *Chasles*: Michel (1793–1880), specialist in geometry and geodesy. *Milne-Edwards*: Henri (1800–85), French zoologist who worked on molluscs and crustaceans, and was amongst the first scientists to dive (in 1844 off Sicily, with Quatrefages). *Tyndall*: John (1820–93), physicist, studied the scattering of light by suspended particles. *Berthelot*: Marcellin (1827–1907), public official, organic chemist and naturalist, author of a note to Frédol about the giant squid the *Alecton* encountered. *Abbé Secchi*: Angelo (1818–78), astronomer; pioneered classifying stars using their spectra. *Commander Maury*: Matthew Fontaine (1806–73), US and Confederate naval officer and hydrographer; author of *The Physical Geography of the Sea* (1855; 1866), discovered the Gulf Stream and the system of ocean circulation, was the first to sound the Atlantic, and invented an electric torpedo. Verne's 'The sea has rivers like dry land' is derived from him. *Agassiz*: Louis (1807–73), Swiss-American zoologist and geologist, pre-Darwinian author of *Research on Fossil Fish* (1833–44) and *Contributions to the Natural History of the United States* (1857–62).

MS1 has a much shorter list, omitting nearly all the French names, but preceded by 'On a table could be seen, half-leafed through, works by Milne Eddvard [*sic*] . . .'

64 *Amongst the books of Joseph Bertrand, Les Fondateurs de l'astronomie*: Joseph Bertrand (1822–1900) taught applied mathematics at the École Normale Supérieure and wrote *Les Fondateurs de l'astronomie moderne* (Hetzel, 1865), described in *From the Earth to the Moon* as a 'fine book by M. J. Bertrand of the Institute'; he advised Verne for that and probably other works; Verne's first cousin, Henri Garcet, was Bertrand's assistant.

the fitting out of the Nautilus did not date from after that: the opposite would be more logical.

66 *a Madonna by Raphael . . . Vernet*: in *Paris in the Twentieth Century*, Verne shows a great interest in paintings. If he visited the galleries in Britain in 1859 and in Scandinavia in 1861, he also entered 'every picture-gallery of any importance in Europe' (interview with Sherard in 1893). These works, mostly Italian, part of the western European canon, generally follow chronological order: *a Madonna by Raphael*: or Raffaello Sanzio (1483–1520), architect and painter, whose works include a number of Madonnas; Verne's *Salon de 1857* (*S57*) devotes a dozen lines to the painting, *Raphaël apercevant la Fornarina pour la première fois* (1856), by François Léon Benouville (1821–59); *a Virgin by Leonardo da Vinci*: (1452–1519), Renaissance engineer, scientist, universal spirit, and painter of *The Virgin of the Rocks* (1483–6) and the *Mona Lisa* (1503–6 and 1510–15); *a nymph by Correggio*: real name Antonio Allegri (1489?–1534), a sensual artist of religious paintings, including many Virgins. *S57* quotes his *Antiope* (n. d.), similar to Nemo's canvas; *a woman by Titian*: (MS2: 'a courtesan by Titian'), originally Tiziano Vecellio (1488?–1576), portraitist, artist of *The Assumption of the Virgin* (1516–18), and whose *La Maîtresse* (n. d.), comparable to Nemo's painting, is described in *S57*; *an Adoration by Veronese*: Paolo, originally Paolo Caliari (1528–88), painter of *The Adoration of the Magi* (1573) and whose *Dalmatic* is quoted in *S57*; *an Assumption by Murillo*: Bartolomé Esteban (1617–82), genre scenes, portraits, and

religious subjects; a *portrait by Holbein*: Hans the Elder (1465?–1524), or Hans the Younger (1497?–1543), gothic painters of religious works; *a monk by Velázquez*: Diego Rodríguez de Silva y (1599–1660), portraits, still lifes, and genre and historical scenes; a *martyr by Ribera*: (Verne: 'Ribeira') José or Jusepe de (1588–1652), baroque religious artist.

Starting from Rubens, the artists are Flemish or Dutch, except three Frenchmen: a *country fair by Rubens*: Peter Paul (1577–1640), baroque painter of portraits and allegorical, historical, and religious scenes; *La Kermesse* (*c.*1630) is in the Louvre. *S57* presents 'a magnificent *Atelier de Rubens*', by Peter Rudolf Karl Herbsthoffer (1821–76); *two Flemish landscapes by Teniers*: David, the Younger (1610–90), landscapes and religious and genre scenes; *Gerrit Dou*: (1613–75), miniatures in the style of Rembrandt; *Metsu*: Gabriel (1629–67), painter of eclectic style and subject; *Paul Potter*: (1625–54), artist of landscape and animal scenes; *Géricault*: Théodore (1791–1824), painted *The Raft of the 'Méduse'* (1819), an important source for Verne's *The Chancellor*; *Prud'hon*: Pierre-Paul (1758–1823), painter of animals and landscapes; *Backhuysen*: (Verne: 'Backuysen'), Ludolphe (1631–1709), painter of ships; *Vernet*: Joseph (1714–89), painter of shipwrecks, sunsets, and conflagrations, including *Jonas* (1753) and *La Visite du cratère de Vésuve* (*c.*1740). It is surely no coincidence that the last name in the list should be a J. Vernet with a strong interest in the sea, ships, monsters, the interiors of volcanoes, and eruptions.

MS2 is again revealing. The religious paintings—Veronese, Murillo, Velázquez, and Ribera—are absent. The Christian pictures indeed seem out of character for a Nemo whose library no longer contains the Holy Scriptures—and may be a sign of Hetzel's imposition of 'moral' values.

Delacroix . . . Daubigny: the moderns are all French, as are the three most recent old masters. All are relatively traditional—no Manet, Monet, or Turner. *Delacroix*: Eugène (1798–1863), Romantic painter of *Liberty Leading the People* (1831) and *La Barque du Dante*, for which *S57* calls him a 'great painter'; *Ingres*: Jean-Auguste-Dominique (1780–1867), artist of classical and mythological works qualified in *S57* as 'master[s] of modern art'; *Decamps*: Alexandre (1803–60), introduced oriental themes and painted animal subjects; *Troyon*: Constant (1813–65), landscapes and animals; *Meissonier*: Jean-Louis-Ernest (1815–91), genre and military scenes, who drew his friend Hetzel; *S57* praises eight of his paintings to the skies, 'a painter without rival in the genre he has in a way created'; *Daubigny*: Charles-François (1817–78), painter of landscapes which influenced the Impressionists, of *Le Printemps*, to which *S57* devotes seven lines, and of *Vallée d'Optevoz*, perhaps 'the most beautiful landscape of the Salon' (*S57*).

MS2 is again quite different. The following are present: Scheffer (Ary, 1795–1858, Franco-Dutch portraitist, including one of Arago); Delaroche (Paul, 1797–1856, historical painter); Courbet (Gustave, 1819–77, portrait and landscape painter); Rosa Bonheur (1822–99, farm and rustic scenes);

Fromentin (Eugène, 1820–76, oriental scenes); and Millet (Jean-François, 1814–75, landscapes). MS1 has 'Daubigny' back in; but only Courbet and Fromentin from the above list.

66 *Weber . . . Gounod*: Verne showed a great passion for music. A good pianist, he occasionally composed music; he says that he could have turned professional had he wanted to do so (interview with Sherard in 1894). Verne's interest in opera dates from his libretto, *La Mille et deuxième nuit* (1850).

The composers cited seem ill-adapted to Nemo's melancholic instrument (they are probably cited for their arias for the piano): six historical Germanic musicians and three French composers of opera, including two contemporaries; Wagner is the only non-French contemporary. *Weber*: Carl Maria von (1786–1826); *Rossini*: Gioacchino Antonio (1792–1868); *Mozart*: Wolfgang Amadeus (1756–91), Austrian; *Beethoven*: Ludwig van (1770–1827); *Haydn*: (Franz) Joseph (1732–1809), Austrian; *Meyerbeer*: Giacomo (1791–1864), German who lived in France after 1824; Verne describes his opera *Les Huguenots*—which his father hummed to one of his sisters while she suckled—a 'masterpiece' ('Doctor Ox'); *Hérold*: Louis-Joseph-Ferdinand (1791–1833), comic opera; *Wagner*: Richard (1813–83), wrote operas including *Tannhäuser* (1845) and *Tristan and Isolde* (1865); *Auber*: Daniel-François-Esprit (1782–1871), operatic works; *Gounod*: Charles-François (1818–93), the opera *Roméo et Juliette* (1867).

'Massé' also appeared in the 1869 edition. Victor Massé (1822–84) composed comic operas, and was a member with Verne of the musical dining club the Onze sans Femmes (Eleven Without Women), founded in 1868.

piano-organ: an instrument of modest width, often equipped with more than one keyboard.

Orpheus: mythological musician and one of the Argonauts; visited the underworld.

MS1 has: 'a Delacroix, an Ingres are merely for me contemporaries of Apelles or Zeuxis, and it seems to me that this world has not long survived them'. Apelles was a fourth-century BC Greek painter; Zeuxis, an innovative fifth-century BC Greek painter. No canvas of either artist has survived, foreshadowing the probable destiny of Nemo's own work.

Captain Nemo fell silent and seemed lost in a deep reverie: immediately before this sentence, MS1 has: ' "Contemporaries of Orpheus, whose success they never equalled in the Stone Age." | "But you love their works." | "Yes, but there is a music I prefer to that of all the ancient and modern artists." | "Which one, captain?" | "My own, sir." | This reply explained to me the indistinct sounds I had heard during the first night spent on the hull of the *Nautilus*.'

Such a dialogue perhaps also explains why Aronnax, who identifies paintings at a glance, is unable to place the music Nemo is playing; and why Nemo's denial that he is an 'artist' seems slightly equivocal. Verne's reference to 'the Stone Age'—a controversial term—fits in with dramatically shortened time-scales, since he has not totally given up the date of Genesis as 4004 BC; it was only in the 1860s that French opinion accepted humanity's existence in prehistoric times.

67 *François I*: (1494–1547), reformist king (1515–47) who founded the Collège de France and laid the foundations of the modern state.

68 *Tavernier*: Jean-Baptiste (1605–89), trader and author of *Six voyages en Turquie, en Perse et aux Indes* (1676–7).

must have spent millions acquiring the different items: one of Aronnax's many erroneous speculations.

69 *Only the barest of necessities*: the introduction to the *Nautilus* shows parallels with Verne's seminal visit in 1859 to a mansion house in Oakley in Fife. Verne's autobiographical *Journey to England and Scotland* describes a difficult sea-journey, climbing a ladder, a surprising welcome in French, a change into dry clothes, and an attendant speaking a mysterious language. The guests enter the dwelling 'without even being able to study its external form', and find 'assembled all the discoveries of modern luxury': 'a magnificent salon' with angled seats, display cabinets, and windows 'allowing extensive views in all directions'. The walls are covered with 'magnificent canvases from the Italian school . . . and a few masterpieces from the Flemish school'; and the salon leads into an 'austere and peaceful library and a natural history room'. There is even illumination of the exterior, a 'plaintive melody', and a 'platform' on the top with a 'powerful telescope'. The guests are in sum 'flabbergasted to find such luxury in the middle of the half-wild countryside', including perfect Gothic plumbing.

70 *on the surface*: MS1 adds a *double entendre*, 'You can see that I am amply equipped'.

That agent is electricity: MS1 adds: 'it steers me, it charges my rifles'.

71 *I could have . . . obtained electricity from the difference in temperature between them*: Nemo does not generate electricity from the water. However, in *Master of the World* (1904) Verne mistakenly says that electricity 'was drawn from the surrounding water by the celebrated Captain Nemo'.

Bunsen: Robert Wilhelm (1811–99), chemist who contributed to the invention of the zinc-carbon battery (1841) and the spectroscope, and improved the Bunsen burner.

Dr Aronnax, you will see me doing so: although we do hear more about the captain's underwater mines, we never in fact see him working there.

72 *wind, water, and steam*: MS1 adds, 'and will on its own meet all humanity's needs'.

The total length was about 35 metres: from centre to end, as confirmed by Nemo's '70 metres' later in the chapter. In the opening pages, Aronnax had rejected 200 feet as the length, although 'reliable' sources had given 350 feet.

73 *crew room . . . But its door remained closed*: Verne's 'poste de l'équipage' is often translated as 'control room'; in other works he uses the term in the

sense of 'living quarters', although the second manuscript describes work going on here: '. . . a score of men . . . were needed to operate the *Nautilus*. I thought therefore that the crew of this strange ship were limited to that number. | About ten seamen were busy working, and did not seem to notice my presence in their room.' In any case, the space is small compared to Nemo's salons.

74 *Ruhmkorff*: Heinrich Daniel (1803–77), physicist, inventor of an induction coil (1850–1).

up to 120 revolutions per second: Nemo means per minute!

'*A speed of 50 knots*': figure that would require many thousand horsepower; MS2: '35 knots', MS1: '30 knots'.

75 *It is a long cylinder with conical ends*: MS1: 'It is long so as to go fast.' In addition to the scientific point, Verne is probably being scurrilous.

These two measurements allow you to calculate the surface area and volume of the 'Nautilus': on the contrary: even assuming a cylinder and two uniform cones, one needs to know their respective lengths.

its volume 1,507.2 cubic metres: (Verne: '1,500.2', amended here; the first manuscript has '1,507.2'); the '1,356.48 cubic metres' of the following paragraph should probably be about '1,350 cubic metres'; also Nemo seems to forget that this is salt water, 2.5 per cent heavier; and two paragraphs below, finally, Verne's '1,356.58 tons' has been amended. It is possible in addition that there is a more serious mistake somewhere. A cylinder only 30 metres long and of radius 4 metres has a cross-section of about 50 square metres and a volume of about 1,500 cubic metres on its own—unless the central part is not cylindrical, but 'spindle-shaped' (term used three times, but to describe the overall shape of the *Nautilus*).

77 *100 atmospheres*: in fact variations in temperature and salinity have a much greater effect on water density than the pressure.

79 *I love it like the flesh of my flesh*: Genesis 2: 23–4: 'And Adam said . . . "[The] flesh of my flesh: she shall be called Woman, because she was taken out of Man".' Nemo's relationship to his submarine is both paternal and carnal.

the Dutchman Jansen: Belgian-born Marin Henry (1817–93), Dutch rear-admiral, translator into Dutch of Maury, and author of works on measuring sea temperatures and on the East Indies.

80 *Le Creusot . . . Hart Brothers of New York*: manufacturing companies. *Le Creusot*: the Schneider iron and steel mills and munition factories (founded 1837) at Le Creusot, Saône-et-Loire. *Penn and Co. of London*: (Verne: 'Pen') John Penn & Sons, of Greenwich; constructed the first treadmill (1817) and patented an important improvement to the screw propeller (1854). *Laird's of Liverpool*: (Verne: 'Leard') Laird Brothers, of Birkenhead, known for its early iron vessels (1829). *Scott & Co. of Glasgow*: shipbuilders, in fact Scotts of Greenock. *Cail and Co. of Paris*: steel works in Denain, near Lille, which constructed locomotives, etc., founded by Jean-François Cail

(1804–71). *Krupp in Prussia*: family of steel manufacturers, including Alfred (1812–87) and Friedrich Alfred (1854–1902). *Motala in Sweden*: a small town producing naval and electrical equipment. *Hart Brothers of New York*: no trace has been found.

1,687,500 francs: Verne: '1,687,000'.

the ten billion francs of France's debts: 1869 and *MÉR*: 'twelve billion', implying that the illustrated edition of 1871 was, surprisingly, prepared before the 1869 ones.

383,255,800 square kilometres, or more than 38 million hectares: modern estimates give 361 million square kilometres; and given that 100 hectares are a square kilometre, the second figure should apparently read 'thirty-eight billion'. Also, the '2,250 million cubic miles' may mean cubic *kilometres*, for modern estimates give 322 million cubic miles. Finally, 'a sphere sixty leagues in diameter' would only give about 40 million cubic miles.

81 *its metal plates overlapped slightly*: earlier, 'The blackish surface . . . had no overlapping sections'.

82 *This reply taught me nothing*: in fact Nemo spontaneously uses the Paris meridian. In the following sentence Verne writes '37° 15˝', a slip corrected here.

83 *Galileo . . . Maury, whose career was ruined by a political revolution*: Galileo Galilei (1564–1642), astronomer and physicist who developed the telescope, observed sunspots, and discovered that all bodies fell at the same speed. In 1633 the Inquisition made him renounce his support of Copernican heliocentric theory. Maury, an American oceanographer, author of *The Physical Geography of the Sea* (1855), an important source for Verne, resigned from the Navy at the beginning of the Civil War, went into exile in Mexico, but returned in 1868 following an amnesty, to become a lecturer.

A brief selection of information shared with Maury would include: the references to Wilkes, Ehrenberg, Humboldt, Faraday, Captains King and Fitzroy, Franklin, Parker, Denham, Dumont d'Urville, and Ross; 'ooze', the expansion undergone by freezing water, undercurrents, the Northwest Passage as demonstrated by whales on the other side having stamped harpoons in them, right whales unable to cross the warm waters of the equator, the use of British miles, burials at sea, messages-in-bottles, sounding techniques, the transatlantic cable over the 'telegraphic plateau' and the bringing up of specimens from it; life under pressure on the seabed, the calm in the deeps, jellyfish as nettles, the sea of milk, luminescence, the salinity of the sea, and the nautilus shell; driftwood coming down the Mississippi (not tree-trunks down the Missouri, as Verne claims), the difference in the level between the Red Sea and the Mediterranean, the Sargasso Sea, the Gulf Stream, the 'Kuro-Siwo' (*sic*) or Black Stream, the large Antarctic landmass needed to produce icebergs, and many of the localities.

Hôtel du Sommerard: a museum in the Latin Quarter, devoted mainly to medieval France; now known as the Cluny Museum.

85 *Ehrenberg*: (Verne: 'Erhemberg'), Christian Gottfried (1795–1876), naturalist
    specializing in coral, author of a study of marine phosphorescence
    (Memoirs of the Berlin Academy, 1835).

86 '*vertebrates . . . designed for life underwater*': text taken from the *Dictionnaire
    français illustré et encyclopédie universelle* (Bureau de la publication and Lévy,
    1847–63), Dupiney de Vorepierre and Jean-François-Marie de Marcoux,
    eds, vol. 2, p. 760, entry on 'Fish'.

91 '*Nautron respoc lorni virch*': (MS1: '. . . restoll loni . . .'), 'Nautron' contains
    the root naut-; 'respoc' is an anagram of 'Crespo' (see following note); and
    'virch' contains the root 'vir' (homme). Aronnax later deduces that the
    phrase means 'We have nothing in sight', but it is not clear which words
    mean what.

92 *a tiny island . . . called Roca de la Plata, meaning 'Silver Rock'*: (Verne:
    'Rocca . . .'); Francisco Sanchez Crespo was captain of the galleon, *El Rey
    Carlos*. Roca de la Plata, or Crespo Island, 'is only a rock lost in the ocean,
    and one of the most isolated of all this Micronesia' (MS1). The feature
    that Crespo claimed to have discovered on 15 October 1801 was deleted
    from most maps from the 1870s.

94 *Rouquayrol–Denayrouze apparatus*: mining engineer Benoît Rouquayrol
    (1826–75) and naval lieutenant Auguste Denayrouze (1838–83), the author
    of *Manuel du matelot plongeur, et instructions sur l'appareil plongeur Rouquayrol-
    Denayrouze* (1867). The most sophisticated version allowed an hour's div-
    ing at 10 metres, or half an hour at 40 metres: much less than Nemo's
    version. Rouquayrol invented an 'aerophore' for rescuing miners (1860),
    then a breathing system that automatically regulated the pressure as dif-
    ferent depths were reached. In collaboration with Denayrouze, he created
    an air tank placed on the diver's back. It was replenished via a tube from
    the surface, which it could dispense with for limited periods. Such a device,
    meaning a flexible suit was no longer needed, was used for collecting
    sponges in the Mediterranean. Verne's contribution is to increase the pres-
    sure of the tank and to add a 'copper sphere', to allow deeper dives.
    However, the pressure in such a combination would reach thirty bars and
    force the blood to the head, with fatal results, unless the suit was absolutely
    waterproof. Since Aronnax takes a nap in it later on (I 17), the 'two tubes'
    must connect to the sphere rather than directly to the mouth.

95 *Ruhmkorff device*: *Journey to the Centre of the Earth*: 'The Ruhmkorff
    apparatus consists of a Bunsen battery . . . an induction coil . . . and a glass
    coil under vacuum . . . producing a continuous white light.'

    Fulton . . . Landi: inventors of naval armaments. *Fulton*: Robert (1765–
    1815), American inventor and engineer. He designed the first commercially
    successful steamboat (1807); and built two different submarines called
    Nautilus, designed to launch explosives against British ships. He success-
    fully demonstrated his three-man 21-foot candle-lit craft on the Seine in
    Paris in 1800–1. The *Nautilus* had a spindle shape, a folding sail, a ballast
    pump, a conning tower with glass ports, rudders and diving planes for

vertical and horizontal control, oxygen from compressed air, a hand-powered propeller, and a torpedo charge on a trailing rope. It was tested by the French Navy at Brest in 1800 or 1801, but the results were mixed. *Britons Phipps Coles and Burley*: (Verne: 'Philippe Coles'), Captain Cowper Phipps Coles (1819–70), inventor of a rotating turret and author of *Letters from Captain C. Coles to the Secretary of the Admiralty on Sea-Going Turret Ships* [1865?]; Bennett (Graham) *Burley* (1840–1914), later Burleigh, Confederate naval officer, inventor with his father of an underwater battery and a mine that had to be screwed to the vessel, and author of a pamphlet, *Lettres patentes pour des perfectionnements relatifs à l'usage des canons sous-marins* (1862). *Furcy*: mechanic from Paris, who exhibited an underwater gun at the 1867 Exhibition, not entirely waterproof however. *Landi*: Tommaso or Thomas (dates unknown), living in Paris, author of a London patent, *Nouveau procédé pour l'immersion du câble télégraphique sous-marin* (1858), and of a pamphlet, *Les Nouvelles Bombes: Bombe à percussion interne et bombe de second éclat* (1860).

96 *small glass capsules, invented by the Austrian chemist Leinebrock*: (Verne: 'Leniebroek'), the form 'Leinebrock', present in the first manuscript, and more in line with German usage, is adopted in this edition. However neither spelling is attested.

   miniature Leyden jars: Verne seems to be confusing balls that carry an electric charge with balls projected by electric means, the only sort attested. A possible source is: 'An Austrian chemist has reportedly discovered an electric bullet that explodes like lightning when it has penetrated the body' (*Les Mondes*, vol. 12, 1866, p. 228). The first manuscript clarifies the nature of Verne's electric bullets: ' "Glass capsules?" | "In which this chemist found a method of storing powerful electric sparks; these capsules are covered with a steel framework which allows them to enter flesh, and they explode at the slightest shock" ' (21). Electrically-projected balls or bullets seem to have been invented in 1746 by Pieter van Musschenbroek (1692–1761), a physicist from Leyden, author of *Elements of Physics* (1726) and co-inventor of the Leyden jar, whose name ends like 'Leniebroek' . . . *Leyden jars*: electrical condensers with a glass jar as a dielectric between sheets of tin foil (1745–6).

97 *about twenty electric bullets*: two pages earlier, Nemo had said 'a fully loaded gun can contain up to ten' electric bullets.

103 *witty naturalist*: Frédol (p. 48).

105 *its species will probably soon become extinct*: sea otters were indeed almost hunted to extinction, but are now protected. Verne's own opposition to hunting is clearly stated on numerous occasions, so it is possible that Nemo's behaviour (plus his companion's a page later, and even the unjustified over-fishing in I 18) is being criticized, if not by Aronnax, at least by the author.

107 *Monstrous fireflies*: 'fiery mouths' ('bouches à feu') in some modern editions must be an error for 'fireflies' ('mouches à feu'). Richard Ellis says

that such sharks do not have a 'phosphorescent substance', but in fact at least one species of dogfish shark is luminescent. (His *Monsters of the Deep* (New York: Knopf, 1994) harshly criticizes Verne for scientific 'errors', but itself contains a number of mistakes.)

108 *I recognized what were clearly Irish, French, a few Slavs, a Greek, and a Cretan*: Aronnax has an amazing, almost racist, ability to discern the different nationalities; but the men's appearance is the only way their varied origins and hence the scale of Nemo's social experiment can be indicated— at the same time as muddying the question of his nationality.

109 *caloric*: an indestructible, all-pervading, undetectable fluid, formerly believed to be responsible for the transfer of heat.

You will see the consequences of this phenomenon at the Poles: Aronnax will see only one Pole (II 13).

4½ million cubic leagues . . . a layer more than 10 metres thick: the first figure is much too large, the second much too small.

110 *15,149 metres*: the great depths quoted in *20T* are based on faulty sounding techniques, with some more than double the real figure. The deepest point is now calculated to be about 10,900 metres.

111 *Captain Cook*: James (1728–79), navigator. He explored the coasts of Australia and New Zealand, and is credited with preventing scurvy through proper diet.

5,000 metres above sea level: in fact 4,205 metres.

112 *Agora . . . Galen*: in Greece, the Ancient Agora, an open space located at the foot of the Acropolis, served as a market and meeting place. *Athenaeus*: Verne seems to be confusing Athenaeus, a Greek physician (late 1st century), and Athenaeus of Naucratis, a Greek historian and grammarian (*c*.170–*c*.230), author of *Banquet of Scholars*, who describes the beauty of argonauts on Roman tables. *Galen*: probably Claudius Galen (AD 130?–200), Greek physician and anatomist (218–68), but perhaps Gallien, or Gallienus, Roman emperor (253–68).

d'Orbigny: Alcide-Charles-Victor-Dessalines (1802–57), creationist geologist who published *Monographie des céphalopodes acétabulifères* (1834) and *Paléontologie française* (1840–54), ordering rock strata by their fossil content and thus equating the past with its visible stages, the metaphor that generates *Journey to the Centre of the Earth*.

113 *Jean Macé*: (1815–94), publicist and author of *Les Serviteurs de l'estomac* (1864). He founded the *Magasin d'Éducation et de Récréation* with Hetzel in 1864 (Verne was also a director from 1866); its inaugural issue started the serialization of *Captain Hatteras*. In *Paris in the Twentieth Century*, Verne calls him 'the most ingenious of scientific popularizers'.

steering the wrecked three-master through the ocean depths: it is not clear if this is a merchant ship or a warship; and no cause of the shipwreck is proposed. It is true that the very presence of the *Nautilus*, 'at most . . . a few hours' afterwards, could be indicative of Nemo's involvement, especially given the 'series of maritime disasters that the *Nautilus* was to encounter on its route' (I 19). However, the first manuscript says the wreck is 'not more than a few days old', meaning that the *Nautilus* may not have sunk it.

114 *'the Florida, Sunderland'*: a merchant ship named *Luida Florida*, from Sunderland, is listed in *The Mercantile Navy List* of 1860; the famous Secessionist *Florida* which sank about thirty-seven ships during the Civil War (1861–5) was at the centre of the Alabama Affair.

on 11 December: it was already 11 December at the end of the previous chapter. Has Verne forgotten; or is he marking the wreck of the *Florida* as at Tuamotu, in the centre of the huge area of the Pacific owned by the French and an unlikely place to meet a British ship?

Bougainville's: Louis Antoine de Bougainville (1729–1811), explorer, naturalist, and geographer. He fought in the American War of Independence, rediscovered the Solomon Islands, and wrote a *Voyage around the World* (1771–2).

Captain Bellingshausen of the Mirny: (Verne: 'Captain Bell of the *Minerve*') Fabian Gottlieb von Bellingshausen (1778–1852), admiral and explorer. He skirted round Antarctica, discovering Peter I and Alexander I Islands. He is mentioned again (as 'Bellinghausen') in the Antarctic episode.

115 *Mr Darwin*: Charles Robert (1809–82), naturalist. From findings accumulated on a circumnavigation on the *Beagle* (1831–6), he formulated the modern concept of evolution, in *On the Origin of Species* (1859, French translation, 1862) and *The Descent of Man* (1871). Verne's mention of him here is the first. Although on this occasion approval is given to Darwin's writings on coral reefs or the ocean depths, on evolution itself Verne remained largely silent or actively disapproving.

A hundred and ninety-two thousand years: the figures quoted in fact give about 10 million years.

116 *Tonga . . . killed*: historical events in the South Pacific. *the final resting-place for the crews of the 'Argo', the 'Port-au-Prince', and the 'Duke of Portland'*: the *Argo* was an Australian brig wrecked on Argo Reef, south-east Fiji, in January 1800; the *Port-au-Prince* was a Liverpool privateer, seized on 23 November 1806 by natives of the Levuka Islands; and the *Duke of Portland* was an American ship seized at Tongataboo in Tonga in June 1802: in each case the crew were killed. *Captain de Langle, La Pérouse's friend*: Paul de Langle (1744–87), captain of the *Astrolabe* and La Pérouse's first officer, killed on 11 December 1787 on Tutuila in the Samoan group. Jean-François de Galaup de *La Pérouse* (1741–88) was an explorer who died on Vanikoro in 1788.

Tasman . . . Torricelli: Abel Janszoon (1603–59), Dutch navigator and explorer, discovered Tasmania and New Zealand and proved that Australia was an island. *Torricelli*: Evangelista (1608–47), mathematician and physicist, disciple of Galileo.

Cook in 1774, d'Entrecasteaux in 1793, and finally Dumont d'Urville: (Verne: '1714'), Antoine-Raymond-Joseph de Bruni d'Entrecasteaux (1737–93), officer and explorer of Australia. The explorer Jules-Sébastien-César Dumont d'Urville (1790–1842) studied terrestrial magnetism, charted the South Atlantic and South Pacific, and discovered Adélie and Clarie Coasts.

116 *Captain Dillon, the first man to throw light on the mystery of La Pérouse's shipwreck*: Peter Dillon (1788–1847), Irish captain and author of *Narrative . . . of a voyage in the South Seas . . . to ascertain the actual fate of La Pérouse* (1829, French translation, 1830).

117 *Seneca's precept*: Lucius Annaeus Seneca, the Younger (*c*.4 BC–AD 65), stoic philosopher, writer, and politician. The precept is found in his *Letters to Lucilius* (letter 78, section 23).

Quiros: Admiral Pedro-Fernandez de (1565–1614), Portuguese navigator.

Vanikoro: or Vanikolo, in the Santa Cruz Islands, south-east Solomon Islands.

118 *the Recherche and the Espérance*: the *Recherche* was a twenty-gun frigate (1787–94) of the Marsouin class; the *Espérance*, a frigate (1781–94) of the Rhône class.

Bowen . . . New Georgia Island: George Bowen declared that he had seen remains from La Pérouse's ship, in December 1791; New Georgia is in the Solomon Islands.

a report by Captain Hunter: John Hunter (1738–1821), later governor of New South Wales. He explored the Furneaux Islands and Bass Strait, showed that Tasmania was an island, and wrote *An Historical Journal . . . of the New Discoveries in the South Seas* (1793).

119 *Tikopia in Vanuatu*: in fact part of the Solomon Islands (Verne: '1824'; 1871: 'Tikipia').

Dumont d'Urville and his Astrolabe: not to be confused with La Pérouse's *Astrolabe*, the ship after which *La Coquille* (1811–51) was renamed so as to search for its remains.

120 *M. Jacquinot*: Charles-Hector (1796–1879), admiral; he edited Dumont d'Urville's *Voyage au Pôle sud et dans l'Océanie . . .* (1842–54).

The Bayonnaise, commanded by Le Goarant de Tromelin: Louis-François-Marie-Nicolas Le Goarant de Tromelin (1786–1867), later rear-admiral. The *Bayonnaise* was a corvette sent in fact to report on the political situation in Hawaii, and thence, via Tikopia and Vanikoro (17 June 1828), back to France.

121 *The Astrolabe . . . Satisfaction*: in this paragraph Verne is weaving fact and fiction, with the story up to and including the departure ('northwards') in the cannibalized ship being what Dillon learned from the islanders. The wreck of the *Boussole* was located in 1964, 500 metres north-west of the *Astrolabe*. The rest still remains an unsolved mystery; Verne's tin box and location are apparently invented—or borrowed from a different narrative.

122 *La Pérouse Island*: Verne has 'le groupe de La Pérouse', but modern texts refer to La Pérouse Island, Vanikoro.

123 *the dangerous reef*: this is the Great Barrier Reef, a very rare term in 1868, more specifically Tribulation Cape, off the Bay of Trinity; in fact only the *Endeavour* touched it, during the night of 10–11 June.

124 *Francisco Serrao . . . Dumont d'Urville in 1827*: all the travellers quoted by Verne are indeed reported, with various degrees of reliability, to have visited New Guinea; Francisco Serrao in 1511: (Verne: 'Serrano'), despatched by Albuquerque from Malacca to the Moluccas; *don Jorge de Meneses in 1526*: (Verne: 'don José de Meneses'), appointed captain-designate of the Moluccas, but was blown off course en route: it is not certain that he found New Guinea; *Grijalva in 1527*: Juan de (1489?–1527), Spanish navigator and explorer of Mexico; *the Spanish general Alvar de Saavedra in 1528*: (d. 1529), relative and friend of Cortez, who sent him to the South Seas in 1527; it is in fact conjectural which landmass he sighted; *Iñigo Ortiz de Retes in 1545*: (Verne: 'Juigo Ortez'), despatched from the Moluccas; *the Dutchman Schouten in 1616*: (Verne: 'Shouten'), Willem (1567?–1625), mariner, discovered the Admiralty Islands, and was the first to sail round Cape Horn, named after his birthplace Hoorn; *Nicholas Struyck in 1753*: (Verne: 'Nicolas Sruick') (1687–1769), author of geographical works; *Dampier*: William (1652–1715), British buccaneer and explorer who reported sea serpents. He sailed round the world three times, and was on the two privateering expeditions when Alexander Selkirk, the model for Robinson Crusoe, was marooned on Juan Fernandez and then rescued; *Funnell*: (Verne: 'Fumel'), William (dates unknown), mate who served with Dampier on the *St George*, author of *A Voyage Round the World* (1707); *Carteret*: Philip (d. 1796), British rear-admiral, explorer, and map-maker, sailed around the world (1766–9); *Edwards*: Captain Edwards of the *Pandora*, despatched to the Pacific to apprehend the *Bounty* mutineers; *Forrest*: Thomas (1729?–1802?), captain and author of *A Voyage to New Guinea, Moluccas* (1774–6), and *A Treatise on the Monsoons in the East Indies* (1782); *McCluer . . . in 1792*: (Verne: 'Mac Cluer'), John (d. 1794?), British explorer and surveyor; *Duperrey in 1823*: Louis-Isidore (1786–1865), navigator, geographer, and author of *Voyage autour du monde . . . dans la corvette . . . 'La Coquille'* (1826), (the same ship, re-baptized the *Astrolabe*, took part in La Pérouse's ill-fated expedition).

the dark-skinned peoples [Noirs] . . . the redoubtable Andamanese: Grégoire-Louis Domeny de Rienzi (1789–1843), navigator and racist author of *Dictionnaire usuel et scientifique de géographie* (1841) and *Océanie, ou cinquième partie du monde* (1836–8). The 'M.' is unusual for past authors. While at the time 'Malaysia' included much of south-east Asia, including a section of the Torres Strait, it did not extend to the Andaman Islands in the Bay of Bengal.

Luis Vaez de Torres: (Verne: 'Louis Paz de Torrès'), Spanish navigator (b. 1565; flourished in 1606): he served under Quiros (see note to p. 117).

Vincendon-Dumoulin and Ensign (now Admiral) Coupvent-Desbois: Clément-Adrien Vincendon-Dumoulin (1811–58) wrote *Îles Marquises, ou Nouka*

Hiva (1843), *Îles Taîti* (1844), and *Hydrographie du voyage au Pôle sud et dans l'Océanie, par Dumont d'Urville* (1843–5). Auguste-Élie-Aimé Coupvent-Desbois (1814–92), ensign in the circumnavigation via Antarctica of 1837–40, co-author with Vincendon-Dumoulin of *Physique* (1850). The 'Map of the route of the corvettes the Astrolabe and the *Zélée* through the Torres Strait' (1840) was published in the *Atlas hydrographique*, a volume accompanying Dumont d'Urville's *Voyage au pôle Sud et dans l'Océanie* (1842).

125 *Captain King's*: Phillip Parker King (1791–1856), admiral, explorer, and author of *A Voyage to Torres Strait* (1837). His 'Chart of the Intertropical and West Coasts of Australia' was published in his *Narrative of a Survey of the Intertropical and Western Coasts of Australia* (1825).

   Toud Island and the Bad Channel: (Verne: 'Tound'), features that appeared in a map dated 1840 in the *Atlas hydrographique*.

   Gueboroar Island: no trace has been found of this archetypal Robinson Crusoe and Swiss Family Robinson-inspired desert island. Given that the reefs in the following paragraph seem to be Warrior Reefs, it is probably Gabba Island or, more frequently, Guebe or Guebé (Two Brother Island, Gerbar in the indigenous language), an Australian island, discovered by Torrès in September 1605; 'Gebar' island appears on some contemporary maps. But in any case the information about Gueboroar is invented, given the variety of fauna and of 'mountains' and 'plains', absent in reality from the low-lying islands around.

128 *two legs and feathers*: allusion to Plato's apocryphal definition of man as a 'featherless biped'.

130 *rima in Malay*: the Malay words of Verne were rarely attested at the time; however, Rienzi gives the translations: 'rima' (breadfruit, vol. 1, p. 106); 'mado' ('leader or respected person' in the language of Murray Island, vol. 1, p. 338); and 'Assai' ('come here', vol. 1, p. 338).

135 *great emerald bird of paradise, one of the rarest*: given Verne's description, this may be the Magnificent Bird of Paradise; in contrast with Verne's 'eight species', more than 40 species of birds of paradise have now been identified.

137 *a species of 'rabbit kangaroos' which normally live in the hollows of trees*: these must be tree kangaroos, hare wallabies, or forest wallabies.

139 *are those that you call savages any worse than the others?*: in a contemporary humorous letter to his father, the novelist maintains that 'savages are more civilized' than others, for they have 'authority over their parents' [March? 1868]. The last two sentences of this very Vernian dialogue, opposing a naive Aronnax to an ironic Nemo, were, however, written by Hetzel in the margin of the second manuscript, Verne merely retracing them in ink.

142 *weight in gold*: this paragraph closely follows Frédol (p. 279). More generally, when Verne cites 'naturalists', he is often referring to the same writer.

146 '*I have given the order to open the hatches*': why? They will be on the open sea in a couple of hours. Are the hatches opened only to demonstrate the power of electricity?

the handrail of the stairs: it seems strange that all the attackers touch the handrail, and that Ned seizes it 'in both hands'.

Ten suffered the same fate: MS2 has a significant variant here: '~~He pressed the switch. A blood-curdling cry was heard outside. I was pale with fright. The hatches had been opened. I looked at Captain Nemo, still impassive, and rushed out of the salon.~~ | ~~I arrived on the platform. Twenty canoes were fleeing, a hundred dead bodies lay over the flanks of the *Nautilus*.~~ | ~~I understood: the platform, insulated by some unknown mechanism and charged with all the electricity on board, had produced the effect of a huge battery. The savages crowded on it had been struck by lightning!~~'

Between his assailants and him, Nemo had extended an electric circuit that none could cross with impunity: the language and the action, here and elsewhere, coincide largely with the device 'Nemo me impune lacessit', for the captain is responding to wrongs.

147 *it left behind the dangerous passes of Torres Strait*: MS2 contains a description of a French three-master observed as the submarine leaves Torres Strait, but this was deleted after Hetzel's reading (see Appendix 1: Inception).

ÆGRI SOMNIA: 'bad dreams', quotation from Seneca and Horace, perhaps via Dumas.

I could not follow its revolutions, let alone count them: hardly surprising, since Aronnax is inside the submarine.

a holy ark: reference to Noah's Ark (Genesis 6: 14–16), ultimate refuge from man's iniquities, rather than to the Ark of the Covenant (Exodus 25: 10–22), containing the Ten Commandments.

the sacred lizards: crocodiles are not of course lizards. But Verne's other facts are authentic, with virgins sacrificed to crocodiles in Timor until at least 1850.

149 *1.018 for the Ionian Sea*: given that the other densities are at least 1.026, '1.018' may be a misprint.

152 *near the front of the platform*: in I 6 the searchlight is implied to be at the rear.

invisible point of the horizon: it will later become clear that Nemo has seen an enemy ship in these Dutch waters on the route to Australia.

155 *19 January*: Verne avoids weighing his climaxes down with dates; this is the last one of the first volume. The second volume opens on 21 January 1868 (the voyage across the Pacific began around 8 November 1867).

Moquin-Tandon: Horace-Benedict-Alfred (1804–63), botanist and doctor, author of *Histoire naturelle des mollusques* (1855) and *Le Monde de la mer* (1865, under the pseudonym of Alfred Frédol), an important source for *20T*.

156 *which struck this man*: *MÉR* and 1869 add: 'The first officer was at his side. He [the injured man] threw himself forward to prevent the collision . . . A brother getting himself killed for his brother, a friend for his friend, what could be simpler! That is the law for everyone on the *Nautilus*.' This passage, with its rather implausible action, is the only real interaction we observe between Nemo's crew members, and illustrates high ideals. It may also contain a slight allusion to Dumas *père*'s 'One for all, and all for one!' Its didactic tone and ineffective altruism suggest that Hetzel at least contributed to it.

Other ideas probably taken from *The Count of Monte Cristo*—to which Verne dedicated his Mathias Sandorf (1885)—include Xenophon, Lucullus, and Château-Renaud; the Mediterranean boat called a 'tartan', 'the famous sea serpent of the *Constitutionnel*', and a large, multilingual library; the notions of Greek liberation from the Turks, of fashioning pen and ink from fish remains while in prison, of cruelly watching fish change colour as they die on the dining table, of the hero keeping a portrait of a young woman on his bedroom wall; and a parading of artists, including Meyerbeer, Delacroix, Decamps, Potter, Dow, Murillo, and Raphael.

157 *something like a funereal plain-chant. Was this the prayer for the dead*: the prayer for the dead is associated with the belief in purgatory; together with the 'plain-chant' and the 'cross' depicted below, an impression is created of Catholicism—and hence of a non-northern origin for Nemo.

the coral kingdom: the *Musée des familles*, to which Verne had contributed regularly, contained an article by Bertsch on coral reefs (March 1863), as well as one, written by Verne's friend, director, and co-author Pitre-Chevalier, on Hallett's trials of the *Nautilus* on the Seine (July 1858).

it was only in 1694 that the Marseillais Peyssonnel: (Verne: 'Peysonnel') Claude-Charles de (1727–90), author of *Traité du corail* (London, 1756; Verne's date should be 1723).

159 *But as one thinker has remarked*: Michelet, in *La Mer*, who entitles a chapter 'Flower of Blood' (II, 4), words reproduced by Verne three paragraphs below.

160 *The clearing was a cemetery*: this powerful burial scene shares elements with the funeral of a sailor similarly killed by machinery on the *Great Eastern* (*A Floating City*, ch. 30).

161 *And in a sudden movement . . . the surface of the waves*: these two paragraphs, together with the more melodramatic parts of the previous lines and most of the Christian symbols, are absent from both manuscripts. They may easily be some of the 'tears' that Verne invites Hetzel to add to the book (14 August 1868); in any case they are in the publisher's style.

163 *PART TWO*: the division is an important one, as MS2 Part One was revised before MS1 Part Two. There was also a gap of a year between the book publication of the two parts, leading Verne to write: 'Paris, 27 December 1869 | My dear father . . . I haven't tried to obtain articles [reviews] for *Twenty Thousand Leagues under the Seas*. I'm waiting for the second volume to appear, as the first alone cannot give an idea of the work.'

Here begins the second part of this voyage under the seas: MS1 adds, obscurely: 'Not that it cannot deviate, either through the space we have covered, or through the time spent covering it.'

Always the same defiance of human society, wild and implacable: MS2 has the stronger: 'Always the same defiance ~~of the human race, or rather the same hatred, implacable and permanent~~, wild and implacable. | ~~That was the true mystery surrounding him, the key to his enigmatic existence . . . Yes, it was in this hatred that the secret was to be sought~~.' Five lines lower, it reads, '. . . the wound of that man, most certainly struck in a violent battle', a clearer hint of Nemo's agenda.

some terrible but unknown sort of revenge: it is hard to see how Aronnax deduces Nemo's mission of vengeance from the existence of a wounded man.

writing, so to speak, at the dictation of events: Aronnax claims to be writing mostly without the benefit of hindsight, the mixture of tenses in these opening pages being a sign. He presumably writes notes every day or at the first opportunity, but has to conceal information (and conceal his concealment). By the time he is able to write up the underwater excursion, for instance, he knows that it is a funeral, but chooses not to reveal this until the end.

164 *could not understand French . . . but he remained mute and impassive*: MS1 adds, 'and yet I sometimes saw his lips purse and his eyes sparkle below their lids', a rare sign of passion in Nemo's crewmen—and another hint at a French nationality.

167 *Remington*: Philo (1816–89), American developer of the breech-loading rifle, with his father Eliphalet Remington (1793–1861); he also improved the typewriter from about 1873.

Captain Fitzroy: (later vice-admiral) Robert (1805–65), hydrographer and meteorologist, captain of the *Beagle* on Darwin's 1831–6 journey and editor of *Narrative of the Surveying Voyages of His Majesty's Ships 'Adventure' and 'Beagle'* (1839). MS1 says Darwin's visit to Keeling Island was in '1858'.

168 *the thermometer still invariably indicated +4°*: modern studies indicate a minimum of 1 degree.

Oppian: Greek poet born in Cilicia (flourished 2nd century AD), author of *Halieutica* ('On Fishing').

169 *raised for the wind like light sails*: according to Léon Renard, *Le Fond de la mer* (pp. 256–7), and Figuier (p. 474), the webbed arms do not serve as sails.

'it never does': only the female does not come out, so as to protect the eggs.

he should have called his ship the Argonaut: the quest of Jason and the Argonauts is to find the Golden Fleece.

171 *28 February*: or January?

a volume by H. C. Sirr, Esq. entitled Ceylon and the Cingalese: (Verne and MS2: '*Ceylan and . . .*'; MS1: '*Ceylon*'), Henry Charles Sirr (1807–72), diplomat: his book was published in 1850, with a chapter on the Mannar pearl fishery.

172 *Treaty of Amiens in 1802*: between Britain and Napoleonic France.

    Percival: (Verne: 'Perceval', MS1: 'Percival'), Robert (1765–1826), author of *An Account of Ceylon* (1803).

    some divers can stay as much as 57 seconds and very good ones, 87: these figures seem very low.

174 *turning the pages automatically*: from about 1867, Verne's writing includes vocabulary of 'automatically', 'instinctively', and even 'subconsciously', signs of an interest in the hidden workings of the mind.

177 *Charles V of France*: (1500–58), reigned over the Holy Roman Empire (1519–57); also known as Charles I of the Spanish Empire, which he founded.

    Caesar gave Servilia a pearl estimated to be worth about 120,000 francs of our money: Servilia was the mother of Brutus, one of Caesar's assassins (44 BC). This gift, reported by Suetonius in *Lives of the Twelve Caesars*, encouraged the rumour that Brutus was Caesar's illegitimate son. Frédol gives the correct sum: 'Julius Caesar offered Servilia a pearl valued at about 1,200,000 francs of our money' (p. 267).

    Cleopatra: Cleopatra VII, Thea Philopator (*c*.69–30 BC), queen of Egypt (51–30), famous for her beauty and her relationship with Julius Caesar.

179 *that etymology derives the French word for shark, requin, from the word requiem*: according to popular belief; the word is probably more akin to 'chien' (dog).

182 *Darwin . . . coconuts*: in *The Voyage of the 'Beagle'*, Darwin describes a crab that splits coconuts.

184 *the phenomenal mollusc*: the giant clam (*Tridacna gigans*) does reach a few feet in size, can weigh 440 pounds, and can trap divers.

188 *Vasco da Gama*: (1469?–1524), Portuguese explorer, the first European to reach India by sea (1497–9).

190 *Idrisi*: (1099?–1164?), Arabian geographer, scientist, and poet. His monumental *Kitab Rujjar* (1154) contains a description of the known Earth.

191 *this classical importance, one which the railways of Suez have already brought back in part*: the British considered the 204-mile Cairo-to-Suez railway (1858) a triumph for their imperial communications, and subsequently opposed the building of the Suez Canal.

193 *The latter method, requiring the use of divers, is preferable*: a few pages previously, pearl fishing had been castigated for its effect on divers' health.

194 *Strabo*: (63? BC–AD 24?), Greek historian, philosopher, volcanologist, and firm believer in monsters in the Mediterranean; author of a *Geographia*.

    Arrian . . . Artemidorus: Greek thinkers. *Arrian*: or Flavius Arrianus, 2nd-century historian, author of the *Indica* and *Anabasis*, a life of Alexander the Great; *Agatharchidas*: flourished 177 BC, general in the Peloponnesian War and author of *On the Erythraean Sea*; *Artemidorus*: flourished 100 BC, author of a systematic geography.

195 *a fourteenth-century chronicler*: the chronicler is named as an untraceable 'Nacos de [of] la Charité sur Loire [a place name in Nièvre]' by Léon de Laborde (1807–69), *Commentaire géographique sur l'Exode et les nombres*.

the Hebrew word "Edom": MS2 and the 1869 and 1871 editions have 'Edrom', corrected here to 'Edom', following the *MÉR* edition. 'Edom' certainly means 'red(dish-brown)' in Hebrew, but the 'Red Sea' in the English Bible is the translation of 'Yam Suf' (literally 'sea of reeds'), not now confirmed to be the modern Red Sea.

The posthumous story 'Eternal Adam', of unparalleled brilliance and ascribed mainly to Michel Verne, is entitled 'Edom' in manuscript form. According to Genesis (36: 8), Edom was Esau's other name; and those reputed to be his descendants were also known as Edom, as was the area they lived in, south-east of ancient Israel.

196 *Sesostris . . . Necho*: probably Sesostris III (1878–1843 BC), the fifth ruler of the twelfth dynasty of Egypt; his work was on the first cataract of the Nile, but also on a separate canal. *Necho*: twenty-sixth-dynasty pharaoh (ruled 610–595 BC), mentioned in the Bible (2 Chronicles 35: 20, 22; 36: 4). He sent Phoenicians on an expedition that may have circumnavigated Africa.

Darius . . . Ptolemy II: ancient rulers. Darius: Darius I (the Great) (*c.*558–486 BC), king of Persia, defeated at the Battle of Marathon (490 BC). *Hystaspes*: (flourished 550 BC), satrap of Parthia. *Ptolemy II*: (*c.*308–246 BC), king of Egypt (285–246 BC); married his sister.

until the century of the Antonines . . . Caliph Umar: Roman emperors Marcus Aelius Aurelius Antoninus (121–80 BC) and Antoninus Pius (AD 86–161). Umar ibn al-Khattab (*c.*586–644), or Umar I, second caliph, who expanded the Muslim empire and probably instituted the haj to Mecca.

filled in once and for all by Caliph al-Mansur to prevent food reaching Mohammed ben Abdallah, who had rebelled against him: Abu Jaafer Abdullah al-Mansur (712?–75), caliph (754–75); it seems to have been in fact in 775 that he filled in the canal. Mohammed ben Abdallah (*c.*712–64), now called Abdulla ibn Ali, was al-Mansur's uncle and governor of Syria; his rebellion apparently took place in 754.

General Bonaparte: Napoleon Bonaparte (1769–1821), emperor of France (1804–14 and 1815); reformed the administration and conquered most of Europe; exiled to Elba and St Helena. In 1799 a survey he ordered concluded that building a sea-level canal between the Mediterranean and Red Sea was impractical.

Hazeroth, the very place where Moses had camped 3,300 years before: the precise location is not in fact known; and of course there is no historical confirmation of much of the Bible. According to Numbers 11: 35, the

Israelites 'camped at Hazeroth', whereas in Numbers 12: 16, they 'moved from Hazeroth and camped in the Wilderness of Paran'.

197 *M. de Lesseps*: Ferdinand-Marie (1805–94), French diplomat who built the Suez Canal (17 November 1869), described in *Around the World* as 'the magnificent work of M. de Lesseps'. Verne's Légion d'honneur of 1870 may have been proposed by Lesseps.

198 *Aures habent et non audient*: 'they have ears and do not hear' (Psalms 6: 115, cf. Mark 8: 18).

200 *dugong*: Ned's 7-metre, 5,000-kilogram dugong is exceptional, as the maximum size is normally 4.5 metres and slightly over a ton.

202 *which formed splayed tusks*: tusks indicate a male dugong, and so Ned could not have seen its breasts two pages previously. Also, dugongs do not have 'fingers'; and they are usually inoffensive.

204 *Mount Horeb, the Sinai on whose summit Moses saw God face to face*: Mount Horeb was indeed where Moses received the Ten Commandments, but its location is uncertain. Although Moses leaves with the intention of seeing God's face, He appears only in the form of a burning bush, since: 'thou shalt see my back parts: but my face shall not be seen' (Exodus 33: 23).

205 *Mississippi or Hudson steamboats*: in New York, Verne took a huge steamboat, the *St John*, up the Hudson to Albany (10–11 April 1867, *A Floating City*, chs. 35–6).

210 *Est in Carpathio Neptuni gurgite vates | Caeruleus Proteus . . .* : 'In Neptune's Carpathian flood there dwells a seer, Proteus, of sky-blue hue' (Virgil, *Georgics*, book 4, lines 387–8).

 The next day, 14 February: this should be '13'. Similarly '19 March' seems to occur on two different days (II 13).

 what had become of the insurrection since then, I had absolutely no idea: the Cretan revolt against Turkish rule broke out in 1866, and continued on and off until 1869.

211 *Vitellius*: (15–69), briefly Roman emperor in the 'year of the four emperors' (69). This paragraph borrows, often verbatim, from the *Life of the Twelve Caesars* (371), by Suetonius, perhaps via Lacépède.

 Mark Antony's vessel at the Battle of Actium, in this way helping Augustus to victory: Mark Antony (83?–30 BC), general and politician, and Cleopatra were defeated at Actium in western Greece (31 BC), leading to the crowning in 27 BC of the first Roman emperor, Augustus.

212 *Pesce*: the diver must be inspired by Nicolas Pesce-Cola (13th century; Italian pesce = fish), a legendary fisherman from Messina, with webbed hands and feet, meant to be able to stay underwater for days; some situate his exploits in Charybdis, a whirlpool that engulfed ships and contained monstrous polyps. This episode, with no clear impact on the story, and where Nemo displays an unusual sociability, is absent from the first manuscript. Hetzel's involvement cannot be excluded; in the other manuscripts, he

adds edifying scenes, designed to inspire young people, but often implausible and badly integrated.

Where had this precious metal come from, representing as it did an enormous sum of money?: no doubt from Vigo Bay.

the captain wrote an address on its lid, using characters that looked like modern Greek: MS2 has Nemo writing, 'in black ink', 'an address in copper-plate as follows:', followed by a page break; in other words it was planned to include the actual address. In MS1, Nemo writes to 'A. P. Leader of the Cretan Insurrection'.

Nemo may be partly based on Gustave Flourens (1838–71), a French revolutionary. He fought in both the 1863 Polish Insurrection and the 1866 Cretan revolt, supported the Irish nationalists, lived in exile in London and Belgium, and wrote distinguished volumes, like *Histoire de l'homme* (1863) and *Science de l'homme* (1865), as well as political works (1863, 1864).

213 *Until five o'clock I wrote up my notes*: if earlier Aronnax referred to the existence of his notes, now he is referring to his own writing. But further levels also exist. Thus Aronnax's 'sort[s] out [his] notes'; recasts them in past-tense, personal-memoir style; submits the result to Ned and Conseil; and in the end publishes it.

we were not at high latitudes: a slip for 'low latitudes'.

214 *Cassiodorus*: Flavius Magnus Aurelius (*c*.490–*c*.585), statesman and historian.

Finally, on 10 March a small island called Reka appeared: to know the name, Nemo must either have launched his submarine after 10 March 1866 or still have some contact with dry land.

215 *the mare nostrum of the Romans*: 'our sea'; Verne visited the Mediterranean twice, in the company of Hetzel: in 1866 and in about January 1868.

Pluto: Greco-Roman god of death and the underworld; here referring to volcanic action.

217 *Lucullus*: Lucius Licinius Lucullus (115–56? BC), general and consul, fond of original banquets.

218 *Arachne*: (Greek for 'spider'), Arachne wove a tapestry depicting the gods' amorous activities. When Athena tore it up out of jealousy, she hanged herself, and was turned into a spider.

219 '*it blocks the whole of the Strait of Libya, and Smyth's soundings prove that the two continents were formerly connected between Capes Bon and Farina*': (Verne: 'Smith's . . . Boco . . . Furina'), Verne's 'détroit de Libye', where 'Libya' meant most of North Africa, seems to correspond to the modern Sicilian Channel. *Smyth*: Rear-Admiral William Henry, author of *The Mediterranean* (1854).

222 *the Atlas, which had disappeared with all hands twenty years before*: in fact a few years: this French liner left Marseilles for Algiers on 3 December 1863.

222 *Strait of Gibraltar*: the *Nautilus* heads from Sicily to Gibraltar, passing not far from Provence, but with hardly a mention of France. The Greek islands having been presented in the preceding chapter, this chapter, 'The Mediterranean in Forty-Eight Hours', consists of little more than long lists of marine life.

223 *the temple of Hercules, sunk, according to Pliny and Avienus*: this mythical temple corresponded approximately to the columns of Hercules, the site of the theft of oxen, one of his twelve works; it was made up of rocks on both sides of the Strait of Gibraltar. Rufius Festus *Avienus* was a fourth-century poet, author of *Ora Maritima* (Sea Coasts), a wild account of the Mediterranean and surrounding areas.

225 *My novel was falling from my hands half-way through*: is Aronnax thinking of novel-reading in general or referring to his own ongoing book? *20 T* is in any case the story of its own writing. As the author of *The Mysteries . . .*, Aronnax is invited to write for the *New York Herald*, producing the written invitation to hunt the monster. Nemo later admits that he too has kept a record, and may entrust it to the waves in a floating container (a favourite Hetzelian trope). At the end, Aronnax will reveal that his new 'study' of the sea, which, turned into 'memoirs', has now become a 'narrative', is somehow already complete. His book thus ends up coinciding with Verne's novel.

226 *in perpetuity*: instead of the words following 'gratitude', MS2 has '~~No, however, for the captain was exceeding his rights in claiming to be able to keep us on board his ship in perpetuity.~~'

227 *Kosciusko . . . John Brown*: heroes who often died defending a liberal or patriotic cause. The list, which was added to the novel after Hetzel had read it, includes one Pole, two Greeks, one anti-Austrian, two anti-Confederates, and two anti-Britons. *Kosciusko*: Thaddeus (1746–1817), Polish general who fought for American independence and in 1794 led a rebellion against Russian and Prussian control of his homeland; at the Battle of Maciejowice (1794), he uttered the cry, 'Poland is finished', a defeat followed by the dismemberment of the country; *Botsaris, the Leonidas of modern Greece*: Markos (1786–1823), who fought in the war of independence against the Turks, and died in the defence of Missolonghi; *Leonidas*: king of Sparta who perished defending the Pass of Thermopylae with only 300 men (480 or 481 BC) in the Second Persian War; *O'Connell, the defender of Ireland*: Daniel, 'the Liberator' (1775–1847), political leader who campaigned for Irish independence; *Washington, the founder of the American Union*: George (1732–99), commander-in-chief in the War of Independence and first president (1789–97); *Manin, the Italian patriot*: Daniele (1804–57), led the Venetians against Austrian rule in 1848 and headed a short-lived republic; *Lincoln, who fell shot by a supporter of slavery*: Abraham (1809–65), sixteenth US president (1861–5); he maintained the Union in the Civil War and issued the Emancipation Proclamation (1863); *John Brown*: (1800–59), abolitionist celebrated in the song 'John Brown's Body'; he used force to liberate Southern slaves, but was finally hanged.

Verne wrote to Hetzel, 'The incident of John Brown [of which no trace has survived] pleases me by its concise form, but in my view, diminishes the captain. His nationality needs to be kept vague, together with the causes which cast him into his strange existence. In addition the incident of an *Alabama* or a false *Alabama* is unacceptable and inexplicable; if Nemo wanted to take revenge on the slavers, he only had to serve in [Ulysses] Grant's army and everything was settled' [17 May 1869]. The *Alabama*, which claimed to have destroyed 75 merchantmen, was sunk by the Unionist *Kearsarge* off Cherbourg on 11 June 1864, and was commemorated in a painting by Manet.

229 *Louis XIV . . . imposed his grandson, the Duke of Anjou*: historical events. *Louis XIV*: (1638–1715), the Sun King (ruled 1643–1715), built the Palace of Versailles. *The Duke of Anjou*: (1683–1746), ruled Spain as Philip V (1700–46).

Admiral de Château-Renaud: (Verne: 'Château-Renault'; MS2: 'Château-Renaud'), François-Louis de Rousselet de (1637–1716). Despite the problems, he was congratulated by Louis XIV.

230 *Vigo Bay*: in the Battle of Vigo Bay (23 October 1702), French ships under Château-Renaud were escorting Spanish galleons. It was not in fact this admiral who gave the order to scuttle the ships, an order which, despite Nemo's account, was only partially executed.

Hernando Cortez: (1485–1547), Spanish explorer who brutally conquered the Aztecs.

231 *the work of a rival company*: following electricity-illuminated searches from 1865 by Ernest Bazin, a society was founded to recover the galleons from Vigo Bay in 1869, meaning that Aronnax cannot know of its founding.

233 *33° 22′ N, 16° 17′ W, that is 150 leagues from the nearest coast*: these coordinates are in fact close to Madeira. Might it be a deliberate mistake by Aronnax to prevent Ned's escape?

236 *and so boldly followed him*: MS2 has the interesting: 'and due to a purely physical effect, the more I rose towards the top strata, the heavier I felt'.

awe-inspiring squid: MS2 has 'giant squid'; the same paragraph in MS2 has 'crustaceans, lurking like tigers' and 'crabs . . . ready to pounce'.

237 *not those of the Creator*: MS2: 'not those of nature'.

'*Come on! Further! Come with me!*': in this imaginary conversation Nemo uses the intimate form ('Viens!'), perhaps in response to Aronnax's seizing of his arm. In MS2 it is Nemo who takes Aronnax's arm to point out the reddish glow.

another Torre del Greco: a port and valley below Vesuvius, destroyed many times.

238 *a whole Pompeii sunk beneath the waters*: Pompeii was destroyed by the eruption of Vesuvius in AD 79, and rediscovered in 1748.

238 *that ancient Meropis . . . d'Avezac*: believers and disbelievers in Atlantis.
Theopompus: (*c*.380–*c*.315 BC), Greek historian. According to the *Varia
Historia* (book 3, ch. 18) of Aelianus (flourished early 2nd century AD),
Theopompus writes of a conversation that Midas, king of Phrygia, has
with the aged satyr Silenus, who tells him of the continent of Meropis (*mer* +
opis ('over or near')), considerably larger than the known world. *Plato*:
(427–347 BC), Greek philosopher, author of *The Republic*. *Origen*: or Origines
Adamantius (185?–254?), Christian philosopher who castrated himself to
ensure celibacy; *Porphyry*: (*c*.232–*c*.305), philosopher who helped found
Neoplatonism; *Iamblichus*: (d. *c*.330), Syrian-born Greek mystic philosopher, author of *De Mysteriis*; *d'Anville*: Jean-Baptiste Bourgignon d'Anville
(1697–1782), geographer and cartographer; *Malte-Brun*: probably Conrad
(1775–1826), Danish geographer, founder of the Société de géographie
(of which Verne was a member); author of *Précis de la géographie universelle*
(1812–29)—praised to the skies in *Journey to England and Scotland*—which
contains a page on Atlantis, characterized as 'uncertain' (vol. 1, p. 56);
Posidonius: (135–50 BC), Greek stoic philosopher, volcanologist, polymath,
and partial believer in Atlantis; *Ammianus Marcellinus*: (*c*.325/330–*c*.395),
Latin historian born in Antioch, prolific continuer of Tacitus; *Tertullian*:
Quintus Septimus Florens (*c*.160–*c*.230), Carthaginian church father,
founder of the schismatic Tertullianists; he describes Atlantis in the
Apologetic and *De Pallio*; *Engel*: Samuel (1702–84), Swiss geographer, author
of *Quand et comment l'Amérique a-t-elle été peuplée d'hommes et d'animaux?*
(Amsterdam, 1767); *Scherer*: (Verne: 'Sherer'), Jean-Benoît (1741–1824),
diplomat, historian, and author of *Recherches historiques et géographiques sur le
Nouveau-monde* (1787), about the origins of the American Indians; he quotes
Plato on Atlantis (pp. 583–4); *Tournefort*: Joseph Pitton de (1656–1708),
botanist and author of *Voyage au Levant* (1717), which discusses Atlantis;
Buffon: Georges-Louis-Leclerc (1707–88), French pre-evolutionary
naturalist. His works include a *Histoire naturelle* (1749–1804), with an
illustration of a cephalopod embracing a frigate, and *Époques de la Nature*,
which describes Atlantis (Sixth Epoch); *d'Avezac*: Armand (1799–1875),
geographer and author of *Les Îles fantastiques de l'océan occidental* (1845).

the land of the powerful Atlanteans: the Atlantis idea has gripped generations
of writers. It is normally taken as being in the Atlantic—Michelet places
it at Tenerife (I, 4), but also englobing Auvergne and the West Indies.
However, it is sometimes situated, following Strabo, in Thira (near modern Santorini), an island buried in a volcanic eruption and 30-metre tidal
wave (*c*.1615 or 1500 BC). Thira's Bronze Age ruins were first explored in
the 1860s, when the French quarried pumice to build the Suez Canal.

Atlantis is also central to 'Eternal Adam' (1910), where remains of 'columns and pottery, such as we had never seen' prove to survivors of a future
cataclysm that they formed part of an indefinite number of civilizations
that emerged and failed.

*His dialogues of Timaeus and Critias were, so to speak, dictated under the
inspiration of Solon, poet and legislator*: Plato used Atlantis to illustrate his

theory of human history as a cyclical rise and fall. His *Timaeus* (*c*.395 BC) describes a large island Utopia on the other side of the Pillars of Hercules: 'There occurred violent earthquakes and floods; and in a single day and night of misfortune all the warlike men sank together into the Earth, and the island of Atlantis similarly disappeared into the depths of the ocean. For this reason, the sea in those parts is impassable and impenetrable, with a shoal of mud blocking the route.'

The information in Verne's next two paragraphs is taken mainly from Plato's *Critias* (18th dialogue onwards), in which Critias, an Athenian politician, philosopher, and poet, provokes Timaeus's response. But whereas Verne describes the unnamed town as 'nine hundred centuries old', Plato says '9,000 years'. *Solon*: (*c*.639–*c*.559 BC), statesman whose constitutional reforms gave rise to the Athenian state. Mentioning 'ruins that were hundreds of thousands of years old' allows Verne to make coevals of 'the contemporaries of the first man', the 'geological epochs', the 'fabulous times', and 'the gigantic inhabitants [who] lived for whole centuries'.

Sais, a town already 800 years old: Sais was the ancient capital of Lower Egypt, with an important temple complex. The '800 years', inconsistent with the figures of 1,000 and 9,000 years, is a misquoting of Plato's '8,000 years'.

239 *Machimos the warlike and Eusebia the holy*: (Verne: 'Makhimos . . . Eusebès'), the source for these two localities is Aelianus, whose *Varia Historia* (book 3, ch. 18) invents the great towns in 'Meropis' of 'Machimos (the warlike) and . . . Eusebia (the holy)'.

241 *Bailly*: Jean-Sylvain (1736–93), scholar and politician, author of *Lettres sur l'Atlantide de Platon* (London, 1779), president of the States-General (1789), and mayor of Paris (1790); guillotined. *Captain Hatteras* refers to the 'astronomer Bailly, who maintained that the Atlanteans, the disciplined lost race of which Plato speaks, lived here [at the North Pole]' (II 24).

242 *I did not know where we were*: the position is important, indicating the location of both Atlantis and the captain's home port. Nemo's invitation to visit the lost continent was issued at 33° 22′ N, 16° 17′ W. Then from dawn until 4 p.m. the *Nautilus* sails 'southwards' at '20 knots', covering about 200 miles, until it nears 'a continent or at the very least an island, perhaps one of the islands of the Canaries or of Cape Verde'. Aronnax is again being duplicitous, for this must be Funchal or the Canary Islands, whereas Cape Verde is a good 1,000 miles away. The submarine then continues more slowly on into the night, covering about 100 miles to reach Nemo's base. (Verne drops heavy hints when he has Aronnax discover bees, 'so common throughout the Canary Islands'.) The Canaries are perfect for the captain, since they are actively volcanic (thus hiding his smoke), partly deserted, and Spanish, an appropriate home port for 'Juan Nemo'.

244 *served me well*: MS2 adds 'Here I am master of the lake!', apparently an allusion to *The Lady of the Lake* (1810), by Walter Scott (1771–1832), who

is referred to at the end of this chapter and forms a major inspiration for *Journey to England and Scotland*.

244 *those of Newcastle*: on the night of 3–4 September 1859, Verne saw these underwater coalmines on the train from Edinburgh to London (*Journey to England and Scotland*, ch. 37).

248 *Walter Scott's hero*: perhaps Darsie Latimer in *Redgauntlet* (1824), almost overtaken by the tide of Solway Firth (letter IV), or Arthur Wardour in *The Antiquary* (1816, French translation, 1857; chs. 6 and 7).

249 *Sargasso Sea*: the calm centre of the clockwise rotation of the North Atlantic. Although nautical lore referred to vessels trapped in dense seaweed, in fact the area was avoided mostly because of the lack of wind. It is now a relatively small area in the western Atlantic, but Maury's Plate VI, 'Gulf Stream and Drift', shows the main Sargasso Sea as centred on 30° W, south-west of the Canaries, with the area around Bermuda as an extension.

250 *sargazo*: (Verne: '*sargazzo*'), the following paragraph quotes Maury approximately. To ensure a faithful translation of Verne, the French version is here translated back into English.

The Physical Geography of the Globe: in reality *Physical Geography of the Sea* (1855, French translation, 1858); the following paragraph is taken from its sec. 688.

252 *horse and its rider*: information taken from Frédol (p. 428), who attributes these observations not to the fishermen, but respectively to navigator and author John Barrow (1764–1848), to French students, and to an unidentified 'Müller'.

a certain gentleman from Copenhagen: Daniel Friedrich Eschricht (1798–1863), a whale specialist.

253 *Captain Denham of the Herald*: (cf. Maury, sec. 688), Henry Mangles Denham (1800–87), naval surveyor, later admiral, who drew navigational charts of the Fijian archipelago (1855–6).

Lieutenant Parker of the American frigate Congress: (Verne: 'Parcker'), quoted by Maury (secs. 466 and 688) as Lieutenant J. P. Parker, in 1852. The '15,140 metres' in this paragraph was '15,149 metres' in I 18; but both figures are faulty.

254 *McClintock, the hero of the polar seas*: (Verne: 'Mac Clintock'), Leopold, author of *The Voyage of the 'Fox' in the Arctic Seas* (1859), who describes the discovery of a cairn proving that John Franklin had died in 1847. The *Bull-Dog* of the following sentence dived in 1855.

255 *below three leagues*: the submarine had previously been at a depth of 'three and a quarter leagues'.

257 BALEEN AND SPERM WHALES: in the first manuscript, the title is 'Scies et baleines' (Sawfish and Whales). Certainly a fight of these two species might seem more dramatic; however, the text of the draft chapter does not

contain such a combat. Both words in French have two meanings; Verne may be making a play on words.

261 *Sinbad the Sailor*: in *The Thousand and One Nights*, he makes seven voyages, encounters sea monsters and the Old Man of the Sea, and is carried aloft by a giant roc; the episode in *20T* echoes the 538th and 539th nights.

50 tons: this should logically be '500 tons'; 'October' below is also a slip.

262 *the Essex sank almost immediately*: the attack and sinking of the *Essex* are related in *Moby-Dick*, similarly forming a prelude to the climax, although Verne describes a '(baleen) whale' and Melville, a sperm whale. Melville's cited source is *Narrative . . . of the Whale-Ship 'Essex'* (1821) by Owen Chase, the first mate, whose account of the incident in 1820 has the sperm whale stopping the ship dead, rather than pushing it backwards, as in Verne.

263 *enough problems with their natural enemies*: if Verne himself is opposed to hunting, *20T* is often ambivalent. The danger of extinction of the sea otter, dugong, and manatee, as well as Ned Land's excesses, are emphasized; but the extermination of the sperm whale seems to be advocated.

Ned whistled Yankee Doodle between his teeth: From the Earth to the Moon calls 'Yankee Doodle' the American 'national song' and compares it to the Revolutionary 'La Marseillaise'. Ned's subtext is apparently anti-colonial and anti-upper class.

264 *twenty-five huge teeth*: inaccurate quotation, since Frédol writes of 20 to 25 teeth on each side of the lower jaw (p. 547); one would expect an even number of teeth. The same author, cited a few lines lower, is named Moquin-Tandon in I 24.

267 *pack-ice . . . 'streams' when they are longer*: (Verne: 'palchs'), the *OED* quotes an 1850 source: 'If the field is broken up into a number of pieces . . . the whole is called a pack, if the pieces are broad they are called a patch; and when long and narrow a stream.'

268 *55th meridian*: at the beginning of the chapter the *Nautilus* was following the '50th meridian'.

269 *73.5 degrees*: a slip for 'centimetres'. The idea of the low barometer reading in the Antarctic is present in Maury.

Hansteen: (Verne: 'Hansten'), Christopher (1784–1873), Norwegian astronomer, researcher in terrestrial magnetism, and author.

18 March: should this not be the 17th?

271 *I can do what I wish with the Nautilus*: MS2 has 'I do what I say', revealing Nemo's self-image.

272 *child's play for the Nautilus*: MS2 has 'child's play for *Nautilus*', as if it were an animate being.

four to one: (MS2: 'one to four'), neither this ratio, nor Nemo's three to one, nor consequently the rest of the following paragraph, are accurate in the 1871 edition. The ratio is now believed to be six or eight to one, depending on the salinity of the water and of the ice. However, some of these figures are correct in the 1869 edition.

274 *Two degrees already gained*: in fact one. Nor does a water temperature of −12° seem plausible.

19 March: in fact the 18th.

275 *900 metres . . . the surface of the ocean*: another evident slip, like that of the previous paragraph. If one accepts Nemo's three to one, these figures are correct in the 18mo editions, again implying they postdate the 1871 edition.

277 *he seemed to take possession of the southern regions*: MS2: 'he appeared as the spirit of the southern regions'.

James Ross: James (Clark) Ross (1800–62), explorer and admiral. He helped locate the North Magnetic Pole in 1831, and discovered the Ross Sea and Victoria Land (1839–43). The information in this paragraph is identical in Maury (sec. 468), who says however that Mount Terror is extinct.

279 *The following day, 20 March*: this should be the 21st.

280 *not be able to surpass . . . tritons*: MS2 has the more misogynist '. . . to equal'. Walruses are not found in the Antarctic (nor are the seals of this chapter). Triton, son of Poseidon, is a minor Greek deity, with a human face and a fish tail; a triton is the male equivalent of a siren.

cetaceans: seals are no longer classified as cetaceans.

283 *less than 100 metres*: in reality of the order of a kilometre.

China: it was possibly near this point in the text that Hetzel made one of his more catastrophic suggestions/instructions, in line with his wish to make Verne's books more commercial: 'Sunday—3 a.m. . . . save some little Chinese kidnapped by Chinese pirates. They are not dangerous. They are funny, they are to be taken home in the dinghy. They are completely taken in [*sic*]. Nemo cannot worry about them [*sic*]. One could be kept on board. No one understands him, he understands no one. He would cheer the *Nautilus* up. But that is your business' (25 April 1869).

284 *southwards*: south and north become increasingly arbitrary as the Pole is approached.

285 *chronometer*: in the margin of MS1 Verne wonders: 'Can one observe under these conditions?'

the Dutchman Gherritz: or Gerritsz (Verne: 'Ghéritk'), Dirck or Derk, navigator. He was swept southwards from South America in a storm, in fact in 1599, and discovered high snow-covered mountains, now thought to be the South Shetlands.

Verne's 'semi-structured' list of the successive latitudes reached by the Antarctic explorers is an echo of his hero, Captain Hatteras, whose only thought is the distance from the North Pole, an obsession which will lead to his madness and death. A compass-direction fixation is also visible in *Journey to England and Scotland*, where the focus of Verne's dreams is the Highlands, and the northwards urge a leitmotiv in every chapter.

286 *Bransfield . . . Balleny*: explorers. *Bransfield*: (Verne: 'Brunsfield'),
Lieutenant Edward (*c.*1795–1852). He and Bellingshausen are generally
thought to have been the first to have sighted the Antarctic mainland.
However, recent cartographic studies have shown that the continent may
have been known about as early as the sixteenth century; *Morrell*: (Verne:
'Morrel'), Captain Benjamin (1795–1835), author of *A Narrative of Four
Voyages . . . to the South Seas . . . and Antarctic Ocean* (1832). He was not in
fact in the Antarctic in 1820; *Powell*: George (1794–1824), a sealer and
captain of three expeditions, in fact 1818–22, he co-discovered the South
Orkneys; *Weddell*: (Verne: 'Weddel'), James (1787–1834), who discovered
the Weddell Sea, in fact in 1823; *Foster, commanding the 'Chanticleer'*:
(Verne: 'Forster'), Henry (1796–1831), author of *Voyage to the Southern
Atlantic Ocean* (1834); *Biscoe*: (Verne: 'Biscoë'), John (1794–1843), RN,
discovered Enderby Land and the Biscoe Islands (1830–2); *Wilkes*: (in fact
American), Lieutenant Charles (1798–1877), led the six-ship Exploration
Expedition (1838–42) and discovered Wilkes Land; *Balleny*: John (*c.*1790–
1857), whaling captain, discovered the Balleny Islands. Verne's '76° 56''' in
the following sentence has been amended to '70° 56'''.

a black flag, carrying a golden 'N' quartered on its bunting: possibly an allusion to Napoleon, whose N adorns French buildings and bridges. The black
flag is traditionally a pirate flag; and black is also the colour of anarchists.
The black on the white ice may in addition be a textual metaphor. But
much of the power of the image derives from the sun's golden rays before
the black six-month night.

my new realm: a footnote to Verne's *The Sphinx of the Ice Realm* (1897)
reads: 'someone had already set foot on this point of the globe, on
21 March 1868' (II 10). The authorial voice summarizes the Antarctic scene
and the approach by 'that mysterious character', before concluding: 'And
at the moment that the horizon, just to the north, cut the solar disc into
two equal parts, he took possession of the continent in his own name, and
unfurled a flag of bunting embroidered with a golden N. Offshore floated
a submarine boat called the *Nautilus*, the name of whose commander was
Captain Nemo. J. V.'

288 *'But where can we find him?' asked Ned*: Ned and Conseil do not know their
way round the library or dining-room (they eat in their cabin).

299 *That day, the sixth of our imprisonment*: 25 March is not noted; 26 March is
the fifth day; 27 March is spent on work. Since a night comes before 'That
day', it must in fact be the seventh day, the 28th, a date confirmed a page
below.

304 *John Davis*: (*c.*1550–1605), discovered the Davis Strait and Baffin Bay.

Richard Hawkins: (1562–1622), admiral who defeated the Invincible Armada
(1588) and commanded an expedition to South America (1583–97), where
he was imprisoned by the Spanish.

305 *the easternmost point of South America, Cape São Roque*: although Cape São
Roque is the point closest to Africa, it is not the furthest east.

305 *the Guyanas, a French possession*: French Guyana in fact coexisted with
British and Dutch Guyana, as Verne recognizes a page later when he writes
of 'the Dutch coast near the mouth of the Maroni'.

308 *at least 4,000 kilograms*: in reality the maximum size of the manatee is
about 5 metres and 700 kilograms.

Toussenel: Alphonse (1803–85), author of *L'Esprit des bêtes: Le Monde des
oiseaux* (1847, reprinted many times) and *L'Esprit des bêtes: Mammifères de
France*, with a preface by P.-J. Stahl (pseudonym of Hetzel—Hetzel, 1868).

311 *Diana*: the virgin goddess of hunting and childbirth, associated with the
moon.

313 *a painting of the said squid*: the church referred to is St Thomas's Chapel;
and the painting is an *ex-voto* from sailors grateful for surviving the
incident described in Montfort's *Histoire naturelle* (see note to p. 318).

and you know what use legends are in natural history: MS2 has '*ex-votos*' instead
of 'legends': anticlerical and showing the connection with St Thomas's
Chapel and Montfort.

but a certain Olaus Magnus speaks of a mile-long cephalopod: (Verne: 'Olaüs
Magnus') (1490–1557), Swedish scholar and archbishop of Uppsala, an
expert on runes and author of a work translated as *Histoire des pays
septentrionaux* (1560, 1561).

one day the Bishop of Nidaros . . . returned to the sea: (Verne: 'Nidros'), Eric
Falkendorff, archbishop of Nidaros (now Trondheim), who wrote a letter
to Pope Leo X about the mass in question.

314 *Captain Paul Bos of Le Havre*: in May 1868 Verne acquired a boat, the
St Michel, built by 'one of my friends, one of the best captains of Le Havre'
[June? 1868, to his father], Charles-Paul Bos (1826–83). Le Crotoy native
Bos, who often stayed there with his brother, a few paces from Verne's
residence, was a former naval officer. He was responsible for the novelist's
navigation accounts, duly recorded in his logbooks.

Captain Bouyer: (Verne: 'Bouguer'), Frédéric (1822–82), author of *La
Guyane française* (1867), with engravings by Riou, one of the illustrators of
20T. A letter to the *Figaro* of 21 August 1871 indicated Verne's misspelling,
which was not however corrected in subsequent reprints. The incident
Aronnax relates, on 30 November 1861, was attested in a letter written to
the French Academy of Sciences by Sabin Berthelot, French consul at
Tenerife. The story was much criticized, including the impracticability of
trying to haul a two-ton mass on board using a single rope, the strange
behaviour of the creature in swimming under the boat and remaining on
the scene for two or three hours, and the general lack of information about
the tail, which apparently weighed 40 pounds.

315 *20 to 25 tons*: this seems a lot for an eight-metre squid, although Verne
may be indicating the length of the body *without* the tentacles. The *Furies*
mentioned a few lines above were terrifying winged goddesses with
serpentine hair.

317 *a spurt of blackish liquid, secreted from a bursa in its abdomen*: the symbolism of this battle scene includes the 'black ink' and the 'quill' of the struggle of writing.

318 *with it my unfortunate compatriot*: the musk smell and dark liquid are visible in descriptions going back to Pontoppidan and Pliny. But this scene resembles what a Captain Jean Magnus Dens told Pierre Denys (de) Montfort (director of the Natural History Museum, but later convicted of forgery). Montfort's *Histoire naturelle, générale et particulière des mollusques* (1802–5) states that 'poulpes' can sink ships, and reports that Dens's men were scraping their ship between St Helena and Nova Scotia, when a huge animal rose from the water and threw a giant tentacle round two of them. Another arm seized a third man, who shouted for help. Several harpoons were driven into the monster, and the crew cut off one arm, 25 feet long, with axes and knives, but to little effect, and the animal carried off the two sailors. The third man died the following night.

red: MS2 has 'red and black', probably an allusion to Stendhal's novel, but also a conjunction of blood and ink.

the author of The Toilers of the Sea: Hugo's novel (1866), which Verne mentions in a letter, depicts a battle with an octopus ('pieuvre') (vol. 2, book 4, chs. 1–3). Despite similarities with Verne, such as the colour change, there are also considerable differences: Hugo emphasizes the tough skin, the phosphorescence when mating, the fact that the mouth and the anus are combined, and so on. Verne's squid has 'eight arms, or legs' (like an octopus), whereas squid are often said to have ten; nevertheless two of these are tentacles, of distinct form and function.

319 *I did not see him for some time*: in the first manuscript Nemo disappears for more than a week; given that the bedrooms are side by side, Aronnax should see or hear him from time to time. Might he have a hideaway on the upper gangway? Or does he sometimes leave the *Nautilus*?

320 *the open sea of the Pole*: the information in this paragraph is taken from Maury. Verne quotes two different speeds for the Gulf Stream, perhaps due to a confusion between miles and kilometres.

321 *fish . . . dedicated to his good lady wife*: the 'mugilomore Anne-Caroline'.

323 *in a small floating container*: MS2 has 'bottle cask' (its final chapter also has 'bottle'); although where such an object came from is unclear. The idea that Nemo will include his name and the story of his life is added in the margin.

at this moment: instead of this phrase, MS2 has 'I shut the thoughts up inside me'; in the next paragraph, it has 'risky' in place of 'crude'.

325 *a second time*: the six paragraphs ending here were added in the margin of MS2, replacing a crossed-out passage: '"But finally, by what right are you holding us?" | "By the right that I accord myself," the captain said firmly. "I have already given you my reasons, and am very surprised to see you returning to the subject." . . . "But we have the right to regain our freedom by any means." | "Regain it. I have not asked for your word that you will never

~~leave the vessel without my authorization." | "We would not have given it to~~
~~you, sir!" | Captain Nemo looked at me, his arms proudly crossed. | "May~~
~~this first time that you have raised the subject", he said, "be also be the last."'~~

Behaviour between nineteenth-century gentlemen demanded that one
kept one's word and maintained some level of courtesy (just as men-of-
war gave warning before attacking). The MS2 dialogue is more forthright
concerning the limits of what either side can do. But the 1871 version adds
Aronnax's important assessment of Nemo, of their position on board, of
his own obscure hopes of a perhaps posthumous fame, and of his incom-
prehension of the captain's life, almost in terms a quarrelling couple might
use. His arguments in this published text are essentially subjective,
amounting to an appeal for mercy. Nemo easily crushes Aronnax by referring
to his absolute power and saying that it was not he who got them into this
situation. His only concession is the flattery he uses of his interlocutor's
ability to 'understand anything'.

325 *18 May*: a slip; it must be about 8 or 9 May.

326 *1854*: Verne: '1864'.

328 *the Solway . . . City of Glasgow*: ships lost at sea; *the 'Solway'*: (constructed
1841), 20 miles west of Corunna, 7 April 1843, 35 lives lost; *the 'Isis'*:
(1842), off Bermuda, 8 October 1842, no lives lost; *the 'Hungarian'*:
Sable Island, 20 February 1860, 237 dead; *the 'Canadian'*: Belle Isle Strait,
4 June 1861, 35 dead; *the 'Anglo-Saxon'*: (1856), near Cape Henry, 27 April
1863, 238 dead; *the 'United States'*: Bird Rocks, Gulf of St Lawrence,
25 April 1861, all lives lost; *the 'President'*: last seen on 11 March 1841,
with 136 people on board; *the 'City of Glasgow'*: (1850), sailed for Delaware
on 1 March 1854, not seen again.

330 *which makes a total of 25 million*: in fact 200 million. (Five lines lower, 'four
cod' should similarly read 'three'.)

331 *Cyrus Field*: Cyrus (West) Field (1819–92), American merchant and finan-
cier. The first transatlantic cable of 1858 failed after three weeks, but the
1866 one was successful. Verne met Field on board the *Great Eastern* on
18 or 19 March 1867, and attended one of his presentations on the laying of
the cable; on 4 April, he gave the novelist a meticulous personal visit of the
ship. The first manuscript contains several additional lines about the route
of the cable and Field's failures, as well as the expense of sending telegrams. It also implies that Nemo knows the story of the cable, successfully
laid only after his embarkation on the *Nautilus*.

Captain Anderson: ch. 3 of *A Floating City* presents a flattering portrait of
this real-life personage, who was captain of the *Great Eastern* on Verne's
own crossings.

the armistice between Prussia and Austria after Sadowa: village in northern
Czechoslovakia, site of a Prussian victory in the Seven Weeks War (1866).

'Glory to God in the highest, and on earth peace, good will to men': Luke 2: 14.
In fact Field sent the telegram on 7 August 1858, the first part being:
'Europe and America are united by telegraph'.

332 *Cape Clear and Fastnet lighthouse*: after a port call in Cork on the *Great Eastern*, Verne saw Cape Clear and Fastnet towards the end of March 1867.

betray the captain's secrets: the first manuscript reinforces the captain's sombre mood. Aronnax wonders if the reason may be because he is close to his homeland; that he may be French; but rejects the idea, without giving any reason; then implicitly supports it, by citing the nationality of the sailor carried off by the squid. Such manoeuvring, which happens elsewhere in the novel, seems to be a stratagem both to undermine Aronnax's credibility and to slip ideas in which, if openly expressed, might be vetoed by Hetzel.

334 *the Marseillais . . . Admiral Van Stabel*: naval officers. *La Poype-Vertrieux*: Jean-François de (1758–1851); *Admiral d'Estaing*: Charles Hector (1729–94), guillotined; *Count of Grasse*: François-Joseph-Paul, Marquis de Grasse-Tilly (1722–88), admiral. His decisive blockade of Chesapeake Bay cut off Cornwallis's retreat in the American War of Independence (1775–83); *Villaret de Joyeuse*: (Verne: 'Villaret-Joyeuse'), Louis-Thomas (1750–1824), admiral who fought courageously in the battle Verne describes, and was later able to escort the convoy of wheat into Brest. In 1802, however, the same officer refused Fulton's request to use his *Nautilus* to attack a British warship positioned off Brest; *Admiral Van Stabel*: Pierre-Jean (1746–97).

rather than surrender: Verne is following the exaggerated French press. In reality, the *Vengeur*, on the point of sinking, surrendered and, out of the 600 or so crew, 367 sailors and seven officers were saved by British ships. However, the huge food convoy, vital for French supplies, did get through.

'The Vengeur!': this warship, built in Toulon, played an important role in the War of Independence. The main message of the episode is Nemo's support for 'the people', the underdog, the Revolution, Republicanism, and left-wing values. Surprisingly, Verne omits to mention that the submarine is off the coasts of France and England.

Yes, monsieur: MS2 has: 'But give it back its real name: Le Vengeur du peuple!' Nemo is at this point opposed to all the great powers; with indications of anti-Turk, anti-Confederate, anti-Russian, and anti-British sentiments. Aronnax surmises that there is a 'coalition of nations against him'.

A fine name: Verne often inserts anagrams of his surname; here 'Vengeur' gives 'Verne' and 'gu' with a soft g: a fine name indeed!

the glorious wreck: MS2 has 'the Republican wreck'. The R word is absent from Verne's major works, even though the novelist, despite becoming increasingly conservative, and even reactionary, would later be elected to Amiens Council on a Republican list.

a monstrous or sublime hatred that time could not diminish: Hetzel imposed drastic alterations on the endings of nearly all the novels, but especially *Captain Hatteras*, *From the Earth to the Moon*, *The Mysterious Island*, and

Hector Servadac, in each case inserting an implausible happy ending that altered the meaning and structure of the novel. In *20T* similarly, he insisted on radical changes to the second manuscript, especially the final chapters.

Verne protested, writing an important account of Nemo's character and motives: 'I can see full well that you're picturing a very different fellow from mine . . . We have agreed on two main points: | 1. to change the horror that the captain inspires in me [*sic*] after his great execution, in the interest of the character. | 2. to speed up the action after the sinking of the double-decker. | This will be done, but, for the rest, all I need to do is to justify the captain's terrible action in terms of the provocation he undergoes. Nemo doesn't run after ships and sink them, he doesn't attack, he responds to attacks. But nowhere, whatever your letter says, have I made him a man who kills for killing's sake. He has a generous nature and his feelings are on occasion brought into play in the environment he lives in. His hatred of humanity is sufficiently explained by what he has suffered, both he and his family . . . I am sure I have followed a very natural crescendo. There are generous sentiments, especially in the second volume, and only the force of events makes our hero into a sombre lawgiver . . . when you read this second volume you were very pleased at the improvement it had undergone and it was the last few pages that appalled you; you are right about the effect produced on Arronnax [*sic*], and I will change it. But vis-à-vis Captain Nemo it's not the same, and when you explain him in a different way you change him to the point that I can't recognize him. | What I mean is that if he was a fellow to be done again—which I feel perfectly incapable of, for I've been living with him for two years, I couldn't imagine him otherwise—it wouldn't be a day that needed spending in Paris, but a month . . . In sum, your letter has tortured me' [17 May 1869].

Reading this letter, one can sympathize with the author, for the essence of Nemo's character seems to have been lost on the publisher, who falls into the trap of judging Nemo's actions without taking into account the reasons. The climax is so much a product of the previous 600 pages that Hetzel's quick-fix changes do seem of a nature to 'torture' his author.

335 *a great warship with a ram: an armour-plated double-decker*: the two French vessels of the Solférino type (or Magenta class) were the only two such ships worldwide; their armour-plating extended more than two metres below the waterline.

336 *had he not attacked some ship?*: MS2 has '~~of a certain nation which he pursued with hatred~~', implying that Nemo's attacks are against a particular country—although it is not considered prudent to name it.

If Aronnax is drugged and imprisoned for the events in the Indian Ocean, why are the panels not even closed now? If a correlation between drugs and attacks is established, why does Nemo administer them when Aronnax first arrives—is he perhaps attacking the *Abraham Lincoln*?

337 *floored by an iron hand and thrown to the deck*: MS1: 'held him bent down to the ground'.

ship of an accursed nation: at an early stage Nemo was Polish, and his enemies Russian—an allusion to the Polish insurrection of 1863 against Russian despotism. Although this would have been popular in France, Hetzel vetoed it as he did not want to upset the Russian government and hence lose sales. Verne protested repeatedly: 'suppose Nemo to be a *Pole*, and the ship sunk a *Russian* one, would there be the shadow of an objection to raise? No, a hundred times no! . . . the first idea of the book, true, logical, complete: a Pole—Russia. But since we cannot say it . . . let's imagine that it can be *that*.' [April? 1869]. 'But, to be frank, I regret my Pole, I had got used to him, we were good friends, and what is more, it was more straight-forward, more sincere' [29 July 1867]. In MS1, Nemo uses stronger language: 'an accursed, disgraced, nation'.

The attack has come: MS2: ~~'It would be the act of a barbarian'~~, producing the response ' "Keep quiet~~, sir~~," replied the captain in an irritated tone, "~~Keep quiet, sir~~ . . . The attack has come! ~~From them!~~ . . ." ' The '~~From them~~' emphasizes that Nemo ripostes to attacks, not launches them himself, ensuring that no one assails him with impunity.

338 *Go down*: MS2: 'Go down~~, I tell you~~.'

'I am the law, I am the justice': perhaps a mocking, anarchistic echo of God's 'I am the first, I am the last' (Isaiah 44: 6) and of Jesus's 'I am the way, and the truth, and the life' at the Last Supper (John 14: 6).

country, wife, children, parents—perished as I watched: by speaking of his country ('patrie') which has 'perished', Nemo seems to imply that it is a European one, Poland being the obvious example.

In the face of Hetzel's obduracy, Verne feels obliged to re-emphasize the reasons for Nemo's actions and his own support for them: 'I refuse to write the letter in question concerning Captain Nemo if I cannot explain his hatred, or I will remain silent about the reason for the hero's hatred and life, his nationality, etc. Or, if necessary, I will change the ending . . . You say: but he performs an evil act! I reply no; imagine again—this was the original idea for the book—a Polish nobleman whose daughters have been raped, wife killed with an axe, father killed with a knout [a whip with leather thongs, used on Russian criminals], a Pole whose friends all die in Siberia . . . In such a situation, I would sink without hesitation. In order not to feel as I do on this matter, one would need to have never hated . . . After all this, I repeat I will act for the best, and if necessary, I will change the ending of the sunk ship' [11? June 1869]. Verne was clearly being told to write a letter to the press to 'explain' Nemo's behaviour—a preposterous idea after 600 pages of justification.

Miller and Walter suggest that Nemo is Indian. It is true that previous hints had included: the ambiguous 'That Indian, Professor, is an inhabitant of an oppressed country. I am his compatriot, and shall remain so to my very last breath!' (II 3); and Aronnax's speculation that Nemo was 'born in the lower latitudes' (I 8). However, Nemo's art collection, preferred composers, and other cultural references are exclusively European—there is little trace of oriental influence in his allusions. Given the attack by the *Abraham Lincoln*, one could as plausibly argue that Nemo was anti-American. Also, the correspondence and the manuscripts seem to preclude any specific interpretation—apart from one (see Appendix 1: Inception). In the same letter, Verne himself wrote: 'Readers will suppose what they want, depending on their character.'

338 *sunk before nightfall*: in fact, it will only sink at dawn.

339 *easy to escape*: how, if the warship is to be sunk? More generally, nearly all of Aronnax's surmisals in this chapter prove misguided.

340 *so as to form a unified line with it*: MS2 has '~~to my great surprise~~'.

five o'clock . . . the Nautilus was slowing: this time is inconsistent with the earlier 'six a.m.'. The location of the final events is not indicated. At noon the day before, the *Nautilus* had found the wreck of the *Vengeur*, at 47° 24′ N and 17° 28′ W. Until six in the morning, it draws the ship eastwards: a distance of about 400 kilometres, since the maximum sustained speed of a double-decker was about 14 knots. The place is, in sum, some 200 kilometres west of Finistère, not far from the naval centres of Le Havre and La Rochelle—a sign of the nationality of the ship?

it was allowing itself to be approached: Hetzel suggested that Nemo 'back the *Nautilus* into a cul-de-sac from which he cannot escape except by sinking the ship'. Verne riposted that the *Nautilus* was too quick and too strong to allow that to happen; and that if it was cornered, it would mean there wasn't enough water to sink the ship' [29? April 1869].

341 *through the vessel*: being eight metres high, against a draft of less than nine metres in armour-plated warships, only part of the *Nautilus* will pass 'through' the vessel—in any case an implausibility, even if it has almost infinite power.

the decks: this plural is an allusion to the ship's class, the Solférino.

342 *the portrait of a woman . . . knelt down sobbing*: a portrait apparently absent on Aronnax's first visit, perhaps an addition after Hetzel's reading of the manuscript. With, a few pages above, 'country, wife, children, my father—perished!', this is a rare reminder of the theme of a Polish Nemo, opposed to Russian tyranny.

The closing words of the chapter in MS1, although partly illegible, differ from the book version and MS2, for Nemo shouts rather than sobs, and his dominant sentiment is disappointment rather than remorse: 'Horrible. | The double-decker cried out . . . to wonder . . . We have experienced a setback. | Woe! Woe!'

at unsurpassed speed: in the published version, this sentence is all we know about the *Nautilus*'s route. It is a frustrating void, since the submarine will pass near Verne's beloved Brittany and Picardy—unless it goes through the Irish Sea—to leave the Channel and the North Sea without a single mention.

MS2, in contrast, has the following passage (most of which is crossed out): 'I saw that we had entered the English Channel, which could not help but reassure me. At this phase of the moon, the tides already displayed some movement. Their current which is 75 centimetres per second between Ouessant and Land's End, must have been 2.50 metres [per second], and carried us on ever more quickly. | The bottom of the Channel is on average 170 metres deep. It is relatively flat, and forms a sandy valley, sunk between Britain and France. That day, the *Nautilus* remained quite close to the coast of north-west France.' Verne cannot resist taking his submarine near his birthplace and demonstrating his familiarity with the Channel.

then the moon rose: in MS2 Verne shows his knowledge of the area round Le Havre (two lighthouses stood at Cap de la Hève; Cap d'Antifer will later be alluded to in the title *Captain Antifer*). He also reveals his powerful visual imagination, stimulated by paintings and by natural complexities (the passage is again largely deleted): 'The condition of the sea would not have allowed it. | By evening, we had covered the whole of the Channel between Brest and the mouth of the Seine [words replaced by: 200 leagues of the north Atlantic]. The clock read seven o'clock, when the light of la Hève sent us its electric brilliance. I recognized the magnificent cliffs of Cap d'Antifer, which took on a fantastic appearance as night fell: their limestone surface, dotted with small patches of grass, produced an interminable procession of strange figures, queens of the Middle Ages arranged with the robustness of the old painters, a Cimabue, a Mantegna, bishops in tall mitres blessing lords in helmets and armour, ladies with long headdresses draped in their robes with broad folds, squires standing behind vast feasting tables; castles with turrets and machicolations, too small and not in the proper perspective, as in the bas reliefs of old cathedrals. Yes, I saw them coming back to life. Then shadows came, the vision melted into the mists of evening.' Cimabue (1240?–1302) was an Italian artist of lifelike New Testament frescoes; Andrea Mantegna (*c.*1436–1506), an engraver and painter who experimented with perspective and spatial illusion.

343 *The time of the clocks on board had been suspended*: perhaps an allusion to Lamartine's 'Oh time! Suspend your flight!', apparently meaning that the clocks have stopped—Verne often takes metaphors literally. Time itself has accelerated dramatically, and indications of date have also disappeared as Aronnax becomes more distraught.

At each moment I expected to see, like the fabulous Gordon Pym, 'a shrouded human figure . . . which defends the approaches to the Pole': Verne is quoting Baudelaire's translation at the end of the main body of Poe's *The Narrative of Arthur Gordon Pym of Nantucket* (1838). However, Poe does not include the phrase 'thrown across the cataract which defends the approaches to the Pole', the final words being: 'And the hue of the skin of the figure was of the perfect whiteness of the snow.'

Verne wrote only one literary study: 'Edgar Poe et ses œuvres' (*Musée des familles*, April 1864, 193–208). This article refers to Baudelaire's translation and preface and explores 'A Descent into the Maelström' ('a vertiginous excursion embarked upon by fishermen from Lofoten') and especially *Arthur Gordon Pym*. Verne's *The Sphinx of the Ice Realm* (1897) is a sort of interpretation, adaptation, and sequel to Poe's only novel.

343 *Not one crew member appeared for a single moment*: how do Aronnax and company receive their meals?

When it went up again to replenish its air, the hatches opened and closed automatically: Verne uses 'panneaux' for both the panels on the windows and the hatches leading to the platform or the dinghy. Here he must be thinking of the hatches, with 'automatically' meaning 'without visible human intervention' or 'by remote control'. Why did we not know about this before? And why was it not used to keep the Papuans and the squid out?

no longer tenable: the last four paragraphs, beginning with 'Starting from . . .', appear in the margin of MS2, replacing a crossed-out visit to the bay on which Le Crotoy is located: 'At about midnight, we passed near the Baie de Somme whose 10,000 hectares of sand are covered by the rising tide.'

what date I cannot say: the date is 'fifteen or twenty days' (II 22) after '2 June' (II 21), or between 17 and 22 June 1868. In MS1, the weeks of wandering are absent, the escape from the submarine taking place the day after leaving the Channel, as confirmed by the date in the margin, '3 June'.

344 *find shelter there*: MS2 has: 'Ned Land who was watching for me to wake up'. Aronnax then replies to Ned, who refers to Great Yarmouth in another deleted passage: '"We must seize the opportunity." . . . "We're past the Straits of Dover. We've sighted the lights of Great Yar and North-Foreland. We're entering the North Sea. No time to be wasted! Who can say where we'll be carried off to."'

without the crew realizing: MS2 adds: 'Depending on the wind, we will land in Scotland or Holland.' Scotland does not really seem to be on their route, but Verne cannot resist the idea of heading back to his ancestral homeland.

I went out . . . a day or even an hour: instead of these three sentences, MS2 has: 'The *Nautilus* was floating a few miles from land, which lay to starboard. A hot day was in store . . . The weather looked as though it was going to favour us. The *Nautilus* stayed close to land as it headed north. Unfortunately it was moving very fast. Would it find the narrow passes of the Kattegat or the Sound? Would it enter that Baltic Sea which has no way out? I did not know what to think. But I imagined that in the event it would move up the west coast of Norway. | Yes, Ned was right . . . After the bearings at noon, the *Nautilus* dived back down.' The only coast aligned north–south is that of Denmark; Verne knows the area: on 5 June 1861, en route for Ystad in Sweden then Norway, he embarks in Lubeck on the steamer *Svea*, a sea-crossing which delights him.

'Crotoy, 15 May 1869 . . . Agreed. The end of the voyage through the English Channel between Calais, Boulogne, and Dover is like the Place de la Bourse in Paris. It needs redoing. You mustn't know where you are. It will be terrifying, and the bombshell of the Maelstrom even more terrifying. | As for a slaver, corsair, or pirate ship, you know full well that they don't exist any more. And if we're sticking as much as possible to contemporary reality, it would be a mistake to suppose the existence of things which do not exist in reality. I'm constantly telling you this, from the point of view of logic. | The best was Nemo battling against the whole of society. A fine situation but difficult to make people believe in, since there was no motive for such a fight.'

345 *He had not gone to bed*: MS2 has the equivocal 'I would have preferred him to be in bed.'

346 *'God almighty! Enough! Enough!'*: Nemo's final words are not easy to interpret. He is anguished ('sobbings'); his appeal or protest to the Christian God—or is it just an exclamation?—is surprising; Aronnax's hypothesis of 'remorse' is undoubtedly more telling about his own mood than the captain's. In sum, it is not clear whether it is his whole life or the recent events that have upset him so much. MS2 has 'Enough! Enough! Enough!': more obsessive, but less religious.

347 *Maelstrom*: Pontoppidan describes the Maelstrom (vol. 1, ch. 77). Verne's episode may also show a slight influence from the ending of Poe's 'MS. Found in a Bottle' (1833), but significant borrowing from his 'A Descent into the Maelström' (1841). This includes such features as the terrifying effect of the name itself, the manner of escape (Poe's first-person narrator lashes himself to a barrel), the period of unconsciousness, and the aid from Lofoten Islands fishermen. Poe writes 'Large stocks of firs and pine trees . . . rise again broken and torn to such a degree as if bristles grew upon them. This plainly shows the bottom to consist of craggy rocks': a clear source for *20T*.

Verne carefully planned the surprise: 'As for the ending, the carrying off into unknown seas, the arrival at the Maelstrom without Aronnax or his companions having any inkling, their idea of remaining when they hear that sinister word, the boat carried away with them despite their efforts, it will be superb, yes superb!' [11? June 1869].

between Vaeroy and the Lofoten Islands: (Verne: 'entre les îles Feroë et Loffoden'), the Faroes are a long way away, and there is only one island of Vaeroy, hence the amendment here.

a whirlpool from which no ship has ever been able to escape: the whirlpool is about 5 miles wide, with a current reaching more than 12 knots, with the strong local winds making it more dangerous.

'navel of the ocean': expression visible in *Les Misérables* by Hugo, referring to 'Paris . . . a maelstrom where all is lost' (1863—vol. 2, book 5, ch. 10).

engaged by its captain: MS2 adds: 'It was jibbing at a dizzy speed.' In addition to the man–machine comparison and phallic and childbirth symbolism, this paragraph is written in the imperfect tense in French. The succession of events is emphasized, as in the adventure novel; but time also drags, giving the impression of being ethereal or drugged, as in the Romantic tradition.

347 *as the Norwegian expression has it*: Verne sometimes resorts to quotation to get his more daring passages through (e.g. the erotic description of Aouda in *Around the World*). Given the similarity with Poe, we may doubt his quoted source, especially as MS2 has 'a Norwegian author poet has said'.

and us with it: MS2 adds 'How long this torture went on, I could not say. What happened, I could not recount. A single incident has remained in my mind.'

we can still get out alive: MS2: ' "We need to get it over!" said Ned. | "Yes!" I exclaimed. "Go on Ned! Undo the last bolt! And let us die far from the *Nautilus*!" | The bolts were loosened, and following a violent impact I was knocked unconscious.' In this version, the three seem to deliberately enter the Maelstrom—Aronnax's suicidal impulse seems to be a further sign of the horror that he now feels for the *Nautilus*.

348 *We embraced warmly*: MS2 adds: 'I was in a bad state.'

we cannot think of returning to France: using the present tense, the narrator is playing a balancing act, with narrative and fictional time converging precariously.

I am revising the tale of these adventures: MS2: 'I revised'. Aronnax has become the author of *20T*, although he does not name the book.

But what became of the Nautilus?: Verne left the ending open: 'Then the mystery, the eternal mystery of the *Nautilus* and its captain!' [11? June 1869].

Verne's submarine and its inventor will have many imitators and admirers over the following century. These include Conan Doyle's *The Maracot Deep* (1929) and Paul Éluard, with Georges Perec and Philippe Sollers both making direct reference to *20T*. Arthur Rimbaud's 'Le Bateau ivre', begun in August 1871, is also derived from this novel, with much borrowing of imagery and themes, including 'monitors', 'phosphorescence', 'lactescent', 'Floridas', 'may my keel explode', 'singing fishes', and 'Maelstrom'.

Is Captain Nemo still alive?: Nemo reappears in *The Mysterious Island*, complete with the *Nautilus*, as the agent who has secretly been protecting the settlers from the dangers of the desert island; and eventually dies. The 'true' nationality of Nemo and his crew is 'revealed' to be Indian (although at least one of them had been French). His victims were, it seems, British; and so on. But this Nemo bears no resemblance whatsoever to the Nemo we know; and the most basic facts do not tally. His age and all the dates, for instance, are wildly off; and he claims, in a strange echo of Hetzel's implausible idea, that he sank the warship 'in a narrow, shallow bay— I needed to get through'.

The Mysterious Island is therefore worse than useless in understanding *20T*. Even 'Nemo's' actions to help the settlers seem suspect, for they nullify the validity of their utopian experiment. Discoveries about Hetzel's interventions have further undermined the validity of the 1874 novel. In the published version, we read of the captain's deathbed remorse and of a bumptious assessment of his life as a 'mistake'. The captain's dying words, the absurd 'God and my country!', were, criminally, added in Hetzel's handwriting. The second manuscript originally had in their place 'Independence!'

Voyage à travers l'impossible (1882), published under Verne and Adolphe d'Ennery's joint names, goes even further in betraying the novelist's thought. 'Nemo', for example, has become a reactionary and a bigot, and declaims: 'you will see emboldened criminals multiplying indefinitely . . . and assassins telling themselves: "We can kill without fear; we will not be executed! . . . remorse is a vain word, for God does not exist! [etc.]" '

It is preferable in sum to forget the two commercially inspired sequels which travesty the restless anarchist we know; and think of Nemo as still prowling the ocean deeps.

the manuscript containing the story of his whole life: 'Eternal Adam' (1910) consists mainly of a manuscript left to fate, recounting a similarly unique experience; and indeed, parallels with *20T* abound. A select list includes: the pleasure of smoking; an allusion to the battle between the *Merrimack* and the *Monitor*; an overwhelming dominance of the oceans and an exclusive diet of sea-food; biblical language; archaeological remains as a way of investigating the truth of legends; a fascination for Atlantis, with its arches and broken columns giving rise to heady contemplations on human destiny; the word 'Edom'; an invented language containing teasing hints of European and non-European languages; a new and totally masculine society; a surprising re-emergence of French to convey a heartfelt message; and the contrast between a scientific composition, written by men of superior learning but destined to be lost, and a personal narration, composed by a slow-witted and self-centred author but surviving many vicissitudes and wielding great influence. 'Eternal Adam' is therefore a brilliant sequel to, and affectionate pastiche of, Nemo's story.

349 *survived where so many ships have perished*: MS2 originally read 'I also believe, I fear that his powerful machine has overcome the sea in its most terrifying abyss, and that his *Nautilus* has survived'. This implies that the submarine does escape, considered an undesirable outcome. An addition complicates matters further: the words 'yet more—for must I hope so?' are inserted after 'fear'; and the subjunctive *ait* is crossed out and replaced with *ait* again. In sum, the hesitation between believing, fearing, and hoping reflects the complexities of Aronnax's feelings—and the disagreements between author and publisher.

'Hast thou walked in the search of the depth?': Verne has, 'Qui a jamais pu sonder les profondeurs de l'abîme?', probably meant to quote 'hast thou walked in the search of the depth?' (Job 38: 16), but translatable as 'Who has ever been able to sound the depths of the abyss?' But he may also be

thinking of 'That which is far off, and exceeding deep, who can find it out?' (Ecclesiastes 7: 24) or 'Who shall descend into the deep?' (Romans 10: 7), or even of 'Hast thou entered into the springs of the sea?' (Job 38: 16).

The title page of Zurcher and Margollé's *Le Monde sous-marin* (Hetzel, 1868) has a similar epigraph: 'Qui sondera les mystères de l'Abîme? Job' ('Who will sound the mysteries of the Abyss? Job'). Furthermore, Renard's *Le Fond de la mer* (also Hetzel, 1868) begins with the words 'Qui pénétrera les mystères de l'Océan?' ('Who will penetrate the mysteries of the Ocean?'), ascribing it however to the Wisdom of Solomon.

Since the seventeenth century, the date of the Creation had been calculated as 4004 BC; and Verne's '6,000 years' implies that he ascribes the same age to Ecclesiastes. But in the 1860s, especially following the discovery of ancient fossil remains, doubt was increasingly cast on the traditional age of Creation; and Ecclesiastes is now dated as third century BC.

349 *Captain Nemo and I*: MS1 is different, closing in particular with a ringing endorsement of Nemo's way of life: 'And now what became of the *Nautilus*? Did it succumb. [*sic*] Perhaps! But perhaps also its formidable construction allowed it to resist and to escape the abyss. | And what became of Captain Nemo? I do not think anyone will ever know. Perhaps he is continuing. | As for the disappearance of the frigate, it will be found out which government has lost it and so its/his [*sa*] nationality will be known, and where he [*il*] comes from, and where he is going! | And I, who have been present at so many scenes, how can I forget him. | And he, if he still lives with his *Nautilus* and his companions, the man of the waters, in his final homeland. The free man!'

Three general features of the publisher's interventions are similarly regrettable: a simplification of the geographical presentations; a reduction in the number of British achievements and an increase in those of the French; and the imposition of a conventional ideology, reducing the social and philosophical commentary and promoting modern industry and science. In the margin: 'But one should take note, he is impregnable! [*imprenable*]'. MS2 ends with '~~Is he not the only man who can reply "I have!" to that question of the Book of Ecclesiastes, "Who has ever sounded [Qui a jamais sondé]~~ . . ."' The published text is then substituted in the margin, apart from two variants: it originally read '~~secrets~~ of the abyss' rather than the published 'depths'; and 'loudly and clearly' instead of 'now'.

The quotation from Job in MS2 is slightly closer to the original. Also, having Nemo take the curtain solo, as in both manuscripts, seems aesthetically preferable. And finally, the idea of Nemo's impregnability, perhaps deleted because of Aronnax's bourgeois values, sounds very much like an ultimate defiance thrown at Hetzel and all conformists.

The conclusion is in fact typical in many ways of the changes visible throughout the process of revision of the novel, from the first draft to the published form. Thus almost all the formal elements, especially the style and the continuity, improve between the uncorrected first manuscript and the published book. At the various stages, a few short passages of lesser interest are also jettisoned or abridged; and one or two mistakes corrected. Some scenes are improved, like the final descent into the Maelstrom.

But in many other cases, the extensive changes, especially those where Hetzel's pencil remarks, additions, and corrections can be seen, are of doubtful or non-existent utility, including those to the following scenes: the mysterious wounding of the crew member while Aronnax is drugged; the preparations for the underwater funeral; the discovery of Atlantis; the fight with the giant squid; the preparations for reaching the South Pole; the final approach of the warship, originally at night and of great beauty; and Nemo's deadly riposte.

Similarly, we can regret the fuller earlier versions of many sections, for example: the humorous discussion about cannibalism; two or three instances in the early chapters, where Ned Land already reveals an underlying violent streak, and tries to escape; frequent junctures where Aronnax is more forthcoming about his own movements and conversations, and above all about his great doubts and anxiety; and a dithyramb to the *Nautilus*, focused on its technical prowess and all-conquering power, and which concludes that Nemo is to be unequivocally praised.

The Oxford World's Classics Website

www.worldsclassics.co.uk

- Browse the full range of Oxford World's Classics online

- Sign up for our monthly e-alert to receive information on new titles

- Read extracts from the Introductions

- Listen to our editors and translators talk about the world's greatest literature with our Oxford World's Classics audio guides

- Join the conversation, follow us on Twitter at OWC_Oxford

- Teachers and lecturers can order inspection copies quickly and simply via our website

www.worldsclassics.co.uk

American Literature

British and Irish Literature

Children's Literature

Classics and Ancient Literature

Colonial Literature

Eastern Literature

European Literature

Gothic Literature

History

Medieval Literature

Oxford English Drama

Philosophy

Poetry

Politics

Religion

The Oxford Shakespeare

A complete list of Oxford World's Classics, including Authors in Context, Oxford English Drama, and the Oxford Shakespeare, is available in the UK from the Marketing Services Department, Oxford University Press, Great Clarendon Street, Oxford OX2 6DP, or visit the website at www.oup.com/uk/worldsclassics.

In the USA, visit www.oup.com/us/owc for a complete title list.

Oxford World's Classics are available from all good bookshops. In case of difficulty, customers in the UK should contact Oxford University Press Bookshop, 116 High Street, Oxford OX1 4BR.